GATEWAY TO NEVER

T0166324

Baen Books by
A. Bertram Chandler

To the Galactic Rim (omnibus)
First Command (omnibus)
Galactic Courier (omnibus)
Ride the Star Winds (omnibus)
Upon a Sea of Stars (omnibus)
Gateway to Never (omnibus)

GATEWAY TO NEVER

A. Bertram Chandler

GATEWAY TO NEVER

Gateway to Never © 1972 by A. Bertram Chandler
The Dark Dimensions © 1968 by A. Bertram Chandler
The Way Back © 1978 by A. Bertram Chandler
"The Dutchman" originally appeared in *Galaxy*, November-December, 1972, © 1972 by A. Bertram Chandler
"The Last Hunt" originally appeared in *Galaxy*, March-April, 1973, © 1973 by A. Bertram Chandler
"On the Account" originally appeared in *Galaxy*, May-June, 1973, © 1973 by A. Bertram Chandler
"Rim Change" originally appeared in *Galaxy*, August, 1975, © 1975 by A. Bertram Chandler
"Doggy in the Window" originally appeared in *Amazing Stories*, November 1978, © 1978 by A. Bertram Chandler
"Grimes and the Gaijin Daimyo" originally appeared in *Dreaming Again*, Harper*Voyager*, Australia, 2008, © 2008 by the estate of A. Bertram Chandler
"Around the World in 23,741 Days" originally published in *Algol*, Spring, 1978, ©1978 by *Algol* Magazine; reprinted by permission of *Algol*.

A Baen Books Original

Baen Publishing Enterprises
P.O. Box 1403
Riverdale, NY 10471

www.baen.com

ISBN 13: 978-1-4767-8047-4

Cover art by Alan Pollack

First Baen printing, May 2015

Distributed by Simon & Schuster
1230 Avenue of the Americas
New York, NY 10020

Library of Congress Cataloging-in-Publication Data

Chandler, A. Bertram (Arthur Bertram), 1912-1984
Gateway to never / by A. Bertram Chandler.
    pages ; cm
ISBN 978-1-4767-8047-4 (omni trade pb)
I. Title.
PR6053.H325G38 2015
823'.914--dc23
                                    2015004392

Printed in the United States of America

9 8 7 6 5 4 3 2 1

CONTENTS

Gateway to Never 1

The Dark Dimensions 151

The Way Back 295

The Dutchman 431

The Last Hunt 461

On the Account 487

Rim Change 517

Doggy in the Window 569

Grimes and the Gaijin Daimyo 601

Around the World in 23,741 Days 621

ACKNOWLEDGEMENT

Thanks to Andrew I. Porter for permission to include
the memoir, "Around the World in 23,741 Days"
by A. Bertram Chandler, which originally appeared
in the Spring 1978 issue of *Algol* magazine.

GATEWAY TO
NEVER

DEDICATION:
For Susan, as usual.

≈ Chapter 1 ≈

COMMODORE JOHN GRIMES did not like customs officers; to his way of thinking they ranked with, but even below, tax collectors. The tax collector, however, is loved by nobody—with the possible exceptions of his wife and children—whereas the customs officer makes his impact only upon the traveling public, among whom professional spacemen are numbered.

Grimes was not at all pleased when his latest secretary, Miss Pahvani, told him that the Port Forlorn Chief of Customs wished to see him. It was not that he was especially busy; the only thing to occupy his attention was the Stores Requisition sent in by the chief officer to *Rim Mandrake*, through most of the items on which he had been happily running his blue pencil.

He looked up from his desk and said irritably, "Tell him I'm busy."

Miss Pahvani treated him to her impersonation of a frightened fawn. "But, sir, he says that it is important. And he is the chief collector."

"And I'm the Chief Astronautical Superintendent of Rim Runners. *And* the officer allegedly commanding the Rim Worlds Naval Reserve."

"But, sir, he is waiting."

"Mphm." Miss Pahvani's brother, Grimes recalled, was a junior customs inspector. How did a pretty girl like this come to have a near relative in a profession like that? "All right," he said. "Show him in."

And what was it this time? Grimes wondered. There had been the flap when an overly zealous searcher had discovered that the master of *Rim Basilisk* had no less than two bottles of duty-free gin over and above his allowance for personal consumption. There had been the unpleasantness about the undeclared Caribbean cigars in the cabin of *Rim Gryphon*'s third officer. And what was he, Grimes, supposed to do about it? Send this-practice-must-cease-forthwith circulars to all ships, that was what. . . . He imagined that he was a Rim Runners' master (as he had been, before coming ashore) and mentally composed a letter to himself as astronautical superintendent. *Dear Sir, Your Circular Number so-and-so is now before me. It will shortly be behind me. Yours faithfully. . . .*

"Ah, Commodore," said Josiah Billinghurst, the chief collector of customs, breaking into his thoughts.

"Mr. Billinghurst." Grimes got to his feet, with an outward show of cordiality. After all, he had to share the spaceport with this man. "Come in, come in. This is Liberty Hall; you can spit on the mat and call the cat a bastard!"

Billinghurst winced, as he was intended to do; Grimes knew very well that he hated the merest suggestion of coarse language. He lowered his bulk into one of the chairs on the other side of Grimes' big desk. He was a grossly fat man and his gold-braided uniform did not become him, and neither did he become the uniform. Grimes wondered, as he had wondered many times before, what perverted genius had first thought of putting these enemies of mankind into naval dress.

"Coffee, Mr. Billinghurst?"

"If I may, Commodore."

Miss Pahvani brought in the tray, poured for the two men. *One more smile like that,* Grimes thought sourly, *and our fat friend will make your brother a chief inspector.* He said, when the girl was gone, "And what can I do you for?"

"Nothing, I hope." Billinghurst permitted himself an apology for a smile, then reverted at once to the appearance of a mournful overfed bloodhound. "But you might be able to do something for me."

"In which of my official capacities?" asked Grimes.

"Both, quite possibly." He sipped noisily from his cup. "This is good coffee."

"Imported. And the duty was paid on it."

"I have no doubt that it was. Frankly, Commodore, it wouldn't worry me much if it were out of ship's stores and not a cent of duty paid."

"You surprise me, Mr. Billinghurst."

Billinghurst sighed. "All you spacemen are the same. You regard us as your natural enemies. Do you think that I get any pleasure from fining one of your junior officers for minor smuggling?"

"That thought had flickered across my mind," said Grimes. "But tell me, who's been naughty now? *Rim Mandrake*'s the only ship in port at the moment. I hadn't heard that any of her people had been guilty of the heinous crime of trying to take an undeclared bottle of Scotch ashore."

"None of them has, Commodore."

"So?"

"I don't make the laws, Commodore Grimes. All that I'm supposed to do is enforce them. The government decides what duty shall be paid on the various imported luxuries, and also what quantities of which commodities may be brought in, duty-free, by passengers and ships' crews. Regarding this latter, you know as well as I do that we are inclined to be lenient."

Reluctantly, Grimes agreed.

"When something, such as liquor or tobacco, is intended for personal consumption only, we often turn a blind eye. When something is smuggled ashore to be sold at a profit, we pounce."

"Mphm."

"And then, Commodore, there are the prohibited imports. You have traveled widely; you know that on many worlds, drugs of all kinds are regarded as we regard tobacco and alcohol, or tea and coffee, even."

"Francisco . . ." contributed Grimes.

"Yes, Francisco. A planet of which I have read, but which I have no desire ever to visit."

"An odd world," said Grimes. "Religion is the opium of about half of the people, and opium is the religion of the other half."

"Neatly put, Commodore. Now, I need hardly tell you that drugs, especially the hallucinogens, are banned on the Rim Worlds."

"We get along without them."

"You do, Commodore, and I do, but there are some who think that they cannot. And where there is a demand there will soon be a supply."

"Smuggling?"

"Yes."

"How do you know it is smuggling? How do you know that somebody miles from any spaceport hasn't a mushroom plot, or that somebody with more than a smattering of chemistry isn't cooking up his own LSD?"

"We are working closely with the police in this matter, Commodore. All the evidence indicates that drugs are being smuggled in."

"And what am I supposed to do about it? I'm neither a customs officer nor a policeman."

"You are in a position of authority. Your captains are in positions of authority. All that I ask is a measure of cooperation."

"It is already laid down in Company's Regulations," said Grimes, "that the penalty for smuggling is instant dismissal."

"The penalty for being *caught* smuggling," said Billinghurst.

"Isn't that the same thing?"

"It's not, and you know it, Commodore."

"All right. I'll compose a circular on the subject."

"I expected more from you than this, Commodore Grimes."

"What more *can* I do?" Then, "And how do you know it's *our* ships? Most of them are running the Eastern Circuit, and to the best of my knowledge and belief no drugs are grown or manufactured on Tharn, Mellise, Stree or Grollor, any more than they are on Lorn, Faraway, Ultimo or Thule."

"*Rim Dingo*," said the chief collector, "is engaged in the trade between Lorn and Elsinore. Drug addiction is no problem on that world, but ships from all over the Galaxy come in to the ports of the Shakespearean Sector. *Rim Wombat* runs mainly to Rob Roy, in the Empire of Waverley. As long as the Waverleyans get their scotch they don't want anything else—but the Waverley ports are open to galactic trade."

"Mphm. But I still can't see why there should be all this fuss about mind-expanding chemicals that can be purchased openly on at least a thousand planets."

"Here," stated Billinghurst, "their use is illegal."

"If people enjoy something," said Grimes, "make a law against it. Who was it who said that the law was an ass?"

"I don't like your attitude, Commodore Grimes," Billinghurst said reprovingly.

"There are times when I thoroughly disapprove of myself," said Grimes, with mock penitence. "Anyhow, I'll get that circular into production."

"Thank you," said Billinghurst. "I'm sure that it will be a great help."

Sarcastic bastard! thought Grimes.

ᔕ Chapter 2 ᔕ

THAT EVENING, Grimes talked things over with his wife. He said, "That fat slob Billinghurst was in to see me."

"What have you done now?" Sonya asked him.

"Nothing," replied Grimes, hurt.

"Then what have your captains and officers been doing?"

"Nothing, so far as I know."

"Our Mr. Billinghurst," she said, "doesn't like you enough to drop in for a social chat."

"You can say that again." The commodore's prominent ears reddened. "I don't like him, either. Or any of his breed."

"They have their uses," she said.

Grimes looked at Sonya in a rather hostile manner. He growled, "You *would* say that. After all, you are an intelligence officer, even if only on the Reserve List."

"Why rub it in?" she asked.

"I'm not rubbing anything in. I'm only making the point that customs officers and intelligence officers have a lot in common."

"Yes, we do, I suppose. To be in either trade you have to be something of a human ferret. And the Survey Service's Intelligence Branch has worked with the customs authorities more than once."

"Has Billinghurst asked you to work with him?" he demanded.

"No. Of course not. He represents the Government of the Confederacy, and my Reserve Officer's Commission is held, as well you know, in the Federation's Survey Service."

"You are a citizen of the Confederacy by marriage."

"Yes, but a private citizen. As far as the Rim Worlds are concerned I'm just a civilian. Of course, if I got orders from my bosses on Earth to work with Billinghurst—just as I've had orders in the past to work with you—I should do just that."

"Mphm. Well, I most sincerely hope that you don't."

"Suppose," she suggested, "that you tell me what all this is about. I know you don't like Billinghurst—but he's only doing the job that he's paid to do."

"Why should the taxpayers be forced to pay for the upkeep of their natural enemies?" asked Grimes rhetorically.

"It always has been so," she told him. "It's just one of the prices one pays for civilization. But suppose you put me in the picture insofar as you and Mr. Billinghurst are concerned."

"All right. As you know very well the Rim Worlds are far less permissive than Earth and the older colonies. By comparison with them, we're practically puritanical."

"Are we? I haven't noticed anybody suffering agonies of repression."

"Perhaps not. But just compare our attitude towards the commoner drugs with that of, say, Earth. On the home planet marijuana can be purchased as openly as tobacco. Here, on the Rim, it is banned. There the more potent hallucinogens can be bought by those who have a license to use them—even that Dew of Paradise they distill on Arrid. Here, they are banned. I could go on . . ."

"Don't bother. So somebody's been drug running, and Billinghurst thinks that it's your boys. Right?"

"Right."

"And he wants you to do something about it. Right?"

"Right."

"And what are you doing about it?"

"I've already done it. I've composed a this-practice-must-cease-forthwith circular, addressed to all masters and chief officers, drawing their attention to Rule No. 73 in Rim Runners' Regulations—the instant dismissal if caught smuggling one."

"And do you think that will be enough?" she asked.

"That's the least of my worries," he said.

"At times—and this is one of them—I find your attitude towards things in general rather hard to understand." Her slender face was set in severe lines, her green eyes stared at him in what could have been accusation.

Grimes squirmed slightly. He said firmly, "I am not, repeat not, a customs officer—and for that I thank all the Odd Gods of the Galaxy. Furthermore, ever since man came down from the trees he has needed an assortment of drugs—tea, coffee, alcohol, tobacco, the juice of sacred mushrooms, the smoke from burning Indian hemp—to take the rough edge off things in general. Most—all, probably—of these things are dangerous if taken in excess. So are plenty of nondrugs. After all, you can kill yourself overeating."

"Talking of that," she said sweetly, "you could stand to lose a pound or three . . . or four . . . or five."

He ignored this. "What Billinghurst is doing is interfering with the most sacred freedom of mankind."

"Which is?"

"Freedom to go to hell your own way. The odd part is that in any culture where this freedom is an undeniable right very few people take advantage of it. But once the law, in its wisdom, says, "You *must* be good," it's a different story. You will recall that Atlantia, only a few years ago, tried to ban the consumption of alcohol. As a result nondrinkers became drinkers, moderate drinkers became heavy drinkers, and those who had been heavy drinkers drank themselves into early graves. And the rum runners made their fortunes."

"Yes," she said, "the rum runners made their fortunes. People like Drongo Kane, who has always ranked high on your list of pet dislikes. And now that some genius has discovered that there's an ideal market for drugs out on the Rim there'll be more fortunes made, and all by the dregs of humanity. Tell me, John, if you knew that Drongo Kane was among the runners would you be content to do no more than write one of those circulars that nobody ever reads anyhow?"

He grinned. "I'll have to toss a coin before I can answer that one. Much as I dislike Drongo Kane I'd hate to be on the same side as Billinghurst!"

⤝ Chapter 3 ⤞

WHEN GRIMES ARRIVED at Port Last, on Ultimo, he was not in a good temper. The matter calling him away from Port Forlorn had been too urgent for him to wait for a regular sailing, so he had pressed the deep space tug *Rim Malemute* into service. She was an enormously powerful little brute, designed to go a long way in a short time. She was an assemblage of highly specialized machinery packed into a tin can, with no waste space whatsoever.

Williams, her skipper, brought her in as spectacularly as usual, applying the thrust of her inertial drive only when it seemed inevitable that the *Malemute* and her people would be smeared over the landing apron. Grimes, who was a guest in the control room, remarked coldly, "I almost lost my last meal. Not that it would have been much loss."

The tug skipper laughed cheerfully. He and Grimes were old friends and shipmates, and he had often served as the commodore's second-in-command in *Faraway Quest*. He said, "You wanted to get here in a hurry, Skipper, and I got you here in a hurry. As for the tucker—this little bitch isn't an Alpha Class liner."

"Isn't she? You surprise me, Williams."

Grimes watched, through the viewport, the ground car that was coming out to the *Malemute*. Through the transparent canopy he could see two men. One was Giles, the port captain, the other was Dunbar, Rim Runners' local astronautical superintendent. As the tug was in from another Rim Worlds port there were no customs, health, or immigration officials. He said, "I'd better go to start sorting things out. I'll let you know where to send my baggage."

"Aren't you living aboard, Skipper?"

"If I'm a sardine in my next incarnation I'll think about it—but not until then."

Grimes went down to the airlock, the doors of which opened as he reached them, and walked down the ramp while it was still being extruded. As he was doing so the ground car came to a halt and Giles and Dunbar, both tall skinny men, got out. Giles was in uniform and saluted. Dunbar bowed stiffly. Grimes bowed in return.

"Glad to see you here, Commodore," said Dunbar.

"Thank you, Captain."

"Perhaps some refreshment before we get down to business. . . ."

"Thank you, but no. We adjusted our clocks to your local time for the last week of the voyage and I had breakfast before we landed." He looked at his watch. "0930 I make it."

"That is correct, sir."

Grimes got into the front of the car with Dunbar. Giles said that he was going aboard *Rim Malemute* to see Williams to handle the arrival formalities. Dunbar drove off, wasting no time.

Grimes looked with interest at the berthed ships as they passed them—*Rim Cougar, Rim Panther*, the Shakespearean Line's *Othello*, the Waverley Royal Mail's freighter *Countess of Ayrshire*. It could have been Port Forlorn, but for the weather. The sky overhead was blue, with a very few white clouds, not a dismal gray overcast—mainly natural, but contributed to by the smoke from the towering stacks of Lorn's heavy industry. Ahead, once they were through the main gates, was the city of Port Last, and beyond the white and red buildings towered the snowcapped pinnacles of the Ultimate Range. The road ran straight as an arrow through fields of wheat, some still green and some already golden. In these latter the harvesters, looking like huge mechanical insects, were busily working.

Ultimo, thought Grimes. *The granary of the Rim Worlds. A planet of farmers. A world where anything, anything at all, is welcome as long as it breaks the deadly monotony. Like Elsinore, another farming world, but dairy products rather than grain, where compulsive gambling is the main social problem. . . .*

He asked Dunbar, "Where have they got young Pleshoff?"

"In the central jail, Commodore. I could have got him out on bail, but thought that if I did he'd be getting into more trouble."

"What are the charges, exactly?"

"As far as we're concerned, mutiny. As far as the civil authorities are concerned, drug addiction. I should have liked to have held Captain Gaynes and his chief officer as witnesses—but, as you know, *Rim Caribou* was already behind schedule and it would have taken too much time to get reliefs for them. But they left affidavits."

"Mphm. What do you think, Captain?"

"What can I think? The young fool was in the control room, testing gear an hour before lift-off, while Gaynes was in my office and the chief officer was seeing the ship buttoned up for space. The engineers had been doing last-minute maintenance on the inertial drive, had made a test run on one-twentieth power and then, with departure time so close, had left it on Stand-By. Pleshoff slammed it into maximum thrust and the old *Caribou* went up like a rocket. Gaynes and I saw it from my office window. It shook us, I can tell you. Then Pleshoff thought he'd try his hand at a few lateral maneuvers. He wiped the radio mast off the top of the spaceport control tower. He buzzed the market place in Port Last—and it was market day, too, just to improve matters. By this time the chief and second officers had managed to break into the control room. They overpowered him and got the ship back into her berth—just as the entire police force came screaming in through the spaceport gates."

"And what does he say?"

"That it seemed a good idea at the time."

"Mphm. I suppose that all of us, as junior officers, have wanted to become instant captains. This drug addiction charge . . . do you think it will stick?"

"It'll stick, all right. Pleshoff was running around with a very unsavoury bunch of kids of his own age, bearded boys and shaven-headed girls. The Blossom People, they call themselves."

"There are Blossom People on Francisco. I suppose they modeled themselves on these originals."

"Probably. The gang that he was mixed up in seem to have a source of supply for—what do they call the muck?—dreamy weed. Ugh!"

"They smoke it?"

"Yes. In long, porcelain pipes. *They* claim that it's not habit forming. *They* claim that it's no worse than alcohol, that its effects are far less injurious. They even have a religion based on it."

"Is this . . . this dreamy weed grown locally?"

Dunbar laughed. "On Ultimo? You must be joking, Commodore. Every square inch of soil on this planet has to nourish the sacred grain. It's smuggled in, from somewhere. The police and the customs are running around in small circles trying to get their paws onto the runners. But even the pushers are too smart for them."

The car had entered the city now, was running through a wide street on either side of which were low, graceful stone houses. The houses gave way to shops, to office buildings, taller and taller as the vehicle approached the centre. And then they were in the great square, with the fountains and the statue of some ancient Greek-looking lady proudly holding a sheaf of wheat. Surrounding the square were the official buildings—town hall, city library, state church, Aero-Space Authority, police headquarters, and prison. The jail was a cylindrical tower, windowless except at ground level. It was well proportioned, graceful even—but it looked grim.

Dunbar said, "I've warned them that we're coming. They'll let us in."

"As long as they let us out," said Grimes.

～ Chapter 4 ～

THE POLICE LIEUTENANT in charge of the ground-floor office eyed Grimes and Dunbar as though they were candidates for admission. "Yes?" he barked.

"I am Captain Dunbar," said the local astronautical superintendent. "This gentleman is Commodore Grimes."

The policeman's manner softened very slightly. He asked, "And what can I do for you gentlemen?"

"We wish to see Mr. Pleshoff. Colonel Warden said that it would be in order."

"Oh, yes. Pleshoff." The swarthy and burly young man leafed through a book on his desk. "We still have him."

Pleshoff, thought Grimes. *With no "Mister." But if you get on the wrong side of the law you soon lose your rank and status.*

"Cell 729," muttered the lieutenant. He raised an imperious hand and a constable obeyed the summons. "Bamberger, take these visitors to see the prisoner Pleshoff."

"It is a work period, sir."

"I know that. But I think that the sovereign state of Ultimo can afford to dispense with his services for half an hour, or even longer."

"Follow me, please, gentlemen," said the brawny Bamberger. He led the way to a bank of elevator doors. He addressed a grille set in the nearest one, said. "Constable Bamberger, No. 325252, with two visitors, Commodore Grimes and Captain Dunbar." Then, to his charges, "Stand beside me, please. One on either side of me." And again to the grille, "Constable Bamberger and party positioned."

There was a flash of intense light, lasting for the briefest fraction of a second. Grimes allowed himself to wonder how he would look in the instantaneous photograph. The door slid open to reveal an empty cage. There was no control panel. The door silently shut as soon as they were all inside. Bamberger said, "Level 33." There was only the slightest tug of acceleration to indicate that they were being slowly carried upwards.

Grimes said, "I take it that your various robots are programmed to obey only the voices of the prison staff."

"I cannot answer that question, sir."

"Mphm. And I suppose, too, that the elevators move very slowly unless some key word or phrase is used, so that any prisoner attempting to escape from an upper level in one cage would find that those on the ground floor had been given ample time to prepare for his reception."

"I cannot answer that question, sir."

"If the machinery running the elevators obeys only the voices of the guards," said Dunbar, "how could a prisoner persuade it to work for him?"

"In the history of penology," said Grimes, "there are many instances of prisoners persuading guards to help them to escape. And not only with a knife or gun in the back."

"I'm afraid that I can't see Pleshoff doing any bribery," said Dunbar. "Not on Rim Runners' third officer's salary. I couldn't do it on mine."

"Mphm," grunted Grimes, and Bamberger looked relieved at the change of subject.

"What work do the prisoners do?" asked Grimes.

"Pleshoff, sir," said the constable, "is in the workroom where playmaster components are assembled. All the convicts receive full Award rates for whatever work they are doing. In the case of a prisoner not yet tried and convicted, even when undeniably guilty of the offense with which he is charged, he is allowed to keep the money he earns after the cost of his keep has been deducted.

After conviction, of course, all his earnings revert to consolidated revenue."

"Mphm." Grimes turned to Dunbar. "I'm surprised that our Mr. Pleshoff hasn't been up before the Beak yet."

"He's had to take his place in the queue, Commodore."

"So they're keeping you busy," said Grimes to Bamberger.

The constable's wooden face at last betrayed some emotion. "It's these Blossom People, sir. They get a lungful of dreamy weed and the things they get up to aren't at all funny. We never have the same trouble with *proper* criminals."

"I suppose not. A proper criminal you just regard as one of the family."

Bamberger gave Grimes a very nasty look, then lapsed into sulky silence.

"But they are becoming a menace," said Dunbar. "The Blossom People, I mean."

"I suppose they are," said Grimes. Performing aerobatics in a 3,000-ton spaceship certainly could be classed as being a menace.

"Floor 33," announced Bamberger. He led the way out through the opening door.

Most of Floor 33 was occupied by the workroom. Through the space ran long, slow-moving conveyor belts. Industriously engaged at these were about a hundred men, each of whom was dressed in drab gray coveralls, each of whom had his number stenciled on to the chest and back of his garment. Blue-and-silver-uniformed guards strolled watchfully along the lines, and other guards stood behind mounted guns of some kind in inward-facing balconies. *Those screwdrivers,* thought Grimes with a twinge of apprehension, *could be used as weapons. And the soldering irons . . . But how long would a prisoner who tried to attack a guard last? Not long.* He transferred his attention to an almost-completed playmaster that was sliding past him. He wondered if the machine in his own home had been assembled in a place like this.

One of the guards who had more silver braid on his sleeves than the others came to meet them. He said, "Commodore Grimes? Captain Dunbar? You wish to see Pleshoff, Number 729. You may use the refreshment room. It will not be required for general use until the next smoke, forty-five minutes from now. Take these gentlemen there, Bamberger."

"Yes, Sergeant."

The refreshment room was grim, gray, cheerless. It contained an ice-water dispenser and dispensers for tea and coffee. Bamberger asked if they wanted a drink. Dunbar refused one. The constable drew paper cups of coffee for Grimes and himself. The fluid was lukewarm, black, and bitter and could have been an infusion of anything at all but what it was called.

Escorted by two guards Pleshoff came in. Grimes remembered the young man, had interviewed him when he applied for a position in Rim Runners. He had been a junior officer in Trans-Galactic Clippers and had met a girl from Faraway when his ship had carried a number of Rim Worlds' passengers on a cruise. He seemed to remember that Pleshoff had married the girl—yes, he had applied for an extension of leave during his honeymoon. And hadn't Pleshoff's captain mentioned to him, not so long ago, that the marriage had broken up?

There are some men who look like spacemen, like officers, no matter what they are wearing. Pleshoff was not one of them. Out of uniform—or in the wrong uniform—he looked like a very ordinary, very frightened young man. *At least he didn't look like a criminal,* thought Grimes.

The commodore said to the guards, "Do you think that you could leave us alone with the . . . er . . . prisoner?"

Bamberger said, "These gentlemen were vouched for by Colonel Warden."

One of the other men asked, "Aren't you Commodore Grimes, sir? *The* Commodore Grimes?"

"There's only one of me as far as I know," said Grimes. "On *this* Continuum."

Bamberger was puzzled by this remark and said doubtfully, "We have to ask the sergeant."

But the sergeant was agreeable, and after a few minutes Grimes, Dunbar, and Pleshoff had the refreshment room to themselves, the two superintendents seated on a hard wooden bench and the young officer facing them, perched on a chair that looked even harder than their own seat.

Chapter 5

"AND NOW, MR. PLESHOFF," said Grimes sternly, "what have you to say for yourself?"

"I suppose it's no good my saying that I'm sorry, sir."

"It's not," Grimes told him. *But,* he thought, *I'm sorry. I'm sorry to see a youngster ruin his career.*

"I suppose, sir, that I'm finished with Rim Runners."

"I'm afraid, Mr. Pleshoff, that you're finished in space. After what you did, your Certificate of Competency will have to be dealt with. There's no way out of it. But I don't think that we shall be pressing the mutiny charge."

"Thank you, sir."

"You haven't much to thank me for, Mr. Pleshoff. You're on the beach. You still have to face the drug charges. But I shall instruct our legal people to do what they can for you."

"Thank you, sir."

"And you might do something for me."

"Anything I can, sir." Pleshoff was pitifully eager.

"I'll be frank with you. Until now I've never taken this drug business seriously. I've thought, if people want to blow their minds, let 'em. It just never occurred to me that anybody in a position of trust, of responsibility, would get . . . hooked? Is that the right word?"

"But I'm not hooked, sir. I tried the dreamy weed only once, and they told me that its effects would be for that night only."

"And who," demanded Grimes sharply, "are *they?*"

Pleshoff's immature features set into a mask of stubbornness. He muttered, "Keep them out of it. They're my friends."

"You mean," said Grimes, "that *she's* your friend."

"Yes," admitted the young man. And then the words poured out. "I've been very lonely, sir. Ever since Sheila and I broke up. Then I met this girl, here, in Port Last. It was in the park. I'd been given the afternoon off and had gone for a walk. You know how it is, sir. You meet somebody and you sort of click. She's like the girls I used to know at home. You know—more free in her talk than the girls out here on the Rim Worlds, more way out in her dress. I took her to dinner that evening. She decided on the place. A little restaurant. Intimate. Candles on the tables, and all that. The menu on a blackboard. I didn't know until then that there were such places out here. That was just the first night, of course. There were other nights. We . . . we became friendly. And with the ship on a regular trade, coming in to Port Last every three weeks or so, I . . ." he grinned weakly, "I had it made.

"She had other friends, of course. All in the same age group. One night she asked me round to a party at one of their places. There was music, of course, and plenty to drink, and things to nibble on, and we were all dancing some of the time, and talking some of the time. You know.

"And then the chap who was throwing the party got up and said, 'Quiet, everybody! Silence in court! I have an announcement!' Then he went on to say that the pusher had come good at last, and that the gateway to never was open. This didn't make any sense to me. He started passing out long, pretty, porcelain pipes, and then brought out from somewhere a can of what looked like a greenish tobacco. 'What is it?' I asked my girl. 'Where were *you* dragged up?' she asked me. After all we mean to each other, don't tell me that you're a block.'"

"A block?" asked Grimes.

"It's what they call stiff and stodgy and conventional people, sir. Well, I told her that I wasn't a block. Then she said that I must be, otherwise I'd recognize dreamy weed when I saw it. Well, I'd heard about dreamy weed, of course, but you never see it in the Academy, although when I was there, for my pre-Space training, two senior cadets were booted out for smoking it. And there's something in TG Clippers' Company's Regulations about it not being allowed aboard their ships. So I wasn't keen on trying it and said that we were lifting off the next day.

"She told me that I'd be right as rain in the morning. She told me, too, that to get the full benefit of it you had to smoke it with somebody, somebody towards whom you felt affectionate. If I wouldn't smoke with her, she was going to smoke with . . . the name doesn't matter.

"You know what it's like, sir. How a girl can make you do things you wouldn't do ordinarily."

"'Lord,'" quoted Grimes, " 'the woman tempted me, and I fell.'"

"Who said that, sir?"

"A man called Adam. Rather before your time, and even mine. But go on."

"It was odd, sir. The smoke, I mean. She and I shared the pipe, passing it back and forth between us. It seemed that I was inhaling something of her, and that she was inhaling something of me. And it was like breathing in a fluid, a liquid, rather than a gas. A warm, sweet, very smooth liquid. And then, somehow, as we smoked we were . . . doing other things." Pleshoff blushed in embarrassment. "The people round us were . . . doing the same. But it wasn't always boys with girls. There were some boys with boys, and there were girls together. And the lights were dim, and dimmer all the time, and redder, and redder, like blood. But it wasn't frightening. It was all . . . warm, and . . . cozy. And there was a pulsing sound like a giant heartbeat. It must have been my own heart that I was hearing, or her heart, or the hearts of all of us. And we were very close, the two of us, all of us. And . . .

"And we reached our climax. It's the usual way of putting it, sir, and the words are the right words, but . . . can you imagine an orgasm that's an implosion rather than an explosion? And after that there was the slow, slow falling into a deep velvety darkness, a warm darkness. . . .

"And . . .

"And then it was morning. Most of the others were waking up too. It should have all looked very sordid in the first light, naked bodies sprawled everywhere, but it didn't. And I felt fine, just fine, as fine as everybody looked, as fine as I knew that I looked myself. Somebody had made coffee, and I'd never tasted coffee as good before. It tasted the way that coffee smells when it's being ground. And my cigarette tasted the way that somebody else's cigar usually smells. I'd have liked to have stayed for breakfast with the others, but I had to be getting back to the ship. After all, it was sailing day. So I got back to the ship. I was still feeling fine—on top of the world, on top of all the worlds. I just breezed through all the things I had to do."

"Including testing the gear," remarked Grimes.

Pleshoff's face lost its animation. "Yes, sir. The gear. I was there, by myself, in the control room. I saw that the inertial drive was already on Stand-By. And then, quite suddenly, the thought came to me, 'Why shouldn't I show the old bastard—sorry, sir, the Old Man, I mean—that he's not the only one who can handle a ship?' I knew that he was still in Captain Dunbar's office, and I thought it'd be a fine joke if he saw his precious *Caribou* lifting off without him."

"Mphm. A very fine joke," commented Grimes. "You may consider yourself highly fortunate that nobody was hurt or killed. Mphm. I suggest that you tell the authorities the name of your host on that unfortunate evening—although no doubt the local detective force is quite capable of finding it out for themselves. The real villain, of course, is the pusher. If you could name him you'd probably get off with a light sentence."

"I can't," said Pleshoff dully. "And if I could, I wouldn't."

Grimes shook his head sadly. "I don't know what trade you'll be entering after the authorities turn you loose—but whatever it is, you'll find that schoolboy code of honor a disadvantage." He got to his feet. "Well, Mr. Pleshoff, we'll do our best for you. We pride ourselves that we look after our own. But I'm afraid that you won't be one of our own for very much longer."

Chapter 6

"I DON'T KNOW what today's young people are coming to," complained Captain Dunbar as he and Grimes left the jail. "Drugs. Orgies."

"I've never taken part in an orgy," said Grimes rather wistfully. "Have you?"

"Of course not!" snapped Dunbar, looking at his superior in a rather dubious manner. Then, apparently having decided that the commodore must have been joking, he went on, "Until now we've been clear of all this sort of thing on the Rim Worlds. I always said that it was a big mistake to open these planets to intergalactic trade."

"Mphm. Where am I staying, by the way?"

"We've booked you into the Rimrock House, Commodore."

Grimes sighed. There was a Rimrock House at Port Forlorn, on Lorn, another one at Port Farewell, on Faraway, yet another at Port Edgell, on Thule. From time to time he had stayed at them all. They were the most expensive hotels on the Rim Worlds—but by no means the best. He would have preferred some place with a less pretentious menu but far better food, with the staff not rigged out like galactic high admirals, but with far better service. But it would be only for a few days, until he had this *Rim Caribou* mess sorted out.

The Rimrock House was one of the huge buildings fronting on to the Central Square. Dunbar drove Grimes the short distance, although he would rather have walked, and promised that he would have the commodore's gear picked up from *Rim Malemute* and sent out to the hotel.

Grimes left the car, walked over the sidewalk to the big doorway, through the force field that prevented the atmosphere of the hotel from being tainted by the excellent fresh air outside. On a world such as Lorn there would have been some point to it, but on Ultimo it was merely a very expensive absurdity. He nodded to the gorgeously uniformed doorman who had saluted him as though he were at least the Federation's first space lord. He went to the huge desk behind which a half-dozen very pretty girls were chirping to each other like colorful inmates of an aviary. Eventually one of them condescended to notice him.

"Sir?"

"My name is Grimes. I am booked here."

"Would that be Commodore Grimes, sir?" asked the tall blonde, statuesque in her form-revealing trouser suit of crimson dermitex.

"Yes."

"There is a Carlottigram for you, sir. It came in only a few minutes ago." She handed Grimes the dark blue envelope.

What now? he wondered as he ran a fingernail along the seal fine. *What now?* The envelope tidily fell apart. He looked at the message it had contained.

From: Officer Commanding Rim Worlds Navy
To: Commodore Grimes, D.S.M., O.C., F.H.S.C., R.W.N.R.
Copies: c/o Rimrock House, Port Last, Ultimo
c/o Tug, Rim Malemute, Port Last, Ultimo
c/o Dock Office, Rim Runners, Port Last, Ultimo
Text: As and from date of origination you are to consider yourself called to Active Service, Rim Worlds Navy, Pay and Allowances as for Commodore First Class, Expenses as requisite. You are to cooperate with Police, Customs and other authorities in investigation of drug smuggling. Indefinite leave of absence from Rim Runners arranged.
(Signed) Kravitz

"Mphm," grunted Grimes thoughtfully. He could imagine what had been happening. High-up politicians must have been getting concerned about the general deterioration of Rim Worlds' morals, and some of them must have demanded that the Navy do something about the smuggling in of drugs. And Admiral Kravitz—Grimes could just picture him—must have said, "We'll put Commodore Grimes on the job. Anything at all off-beat is right up his alley." And if Grimes were successful in stopping the traffic the Navy would take the credit. If he made a mess of things, it would be pointed out that, after all, he was only a reserve officer, not Navy proper. On past occasions Sonya had worked with him—but that had been when the Federation and the Confederacy had been acting in concert. On this occasion they would not be. The majority of Federated Planets approved the permissive society. The Rim Worlds did not, repeat not.

Oh, well, thought Grimes, *I suppose I'd better do something about something. For a start, I'd better organize transport for myself. Billy Williams is a reserve commander, and* Rim Malemute *is rated as a naval auxiliary vessel. And the Navy has a yard here, at Port Last, and an armory. It's time I did some telephoning. It's just as well that the Admiralty will be footing the bills.*

A smartly uniformed boy took him up to his suite. Once there Grimes called *Rim Malemute,* by now hooked into the planetary telephone service, and told Williams to come out to see him as soon as possible. Then he spoke to Rim Runners' Port Last manager, telling him that he, Grimes, had been called to Active Service. He dictated a Priority Carlottigram to be sent to Admiral Kravitz, requesting the services of the *Malemute* and her personnel. He rang the O.I.C. Port Last Base, introducing himself and warning the officer that probably he would require some modifications made to the tug. He sent another Carlottigram, this one to Sonya, saying, *Involved in fun and games. See if you can get yourself asked to the party.* He caught Captain Dunbar at his office, and told him what was happening. Finally he rang the Port Last chief collector of customs.

"Grimes here. Commodore Grimes. I've been instructed to work with you people on this drug running business."

"Oh, yes, Commodore. The Navy told us that they were putting a senior officer on to it. Hang on a moment, will you? There's a friend of yours here would like a word with you."

A *friend?* thought Grimes. *If I had any friends on this world they wouldn't be in the customs department.*

But he recognized the face that appeared in the little screen of the telephone. It was Billinghurst, who said, "A very good day to you, Commodore. I suppose you came here over the *Rim Caribou* affair. I was here when it happened. There's been a conference of all the senior customs officers of the Rim Worlds. Yes, about this drug business." He laughed fatly. "I think you'll admit, now, that sending out circulars isn't quite good enough!"

Chapter 7

IN THE DAYS that followed, Grimes was busy. The modifications to *Rim Malemute*—mainly the fitting of weaponry—he left in Williams' capable hands, concerning himself with setting up some kind of an organization and with reading all the official reports that were made available to him. Pleshoff, he learned, had been very unlucky. In the vast majority of cases those who smoked dreamy weed functioned normally on awakening. He learned, too, that the drug was not one on which one became hooked, although those who had participated in a dream time, as it was called, wished to repeat the experience as soon as possible. But, as far as he could determine, the stuff was no more dangerous than alcohol, and its overall effects were far less damaging. Still, he had been ordered to help stamp out the traffic—and, as Sonya had said, there were far too many utterly unworthy people making far too big profits from it.

For much of the time he was having to work with Billinghurst who, even though Port Forlorn was his own bailiwick, had been put in general charge of the investigation by his Department. Grimes acquired a grudging respect for the man's capabilities although it was still impossible to like him. Billinghurst, however, insisted on treating Grimes as an old friend. His attitude was, we're both Lorners. We have to stand together against these Ultimo hicks.

He said, "We'll not be able to rely too much on the police, Commodore. They're like all policemen, everywhere. When it comes to dealing with members of the criminal classes they're quite efficient, but when they tangle with students, or spheres, they go all hysterical."

"Spheres?" asked Grimes.

"You should study the jargon. They call themselves spheres. They call people like us blocks. We block the spheres from rolling."

"And just how do the . . . er . . . spheres roll, Mr. Billinghurst?"

"Doing anything tonight, Commodore? There's a roll around at the Dominey Hall. You and I will have to wear false beards and dress the part; spheres come in all ages and sizes. Young Pahvani—his sister is in your office—will be with us. He's been growing his own beard so he can play the part of a sphere if necessary. He'll tell you what to wear, and all the rest of it."

Grimes changed into his sphere outfit in Pahvani's room, in the unpretentious hotel in which the young customs officer was living. He surveyed himself rather dubiously in the full-length mirror. Black leather shorts—but that part of it wasn't so bad, he was used to wearing shorts with uniform. Bare legs—well, at least he maintained a good tan. Ornate, metal-studded sandals, looking like the sort of footwear that Roman legionaries must have worn. A short shirt, worn outside the shorts, basically dark green but liberally decorated with improbable scarlet and orange blossoms. A string of glass beads, each one a different shade of blue, and each one perfectly spherical. And the beard . . . it matched the hair of his head perfectly, but that was all that could be said in its favour. It was not the sort of beard that Grimes would ever have grown. It was too long, too untidy, untrimmed, uncombed.

There was one consolation; Billinghurst, who did not have the build for this sort of rig, looked even worse than Grimes, his spindly legs offensively incongruous under the gross bulk of his body. Sub-Inspector Pahvani looked quite good. His beard suited him. He could have been an old-time Indian mystic.

It was only a short walk from the hotel to the Dominey Hall, which was situated in the Old Town suburb of Port Last, differing from the ancient sheet metal buildings around it only in size. It was a huge barn of a place with no pretentions to architectural style. Projected into the air above it, in huge, shimmering letters of blue fire, were the words:

TONITE! TONITE!
ROLL-AROUND
TONITE!

Already there were crowds converging on the hall—men, of all ages, dressed as Grimes and his companions were dressed; girls and women, shaven-headed, most of them, similarly attired although their shorts were much shorter and many of the shirts were practically transparent.

There were police, too, obvious in their blue and silver uniforms. One of them, when Grimes stopped to stare at the crowd, poked him quite painfully with his club, snarling, "Move along there, you bearded wonder! Move along!" Grimes decided to move along. Billinghurst chuckled and murmured, "You see what I mean about the police force, John."

"I see, Joe. And I feel it!"

They reached the door, where Pahvani paid the admission for all three of them. There were no seats in the hall. There was a platform in the centre of the floor, as yet unoccupied. The glaring lights overhead were red and green, blue and yellow. The air was hot and already heavy with the odour of perspiring and not overly clean humanity. Many of the women had already removed their shirts and a few of the men had done so.

"What band tonight, Francis?" asked Billinghurst casually.

"The Music of the Spheres, sir."

"Watch it!" snarled Billinghurst.

"The Music of the Spheres, Joe."

"Appropriate, I suppose," commented Grimes. He saw that a circle of flooring in the centre of the platform was sinking, was vanishing from sight. Some sort of elevator, he supposed. It would have been impossible for the bandsmen to struggle to their places through this crowd.

Yes, it was an elevator. It brought up the instrumentalists—three bearded men with electric guitars, three more with small drums, one seated at a piano, and an enormously fat blonde girl who was holding a microphone.

They started almost at once—the guitars snarling, the drums

thudding, the piano holding the tune together. The fat girl yelled into the microphone and her voice, vastly amplified, came at them from all corners of the hall.

> *"Driftin'*
> *"An' dreamin',*
> *"No lyin',*
> *"No schemin'*
> *"Just you, an' me,*
> *"An' he, an' she,*
> *"Just we,*
> *"Ain't yer gonna drift an' dream some time with me?"*

So it went on, for quite some time. Grimes was not enjoying himself much. He suspected that Billinghurst was not either. But young Pahvani was reveling in the music with its odd, broken rhythm—*like an inertial drive unit slightly on the blink,* thought Grimes nastily—as were most of the others in the crowd. But the real Roll-Around had not yet started.

When it did there was, at last, some rhythm in the music—unsubtle, compelling. As though stirred by a giant spoon the crowd began to move, clockwise, around the hall, marching in step to the insistent drums, stepping high, bringing feet thudding down on the reverberant floor. It was impossible not to join in, physically as well as psychologically. To the snarling guitars and growling drums they marched, to the amplified bass beat of the flogged piano, to the words that the fat woman was belting out in an almost baritone.

> *"Rolling free, rolling free!*
> *"Give a shock to the blocks—One, two, three!*
> *"Oh, we'll roll the bastards under*
> *"And we'll break them all asunder,*
> *"Rolling free, rolling free, rolling free!"*

Grimes was singing as loudly as anybody. So was Pahvani. Billinghurst was merely muttering the words, without enthusiasm.

Round, and round, and round again. Pahvani had got his shirt off somehow. Grimes, sweating profusely, would have liked to have done the same, but in this crush it was impossible. He saw that some of the women had, with fantastic agility, contrived to strip themselves stark naked.

> *"Over land, over sea, we go rolling, rolling free,*
> *"And we'll always go rolling along!*
> *"Over hill, over dale, you will see our dusty trail,*
> *"As we always go rolling along."*

Round, and round, and round again. Tramp, stamp, tramp, *stamp!* Overhead the lights were swinging to the percussive heat of the music.

> *"An all you blocks stop growlin',*
> *"Or this is what we'll do!*
> *"The spheres was made for rollin,*
> *"They'll roll right over you!"*

"I was hoping," gasped Billinghurst, contriving to whisper and pant simultaneously, "to pick something up here."

"That one looks quite nice," suggested Grimes, who had got his second wind. "A bit sweaty, but aren't we all?"

"No . . . not . . . *that!* Information."

"A rolling sphere gathers no moss," Grimes told him.

Round, and round, and round again. Tramp, tramp, tramp! Stamp, stamp, *stamp!*

> *"When the spheres come rolling in,*
> *"When the spheres come rolling in,*
> *"We're gonna be in that number*
> *"When the spheres come rolling in!"*

To Grimes' right there was a skinny, half-naked, almost-breastless girl who had been edging closer and closer to him with every circuit of the floor. He was beginning to wonder if a pick-up were intended, was trying to work out ways and means of achieving a painless brush-off. She just wasn't his type. And then he saw that a plump, copiously perspiring young man had joined her in this dance that was more like a march. He heard him whisper to her, "0200 hours at the Fitzroy Crossing. Pass it on!" His message delivered, he vanished into the mass of dancers.

Somehow the skinny girl had inserted herself between Grimes and the almost-exhausted Billinghurst. She was singing softly, in time to the music,

> *"When the weed comes dropping in,*
> *"When the weed comes dropping in,*
> *"Oh two hundred, Fitzroy Crossing,*
> *"When the weed comes dropping in!"*

The music changed, but she went on singing,

> *"Dreamy free, dreamy free,*
> *"Dreamy weed, dreamy weed, dreamy free . . ."*

She made a face at Billinghurst, flashed a smile at Grimes, and wriggled away through the crowd.

Round, and round, and round—but with every circuit edging closer to the exit.

> *"Oh, we'll roll, away up yonder!*
> *"Oh, we'll roll, away up yonder!*
> *"Oh, we'll roll, away up yonder!*
> *"When they roll away up yonder we'll he there!"*

And Billinghurst, getting his wind back, sang the final, "We'll be there!" with great emphasis.

⮜ Chapter 8 ⮞

BUT THEY ALMOST WEREN'T THERE.

There was a minor riot outside the Dominey Hall. Accounts as to its cause differed. One morning paper said that a crowd, singing, "We'll roll the bastards under!" had charged a group of policemen. The other paper said that the police had charged a small group of people from the Roll-Around who were going their ways quite peacefully.

Actually it had been Grimes' fault. Those noisy songs, with their primitive rhythm, had carried him back in time, to when he was a young and normally rowdy cadet in the Federation's Survey Service. He had remembered something that he and his shipmates had been fond of singing whenever there was a minion of the law within earshot. He had insisted on teaching the words to Billinghurst—who was not amused—to Pahvani—who was—and to a half-dozen young men and girls who were going the same way as themselves.

"There's a policeman on his beat,
"Over there, over there!
"There's a policeman on his beat,
"Over there!
"There's a policeman on his beat,
"I can smell his sweaty feet,
"There's a policeman on his beat,
"Over there!"

During the third, noisy rendition of this ditty a dozen policemen tried to silence the songsters. Punches were thrown. Stunguns were used, set so as to inflict the maximum pain without causing unconsciousness. A large body of revelers rushed to the aid of Grimes and his companions. Police air cars clattered overhead, dropping arrest meshes, wire nets that ignored the specially treated police uniforms but that clung to everything else in a tight grip. The air cars ranged over the street like seine net fishermen over a school of fish. Their catch, dangling under the aircraft, was hauled ignominiously to the station house. Grimes, Billinghurst, and Pahvani would have spent the night in cells had not Pahvani, who had been acting as liaison officer between police and customs, been recognized by the lieutenant in charge. He had the three Lorners hustled away from the other prisoners, ostensibly for interrogation. Shouts of sympathy and encouragement followed them.

As soon as he could safely do so Billinghurst snarled, "You almost ruined everything, Commodore!"

"When among spheres—roll!" replied the unrepentant Grimes.

"You, Lieutenant Whatever-Your-Name-Is," snapped Billinghurst to the police officer. "I am the chief collector of customs for Port Forlorn, in overall charge of this drug investigation. This is Commodore Grimes, of the Rim Worlds Navy, who's working with me." He glared at the commodore. "Or against me, to judge by tonight's little effort. Sub-Inspector Pahvani you already know."

"And what can I do for you, sir?"

"I want vehicles, and I want men. Armed men."

"And a map," contributed Grimes. "And all the geographical information you can give us." He waited for Billinghurst to say something, then added, "It seems that there's to be a drop at Fitzroy Crossing. At 0200 hours tomorrow."

"There's a wall map in the Captain's office," said the lieutenant. "Follow me, please."

The map was a large-scale topographical one, covering Port Last and the surrounding countryside to a distance of fifty kilometres from the City Centre. "The Fitzroy Crossing is not far from here," said the police officer, jabbing with his finger. "There's a bridge, as you see, both road and monorail. On the north side of the bridge there's Davidsham Village—with one senior constable who, by this time, will be tucked up warm and snug in his little bed." He laughed. "I was stationed there myself before I was promoted to sergeant. Nothing ever happens in Davidsham. Even so, I should hardly think that the drop will be to the north of the Crossing.

"Now, on the south side we have the wheatfields. And," his finger jabbed again, "*here* we have the racecourse. I hope you gentlemen can manage to be here for the Ultimo Cup Week—it's really something."

"Landing facilities?" asked Grimes, who was not at all interested in horses.

"You could set a cruiser down there, Commodore. And a couple of destroyers. No G.C.A. of course. Ha, ha."

"There probably will be," said Grimes. "A small beacon, mounted on a car. Mphm. Now, Mr. Billinghurst, if we go charging out there in police vehicles we'll scare off the reception committee—and whoever's making the delivery. I suggest that we land somewhere to the north of the racecourse, well away from the road, and make our way to the landing site on foot. We shall want a guide. Do any of your men know the district, Lieutenant?"

"I do, sir."

"Good. And have you any quiet cars? Inertial drive kicks up one helluva racket, especially on a still night like this."

"We have the blimps, sir. They have been developed especially for police use on this planet."

"They should do." And, Grimes thought, *Once again the airship comes back into service.* He said, "But I thought you had no really serious crime on Ultimo."

"There are gambling schools, sir, very often meeting out in the country. They play a game of chance, tossing two coins. When it comes to catching the gamblers red-handed we find the silent approach technique very useful. The blimps are propeller-driven, with almost noiseless electric motors."

"Make it blimps, then."

"Very good, sir. And now, if you'll excuse me, I'll ring the precinct captain and start getting things organized."

"Before you do, Lieutenant, is there a washroom handy? I'd like to get this artificial foliage off my face. I'd just hate to get it wound round a blimp's propeller."

≈ Chapter 9 ≈

AIRSHIPS had always fascinated Grimes. Now and again, on worlds lagging in technological development, and on planets whose people had a commonsense attitude towards unnecessary power consumption, he had been a passenger in such craft. The Shaara, for example, could build spaceships at least as good as anything built by man, but for atmospheric flights they favored lighter-than-air machines.

The blimps of the Ultimo police were well conceived, well designed, well constructed. They were semirigid ships rather than true blimps, however. They had heating coils inside their balloons to give the helium additional lift, and there was an arrangement of bands and nets whereby the lift could be reduced by compression of the gas. Water ballast was carried, but except in emergencies there would be no need for any valving of helium or dumping of ballast. Below the rigid spines were slung the gondolas, one to each ship, and each with a single pusher screw.

Grimes, Billinghurst, and Pahvani rode in the leading ship, the one piloted by the police lieutenant. With them were four constables. Grimes sat with the pilot in the little control cab at the fore end of the gondola, watching everything with interest. Mooring lines were cast off by the ground crew, but the ship still sat stolidly on its skids, although above the gondola the gas bags, enclosed in their sausage-shaped integument, were swaying and creaking. The lieutenant's hand went to a switch on the control panel and almost immediately there was the subdued hum of an electric motor. *Decompression?* wondered Grimes. But apart from the mechanical noise, which soon stopped, nothing at all seemed to be happening.

The lieutenant swore under his breath. Then he called back into the main cabin, "Excuse me, Mr. Billinghurst, how much do you weigh?"

"I . . . I haven't checked lately, Lieutenant."

"Then it's time you did!" muttered the young man.

There was a fresh sound, the splashing of water on to the concrete of the blimpyard. Now the ship was rising, smoothly, silently, up past the lighted windows of the police barracks, up, up, until, a checkered pattern of crisscrossing street lights, Port Last lay below her. Grimes poked his head out of an open side window, looked astern. One by one, great dark shapes, their black bulks in silhouette against the glow of the city lights, the other five airships were swimming upwards.

The lieutenant started his motor then. It was almost silent, and only a faint swishing sound came from the propeller. Slowly he brought the ship round to her heading, explaining, "We have to be careful how we handle these things. They're just a little flimsy." Gradually the lights of the city, of the scattered outer suburbs, drifted astern.

It was a fine night, clear, almost windless. The single moon of Ultimo, named Ceres, was hanging high in the black sky, the empty sky of the Rim Worlds. It was just past its full but did not give much light; satellites so large as to be almost sister planets are rare throughout the Galaxy. Nonetheless, the surface of the Fitzroy River reflected what little illumination there was, a faintly gleaming silver ribbon winding through formless masses of darkness. On the horizon was the dim cluster of yellow lights that was Davidsham.

Silently the squadron flew on, invisible from the ground now that it was clear of the glare from the city, keeping the river to starboard, the distant village fine on the starboard bow. Grimes borrowed the pilot's night glasses. He could see, now, the straight black line that cut the silver ribbon. The bridge . . . He looked more to his left, trying to pick out the racecourse, but without success.

"You'll not find it, sir," laughed the lieutenant, "unless you've eyes like a cat. But you see the horseshoe bend, just this side of the village?"

"Mphm. Yes."

"There's a field there that's been harvested. That's where we're landing."

"And then we get out and walk."

"Yes. Then we get out and walk."

The airship was losing altitude as the pilot applied negative dynamic lift. Grimes could make out features on the ground below now, as long as they were not too far distant. He could see the paleness of the fields that were yet to be harvested, the darkness of those where reaping had already taken place. Another electric motor started up, and from above came a faint creaking as the gas bags were compressed. The ground seemed very close now, and seemed to be rushing past at a fantastic speed. Grimes started to worry about tall trees and the like, but told himself that the lieutenant knew what he was doing. In any case, it would be unlikely that there would be any trees in the wheatlands to rob the precious grain of its nutriment.

The pilot snapped rapid orders to the other ships on his radio, then stopped the main motor, restarting it almost at once in reverse. The ground below slowly lost its retrograde progression relative to the ship, but was coming up to meet her as the buoyancy was squeezed out of her balloons. There was a dry crackling from under the gondola as the skids brushed the stubble. Then, with all motors stopped, she landed. Men jumped from the side doors, quickly and efficiently moored her with screw pegs.

"All ashore!" ordered the lieutenant cheerfully.

Grimes jumped down from the gondola to the ground, cursing to himself as the stubble scratched his bare calves and shins. He should have changed out of this absurd rig; getting rid of that insanitary beard had been a step in the right direction, but not far enough. It was fortunate that the correct footwear for a Roll-Around consisted of very heavy sandals. He was joined by Billinghurst and Pahvani. He stood with them to watch the other airships coming in. He wondered how those landing managed to avoid those already down, and was told by the lieutenant that on occasions such as this dim lights were shown on the tops of the gas bags.

There was a very cautious flashing of down-pointed, shielded torches. The lieutenant detailed a man to stay with each ship, then said to Grimes, "You and the other two had better stay close to me, Commodore. We'll walk to the racecourse from here, making as little noise as possible. Before we get there we'll spread out to surround the position—just in case there's anybody there. If there's not—some of us will wait in the Owners' Stand, some by the Saddling Paddock and the rest by the Tote. That'll give us a good coverage."

"And good odds?" asked Grimes.

He did not much enjoy the walk over the fields. There was enough moonlight to make the going not too difficult, but the sharp spiny stubble was drawing blood with almost every step. And the air, despite the lack of wind, was decidedly chilly. And *things* were rustling in the dry stalks. He had visions of venomous reptiles, insects or the like, and was only slightly reassured when his guide whispered to him that it was only cats—of Terran origin—hunting a small and harmless (apart from its appetite for grain) indigenous rodent.

Behind him, despite his bulk, Billinghurst was moving silently, as was Pahvani, and as far as noise was concerned the policemen might not have been there at all. Grimes murmured something complimentary to the lieutenant and was told that this was the Gaming Squad, used to creeping up on parties of gamblers. He asked if the fines collected from such desperate criminals sufficed to pay for the airships and other equipment, and was answered by a pained silence.

Whispered orders were passed back and the policemen spread out to surround the racecourse. Grimes could just hear the faint voices from the lieutenant's wrist radio as the members of his force reached their assigned positions. Then the order was given to advance, with caution. Ahead, rails glimmered whitely in the faint moonlight. Grimes, following the leader, ducked under them and on to the track. There were vague shapes in front of them, moving towards them—but it was only the men who had entered the course by the Owners' Stand and who were now on their way to the Tote.

They reported briefly to their officer that they had seen nobody, and that nothing larger than a cat had registered on their biodetectors.

Grimes looked at his watch. An hour to wait. Probably the receivers would not be here until just before the drop was due—assuming, of course, that this was the drop site.

He hoped that the benches in the stand would be padded.

They were—but the padding had long since lost any softness it had ever possessed.

❧ Chapter 10 ❧

IT WAS A LONG WAIT, in the cold and the dark, while the little moon, now past the meridian, slowly slipped down the starless sky. The policemen—and, to an only slightly lesser degree, Billinghurst and Pahvani—were used to vigils beside yet-to-be-sprung traps; Grimes was not. He wanted to be *doing* something. Finding that the lieutenant had a pass key that fitted the lock of the toilets under the stand he borrowed it, although what he really wanted was a smoke. His battered, stinking pipe was very comforting after he got it going and he was in no hurry to rejoin his comrades. Then, looking at his watch, he decided that he had better. The time was 0155 hours.

As soon as he was back outside he heard the noise. Something was approaching from the direction of the city, something in the sky. The irregular stuttering of a small inertial drive unit was unmistakable. He looked up, in the direction from which the sound was coming, but saw nothing. But it was not likely that the smugglers' aircraft would be showing running lights.

It was visible at last, but only when it dropped to a landing in the centre of the ellipsoid formed by the track. It just sat there, but nobody came out of it. Its crew was waiting, just as the police were waiting.

Grimes looked at his watch again. 0201 . . . 0202 . . .

"Here it comes!" whispered the lieutenant.

Here it came.

At first it was no more than a barely audible, irritable muttering drifting down from the zenith. It became louder, but not much louder. The machine that finally dropped into sight was no more than a toy, no more than a model of a ship's boat. It might have accommodated the infant child of midget parents who had bred true, but nobody larger. But it could carry quite a few kilos of dreamy weed.

The police had their stunguns ready, trained on the smugglers' aircraft and on the robot, which were covered from three points— from the Owners' Stand, from the Saddling Paddock, from the Totalizator. The lieutenant had stationed his men well; whoever had come to pick up the consignment would be inside the effective range of the weapons, but each police party would be just outside the range of the guns of the others.

Somebody was coming out of the aircraft at last, walking slowly and cautiously towards the grounded robot spaceboat, hunkering down on the grass beside the thing.

"Fire," said the lieutenant in a conversational tone of voice, speaking into his wrist transceiver.

The air was alive with the vicious buzzing of the stunguns. The smuggler was frozen in his squatting posture, paralyzed, unable to stir so much as a finger. But the robot moved. Its drive unit hammered shockingly and unrhythmically and it shot straight upwards. Beams from hastily switched on police searchlights swept the sky like the antennae of disturbed insects—then caught it, held it, a tiny bright star in a firmament that had never known any stars. At least four machine rifles were hammering, and an incandescent tracer arched upwards with deceptive slowness. The lieutenant had drawn his laser pistol and the purple beam slashed across the darkness, power wasting and desperate. Some hapless night-flying creature caught by the sword of lethal light exploded smokily.

It might have been the machine rifles that found their mark, it might have been the laser pistol. Nobody ever knew. But the broken beat of the inertial drive ceased abruptly and the robot was falling, faster and faster, still held in the searchlight beams. It hit the ground almost exactly at the point of its initial landing.

It hit the ground—and, "Down!" shouted somebody. "Get down!"

It hit the ground, and where it struck an instantaneous flower of intolerable flame burgeoned, followed by a *crack!* that sounded as though the very planet were being split in two. The blast hit the grandstand, which went over like a capsizing windjammer—but, freakishly, the structure remained intact. Had it not done so there would have been serious injuries, at least to those upon it. Dazed, deafened, Grimes struggled to his feet, crept cautiously along the back of the bench upon which he had been sitting. Lights were flashing as men helped each other from the wreckage.

Billinghurst got clear of the stand before Grimes. He had found a torch and was running clumsily across the grass to the still smoking crater. The commodore followed him. He gagged as the customs officer's light fell on the tangle of broken limbs and spilled entrails that had been the smuggler who had come out from the air car. The head was missing. After a cursory glance Billinghurst ignored the dead man, carried on to the wrecked vehicle, which had been blown on to its side. He shone his light in through the open door. The girl inside appeared to be uninjured, but she was very still. A strand of hair glowed greenly across her white face. Her hair? Grimes could see the beam of the torch reflected from her shaven, polished scalp. The fat man stooped, lifted the hank of green fibre, twisted it between his thick fingers, sniffed it.

"Dreamy weed," he said flatly. Then, "The poor little bitch got what she came for. It's the very last thing that she did get." He shifted the beam of his torch and Grimes saw that the girl's body, below the waist, was no more than a crimson pulp.

The commodore looked away hastily, up to the empty blackness of the sky. Somewhere up there was a ship. Somewhere up there was somebody who had killed, ruthlessly, to destroy all evidence that could be used to stop his profitable racket.

"Losing your neutrality, Commodore Grimes?" asked Billinghurst.

~ Chapter 11 ~

PETER FELLINI, STUDENT.
Aged 19.75 Years, Local, 18.25 Years, Standard.
Inga Telfer, Artist.
Aged 25.50 Years, Local, 23.05 Years, Standard.

The identification of the bodies had presented no problems. Ultimo is one of those worlds where everybody is fingerprinted, where a record is made of everybody's retinal patterns and where coded information, including allergies and blood group, is tattooed in everybody's armpits.

The two victims were known to have been Blossom People. Fellini had been brilliant in his studies. Inga Telfer's swirling abstracts had been in great demand and had fetched good prices. Their deaths had been remarkably pointless; they had suffered the misfortune of being at the wrong place at the wrong time.

The identification of the ship that had made the drop was also easy. Immediately on return to Port Last Grimes and Billinghurst had gone to Aero-Space Control. The duty officer had at first been uncooperative—as far as he was concerned here were two spheres, albeit beardless ones, invading his office. But once credentials were produced he was very helpful.

Yes, the Tanagerine tramp *Ditmar* was at present in orbit about Ultimo, having signalled her intention of landing at first light. Her master, one Captain Reneck, did not like pilotage in the dark. He had brought his ship into Port Last on quite a few occasions, but always during daylight hours. Yes, *Ditmar* was on a regular run between Ultimo and Eblis. She was chartered to bring shipments of minerals from the so-called Hell Planet, and to carry assorted foodstuffs back to the holiday resort in Inferno Valley. And where was she relative to Port Last, to the Fitzroy Crossing, shortly after 0200 hours? To judge by the elements of her orbit, constantly checked by ground radar, she must have been on the other side of the planet.

"Mphm," grunted Grimes doubtfully on learning this. At the time of the attempted escape of the robot, at the time of its destruction, line of sight communication between it and the mother ship would have been impossible. But there was no reason why *Ditmar* should not have left at least one relay station in orbit. If this were so, then she ran to a line of highly sophisticated electronic gadgetry not usually, if ever, found aboard a merchant vessel, a tramp freighter at that.

And Tanager . . .

It was one of the older colonies, having been settled during the Second Expansion. It was a Federated Planet, but rather peculiarly situated, being only world with a human population in a sector of space that had been colonised by the Shaara. There was a Federation Survey Service base on Tanager, a base that could be of vital strategic importance should Man and Shaara ever fall out again. The Tanagerines knew this, and every now and again talked of the economic advantages that would accrue if their world became part of the Shaara Empire—so the Federation went to great pains to try to keep them happy. And for many years now the foreign policy of the Rim Worlds Confederacy had been geared to that of the Interstellar Federation.

Don't let's be nasty to the Tanagerines, thought Grimes, *but if* Ditmar's *Master had broken Rim Worlds laws he must expect some nastiness.*

Grimes and Billinghurst were out at the spaceport at dawn to see *Ditmar* come in. The battered tramp dropped down carefully, with a caution that would not have been amiss in a vessel ten times her size. Although she was from one of the other Rim Worlds she was a foreign ship, so officials from port health, immigration, and customs were waiting for her. The customs officers were, in fact, out in force.

Ditmar bumbled in hesitantly, at last hovering a few feet over the beacons that marked her berth. Her inertial drive unit was a particularly noisy one. When at last it was stopped the short-lived silence was deafening—and broken by the tinny crash as the ship's tripedal landing gear hit the concrete. There was a long delay, and then the after-airlock door opened slowly and the ramp extruded. Billinghurst pushed himself to the head of the group of waiting officials, tramped heavily aboard. Grimes followed him.

Ditmar's mate, a burly, swarthy young man in shabby uniform, received them. He mumbled, "You'll find all the papers in the purser's office, as usual."

"Take us to the Captain," snapped Billinghurst.

"This . . . This isn't usual."

"I know it's not usual." Billinghurst turned to give orders to his officers. "Spread out through the ship. Living quarters, control room, engineroom, everywhere."

"But, look, mister. We're in from Eblis. *Eblis.* That's one of *your* bloody Rim Worlds, isn't it?"

"Take us to the captain," repeated Billinghurst.

"Oh, all right, all right. You'll have to use the stairway, though; the elevator's on the blink."

Grimes and Billinghurst followed the officer up the internal spiral staircase. It didn't worry Grimes much, but by the time they got up to the captain's flat the fat man was soaked with sweat, his face purple. The mate knocked at the open door, said, "Two customs officers to see you, sir." Grimes glared at him. Admittedly his uniform, which he had put on for the occasion, was similar to Billinghurst's, but if this young oaf could not distinguish between different cap badges it was time that he started to learn.

"Come in, come in." Captain Reneck looked up from his desk. "The cargo manifest and the store sheets are in the purser's office. I don't have them here."

"I am the chief collector of customs at Port Forlorn," began Billinghurst.

"Haven't you got your ports mixed?"

"And I am in overall charge of an investigation. This gentleman with me is Commodore Grimes, of the Rim Worlds Navy."

"Indeed?" Captain Reneck's bushy black eyebrows, the only noticeable feature of his pale, smooth face, lifted. "Indeed? A customs officer *and* a commodore of the Rim Worlds Navy. Please be seated, gentlemen."

"Captain Reneck," said Billinghurst, "I'll waste no words. At approximately 0200 hours this morning, Port Last time, a powered container of dreamy weed—a powered, booby-trapped container of dreamy weed—made a landing at the Fitzroy Crossing."

"So? But at 0200 hours this morning I was not over Port Last, or the Fitzroy Crossing."

"Does your ship carry probes?" demanded Grimes. "Robot probes, remote-controlled? Is she fitted with the equipment to launch and guide and recover such probes?"

Reneck grinned. His ugly teeth showed yellow in his white face. "As a matter of fact she does, and she is. Tanager is a poor world and cannot afford specialized survey craft. All of our merchant ships—all of them tramps like this vessel—are so fitted as to be able to carry out survey work if required."

"Two people were killed this morning," said Billinghurst. "A young man and a young woman."

"I am very sorry to hear that," said Reneck, neither looking nor sounding sorry.

"What do you know about the container of dreamy weed that was dropped?" blustered Billinghurst.

"What should I know?"

"It must have come from your ship," said Grimes.

"How could it have done so? I was nowhere near the scene of the alleged smuggling."

"And murder."

"Murder, Commodore? Strong word. How could I, a law-abiding shipmaster, be implicated in murder? A naval officer like yourself, maybe, but not a merchant spaceman." He sighed. "Murder . . ."

"Who's paying you?" snapped Billinghurst suddenly.

"The TSSL, of course. The Tanager State Shipping Line." He grinned with another display of discolored teeth. "Between ourselves, gentlemen, they could pay much better than they do."

"So something a little extra, over and above your salary, tax free," suggested Grimes.

"Really, Commodore . . . you wouldn't suggest that, surely."

"How many robot probes do you carry?"

"Three. You will find that number shown on my store sheets, and you will find that number in the launching bay."

Billinghurst lumbered to his feet. "Let's get out of here, Commodore Grimes." He turned to Reneck. "My men are taking the ship apart. If they find so much as one strand of dreamy weed, may all the Odd Gods of the Galaxy help you. Nobody else will."

∽ Chapter 12 ∾

THE ODD GODS OF THE GALAXY did not have their peace disturbed. *Ditmar* was a clean ship—clean, that is, from a custom officer's viewpoint, although not necessarily from that of a spaceman. She was far scruffier than the generality of tramps. Painted surfaces were not only crying out for a fresh coat of paint but for the washing of what had been applied sometime in the distant past. The ghosts of every meal that had been cooked in her galley since her maiden voyage still haunted her accommodation; the dirt of unnumbered worlds was trodden into her deck coverings.

But she was *clean*. There was not even any pornography in her officers' cabins. Nobody had a drop of liquor or a fraction of an ounce of tobacco over and above the permitted duty-free allowance. Her papers were in impeccable order. She was so clean, in fact, as to invite suspicion.

From the viewpoint of the authorities it was unfortunate that she was of Tanagerine registry. Had she been under any other flag it would have been possible to clap some of her personnel into jail on some trumped-up charge or another. A fight in a bar, started by a provocateur . . . The imprisonment of all participants and, if necessary, innocent bystanders. The administration of "blabberjuice" in food or water . . . Oh, it *could* have been done, but little, otherwise unimportant Tanager was a pet of the United Planets Organization. Billinghurst and the Port Last chief of police would have liked to have done it regardless, but orders were given to them to handle *Ditmar* with kid gloves before they could give orders of their own to their undercover agents.

Bugs, of course, were planted in the places of entertainment and refreshment frequented by *Ditmar*'s crew. They picked up nothing of interest. The Tanagerines seemed to be enthusiastic amateur meteorologists to a man and discussed practically nothing except the weather. Bugs were planted aboard the ship herself—a customs searcher, of course, knows all the good hiding places aboard a vessel. The only sound that they recorded was a continuous, monotonous *whirrup, whirrup, whirrup*.

All that could be done was to delay the ship's departure on her return voyage to Eblis. At Grimes' suggestion the Port Last Department of Navigation surveyor checked up on *Ditmar*'s life-saving equipment. One of her lifeboats was not airtight, and was condemned, and the stores in one of the others were long overdue for renewal. The faulty boat could have been repaired, of course, but the surveyor's word was law. And, oddly enough, lifeboat stores were practically unprocurable at Port Last and would have to be shipped from Port Forlorn. So it went on. The master of a merchant vessel is peculiarly helpless when the authorities of any port take a dislike to him.

Meanwhile, *Rim Malemute*, her armament fitted, was almost ready for space. Grimes was taking her to Eblis. Officially he was visiting that world to inspect port facilities, as the Rim Worlds Navy was thinking of opening a base there. Billinghurst wanted to come with him, saying that he wished to make arrangements for the setting up of a customs office at Inferno Valley. Grimes told him that this would look too suspicious, both of them leaving Port Last in the same ship. This was true, of course, but the real reason for the commodore's refusal to cooperate was that he did not wish to share the cramped quarters aboard the little *Malemute* with a man of Billinghurst's bulk. Alternative transport was available, although not at once. TG Clippers' cruise liner, *Macedon*, was due shortly at Port Last, and Inferno Valley was her next port of call.

"Eblis," said Billy Williams, when he and Grimes were discussing matters prior to departure. "I've never been there, Skipper. What's it like?"

"Its name suits it, Commander Williams, very well indeed. It's mainly red desert, with rocks eroded by wind and sand into all sorts of fantastic shapes. It has volcanoes—big ones and little ones—like other worlds have trees. The atmosphere is practically straight sulphur dioxide. The inhabitants look like the demons of Terran mythology—horns and tails and all—but they're quite harmless, actually. Earth tremors are more common than showers of rain on normal worlds. The odd part about it is that as long as you keep away from the really dangerous areas you're as safe there as you are anywhere in the Galaxy. The planet is like a huge amusement park with all sorts of hair-raising rides; you get the illusion of risk with no real risk at all. That's why it's such a popular holiday resort."

"Inferno Valley . . . isn't that owned by a retired space captain?"

"Yes. Captain Clavering. He came out to the Rim quite some years ago, owner/master of a ship called *Sally Ann*. She was—of all things!—an obsolescent Beta Class liner. Far too big and expensive in upkeep for a little, one-ship company. He'd been getting by somehow, just making ends meet, but when I met him he'd come to the end of the line. I was able to put a charter in his way; the Rim Worlds Universities were sending a scientific expedition to Eblis and we, Rim Runners, hadn't any ships either handy or suitable.

"So he went to Eblis. He and his wife, he told me later, quite fell in love with the valley in which the expedition set up its main camp. There are these quite fertile valleys all over the planet, actually, not too hot and the air quite breathable if you don't mind the occasional whiff of brimstone. But what gave him the idea of a holiday resort was a remark that he'd heard somebody—it may have been me—make: 'Anybody who comes out to the Rim to earn a living would go to hell for a pastime!'

"That was his start. He had people living in tents at first, with quite primitive facilities. He used his own *Sally Ann* to carry holidaymakers from the Rim Worlds to this amusement park inferno. Then TG Clippers, when they started cruising, got into the act. Then the Waverley Royal Mail. Even the Dog Star Line. And Clavering never looked back.

"His old *Sally Ann* is still there, I believe. He doesn't use her himself—he's too busy being a resort manager. And I don't think he's sufficiently sentimental to hang on to her for old time's sake—it's just that the market for secondhand ships of that size is a very limited one."

Grimes carefully filled and lit his pipe. When it was going he said, "I rather liked Clavering, and I'm pleased that he's done so well. I only hope that he's not mixed up in this dreamy weed business."

"I don't see why he should be, Skipper. He must be coining money in his legitimate business."

"Nobody is so rich that he can't use a few extra credits—especially when they're tax free. Too, very few people from the Inner Worlds would consider the possession, use, or even peddling of a drug like dreamy weed a crime. I'm not at all sure that I do myself. It's when the racketeers get mixed up in the trade that it's bad. It's when two young people get blown into messy tatters by the bastards they're working for."

"And it's when people make a religion out of what is, after all, just a pleasure," said Williams, who had his puritanical moments.

"If all religions had been like that," Grimes told him, "they'd have done far less harm over the ages."

Williams was not convinced.

~ Chapter 13 ~

WILLIAMS PILED ON THE LUMES all the way from Ultimo to Eblis. Grimes was in a hurry; he wanted to get there before Reneck's principal was fully advised as to what had been happening at Port Last. *Ditmar*, of course, could not legally use her deep space radio while in port, so any Carlottigrams originated by her master would have to be handled by the Port Last G.P.O. And the Port Last post office telegraphists were on strike. Grimes did not know how much Billinghurst had to do with this, but suspected that it was plenty. The cause of the stoppage had been the quite justifiable dismissal of a shop steward for insolence. Who was Billinghurst's undercover man—the shop steward or the overseer who had fired him? Perhaps they were both customs agents. Perhaps—but this was unlikely—the strike was coincidental.

The more Grimes thought about it the more sure he became that Ebbs was the source of dreamy weed shipments to the other Rim Worlds. Inferno Valley was not a Rim Worlds' port of entry, therefore there was no customs office on Eblis. In theory any ship bound for Eblis was supposed first to land on one of the worlds from which she could be entered inwards. *Ditmar*, for example, when she had first come out to the Rim had arrived at Port Edgell, on Thule, with a cargo of cheese from Elsinore. She had then loaded general cargo for Inferno Valley, and thereafter had shuttled between Eblis and the other Rim Worlds, mainly Ultimo, with regularity. As a foreign ship she had been liable to customs inspection every time in, but as she was not from a foreign port the inspection, until this last time, had been a mere formality. And as her contraband was always dropped before she entered the atmosphere even a rigorous going over, as on this last occasion, would have revealed nothing.

Insofar as Eblis was concerned, you could land a battle fleet unobserved as long as it was well away from any of the widely spaced centres of population. There was Aero-Space Control, of a sort, but it had no radar and talked only when talked to.

The dreamy weed was grown and processed on quite a few of the Inner Worlds, the Federated Planets. As far as the Federation was concerned anybody could smoke the stuff who wished. It was regarded as a rather superior marijuana, the use of which had been legalized, for centuries, on practically every planet of the Federation. If any world government, inside or outside the Federation, cared to make its use illegal it was up to that government to enforce its own laws. The Federation couldn't care less, one way or the other, as long as it received whatever taxes and duties were due.

Grimes had his plan of campaign, such as it was, mapped out. He would land at Inferno Valley. He would tell Clavering, who had been made, some time ago, planetary commissioner on Eblis, that he was conducting a survey prior to the possible establishment of a naval base on the Hell Planet. He would use *Rim Malemute* for his excursions—she was a handy little brute and suitable for work inside an atmosphere—or, if necessary, he would hire air or ground transport. If Clavering were among the smugglers he would be liable to betray himself; if he were not he would afford every possible assistance to Grimes. The owner of a pleasure resort would profit rather than otherwise by the presence of recreation-hungry naval officers and ratings.

A subjective week after her lift-off from Port Last *Rim Malemute* was in orbit about Eblis. She circled the fiery world, her people gazing down in wonderment at the cloud envelope of black and brown and yellow smoke that, now and again, was riven by hurricane-force winds to uncover the fire-belching volcanoes on the surface. The night side was even more spectacular, in a frightening sort of way, than the day side. It seemed that life as we know it could not possibly survive in that caldron of incandescent gases.

Williams asked wryly, "Sure we've come to the right place, Skipper?"

"Quite sure, Commander Williams," Grimes told him. "Call Aero-Space Control, will you?"

"*Rim Malemute* to Aero-Space Control. *Rim Malemute* to Aero-Space Control. Do you read me? Over."

After the seventh call the Inferno Valley duty officer came through.

"Eblis Aero-Space Control here. Vessel calling, say again your name, please. Over."

"*Rim Malemute*. Repeat, *Rim Malemute*. Over."

"*Rim Malemute*? Aren't you the tug? Over."

Grimes took the microphone from Williams. "This is the Rim Worlds Naval Auxiliary *Rim Malemute*, requesting berthing instructions. Over."

"Have you been here before, *Rim Malemute*? The spaceport's at the eastern end of Inferno Valley." There was a long pause. "Latitude one three degrees, four five minutes north. Longitude oh, oh, oh degrees east *or* west. We reckon from the Inferno Valley meridian. The time here is 1149 hours, coming up for Mean Noon. Equation of Time zero as near as dammit. That any help to you? Over."

"Yes, thank you. Now, if you'll switch your beacon on . . ."

"Give me time, man, give me time. Nobody was expecting you. On now."

"*Rim Malemute* to Aero-Space Control. Beacon signal coming in. We are almost directly above you. Have you any further instructions for us? Over."

"Yes. Listen carefully. Berth Number One—that's the pad furthest to the east—has *Sally Ann*. She's our ship. Berth Number Three—that's the one furthest to the west—has Trans-Galactic Clipper's cruise liner *Sobraon*. You should be able to get into Berth Number Two. I suppose you *are* the tug and not some dirty great battle cruiser with the same name? Over."

"Yes, we are the tug. Over."

"Watch the wind, *Rim Malemute*. In the Valley it is calm, but overhead we have west at seventy knots. Over."

"Thank you, Aero-Space Control. We are coming in. Over."

"We're coming in," repeated Williams. He cut the inertial drive and the little ship fell like a stone, applied vertical thrust to slow her descent only when her hull began to heat as she plunged into the outer atmosphere. He explained. "Have ter make it fast, Skipper. With all these bloody winds at umpteen knots we'll be all over the place unless we get downstairs in a hurry."

"Mphm," grunted Grimes, who had almost swallowed his pipe.

They were into the first cloud layer now, rolling black vapor slashed by dazzling lightning flashes. They were through it, and dropping through a stratum of clear air—and through turbulence that shook the tug like a terrier shaking a rat. Below them a cloudscape of fantastic castles in black and brown and yellow rushed up to meet them. Williams had no eye for the scenery; he was watching his radar altimeter and the shifting blip of the beacon signal. The ship shuddered as he applied lateral thrust to compensate for the fast drift to leeward.

They were under the cloud ceiling at last. Inferno Valley lay almost directly beneath them, a rift in the red rocks, a canyon, but one formed by geological upheaval than by erosion. To the north and to the south towered the volcanoes, classical cones, the smoke and steam from their craters streaming out almost horizontally. At the eastern end of the valley stood a great monolith, a fantastic needle of rock. The spaceport must be to the west of this formation.

Lower dropped *Rim Malemute* and lower, with Williams fighting to keep her in position relative to her landing site, with his officers calling out instrument readings in voices that, for all their studied calmness, betrayed fear. The nearer of the volcanoes emitted a great burst of smoke and incandescent molten matter and the dull *boom!* was felt and heard through the insulated hull. A shift of wind blew the *Malemute* away from the valley, at right angles to the rift—and once again she shuddered and complained in every member as lateral thrust drove her back on to her planned line of descent.

Then, quite suddenly, she was below the rim of the canyon.

Below, deep, deep below, there was a silvery ribbon of water, the dark green of vegetation, the pastel colours of buildings. Below, looking from this altitude to be right alongside each other, were the metallic spires that were *Sally Ann* and *Sobraon*.

But there was room enough, and in this windless valley maneuvering was easy. Neatly, with no fuss and bother at all, Williams dropped *Rim Malemute* between the other two ships, in the exact centre of the triangle of brilliant red lights that marked his berth.

~ Chapter 14 ~

"**AERO-SPACE CONTROL** to *Rim Malemute*. Leave your inertial drive on Stand-By until your stays have been rigged and set up. Over."

"Stays?" asked Williams. *"Stays?"*

"Yes," Grimes told him. "Stays. Lengths of heavy wire rope, with bottle screws and springs. Necessary in case there's an exceptionally heavy earth tremor."

"And I suppose if there is one, before I've been tethered down, I have to get upstairs in a hurry."

"That's the drill."

Grimes, Williams, and *Rim Malemute*'s officers looked out through the control room viewports. A man had come on to the apron, dressed in white shirt and shorts that were like a uniform, although they were not. He was giving orders to a squad of about a dozen natives. These looked as though they should have been carrying the traditional pitchforks instead of spikes and spanners. In appearance they were more like kangaroos than dinosaurs—but scaled kangaroos, with almost human heads. Almost human—their goatlike horns and the gleaming yellow tusks protruding from their mouths made it quite obvious that they were not. They wore no clothing, and their reptilian hides ranged in colour from a brown that was almost black to a yellow that was almost white. Three of them climbed up the *Malemute*'s smooth sides, using the sucker pads on their hands and feet, carrying the ends of the wire cables after them with their prehensile tails. Swiftly, efficiently, they shackled these ends to conveniently situated towing lugs. Then they scampered down to join their mates on the ground. The stays were stretched, set up taut. From the transceiver came the voice of Aero-Space Control, "*Rim Malemute*, you may shut down your engines and leave your ship at your discretion."

Grimes had been using binoculars to study the face of the man who had directed mooring operations. "Yes," he said at last. "That's Clavering. He's put on weight, lost that lean and hungry look, but he hasn't changed much."

He led the way down from the control room, followed by Williams. He was first down the still extruding ramp. Clavering came to meet him, threw him a sort of half salute. "Welcome to Inferno Valley, sir," he said not very enthusiastically. Then recognition dawned on his face. "Why, it's Commodore Grimes!" Then, with an attractive grin, "I'd have expected you to be in command of something bigger than *this!*"

"I'm not in command of *Rim Malemute*," Grimes told him. "I'm just a passenger. This is Commander Williams, Captain Clavering, who had the dubious pleasure of bringing me here."

There was handshaking all round, then Clavering said, "Come to my office, and tell me what I can do for you."

Grimes and Williams looked about them curiously during their walk from the spaceport. It should have been gloomy in the deep ravine, with the murky yellow sky no more than a thin ribbon directly overhead, but it was not. The canyon walls—red, orange, banded with gold and silver—seemed to collect all the light that there was and to throw it back. Here and there on the sheer cliff faces vegetation had taken hold, static explosions of emerald green in which glowed sparks of blue and violet. Similar bushes grew from the firm, red sand that was the valley floor.

Two natives passed them, bound on some errand. They waved to Clavering, grinning hideously. He waved back. He said, "You get used to their horrendous appearance. They're good, cheerful workers. They like to be paid in kind rather than cash, in all the little luxuries that cannot be produced on this planet. Candy, they love. And they've acquired the taste for the more sickly varieties of lolly-water. Which reminds me—you are in from Port Last, aren't you? Did you see anything there of *Ditmar?* She brings my supplies in, and takes back the chemicals produced at my plant on the Bitter Sea, not far from here."

"I'm afraid she's going to be late," said Grimes. "She ran into all sorts of trouble with the Department of Navigation. Safety equipment was in a shocking state."

"I'm not surprised, Commodore. But you can't blame Captain Reneck entirely. His owners seem to be a bunch of cheeseparing bastards. Still, he might have let me know he was delayed."

"You can't blame him for that, either," said Grimes. "The post office boys on Ultimo are playing up."

"Oh. And I shall have a strike on *my* hands if I try to pay my devils in cash instead of kind. Still, if worst comes to the worst I shall be able to do a deal of some kind with *Sobraon's* catering officer. Now, this is the Devil's Stewpot that we're coming to. Between ourselves the story that the waters have marvelous rejuvenating properties is just a story—but a good soak and a good sweat never did anybody any harm."

The heat from the huge, circular, natural pool was almost overpowering even though they passed several meters from its rim. The people in it were not engaged in any violent physical activities. They just lay there in the shallows, only their faces, the breasts of the women and the protuberant bellies of both sexes appearing above the steaming surface.

"There are times," said Clavering, "when I wish, most sincerely, that *young* people could afford to come on these TG cruises."

"That one's not bad," said Grimes, nodding towards a woman who had just emerged from the water and who was walking slowly towards the next pool.

"Not bad at all," agreed Clavering. "She's old Silas Demarest's secretary, quote and unquote. You know—Demarest, the boss cocky of Galactic Metals. Now, this next bath, the Purgatorial Plunge, is not natural. Quite a few of my . . . er . . . customers give it a miss after they've sweated all the sin out of themselves. But it's amazing the extremes of cold that the human body can take after it's been well and truly heated."

"Mphm." Grimes watched with appreciation as the naked girl dived into the clear, blue-green, icy water and propelled herself to the other side with swift, smooth strokes.

"And after the Purgatorial Pool you have the choice of swimming back to the Lucifer Arms—that's my hotel—in the River Styx, or walking along its banks. Or, if you're really keen, jogging along its banks. The temperature of the Styx is normal, by the way, what we refer to as pee-warm."

The girl, Grimes saw, was swimming back, which was rather a pity, especially as she was a fast swimmer.

"Just around this bend you'll see the Lucifer Arms and the other buildings. Or 'inflations.' I had an architect staying here who tried to convince me that 'inflation' was a more correct word. This is earthquake country—this is an earthquake planet—and any normal construction wouldn't last long."

And there, on the north bank of the Styx, was the Lucifer Arms. Imagine an igloo. Color it. Put another one beside it and color that, being careful to avoid a clash. Put another one beside the first two. Put one on top of the triangular base. And so on, and so on, and so on . . .

Dome upon dome upon dome, and every one a bubble of tough, stiffened plastic, its double skin filled with pressurized gas. It was as though some giant had emptied tons of detergent into the sluggishly flowing river and then stirred it violently so that the iridescent froth was flung up on to the bank. The edifice should have been an architectural nightmare—but, fantastically, it was not. Those soft-hued demispheres should have been in violent contrast to the harsh, red, towering walls of rock on either side of the rift valley—but in some weird way they matched the awe-inspiring scenery, enhanced it, even as did the ghost gums that Clavering had planted along the banks of the river, raised from saplings brought all the way from distant Earth. (But the management of TG Clippers, of course, had probably charged only nominal freight on them.)

The ex-captain led the way to the hotel's main entrance, through the force screen into the air-conditioned interior. It was only then that Grimes realized how sulphurous the hot air outside had been. It was a matter of contrasts. After the atmosphere of *Rim Malemute*, far too small a ship for any sort of voyage, even the natural air of Eblis had smelled and tasted good.

Clavering took Grimes and Williams to his office, itself a dome within the assemblage of domes. The three men seated themselves in very comfortable chairs that, too, were inflated plastic. A grinning devil, his scales highly polished, came to take their orders for drinks. Save for a tendency to hiss his sibilants his Galactic-English was very good.

Clavering sat back in his chair, which molded itself to the contours of his body. Save for his almost white hair he had aged very little since Grimes had seen him last—how many years ago? He was as smooth and as smug as a well-fed cat—in that, he had changed.

After the native had brought the tray of drinks, in tall glasses misted with condensation, he asked, "And now, Commodore Grimes, just what can I do for you?"

Chapter 15

"I THOUGHT YOU KNEW," said Grimes innocently.

"How the hell could I know?" countered Clavering. "I'm not a telepath."

"Didn't you get the letter, Captain?"

"What letter?"

"From the Admiralty."

"No. Was there supposed to be one?"

"Yes. I was shown a copy. But the mail services are getting worse than ever these days. The original will probably be in the mail brought by *Ditmar*, when she finally lifts off Ultimo."

"And just what is this famous letter about?"

"The base."

"What base?"

"Sorry, I was forgetting that you don't know. I'll put you in the picture. The Space Lords of the Confederacy, with a surplus of the taxpayers' money to play with, have decided that it might be a good idea to establish a naval base on Eblis."

"What in the Universe for? It would have no strategic value whatsoever."

"Just what I tried to tell them, Captain Clavering. But ours not to reason why, and all the rest of it."

"I suppose not." Then, "I'm glad to see you again after all these years, Commodore Grimes, but you might have let me know that you were coming. An ETA would have been useful. As it was, you just appeared out of nowhere and, between ourselves, young Lingard who's supposed to be in charge of Aero-Space Control isn't the brightest. He should have told you to stay in orbit until sunset or dawn, when there's always an hour or so of flat calm. He should have asked you if you wanted a pilot in. I do the piloting, as a matter of fact. I go up in one of *Sally Ann*'s boats and board outside the atmosphere."

"Keeping your hand in . . ."

"Yes." Then Clavering returned to his original complaint. "I know that the Navy always does as it damn well pleases, but an ETA would have been useful."

"You'd have got one," lied Grimes, with a warning glance at Williams, "if the Carlotti gear hadn't gone on the blink. I'm afraid that the poor little *Malemute*'s showing her age. If it's not one thing broken down, it's something else." Then, as a SOP to *Rim Malemute*'s skipper, "Of course, she's very hardworking."

"But this base, Commodore," said Clavering. "The idea's crazy. Eblis is absolutely unsuitable. There's a shortage of suitable landing sites, and the climate is quite impossible, and . . ."

"You made out all right, Captain." Grimes smiled. "And look at the trade that *you'd* be doing, as owner of the only recreational facilities on the planet."

"And look at the headaches I'd be getting! The natives spoiled by the big money, or its equivalent, splashed around by a spendthrift government. Brawls in my bars . . ."

"Come, come. I'll not say that our officers and ratings are fit and proper personnel for a Sunday school treat—but they are quite well behaved."

"They may be, Commodore, but are the tourists? I can just imagine it. Mr. Silas Q. Moneybags is staying here with his latest blonde secretary. A handsome young lieutenant, all prettied up in his go-ashore uniform, does a line with the blonde. Mr. Moneybags, after a drink or three too many, takes a swing at the lieutenant. Oh, no, Commodore. That sort of carry on is not for me if I can possibly avoid it."

"Mphm. I see your point, Captain. But I was sent here to make a survey, and a survey I have to make. To begin with, I suppose you have Eblis pretty well charted?"

"Of course. I was a navigator before I became a hotel manager. Suppose you and Commander Williams come with me to my map room."

"Thank you," said Grimes.

Chapter 16

THE MAP ROOM was in another of the plastic bubbles. It contained a mounted globe, a huge table upon which flat charts could be spread, a projector, and a wall screen.

Clavering went first to the sphere, sent it spinning with a touch of a finger, slowed its rotation with another touch, stopped it. "Here," he said, "is Inferno Valley. A typical rift formation, as you will already have realized. To the north we have the Great Smokies, and to the south the Erebus Alps. North of the Smokies you find the Painted Badlands—and the sandstorms there can strip even one of my armor-plated devils to bare bones in minutes. South of the Alps there's mountain range after mountain range—the Devil's Torches, the Infernal Beacons, the Lucifers. . . ." He rotated the globe twenty degrees. "To the west of Inferno Valley there's the Bitter Sea. Our chemical extraction plant is there. Even if the tourist trade died on us—and it shows no signs of ever doing so—we'd get by. And to the north we still have the Smokies, and to the south the Torches, the Beacons and the Lucifers." The globe rotated again. "And here there's a quite remarkable formation, stretching practically from pole to pole. The Satan's Barrier Range. Worth visiting just to see the fantastic rock formations, such as the Valley of the Winds and the Devil's Organ Pipes. When conditions are right you'd swear that some supernatural being was playing a gigantic organ—a little light music for Walpurgis Nacht.

"West of the Barrier there're the Fire Forests and the Burning Pits.

The Fire Forests are . . . clumps of young, new volcanoes, and their number grows every year. The Burning Pits are just what their name implies. Further west still, and we begin to pick up the foothills of the east-west ranges—the Great Smokies, the Torches and all the rest of them. There are, of course, valleys like this one, but smaller. There's nothing that could accommodate a base, with its barracks and workshops and repair yards."

"Mphm. Quite a world you have here, Captain Clavering. I suppose you run tours from Inferno Valley for your customers?"

"Yes. Unluckily the Organ Pipes Tour was a couple of days ago, and my air cars are now undergoing maintenance. You will appreciate that the abrasive winds make this essential after every outing. I'll not be running another tour until *Macedon* comes in. *Sobraon*, of course, lifts off first thing tomorrow morning."

"Taking her out?"

"Yes. Her master's newly appointed and would like to see the Eblis pilotage both ways, arrival and departure, before he makes a stab at it himself. And now you really must excuse me. There's always something to be done around a place like this. But you'll have dinner with us tonight, of course. Sally will be wanting to see you again. You too, of course, Commander Williams, are invited." He paused. "Come to that, why don't you and all *Rim Malemute*'s people stay at the Lucifer Arms? I've plenty of accommodation."

"And I'm entitled to reasonable expenses," said Grimes.

Clavering laughed. "I should have made it clear that I want you as nonpaying guests. But I'm not averse to taking the government's money."

"And I'm not averse," said Grimes, "to having some small percentage of what I pay in income tax and customs duty spent of my comfort."

And had a flicker of apprehension showed on Clavering's face when Grimes used the words "customs duty"?

Damn it all! thought the Commodore. *I'm neither a policeman nor a customs officer.*

Then he remembered young Pleshoff, whose career had been ruined, and Peter Fellini and Inga Telfer, who were dead.

Chapter 17

THE DINING ROOM of the Lucifer Arms was yet another plastic hemisphere, but a huge one. Clavering and Sally, his wife, had their table in the exact centre of the circular floor. It was on a low dais, raised above the level of the others so that the ex-captain could oversee everything that was going on. Not that his supervision was really necessary; his devils, looking more than ever like refugees from a black humor cartoon in their stiff white shirts, black ties and black jackets, were superbly trained, attentive without being obtrusive. And there were three human headwaiters, circulating slowly among the diners, watching everything.

Grimes enjoyed his meal. For almost as long as he could remember he had liked highly spiced, exotic foods, and every item on the menu was either deviled or flambèed—or both. Williams, who preferred good plain cooking, was not so happy—but to judge by his rate of consumption he found nothing at all wrong with the excellent chilled hock. Neither did Captain Gillings of *Sobraon* who, with his chief officer Mr. Tait, made up the party. So far he was showing no effects, but—*Any moment now!* thought Grimes. And—*It's none of my business.*

Yet when Gillings put his hand firmly over the top of his empty glass, saying, "I lift off at dawn," Clavering persuaded him to accept a refill, remarking, "I'm taking your ship up for you, Captain. As long as *I'm* on the ball in the morning." Mrs. Clavering, a tall, very attractive blonde, looked as though she were about to interfere,

70

especially when she saw that her husband's glass was also being refilled. She asked Grimes rather pointedly, "What are the rules about drinking in the Navy, Commodore?"

Grimes said, "It all depends. Sometimes you know that you can afford to relax, at other times you know that you can't. Mphm. But drink is not the major problem. You can always tell if a man is under the influence. With other drugs you can't tell if a man's judgment has been seriously impaired. Not so long ago—in my civilian capacity as Rim Runners' Chief Astronautical Superintendent—I had to try to sort out a most distressing business. The third officer of one of our ships had been among those involved in a dreamy weed orgy. The next morning, apparently quite normal, he was testing the gear prior to his vessel's lift off from Port Last. The inertial drive, which had been given a trial run by the engineers after maintenance, was on Stand-By. The officer noticed this—and thought it would be a good idea to take the ship up, himself, for a joyride."

"And what happened?" asked Sally Clavering.

"General alarm and despondency. Luckily there was nobody hurt, and no serious damage. The young man, I'm afraid, will have to serve a jail term—the Rim Confederacy takes a very dim view of drugs in general. And his spacegoing career is ruined."

"If your government," said the TG Clipper Captain, "weren't so many years behind the times that sort of thing wouldn't happen. In the Federated Planets we accept the consciousness-expanding drugs. We know that there are some people affected more strongly than others, just as there are some people more strongly affected by alcohol than others. On Austral—my home planet—a smoker has to take out a license and is subjected to various physical and psychological tests. He knows just what effect marihuana, dreamy weed or anything similar will have on him, and regulates his activities accordingly. In my own case, for example, I know that if I were enjoying a pipe instead of Captain Clavering's excellent wine I should be, no more than two standard hours after the last inhalation, perfectly capable of taking my ship into or out of any spaceport in the Galaxy—more capable, in fact, than if I had not smoked. This third officer of yours was unlucky."

"You can say that again, Captain Gillings," agreed Grimes. He looked casually around the table. Sally Clavering was showing interest in the conversation. So was Mr. Tait, Gillings' chief officer. Williams looked as though he were interested only in the wine. And Clavering was suddenly taking great interest in a party of rather noisy revellers six tables away.

He said, "I hope those people don't carry on like that aboard your ship, Captain Gillings."

"Not all the time, Captain Clavering. They're usually quite quiet at breakfast."

"Black coffee and two aspirins, I suppose. Talking of coffee, shall we adjourn to the Grotto? I've some rather decent Altairian Dragon's Blood that we could have as a liqueur."

He got up from the table and, as soon as his wife and his guests were on their feet, led the way from the dining room, pausing slightly now and again to exchange salutations with the people at the other tables.

A short tunnel led to the Grotto, its walls coloured and shaped in the likenesses of rough granite. Grimes had to put his hand out to convince himself that they were not granite and was almost surprised by the soft spongy texture under his fingers. In the Grotto itself amazingly realistic stalactites hung from the high ceiling, and stalagmites grew upwards from the floor. But if there should be an earth tremor there would be no danger of frail human flesh being crushed and torn by falling masses of jagged limestone. Should, by any chance, a stalactite be shaken adrift from its overhead anchorage it would float gently downwards like the plastic balloon that in actuality, it was. Nonetheless, the effect was convincing, enhanced by the dim green and blue lighting, by musical trickling of water somewhere in the background.

They sat around a table that could have been a slab of waterworn limestone, on surprisingly comfortable chairs simulating the same material. A devil brought a tray with coffee pot and cups, another devil the teardrop decanter and the slim glasses. Sally Clavering poured the coffee, her husband the liqueur.

"Here's to crime," said Grimes, raising his glass.

"An odd toast, Commodore," said Clavering.

"A very old one, Captain."

"It all depends," said Captain Gillings, whose speech was becoming a little slurred, "on what you mean by crime."

"Too," said Williams, who enjoyed an occasional philosophical argument, "one has to distinguish between crime and sin."

"Smuggling, for example," said Grimes, "is a crime, but is it a sin?"

"Depends on what you smuggle," said Gillings.

"Too right," agreed Williams.

"Take gambling," said Clavering a little desperately. "It's a crime—I mean, it's classed as a crime—when the state doesn't get its rake-off. But as long as the government gets its cut it's perfectly all right."

"I 'member once on Elshinore . . ." began Gillings. "Ticket in Shtate Lottery . . . only sheventeen off million creditsh . . ."

"I always think," said Grimes, "that the people of these very agricultural planets, like Elsinore and Ultimo, need such outlets as gambling and, perhaps, drug-taking. The essentially rural worlds tend to be more—sinful, shall we say?—more sinful than the heavily industrialized ones."

"Who shaid gambling wash a shin, Commodore?" asked Gillings.

"It's only a sin," said Clavering thoughtfully, "if somebody else, somebody apart from the gambler himself, is hurt. That can be said about most crimes, so-called."

"Take forgery," contributed Williams. (*Blast you!* thought Grimes. *Why must you go changing the subject?*) "Take forgery. S'pose I print a million Ten Credit notes. S'pose they're all perfect. Undetectable. I win. But who loses?"

"I'll go into partnership with you, C'mander Williamsh," said Gillings. "When d' we shtart?"

"Time we started getting back to the ship, sir," said Mr. Tait, looking pointedly at his watch.

"A nightcap, Captain Gillings?" asked Clavering.

"Thank you, Captain Clavering. I will take jusht one li'l hair o' the dog thash bitin' me. After all, it'sh a long worm that hash no turning. Thank you. Thank you. Your very good health, shir. An' yoursh,

Mishess Clavering. An' yoursh, Commodore Grimesh. An' yoursh, Commander Williamsh. An' . . . an' . . . Shorry, Mishter Tait. Glash's empty. Musta 'vaporated. Very dry climate here. Very dry . . ."

Somehow Tait got his captain out of the Grotto. Mrs. Clavering looked at her husband angrily. "You know he can't take it. That Dragon's Blood on top of what he had before and with dinner." She looked at Grimes. "I'm sorry, Commodore. But this sort of thing makes me angry."

"It's not as though he were taking his ship up himself," said Clavering.

"It makes no difference. As *you* were always telling me, before you came ashore, the master is *always* responsible for his ship. You should have known better than to encourage him."

"He'll be all right in the morning, Sally." He yawned. "Time I was getting some shut-eye myself. And I'm sure that you and Commander Williams must be tired, Commodore. I'll show you to your rooms."

"Thank you, Captain. Oh, I'd rather like to see you take *Sobraon* up tomorrow. Both of us would, in fact. Do you think you could have us called in time?"

"Surely. You can come along for the ride, in fact. I put her in orbit, then my boat will pick us up and bring us back. I'll tell the devil in charge of your level to call you in good time. What do you want with your morning trays? Tea? Coffee? Or whatever?"

"Coffee," said Grimes and "Tea," said Williams.

Clavering took them to a lift shaft that was one of the very few really rigid structural members in the hotel, accompanied them to their levels, and then took them to their rooms. Williams, who was not quite sober, looked at the inside of his hemispherical sleeping compartment and said that he wanted Eskimo Nell to keep his bed warm. Clavering told him that the devils who looked after the bedrooms were female devils. Williams said that, on second thoughts, he would prefer to sleep alone. He vanished through the circular doorway.

Grimes said goodnight to Clavering then went into his own bedroom. It looked to be very comfortable, with an inflated bed and matching chair, a shower and toilet recess and—the only solid furnishing—a refrigerator. Suddenly he felt thirsty. He looked in the refrigerator, found fruit and several bottles of mineral water, together with plastic tumblers. He opened one of the bottles, poured himself a drink. But he only half-finished it. It was deliciously cold but, after the first few swallows, its flavor was . . . wrong. The water from the tap in the shower recess was lukewarm and tasted of sulphur, but it was better. Grimes drank copiously—the dinner had been conducive to thirst—then undressed and got into the soft, resilient bed.

No sooner had his head hit the pillow than there was an earth tremor, not severe but quite noticeable. He grinned to himself and muttered, "I don't need rocking." Nor did he.

Chapter 18

LIKE MOST MEN who are or who have been in active command Grimes possessed a built-in alarm clock. This woke him promptly at 0500 hours Local, the time at which the domestic devil was supposed to be calling him, with coffee. Although Grimes had awakened he was in a rather confused state and it took him many seconds to work out where he was and what he was supposed to be doing. He was on Eblis. He was shut up in a pneumatic plastic igloo. He was supposed to be aboard *Sobraon* before she lifted off at 0600 hours. He wanted his coffee. Even when there had been no night before the morning after he wanted his coffee to start the day with. He thought about coffee the way that it should be—hot as hell, black as sin and strong as the devil. Talking about devils—where the hell was the lazy devil who should have called him?

Grimes found a bell push among the inflated padding that backed the bed. He pushed it. He pushed it again. He pushed it a third time. Eventually the pluglike door opened and the chambermaid, if you could call her that, came in. The white frilly cap looked utterly absurd perched on top of her horns. She asked in a well-modulated voice, with only the merest hint of croak or hiss, "You rang, sir?"

"No. My physiotherapist told me that I should exercise my right thumb more."

"My apologies for the intrusion, sir." She turned to go. The long claws of her kangaroolike feet indented the padded floor.

"Wait. I was joking. Word was left for me to be called at five, with coffee. It is now 0515."

"Nobody told me, sir. Do you wish coffee?"

"Yes, please."

"Black, sir, or white? With sugar or without? Or with mintsweet, or lemonsweet, or honey? And do you wish toast, sir, or a hot roll? With butter, or with one or more of our delicious preserves? Or with butter and preserves?"

"Just coffee. In a pot. A big one. Better bring a cup as well. Sugar. No milk. Nothing to eat."

"Are you sure that you would not care for the full breakfast, sir? Fruit, a variety of cereals, eggs to order, ham or bacon or sausages. . . ."

"No!" He softened this to "No, thank you." After all, the demon-girl was doing her best. "Just coffee. Oh, and you might look in the room next door to see if Commander Williams is up. He wanted tea, I think."

Grimes showered hastily, depilated, then dressed. While he was doing this latter the coffee arrived. It was good coffee. After he had finished his first cup he thought he had better see how Williams was getting on.

The tray, with its teapot and accessories, was on the commander's bedside table. The commander was still in the bed. He was snoring loudly and unmusically.

"Commander Williams!" said Grimes. "Commander Williams!" snapped Grimes. "Commander Williams!" roared Grimes.

In any Service it is an unwritten law that an officer must not be touched in any way to awaken him—even when the toucher is superior in rank to the touchee. Grimes knew this—but he wanted Williams on his feet, *now*. He took hold of the other man's muscular shoulder, shook it. Williams interrupted his snoring briefly and that was all. Grimes hammered on the headboard of Williams' bed—but it, like everything else except the refrigerator, was pneumatically resilient, emitted no more than a soft, slapping sound.

Grimes thought of hammering the refrigerator door with something hard and heavy and had his right shoe half off before he thought of a better idea. Presumably this cold box, like the one in his room, would contain a few bottles of mineral water.

It did. There were six bottles, and five of them were empty, put back after they were finished by Williams, who had a small ship man's necessary tidiness. Grimes pulled the seal of the sixth bottle, inverted it over the commander's head. The icy fluid gurgled out, splashed over hair and face and bare chest and shoulders.

Williams' eyes opened. He said, slowly and distinctly, "Mr. Timmins, you will fix the thermostat *at once*. This is a ship, Mr. Timmins, a *ship*-not an orbital home for superannuated polar bears. I want her warm as a busty blonde's bottom, not cold as the Commodore's heart."

"Williams, wake up, damn you!"

"Brragh."

It was hopeless. And Williams' sleep was far deeper than could be accounted for by the previous night's drinking. He had taken nothing like as much as Captain Gillings—and, presumably, *he* was up. Those bottles of mineral water, only one of which Grimes had no more than tasted, five of which Williams had quaffed . . .

But who . . ?

And why. . . ?

Grimes looked at his watch. If he hurried he would get to the spaceport before *Sobraon* lifted. He tried to hurry, but considerable local knowledge was required to find a quick way out of the vast honeycomb that the Lucifer Arms resembled. At last he was clear of the building and running along the path of coarse red sand beside the Styx. It was dark still, it would be some time before Inferno Valley received the benefit of the rising sun. But there was light enough from the luminescent lichenous growths that grew, here and there, on the granite cliffs. Past the Purgatorial Pool he ran, past the Devil's Stewpot, blundering through the white, acrid fog that, at this hour of the morning, shrouded its surface.

And there were the ships at last—Clavering's *Sally Ann* in the background, dwarfed by the towering Devil's Phallus, and *Sobraon*, hiding with her bulk the little *Rim Malemute*. The TG Clipper's atmosphere running lights were on, and at the very tip of her

needle-pointed stem an intensely bright red light was winking, the
signal that she was ready for lift-off. Loud in the morning calm was
the irritable warming-up mumble of her inertial drive. Well clear of
her vaned landing gear the mooring gang—the unmooring gang—
was standing in little groups. The last airlock door was shut, the
boarding ramp in.

The note of the liner's inertial drive deepened, became
throbbingly insistent. A siren howled eerily. Then she was lifting,
slowly, carefully. She was lifting, and her drive sounded like the
hammers of hell as it dragged her massive tonnage up to the distant
ribbon of yellow that was the sky.

She lifted—then suddenly checked, but there was no change in
the beat of her engines, no diminution of the volume of noise. Yet
she hung there, motionless, and those on the ground, human and
native, started to run along the valley toward Grimes.

There was a sound like that of a breaking fiddle string—a fiddle
string inches in diameter plucked to destruction by a giant, a ship-sized
giant, a ship. . . . *Sobraon*, suddenly freed, surged upwards, and astern
of her the broken ends of the mooring cable that had fouled one of her
vanes lashed out like whips, striking sparks from the granite rocks.

And *Rim Malemute*, whose mooring wire it was that had been
snagged, teetered for long seconds on two feet of her tripedal landing
gear, teetered—and toppled.

"Cor!" muttered somebody. "They haven't half made a mess of
the poor little bitch."

Grimes looked at him. It was Rim *Malemute*'s shipkeeping officer,
who had turned out to watch the big TG Clipper's lift-off.

The commodore said, "You're a witness. Come with me to the
control tower and we'll slap a complaint on the duty controller's desk
before he has time to think of suing us for having our lines too close
to *Sobraon*'s stern vanes."

"But he can't, sir. The port captain himself saw the moorings set
up."

"Port Captains," Grimes told him, "are like the kings in olden
days. They can do no wrong."

Chapter 19

THE CONTROL TOWER was a shack on stilts and had little in the way of electronic equipment—just a normal space-time transceiver, a Carlotti transceiver and, logically enough for this planet, a seismograph. The duty Aero-Space Control officer was little more than a boy, and a badly frightened boy at that. He looked around with a start as Grimes and the *Malemute*'s third engineer burst in. He said, in a shaken voice, "Did you see that, sir? Did you see that?"

"Too right I saw it!" Grimes told him. "Stick a piece of paper in your typewriter and take this down. Ready? 'I, John Grimes, Commodore, Rim Worlds Naval Reserve, Senior Officer of the Rim Worlds Navy on Eblis, hereby lodge a complaint, as follows.' Got all that? 'At 0600 hours this morning'—put the date in, will you?—'the cruise liner *Sobraon*, under the pilotage of Captain Clavering, Port Captain, Inferno Valley, fouled the moorings of the Rim Worlds' Naval Auxiliary Vessel *Rim Malemute*, as a result of which *Rim Malemute* sustained severe damage, the extent of which has yet to be determined. I, Commodore John Grimes, hold the Inferno Valley Port Authorities responsible for this accident.' That's all. Give it to me, and I'll sign it. Take copies and let me have three."

"But, sir, it was an accident. I saw it too. When *Sobraon*'s vane fouled Rim *Malemute*'s moorings, Captain Clavering had to keep on going. The ship was off-balance. If he'd tried to land there'd have been a shocking disaster."

"I *said* it was an accident," stated Grimes. "But that has no bearing at all on the question of legal liability. Somebody will have to pay for the repairs to the *Malemute*. I suppose that it will be Lloyd's, as usual."

But was it an accident? Grimes asked himself. This *Sobraon* was practically a sister ship to Clavering's own *Sally Ann*, his last space-going command. Too, Clavering had piloted *Sobraon* inwards. He would know the second/foot/tons developed by her inertial drive. As port captain he would know, too, the breaking strain of *Rim Malemute*'s moorings. His motive? Plain enough. He didn't want Grimes ranging far and wide over the surface of Eblis, ostensibly conducting a survey. Deliberately, knowing Gillings' weakness, he had got the TG Clipper's master drunk the night before lift-off. And Gillings, knowing that he was morally as well as legally to blame for the alleged accident, would tend to back up Clavering in any story that did not show him and his pilot in a bad light. After all, insofar as his owners were concerned *he* was there, and *they* were not.

Just then Clavering came through on the transceiver. His face, in the little screen, was surprisingly calm. Behind him, Gillings seemed to have aged years in as many minutes. "*Sobraon* to Eblis Aero-Space Control . . . I don't think we sustained any damage, but I'm putting the ship in orbit until we're sure. Expect me when you see me. Over."

"Commodore Grimes is here, sir."

"Put him on, will you? Good morning, Commodore. I'm afraid we damaged your *Malemute*. I saw her come a clanger in the rear vision screen. I'm sorry about that."

"So am I," Grimes said.

"I'm Lloyd's Agent on Eblis. I'll survey *Malemute* as soon as I get back."

"That's uncommonly decent of you," said Grimes.

"Don't take it so hard, Commodore. Excuse me, please. I've some pilotage to do. Over and out."

"Mphm," grunted Grimes. After this unsatisfactory conversational exchange he could continue with his thoughts. There was the failure, the deliberate failure, he was sure, to have Grimes and Williams called so that they could be in *Sobraon*'s control room during lift-off. There were the bottles of drugged mineral water—very tempting after a thirst-inducing meal—in the bedroom refrigerators. Of course, he did not know that the mineral water had been drugged, but it certainly looked that way. He should have kept a sample—but what good would that have been? On this world there were no police, no forensic laboratories. Clavering was the law—such as it was.

Clavering came back on the NST transceiver. "In orbit," he announced. "The chief officer's making an inspection now. Is Commodore Grimes still with you?"

"Grimes here."

"For your report, Commodore, the wind caught us just as we were lifting."

"There wasn't any wind, Captain Clavering. I saw the whole thing happen."

"Oh, there wouldn't be any wind at ground level. But there are some odd eddies in the higher levels of the canyon."

"As low as only one hundred meters up?"

"Yes."

And you're the expert on this bloody world, thought Grimes. *Your word'd be better than mine if I tried to raise any kind of a stink.*

"For the remainder of your stay on Eblis," went on Clavering, "you and your people must stay free of charge at my hotel. I cannot help feeling that I'm to blame for what happened."

Too right you are, thought Grimes.

"We'll talk things over as soon as I get back."

We'll do just that, thought Grimes.

"I'll be seeing you, then."

"I'll be seeing you, Captain Clavering," said Grimes, trying to inject the slightest touch of menace into his voice. If he got Clavering worried he might start making mistakes.

And—*Damn it all,* thought Grimes, *I'm not a policeman!*

He said to the duty officer, "Ring the hotel, please, and see if Commander Williams is available."

Commander Williams, it seemed, was not. When he finally did wake up, thought Grimes, he'd be sorry that he hadn't stayed asleep. He loved his little *Malemute* as other men loved a woman.

Chapter 20

LATE IN THE MORNING Williams broke surface. When he heard what had happened to his ship he snapped from a muzzy semiconsciousness to a state of energetic alertness with amazing rapidity. As soon as he was dressed he hurried to the spaceport to assess the damage.

Grimes waited for him in the spacious lounge of the Lucifer Arms that now, after the cruise liner's departure, was almost deserted. Sally Clavering found him there. She sat down, facing him over the small table with its coffee service, said. "I heard what happened, Commodore."

"You probably heard it happen," said Grimes, who was in a bad mood. "There was quite a crash."

"But Ian's such a *good* shiphandler."

Grimes relented slightly. He had always found it hard to speak unkindly to really attractive women. He said, "The best of us have our off days. And, sooner or later, accidents just have to happen."

"Do you think it *was* an accident?" she asked.

"Mphm," grunted Grimes noncommittally.

She said, "I'm worried, Commodore. I've a feeling—it's more than just a feeling—that Ian's got himself into some sort of trouble. Over the past year or so he's . . . changed. I've asked him, more than once, what it is, but he just laughs it off."

"Money trouble?" asked Grimes.

She laughed. "That's the least of our worries. I was, as you know, *Sally Ann*'s Purser—and now that I'm ashore, I carry on pursering. I keep the books for the hotel and all the rest of it. I hope you don't think that I'm boasting when I say that we're doing *very* nicely."

"Income tax?"

"No. Really, Commodore, we have it made. Eblis is one of the Rim Worlds, and legally speaking is part of the Confederacy, but *we*, *Sally Ann*'s crew, were the first settlers, the only permanent settlers. How did our lawyer put it? 'You're *of*, but not *in*, the Confederacy.' Sooner or later the Grand Council of the Confederacy will get around to passing laws to bring us in properly, so we have to pay taxes, and duty on everything we import. What's holding up such legislation is the squabbling over which of the Rim Worlds shall take us under its wing—Lorn or Faraway, Ultimo or Thule. Another complicating factor, which we shall drag in if we have to, is that *Sally Ann*, still in commission, is under Federation registration, and all of us, *Sally Ann*'s original crew, are still Federation citizens."

"Complicated," admitted Grimes.

"Yes, isn't it? Of course, if the Navy decides that it *must* have a base here there's not much that we can do about it." She smiled. "But we have reduced rates at the hotel for legislators. That should help."

"You shouldn't have told me that."

"Everybody knows. Everybody knows, too, that a holiday here would be impossibly expensive if our profits were eaten away by taxes. Our guests from the Rim Worlds aren't in the same financial brackets as those in the cruise liners, from the Federation's planets. The next cruise ship in will be *Macedon*. While she's still here Ian will be taking *Sally Ann* to Ultimo to pick up a large party of Rim Worlders. A religious convention, as a matter of fact."

"Odd," commented Grimes. "This is hardly the sort of world to inspire the fear of hell fire."

"It is in parts, Commodore, make no mistake about that. But these people who're coming don't belong to any of the old religions. They're members of some new cult or faith or whatever. What do they call themselves? The Gateway? Something like that."

"All religions are gateways, I suppose, or make out that they're gateways—gateways to . . . something." He tried to steer the conversation back on to its original track. "With all this trade I can't see how you or Captain Clavering have anything to worry about."

"That's it, Commodore. We shouldn't have any worries. But Ian's been . . . odd lately. Forgive me for suggesting it, but I thought that you, as a fellow shipmaster, might be able to pull him out of it. He'll tell you things that he wouldn't tell me."

Is there a marriage guidance counsellor in the house? thought Grimes. He said, "Just a phase, probably. All marriages pass through them. There are times when Sonya—you must meet her some time—when Sonya and I are hardly on speaking terms. But we get over it." *Another woman?* he asked himself. *Or . . . ?*

She read his thoughts, partially at least. She said, "It's not another woman. He has his opportunities, running a resort like this. He may have taken an occasional opportunity. But his . . . his secrecy is worse between ships, at times like this when the hotel is empty. There's something on his mind. He hardly slept at all last night, and when he did sleep he was muttering to himself. And it wasn't a woman's name, either. It was, I think, just technicalities. 'Thrust' came into it. And 'breaking strain'."

"Mphm. Just a technician's nightmare. I get 'em myself sometimes." He remembered the dream that Williams must have experienced when he, Grimes, tried in vain to awaken him. "So do other people. Oh, by the way, do you bottle your own mineral water?"

She looked surprised at the abrupt change of subject, then said, "Yes. As a matter of fact we do. We have a small plant on the bank of the river, the only river, running into the Bitter Sea. Its water's not quite as rich in assorted chemicals as the Sea itself. Rather an acquired taste, actually, although it's supposed to have all sorts of medicinal qualities. The tourists drink it religiously. We import soft drinks too—but they're mainly for the devils, who enjoy anything as long as it's really sweet."

"I had some of your own mineral water last night, when I turned in. I thought it tasted a bit . . . odd."

"It most certainly does, Commodore. I never touch it myself. But the bottling plant is one of Ian's hobbies." She lapsed into a short, brooding silence. "If ever a man *should* be happy, it's him."

"Men are unwise and curiously planned," quoted Grimes.

"You can say that again, Commodore. But here comes your Commander Williams. He looks as though *he* has real worries. I'll leave you to him."

Williams dropped into the chair vacated by Sally Clavering, so heavily that Grimes feared that he would burst it. He said, "She's had it. She's really had it, Skipper. The inertial drive unit sheared its holding-down bolts. The Mannschenn Drive looks like one of those mobile sculptures—an' about as much bloody use! Even the boats are in a mess—the inertial drive units again. The work boat is the least badly damaged."

"Radio gear?"

"We can fix the NST transceiver, I think, but not the Carlotti. We haven't the spares. But the *Malemute* herself . . . we have to get her sitting up properly before we can start any major repairs, an' there's no heavy lifting gear on the bloody planet. We could do it by using a tug—but *Rim Malemute* is the only tug we have in commission—*had* in commission—on the whole bloody Rim. Oh, yes, there's *Rim Husky*, but she's been laid up for so long that she's just part of the Port Edgell scenery—an' at her best she couldn't pull a soldier off her sisters!"

"We can ask Captain Clavering to hook on to the *Malemute* when he takes his *Sally Ann* out."

"Yes, we can, I suppose. He's *very* good at towing, isn't he? Ha, ha! An' when'll that be, Skipper?"

"Not until *Macedon*'s arrived here. Mphm. I doubt if he'll come at it. Too much chance of damaging *Macedon*."

"He didn't mind damaging *Sobraon*. Although I did hear, from that young puppy in Aero-Space Control, that she got away with no worse than a few scratches an' some dented fairing. Clavering's on his way back down from orbit now, an' Captain Gillings, the pride of TG Clippers, is on *his* way rejoicing. What a pair! What a bloody pair! He an' Clavering. . . ."

"You weren't too bright yourself this morning."

Williams grinned ruefully. "No, I wasn't, was I? Do you know what I think it was?" He obviously did not expect that his story would be believed. "I had one helluva thirst when I turned in, and all that was in the 'fridge was a half-dozen bottles of lolly-water. It tasted like it'd been drunk before, but it was cold and wet. You know, Skipper, I think it must have gone bad."

"You could be right," said Grimes, "although not in the way you mean."

⇜ Chapter 21 ⇝

CLAVERING CAME IN FROM ORBIT. As soon as his boat had landed he sought out Grimes. He said, "I'm afraid I made a mess of your *Rim Malemute*."

"You did just that, Captain Clavering. I take it you've seen my letter on the subject?"

"I have, Commodore. Don't you think it was rather unnecessary?"

"No. I represent the Rim Worlds Navy, and when one of their ships is damaged I have to make sure that the person responsible, or his insurance company, foots the bill for repairs."

Clavering grinned without mirth. "I suppose you read the copy of Inferno Valley Port Regulations I had put aboard your *Malemute*? One of the rules is that anybody who lands on this planet does so at his own risk. But we're both of us spacemen, Commodore. Suppose you enjoy your holiday here, and let the lawyers argue about who pays whom for what." His grin was friendly now. "I'm sure that you and Commander Williams will join me in a drink to show that there's no hard feelings."

"Smoke the pipe of peace," said Grimes.

Clavering looked at him, hard, but Grimes kept his face expressionless, thinking, *I shouldn't mind betting that he could produce a pipe of dreamy weed if it were called for.*

A devil brought cold drinks. The commodore sipped his, then said, "I'm not sure that I should be having this. And I'm sure that

Williams should lay off the grog after his effort last night. We both of us slept in. Of course, if we'd been called on time . . ."

Clavering flushed—guiltily? He said, "I seem to be doing nothing else but apologize. It was my fault. I should have seen to it personally that your level devil understood the instructions. I should have checked up on you before I left the hotel. But I overslept myself, and had to rush down to the ship almost as soon as I was out of bed. With these big brutes the only safe time to lift off or land is during the dawn or sunset lull."

"And even then it's not all that bloody safe," remarked Williams.

"Nothing is safe, Commander, ever. You should know that by this time."

"If anything can go wrong, it will," contributed Grimes.

"You said it, Commodore. It's really surprising that things don't go wrong more often."

"Mphm. And now, Captain Clavering, much as we're enjoying your hospitality I have to remind you that we're here on business."

"Business?" Was there a flicker of fear in Clavering's eyes?

"Yes. This survey for the projected base. Had you forgotten? I was wondering if we could hire transport from you."

Clavering did his best to look apologetic. "Normally I'd be only too pleased to let you have something suitable, Commodore. But this request of yours comes at an awkward time. Apart from *Sally Ann*'s boats I have only two heavy-duty atmosphere craft. They were both used extensively for tours during *Sobraon*'s stay on Eblis, and with maintenance staff working flat out they'll be ready for use again just when *Macedon* comes in."

"What about *Sally Ann*'s boats?"

"Once again, out of the question. I've just finished getting them up to the required standard for my charter trip. You know as well as I do—better than I do, probably—what sticklers for regulations the Department of Navigation surveyors are at Port Last, and that's where I shall be going. I don't want to be held up the same as *Ditmar* has been."

"I suppose not. How about ground cars?"

"We don't have any—not for passenger transport. We have the trucks bringing chemicals from our plant on the Bitter Sea."

"And bottles of mineral water."

"Yes. Have you tried our Bitter Soda yet? You should. A universal panacea for all the ills afflicting man."

"Including insomnia?"

"Possibly. I don't drink the muck myself."

"You just make it."

"Yes."

"I often wonder what the vintners make," quoted Grimes, "one half so precious as the stuff they sell. Or should it be 'buy,' not 'make'? No matter."

"What are you driving at, Commodore?" demanded Clavering.

"I'm not sure myself, Captain. Just thinking out loud. Sort of doodling without pen or paper. And as I can't be getting on with my survey I shall be doing a lot of thinking, just to pass the time. Call me Cassius."

"Cassius?" asked Williams, breaking the silence.

"Yes. He had a lean and hungry look. He thought too much. He was dangerous."

"You'll be able to go on the tours when *Macedon* comes in," said Clavering. "The Painted Badlands. The Valley of the Winds and the Organ Pipes. The Fire Forest . . ."

"From what I've already learned," said Grimes, "none of them at all suitable sites for a naval base."

"There just aren't any suitable sites. Period."

"Looks as though I was wasting my time coming here, doesn't it?"

"*Sally Ann* will be empty on the run from here to Port Last," said Clavering a little too eagerly. "I'll be pleased to give passage to you and Commander Williams and the rest of *Rim Malemute*'s officers."

"Thank you, Captain. But we can't accept. Traditions of the Service, and all that. Don't give up the ship. She's our responsibility. I'm afraid we're stuck here until she's repaired."

"I suppose I might tow her back to Port Last for you," suggested Clavering doubtfully.

Grimes went through the motions of considering this. Then, "Too risky. Deep space towing's a very specialized job, as Williams, here, will tell you. And the most awkward part would be getting the *Malemute* off the ground. You've all damn room to play within your spaceport at the best of times, and when your *Sally Ann* lifts off you'll have *Macedon* cluttering up the apron, with mooring wires every which way. No. Not worth the risk."

"At least," said Clavering, "I shall be having the pleasure of your company for quite some time." He was obviously trying to convey the impression that the prospect was a pleasurable one. He essayed a smile. "So, gentlemen, make yourselves at home. This is Liberty Hall. You can spit on the mat and call the cat a bastard."

The literal-minded Williams looked around him, at the pneumatic furniture, the inflated walls. He grinned, "If you did have a cat you *would* be calling him a bastard, or worse, I can just imagine one racing around in here, digging his claws into everything."

Clavering smiled, genuinely this time. He said, "This plastic is tougher than it looks. It has to be, as the devils just refuse to cut their toenails. But it is a nightmare I have sometimes, the skins of the bubbles pricked and the whole damn place just collapsing on itself like a punctured balloon. But it can't ever happen."

"Famous last words," said Grimes cheerfully. "It can't happen here."

"It can't," Clavering told him forcefully.

∽ Chapter 22 ∽

GRIMES WAS FAR FROM HAPPY and was wishing, most sincerely, that the Navy had assigned somebody else to work with the Customs in this drug-running investigation. What put him off the job more than anything else was being obliged to accept Clavering's hospitality—it was impossible to live aboard *Rim Malemute* until such time as she was righted. He had insisted that the ex-captain send the bills for himself and the tug's officers to the Rim Worlds Admiralty, but there were still the rounds of drinks on the house and, with Williams, dining every night at Clavering's table. He was more than ever sure that he was not cut out to be a policeman. But the memories of those three young people—two dead and one with his career ruined—persisted.

He talked matters over with Williams while the two of them paced slowly along the left bank of the Styx. The tug skipper was but a poor substitute for Sonya on such an occasion, but he was the only one in whom Grimes could confide.

He said, "I don't like it, Commander Williams."

"Frankly, Skipper, neither do I. Clavering ain't all that bad a bastard, an' his wife's a piece of all right, an' here we are, sleepin' in his beds, eatin' his tucker an' slurpin' his grog. An' if all goes well, from our viewpoint, we'll be puttin' him behind bars."

"Mphm. Not necessarily. His legal status, like that of his world, is rather vague. Even so, the Rim Worlds governments, both overall and planetary, could make life really hard for him. For example, somebody might decide that Inferno Valley is *the* site for a naval base. But I'm not concerned so much with the legalities. It's the personal freedom angle. If somebody wants to blow his mind, has any government the right to try to stop him?"

"I see what you mean, Skipper. But when that same somebody is in a position of responsibility, like young Pleshoff, he has to be stopped. Or when somebody, like Clavering, is making a very nice profit out of other people's mind-blowing . . ."

"In most of the Federated worlds it's the governments that make the profits, just as they do from every other so-called vice—liquor, tobacco, gambling. . . . Damn it all, Williams, is Clavering a sinner, or is he just a criminal, only until such time that somebody sees fit to liberalize our laws?"

"I'm not a theologian, Skipper."

"Neither am I. But both of us, when sailing in command, have been the law *and* the prophets. Both of us have deliberately turned a blind eye to breaches of regulations, whether Company's or Naval."

"When you're Master Under God," observed Williams, "you can do that sort of thing an' get away with it. The trouble now is that we have far too many bastards between us an' the Almighty. It's all very well our hearts fair bleedin' for Clavering—but we have to keep our own jets clear."

"Mphm. All right, then. You suggest that we regard ourselves as policemen, pure and simple."

"I've known a few simple ones," said Williams, "but I've yet to meet one who's pure."

"You know what I mean!" snapped Grimes testily. "Don't try to be funny. Now, we *think* that the dreamy weed is coming in through Eblis, and that it's transshipped from here to Ultimo or wherever in *Ditmar*. Clavering tells me, by the way, that she's still held up. Her yeast vats were condemned. But where was I? Oh, yes. We think that the contraband is shipped from somewhere to Eblis. Through the spaceport? No, I don't think so. Too many people around, even when there's no cruise ship in, who might talk out of turn. Only a dozen of the people here are *Sally Ann* originals; the rest are Rim Worlders.

The head waiters, the chef and his assistants, the mechanics in the repair shops . . . So. So this is a fair hunk of planet, and I'd say that the only man who really knows it is Clavering, and Clavering, by putting the *Malemute* and her boats out of commission, has made sure that we don't get really to know it.

"Our fat friend Billinghurst is due here shortly, in *Macedon*, and he'll be relying on us to lay on transport. And we can't lay it on, and I can't see the master of *Macedon* lending us one of his boats."

"So we just go on sittin' our big, fat butts doin' sweet damn' all," said Williams. "Suits me, Skipper."

"It doesn't suit me, Commander Williams. Much as we may dislike it we have a job to do. And as long as we're the ones who're doing it we stand some chance of protecting Clavering from the more serious consequences."

"That's one way of lookin' at it, Skipper. *And* Mrs. Clavering, of course. Pardon me bein' nosey, but she an' you seem to be gettin' on like a house on fire. Long walks by the river after dinner while Clavering's in his office cookin' his books."

"If you must know, Commander Williams, she has asked my help, *our* help. She knows that her husband is mixed up in something illegal, but not what it is. She has told me about the prospecting trips that he makes by himself, and about the Carlotti transceiver that he keeps, under lock and key, at his bottling plant by the Bitter Sea."

"Nothin' wrong with that. When he's out there he has to keep in touch with home."

"Yes, but an NST transceiver would do for that. You should know by this time that a Carlotti set is only for deep space communications."

"Just a radio ham," suggested Williams. "When he gets tired of hammering the stoppers on to bottles he retires to his den and has a yarn with a cobber on Earth or wherever."

"Mphm. I doubt it. Anyhow, Mrs. Clavering is far from happy. She'd like to see her husband drop whatever it is he's doing, but she wouldn't like to see him in jail. If we can catch him before that fat ferret Billinghurst blows in we shall be able to help him to stay free. If Billinghurst gets *his* claws into him, he's a goner."

"You sure make life complicated, Skipper," complained Williams.

"Life *is* complicated. Period. Now, your work boat . . ."

"In working order. But if you intend a long trip it'll be so packed with power cells that there'll be room for only one man."

"Good enough. And your engineers, I think, have been passing the time doing what repairs they can to *Malemute*, and have been in and out of Clavering's workshop borrowing tools and such."

"Correct."

"By this time they should be on friendly terms with Clavering's mechanics."

"If they don't know by this time which of the boats it is that Clavering takes out to the Bitter Sea, they should."

"They probably do know."

"I'd like a transponder fitted to Clavering's boat, and the necessary homing gadgetry to your workboat. I don't know quite how Clavering's boat can be bugged without somebody seeing it done—but, with a little bit of luck, it should be possible. Mphm. Suppose, say, that the inertial drive main rotor has to be carried to the shop so that work can be done on it with one of the lathes. Suppose that everybody—everybody but one man—is clustered around the thing, admiring it. And suppose this one man manages to stick the transponder to the underside of the hull of Clavering's boat when nobody is looking."

"Possible, Skipper, just possible. We already have transponders in stock; they're used quite a lot in salvage work. We've plenty of tubes of wetweld in the stores. An' if Clavering's mechanics know nothin' about the drug racket they'll not be expecting any jiggery pokey from my blokes. Yair. Could be done."

"And how's the repair work on our Carlotti set coming on?"

"Not so good."

"A pity. I'd like to do some monitoring. Just who does Clavering talk to?"

It was some time before the plan could be put into effect. The boat that Clavering usually used for his trips to the Bitter Sea—and for his prospecting trips—was undergoing an extensive and badly needed overhaul. Even without wind-driven abrasives to severely damage the exterior of an atmosphere craft, the air itself was strongly corrosive. Too, most of the work force was engaged on necessary maintenance to make *Sally Ann* thoroughly spaceworthy for her charter trip.

Macedon came in, and aboard her, as a passenger, was Billinghurst. Sub-Inspector Pahvani was with him, and a half-dozen other customs officers. Unlike policemen, customs officers, when out of uniform, look like anybody else. Billinghurst and his people had no trouble in passing themselves off as ordinary tourists.

Chapter 23

"**LOOKS LIKE** you've been having trouble, Commodore," commented Billinghurst to Grimes as the pair of them stood by the Devil's Stewpot watching what seemed to be the majority of *Macedon*'s passengers wallowing in the murky, bubbling, steaming water. "Sabotage?"

"Accident," replied Grimes. "*Sobraon* was lifting off, and one of her stern vanes snagged one of Rim *Malemute*'s mooring wires."

"Accident? You don't really believe that, do you?"

"I've handled ships for long enough, Mr. Billinghurst, to know that accidents do happen."

"All the same, Commodore, it's suspicious," stated Billinghurst.

"How so?" asked Grimes, just to be awkward.

"As I recollect it, the idea was that you were to run a survey of the planet, officially looking for sites for the naval base, and actually looking for places where dreamy weed might be brought in. I don't suppose that you've even started to do that."

"How right you are."

"Meanwhile, you're living in the lap of luxury, and the taxpayer is picking up the tab for your hotel bills."

"The taxpayer forked out for your fare in *Macedon*, and will be picking up the tab for *your* hotel bills."

"That's different."

"How so?"

"Because, Commodore, in matters of this kind I'm a trained investigator. You're not. *You* can't do anything unless you've a ship under you. When *Rim Malemute* was *accidently* knocked out of the picture you were knocked out of it too. I did expect some cooperation from you in the way of transport, but now I'll have to manage as best I can by myself. Don't worry; I've done it before."

"I'm not worrying," said Grimes. He looked with some distaste at an enormously fat, naked man waddling down to the hot pool like a Terran hippopotamus. He asked, "Why don't *you* try the Stewpot, Mr. Billinghurst? You could afford to lose some weight."

"Because I've more important things to do, that's why. *I'm* not here on holiday."

"Neither am I, unfortunately."

"So you say."

"So I say. But tell me, just how do you intend to go about things? I realize that I'm just an amateur in these matters, so I'd like to know how a real professional operates."

Billinghurst lapped up the flattery. He said, "In any sort of detective work the human element is, in the final analysis, far more important than all the fancy gadgetry in the laboratories. One informer—voluntary or involuntary—is worth ten scientists. I have chosen to accompany me young, keen officers who are not unattractive to the opposite sex. Sub-Inspector Pahvani you, of course, already know. That is Sub-Inspector Ling just coming out of this absurdly named hot pool."

"Certainly a tasty dollop of trollop," remarked Grimes as the golden-skinned, black-haired, naked girl passed them.

"She is a very fine and capable young woman," said Billinghurst stiffly. "Anyhow, I have young Pahvani and three other men, Miss Ling and two other women. All of them are provided with ample spending money. All of them are to pass themselves off as members of well-to-do families on Thule—they'd have to be well-to-do to afford the fares that TG Clippers charge *and* a quite long holiday here—enjoying a vacation. Captain Clavering has quite a few unattached men and women among his staff here, and my officers have been instructed to . . . to make contacts."

"All-over contacts," said Grimes.

"Really, Commodore, you have a low mind."

"Not as low as the mind of the bastard who first thought of using good, honest sex as an espionage tool. But go on."

"Well I'm hoping that some of Clavering's people become . . . er . . . infatuated with some of my people. And I hope that they—Clavering's people—talk."

"So you can build a case on bedtime stories."

"You put things in the most crude way, Commodore Grimes."

"I'm just a rough and tough spaceman, Mr. Billinghurst. It has been rumored that my rugged exterior hides a heart of gold—but there are times when even I am inclined to doubt that."

"Who's that young man whom Miss Ling is talking to?"

"That's Clavering's chef. Like all good chefs he is always tasting as he cooks. A daily session in the Devil's Stewpot helps him to keep his weight down. He's a Farawegian. He started his career in the kitchen of the Rimrock House at Port Farewell. Mphm. Your Miss Ling is coming back with him for another good sweat session. She must be conscientious. I hope she doesn't lose any weight; she's just right as she is."

"And does this chef *know* anything?"

"He certainly knows cooking. Ah, there's your Mr. Pahvani, getting on with the job. Does he use steel wool on his teeth, by the way? That smile, against his brown skin, is really dazzling. The recipient of the charm that he's turning on is Clavering's head receptionist. She's from Thule, but she prefers it here. Oh, looks like my Commander Williams is making a conquest from among *Macedon*'s customers. I must say that I applaud his good taste."

"That," said Billinghurst, "is *my* Miss Dalgety that he's talking to. I'll have to warn her off him."

"Mistakes will happen. After all, you can hardly expect Williams to wear uniform for his daily dip, can you? Any more than you can expect Miss Dalgety to appear in her sub-inspector's finery."

"You seem to have made *some* enquiries, Commodore," admitted Billinghurst reluctantly. "Perhaps you will oblige me with thumbnail sketches of all Clavering's staff here."

"All? Devils as well as humans? I'm afraid you're out of luck as far as the devils are concerned. At first I thought I was getting them sorted out by the colour of their scales—and then I found out that this varies from day to day. If you look really hard you can tell which are males and which are females, though."

"Humans, of course, Commodore."

"Well," began Grimes, "there's Clavering himself. Spaceman. Hangs on to his Federation citizenship. Still makes an occasional voyage in command of *Sally Ann*, also brings in and takes out ships whose Masters want a pilot."

"I suppose he was piloting *Sobraon* when she fouled your *Malemute*."

"*As* a matter of fact, he was. Wife, Sally Clavering. Tall blonde, very attractive. Ex-purser, and looks after the books of the hotel, the chemical works on the Bitter Sea and the bottling plant. Then there's Larwood, another Federation citizen, chief officer of *Sally Ann* and assistant port captain, assistant hotel manager and assistant everything else. Very quiet. Doesn't drink, doesn't smoke, has no time for women. I think there was a marriage once, but it broke up. Ah, here's Mrs. Clavering. Sally, this is Mr. Billinghurst, an old acquaintance from Port Forlorn. Mr. Billinghurst, this is Mrs. Clavering."

Billinghurst bowed with ponderous dignity. He said, "I am very pleased to meet you." Then, "This is quite a place you have here. I'd heard so much about it that I just had to come and see it for myself."

"I hope you enjoy your stay, Mr. Billinghurst. We do our best to make our guests feel at home."

Home was never like this, thought Grimes. A slight earth tremor added point to his unspoken comment.

Billinghurst was unshaken. It would have taken a major earthquake to unsettle him. He asked, "Do you have these tremors often, Mrs. Clavering?"

"Quite frequently. You soon get used to them."

"I hope you're right. I hope that I shall. Some people never get used to motion of any kind, and have to take all sorts of drugs to help them to maintain their physical and psychological equilibrium."

She laughed. "We dispense one very good drug for that purpose ourselves, Mr. Billinghurst. You can get it in the bar. It's called alcohol."

"I think I could stand a drink," admitted Billinghurst. "Will you join me, Mrs. Clavering? And you, Commodore?"

"Later, perhaps," she said. She dropped the robe that was all she had been wearing. "I always have my daily hot soak at this time."

Grimes got out of his own dressing gown. "And so do I."

He followed the tall, slim woman into the almost-scalding water. They found a place that was out of earshot from the other bathers. She turned to face him, slowly lowered herself until only her head was above the surface. Grimes did likewise, conscious of the stifling heat, of the perspiration pouring down his face.

She said, "I don't like your fat friend, John."

"Neither do I, frankly."

"I never have liked customs officers."

"Customs officers?"

"Don't forget that I was once a spacewoman, a purser. I know the breed. But what were all those not so subtle hints about drugs? Did he expect me to offer him a pipeful of dreamy weed?"

"Perhaps he did," said Grimes. "Perhaps he did."

"Surely you don't think . . . ?"

"I wish I didn't."

"But . . ."

"But the bloody stuff is coming into the Rim Worlds from somewhere, Sally. I know of one young man, an officer in our ships, who got himself emptied out because of it. I know of two other young people who were killed because the container of the weed, dropped from *Ditmar*, was destroyed, by remote control and by explosion, to stop it from falling into customs' hands. I'm not saying that Ian knew anything about that; I'm sure that he didn't. But—on this world of all worlds!—he should bear in mind the old proverb: He who sups with the devil needs a long spoon."

"You're . . . accusing Ian?"

"The evidence—and what you yourself have told me—point to his being somehow implicated. If he gets out from under now I shall be able, I think and hope, to shield him from the consequences. If he doesn't . . ."

She looked at him long and earnestly. Then, "Whose side are you on, John?"

"I'm not sure. There are times when I think that stupid laws breed criminals, there are times when I'm not certain that the laws are so stupid. When it comes to things like dreamy weed there's too much hysteria on both sides. It's far easier to handle drugs like alcohol, because nobody has made a religion of them."

"Have you talked to Ian yet, as I asked you to?"

"I've tried once or twice, but he's very hard to pin down."

"Don't I know it! But I think he realizes that the game's up and that he's let whoever has been bringing the stuff in that the trade is finished."

"He hasn't been able to get out to his bottling plant where he has his private transceiver. His air boat is still under repair, and it would take too long by road."

She said, "Surely the port captain is allowed to play around with the Carlotti equipment in the control tower in his own spaceport."

"Oh, well," said Grimes, "I'll shed no tears if it turns out that I've come here for nothing."

~ Chapter 24 ~

SEEING A PLANET as a tourist is not the same as running your own survey, but it is better than not seeing a planet at all. *Macedon*, with all her experience-hungry passengers, was in, and the three large atmosphere fliers, the aircoaches, were now completely overhauled and ready for service.

Billinghurst sneered at Grimes and Williams, saying they were having a glorious holiday at public expense. He preferred to stay in Inferno Valley, keeping his eyes and ears open. The only one of his officers to go on the tours was Denise Dalgety—but not so that she could continue to turn her considerable charm on to Williams. She had transferred her attentions to Larwood, who was in charge of the sightseeing expeditions. Grimes felt sorry for the dark, morose assistant manager. He would liked to have warned him. More and more it was becoming obvious that he appreciated the company of the plump redhead who, ever more frequently, was able to coax an occasional smile from him. Sooner or later there would have to be a rude awakening.

The first trip was to the Painted Badlands. Grimes and Williams rode in the leading aircoach, the command vehicle, which was piloted by Larwood. They had been given seats right forward, on the starboard side, immediately abaft the pilot. In the corresponding seats to port were an elderly Terran businessman and his wife, both looking slightly ludicrous in the heavy-duty one-piece suits, as much metal as fibre, that were mandatory wear. There was a single seat to port of that occupied by Larwood; in this, of course, sat Denise Dalgety. In any form of transport whatsoever rank hath its privileges. She, apart from Williams, was the only young passenger in the coach. Her companions had said, rather too loudly, at the bar the previous night, that they didn't want to be herded around with a lot of old fossils.

Dawn was just coming in when the three coaches lifted from the landing field close by the hotel. Their inertial drives hammering erratically, they climbed slowly, drifting a little to the west so that the fantastic bubble structure, multihued and luminescent, lay beneath them. Grimes permitted himself to wonder what would be the effect of a few handfuls of heavy steel darts dropped from the aircraft.

Slowly they climbed, hugging the north wall of the canyon which, in this light, was blue rather than red, splotched with opalescent patches where grew the phosphorescent lichen and fungi. Slowly they climbed, and with every meter of altitude they gained the orange ribbon of sky directly above them widened. "Aero-Space Control to Painted Badlands Tour," came a matter-of-fact voice from the transceiver. "There's as much of a lull as you're likely to get. Keep clear of the Devil's Phallus. There's turbulence. Over."

"PB Tour to Aero-Space Control. Roger. Over."

Grimes grinned to himself. This, he knew, was all part of the window dressing.

Larwood said into his microphone, "Make sure your seat belts are fastened, folks. We may get a few bumps when we clear the canyon rim."

There were a few bumps, but very minor ones. The coaches were lifting under maximum thrust now, and below them was Inferno Valley, a deep, dark slash in the face of the planet. To the south towered the Erebus Alps, peak after conical peak, from each of which a pillar of flame-shot smoke rose almost vertically. Dim in the distance were the Devil's Torches, volcanoes even more spectacularly active than those of the Alps. And beyond those? The Infernal Beacons? It was hard to be sure. Already the early-morning clarity of the atmosphere was becoming befouled.

The note of the inertial drive changed as Larwood brought his coach around to a northerly heading. He announced, "If you look hard, folks, you'll see the Bitter Sea out to port, on our left. We shall be stopping there overnight on our way back. Most of the day we shall be spending in the Painted Badlands, of course."

"Pilot!" This was an old lady well back in the coach. "We've come all this way and you've shown us practically nothing of the Erebus Alps and the other ranges."

"I may wear wings on my uniform, madam," Larwood told her, "but they aren't bat's wings. A devil, one of those mythological devils out of the mythological hell, might survive there, but we certainly shouldn't. Updraughts, downdraughts, red hot boulders hurtling through the air—you name it, the Erebus Alps and the other ranges have got it. But I promise you that the Painted Badlands will be an experience none of you will ever forget. Now, all of you, you can either look astern, behind you, or at the stern view screen that is in front of every seat. I've just switched it on. The screen might be clearer. You will realize the sort of muck and rubbish we should have to fly through. The wind's just starting to rise."

Muck and rubbish, thought Grimes, peering into the screen that he shared with Williams. *A good description.* The pillars of fiery smoke from the multitudinous craters were leaning towers now, blown ever further and further from the vertical until they approached the horizontal. The sharp outlines of the peaks were blurred, were obscured by the wind-driven fumes and dust. Overhead the sky was no longer orange but a glowing yellow across which scudded the low black clouds. And below, the whirling flurries of red dust were blotting out all landmarks. Then, through some meteorological freak, the air ahead of them cleared and, brooding sullenly over the red plain, the Great Smokies appeared, almost black against the yellow sky, belching volumes of white steam and dark brown smoke.

"But you're flying over *them*, Pilot!" complained the old lady accusingly.

"Not over, madam. Through. Just fine in our starboard bow, a little to the right of dead ahead, you'll see the entrance to Dante's

Pass. Also, if you will look at the smoke from the volcanoes, you will see that the wind is nowhere near as bad as it is to the south'ard. The Smokies are in the lee of the highest part of Satan's Barrier."

"But these mountains are only *smoking*," muttered the old lady.

"If we'd only known," whispered Williams to Grimes, "we could have brought along a couple of nuclear devices just to keep the old dear happy."

"Mphm. Smoke or flame—this is a good place for a holiday, but I wouldn't want to live here."

"Don't mention holidays, Skipper. Glamorpuss up ahead might hear you."

Denise Dalgety turned in her seat, smiled sweetly at Williams. "I'm enjoying *my* holiday," she said.

"What was all that about, Denise?" asked Larwood.

"Nothing much, Ron. Nothing much. Just something that Commander Williams said."

"Oh," grunted Larwood. Then, into the microphone again, "Coming up to Dante's Pass now, folks. To port, Mount Dante. To starboard, Mount Beatrice. Looks like Dante's a heavy smoker still, but Beatrice seems to have kicked the habit. Ha, ha."

Ha, ha, thought Grimes. *I'm rolling in the aisle in a paroxysm of uncontrollable mirth.*

But his irritation faded as he stared out at the spectacular scenery. The coach had dropped to an altitude well below that of the peaks, seemed to be barely skimming the numerous minor craters that pocked the valley floor. Smoke was issuing from almost all of them— in some cases a trickle, in others as a billowing cloud. And all up the steep, terraced side of Dante were similar small craters, most of them active. The slopes of Mount Beatrice were also pockmarked but, for some reason, only an occasional wisp of vapor was evident.

"You could do better, Skipper," whispered Williams.

Grimes, who had brought out his pipe and was about to fill it, changed his mind and put the thing back in his pocket.

On they flew, and on, the three coaches in line ahead, the Great Smokies to either side of their course and at last falling astern. On they flew, and the smoldering mountain range dropped astern, and the foothills, each of which was a volcano. Smoke eddied about them, restricting visibility, often blotting out the view of the tortured landscape below them. Turbulence buffeted them, and once the coaches had to make a wide alteration of course to avoid a huge red tornado.

Desert was below them at last—huge dunes the faces of which displayed all colors from brown through red to a yellow that was almost white, with streaks of gray and silver and blue. Beyond the dunes was a region where great rock pillars towered like the ruins of some ancient devastated city, sculpted by wind and sand into fantastic shapes, glowing with raw color.

"The Painted Badlands," announced Larwood unnecessarily. "The wind's from the west still, so it's safe to land."

"What if the wind was from the east?" asked the old lady.

"Then, madam, we shouldn't have the protection of Satan's Barrier. There'd be a sandstorm that'd strip us to our bare bones. You can see what wind and sand have done to those rocks down there."

The irregular hammering of the inertial drive became less insistent. The coach slowed, began losing altitude. It dropped at last to coarse red sand in what could have been a city square, a clear space with the eroded monoliths all about it. The second vehicle landed in a flurry of ruddy dust, then the third.

"Welcome to Dis," said Larwood. "You may disembark for sight-seeing. Respirators will be worn; I wouldn't say that the atmosphere's actually poisonous, but too much of it wouldn't do your eyes, throat or lungs any good. You will all stay with me and not go wandering off by yourselves. You may pick up souvenirs—pretty pebbles and the like—within reason, but I warn you that this wagon doesn't develop enough thrust to carry home one of the monoliths. Ha, ha."

One by one the passengers passed out through the airlock, jumped or clambered down to the windswept sand.

"If it wasn't for the easterlies," said Williams to Grimes, his voice muffled by his breathing mask, "this'd be a good spot for a Base."

"At least," said Grimes, "we shall be able to write some sort of report on this base business now. Just in case somebody actually asks for it."

~ Chapter 25 ~

IT WAS A LONG DAY, and a tiring one. A heavy protective suit complete with respirator is not the most comfortable wear for sightseeing, and Larwood was determined that they should see everything.

They looked at the Venus de Milo—which, if one used one's imagination, just could have been a giant statue of a woman, carved from black basalt minus her arms. Their guide made the inevitable joke about the consequences of fingernail biting. They saw the Leaning Tower of Pisa. It did lean, but there all resemblance ceased. They saw the Sphynx, which was not too unlike a great, crouching cat if looked at from the right angle and the Great Pyramid. They returned to the comparative luxury of the coaches for a sandwich meal and very welcome cold drinks. After lunch a short flight took them away from the so-called City Square of Dis to another part of the Badlands. Here they saw the Colossus of Eblis, which vaguely resembled a man standing arrogantly with his legs apart, the Thinker (Larwood, of course, had to say that a huge stone toilet roll was being carved to hang alongside the seated, brooding figure), Mount Olga and Ayers Rock. Grimes made himself unpopular by saying that the originals of these last two named gained greatly in majesty by being situated in a vast empty desert with no surrounding clutter to distract attention from them.

They saw the Devil's Launching Pad, a low plateau surmounted by a remarkably regular row of what, from a distance, could have been archaic space rockets. They saw the Dinosaurs, and St. Paul's Cathedral, and St. Bazil's Cathedral, and the Rainbow Bridge. They saw . . . But it was all too much, much too much, at the finish. They stumbled through the surrealistic landscape, the rockscape, with its great contorted masses of garishly coloured stone, behind their guides. Even Larwood was running short of witticisms, although he did say that it just required one good crash to make the Lorelei look happy.

Tired, perspiring in their suits and behind their masks, they stumbled back into the coaches, gratefully loosening clothing and removing respirators. The irregular blotch of brightness in the yellow sky that was the sun was low in the west when they lifted, but there was daylight enough for the coaches to negotiate Dante's Pass without trouble, and Mount Beatrice honoured them with a salute, a huge, spectacular smoke ring, as they flew past. The sun was not yet down when they approached the western shores of the Bitter Sea and the white buildings of the bottling plant, on the bank of the River of Tears, stood out against the dusky red of the desert like a handful of white pebbles dropped there. As they approached they could see that these were of the by now familiar bubble construction—although, Larwood told them, the skins were centimeters instead of mere millimeters thick, and had frequently to be renewed.

He announced, on his public address system, "We shall be staying here overnight, folks. One dome has been fitted out as a dormitory for tourists, and the one adjoining as a mess hall. At dark floodlights will be turned on so that you may all enjoy a swim in the Bitter Sea. You will have time for another one in the morning, before we leave for Inferno Valley. Oh, before forget, there are fresh water showering facilities at the Bottling Plant. I advise you all to take a shower after swimming in the Bitter Sea."

"Swimming, the man said," complained Grimes, his voice muffled by the respirator that, now, was all that he was wearing.

"Walkin' on the water's just the thing for a high an' mighty Commodore," laughed Williams.

"But not for a mere commander, like you."

"I wonder if one could really walk on it," murmured Williams. He managed a sitting posture and then overbalanced, finishing up flat on his back. He said, "Any bastard tryin' to commit suicide in this soup'd die o' frustration."

"Mphm." Grimes managed a kind of squat and looked around him. The other passengers were enjoying themselves, splashing and squealing in the harsh glare of the floodlights. But the one he was looking for—the only one who would have been worth looking at—was not there. Neither was Larwood, although the other two coach pilots were disporting themselves with their charges.

"Mphm," grunted Grimes again. So Billinghurst's pet blonde spy was earning her keep whilst he and Williams were having a good time. But perhaps she was having a good time too.

"Lookin' for Denise?" asked Williams.

"As a matter of fact, yes."

"She went off with that frosty-faced sidekick o' Clavering's just before we all got undressed for our dip. I suppose he's showin' her his etchings. Unless I get outer this hellbroth soon I'll be able to show all the girls my itchings!"

"Yes, it does seem to be mildly corrosive. I'd hate to swallow any. Coming out?"

"Too bleedin' right, Skipper. When I want a swim I have a swim, when I want a walk I have a walk. What we're doin' now is just a compromise."

Clumsily the two men splashed ashore. Once they were through the airlock of the bottling plant they removed their respirators, handing them to attentive attendant devils. They followed one of the natives to the showers, where others of his kind were scampering around in the clouds of steam armed with long-handled brushes, enthusiastically scrubbing down the naked humans. The red lighting of the place made it all look like a scene from a mythological inferno—and, muttered Grimes, some of the tourists looked like refugees from the canvases of Hieronymus Bosch.

After their showers—hot water and detergent to remove the salty scum, cold water for refreshment—the two men got into clean coveralls provided by the management, collected personal belongings from their lockers in the change room, then strolled into the dormitory. There was no sign of either Denise Dalgety or of Larwood. They walked into the mess hall, where a few people were sitting over cold drinks. The girl and Clavering's assistant were not there either.

Grimes wasn't worried—what Billinghurst's officers did with themselves, or had done to them, was none of his concern—but he was curious. Perhaps "curious" is not quite the right word. He had the feeling that the girl was finding out something and he would have liked very much to know what it was. Perhaps pride was involved. He could imagine Billinghurst telling his story to an appreciative audience: "There was the famous Commodore Grimes, and all that *he* did was to get his ship wrecked and then, with nothing at all that *he* could do, have one helluva good time like a tourist, at the taxpayer's expense. One of *my* sub-inspectors, a girl at that, did much better than *he* did."

"Denise Dalgety, the Beautiful Blonde Spy," muttered Williams.

"Jealous, Commander?"

"My oath, yes. I still haven't forgiven that bastard Billinghurst for calling her off me. He ruined the beginnings of what promised to be a beautiful friendship. I wonder where he's taken her? Larwood, I mean."

"Clavering has an office here. Presumably his second-in-command has a set of keys to it."

"An' now he's chasin' her round the water cooler . . . or she's chasin' him round the water cooler."

"The chasing part," said Grimes, "must be well over."

"Some people are slow starters. All right, then. He's sittin' there, with a silly smile on his face, while she photographs the plans of the fortifications with the miniature camera hidden in one of her ear clips, which are the only things she's wearin' at the moment. There's a recorder in the other clip."

"Try to be serious, Williams."

"What about, Skipper? It'd be a lot easier for me if I knew which side you were on. Are you pro- or antismuggler? I know damn well that you're anti-Billinghurst—but who's not? Ever since we've been on this bloody job you've been obscuring the issue with a fog of moral principles. And we aren't concerned with the moral side of it, only with the legal side."

"And that," Grimes told him, "is even more obscure. Whose laws apply on this planet—the laws of the Confederacy or the laws that Clavering makes up as he goes along? The Confederacy, don't forget, didn't want Eblis. Clavering saw its possibilities."

"And so what? As planetary ruler he pays his taxes to the Confederacy rather than to the Federation—because that way he pays less. But, by so doing, he has admitted Confederate jurisdiction."

"Here she comes," said Grimes in a low voice.

Here she came. She saw Grimes and Williams, walked to the table where they were seated. An attentive devil clattered up to take her drink order. She waved the native away.

"Commodore," she said, smiling sweetly, "I understand that you're attached to this investigation as an astronautical expert."

"Mphm. I suppose so."

"Ron showed me round the bottling plant. He said that I should see more if I had his undivided attention, that it would be better than going on the conducted tour of inspection later this evening."

"Mphm."

"It wasn't very interesting really. Just machines doing things, washing bottles, filling bottles, sealing bottles. . . ."

"Mphm."

"And then he took me into the office."

Grimes, looking at Williams' face, had trouble in keeping his own straight.

"I'm not very well up on ships' instruments. Usually I'm concerned with passengers' baggage. Tell me, Commodore, that radio with an antenna like a Mobius Strip, formed as a long ellipse, universally mounted, is a Carlotti transceiver, isn't it?"

"It is." (But he knew already that there was one in the bottling plant.)

"And it's never used for short-range signalings? Only ship to ship, ship to planet, planet to ship, planet to planet?"

"As a general rule."

"A message came through while we were . . ." She blushed. "Well, a message came through. Ron said that I'd have to leave the office, as it was probably Captain Clavering calling about some important business and, even though he trusted me, some matters regarding the bottling of the River of Tears water were a commercial secret. Luckily I'd taken my ear clips off, and left them behind when I went out. And then, after . . ." She blushed again. "And then after I left Ron—he let me back inside when whoever it was had finished sending—I played it back when I went into the toilet."

She detached the ornament of interlocking golden rings from her right ear, put it on the table. She said, "I have it set for the lowest volume. You'll have to pretend to be looking at it closely. Press the spring clip."

"An interesting piece of jewelry," commented Grimes, picking it up. "Very fine workmanship."

He heard, "Damn! The Old Man's calling from Inferno Valley!" (Presumably earlier conversation had been censored by one of those involved.) "Let him call." "But darling, it could be important." "Answer it then, and get it over." "Denise, it's not that I don't trust you, but it could be something confidential." "All right then, I'll go out into the main office. Give me time to put something on." "There's no need, all the doors are locked." "Do you think more of your boss than you do of me?" "Please, Denise, just leave me and let me answer this call." "All right, all right. I bet Billy Williams wouldn't drop me like a hot cake and come a-running if Commodore Grimes whistled for him!" A hissing silence, then, "SB Three calling IC. Anyone there? I repeat, anyone there?" The voice was oddly familiar. "IC answering SB Three. This is RL receiving you." "I've a shipment for you, IC. Will advise later when. Presumably usual place. Over." "But, SB Three, the heat's on." "You'll want this shipment for the Convention, won't you? Over, and most definitely out." Silence, then Ron Larwood's voice again, presumably on a normal telephone. "That you, Sally? Can I get hold of the captain? I'll call later then. No, no trouble with the tour. Very well-behaved bunch of customers. See you tomorrow. Goodnight."

And that was all. There are more secrets than commercial ones.

✑ Chapter 26 ✑

BEFORE THEY COULD ALL SIT DOWN to their evening meal there was the conducted tour of the bottling plant—all very boring unless one happened to be an engineer. Larwood pointed out with pride the way in which the machinery was mounted on floating platforms so that it would suffer no damage, and even go on functioning, in the event of an earth tremor. There were free samplings of the mineral-rich water, from which Grimes and Williams abstained. What had happened during their first night on Eblis had put them off the stuff.

Grimes, more out of spite than from any desire to know, asked, "And what's behind that door, Mr. Larwood?"

"Just the office, Commodore Grimes. Nothing of any interest whatsoever."

"I'd rather like to see it, Mr. Larwood. As I spend most of my days behind an office desk I might get some ideas as to how to make myself more comfortable. If your office is like the plant it'll be up to the minute."

"I'm sorry, Commodore. Only Captain Clavering has the keys. In any case, there's nothing at all to see."

"Some other day, perhaps?" said Grimes vaguely.

"Yes, Commodore. Some other day."

And then they were all sitting down at the tables in the mess hall, and the devils were bringing in steaming platters of food and bottles of cold wine, and everybody was tucking in to the bouillabaisse made from various denizens of the Bitter Sea as though none of them had eaten for at least a week. Even Williams enjoyed it, leaving nothing in his bowl but empty shells and cracked claws. Denise Dalgety, who was at the next table, was eating with a very good appetite, but Larwood was off his feed.

It was bedtime then, and the tourists retired to the dormitory. The air mattresses were very comfortable, and even the chorus of snores from all around him could not keep the commodore awake. He was vaguely conscious of a slight earth tremor just before he dropped off, but it did not worry him.

Music over the public address system woke the tourists. Most of them went out for a last swim in the Bitter Sea, but Grimes and Williams did not. Apart from anything else there was privacy for conversation in the shower room.

"I wonder just who SB Three is," said Grimes. "That voice sounded familiar. I've heard it before, but a very long time ago. It made quite an impression on me."

"One o' the Australoid accents, Skipper," said Williams.

"Pots and kettles, Commander. Pots and kettles. But it hadn't got that peculiar Rim Worlds twang, like yours."

"Austral?" suggested Williams doubtfully.

"Mphm. Yes. Could be. And those initials, SB, ring some kind of bell too. IC is obviously Ian Clavering, and RL is Ron Larwood. Do we know anybody who has SB for initials?"

"*I* don't, Skipper, 'cept for a sheila back on Lorn called Susan Bartram. It couldn't have been her."

"How do you know? In this sort of business all sorts of odd people may be implicated."

"It wasn't a woman's voice," began Williams, then realized that Grimes was not entirely serious.

"Yes, as you say, Commander, it was a man's voice. But whose?"

"There're one helluva lot o' men in this Galaxy—an' you, in your lifetime, have met at least your fair share of 'em."

"Too right."

And then the first of the bathers came in from the Bitter Sea, and the attendant devils got busy with detergent and long-handled brushes, and there was no more opportunity for conversation.

After a good breakfast the tourists got back into the coaches. The first pallor of dawn was showing in the eastern sky, with the black plumed Great Smokies in silhouette against the yellow luminosity, when the vehicles lifted. To the south'ard the low clouds reflected the glare from the Erebus Alps and the Devil's Torches. The wind had yet to rise, although the Bitter Sea was well enough in the lee of Satan's Barrier to be shielded from the full fury of the westerlies.

Larwood and the other two pilots wasted no time. Was he in a hurry, wondered Grimes, because he wanted to report that odd deep space radio call to Clavering, or because he wanted to get back to Inferno Valley while the dawn lull lasted? But he must have called Clavering again last night, after he had got rid of Denise Dalgety. And Clavering was to lift off at sunset in *Sally Ann* on his charter voyage, so Larwood must have made sure of getting in touch with him as soon as possible.

The sun came up—and there, ahead, was the dark gash in the ochre desert that was Inferno Valley. From its eastern end white steam, from the Devil's Stewpot, was lazily rising, curling in wreaths about the Devil's Phallus. *One thing about this world,* thought Grimes, *there's no need to go the trouble and expense of putting up wind socks.*

Larwood started to lose altitude as the coaches approached the western end of the valley, dropped below the lips of the canyon as soon as possible, skimmed over the placid waters of the Styx at reduced speed, almost brushing the upper branches of the ghost gums along its banks.

He grounded just in front of the main entrance to the Lucifer Arms, said into his public address microphone, "Well, that's all, folks. Thank you for your company and cooperation."

Williams looked at the back of Denise Dalgety's blonde head and whispered,

"She and the Mate

"Would cooperate

"Upon the office table."

"There's probably a settee in there," said Grimes, taking a malicious pleasure in seeing the girl's ears redden.

"All ashore what's going ashore!" said Larwood with spurious heartiness. "This is the end of the penny section!"

Clavering, Grimes noticed, was waiting just inside the hotel entrance. He looked impatient. Grimes could not see Larwood's face, but the back of his neck looked impatient too. Slowly, clumsily, the tourists extricated themselves from the coach. Grimes and Williams politely held back to let Denise Dalgety out first. She said sweetly, "After you, Commodore," but Larwood seemed anxious to be rid of her.

At last they were all out, standing in gossiping groups on the firm red sand. Larwood, his responsibilities at an end, went straight to Clavering. The two men exchanged a few brief words and then went into the hotel, brushing past Billinghurst, who was on his way out. Denise Dalgety walked swiftly towards the fat customs chief to make her report.

"Nobody loves *us*, Commander," said Grimes sadly.

"Is it surprising, Skipper?" countered Williams.

Chapter 27

GRIMES MANAGED to have a few words in private with Clavering before his departure for Ultimo. It was natural enough that he should wish to have a look over *Sally Ann*, and that vessel's master could not very well refuse his request.

When they were in the old liner's control room Grimes said seriously, "I'm warning you, Captain."

"What about, Commodore?" Clavering's voice was altogether too innocent.

"You know."

"All right. So I know. So what?"

"Try to get out of this mess that you've gotten into, man. Tell whoever's behind the racket that he'll have to find some other way of bringing the stuff in. The risk, for you, just isn't worth it. You've built up a very nice little business here—a not so little business, rather. How long will it last if the Confederacy gets really hostile?"

Clavering said stiffly, "For your information I *am* pulling out." His face worked strangely. "Also for your information—I knew Inga Telfer. I . . . I knew her well. I don't need to tell you, Commodore Grimes, that the owner and manager of a holiday resort has even better opportunities than a passenger ship officer. Did you see any of Inga's work? There's a lot of Eblis in it; she was always saying that this planet is a painter's paradise. Eblis and dreamy weed, and all splashed down on canvas. When I heard of her death

I was . . . shocked. I want nothing more to do with the traffic that killed her. Satisfied?"

"Mphm. What about the consignment that's on the way?"

"What consignment?" countered Clavering.

"I just assumed that there would be one," said Grimes. He could not say more for fear of blowing Denise Dalgety's cover.

"Assume all you like," said Clavering.

And then his chief officer—not Larwood, who would be staying behind to run things in his captain's absence—came in to report that he had completed the pre-lift-off inspection.

"Thank you, Mr. Tilden," said Clavering. "And now, if you'll excuse me, Commodore, I have to start thinking about getting this old lady upstairs. Mr. Tilden will show you to the after airlock."

"This way, sir," said the mate.

"A pleasant voyage, Captain," said Grimes.

"Thank you. Enjoy your stay on Eblis, Commodore."

"I'll do just that," promised Grimes.

Not so very long later, he stood with Billinghurst and Williams, a little apart from *Macedon*'s passengers, and watched *Sally Ann* lifting off. The big ship climbed slowly and, it seemed, laboriously— although this impression may have been due to the way in which the irregular hammering of her inertial drive was echoed back from the red basalt cliffs of the canyon walls. Slowly she climbed, clambering up towards the strip of darkling yellow sky far overhead, her far from inconsiderable bulk dwarfed by the towering monolith of the Devil's Phallus. Slowly she climbed at first, then faster and faster, hurrying to get clear of the atmosphere during the sunset lull.

Abruptly Billinghurst asked, "Did *you* find anything out, Commodore?"

"Eh? What?"

"I asked," repeated the fat man patiently, "if *you* found anything out?"

"I don't wear ear clips," said Grimes.

"Ha, ha. Very funny. But, talking of electronic gadgetry, it's a bloody pity you haven't got *your* Carlotti receiver repaired yet."

"Why?"

"Do I have to spell it out? Because then we could monitor all incoming and outgoing signals."

"Not necessarily," Grimes told him. "This mysterious SB Three could be sending on a very tight beam, aimed directly at the bottling plant. I didn't get a look at the transceiver there myself, but probably it's designed for tight beam transmission."

"Not that it makes any difference," said Billinghurst, "since *you* can't do anything about it, anyhow."

I've got Clavering's word that he's pulling out, thought Grimes. *For what it's worth . . .* How many times have men engaged in illegal activities said, "Just one more time?" Too many. Far too many. And was Clavering already using his ship's Carlotti equipment to establish communication with SB Three? All too likely.

"I don't suppose anything will happen until Clavering gets back," said Billinghurst.

"If then," said Grimes.

"Are you helping me or not, Commodore?"

"I was merely expressing an opinion. For your information, Mr. Billinghurst, as you should have gathered from the conversation your Miss Dalgety recorded, everybody on this planet knows who you are and what you're here for, and they suspect that my story about the projected naval base is just a blind. The way in which *Ditmar*'s been held up at Port Last stinks to high heaven. It's obvious, as Larwood said, that the heat's on."

"When the heat is on, Commodore, people get panicky and make silly mistakes."

"Some people do, but not all."

"These ones will," said Billinghurst flatly, and waddled off.

"The old bastard really loves you, Skipper," commented Williams.

"Doesn't he? Damn it all, Commander, I rather envy him. To be in a job where there's no question of rights or wrongs or personal freedoms, just what's legal and what's illegal. . . ."

"Remember Pleshoff and Fellini and Inga Telfer."

"Pleshoff's a young idiot, and unlucky to boot. Fellini and the girl were killed by H.E., not by dreamy weed. Too, we're just assuming that the charge in the drop container was detonated deliberately. Don't forget that it was under fire from laser and projectile weapons."

"If you were takin' a more active part, Skipper, you'd be far happier. You wouldn't be carryin' on as if yer name was Hamlet, not Grimes."

"Perhaps you're right. If only we had the *Malemute* in running order. . . ."

"But we haven't. But we still have the work boat, and that transponder is still stuck to Captain Clavering's pet atmosphere flier."

"For all the good it is," said Grimes.

Chapter 28

IT SEEMED SAFE TO ASSUME that nothing would happen until Clavering's return from Ultimo, if then. Billinghurst condescended to explain to Grimes the part that the commodore would have to play should the mysterious SB Three land on Eblis to discharge a consignment of dreamy weed.

"We have to bear in mind," he said, "that we're surrounded by legal complications. We can't touch Clavering—or, if we do, his legal eagles are going to raise a scream that'll be heard from here to the Magellanic Clouds. Given time, no doubt, we could nail something on him. But what? No matter. SB Three, however, is most definitely a lawbreaker. He—or she, or it, for all I know—is landing on one of the Rim Worlds without going through the formalities of obtaining an Inward Clearance. He and his ship are liable to arrest. I have the legal power to make such an arrest, of course—but usually, in such cases, the Navy is called upon to seize on behalf of the customs department. You, even with the small handful of *Rim Malemute*'s officers at your disposal, will be able to put a prize crew aboard the seized vessel and take her to Port Last."

"I suppose so," admitted Grimes. "I'd be happier if I had the *Malemute* at my disposal as well as her officers, though. I had the little bitch fitted with a good set of teeth, and now she won't be able to show them, let alone use them."

"This isn't a naval action, Commodore. This is merely the seizure of a smuggler."

"Mphm. Some quite respectable merchant vessels are armed like young cruisers. I shouldn't be at all surprised if SB Three, if he shows up, packs an even heavier wallop."

"When SB Three shows up," said Billinghurst firmly, "we will arrest him."

"And meanwhile?"

"My people will continue to cultivate the friendships they have made. So far the only one to have got results is Miss Dalgety. As you know. It isn't up to me to give you orders, Commodore, but perhaps if you continued making your sightseeing tours you might learn something."

"Thank you," said Grimes, with mock humility.

So he saw the Valley of the Winds and listened to the Devil's Organ—which, he said, reminded him of the lowing of a sick cow. He visited the Burning Pits, and he and Williams amused themselves by imagining Billinghurst being reduced to a puddle of grease at the bottom of the Wishing Well, into which they threw coins to watch them become blobs of molten silver in seconds. They were flown over the Fire Forests on a day when conditions were suitable, and applauded with the rest of the tourists when Larwood solemnly named a new volcano Mount Denise, swooping low to drop a bottle of champagne (he always carried a few on this trip for such occasions) into the bubbling crater.

They dined and danced in the Lucifer Arms, they perspired in the Devil's Stewpot and even, eventually, got into the habit of running straight from its almost boiling waters into the artificially cooled Purgatorial Pool. They spent evenings in the Gambling Hell and soon learned to avoid the One Fingered Bandits so as to make their money last longer at the TriDi Roulette tanks. Insofar as the smuggling was concerned they saw nothing, heard nothing, learned nothing. As far as they could gather Denise Dalgety, although enjoying herself even more than they were, had learned nothing further, and neither had the other undercover Customs agents.

Finally *Macedon* departed on the next leg of her galactic cruise and the hotel was almost empty again, the only guests being Billinghurst and his people and *Rim Malemute*'s crew. Larwood busied himself with the overhaul of the tourist coaches and Denise Dalgety, left to her own devices and not liking it, took up with Williams. Grimes spent much of his spare time in the company of Sally Clavering. Billinghurst sat around and sulked.

Then, with the ship *Sally Ann* on her way back from Port Last, there was an outbreak of fresh activity. The main lounge was converted into a dining room, and the vast, domed dining hall was stripped of its furniture—an easy job, since it had merely to be deflated and stowed—and hung with somber black drapes.

"I don't like it, John," confessed Sally Clavering to Grimes. "But this is the way *they* want it, and *they're* paying."

"*They*, I take it, being the Church of the Gateway."

"Yes. They must be going to hold services in here. But . . . all this black. No crucifixes, or stars and crescents . . . not even a Crux Ansata."

"Not even an alarm clock," said Grimes. "I was on Darsha once, and went to a service in the famous Tower of Darkness. The clock is running down, and all that. Made quite an impression on me. I suppose Entropy is as good a god as any, although not to my taste."

"Do you know anything about these Gateway people, John?"

"Hardly a thing, Sally. It's a new cult that's sprung up on Ultimo, quite recently." *And,* he thought, *dreamy weed's mixed up in it somehow. The hallucinogens have been part and parcel of quite a few freak religions.*

She said, "I don't think I shall like them. I wish Ian hadn't agreed to let them hold their convention here. But they're paying well."

"Thirty pieces of silver?" asked Grimes.

She snapped, "That's not funny."

"I'm sorry, Sally. But . . . I could be wrong, I probably am, but it often seems to me that religion has betrayed man more times than it has led him upwards."

"I don't agree."

"You don't have to. Even so, what Marx said seems, to me, to have validity. Religion is the opium of the people." *And opium is the religion of some people.*

"Marx . . . there's a false prophet for you."

"Not altogether false." He laughed. "I'm a spaceman and you're an ex-spacewoman, and the pair of us should know better than to discuss two of the subjects that are taboo in space—religion and politics."

She said, "We're not aboard ship now."

"We might as well be. Just a handful of men and women living in one little valley on a hostile planet. . . ."

"You'll be serving out the rifles and the revolvers next, to fight off the hostile natives."

"Are they restless tonight?" *I know that I am,* he thought. *I can't help feeling that Clavering's going to do one last piece of drug running—and, as far as he's concerned, it will be quite legal. But SB Three will be on the wrong side of the fence as far as the law's concerned.*

He excused himself as soon as he decently could, went to find Billinghurst, told him what he suspected. The customs officer was scornful. He said, "You only see the obvious, Grimes, when your nose is rubbed in it. The convention was mentioned in that Carlotti call recorded by Miss Dalgety. You and your officers had better be on their toes when Clavering gets back with his shipload of cranks. I've already warned my people."

"I don't think, somehow," said Grimes, "that SB Three will be landing in Inferno Valley."

"Are you sure you can't get your bloody ship fixed in time?" demanded Billinghurst.

"Quite sure," Grimes told him.

Chapter 29

SALLY ANN came in from Ultimo, dropping down through the morning twilight the dawn lull, the eddying streamers of white mist rising sluggishly from the Devil's Stewpot. *Sally Ann* came in, and all Clavering's staff, as well as the guests at his hotel, were out to watch the berthing. The big ship settled gently to her pad just beyond the crippled *Malemute*. Almost immediately the mooring crew of devils, under Larwood's direction, swarmed over her, shackling on and setting up the wire stays. Only when this job was completed did the last mutterings of the liner's inertial drive fade into silence. Then, up and along her towering hull, airlock doors opened and ramps were extruded.

Disembarkation at a port like Inferno Valley—as Grimes took pleasure in pointing out to Billinghurst—was not a lengthy procedure. There were no port health, immigration, or customs officials to slow things up. Within seconds the first passengers were trooping ashore.

Grimes looked at them curiously. They were like—yet markedly unlike—the spheres with whom he had rolled at Port Last. The women's heads were shaven, the men all had long hair and beards. But most of them belonged to a different age group, were older, and wore long dark robes instead of form revealing clothing.

Larwood came to greet the first group down the ramp. He saluted the man who seemed to be in charge. He asked courteously, "Are you the . . . er . . . leader, sir?"

The tall, gray-haired and gray-bearded man replied, "Yes, my son. I am the Guru William. Is all prepared for us?"

"All is prepared, Your . . . Your Reverence. Accommodation for two hundred people. Our main hall converted into a temple, to your specifications."

"It is good," said the Guru.

"It is good," echoed those of his followers within earshot.

"Somethin' odd about these bastards, Skipper," whispered Williams to Grimes.

"Mphm. Yes." The commodore looked at the members of the Church of the Gateway as they trooped past him. They walked as though they were in a state of trance, gliding over the hard-packed red sand somnambulistically. Every face, young, not so young, or old, male or female, wore the same expression of . . . of beatitude? *When the saints go marching in,* thought Grimes irreverently, *I don't want to be of their number.*

Clavering came down the ramp from the forward airlock, letting the escalator do all the work. He looked very worried. He started to walk to where Larwood was still talking with the Guru and his party, then paused where Grimes, Williams, and Billinghurst were standing.

Grimes said, "Nice Sunday school outing you have here, Captain."

Clavering almost snarled, "That's not funny, Commodore!" then hurried on.

"What's bitin' *him?*" asked Williams.

"The same as what's just starting to nibble me, probably," Grimes told him. "Are you like me, Commander Williams? Do *you* feel uncomfortable when you're among really pious people, men and women who evince a passionate belief in something utterly irrational? Have you ever tried to argue with some fanatical true believer who's doing his damnedest to convert you to his own brand of hogwash? That's the way I feel now, looking at this bunch."

"Live an' let live," said Williams airily.

"I quite agree. That's the viewpoint of the cynical, tolerant agnostic. But don't forget that it's always been the overly religious who've taken a righteous delight in the slaughter of nonbelievers.

Crusades, Jihads, bloody revolutions to establish the dictatorship of the proletariat—you name it, they've done it."

"I think these are a harmless bunch, Skipper, even if they are a bit odd. No more than rather elderly Blossom People with a few extra trimmings. Just spheres who're a bit too stiff in the joints for any really hearty rolling."

"Mphm. You could be right. I hope you are right." He turned to look at the devils who were bringing passengers' baggage ashore. "They don't seem to have much gear with them, do they?"

"Don't suppose they need much," said Williams. "Just a change of robes an' a spare pair o' sandals. A tube of depilatory cream for the sheilas. That's all. Somethin' to be said for travellin' light."

Billinghurst broke into the conversation. He said, "Well, Commodore, the balloon should be going up at any time now."

"What balloon?" asked Grimes, just to be awkward.

"You know," growled the fat man. "As long as you're ready to do what has to be done when it goes up."

"If it goes up," corrected Grimes.

"It will, Commodore, it will."

Grimes said to Williams as the chief collector moved ponderously away, "I hate to have to say it, but I'm afraid he's right."

It was, however, all of five days before the balloon did go up.

Those five days were . . . interesting. The People of the Gateway did not behave as the previous tourists had done. They went on no sightseeing tours. They did not frequent the Gambling Hell, neither did they simmer and freeze themselves in the hot and cold pools. They infuriated the chef by demanding very plain foods, although their consumption of alcoholic drinks was far from low. Morning, afternoon and evening they met in the made-over dining hall, which they called their temple. They made no attempt to convert outsiders, but neither did they refuse admission to the curious.

Grimes attended one or two services, of course, as did Williams and *Rim Malemute*'s officers, and Billinghurst and his people, and the human staff of Inferno Valley. There was no singing, no sermonizing. The worshippers sat on the floor, in near-darkness, around the central dais on which the Guru William was seated. Every time he would open proceedings by saying, "Brethren, let us meditate. Let us open our minds to the true reality." There would be silence, often a long silence, broken only by the subdued sound of breathing. Then somebody would utter a single word, such as, "Peace." Another silence. "Darkness everlasting." Silence again, and a growing tension. "The end of light." "The end of life." "Not-life, not-death." More silence. "The Gateway to Infinity." "Open the gate, open the gate, open the gate!" "The Gateway to Never." "Open the gate!"

"Gives me the willies, Skipper," Williams confessed to Grimes.

"I prefer religions that go in for Moody- and Sankey-style hymns," said the commodore.

"Yeah. At least you can fit your own kind o' words to most o' the tunes." He began to sing untunefully,

"Whiter than the whitewash on the wall!
"Whiter than the whitewash on the wall!
"Wash me in the water
"Where yer wash yer dirty daughter
"An' I shall be whiter than the whitewash
"On the wall!"

"Please, Commander."

"Sorry, Skipper. But sittin' crosslegged among that bunch o' morbid hopheads makes me wanter relax with a spot o' light blasphemy when I get outside. An' you said that you liked Moody an' Sankey."

"I'm not so sure that I do, now. Meanwhile, what do our spies report?"

"Captain Clavering's aircar is ready to lift off at a second's notice. So are all the coaches. An' so is our work boat. Clavering's buggy is still bugged. Absolutely no joy with any of our radio equipment. But I have the boys on watches, an' they'll let us know at once if an' when anything happens."

"And our friend Billinghurst has his boys and girls on watches too. But I think that if Clavering does lift off to a rendezvous with SB Three it will be either around dawn or sunset."

"An' Mrs. Clavering? What's she sayin' these days?"

"Nothing much. Nothing much at all. She's worried stiff, of course. She did sort of hint that this would be the very last time, and that if I called my dogs off I should be . . . er . . . adequately recompensed." He grinned wrily. "Unluckily Billinghurst's dogs are in the hunt as well as mine, and I can't imagine any woman wanting to be nice to Billinghurst."

"People have probably said the same about you, Skipper."

"Remind me, Commander," said Grimes, "to have you busted down to spaceman fourth class when we get back to civilization."

Chapter 30

THE BALLOON WENT UP AT DAWN.

Substituting literal for metaphorical language, Clavering's private atmosphere flier lifted off at dawn. Grimes and his officers were already standing to, although none of them had incurred suspicion by venturing outside their hotel rooms with the exception of the watchkeeper aboard *Rim Malemute*. The young man hurried to the Lucifer Arms to inform the others that Clavering was on his way—to where?—but Grimes, even through the double, air-filled skin of his sleeping quarters, had heard the unmistakable irregular beat of an inertial drive unit.

The plan of operations was put into effect at once. The watch officer ran back to *Rim Malemute* and switched on the NST transceiver. This was still useless insofar as the reception or transmission of messages were concerned, but it was capable of jamming. He then carefully jockeyed the tug's work boat out of its bay, brought it to the landing ground in front of the Lucifer Arms.

Meanwhile Williams and his chief officer, both armed with stunguns, had gone to the hangar in which the resort's aircoaches were garaged. When Grimes and Billinghurst entered the building it was to hear Williams saying to Larwood, "I hereby requisition these vehicles for service in the Rim Worlds Navy."

"Stop playing at pirates, Commander Williams!" growled Larwood. "You've no legal right to do anything of the sort. These coaches are the property of a citizen of the Federation!"

Grimes intervened. "Mr. Larwood," he said, "I can, quite legally, requisition these vehicles—and I am doing so. I shall give you a receipt, and there will be adequate compensation."

"Legally? Come off it, Commodore."

"Yes. Legally. I am empowered to requisition any air or space vehicles of Rim Worlds' registration for naval service. I can't touch your precious *Sally Ann* or her boats—she's Federation registry. But your coaches . . . *they* are licensed to carry passengers by the Confederacy."

"You bloody space lawyer!"

Sally Clavering had appeared on the scene. Her face was pale and drawn. She said, "Don't argue, Ron. It'll get us nowhere. *He* has the law on his side." The look she shot at Grimes should have shriveled him up where he stood.

He said, meaning it, "I'm sorry, Sally."

"You should be. For your information, just in case you're interested, Ian has gone to have it out with Drongo Kane, to tell him to find somebody else to handle his trade at this end, on one of the other Rim Worlds." She addressed herself to Billinghurst now, as well as to Grimes. "But Ian has broken no laws, and you know it."

"Did you say Drongo Kane?" demanded Grimes. *So his had been the oddly familiar voice recorded by Denise Dalgety.*

"Yes."

"And would the name of his ship be *Southerly Buster?*"

"Yes. *Southerly Buster III.*"

"Come on, Commodore." Billinghurst was impatient. "We can't afford to waste any time."

"I know, I know. And I know now whom we're up against. And I don't like it." He grinned. "Or perhaps I do. There're a few old scores to settle!"

Grimes took the work boat up. He hoped that by this time Clavering would be sufficiently distant for the small craft to be beyond the range of his radar. He hovered above Inferno Valley, making altitude slowly, until the commandeered air coach had lifted above the canyon rim. It was not possible for him to exchange any words with Williams, who was piloting the vehicle; the interference being broadcast by Rim *Malemute*'s defective transceiver inhibited any sort of communication. In any case, it would have been advisable to maintain radio silence. Would this jamming effect the functioning of the transponder? Grimes had been assured that it would not, but he was not sure until he saw that the needle of the compasslike indicator had steadied on to a definite heading. He looked into his radar screen. There was nothing but ground clutter. Good. If he could not "see" Clavering, then Clavering could not "see" him.

He turned the boat on to the indicated heading, gave her maximum forward thrust. She vibrated frighteningly, excessively, but she went. He put her on to automatic pilot. It was awkward, he was beginning to find, to have to do everything himself. He had become far too used, over the years, to the control rooms of ships, with attentive officers at his eyes and hands. He felt that he could do with at least three pairs of the former and two of the latter. He looked into his radar screen again. The coach was following him. He transferred his attention to the gyro compass, then to the chart. Clavering, it seemed, was making for Dante's Pass. So Kane's landing place was somewhere in the Painted Badlands.

He looked out through the viewscreens—out, ahead and down. The dawn lull wasn't lasting. Below him the surface of the desert was obscured by driving clouds of red sand; ahead, the Great Smokies were all but invisible. It was obvious, too, that the boat was sagging very badly to leeward. He returned to his instruments to make the necessary course adjustment. He knew that Williams, an excellent pilot, would be doing the same—if he had not already done so.

Another course adjustment . . .

He thought, *The little bitch is going sideways.*

And was that the Great Smokies showing up in the radar screen? It must be. Still there was no sign of Clavering, although the indicator needle jerked to starboard, showing that he had entered the Pass.

And if I keep him ahead, thought Grimes, stopping himself from changing course, *I shall pile up on Mount Beatrice.*

He made the necessary adjustments to his radar. Yes, there they were, Dante and Beatrice, marking the entrance to the Pass, steadily approaching the centre of the screen. He changed to a shorter range setting, and a shorter one, put the boat back on to manual steering. The wheel, mounted on the control column, bucked in his hands. The little craft had been designed to be used in airless space rather than in an atmosphere, a turbulent atmosphere at that. Williams, he thought with a twinge of jealousy, would be having a far better time of it in his air coach.

Hell! That's too bloody close!

Grimes yanked the control column violently to port, applying lateral thrust. Through his starboard window he saw black, steaming rocks dropping away from him. He must have missed them by the thickness of a coat of paint. He jerked the column to starboard as he saw, through a rift in the billowing smoke and steam, one of Mount Dante's minor craters almost below him. Hastily he reduced speed, hoping that Williams would not overtake him and crash into his stern.

He threaded his way through the pass on radar, breathed a great sigh of relief when he was out and clear. He would have liked to have got out his pipe, but he dared not take his hands from the controls. He flew through the last of the heavy smoke and steam into relatively clear air—but only relatively clear. Although on this side of the Smokies it was almost calm, some freak of atmospheric circulation had brought down a thick haze, a yellow murk through which the fantastic rock formations looked menacingly. And Grimes was obliged to make a rock-hopping approach, as was Williams astern of him. If they flew above the eroded monoliths they would be picked up by Drongo Kane's radar. The master smuggler was not a man to neglect precautions.

Grimes watched his indicator needle, keeping Clavering ahead as much as possible. At the same time he watched his radar screen and tried to keep a visual lookout. Afterwards, when he told the story, he would say, "If the Venus of Milo had been equipped with arms I'd have knocked them off—and I as near as dammit castrated the Colossus of Eblis!" This was exaggeration, but only slightly so.

On he flew, and on, perspiring inside the protective suit that he was wearing, his hands clenched on the wheel, his attention divided between the indicator needle, the radar screen, the forward window of his cramped cabin and the chart of the area, one blown up from the brochure issued to tourists. He passed as close as he dared to the rock formations so that he could sight them visually and identify them. Now and again, caught by a freak eddy, he had to apply vertical or lateral thrust, or both together. The work boat complained but kept on going.

Then, ahead on the radar screen but still obscured by the haze, loomed a great mass. There was only one formation that it could be, and that was Ayers Rock. But surely the Rock did not have a much smaller monolith just over a kilometre to the east of it.

Grimes decided not to reduce speed. By so doing he could well forfeit the advantage of surprise. He ignored his radar, concentrated on a visual lookout. And, at last, there, on his port bow, was the sullenly brooding mass of red granite and, right ahead, indistinct but clearer with every passing second, the silvery spire of a grounded spaceship. By the foot of the ramp from her after airlock was a small atmosphere craft.

The commodore applied maximum forward thrust and, at the same time, using one hand, worked his respirator over his head. He put the boat on full reverse when he was almost up to and over Clavering's craft. He cut the drive, slammed down heavily on to the red sand. He was out of the door and running for the ramp before the dust had settled. He was dimly aware that Williams, just behind him, had brought the coach in to a hasty landing.

It was too much to hope for—but it seemed that his arrival had been neither seen nor heard. The airlock outer door remained open, the ramp remained extended. He pulled his stungun from its holster as he ran up the gangway. Impatiently he waited for Williams and Billinghurst to join him in the chamber of the airlock; it was too small to hold more than three men. The others—*Rim Malemute*'s people and the customs officers—would have to wait their turn.

Williams used the standard controls to shut the outer door, to evacuate the foul air of Eblis and to introduce the clean air of the ship into the chamber. All this must be registering on the remote control board in the control room, but perhaps there was no officer on duty there. He pushed the knob that would open the inner door. It opened.

A tall figure stood on the other side of it to receive them—a big man who, if he lost only a little weight, could be classified as skinny. His face, under the stubble of grayish-yellow hair, was deeply tanned and seamed, and looked as though at some time in the past it had been completely shattered and then reassembled not too carefully.

He said, "Welcome aboard, Commander Grimes! I beg your pardon, *Commodore* Grimes. But I always think of you as that boy scoutish Survey Service lieutenant commander who was captain of *Seeker*."

Grimes removed his respirator with the hand that was not holding the gun. "Captain Kane," he said, "you are under arrest, and your ship is seized."

"Am I, now? Is she, now? Let's not be hasty, Commander— Commodore, I mean. What will the Federation say when it hears that a breakaway colonial officer has arrested one of its shipmasters? Suppose we have a yarn about old times first, Commodore. Come on up to my dogbox to see how the poor live. This is Liberty Hall—you can spit on the mat an' call the cat a bastard!"

"I'd rather not accept your hospitality, Captain Kane, in these circumstances. Or in any circumstances."

"Still the same stuffy bastard, ain't yer, Grimes? But if yer seizin' *Southerly Buster III*—I still haven't forgiven yer fer what yer did ter the first *Southerly Buster*—yer'll have ter see her papers. Register, Articles o' Agreement an' all the rest of it."

"He's right," said Billinghurst.

"Ain't yer goin' ter introduce me to yer cobbers, Commodore?"

"This is Mr. Billinghurst," said Grimes curtly, "chief collector of customs for the Confederacy. And this is Commander Williams, of the Rim Worlds Navy."

"The way I'm surrounded," drawled Kane. "I suppose I should surrender. But I ain't goin' to. I . . ."

Whatever else he said was drowned by the sudden clamour of *Southerly Buster*'s inertial drive as she lifted with vicious acceleration, as she staggered under the sudden application of lateral thrust that threw the three unprepared men heavily to the deck.

Kane's stungun was out, and a couple of tough-looking characters, similarly armed, had put in an appearance.

Speaking loudly to be heard above the irregular beat of the drive Kane said cheerfully, "An' if he's doin' what he was told ter do, my gunnery boy's just in the act o' vaporizin' your transport with his pet laser cannon. I hope none o' your nongs are still inside that coach they came in."

But he didn't seem to be worrying much about it.

~ Chapter 31 ~

"AN' NOW," drawled Drongo Kane, "what am I goin' ter do with you bastards?"

"Return us to Inferno Valley!" snapped Grimes.

Kane lazily surveyed his prisoners—Clavering, Grimes, Billinghurst, and Williams, the officers from *Rim Malemute*, the customs sub-inspectors. He said, leering in Denise Dalgety's direction, "Seems a cryin' shame ter throw a good blonde back ter where she came from, don't it?"

The girl flushed angrily and Williams snarled, "That's enough o' that, Kane!"

"Is it, now, Commander? Get it inter yer thick head—an' that goes for all o' yer—that there ain't a thing any o' yer can do."

And there's not, thought Grimes. *Not until this paralysis wears off. And it won't, as long as these goons keep giving us extra shots with their stunguns as soon as it looks like doing so.*

"In fact," Kane went on, "I think I deserve some reward for goin' back, for not leavin' Blondie an' the others wanderin' around in the desert." He extricated a gnarled cigar from the breast pocket of his uniform coverall, ostentatiously lit it with his laser pistol. It stank as bad as it looked.

"Release us at once!" blustered Billinghurst.

"An' wouldn't yer be peeved if I did, Chief Collector? What if I took yer at yer word, an' dumped yer down in the Painted Badlands, miles from anywhere, an' with no transport but yer own bleedin' hooves?" He exhaled a cloud of acrid smoke. "But yer dead lucky. Clavering here won't play ball, so I have ter go all the way ter Inferno Valley in person, singin' an' dancin', ter make me own deal with the boss cocky o' that bunch o' holy joes. Church o' the Gateway, ain't it? They want dreamy weed, I've got it. They can have it, at my price." He fixed his attention on Grimes. "Ever hear o' Australis, Commodore? Not Austral. Australis. A frontier planet like these worlds o' yours, only 'stead o' bein' on the Rim it's way out to hell an' gone beyond the south rotor bearin' o' the Galaxy. Did a sim'lar deal there, wi' some bunch o' religious nuts. They had a guru, too. Often wonder what happened. Been no news out o' Australis fer quite some time. Could be that the world itself ain't there any more. After I heard the guru's advance spiel about what he said was goin ter be the final act o' worship, acceptance an' all the rest of it I decided ter get the hell out." He grinned. "Tell yer what. I'll return yer all ter Inferno Valley, an' insist that this Guru William try ter make converts o' yer. If he won't play he gets no dreamy weed."

"The users of it," remarked Billinghurst, "claim that dreamy weed is nonaddictive."

Keep out of it, you stupid, fat slob! thought Grimes.

"So 't'is, Chief Collector. So 't'is. Smoked it once myself—try anythin' once, that's me. Guess I've the wrong kind o' mind. Didn't see visions or dream dreams. But I'm a baddie, an' you're all goodies."

Clavering said, "There will be no business transactions of any kind on *my* world."

"An who's goin' ter stop me from doin' business? Not you, fer a start. You were pleased enough ter take yer rake-off from my deals until that silly bitch got blown up, weren't yer? Oh, well, go an' stew in yer own juice with the other goodies."

Grimes realized that sensation was coming back into his hands and feet, that he could move his fingers and toes. He mentally measured the distance between himself and the arrogant Drongo Kane, and between Kane and the three armed spacemen lounging negligently in the doorways of the ship's saloon. There was a chance, he thought. There was a chance, and if he could use Kane's body as a shield it might be a good one.

"Mr. Welland," drawled Drongo Kane, "yer might give the . . . er . . . passengers a sprayin' over with yer stungun. I noticed the commodore twitchin' his pinkie just now."

The weapon, set on low power, buzzed softly. Grimes' nerves tingled, then went dead. He could breathe, he could move his eyes, he could speak, even, but that was all.

"I'll give yer all a stronger dose before we land," Kane promised them. "The guru an' his boys an' girls can carry yer off me ship."

"You'll be sorry for this," promised Grimes.

"I shan't be when I count the foldin' money that Guru William's goin' ter hand over ter me," Kane assured him. "Or, if I am, I shall cry all the way ter the bank."

~ Chapter 32 ~

KANE LEFT THEN, presumably to take over the pilotage of his ship. The three guards remained. They sneered at Billinghurst's offer of a free pardon, a reward even, if they assisted the forces of law and order. They laughed loudly when Denise Dalgety made an appeal to their decency as human beings. Welland, who seemed to be Kane's second mate, exclaimed, "We ain't decent, lady; if we were we wouldn't be in Drongo's rustbucket. If yer want ter find out just how indecent we can be . . ."

"No!" she cried. "You wouldn't!"

"Wouldn't I, honey?"

But he didn't, though it was obvious that it was fear of Kane that restrained him rather than any respect for the girl.

Grimes, listening to the varying beat of the inertial drive, was trying to work out where they were. They were flying through severe turbulence, that much was obvious. He said to Clavering, "Has Kane been to Inferno Valley before?"

"Only as a passenger, Commodore. And only in my flier, usually during the evening lull."

"Mphm. Will he be able, do you think, to get down into the valley with the winds on top at gale force, at least?"

"You did, Commodore."

"In a much smaller ship."

Welland guffawed scornfully. "The Old Man could take this bitch through hell without singeing her hide! But stow the gab, will yer? Yer none o' yer sparklin' conversationalists!"

"For the last time . . ." began Billinghurst, making a final attempt to enlist aid from this unlikely quarter.

"Aw, shaddup!"

The stunguns buzzed, and breathing became almost impossible, and talking quite impossible.

Grimes could still think, and he could hear. There were surges of power as lateral thrust was applied one way and the other, then a diminution of the irregular beat as vertical thrust was reduced.

Southerly Buster III was coming in for a landing.

➢ Chapter 33 ➣

THOSE WHO HAD BEEN KANE'S PRISONERS were seated in a group to one side of the huge dining hall, and with them were Sally Clavering and the members of Clavering's staff. These, too, had been incapacitated by judicious use of the stunguns. Drongo Kane had collected his payment from the Guru William and had gone, the noisy hammering of his inertial drive echoing back and forth between the sheer cliffs of the valley's walls until it had suddenly faded into silence.

Kane was gone—but the Guru William remained.

He was a harmless man—to judge by his appearance—saintly, even. He had stood over the nonbelievers after they had been dragged and carried into his temple and had looked at them for long minutes, a faint smile curving his mouth, his huge, brown eyes looking through and beyond the helpless men and women. He murmured, "Peace."

Grimes tried to say something, anything, but could not. He would be voiceless until the paralysis wore off.

"Peace," murmured the guru again, but in a louder tone. "Peace. The last, the everlasting, peace. And you, my sons and my daughters, are blessed, for you shall see, with us, the cessation of all that is harsh, all that is discordant."

Billinghurst managed to make some sort of noise. "Blahh . . . blahh."

"I must leave you, my sons and my daughters, my brethren, my sisters. The worship, the last act of worship, of acceptance, is to begin. Surrender yourselves. Join with us, the People of the Gateway. The gateway is about to be opened."

On to what? Grimes demanded of himself desperately. *On to what?* More than any of the others, with the possible exception of Williams, he was starting to realize the implications of it all. He tried to hold his breath as he smelled the sweet yet acrid taint that was beginning to pervade the air in the dome, reasoning that the smoke of burning dreamy weed was being blown in through the air-conditioning system. He wondered how much the Guru William had paid for the consignment. A small fortune—or a large one—must be smoldering away somewhere behind the scenes.

William had mounted the dais and, surrounded by acolytes, was squatting there in the lotus posture. The bald heads of the women glimmered eerily in the dim light. Their eyes, and the eyes of the men, seemed to be self-luminous. Drifting streamers of gray fog curled about them.

"We accept . . ." intoned the Guru.

"We accept . . ." repeated his flock. The words had a faraway sound, like a thin, cold wind rustling the detritus of long dead years.

"The nothingness . . ."

"The nothingness . . ."

"Beyond the stars."

"Beyond the stars."

The nothingness, or the otherness, thought Grimes. Here, out on the Rim, on the very edge of the expanding galaxy, the skin of the bubble that held the continuum was stretched almost to bursting, the barriers between the dimensions were flimsy, almost nonexistent. There were, Grimes knew all too well, the other time tracks, the alternate universes. And what—if anything—lay between the time tracks, the universes?

"Open the Gateway . . ."

"The Gateway to Never . . ."

I will not believe, Grimes told himself. *I will* not *believe.*

The effects of the last stungun shock were wearing off now, but the fumes of the consciousness-expanding drug were taking effect. On the dais the guru's form was outlined by an aura, not of light, nor yet of darkness, but of *nothingness*.

And the word beat in the Commodore's mind, *Never ... never ... never....* Those about him were becoming insubstantial, filmy.... He lifted his hand—and realized with horror that he could see through it, that he was looking through skin and flesh and bone at the calm, the impossibly calm face of Pahvani.

"Nirvana . . ." the young sub-inspector was murmuring. "Nirvana...."

And was this what had happened on Australis, *to* Australis? Was this why Drongo Kane had gotten away and clear like a bat out of hell? The picture that formed in Grimes' mind of a huge, black, winged mammal beating its way through and between towering columns of crimson fire was as real as though he were actually seeing it—and it was better than that *nothingness* which was showing through the widening rents in the very continuum.

"Open the Gateway . . ."

"The Gateway to Never . . ."

"Accept, accept . . ."

I'm damned *if I'll accept*, thought Grimes.

Light was beating upwards in waves—red, orange, dazzling blue-white—from the core of the planet, washing over and through Grimes' body like cool water, dissipating itself in the utterly starless dark, the dark that was a negation of everything, all around, light that fought a losing battle against the nothingness, that faded, faster and faster, to a faint, ashy glimmer. He put out his hand, or thought that he put out his hand, to catch one of the last, feeble photons, held it in his cupped palm, stared at the dying, weakly pulsating thing and willed it to survive. It flared fitfully, and . . .

Somebody had hold of his sleeve, was shaking it. Somebody was saying, almost hissing, "Sir, sir!"

Grimes stared at the intrusive being. So this was what lay in the nothingness between the time tracks. It was hell, the old-fashioned hell of the fundamentalist faiths at which he had always sneered, a hell peopled by horrendous, horned and tailed demons. . . .

"Sir! Sir! Come back, please!"

Come *back?* What the hell was this stupid devil yapping about? How could he come back when he was only just getting there?

"Sir! Earthquake. Bad one!"

"Go away . . . go away. . . ."

The scaled, clawed hands were at his face, were forcing something over his head. Grimes drew in a panicky breath, and the sudden inhalation of almost pure oxygen nearly choked him. He put up his hands to try to tear off the respirator, but there were devils all around him, restraining him. He was aware that the floor was heaving underfoot, and he was fighting as much to retain his balance as to throw off his assailants.

His assailants?

His saviors.

The floor was like a calm sea over which a long, low swell was rolling, and the walls of the dome were bellying inwards. But only Grimes and his attendant demons were aware of this—and he still wondered if this were actuality or some drug-induced vision. Billinghurst squatted there like a Buddha, and beside him young Pahvani was staring into—or *at*—nothingness, a supernaturally sweet smile on his thin face. Williams was muttering, "The Outback. The last Outback . . ." And Sally Clavering . . . was that a halo faint-gleaming about her head, or was it merely a wreathing streamer of dreamy weed smoke?

And were Billinghurst and Williams and the others as insubstantial as the guru and his people? They were all fading, fading fast, as they swayed in time to the waves that swept across the floor in regular undulations. They were fading—and again, through rents in the very fabric of space-time, that ultimate, horrifying *nothingness* was increasingly evident.

If only the simple, three-dimensional fabric of the dome would rend, to release the hallucinogenic fumes. . . .

What was hallucination, and what was not?

"Sir, sir!" It was the devil who had first pulled Grimes back to reality, or to what passed for reality. "Sir, sir! *Do* something, please! We are frightened."

You aren't the only one, thought Grimes.

He looked at the native. He must have been a kitchen helper of some kind. He was wearing an incongruous white apron, and a belt with a pouch into which were thrust various tools.

"Give me your knife," ordered the commodore.

He grabbed the implement, used it to tear away the black hangings shrouding the interior wall of the dome. Behind these the plastic was tough, too tough, even though the knife was razor-sharp. And then . . . and then the wall bellied inwards as there was a particularly severe tremor and the skin was stretched almost to bursting.

The knife penetrated, and tore the outer skin as well. There was a great *whoosh* as the air rushed out, and Grimes and his helpers were blown through the opening into the night, into the night that was blessedly normal despite the earthquake shocks that continued, with increasing severity. He stood there, keeping his balance somehow, and watched in fascination as the fantastic bubble structure that was the Lucifer Arms collapsed upon itself, as balloon after glowing balloon deflated, some with explosive suddenness, some slowly. The generators kept working until the very end, and the darkness—the real darkness, the natural darkness—did not sweep in until the last bubble had burst.

Grimes had battery powered emergency lights brought from *Rim Malemute*, and then the rescue work began.

☙ Chapter 34 ❧

"I'VE JUST HEARD FROM CLAVERING," said Grimes to Sonya. "He and Sally didn't come out of it too badly. The Lucifer Arms was insured against earthquake damage, and Lloyd's paid up."

"Earthquake damage!" she scoffed. "Earthquake damage! When *you* were running amok with a long knife!"

"It wasn't all that long. And there was an earthquake, after all."

"Joking apart, John, what do you make of it all?"

"You've read my report."

"Yes. But I sort of gained the impression that you were too scared, still, to write what you really thought."

"Could be. Could be. You know, I keep thinking of the Lucifer Arms as a microcosm of the universe in which we live, our space-time continuum. What would have happened if the Guru William had succeeded in bursting the bubble of what we think of as reality, just as I burst that bubble of inflated plastic?"

"I can't see us all going whooshing out into nothingness."

"Can't you? The guru's body was never found, you know, or the bodies of about a hundred of his disciples. Or that of young Pahvani. They *could* have fallen into one of the fissures that opened and closed again—but it's odd that, apart from the utterly missing people, there were no casualties." He slowly filled and lit his pipe. "An unfortunate business. Clavering and his people will have to leave the Rim, of course. Billinghurst's a vindictive bastard. Drongo Kane'll get away scot free. He broke no Federation laws, and I doubt very much if we could get him extradited to any of our worlds."

"And the Confederacy," she said, "will be confirmed in its archaic puritanism insofar as the permissive practices of the Federated planets are concerned."

"I hope that you're right," he said. I sincerely hope that you're right." She looked at him in some amazement. He laughed. "No, I'm not becoming a wowser in my old age. It's just that I've been made to realize that even if what you do doesn't much matter, *where* you do it does.

"To use the so-called mind-expanding drugs out here, on the Rim, is like smoking over a powder barrel!"

"The sort of thing you'd do," she jeered, but without malice.

"But only tobacco," he told her, puffing away contentedly on his pipe. "But only tobacco."

THE
DARK
DIMENSIONS

～ Chapter 1 ～

"I'VE ANOTHER JOB FOR YOU, Grimes," said Admiral Kravitz.

"Mphm, sir," grunted Commodore Grimes, of the Rim Worlds' Naval Reserve. He regarded the portly flag officer with something less than enthusiasm. There had been a time, not so very long ago, when he had welcomed being dragged away from his rather boring civilian duties as Rim Runners' astronautical superintendent, but increasingly of late he had come to appreciate a relatively quiet, uneventful life. Younger men than he could fare the starways, he was happy to remain a desk-sitting space commodore.

"Rim Runners are granting you indefinite leave of absence," went on Kravitz.

"They would," grumbled Grimes.

"On full pay."

Grimes' manner brightened slightly. "And I'll be drawing my commodore's pay and allowances from the Admiralty, of course?"

"Of course. You are back on the Active List as and from 0000 hours this very day."

"We can always use the extra money . . ." murmured Grimes.

Kravitz looked shocked. "I never knew that you were so mercenary, Grimes."

"You do now, sir." The commodore grinned briefly, then once again looked rather apprehensive. "But it's not Kinsolving's Planet again, is it?"

The admiral laughed. "I can understand your being more than somewhat allergic to that peculiar world."

Grimes chuckled grimly. "I think it's allergic to me, sir. Three times I've landed there, and each time was unlucky; the third time unluckiest of all."

"I've read your reports. But set your mind at rest. It's not Kinsolving."

"Then where?"

"*The Outsider.*"

"*The Outsider . . .*" repeated Grimes slowly. How many times since the discovery of that alien construction out beyond the Galactic Rim had he urged that he be allowed to take *Faraway Quest* to make his own investigation? He had lost count. Always his proposals had been turned down. Always he could not be spared or was required more urgently elsewhere. Too, it was obvious that the Confederacy was scared of the thing, even though it swam in space that came under Rim Worlds' jurisdiction. The Federation was scared of it, too. "Let well enough alone," was the attitude of both governments.

"*The Outsider . . .*" said Grimes again. "I was beginning to think that it occupied top place on the list of untouchables. Why the sudden revival of interest?"

"We have learned," Kravitz told him, "from reliable sources, that the Waldegren destroyer *Adler* is on her way out to the . . . *thing*. I needn't tell you that the Duchy of Waldegren is making a comeback, or that Federation policy is that Waldegren will never be allowed to build its fleet up to the old level. But sophisticated weaponry can give a small navy superiority over a large one."

"The Outsiders' Ship, as we all know, is a storehouse of science and technology thousands—millions, perhaps—of years in advance of our own. *Your* Captain Calver got his paws on to some of it, but passed nothing of interest on to us before he flew the coop. Since then we, and the Federation, and the Shaara Empire, and probably quite a few more, have sent expeditions. Everyone has ended disastrously. It is possible, probable even, that this Waldegren effort will end disastrously. But we can't be sure."

"It should not take long to recommission your *Faraway Quest.*

She's only just back from the Fleet Maneuvers, at which she was present as an auxiliary cruiser. . . ."

"I know," said Grimes. "I should have been in command of her."

"But you weren't. For all your early life in the Federation's Survey Service, for all your rank in our Naval Reserve, you don't make a good naval officer. You're too damned independent. You like to be left alone to play in your own little corner. But—I grant you this—whatever sort of mess you fall into you always come up smelling of roses."

"Thank you, sir," said Grimes stiffly.

Kravitz chuckled. "It's true, isn't it? Anyhow, you should be on the spot, showing the flag, before *Adler* blows in. You'll be minding the shop. Play it by ear, as you always do. And while you're about it, you might try to find out something useful about *The Outsider*."

"Is that all?" asked Grimes.

"For the time being, yes. Oh, personnel for *Faraway Quest* . . . You've a free hand. Make up the crew you think you'll need from whatever officers are available, regulars or reservists. The Federation has intimated that it'd like an observer along, I think I'm right in saying that Commodore Verrill still holds a reserve commission in the Intelligence Branch of their Survey Service. . . ."

"She does, sir. And she'd be very annoyed if she wasn't allowed to come along for the ride."

"I can well imagine. And now we'll browse through *The Outsider* files and try to put you in the picture."

He pressed a button under his desk, and a smartly uniformed W.R.W.N. officer came in, carrying a half-dozen bulky folders that she put on the admiral's desk. She was followed by two male petty officers who set up screen, projector and tape recorders.

Kravitz opened the first folder. "It all started," he said, "with Commander Maudsley of the Federation Survey Service's Intelligence Branch. . . ."

$\approx$ Chapter 2 $\approx$

"IT ALL STARTED," said Grimes, "with Commander Maudsley of the Federation Survey Service's Intelligence Branch. . . ."

As soon as he had spoken the words he regretted them. Sonya, his wife, had known Maudsley well. They had been more, much more, than merely fellow officers in the same service. Grimes looked at her anxiously, the reddening of his prominent ears betraying his embarrassment. But her strong, fine-featured face under the high-piled, glossy, auburn hair was expressionless. All that she said, coldly, was, "Why bring that up, John?"

He told her, "You know the story. Mayhew knows the story. I know the story. But Clarisse doesn't. And as she's to be one of my key officers on this expedition it's essential that she be put in the picture."

"I can get it all from Ken," said Clarisse Mayhew.

"Not in such detail," stated Sonya. "We have to admit that my ever-loving husband has always been up to the eyebrows in whatever's happened on the Rim."

"You haven't done so badly yourself," Grimes told her, breaking the tension, returning the smile that flickered briefly over her face.

"One thing that I *like* about the Rim Worlds," murmured Clarisse, "is that the oddest things always seem to be happening. Life was never like this on Francisco. But go on, please, John."

"Mphm," grunted Grimes. "Talking is thirsty work."

He raised a hand, and on silent wheels a robot servitor rolled into the comfortable lounge room. Most people who could afford such luxuries preferred humanoid automatons and called them by human names, but not Grimes. He always said, and always would say, that it was essential that machines be kept in their proper place. The thing that had answered his summons was obviously just a machine, no more than a cylindrical tank on a tricycle carriage with two cranelike arms. It stood there impassively waiting for their orders, and then from a hatch in its body produced a tankard of cold beer for Grimes, Waverley Scotch and soda for Mayhew, iced Rigellian dragon's milk for the ladies.

"Here's to all of us," said Grimes, sipping appreciatively. He looked over the rim of his glass at his guests—Mayhew, tall, gangling, deceptively youthful and fragile in appearance; Clarisse, attractively plump in face and figure, her rich brown hair hanging down to waist level. On Francisco, the world of her birth, she had been one of the so-called Blossom People, and still looked the part.

"Get on with it, John," said Sonya after sampling her own drink.

"Very well. It all started, as I've already said, with Commander Maudsley. As well as being a fully qualified astronaut, he was an Intelligence Officer. . . ."

"It didn't start with Maudsley," said Sonya sharply. "No one knows *when* it started."

"Oh, all right. I'll go back a few more years in time. It was suspected for quite a long while that there was *something out there.* Many years ago, long before the Rim Worlds seceded from the Federation, Faraway was a penal colony of sorts. The Survey Service actually manned a ship with the sweepings of the jails and sent her out to find that . . . *something.* What happened to her is not known to this day. After we'd established our own Confederacy, the Federation's Survey Service was still snooping around the Rim—and Maudsley, passing himself off as the master of a star tramp called *Polar Queen,* did quite a lot of work out there. So far as we know he was the first *human* spaceman to set eyes on The Outsiders' Ship. Shortly thereafter he crashed his own vessel coming in to a landing at Port Farewell on Faraway. He was the only survivor. After that he stayed out there. He served in a few of our Rim Runners' ships, but he was practically unemployable. We didn't know then that he was a Survey Service Commander, Intelligence Branch at that, but it wouldn't have made any difference. He finished up as mate of a ship called, funnily enough, *The Outsider*. Her master, Captain Calver, had been master in our employ, but he and his officers made a pile of money out of the salvage of the T.G. Clipper *Thermopylae* and invested it in an obsolescent Epsilon Class tramp, going into business as shipowners. To comply with regulations, Calver had to ship a chief officer with at least a Chief Pilot's Certificate—and Maudsley was the only one that he could find on Nova Caledon.

"Maudsley was hitting the bottle, almost drinking himself to death. (Forgive me, Sonya, but that's the way that it was.) He talked in his drunken delirium. He talked about The Outsiders' Ship, the finding of which had somehow wrecked his life. Then he committed suicide. . . ."

Grimes paused, looking at his wife. Her face was expressionless. He went on, "For quite a while after that Calver got by in his *Outsider*. Toward the finish, Sonya was his chief officer—she holds her Master Astronaut's papers, as you know. Trade on the Rim was expanding faster than Rim Runners' fleet and there was plenty of cargo for an independent operator. But, eventually, times got bad for Calver. Rim Runners had sufficient tonnage for all requirements, and a small, one ship company just couldn't compete. It was then that he and his co-owners remembered Maudsley's story, and decided to find The Ship from Outside for themselves. They knew that there was something out beyond the Rim that could make them impossibly rich. They had Maudsley's sailing directions, such as they were. The Confederacy evinced some slight interest in the matter, and I was able to help out with the loan of a Mass Proximity Indicator—which, in those days, was a *very* expensive hunk of equipment. Even the Federation chipped in. As *you* know, my dear.

"Calver found The Outsiders' Ship. He and his people boarded . . . her? . . . it? A ship? A robot intelligence? A quarantine station? Who knows? But they found the thing. They boarded it. But I'll let Calver speak for himself. This is a recording of the report he made to me."

Grimes switched on the small recorder that was standing ready on the coffee table. He hated himself for raising so many ghosts from Sonya's past—she and Calver had been lovers, he knew—but these ghosts were bound to have been raised during the expedition. Her face was stony, expressionless, as the once-familiar voice issued from the little machine.

Did you ever read a twentieth-century Terran author called Wells? He's recommended reading in the 'Fathers of the Future' course they have at most schools. Anyhow, there's one of his stories, a fantasy, called A Vision Of Judgment. *Wells imagined a Judgment Day, with all living and all who have ever lived called by the Last Trump to face their Maker, to be tried and punished for their sins or, perhaps, to be rewarded for their good deeds. Everyone has his session of Hell as his naked soul stands in full view of the multitude while the Recording Angel recites the long, long catalog of petty acts of meanness and spite. . . . All the trivial (but not so trivial) shabby things, all the things in which even the most perverted nature could never take pride, and even the spectacular wrongdoings made to look shabby and trivial. . . .*

It was left there, The Outsiders' Ship, *out beyond the Rim, in the hope that with the development of interstellar flight techniques it would be discovered. It was left there, in the far outer reaches of this galaxy, to test the fitness of its discoverers to use the treasures of science and technology that it contains, to build ships capable of making the Big Crossing. We passed the test without cracking . . . quite. Had we cracked there is little doubt that we should have been bundled off the premises as unceremoniously as Maudsley must have been, bundled outside with memories of fear and of horror, and of loss, and with some sort of posthypnotic inhibition to stop us from ever talking about it. It's possible, of course, that some of Maudsley's crew did pass the test—but they died with* Polar Queen.

The test . . . yes, it's ingenious, and amazingly simple. It's . . . it's a mirror that's held up to you in which you see . . . everything. Yes, everything. Things that you've forgotten, and things that you've wished for years that you could forget. After all, a man can meet any alien monster without fear, without hate, after he has met and faced and accepted the most horrible monster of all. . . .

Himself.

Grimes switched off, then busied himself refueling and lighting his pipe. He said, through the acrid smoke cloud, "Calver came back, as you've gathered, and then he and his engineers did a few odd things to his ship's Mannschenn Drive, and then they all pushed off to . . . ? Your guess is as good as mine. To the next galaxy but three? The general impression was that they had some sort of intergalactic drive. Calver was decent enough to leave me a pile of things—notes and diagrams and calculations. Unfortunately I'm no engineer. . . ."

"You can say that again!" interjected Sonya.

Grimes ignored this. "Our own bright boys tried to make something of them. They actually rebuilt a Mannschenn Drive unit as allegedly specified, but it just won't work. Literally. Every moving part has absolute freedom to move on bearings that are practically frictionless, but . . ." He grinned. "Mayhew reckons that the thing won't work unless its operator is approved by it. Frankly, I can't approve of a *machine* that thinks it has the right to approve or disapprove of me!"

"That's only my theory, John," put in Mayhew.

"But you believe it, don't you? Where was I? Oh, yes. After the Calver affair there was quite a flurry of interest in The Outsiders' Ship. The Federation, with our permission, sent *Starfinder* to nose around. She located quite a few derelicts in the vicinity—a Shaara ship, an odd vessel that must have belonged to some incredibly ancient culture, a Dring cruiser. Then she became a derelict herself. When her Carlotti transmissions suddenly stopped we sent *Rim Culverin* to investigate. The *Culverin*'s captain reported that he had boarded *Starfinder* and found all hands very dead; a few had been shot and the rest wiped out by a lethal gas in the air circulation system. Whether or not any of *Starfinder*'s people boarded The Outsiders' Ship we don't know. Probably some, at least, did. *Rim Culverin* was ordered not to investigate *The Outsider* but to tow *Starfinder* in to Lorn. She did just that. Then our big brothers of the Federation tried again, this time with a Constellation Class cruiser, *Orion. Orion* blew up with no survivors. *Rim Carronade* was with her and saw it happen. *Orion* had put quite a large boarding party onto—or into—The

Outsiders' Ship, and it was after their return to their own vessel that the big bang happened. *Rim Carronade* was damaged herself, with quite a few casualties, and returned to Lorn.

"All of you here know me. I'm not one of those people who say, in a revoltingly pious voice, that there are some things that we are not meant to know. For years I've been wanting to take my own expedition out to investigate that hunk of alien ironmongery. I've got my chance at last—and I'm just a little scared.

"And I'm damn glad that I shall have all of you with me."

⤳ Chapter 3 ⤳

SHE WAS AN OLD SHIP, was *Faraway Quest*, but in first-class condition. She had started life as an Epsilon Class tramp, one of those sturdy workhorses of the Federation's Interstellar Transport Commission. Sold to Rim Runners during the days when practically all of the tonnage out on the Rim was at best secondhand, she had been converted into a survey ship. In her, Grimes had discovered and explored the worlds of the Eastern Circuit: Tharn, Mellise, Grollor and Stree. In her he had made the first contact with the antimatter systems to the galactic west.

After secession, the setting up of the Rim Worlds Confederacy, she had been subject to further conversion, this time being fitted out as an auxiliary cruiser. Even though the Rim Worlds Navy now possessed a sizable fleet built to its own specifications, this was still her official status. Nonetheless, Commodore Grimes regarded her as *his* ship.

As Admiral Kravitz had told him, she was practically ready to lift off at once to where *The Outsider* drifted in the intergalactic nothingness. She was almost fully stored. Her "farm" was in a flourishing state; her tissue culture, yeast and algae tanks were well stocked and healthy. Main and auxiliary machinery were almost fresh from thorough overhaul. Sundry weaponry had been mounted so that she could play her part in the fleet maneuvers, and this Grimes decided to retain. He liked to think of himself as a man of peace these days but was willing to admit that it is much easier to be peaceful behind laser projectors and rocket batteries than in an unarmed ship.

The selection of personnel for the expedition posed no great problems. Billy Williams, normally skipper of the deep space tug *Rim Mamelute*, was available. On more than one occasion he had served as Grimes' second-in-command. James Carnaby, second officer with Rim Runners and an outstandingly competent navigator, had just come off leave and was awaiting reappointment. Like Williams, he held a commission in the Reserve, as did Hendrikson, another Rim Runners' second officer, just paid off from *Rim Griffon*. There was Davis, an engineer whom Grimes knew quite well and liked, and who was qualified in all three Drives: Mannschenn, inertial and reaction. There was Sparky Daniels, currently officer-in-charge of the Port Forlorn Carlotti Station but who frequently pined for a deep space appointment. And there was Major Dalzell of the Rim Worlds Marines. Grimes had heard good reports of this young space soldier and, on being introduced to him, had liked him at once.

There was what Grimes described as a brain trust of buffoons from the University of Lorn. There was a team of technicians.

There was an officer of the Intelligence Branch of the Federation's Survey Service—just along, as she said, "to see how the poor live." This, of course, was Commander Sonya Verrill, otherwise known as Mrs. Grimes, who, in spite of her marriage to a Rim Worlder, had retained both her Federation citizenship and her Survey Service commission.

There were the psionicists—Ken Mayhew, one of the last of the psionic communications officers, and Clarisse, his wife. He was a highly trained and qualified telepath. She, born on Francisco, was a descendant of that caveman artist from the remote past who, somehow, on Kinsolving's Planet, had been dragged through time to what was, to him, the far future. Like her ancestor, Clarisse was an artist. Like him, she was a specialist. Inborn in her was the talent to lure victims to the hunter's snare. Twice, on Kinsolving itself, she had exercised this talent—and on each occasion the hunters had become the victims.

The work of preparing the ship for her voyage went well and swiftly. There was little to be done, actually, save for the rearranging of her accommodations for the personnel that she was to carry, the conversion of a few of her compartments into laboratories for the scientists. Toward the end of the refit Grimes was wishing that on that long ago day when the Rim Worlds had decided that they should have their own survey ship somebody had put up a convincing case for the purchase of an obsolescent Alpha Class liner! Not that there was anything wrong with *Faraway Quest*—save for her relative smallness. And it was not only the civilians who demanded space and yet more space. Officer Hendrikson—who, as a reserve officer had specialized in gunnery—sulked hard when he was told that he could not have the recreation rooms as magazines for his missiles. (Dr. Druthen, leader of the scientists, was already sulking because he had not been allowed to take them over as workshops.)

Grimes knew that he could not hasten matters, but he chafed at every delay. As long as the *Quest* was sitting on her pad in Port Forlorn far too many people were getting into every act. Once she was up and outward bound he would be king of his own little spaceborne castle, an absolute monarch. Admiral Kravitz had made it clear to him that he would be on his own, that he was to act as he saw fit. It was a game in which he was to make up the rules as he went along.

It was a game that Grimes had always enjoyed playing.

ᘳ Chapter 4 ᘰ

FARAWAY QUEST lifted from Port Forlorn without ceremony; it could have been no more than the routine departure of a Rim Runners' freighter. Grimes had the controls; he loved ship handling and knew, without false modesty, that he was a better than average practitioner of this art. In the control room with him were Sonya, Billy Williams, Carnaby, Hendrikson and Sparky Daniels. Also there, as a guest, was Dr. Druthen. Grimes already did not like Druthen. The physicist was a fat slug of a man, always with an oily sheen of perspiration over his hairless skin, always with an annoyingly supercilious manner. He sat there, a silent sneer embodied. Had he been a crew member he would have faced a charge of dumb insolence.

Daniels was at the NST transceiver, a little man who looked as though he had been assembled from odds and ends of wire, highly charged wire at that. Williams—bulky, blue-jowled, with shaggy black hair—lounged in the co-pilot's seat. He slumped there at ease, but his big hands were ready to slam down on his controls at a microsecond's notice. Slim, yellow-haired, a little too conventionally handsome, Carnaby was stationed at the radar with Hendrikson, also blond but bearded and burly, looking as though he should have been wearing a horned helmet, ready to take over if necessary. He managed to convey the impression that fire control was his real job, not navigation.

And Sonya conveyed the impression that she was just along as an observer. She was slim and beautiful in her Survey Service uniform, with the micro-skirt that would have been frowned upon by the rather frumpish senior female officers of the Confederacy's Navy. She was a distracting influence, decided Grimes. Luckily he knew her well; even so he would find it hard to keep his attention on the controls.

"Mphm," he grunted. Then, "Commander Williams?"

"All stations secured for lift-off, Skipper. All drives on Stand-By."

"Mr. Daniels, request clearance, please."

"*Faraway Quest* to Tower. *Faraway Quest* to Tower. Request clearance for departure. Over."

The voice of the Aero-Space Control officer came in reply. "Tower to *Faraway Quest*. You have clearance." Then, in far less impersonal accents, "Good questing!"

Grimes grunted, keeping his face expressionless. He said into his intercom microphone, "Count down for lift-off. Over to you, Commander Williams."

"Ten . . ." intoned Williams. "Nine . . . Eight . . ."

"A touching ritual," muttered Dr. Druthen. Grimes glared at him but said nothing. "Five . . . Four . . ."

The commodore's glance swept the control room, missing nothing. His eyes lingered longer than they should have done on Sonya's knees and exposed thighs.

"Zero!"

At the touch of Grimes' finger on the button the inertial drive grumbled into life. The ship quivered, but seemed reluctant to leave the pad. *I should have been expecting this,* he thought. *The last time I took this little bitch out I wasn't inflicted with this excess tonnage of personnel* . . . He applied more pressure, feeling and hearing the faint *clicks* as the next two stages were brought into operation. The irregular beat of the drive was suddenly louder.

"Negative contact, sir," stated Carnaby. "Lifting . . . lifting . . ."

Grimes did not need to look at the instruments. He was flying by the seat of his pants. He could feel the additional weight on his buttocks as acceleration, gentle though it was, augmented gravity. He did not bother to correct lateral drift when the wind caught *Faraway*

Quest as soon as she was out of the lee of the spaceport buildings. It did not really matter at which point she emerged from the upper atmosphere of the planet.

Up she climbed, and up, and the drab, gray landscape with the drab, gray city was spread beneath her, and the drab, gray cloud ceiling was heavy over the transparent dome of the control room. Up she climbed and up and beyond the dome; outside the viewports there was only the formless, swirling fog of the overcast.

Up she climbed—and suddenly, the steely Lorn sun broke through, and the dome darkened in compensation to near opacity.

Up she climbed. . . .

"Commodore," asked Druthen in his unpleasantly high-pitched voice, "isn't it time that you set course or trajectory or whatever you call it?"

"No," snapped Grimes. Then, trying to make his voice pleasant or, at least, less unpleasant, "I usually wait until I'm clear of the Van Allen."

"Oh. Surely in this day and age that would not be necessary."

"It's the way that I was brought up," grunted Grimes. He scowled at Sonya, who had assumed her maddeningly superior expression. He snapped at Carnaby, "Let me know as soon as we're clear of the radiation belt, will you?"

The sun, dimmed by polarization, was still directly ahead, directly overhead from the viewpoint of those in the control room, in the very nose of the ship. To either side now there was almost unrelieved blackness, the ultimate night in which swam the few, faint, far nebulosities of the Rim sky; the distant, unreachable island universes. Below, huge in the after vision screen, was the pearly gray sphere that was Lorn. Below, too, was the misty Galactic Lens.

"All clear, sir," said Carnaby quietly.

"Good. Commander Williams, make the usual announcements."

"Attention, please," Williams said. "Attention, please. Stand by for free fall. Stand by for free fall. Stand by for centrifugal effects."

Grimes cut the drive. He was amused to note that, in spite of the ample warning, Druthen had not secured his seat belt. He remarked mildly, "I thought that you'd have been ready for free fall, Doctor."

The physicist snarled wordlessly, managed to clip the strap about his flabby corpulence. Grimes returned his full attention to the controls. Directional gyroscopes rumbled, hummed and whined as the ship was turned about her short axis. The Lorn sun drifted from its directly ahead position to a point well abaft the *Quest*'s beam. The cartwheel sight set in the ship's stem was centered on . . . nothingness. Broad on the bow was the Lens, with a very few bright stars, the suns of the Rim Worlds, lonely in the blackness beyond its edge.

Williams looked toward Grimes inquiringly. The commodore nodded.

"Attention, please," Williams said. "Stand by for resumption of acceleration. Stand by for initiation of Mannschenn Drive."

Grimes watched the accelerometer as he restarted the engines. He let acceleration build up to a steady one G, no more, no less. He switched on the Mannschenn Drive. Deep in the bowels of the ship the gleaming complexity of gyroscopes began to move, to turn, to precess, building up speed. Faster spun the rotors and faster and their song was a thin, high keening on the very verge of audibility. And as they spun they precessed, tumbling out of the frame of the continuum, falling down and through the dark dimensions, pulling the vessel and all aboard her with them.

The commodore visualized the working of the uncanny machines—as he always did. It helped to take his mind off the initial effects: the sagging of all colors down the spectrum, the wavering insubstantiality of the forms, the outlines of everything and everybody, the distortion of all the senses, the frightening feeling of déjà vu. He said, making a rather feeble joke of it, "This is where we came in."

The others might be paid to laugh at their commanding officer's witticisms, but Dr. Druthen made it plain that he was not. He looked at Grimes, all irritated and irritating inquiry. "Came in *where*?" he demanded.

Sonya laughed without being paid for it.

Grimes glared at his wife, then said patiently to the scientist, "Just a figure of speech, Doctor."

"Oh. I would have thought that 'this is where we are going out' would have been more apt." Druthen stared out through the viewport, to the distorted Galactic Lens. Grimes, seeing what he was looking at, thought of making his usual remark about a Klein flask blown by a drunken glassblower, then thought better of it. He found it hard to cope with people who had too literal minds.

"And talking of going out," went on Druthen, "why aren't we going out?"

"What do you mean, Doctor?"

"Correct me if I'm wrong, Commodore, but I always understood that The Outsiders' Ship lay some fifty light years out beyond the outermost Rim sun. I'm not a spaceman, but even I can see that we are, at the moment, just circumnavigating the fringe of the Galaxy."

Grimes sighed. He said, "Finding *The Outsider* is like trying to find a tiny needle in one helluva big haystack. At the moment we are, as you have said, circumnavigating the Lens. When we have run the correct distance we shall have the Lead Stars in line or almost in line. I shall bring the Leads astern, and run out on them for fifty light years. *Then* I shall run a search pattern. . . ."

Druthen snorted. What he said next revealed that he must have acquainted himself very well with Grimes' history, his past record. He said sardonically, "What a *seamanlike* like way of doing it, Commodore. But, of course, you're an honorary admiral of the surface navy on Tharn, and your Master Mariner's Certificate is valid for the oceans of Aquarius. I would have thought, in my layman's innocence, that somebody would have laid a marker buoy, complete with Carlotti beacon, off *The Outsider* years ago."

"Somebody did," Grimes told him tersely. "No less than three somebodies did. According to last reports those buoys are still there, but none of them is functioning as a Carlotti transmitter. None of them ever did function for longer than three days, Galactic Standard."

"Steady on trajectory, Skipper," announced Williams.

"Thank you, Commander. Set normal deep space watches," replied Grimes. Slowly he unbuckled himself from his chair. It was customary for the captain of a ship, at this juncture, to invite any important passengers to his quarters for an ice-breaking drink or two. He supposed that Druthen was a passenger of sorts—he had signed no Articles of Agreement—and, as leader of the scientific team he was important enough. Too important.

"Will you join me in a quiet drink before dinner, Doctor?" Grimes asked.

"Too right," replied Druthen, licking his thick lips.

Sonya's eyebrows lifted, although her fine-featured face showed no expression.

✥ Chapter 5 ✥

DRUTHEN DRANK GIN, straight, from a large glass. Sonya sipped a weak scotch and soda. Grimes drank gin, but with plenty of ice and a touch of bitters. Druthen managed to convey the impression of being more at home in the commodore's day cabin than its rightful occupants. He talked down at Grimes and Sonya. It was obvious that he considered himself to be the real leader of the expedition, with the astronautical personnel along only as coach drivers.

Patronizingly he said, "Your trouble, Grimes, is that you're too old fashioned. You don't move with the times. I really believe that you'd have been happy in the days of wooden ships and iron men."

"You can say that again," agreed Grimes. He was pleased to note that Sonya was not taking sides against him, as she usually did when the conversation got on to these lines. He went on, "Then, the shipmaster wasn't at the mercy of his technicians to the extent that he is now."

"And you really believe that . . ." Druthen's pale eyebrows were almost invisible against the unhealthy pallor of his skin, but it was obvious that they had been raised. "But why, my dear Grimes, must you persist in this passion for the archaic? To take just one glaring example—the invention and subsequent development of the Carlotti deep space communications system should have put every over-glamorized but unreliable psionic communications officer out of a job. And yet I was amazed to discover that you carry a representative of that peculiar breed aboard this very vessel."

"Ken Mayhew—Commander Mayhew—is an old friend and shipmate. . . ."

"Sentiment, Grimes. Sentiment."

"Let me finish, Druthen." Grimes was childishly pleased to note that the physicist had been offended by the omission of his title. "Let me finish. Commander Mayhew is outstanding in his own field. As long as I have him on board, as well as the Carlotti gadgetry, I shall never be at the mercy of a single fuse. Throughout this voyage he will be in continuous touch, waking and sleeping, with his juniors at the PC Station at Port Forlorn. Too . . ." But Grimes suddenly decided not to come out with what he had been going to say.

"Go on, Commodore."

I always like to keep at least one ace up my sleeve thought Grimes. He said nothing further about Mayhew's abilities, but went on, "Too, it's just possible that we shall be able to make use of his wife's talents."

Druthen laughed sneeringly. "What sort of outfit *is* this? A telepath and a ghost raiser considered essential to the success of a *scientific* expedition." He raised a pudgy hand. "Hear me out. I've done my homework Grimes. I've read the reports written by you and about you. I know that you experienced some odd hallucinations on Kinsolving's Planet—but surely you can distinguish between the objective and the subjective. Or can't you?"

"He can," put in Sonya. "And I can. I was there too, one of the times."

"And on the second occasion," said Grimes nastily, "we had a scad of scientists along."

"Agreed," remarked Druthen smugly. "But second-raters, all of them. On the first occasion—correct me if I'm wrong—it was an expedition organized by a group of religious fanatics. On the third occasion there was, with the commodore and you, Mrs. Grimes, a shipload of fellow spacemen and—women. So . . ."

Grimes managed to keep his temper. "So it all never happened, Doctor?"

"That is my opinion, Commodore." He refilled his glass without invitation. "Frankly, I maintain that *this* expedition should have been under the command of a hard-headed scientist rather than a spaceman who has shown himself to be as superstitious as the old-time seamen regarding whom he is such an expert."

Grimes grinned mirthlessly. "But I am in command, Doctor."

"That is quite obvious. For example, this wasting of time by running to bring your famous Lead Stars in line rather than steering directly for the last reported position of *The Outsider.*"

Grimes laughed. "As long as I'm in command, Dr. Druthen, things will be done my way. But I will tell you why I'm doing things this way. *The Outsider* . . . wobbles. Unpredictably. Sometimes it is this side of the Leads, sometimes the other. Sometimes it is further in, toward the Rim, sometimes it is further out. In the unlikely event of its being in the vicinity of the position at which I shall bring the Lead Stars in line it will be within the detection range of several planet-based observatories. It just might be there, but the chances are that it will not be. So I stand out, and out, until I've run my distance, and then if I've picked up nothing on the Mass Proximity Indicator I just cruise around in circles, through an ever-expanding volume of space. Quite simple, really."

"Simple!" snorted Druthen. He muttered something about people who must have learned their navigation in Noah's Ark. He splashed more gin into his glass. Grimes was pleased to see that the bottle was empty.

Sonya made a major production of consulting her wristwatch. She said, "It's time that we got dressed for dinner."

Surily, Druthen took the hint. He finished his drink, got up clumsily. "Thank you, Commodore. Thank you, Mrs. Grimes. I suppose I'd better freshen up myself. No, you needn't come with me. I can find my own way down."

When the door had shut behind him Grimes looked at Sonya, and she looked at him. Grimes demanded, of nobody in particular, "What have I done to deserve this?"

"Plenty," she told him. Then, "Pour me a drink, a stiff one. I just didn't want to be accused of setting that bastard a bad example."

He complied. "I don't think that anybody could possibly."

She laughed. "You're right." Then, "But don't underestimate him, John. He wasn't the only one doing his homework before we lifted off. I did, too, while you were getting the ship ready. I was able to get my paws on his dossier. To begin with, he's brilliant. Not quite a genius—although he likes to think that he is—but not far from it. He is also notorious for being completely lacking in the social graces."

"You can say that again!"

"But . . . and it's an interesting 'but'. But this he turns to his advantage. When he wants to pick anybody's brains he goes out of his way to annoy them—and, as like as not, they spill far more beans than they would do normally."

"Mphm," grunted Grimes, feeling smugly pleased with himself. "Mphm."

"He resents all authority. . . ."

"Doesn't he just!"

"He feels that he has not received his just due."

"Who doesn't? But since when was this a just universe?"

"In short, he's dangerous."

"Aren't we all in this rustbucket? Aren't we all?" he refilled his glass from the whiskey bottle. "Here's tae us. What's like us? De'il a yin!"

"And thank all the Odd Gods of the Galaxy for *that*," she riposted.

~ Chapter 6 ~

THE RUN OUT to the departure position was uneventful and reasonably pleasant. It could have been more pleasant; spacemen welcome company aboard their ships whom they can impress with their shop talk. But the scientists and technicians each had their own mess and, obedient to Druthen, kept themselves to themselves. It could have been unpleasant, Grimes conceded, if Druthen had forced his company upon Sonya and himself. He was content to let well enough alone.

Meanwhile, he could and did enjoy the society of Mayhew and Clarisse, of Billy Williams, of young Major Dalzell, of the other officers. But during the drink and talk sessions it was hard to keep the conversation away from the purpose of their expedition, from the findings and the fates of earlier expeditions.

Why had Calver been successful (if he had been successful)? Why had those before him and after him met disaster? "There's only one way to find out, Skipper," Williams had said cheerfully. "We'll just have to see what happens to *us!* And if you're around, the fat always gets pulled out of the fire somehow!"

"There has to be a first time for everything," Grimes told his second-in-command with grim humor. "There'll be a first time when the fat won't be pulled out of the fire."

"She'll be right," Williams told him. "Mark my words, Skipper. She'll be right."

And all of them studied the sailing directions, such as they were, until they knew them by heart. "Put Macbeth and Kinsolving's sun in line," the long-dead Maudsley had told somebody. "Put Macbeth and Kinsolving's sun in line, and keep them so. That's the way that we came back. Fifty light years, and all hands choking on the stink of frying lubricating oil from the Mannschenn Drive . . ." And for fifty light years Calver had run, but with the Lead Stars in line astern. He had logged the distance, but found nothing. He had initiated a search pattern, and at last he had been successful. Those following him had not experienced the same difficulties—but each successive ship had been fitted with an improved model of the Mass Proximity Indicator. Calver's instrument had been no more than a prototype, capable of detection at only short ranges.

On the ship sped, running the Rim, and Carnaby checked and rechecked the fixes that he got from the Carlotti beacons set along the very edge of the Galaxy. They were not very accurate fixes; the navigational aids had been positioned to assist vessels running under Mannschenn Drive from known world to known world, not a ship out where no ship, normally, had any business to be. But Carnaby was a good navigator, possessing the valuable quality of intuition. He could look at a spider's web of intersecting lines and mutter, "That can't be right." He could look at another one and say, "That could be right." Now and again he would state, "This *is* right."

He said firmly, "This *is* right."

Grimes and Williams were with him in the control room. The Commodore did not hesitate. "All right, Commander Williams," he ordered. "You know the drill."

Williams spoke into the most convenient intercom microphone. "Attention, attention. All bridge officers to Control. All hands stand by for shutdown of Mannschenn Drive, free fall and centrifugal effects." Throughout the ship the alarm bells that he had actuated were ringing.

Sonya came in, followed by Hendrikson and Daniels. Each of them went to a chair, strapped himself securely. Druthen came in, bobbing up through the hatch like some pantomime monster. His normally pale face was flushed. He sputtered, "What is the meaning of this, Commodore? We were in the middle of a most important experiment."

"And we, Doctor, are in the middle of a most important piece of navigation."

"There should have been warning."

"There was warning. Three hours ago the announcement was made that the adjustment of trajectory would be at about this time."

"Sir, we shall overrun . . ." warned Carnaby.

"Get into a chair, Druthen!" snapped Grimes.

The scientist, moving surprisingly fast for one of his build, complied, sat there glowering.

"Inertial drive—off!" Grimes ordered.

"Inertial drive—off!" repeated Williams.

The irregular throbbing slowed, ceased. There were weightlessness and loss of spacial orientation.

"Mannschenn Drive—off!"

Down in the Mannschenn Drive room the spinning, precessing gyroscopes slowed to a halt, their thin, high whine dropped to a low humming, a rumble, then was silenced. Sight and hearing were distorted; the time sense was twisted. Grimes heard Sonya whisper, "Odd, very odd. This is the first time I've seen double. Is it *me*, or is something wrong with the Drive?"

"Did you see double?" asked Carnaby, with professional interest. "*I* didn't, Commander Verrill."

She laughed shakily. "It must have been a manifestation of wishful thinking, or something. It was only my husband, the commodore, that I saw two of . . ." She was recovering fast. "And did you see two of *me*, John?"

"One is ample," he replied.

But he had not seen even one of her. The woman who, briefly, had occupied Sonya's seat had not been Sonya, although it was somebody who once had been as familiar to him as Sonya was now.

"I would have thought," commented Druthen, "that you people would have been accustomed by now to the psychological effects of changing rates of temporal precession."

"It's just that we haven't lost our sense of wonder, Doctor," Grimes told him.

He looked out through the viewport. The Lens was there, looking as it should look when viewed in the normal continuum, a glowing ellipsoid against the absolute blackness. Visible against the pearly mistiness were the Rim suns, sparks upon the face of the haze. Carnaby was busy with his instruments. "Yes," he muttered, "that's Kinsolving all right. Its spectral type can't be confused with anything else . . . Macbeth must be obscured, directly in line with it . . . yes . . ."

"Set trajectory, Mr. Carnaby?" asked Grimes.

"Yes, sir. You may set trajectory."

"Good." Grimes gave the orders decisively. *Faraway Quest* turned on her directional gyroscopes until the Kinsolving sun was directly astern. Inertial and Mannschenn Drives were restarted. She was on her way.

"I saw two of you again, John," said Sonya in a peculiarly flat voice.

Druthen laughed sneeringly.

And Grimes asked himself silently, *Why did I see her?*

❧ Chapter 7 ❧

EVER SINCE THE FIRST SHIPS, captains have had their confidants. Usually this role is played by a senior officer, but very rarely is it the second-in-command. Ship's doctors, with their almost priestly status, have enjoyed—and still do so enjoy—the status of privileged listeners. But it was not *Faraway Quest's* doctor whose company Grimes sought when he wished to talk things out. It was Mayhew.

Grimes sat with the psionic communications officer in the cabin that had been put to use as the ship's psionic communications station. As a general rule PCOs used their own living quarters for this purpose, but PCOs did not often carry their wives with them. On this voyage Mayhew was accompanied by Clarisse. Clarisse did not think that the psionic amplifier—the so-called "dog's brain in aspic"—was a pleasant thing to have in plain view all the time, to live with and to sleep with. So Lassie—the name by which Mayhew called his disembodied pet—was banished to a spare cabin that was little more than a dogbox anyhow.

Those wrinkled masses of cerebral tissue suspended in their transparent tanks of nutrient solution gave most people the horrors, and the commodore was no exception. As he talked with Mayhew he was careful not to look at Lassie. It was hard, in these cramped quarters, to avoid doing so.

"We're on the last leg, Ken," he remarked.

"Yes, John."

"Have you picked anything up from anybody—or anything?"

"I've told Lassie to keep her telepathic ears skinned for any indication that the Waldegren destroyer is in the vicinity. So far—nothing."

"Mphm. Of course, she mightn't have any telepaths on board. Let's face it, Ken, you're one of the last of a dying breed."

"We aren't quite extinct, John, as well you know. Too, everybody transmits telepathically, to a greater or lesser extent. People like myself and Clarisse are, essentially, trained, selective receivers."

"I know." Grimes cleared his throat. "You must have been receiving quite a few things from the personnel of this vessel. . . ."

Mayhew laughed. "I can guess what's coming next. But, as I've told you on quite a few past occasions, I'm bound by my oath of secrecy. We just don't pry, John. If we did pry—and if it became known, as it certainly would—we'd find ourselves the most popular guests at a lynching party. And, in any case, it's not done."

"Not even when the safety of the ship is involved?"

"The old, old argument. All power corrupts, and absolute power corrupts absolutely. I'll not be a party to your corruption."

But Grimes was persistent. "Even when you're not actually prying you must pick a few things up, without trying to, without meaning to. . . ."

"Well, yes. But it's just—how shall I put it?—background noise. Here's a good analogy for you, and one that you'll understand. After all, you're the Rim Worlds' own authority on Terran sea transport from Noah's Ark to the dawn of the Space Age. Think of the early days of radio—or wireless telegraphy as it was then called. Telegraphy, not telephony. Messages tapped out in Morse code, with dots and dashes. There'd be one of the old-time Sparkses on watch, his earphones clamped over his head, listening. He'd hear the crash and crackle of static; he'd hear relatively close stations booming in, and thin, mosquito voices of distant ones. But—the only one that he'd actually hear would be the one that he wanted to hear."

"Go on."

"It's like that with Clarisse and myself. We hear a horrid jumble of thoughts all the time but ignore them. But if there were the faintest whisper from the Waldegren ship or from *The Outsider* we'd do our damnedest to read it loud and clear."

"Yes, I see, but . . ."

"Something's worrying you, John."

"You don't have to be a telepath to realize that."

Mayhew scowled. "Unless you can convince me that the ship—or anybody aboard her—is in danger I'll not pry."

"Not even on me?"

"With your permission I might. But what seems to be the trouble? Tell me out loud. I'll not put on my thought reading act unless I have to."

"It was during the alteration of trajectory. You know as well as any of us that there are all kinds of odd psychological effects when the Mannschenn Drive is stopped or restarted."

"Too right."

"This time they were odder than usual. To two of us, at least. To Sonya and myself."

"Go on."

"Sonya . . . saw two of me. No, she wasn't seeing double. There was only one of anybody and anything else in the control room."

"Interesting. I'd have thought that one of you would be ample. And what did you see?"

"Whom did I see, you should have said. I was looking at Sonya. But it was not Sonya whom I saw. Years ago I knew a woman called Maggie Lazenby. She was a specialist officer in the Survey Service, an ethologist, with a doctorate in that science, and commander's rank. Very similar to Sonya in appearance. She married a bloke called Mike Carshalton. He's an admiral now, I believe."

"Local girl makes good. If she'd married you she'd only be Mrs. Commodore—and a commodore of the Reserve at that."

"I *like* being a commodore of the Reserve. I don't think I'd like being an admiral. But—it was all rather oddish . . ."

Mayhew laughed. "You, of all people, should be used to the odd things that happen out on the Rim. Don't tell me that you've forgotten the wild ghost chase, in this very ship!"

"Hardly. It was during that when Sonya and I decided to get hitched. But I just don't like these odd things happening at this time."

"Getting choosy in your old age."

"Who's old? But what I'm driving at is this. There's some sort of tie-in with The Outsiders' Ship and Kinsolving's Planet. After all, this business of the Lead Stars—Macbeth and Kinsolving in line. Kinsolving—*and* Macbeth. Years ago, long before our time, there was that odd business on one of the Macbeth planets. A ship from nowhere, old, derelict. A gift horse for the colonists, who didn't look the gift horse in the mouth carefully enough. It came from nowhere and it went back to nowhere—with a few hundred men and women aboard."

"Yes. I've read the story."

"So . . ." murmured Grimes softly.

"So what?"

"I was hoping you'd have some sort of a clue."

"I only work here, John."

"But you're a sensitive."

"A selective sensitive. Do you think it would help if I . . . pried?"

"Go ahead. It's my mind."

"Then . . . relax. Just relax. Don't think of anything in particular. . . ."

Grimes tried to relax. He found that he was looking at that obscenely named animal brain in the transparent container. He tried to look elsewhere, but couldn't. And *it* was aware of him. A dim, wavering image formed in his mind—that of a large, furry dog of indeterminate breed, a friendly dog, but a timid one. What was in his mind's eye was far better than what was in his physical eye, and he was grateful for it. He saw his hand go out and down to pat, to stroke the visionary dog. He saw the plumed tail waving.

Maggie had liked dogs with a sentimentality rare in one qualified in her science. Maggie would like this dog—if she were here. But she was not. She was who knew how many light years distant, and probably very happy as an admiral's lady. But what of all the other Maggies? What of the Maggie whom he had met again, briefly, in that other universe, the doorway into which he had stumbled through on

Kinsolving's Planet? How many universes were there—and how many Maggies?

He was jerked back to reality with a start.

Mayhew's voice was coldly censorious. He said, "I wish that you hadn't asked me to do this, John. It's time you realized how bloody lucky you are."

"Eh, what?"

"Lucky I said—and mean. Lucky being married to Sonya. *Her* temporal precession hallucination was just *you*, in duplicate. Yours was an old flame. You're still hankering after her."

"Some men are naturally monogamous, Ken. . . ."

"And some, like you, are not." He laughed. "Oh, well, it takes all sorts to make a universe. Forgive me if I sounded shocked, but I'd always thought of you and Sonya as being as close as it's possible for two nontelepaths to be. Even a mind reader can be wrong."

"Why shouldn't a man have bread *and* cake?" asked Grimes reasonably." But the odd part is that Sonya and Maggie are as alike as two slices from the same loaf. They'd pass for sisters. Almost as twin sisters."

Mayhew allowed himself to smile. "I suppose you're in love with a type, John, rather than a person. Oh, well."

Grimes changed the subject. "And how do you find our scientific passengers? Dr. Druthen, I'm sure, regards you and Clarisse as sort of commissioned teacup readers."

"He would. But that's one mind, John, that I wouldn't care to pry into. The man just oozes bigotry. He's a second-rater, and although he'd hate to admit it, he knows it. That accounts for his attitude toward the universe in general. He has this driving ambition to be on top, no matter what the cost to other people."

"And you haven't pried?"

"No. I have not pried. But every trained telepath is something of a psychologist—not that one needs to be one to figure out what makes a man like Druthen tick."

"Mphm." Slowly Grimes filled and lit his pipe. "Well, thanks, Ken. There're one or two things I'd like to check in Control. I'll see you later."

He let himself out of the little cabin and then, by way of the axial shaft, made his way to the control room. He chatted there for a while with Billy Williams, then went to his own quarters to join Sonya for a drink or two before dinner.

"Why are you looking at me like that?" she asked him.

"There are times," he told her, "when I realize how lucky I am."

≈ Chapter 8 ≈

THERE WERE TIMES—rather more frequent than he cared to admit—when Grimes was lucky. This was one of them. Part of his luck, perhaps, was in having a really outstanding navigator aboard his ship. Carnaby's last captain had said of him, "He could find a black cat in a coal mine at midnight in three seconds flat." This was not far from the truth.

There had been no need whatsoever for *Faraway Quest* to run a wearisome search pattern after the fifty-light-year plunge outward from the Lead Stars. Carnaby had applied this course correction and that course correction, each time a matter of seconds rather than of minutes or degrees, had played a complicated game of three-dimensional—or four dimensional, even—noughts and crosses in the plotting tank, had overworked the ship's computer to such an extent that Williams had said to Grimes, "If the bloody thing had a *real* brain it would go on strike!"

And then the Mass Proximity Indicator had picked up a target just inside its one-light-year maximum range. Almost directly ahead it was, a tiny spark, a minute bead on the thin, glowing filament that was the extrapolated trajectory. It was time to slow down, although there was no danger of collision. Two solid bodies cannot occupy the same space at the same time—but when one of those solid bodies is proceeding under Mannschenn Drive it is in a time of its own.

Grimes took over personally as the range closed. The tiny spark in the screen slowly expanded to a globe, luminescent, with other tiny sparks in orbit about it. There could be no doubt as to what it was.

The Mannschenn Drive was shut down and *Faraway Quest* proceeded cautiously under inertial drive only, a run of about twelve hours at one G acceleration. The commodore stayed in Control, smoking, drinking coffee, nibbling an occasional sandwich. His officers, their control room watches completed, stayed on with him. Sonya was there, of course, and so were Mayhew and Clarisse. Major Dalzell was there for most of the time, and even Druthen, uninvited, came up.

The Outsiders' Ship was within radar range now, it and the derelicts circling it. It was within radar range and it could be seen visually at last, a tiny, not very bright star in the blackness where no star had any right to be. The powerful telescope was trained on it, adjusted, and its picture glowed on the forward vision screen. It was . . . There was only one word for it. It was fantastic. It shone with a light of its own, a cold luminosity, bright but not harsh. It was not a ship so much as a castle out of some old fairy tale, with towers and turrets, cupolas and minarets and gables and buttresses. It should have looked absurd, but it did not. It should have looked grotesque, and it did, but for all the grotesquerie it was somehow . . . right. Its proportions were the only possible proportions.

Grimes stared at the picture, the somehow frightening picture, as did the others. He felt Sonya's hand tighten on his shoulder. The very humanness of the gesture helped him, brought him back to the prosaic reality of the control room of his own ship. There were things to be done.

"Mr. Carnaby," he snapped, "let me have the elements of a stable orbit about this . . . *thing*. Mr. Hendrikson, see if you can ascertain how many derelicts there are in this vicinity. Plot their orbits."

"And have the weaponry in a state of readiness, sir?" asked Hendrikson hopefully.

"Use your tracking system for plotting those orbits," Grimes told him coldly. "It can be used for other things besides gunnery, you know."

Daniels, the radio officer, had not waited for specific orders. He was dividing his attention between the normal space-time equipment and the Carlotti transceiver. He reported to Grimes: "I think there's the faintest whisper on the Carlotti, sir. I have it on broad band, but I'll try to get a bearing."

Grimes looked at the pilot antenna, at the ellipsoid Mobius Strip rotating about its long axis and quivering, hunting, on its universal mount. There was something there, *something*, but it didn't know quite where. He was about to get up from his chair to join Daniels at the communications equipment when, to his annoyance, Druthen remarked, "So you got us here, Commodore." The tone of his voice implied more than mild surprise.

"Yes. I got us here. Excuse me, I'm busy. . . ."

"Sir. . . ." It was the navigator.

"Yes, Mr. Carnaby?"

"All ready, sir. But we'd better not bring her in closer than a couple of miles. That *thing* has the mass of a planetoid."

"Mphm." Carnaby was exaggerating, of course. It was one of his failings. Even so . . . an artificial gravitational field? A distortion of the framework of space itself?

"Sir, I think I have something . . ." broke in Daniels.

"Commander Williams, take over the pilotage, please. Be careful not to run into any of the derelicts that Mr. Hendrikson is using for his make-believe target practice!"

"Good-oh, Skipper."

Grimes unsnapped his seat belt, strode swiftly to the vacant chair beside Daniels, buckled himself in just as the inertial drive was stopped and the ship went into free fall. He saw that the pilot antenna had stopped hunting, was now steady on a relative bearing almost dead astern of *Faraway Quest*, a bearing that slowly changed as Williams began to put the ship into her orbit.

Yes, he could hear a whisper, no more than a faint, faraway muttering, even though the volume control was turned full on. He could not distinguish the words. He did not think that the speaker was using Standard English. He regretted, as he had done before, that he was and always had been so distressingly monolingual.

"New German, I think . . ." Daniels said slowly.

"Sonya," called Grimes, "see if you can get the drift of this!"

But when she joined her husband and Daniels the set was silent again. *Perhaps*, thought Grimes, *Mayhew might be able to pick something up*. It was not necessary for him to say it aloud.

"Yes, sir," the telepath almost whispered, "there *is* something, somebody. No, it's not the Waldegren warship you're expecting. . . . It's . . . it's. . . ."

"Damn it all, Commander, who the hell is it?" demanded Grimes.

Mayhew's voice, as he replied, held reproof. "You've broken the very tenuous contact that I'd just begun to make."

"Sorry. But do your best, Commander Mayhew."

"I'm . . . trying. . . ."

"Orbit established, Skipper," reported Williams.

"No dangerous approach to any of the other orbits, sir," reported Carnaby and Hendrikson, speaking as one.

"Yes, yes. Commander Mayhew?"

"I'm trying . . . to try." Mayhew's expression was both very faraway and more than a little pained. "But . . . so much interference. There's somebody we know. . . and there are strangers. . . ."

"Are they in these derelicts? Aboard *The Outsider*?"

"No, sir. If they were close, I should know. But they are distant still. But please, please try not to interrupt any more. . . ."

"Let him go into his trance and get on with the clairvoyance," sneered Druthen.

"Shut up, Doctor! Do you want to be ordered out of Control?" snarled Grimes.

The scientist subsided.

"Please . . ." pleaded Mayhew.

Then there was silence in the control room, broken only by the sibilant whisperings of such machines as, with the ship now in free-falling orbit, were still in operation. The soughing of fans, the whining of generators, the very occasional sharp click of a relay. . . .

"Metzenther . . ." muttered Mayhew.

Grimes and Sonya exchanged glances. They were the only two, apart from the psionic communications officer, to whom the name meant anything.

"Trialanne . . ." He was vocalizing his thoughts for Grimes' benefit. "Metzenther, Trialanne . . . Where are you bound?" He seemed to find the answer amusing. "No, *we* haven't any company yet, apart from a half dozen or so derelict ships. . . . Be seeing you . . . Or shall we . . . *I* wouldn't know, I'm not a physicist or a mathematician. . . . And can *you* pick up anybody else . . .? We think we heard a Waldegren ship on our Carlotti. . . . And *I* got the faintest mutter from somebody else. . . . No, not a telepath, just unconscious broadcasting. . . . A servant of some empire or other. . . . Not *yours,* by any chance . . . ? No . . .?"

"And are we to have the pleasure of meeting that big, blonde cow again?" demanded Sonya coldly.

"She was quite attractive, in a hefty sort of way," Grimes told her.

"You *would* think so."

Mayhew grinned. "I rather think, Commander Verrill, that we shall shortly experience the pleasure of renewing our acquaintance with the ex-Empress Irene, and Captain Trafford, and all the rest of *Wanderer's* people."

"But they're on a different time track," said Sonya. "And thank all the Odd Gods of the Galaxy for that!"

"Mphm," grunted Grimes. "Mphm." He gestured toward the viewport through which The Outsiders' Ship was clearly visible. "But here, I think, is where all the time tracks converge."

"I hope you're wrong," said Sonya. "I hope you're wrong. But I'm rather afraid that you're not."

"He's not," confirmed Mayhew.

Chapter 9

"MPHM." Grimes made a major production of filling and lighting his foul pipe. "How long before your odd friends get here, Commander Mayhew?"

"*My* friends, sir?"

"Yes. Your friends. Metzenther and his ever-loving. You telepaths always seem to stick together." Grimes grinned. "Frankly, I regarded that ex-empress woman and her bunch of Imperial Navy throwouts as a pain in the arse. . . ."

Mayhew grinned back. "They thought about you and Commander Verrill in rather the same way."

"Good. But when do they get here?" The psionic communications officer shut his eyes, concentrated. He said slowly, "In about three hours fifteen minutes Standard."

"That gives us time . . . Commander Williams, I think you'll find one or two Confederate ensigns in the flag locker. You'll want one with wire stiffening, and a pole with a magnetic base. We'll plant our colors on the . . . *The Outsider*. I doubt if the legality of the claim will be recognized in a court of interstellar law, but it will give us some sort of talking point.

"Meanwhile, probably quite a few of you are wondering what this is all about. *You* know, Commander Williams, and Mayhew knows, but none of the rest of you will have heard the full story. It'll be as well if I put you in the picture." He turned to Williams. "You'd better get your flag planting under way, Commander, just in case Mayhew's ETA is out. And could you lend Commander Williams a couple or three hands for the job, Major Dalzell? And Mr. Daniels, I shall want everything I say put through on the intercom. Thank you."

Williams and Dalzell left the control room. Grimes cleared his throat. He said into the microphone that Daniels handed him, "Attention, all hands. Attention, all hands. This is important. You will all have seen, in the public information screens, our objective, The Outsiders' Ship. Most of you will have realized that we are now in orbit about it. Shortly you will see a landing party jetting off from this vessel toward *The Outsider*. They will be planting a flag on it. The reason for this is that we shall soon be having company. This will not be the Waldegren warship that we have been expecting—although she, probably, will be along before very long.

"A few years ago," Grimes continued, "I was instructed to take *Faraway Quest* out to investigate some strange, drifting wreckage—wreckage that, obviously, had not originated in *this* universe. It was the remains of a lifeboat that had belonged to a ship called *Star Scout*, and *Star Scout* had been a unit of the Imperial Navy. The only empire that *we* know is the Empire of Waverley, and its navy is officially called the Imperial Jacobean Navy. So . . .

"So we were stooging around, trying to find a few further clues, when this ship, quite literally, appeared from nowhere. Her name was *Wanderer*. She was quite heavily armed, the equivalent to one of our destroyers, but she was privately owned. She had been the yacht of the Empress Irene. She was still owned by the ex-Empress Irene, who was married to her captain. She carried only a small crew—this Irene woman was mate, as well as owner; a Mr. Tallentire, who had been a gunnery officer in the Imperial Navy was second mate, and his wife, Susanna, had been lady-in-waiting to the empress, and was now radio-officer-cum-purser. The psionic communications officer was—and still is—a Mr. Metzenther, almost the double of *our* Commander Mayhew. This Metzenther had—has—an Iralian wife called Trialanne. We don't have any Iralians on this time track. They were all wiped out by a plague. Bronheim was the engineer. He, too, had an Iralian wife—Denelleen . . ."

"Not now he doesn't," Mayhew said soberly. "I've been catching up on past history with Metzenther. Do you mind if I take over, sir?"

"Go ahead, Commander."

"Mayhew speaking. As you all will, by this time, have gathered, I am in psionic touch with the yacht *Wanderer*. She was thrown, somehow, onto this time track when she attempted the passage of the Horsehead Nebula. She was pursued by two New Iralian cruisers—the New Iralians being insurgents. She was carrying Iralian passengers, some of whom were in sympathy with the rebels. With our help she shook off pursuit, and then tried to get back into her own universe by running back through the Nebula. She was overtaken, but came out on top in the running fight. But the rebels among the passengers tried to take over the ship. Denelleen was one of them. . . . Anyhow, the mutineers were defeated. And that's about all."

"That was *then*," said Grimes. "What are these people doing here *now*?"

"You may remember, sir," Mayhew told him, "that when we last met them they were on charter to an organization called GLASS—Galactic League Against Suppression and Slavery. They're still on charter to GLASS. GLASS has the idea that the science and technology in The Outsiders' Ship will be useful to them in their work."

"So *they*: the ex-empress, GLASS and all the rest of 'em have an Outsiders' Ship in *their* universe. So—as I've already guessed—it's not a different one, but the same one as we have. So the time tracks meet and mingle right here." The commodore laughed. "Who else shall we meet, I wonder. . . ."

Sonya said flatly, "Williams has planted the flag."

"And so we, more or less legally, own *it*," said Grimes. He added softly, "Unless *it* owns us."

"Rubbish!" sneered Druthen.

Grimes ignored the man.

～ Chapter 10 ～

"I JUST MIGHT," suggested Daniels diffidently, "be able to establish Carlotti contact with *Wanderer*. I think that the time tracks will almost have converged by now."

"Mphm," grunted Grimes, giving thought to the possibility. Technologically his universe and the universe of the ex-Empress Irene were almost twins. At the time of his previous encounter with the so-called yacht she had possessed Carlotti equipment almost identical to his own. "Mphm." Then, "No, Mr. Daniels. Concentrate on that Waldegren destroyer. She's our main worry." He looked out through the viewport and was relieved to see that Williams and the two marines, silvery figures trailing luminous blue exhausts, were almost back to the ship.

"Looks like being quite a party," commented Sonya. "The big, fat blonde, Irene, with her playmates, *and* our dear friends from Waldegren. . . ."

"No friends of mine," growled Grimes. "I was at the Battle of Dartura. . . . Remember?"

"Long before my time, dearie," she commented.

"Commodore! Sir!" broke in Carnaby. "A target, on the radar!"

"Not one of the derelicts, Mr. Carnaby?"

"No. It just appeared out of nothingness. It's closing on us, fast."

"Mr. Hendrikson—all weapons to bear. Do not open fire without orders. Mr. Daniels, try to establish contact. Commander Mayhew—is it *Wanderer*?"

"No, sir."

"Then who the hell . . . *or what* the hell . . . ?"

"Locked on, sir," reported Hendrikson.

"Good."

"Range still closing, but less rapidly. We should have her visually in a few seconds." said Carnaby.

"Thank you. Commander Williams, the telescope."

"Aye, aye, Skipper!"

"No contact, sir," murmured Daniels. "But I *can* hear the Waldegren ship again. She's still distant."

"I've got her in the telescope," drawled Williams. "Odd-looking bitch . . . she's on the screen now, if you care to take a butcher's."

Grimes took a "butcher's hook," reflecting that life was already sufficiently complicated without his second-in-command's rhyming slang. The strange ship was there, exactly in the center of the circle of blackness, a silver moth pinned against the backdrop of the night. As she approached, her image expanded rapidly. She was a gleaming disc—but, Grimes realized, he was looking at her head on—from which sprouted a complexity of antennae. And then, slowly, she turned, presenting her profile. Apart from that veritable forest of metallic rods she was not unlike the Survey Service courier that had been Grimes' first command long ago, so very long ago, one of the so-called "flying darning needles." As yet she had made no hostile move. But, assuming that she was alien, captained by a nonhuman or, even, by a nonhumanoid, would a hostile move be recognized as such before it was too late?

Grimes flashed a glance at Hendrikson, hushed intently over his console. *He* was ready; possibly rather too ready. He looked back at the screen. He thought, he was almost sure, that the lines of the strange vessel showed a human sense of proportion. He snapped at Daniels, "Haven't you raised her yet?"

"I'm . . . I'm trying sir. I've tried every frequency known to civilized Man, and a few that aren't . . . Ah! Got it!"

There was a babble of sound from the speaker of the NST transceiver. Alien gibberings? No . . . It sounded more like human speech, but horridly distorted, garbled.

Daniels spoke very slowly and distinctly into his microphone. "Rim Worlds Confederacy's cruiser *Faraway Quest* to unknown vessel. *Faraway Quest* to unknown vessel. Come in, please. Come in, please. Over."

In reply came the meaningless gabble.

Daniels was patient, carefully adjusting his tuning. "*Faraway Quest* to unknown vessel. Please identify yourself. Please identify yourself. Over."

"A shi? A shi?"

What ship? What ship? It could be, thought Grimes.

"A shi? A shi? Dringle na puss. Gleeble."

Tickle my puss? Hardly.

"We'll try visual," said Grimes. "Pass me the key, will you? I don't think that my Morse is too rusty."

Williams passed him the Morse key on its long lead. Grimes took it in his right hand, his thumb on the button. He sent a series of "As", the general calling sign. He assumed that somebody, by this time, would have the *Quest's* big searchlight trained on the stranger. He kept his attention on the image in the telescope screen.

Yes, he, whoever (or whatever) he was seemed to know Morse. The acknowledgment, the long flash, the Morse "T", was almost blindingly obvious.

"What ship?" sent Grimes. "What ship?"

From the other came a succession of "As". Grimes replied with "T". Then, "What ship?" he read. "What ship?"

So . . . so was the stranger repeating parrot fashion, or was he being cagey?

"What ship?" sent Grimes again. "What ship?"

"What ship?" he received.

He sent, not too slowly but carefully, making sure that each word was acknowledged, "Identify yourself, or I open fire."

He grinned when the reply came, "You'd better not."

He said aloud, "Not only human, but our sort of people." He flashed, "This is the Rim Worlds Confederacy's cruiser *Faraway Quest*. You are intruding into our sector of space. Please identify yourself."

"Imperial Navy's armed scout *Vindictive*. Rim Worlds Confederacy's Navy not listed in Jane's. Never heard of Rim Worlds Confederacy. Who the hell are you?"

"Commander Williams," said Grimes, "*Jane's Fighting Ships* is in the computer's library bank. Check *Vindictive*, will you? And the Imperial Navy."

"Will do, Skipper. But the only Imperial Navy *we* have is the Waverley one."

"I know. But check it, anyhow." Again his thumb worked rhythmically on the key. "This is *Faraway Quest*. This is Rim Worlds' space. You are intruding."

"You are intruding."

Grimes grinned again, sent, "Can't we talk this over?"

For long seconds there was no reply. Carnaby reported that the stranger was no longer closing the range, was maintaining her distance. Hendrikson announced, unnecessarily, that his weaponry was still in a state of readiness.

Daniels asked, "Can I have the key, sir? If I have a yarn with her radio officer I shall be able to find out what frequencies to use. . . ."

And then *Vindictive* started flashing again. "Request permission to board."

"One man only," Grimes replied.

More time passed. Then, "Please prepare to receive my boat."

Oh, no, thought Grimes. *Oh, no.* The dividing line between a boat and a torpedo is a very narrow one. He was satisfied by now that *Vindictive*'s people were humans; but the human race has a long record of viciousness and treachery, far too often actuated by the very highest motives.

"One man in a suit," he sent, "will meet one man in a suit, midway between our two vessels. They will return to *Faraway Quest* together. You may close the range between ships to ten miles. Do not forget that all my weapons are trained on you, and that my gunnery officer has a very itchy trigger finger." He said aloud, "And I have a very sore thumb."

"Agreed," sent *Vindictive* at last. "Closing. Please remember that you are a big target."

"Commander Mayhew," asked the commodore, "can you pick up anything, anything at all, from those people?"

"Faintly . . ." replied the telepath slowly. "Very faintly. I sense suspicion, distrust. They will fire if they think that they are about to be fired upon."

"And so will we. And now—who's for the space walk? Don't all answer at once."

There was no shortage of volunteers, but Mayhew's rather high voice was distinctly heard above the others. "There's only one possible choice, sir. Me. When I get close to whoever *they* send I should be able to read his thoughts more easily. And Clarisse can look after the shop in my absence."

"Mphm. Very well, Ken. Get suited up. And—look after yourself."

"I always have done, John, all the years that you've known me." He said nothing to Clarisse, but it was not necessary. Accompanied by Williams he left the control room.

"Please let me know when you are ready," flashed *Vindictive*.

"Willco," replied Grimes.

∽ Chapter 11 ∽

"**I SUPPOSE** that it has occurred to you," said Sonya, "that this *Vindictive*, of which no mention is made in *our* version of *Jane's Fighting Ships,* could be from that Irene woman's universe. After all, she is supposed to be a unit of the Imperial Navy."

"The thought had flickered across my mind," admitted Grimes, "even though I'm not, and never have been, an intelligence officer." In spite of the absence of gravity he contrived to lay back in his chair. "We rather gathered, the last—and the only, so far—time that we met the ex-empress that her employers, these GLASS people, were regarded by the Imperial Government as more than somewhat of a nuisance. Shit stirrers, if you'll pardon the expression."

"I've heard worse. Continue."

"So it is reasonable to suppose that if GLASS want to get their paws on *The Outsider* and *The Outsider*'s secrets, the Imperial Navy could be sent out to make sure that they didn't. But . . ."

"What is your 'but'?"

"But I don't think that *Vindictive* was built by the same technology as Irene's *Wanderer*. *Wanderer*, like *Faraway Quest*, had all sorts of odd lumps and bumps on her hull, but she didn't look like a deep space hedgehog. Too, neither *Wanderer* nor ourselves experienced any trouble in initiating either Carlotti or NST radio telephone hookups."

"H'm. I suppose we could get Clarisse to ask that man

Metzenther, aboard *Wanderer*, if they're being followed. Not that you can call it being followed when the pursuer gets there hours before the pursued."

"That, my dear, is very sound tactics, when you can manage it."

Williams' voice came over the intercom. "Commander Mayhew suited up an' in the after airlock."

Then, over the transceiver that was operating on the suit frequencies, Mayhew reported, "All ready, sir."

Grimes flashed the signal to *Vindictive*, read the reply, "The captain is on his way."

"A do-it-yourself-trust-nobody type," commented the commodore. "Tell Commander Mayhew to shove off."

He felt a slight twinge of anxiety—but, after all, Mayhew was a spaceman as well as a telepath, and Williams would have given him a thorough briefing. It would be simple enough; just switch on the suit's reaction unit and steer straight for the other ship, keeping eyes skinned for the blinker that would be flashing from *Vindictive*'s captain's helmet. But did this peculiar Empire in some peculiar universe observe the same rules of spacemanship as were observed in Grimes' continuum?

Obviously it did. All the lights of *Vindictive* went out, as had all the lights showing from *Faraway Quest*. This would make it easier for the space walkers; each of them now would see only the little, but bright beacon toward which he was steering.

Carnaby had the radar on short range, was tracking both space-suited men. He was speaking into the microphone of the transceiver. "That's fine, Commander. Steady.... Steady as you go.... Better shut off your propulsion.... Be ready for a retro-blast...."

Grimes, staring through the viewport, could see the two blinking lights almost as one, so nearly in line were they. Surely Mayhew hadn't much further to go....

"Brake, Commander," came Carnaby's voice. "Brake! Yes, he's braking too. Now ... just a nudge ahead ... that's it!"

And from the transceiver's speaker came Mayhew's whisper. "Contact. Contact established. He's tough, Commodore. Hard to get inside.... But... I can assure you that he intends no treachery."

Grimes took the microphone. "Does he know that you're . . . prying?"

"I don't think so."

"Can he hear you? Me?"

"No, sir. I'm careful that our helmets don't come into contact."

"Good. Go through the motions of searching him for any weapons that he may have outside his suit. Then you can touch helmets and talk to him."

"Very good, sir."

There was a silence that seemed to drag on and on. At last Mayhew said, "Be ready to receive us on board, Commodore."

Williams called up from the after airlock to say that Mayhew and the man from *Vindictive* were aboard, and that he was bringing them up to Control. Grimes found himself wondering what his visitor would be like. He was an officer in the armed forces of an empire— and empire sounded far more glamorous than federation or confederacy. *He's probably got a title,* thought Grimes idly, *and a string of letters after his name half a light year long.* He glanced around his control room, missing nothing. All of his officers were in correct uniform, although some of them were more than a little untidy in appearance. Druthen, of course, was his usual slovenly self—but he was a mere civilian, a passenger.

Williams came up through the hatch. "Commander Mayhew, Skipper," he announced cheerfully. Mayhew, still suited up but carrying his helmet under his left arm, followed Williams. "And Captain Sir Dominic Flandry, of the Imperial Navy. Sir Dominic, may I present Commodore John Grimes, of the Rim Worlds Naval Reserve?" Commander Williams was plainly enjoying himself.

Grimes looked at Flandry. He was not at all sure if he liked what he saw. The captain of *Vindictive* was a tall man, and conveyed the impression of slimness even in his bulky spacesuit. The suit itself was gleaming black with gold trimmings. The helmet that Flandry carried tucked under his arm was also black, with a wreath of golden oak leaves on its visor, with, as an ornate badge, a golden eagle with outspread wings gripping a conventionalized planetary globe in its talons. His face was harsh, with a fierce beak of a nose, and the pencil line black moustache over the sensual mouth should have looked foppish—but somehow didn't. The glossy black hair was touched with gray at the temples. The eyes were a pale blue, and very bleak.

"Your servant, Commodore," said Flandry stiffly.

That'll be the sunny Friday when you're any man's servant, thought Grimes. He said, "Good to have you aboard, Captain. Or should I say, 'Sir Dominic'?"

"Either will do, Commodore." Flandry's sharp eyes were flickering around the control room, missing nothing, missing nobody. They lingered for a few seconds on Clarisse—and for longer on Sonya. *Of course,* thought Grimes, *she would be wearing that indecent micro-skirted Federation uniform.* Flandry said, "You carry a mixed crew, Commodore."

"Mphm. Yes. Although the ladies are specialist officers. Mrs. Mayhew. . . ." Clarisse unbuckled herself from her chair, came forward. "This is Captain Flandry, of *Vindictive*. Captain Flandry, this is Mrs. Mayhew, our assistant psionic communications officer . . ."

"Psionic communications? A telepath . . . and I take it that Commander Mayhew, whom you sent out to meet me, is your chief psionic communications officer. . . ."

He looked at Clarisse again, and suddenly she flushed. Flandry laughed. "Sorry," he said. "Sorry, my dear. I should have had the sense to keep my thoughts under proper control." But he did not sound sorry, and Clarisse, although embarrassed, did not look at all resentful.

"And this is Commander Verrill, of the Federation's Survey Service. She is acting as the Federation's observer on this expedition."

"And not a telepath, I take it," murmured Flandry. He looked as though he were undressing Sonya with his eyes—not that she needed much undressing, thought Grimes, in that apology for a uniform. And he did not like the way that she was looking back at the Imperial captain.

Grimes introduced his other officers, and then Druthen. He said, "And now, Sir Dominic, I suggest that we withdraw to my quarters for discussion. Commander Williams, please accompany us.

Commander Mayhew, Mr. Daniels—please let me know at once if either of you hear anything further from *Wanderer* or Adler."

"*Wanderer*?" asked Flandry, with a lift of one eyebrow.

"One of yours, possibly. She's the private yacht of the ex-Empress Irene."

"Then *not* one of ours," laughed the other. "We don't have an empress. We never have had an empress. I, sir, have the honor." and he made it sound a dubious honor, "of serving His Imperial Majesty Edouard XIV. And this *Adler*?"

"A destroyer sailing under the flag of the Duchy of Waldegren."

"The Duchy of Waldegren? Never heard of it."

The officers were looking at Grimes and his visitor curiously. The commodore decided that they had better continue their discussion in greater privacy. He said, "This way, please, Sir Dominic."

On the way to his suite he noticed that Flandry did not handle himself very well in free fall. So, probably, *Vindictive* ran to some sort of artificial gravity, and when in orbit her officers did not have to cope with the problems of weightlessness. He decided to get one of his engineers aboard the armed scout if it were at all possible. There must be quite a few technologies aboard her well worth copying.

The sliding door opened as Grimes approached it. He stood to one side, waving the others into his day cabin ahead of him. Flandry moved clumsily, shuffling his feet, in their magnetically soled boots, on the deck.

Grimes said, "This is Liberty Hall. You can spit on the mat and call the cat a bastard."

Sonya looked at him coldly. "This is the first time I've heard you say that for quite some time, John. I'd hoped you'd forgotten it."

Flandry flashed her a smile. "It *is* a vivid figure of speech, Commander Verrill. Have you known the Commodore for a long time?"

"Yes. I'm married to him."

"Commodore Grimes, have you any *unmarried* ladies among your crew as attractive as the two ladies I have already met?"

"No, I haven't." Then, in a less surly tone of voice, "Sit down, Captain. And perhaps you will take a drink with us. . . ."

"I'll be glad of the drink—but this suit's not made for sitting in. And when in a strange ship, quite possibly a hostile ship, I prefer to keep it on."

"As you please, Captain Flandry. And you'll have to take my word for it that the drinks aren't drugged or poisoned." Grimes pulled himself into his own chair, strapped himself in. Sonya followed suit. Williams was about to do likewise when Grimes told him to look after the refreshments. Efficiently the commander produced bulbs of the drink required. Flandry asked for scotch.

"Your health, Captain Sir Dominic!"

"Your health, Commodore Grimes." Again there was that sardonic smile. "But should I, as a loyal servant of His Imperial Majesty, be drinking your health?"

"And why the hell shouldn't you be?" demanded Grimes crustily.

"And why should I, Commodore—if you *are* a commodore. Oh, I'll let you have your rank. Even pirates must have officers."

"Pirates? What the hell are you getting at?"

"Pirates." Flandry's voice was harsh. "Pirates, setting themselves up as petty kings on the fringes of a disintegrating empire. Laying their grubby paws on Imperial property, even planting their absurd flag on it. Tell me, Commodore Grimes, what genius thought up that black banner with a golden wheel on it? What does it signify?"

Grimes didn't answer the question directly. He snapped. "*Imperial* property? I suppose you're referring to that heap of alien ironmongery that somebody left in *our* backyard. The Outsiders' Ship, as we call it, lies within Rim Worlds' territorial space."

"Does it? And who, or what, are the Rim Worlds? *The Outsider*, as we call it, was first discovered by Admiral Lord Wolverhelm, who commanded the *Fringe Sweep*."

Grimes eyed Flandry cautiously. He thought, *The bastard's enjoying himself. He's trying to make us lose our tempers.* He said, "Neither the Federation nor the Confederacy runs to 'sirs' and 'lords.' The Empire of Waverley does, of course—but it would never dream of sending an expedition out here without our permission."

"Odd name for a ship—the *Fringe Sweep* . . ." commented Williams.

"That, sir, was the designation of the mission," Flandry told him coldly.

"In any case," put in Sonya, who had been silent for too long, "The Outsiders' Ship was first discovered by Commander Maudsley of the Federation's Survey Service. But the Federation recognizes the territorial rights of the Confederacy."

"Somebody," grinned Flandry, "is going to have a good laugh over this conversation." He lifted a gloved hand to tap the collar of his suit, just below the throat. Grimes thought with no surprise, *A concealed microphone.* "In the unlikely event of my not getting back to my ship, all that's being said is being recorded aboard *Vindictive*. It is also being relayed to our nearest base. My masters will already have come to the conclusion that I have blundered into a nest of pirates. . . ."

"Watch it, mate," growled Williams. "Watch it!"

In a blur of motion Flandry snapped on his helmet. His voice, only slightly distorted, issued from a diaphragm. He said, "This suit, gentlemen—and Commander Verrill—is proof against anything that you can throw at me. Probably I should not survive a nuclear blast—but neither would you. And now, if you will excuse me, I must return to my own vessel. I strongly advise that nobody try to stop me."

Grimes said dryly, "As I recollect it, Captain, the main purpose of this meeting was that we should talk things over. I suppose that you can hear what I'm saying inside that gaudy carapace of yours."

"Of course. Say what you must say."

"Well, Captain Flandry, we haven't talked things over. You've jumped to conclusions, assumed that I'm a pirate king or some such. If I were, I'd not be content with the rank of commodore! It's a wonder that you didn't see that wheel of ours on the black flag as a skull and crossbones! Just try to understand this: as far as *we* are concerned, *you* are the intruder."

"And how can that be, Commodore?"

"Been out on the Rim before, Captain Flandry? Or the Fringe, as you people call it?"

"Nobody comes out here but outlaws."

"And yourself, of course. And that Admiral Lord What's-His-Name before you. But we live on the Rim. We *know* that here, at the very edge of the expanding universe, the walls between the alternate time tracks are very thin indeed, at times nonexistent. We have good reason to believe that The Outsiders' Ship has warped the continuum about itself so that this small volume of space is common ground for ships—and people—from all the universes. . . ."

"You tell a good fairy story, Commodore."

The intercom buzzed sharply; then Carnaby's voice came through the speaker. "Commodore, sir. *Wanderer* has just broken through! And Mr. Daniels thinks that *Adler* is very close. She is reporting back to her base in some sort of code."

"Reinforcements, Commodore Grimes?" asked Flandry coldly.

Briefly Grimes was tempted to say yes. But that could have been dangerous. This Flandry, feeling himself to be outnumbered, would be quite capable of ordering his ship to lash out with all weapons like a vicious cornered animal. "No," he said slowly. "No. Just old friends—or acquaintances, rather—and old enemies."

"Commodore, sir!" It was Carnaby again. "Mr. Daniels says there's *another* ship using a Carlotti transmitter!"

"Cor stone me Aunt Fanny up a gum tree!" marveled Williams. "How many *more* are goin' to turn up at the Vicar's flamin' afternoon tea party?"

"So," said Flandry, "we seem to have met at the crossroads of the universe. If you are to be believed, that is. . . . But I think you will agree that I should return to my own vessel."

"If I were in your shoes I should be saying the same," agreed Grimes. "Commander Williams, escort Captain Flandry to the airlock."

"And how shall I keep in touch—assuming, of course, that I wish to do so? By flashing lamp?"

"Get your radio officer to talk to mine on the blinker. Perhaps, between the pair of them, they'll be able to cook something up."

"I'll tell him now." Grimes could see, through the frontal transparency of Flandry's helmet, the man's lips moving, but he could hear nothing. Then: "Before I go, just one more question. These people in *Wanderer* . . . are they friendly or hostile?"

"They could be either. And, to save you the trouble of asking another question, I haven't a clue as to who or what this other strange ship is."

"If this is the Rim," said Flandry, "you're welcome to it." He bowed stiffly to Sonya. "Although life out here seems to have its compensations."

Then he followed Williams out to the axial shaft.

∼ Chapter 12 ∼

GRIMES AND SONYA hurried back to the control room.

As Carnaby had told him, *Wanderer* had arrived. She was hanging there in the blackness, slim, sleek and deadly looking, no more than a couple of cables from *Faraway Quest*. Typical, thought Grimes, of Irene Trafford or the ex-Empress Irene or whatever she called herself these days. But the commodore, over the years, had become more of a merchant officer than a naval officer in his outlook and just could not see the point of exposing a vessel, any vessel, to unnecessary hazard.

Anyhow, there she was, and close, too close. Grimes thought of actuating his inertial drive to put more distance between himself and the armed yacht—but, damn it all, he was here first. Why should he shift?

The screen of the NST transceiver glowed into life. Colors swirled, coalesced; and then Grimes was looking into the control room of the other ship. Yes, there was Irene, big and brassy as ever, with the careful touch of nonuniform color, the crimson cravat with the white polka dots, added to her otherwise correct attire. Before she became empress, she had been a tough mate in the Dog Star Line, and this outfit, in Grimes' universe as well as in hers, was notorious for its rough-and-ready star tramps. She had been mate in the Dog Star Line, and was determined that nobody should ever be allowed to forget it. Beside her sat Benjamin Trafford, officially, master of *Wanderer*.

The little, wiry, sandy-haired man was as neat and correct as he would have been had he still been serving in the Imperial Navy. And behind them Grimes saw the dark, dapper Tallentire, alert at his fire control console; and with him was Susanna: tall, slender and with high-piled and glossy auburn hair. There was Metzenther who, if he shaved off his beard, would be almost the double of Grimes' Mayhew. There was Trialanne, the Iralian woman: frail, willowy, beautiful, looking as though she had been blown from translucent glass by a master craftsman who was also a superb artist.

And there was a stranger, a most undistinguished-looking man of medium height, dressed in a drab, gray coverall suit. Normally one would not look at him twice. But in *Wanderer*'s control room he was a sparrow among hawks and drew attention. Grimes decided suddenly, *He's hard and dangerous, whoever he is. . . .*

"Commodore Grimes," said Irene in the voice that was almost a baritone.

"Your servant, ma'am," replied Grimes politely—after all, she had been an empress—while, behind him, Sonya snorted inelegantly.

"Come off it, Commodore. Nature never intended you to be a courtier."

"You can say that again," remarked Sonya quietly.

"Commodore Grimes, may I ask what the hell you and your spaceborne junk heap are doing in *our* universe?"

"I might ask the same question of you, Mrs. Trafford."

"Just because I jumped time tracks once—and that accidentally— you needn't think that I make a habit of it."

"Neither do I," said Grimes flatly. This was not quite true, but Irene and her people would not know this.

"And what's that odd looking ship like a tin sea urchin? You must know. We saw a man in a space suit jetting off from your vessel to her."

"One of yours, isn't she? Her captain says that she's the Imperial Navy's armed scout *Vindictive*."

"*Not* one of ours," said Trafford firmly. "We *do* have a *Vindictive*, Commodore, but she's a light cruiser. I should know. I've served in her."

"Irene," asked that drab, too-ordinary man in a voice that matched his appearance, "would you mind putting me in the picture? Who *are* these people?"

"Mr. Smith," said the big blonde, "allow me to present Commodore Grimes, of the Rim Worlds Naval Reserve. In *his* cockeyed continuum the Rim Worlds are self-governing. And Commander Sonya Verrill, who is also Mrs. Grimes, of the Federation's Survey Service. Their Federation is roughly analogous to our Empire. The only other person I know is Mr. Mayhew, who is *Faraway Quest's* psionic communications officer.

"And this gentleman, Commodore, is Mr. Smith, managing director of GLASS. We have been chartered by him to lay claim to and to investigate The Outsiders' Ship."

"The Outsiders' Ship," Grimes told her firmly, "is in the territorial space of the Rim Worlds' Confederacy. Furthermore, we have planted our flag on it."

"According to Space Law," stated Irene, "the mere planting of a flag is not sufficient for laying claim to any planet, planetoid, satellite or whatever. For a claim to be valid a self-sustaining colony must be established. I doubt very much if you have gone so far as that. In any case, The Outsiders' Ship is within Imperial territorial space."

"And *which* Empire, madam?" demanded a sardonic voice.

Daniels whispered, "I've managed a hookup with *Vindictive,* sir. That was Captain Flandry."

"Who the hell was that?" demanded Irene.

"The captain of *Vindictive,*" Grimes replied. "But let us continue our discussion of the finer points of Space Law. As I see it, that *thing* is neither a planet, a planetoid nor a satellite. It is a derelict. . . ."

"It could be held to be a satellite," insisted Irene. "An artificial satellite. . . ."

"A satellite must have a primary."

"Oh, all right, you bloody space lawyer. It's a derelict. But have you put a prize crew on board? Have you got a towline fast to it?"

"My flag . . ."

"You know what you can do with that!"

In the little screen Trafford looked both shocked and

embarrassed. Tallentire tried to hide a grin. Smith did not try to hide his.

"Mphm," grunted Grimes disapprovingly.

"What charming friends you have, Commodore," commented Flandry.

"Acquaintances, Captain," Grimes told him.

"As you wish. But might I suggest, sir, that all three parties convene to discuss matters in a *civilized* fashion?"

"That could be worth considering," admitted Grimes reluctantly.

"And might I urge that we do it as soon as possible, if not before? As yet our three ships haven't opened fire on each other—but who knows what might happen when the other two vessels in the vicinity put in an appearance?"

"He's talking sense," said Sonya.

"*What* other two vessels?" demanded Irene. "We only know of the Waldegren destroyer, *Adler*. Who is the other one?"

"I wish I knew," sighed Grimes.

"Well, Commodore?" snapped Flandry. Grimes was sorry that Daniels had not been able to arrange a visual as well as an audio hookup. He would have liked to have been able to read the other's expression.

"Well, Commodore?" echoed Irene.

"Your place or mine?" asked Grimes, with an attempt at humor.

"Neutral territory," said Flandry. "While all the nattering was going on my first lieutenant sent a boarding party to that odd, dome-shaped derelict about ten kilometers beyond *Vindictive* from your viewpoint. Its late owners were oxygen breathers, although not human. All its life-support systems were intact, and are now functioning. . . ."

"A Shaara ship," stated Grimes.

"The *Shaara*?" asked Irene and Flandry simultaneously. And then Flandry demanded, "And who the hell are they when they're up and dressed?"

"Never mind," said Grimes. "The Shaara ship will do very nicely."

❧ Chapter 13 ❧

THE SHAARA DERELICT was a good place for a meeting. The ship was in good order and condition; her interior lighting glowed brightly; her humming fans kept the clean, untainted air in circulation. How long had they been doing so? Not for too long. The mosslike growth in the hydroponics tanks that the Shaara used for atmospheric regeneration was neither running wild nor withering for lack of the organic wastes that were its food. But of her crew: of the queen-captain, the princess-officers, the drones, the workers, there was no sign—not even so much as a dry exoskeleton. The logbook was still on its ledge in the control room; but no human could hope to read that straggling script.

She was a latter-day *Mary Celeste*. She was one of several *Mary Celestes* in orbit about *The Outsider*.

Boats from the three ships had rendezvoused at the airlock of the derelict. Grimes himself had piloted *Faraway Quest*'s pinnace. With him he had Sonya and Mayhew. Irene had brought with her Trialanne and Stanley Smith, the man from GLASS. Flandry was accompanied only by a simian young officer, almost as broad as he was tall, whom he introduced as Ensign Bugolsky.

This, of course, was when they were all assembled in the Shaara ship's control room, standing among the equipment and instruments, some familiar (although modified to suit arthropodal claws instead of human hands) and some weirdly alien. There were cradles of flimsy-looking webbing but no seats. As the vessel was in free fall, to stand was no hardship.

Flandry, resplendent in his black and gold space armor, removed his helmet. The others removed theirs. Grimes didn't like the way that the man looked at Irene and Trialanne. He most certainly didn't like the way that the man looked at Sonya. And he disapproved most strongly of the way in which the three women looked at Flandry. Mental undressing can be a two-way process.

"And now," announced Flandry with a wide grin, "I declare this meeting open."

"Not so fast, Captain," Grimes told him. "As the senior officer present I feel that that should be my privilege."

"Senior officer? But *I* represent the Imperium."

"*What* Imperium?" demanded Irene nastily.

"Commodore!" Mayhew's usually soft voice was sharp with urgency. "Commodore! Sir!"

Grimes waved him aside. "Later, Commander Mayhew—unless my ship's in danger. She's not? Good. Then let's get this business settled first." He turned to the others. "I'm not overly rank conscious, and I'm insisting on my seniority only because Rim Worlds' sovereignty is involved. To begin with—we are in Rim Confederacy's territorial space. Secondly, I outrank everybody present in this control room. . . ."

"In a pig's arse you do!" flared Irene.

"But I do, madam. I concede that you *were* an empress, but you're not now. Legally speaking you're only the chief officer of *Wanderer*. . . ."

"And the owner of *Wanderer*, Grimes! Which is more than you can say regarding yourself and your precious rustbucket!"

"And *I* still claim," stated Flandry, "that *Wanderer* and *Faraway Quest* are no better than pirates, attempting to steal Imperial property."

"It's a great pity that GLASS is not operative in *your* universe," said Smith in a flat voice. "But since we are discussing legalities, I feel that I, as the charterer of Mrs. Trafford's vessel, should have some voice in the matter."

"Irene!" Trialanne was trying to gain the attention of the ex-empress. "Irene!"

"Pipe down, damn you! Can't you see I'm busy?"

"Obviously," said Sonya coldly, "it would be pointless to put it to the vote who should be chairman of this meeting. Everybody is quite convinced that he has a more valid claim than anybody else. I could say—and, come to that, I *do* say—that I represent the Federation, but I have no desire to be yet another complication. . . ."

"But a very charming one," murmured Flandry, flashing that dazzling grin.

"Thank you, Sir Dominic."

"Very charming, and, I feel, highly competent. For the record, I do not recognize the Interstellar Federation. Nonetheless, I feel that Mrs. Grimes—or, if you prefer it, Commander Verrill—should preside over this meeting. She appears, in spite of her marriage . . ." he made it sound as though he meant "disastrous marriage" . . . "to be the nearest thing we have to a neutral. Will you, then, take charge, Commander Verrill?"

She smiled at him. "Thank you, Sir Dominic. I will." She raised her voice slightly. "To begin with, all of you, this situation calls for straight thinking. We are met together in what is, to all of us, an alien ship. We represent, between us, three different cultures, at least four different governments. But we are all—and I include you, Trialanne—human. . . ."

"So *you* say," growled Irene.

Sonya ignored this, went on. "As an aid to straight thinking, recapitulation will be in order. We are all of us *here*, all of us *now*—that much is obvious. But it should be obvious, too, that *The Outsider*, The Outsiders' Ship, warps normal space time. It exists simultaneously in our universe, and in yours, Sir Dominic, and in yours, Irene—and yet it is from outside all our universes. . . ."

Somebody was grabbing Grimes' arm, the pressure evident even through the thick sleeve of his suit. It was Mayhew. The telepath was pointing to the hatch which gave access to the control room from the body of the ship. Through it a helmeted head was rising slowly.

"I—we—were trying to tell you!" muttered Mayhew.

"Tell me *what*?" growled Grimes.

In reply the other shrugged—no easy feat in a space suit—infuriatingly. *Bloody prima donna!* thought Grimes. *But it can't be all that important. Probably somebody from one of the ships with some trivial message.*

"It could be," Sonya was continuing, in a schoolmistress voice, "that we are all of us here on sufferance. . . ."

The shoulders of the new arrival were now visible, but the faceplate of his helmet was almost opaque. Grimes stared at those armored shoulders. They carried the broad gold stripe of a commodore, the winged wheel of the Rim Worlds Navy. Who the hell could it be? Lannigan? DuBois? Why should either of them be sent out here to interfere with him, Grimes? And this interloping commodore had somebody with him, wearing commander's badges of rank, and the stylized star cluster of the Federation. . . .

Sonya's voice trailed off into silence. She had seen the newcomers at last. So had all the others.

The stranger put gloved hands to his helmet, twisted, lifted. He stared at Grimes—and Grimes stared at him. It was long seconds before Grimes recognized him. One is used to seeing one's own face in a mirror, but one spends very little (if any) time studying solidographs of oneself. Dimly, Grimes was aware that the other stranger, standing to one side and a little behind the commodore, had removed her helmet. He didn't really notice her until she spoke.

"This is a surprise, John," said Maggie Lazenby.

Flandry laughed. "Getting back to our original argument—just which of you two gentlemen is the senior?"

∼ Chapter 14 ∼

"MPHM," grunted Grimes.

"Mphm," grunted Grimes.

Slowly he opened the pouch at his belt, took from it his tobacco tin and his battered pipe. Carefully he filled the pipe, returned the tin to the pouch, brought out a lighter. He lit the pipe. He squinted at Grimes through the swirl of blue, acrid smoke.

Slowly he opened the pouch at his belt, took from it his tobacco tin and his battered pipe. Carefully he filled the pipe, returned the tin to the pouch, brought out a lighter. He lit the pipe. He squinted at Grimes through the swirl of blue, acrid smoke.

Sonya made a major production of a lung-wracking cough.

Maggie said, "Let the man have his little pleasures—and his aid to cerebration."

Sonya demanded, "What are *you* doing with *him*?"

Maggie replied, "I could ask you the same, duckie."

Grimes demanded, "How the hell did *you* get here?"

Grimes replied, "The same way as you." He gestured toward the nearest hexagonal viewport with the hand that held the pipe.

Grimes stared out into the blackness. There had been three vessels there: Flandry's *Vindictive*, Irene's *Wanderer*, his own *Faraway Quest*. Now there were four. He asked, "And what is the name of *your* ship?"

"*Faraway Quest*, of course. She was *Delta Puppis* before the Federation flogged her to us."

"Mphm," grunted Grimes again, feeling a twinge of envy. His *Faraway Quest* was an ex-Epsilon Class tramp. He turned to Mayhew. "You might have kept me better informed, Commander."

"Sir, both Trialanne and I tried to tell you as soon as this other *Faraway Quest* broke through. I couldn't tell you anything before then as she does not carry a psionic communications officer."

"Unfortunately, no," agreed Grimes II. "I tried to convince my masters that a good PCO is worth ten thousand times his weight in Carlotti transceivers—but *they* know best." He added after a pause, "I can never understand this craving to put oneself at the mercy of a single fuse. . . ."

"And how many times have you heard *that* before, Maggie?" asked Sonya.

"I've lost count," said Maggie Lazenby.

"But this question of seniority . . . ?" hinted Flandry, obviously determined to extract the utmost in amusement from the situation.

"*I* am the senior," stated both Grimeses.

"I was here first," said Grimes I.

"Mine is the larger ship," said Grimes II.

Grimes I laughed. "This is bloody absurd, Grimes. Before we get involved in any futile arguments would you mind putting me—us— into your picture?"

"I'll try, Grimes. My masters decided that it was time that somebody took another expedition out to The Outsiders' Ship, and I was given the job. Maggie—you *do* know Maggie, of course . . .?"

"I do. And so does Sonya."

"And I know Sonya. Quite a family party, isn't it? But where was I? Oh, yes. Maggie, although she's married to me, has retained her Federation citizenship and her commission in the Federation's Survey Service. She's along as an observer for the Federation."

"As Sonya is. But go on."

Grimes II carefully relit his pipe. "Well, we rather suspected that there would be other ships, in addition to the known derelicts, in orbit about *The Outsider*. But we were certainly surprised to find that one of those other ships, like mine, was named *Faraway Quest*. Your second-in-command, Commander Williams, was even more surprised. It must have been a shock to him to see my face looking out of the screen when we started nattering over the NST radio. It put him in rather a dither. There he was, conditioned to say, 'Yes, sir; no, sir,' to Commodore Grimes. . . ."

"That doesn't sound like Williams!" said Grimes II.

"Well, as a matter of fact he called me 'Skipper.' But he was in a fine tangle of conflicting loyalties. He suggested that I'd better make contact with you to get things sorted out, and told me where I'd find you. And now, Commodore Grimes, suppose you introduce your friends to me. . . ."

"Certainly, Commodore Grimes," said Grimes who, in a dazed sort of way, was beginning to enjoy himself. "Irene, Trialanne, this, as you see, is Commodore Grimes, who obviously is from a time track not too far divergent from my own. And the lady is Commander Lazenby, of the Federation's Survey Service, and also Mrs. Grimes. Commodore, may I present Mrs. Trafford, who is chief officer *and* owner of the so-called yacht *Wanderer*, and Trialanne, one of her PCOs. Oh, yes, before I forget—Mrs. Trafford is also the ex-Empress Irene."

"I am honored," said Grimes II, with a stiff little bow.

"You bloody well should be," growled Irene.

"And Mr. Smith, the managing director of GLASS, charterer of *Wanderer*. GLASS is an acronym for Galactic League Against Suppression and Slavery. It is, I imagine, a severe pain in the neck to quite a few governments in Irene's universe. . . ."

"We try to be just that," agreed Smith modestly.

"And this, Commodore, is Captain Sir Dominic Flandry, of the Imperial armed scout *Vindictive*. The young gentleman with him is Ensign Bugolsky."

Flandry smiled, but his eyes were cold, wary. "I am glad to meet you, Commodore. And *you*, Commander Lazenby."

You would be, thought Grimes.

"In one way your arrival, sir, is welcome. Until now I have been inclined to doubt your alter ego's stories of alternate time tracks and all the rest of it. But now . . ." Flandry shrugged. He went on, "You are welcome to join our discussion."

"What discussion?" asked Grimes II.

"As to who can lay claim to *The Outsider.*"

"You will agree with me," said Grimes I, "that it lies within Rim Confederacy's territorial space."

"Of course," said Grimes II.

"But *whose* Rim Confederacy?" demanded Flandry and Irene simultaneously. "Yours or his?"

"It's *my* flag that's planted on it," stated Grimes I stubbornly.

"You and your bloody flag!" snarled Irene.

"As I see it," said Grimes II judiciously, "this is a matter to be decided between Commodore Grimes and myself."

"Definitely," said Grimes I.

"We're *surrounded* by the bastards," muttered Irene. Then, to Flandry, "You'll not stand for that, Sir Dominic?"

"*You,*" said Sonya, "can fight it out between yourselves which Empire has a claim to ownership."

Flandry flashed a charming smile at Irene. "I really think, ma'am, that we imperialists should stick together."

"GLASS has never approved of imperialism," stated Smith. "In any case, *Wanderer* is on charter to my organization."

"I seem to remember," said Sonya coldly, "that quite some time ago it was decided that I should preside over this meeting. Even though my husband has been duplicated, I have not. Therefore I suggest that we carry on from where we left off."

"And just why were you so honored, Sonya?" asked Maggie curiously.

"Because I, as an officer of the Federation's Survey Service, am the only one who can claim neutral status."

"But I, too, am an officer of the Federation's Survey Service, dearie."

"Commodore Grimes!" Mayhew called excitedly.

Both Grimeses turned to look at him.

"Yes, Commander?" asked Grimes I.

"*Faraway Quest* . . . She's . . . gone!"

"I was in touch with Clarisse," confirmed Trialanne. "But the contact has been broken."

From Flandry's suit radio came a small, tinny voice. "Captain, sir, *Faraway Quest*, the first *Faraway Quest*, has vanished."

There was no need for Grimes to stare out through the viewport, but he did so. There, hanging in nothingness, were the three ships, three only: *Vindictive*, *Wanderer* and what must be the other *Quest*, the wrong *Quest*.

He turned to look at the elaborately grotesque Outsider with something akin to hatred. "That bloody thing!" he muttered. "That bloody thing!" And he thought, *My ship, my people . . . where are they? Where or when has It thrown them?*

The Iralian woman said softly, "Commodore, *It* is not responsible. Your vessel's Mannschenn Drive was restarted just before she vanished. So I am told by Mr. Tallentire, aboard *Wanderer*."

"Trialanne! Mayhew! Get in touch with Clarisse. Find out what's happening!"

"Don't you think that I'm bloody well trying already?" snarled Mayhew. "Damn your ship. It's my woman I'm worried about!"

"Sorry, Ken," said Grimes. "I needn't tell you to do your best, and better. . . ."

"Mutiny?" asked Grimes II quietly.

"Be your age, Commodore!" flared Grimes I. "With a handpicked crew, like mine, it's impossible."

"The passengers weren't handpicked, John," Sonya told him somberly. "At least, not by you."

Mayhew, his face white and strained, whispered, "The blame is mine, John. I should have disregarded the Rhine Institute's Code of Ethics. I should have pried."

"But you didn't. And I didn't order you to. . . ." He looked around him at the faces of the others in the control room. All realized the gravity of the situation.

Grimes II broke the silence. He said, "Much as I hate to leave The Outsiders' Ship to these . . . outsiders, my *Faraway Quest* is at your disposal, Commodore. After all, we may as well keep this in the family."

"Mutiny is a crime," stated Irene. "All law-abiding citizens should combine to capture and to punish the criminals. I am with you. I am sure that I speak for my officers."

"And count me in," said Flandry, not without a touch of regret.

"Thank you," Grimes said. "Thank you. All of you."

"And where," asked Maggie Lazenby, "do we go from here?"

~ Chapter 15 ~

WHERE DID THEY GO FROM THERE?

Where had *Faraway Quest* gone?

And where was that Waldegren destroyer, *Adler*?

But the discussion, the consideration of these problems was better than the rather childish squabbling as to who had prior claim to The Outsiders' Ship.

It was decided that Grimes, Sonya and Mayhew should take passage in the second *Faraway Quest*, and that Flandry should accompany them. Flandry's own ship, *Vindictive*, was unsuitable for the pursuit of the original *Quest*. She had faster-than-light drive, of course, and faster-than-light deep space communications equipment, but neither of these operated on the principles of the Mannschenn Drive or the Carlotti beacon. She could proceed from Point A to Point B at least as fast as *Faraway Quest* or *Wanderer*, but until she reemerged into normal space time she would be completely out of touch with them.

Vindictive, therefore, would remain in orbit about The Outsider as a guard ship. Flandry impressed upon her acting captain that he was to counter any hostile move made by *Adler*, should she put in an appearance, without hesitation, but that he was to be careful in his dealings with *Faraway Quest I* should she return. As long as there was any possibility that her rightful crew were still alive, as prisoners, as hostages, their safety must be considered at all times.

All this took time, but not too much time. And then Flandry, with his aide, returned briefly to his own vessel, while Irene and her party made their way back to *Wanderer*, and while Grimes I in his pinnace followed his other self, in his pinnace, to *Faraway Quest II*. The stowage of this extra boat in the *Quest*'s cargo hold presented no great problems. By the time that it was secured Captain Flandry was alongside, at the airlock, and was being admitted.

And then the control rooms of *Wanderer* and *Faraway Quest* were manned. Grimes sat in one of the spare acceleration chairs, with Mayhew to one side of him and Sonya to the other, and with Flandry beside Sonya. He watched the other Grimes enviously. *He* still had a ship of his own. He looked curiously at the officers at their stations— and they looked curiously at him and at Sonya and at Flandry. He felt that he almost knew them. Almost certainly their counterparts lived in his continuum; he must have met some of them, however briefly. The communications officer, beside whom Mayhew had taken a seat . . . Surely that was young Carradine, who held the same rank in Rim Runners in Grimes' universe. . . .

Grimes II was giving his orders unhurriedly, decisively; they were acknowledged smartly. In the little screen of the NST transceiver, Captain Trafford in *Wanderer*'s control room was doing likewise. Then Trafford said, facing the iconoscope, "All machinery on full stand by, Commodore."

"Thank you, Captain," replied Grimes II, just a fraction of a second before Grimes I could do so. (*I'll have to watch myself,* he thought. *I'm only a passenger. . . .*)

"Execute on the count of zero."

"Aye, aye. Execute on the count of zero."

"Five . . ." intoned Grimes II. "Four . . . Three . . . Two . . . One . . . Zero!"

From below came the high, undulating whine of the Mannschenn Drive, and with it the temporal disorientation, the sense of unreality. Grimes looked at Sonya and asked himself, with wry humor, *How many of me is she seeing now?* The picture of *Wanderer*'s control room faded from the NST transceiver screen, was replaced by that in the screen of the Carlotti set. Beyond the viewports the brightly lit *Vindictive* and the distant Shaara derelict faded into invisibility—but the cold-gleaming intricacy of The Outsiders' Ship persisted stubbornly.

It is in every space, thought Grimes. *It is in every time. But how is it that nobody else has ever reported this phenomenon?* He answered his own question. *Dead men and missing men do not tell tales.*

And then, suddenly, things were normal—or as normal as they ever are, as they ever can be while the Drive is in operation.

Flandry looked at Grimes. His face was pale. He said, "So this is your Mannschenn Drive. I think I prefer our Standing Wave."

"You get used to it," Grimes told him.

"Speak for yourself," snapped Sonya.

But Grimes II—after all, this was his ship—was taking charge. "Mr. Carradine," he ordered, "keep your ears skinned for the faintest whisper from *anybody* on the main Carlotti. Grab a bearing if you can. Mr. Danby, let me know if you see even the merest flicker in the MPI. And you, Commander Mayhew, I needn't tell *you* what to do. I'm sorry that this ship doesn't run to psionic amplifier, but Mr. Metzenther and Trialanne in *Wanderer* have one."

Flandry said something about trying to find a black cat in a coal mine at midnight. Grimes II laughed. "Yes, Captain, that just about sums it up. And once we do find it we may not be much better off. For any physical contact to be made between ships while the Mannschenn Drive is operating there must be exact synchronization of temporal precession rates. There have been devices whereby one vessel can induce synchronization in the Mannschenn Drive unit of another vessel with her own. But most ships today—certainly all warships—are fitted with special governors which make this impossible unless the captain so desires."

"And when do you start accelerating, Commodore? I'm finding all this free fall rather boring."

"As soon as we know where to accelerate to."

Flandry shrugged. The gesture, now that he was out of his space suit and attired in a close-fitting, beautifully tailored, black and gold uniform, was much more effective.

Irritated, Grimes II asked sharply, "And do *you* have any ideas, Captain Flandry?"

"Why, yes. People don't hijack ships just for the fun of it. We don't have any Duchy of Waldegren in *my* universe—but, from what I have gathered, the Waldegrenese are baddies. The people who have seized the *Faraway Quest*, the *first Faraway Quest* that I was aboard, are also baddies. Could this hijacked *Faraway Quest* be making a rendezvous with *Adler*?"

"What do *you* think, Commodore?" asked Grimes II.

"I think that Captain Flandry could be right, Commodore," replied Grimes I.

"Of course I'm right," said Flandry.

"Mphm," grunted Grimes II thoughtfully. He turned to his navigator. "Mr. Danby," he said, "run up a trajectory for Waldegren. We'll just have to assume that she's coming out by the most direct route, the same as we did from *Faraway. . . .*"

"No," Grimes told him. "She's running out on the Leads astern, the same as we did."

"The *Leads*?" demanded Grimes II.

"Yes. Macbeth and the Kinsolving sun in line."

"You have some most peculiar ideas about navigation on your time track, Commodore. However, this *Adler* also belongs to your time track, so . . . All right, Mr. Danby, do as the carbon copy Commodore Grimes says. And Mr. Carradine, inform *Wanderer* of our intentions."

Carbon copy . . . thought Grimes indignantly. But, original or not, this was not his ship. He—or his own version of himself—was not giving the orders. He could only suggest and be thankful that this other Grimes did not seem to be as pigheaded as he, more than once, had been accused of being.

Briefly the Mannschenn Drive was shut down, and the big, directional gyroscopes rumbled, hummed and then whined as the ship turned about her short axis. Directly ahead—overhead from the viewport of those in Control—the dim, misty Galactic Lens swam into view and was almost immediately distorted beyond recognition as the interstellar drive was restarted. The irregular throbbing beat of the inertial drive made itself felt, and there was gravity again, and weight, and up and down.

"Now we're getting someplace," murmured Flandry a little smugly.

Grimes glared at him and was even more annoyed when he saw that Sonya was looking at the imperial captain with what could have been admiration.

~ Chapter 16 ~

IT WAS NOT A LONG PURSUIT, and it ended in stalemate.

Falling through the nonspace, nontime between the dimensions were the four ships: *Adler*, *Wanderer*, both versions of *Faraway Quest*. Trajectories had been matched, in spite of the initial efforts of *Adler* and *Faraway Quest I* to throw off their pursuers; but it was only those two vessels that had synchronized temporal precession rates.

Back toward *The Outsider* they ran, all four of them, a mismatched squadron. And they would run past their objective, and go on running, until somebody did something, somehow, to break the deadlock.

Meanwhile, Grimes had learned that his crew was safe, although they were now prisoners. At last, at long last, and with assistance from Metzenther and Trialanne, Mayhew had been able to reestablish his *rapport* with Clarisse. It had not been easy, but after many hours of concentrated effort the three telepaths had been able to drag her mind up out of its drugged sleep to a condition of full awareness. She was able, then, to supply the details of Druthen's take-over of the ship. It had been done with surprising ease, merely by the introduction of an instantaneously anesthetic gas into the air circulatory system. In theory, this should have been impossible. Alarms should have sounded; pumps and fans should have stopped; baffle plates should automatically have sealed off the ducts. But Druthen was a scientist,

226

and his people were scientists and technicians. He had a very well-equipped laboratory at his disposal. And, most important of all, Mayhew and Clarisse had obeyed that commandment of the Rhine Institute: Thou shalt not pry into the mind of a shipmate.

"It's no use crying over spilt milk, Ken," Grimes told his psionic communications officer. "At least we know that Clarisse and the others are unhurt. . . ."

"What the hell's the use of having these talents if you don't use 'em?" wondered Flandry, all too audibly.

"Some of us," Grimes told him coldly, "subscribe to ethical codes."

"Don't we all, Commodore? Do unto others as they would do unto you—but do it first!"

"Captain Flandry is right, John," said Sonya.

Yes, thought Grimes, *I suppose the bastard is right. And, come to that, I've tried often enough, and sometimes successfully, to get PCOs to pry for me. . . . Like Spooky Deane, who loved his gin—or my gin. . . . Even so. . . .*

Anyhow, there was now telepathic communication between the two *Faraway Quests*, and communication regarding which neither Druthen nor the captain of *Adler* was aware. Not that it would have worried them much if they had known about it. Clarisse was locked up in the quarters that she had shared with her husband. There was little that she could tell him, and nothing that she could do. She could not communicate with the other prisoners, who were nontelepaths. She could not even pry into the minds of Druthen and his people— and neither could Mayhew and Metzenther and Trialanne. The scientist had, somehow, succeeded in stimulating Mayhew's psionic amplifier—it could, of course, have been just a side effect of the anesthetic gas that had been used during the takeover—and the continual howling of that hapless, disembodied dog's brain blanketed all stray thoughts. Trained telepaths could punch their signals through the psionic interference, but that was all.

In any case, Druthen was willing enough to talk.

He, fat and slovenly as ever, glowered out at Grimes from the screen of the Carlotti transceiver. Grimes stared back at him, trying to keep his own face emotionless. It was all wrong that he should be looking into his own control room this way, from outside, that he should see the nerve center of his own ship in the hands of strangers, of enemies. With Druthen were two of the scientist's own people, and in the background were three uniformed men: large, blond, obviously officers of the Waldegren Navy.

The senior among them, a full commander by his braid, came to stand beside Dr. Druthen. Druthen seemed to resent this, tried to push the officer out of the field of the iconoscope. He muttered, "Nehmen Sie mal Ihre Latschen weg."

The other replied, "Sie sind zwar dick genug für zwei, aber Sie haben nur für einen Platz gezahlt Rücken Sie weiter."

Sonya laughed. Grimes asked her, "What's the joke?"

"Just that they don't seem to love each other. Druthen told the commander to get his big feet out of his way, and the commander told *him* that even though he's big enough to fill two seats he's only paid for one. . . ."

"Paid?" asked Grimes.

"Obviously. He's bought his way into the Duchy of Waldegren."

"Ja," agreed the Waldegren commander. And then, speaking directly to Grimes, "And you the captain of this ship were? But . . ." His eyes widened. "*Vich* of you der kapitan vas?"

"I suppose we're twins, of a sort," grinned Grimes I. "The gentleman standing behind me is Commodore Grimes, commanding *Faraway Quest*. And I am Commodore Grimes, commanding *Faraway Quest*—the *Faraway Quest* aboard which you, sir, are trespassing."

"But I am the captain now," stated Druthen, smugly.

Grimes ignored this. He asked coldly, "Where are my people?" (There was no point in letting Druthen and the officers of the prize crew know that he was already fully informed on that subject.)

"Do you want them back?" countered Druthen, with an infuriating expression of deliberate incredulity.

"Yes. And my ship."

Druthen laughed sneeringly. "You don't want much, Commodore. Or should I say, ex-Commodore? Your masters will not be very pleased with you. The ship—*I* keep. Doubtless the Duchy will pay me a fair price for her. The crew . . . They are useful hostages. You and your allies dare make no hostile move for fear of hurting them." The fat face was suddenly gloating, evil. "And, perhaps, I can use them to persuade you to call off this futile chase. Suppose I have them thrown, one by one, unsuited, out of the airlock . . . ?"

"Herr Doktor!" snapped the commander. "Enough. That I will never countenance. I am an officer, not an executioner."

"Sie glauben wohl Sie sind als Schiffsoffizier was besonderes!"

"Hau'ab!" The commander struck rather than pushed Druthen away from the screen. Those in the control room of *Quest II* watched, fascinated, a brief scuffle in the control room of the other ship. And then the senior officer of the prize crew was addressing them again. "Herr Commodore, my apologies. But I my orders must follow, even when I am told to cooperate with *schwein. Aber*, my word I give. I, Erich von Donderberg, promise you that your crew will be treated well as long as I in this ship am."

"Thank you, Commander," said Grimes stiffly.

Druthen, with one eye puffed and almost shut, bleeding from the corner of his mouth, reappeared.

"Officers!" he spat. "Gold-braided nincompoops, survivals from a past age who should have become extinct millennia ago! I'm cutting you off, Grimes. I want the transceiver so that I can call Captain Blumenfeld in *Adler*. There'll be some changes made in the composition of this so-called prize crew!"

The screen went blank.

"What now?" asked Flandry. "You know these Waldegren people. I don't."

"They're naval officers," said Grimes at last. "They're professional naval officers. They can be ruthless bastards—but they do, at times, subscribe to a rather antique code of honor. . . ."

"I concur," said Grimes II.

"Would you mind," asked Grimes I, "passing the recording of this rather odd interview on to *Wanderer?* Irene and her people may have some comments."

"Certainly, Commodore."

"And you should be able to let us know, Ken, if Druthen is able to persuade Captain Blumenfeld to let him play the game his way?"

"I'll try," said Mayhew doubtfully. "I'll try. With Clarisse alert and with Metzenther and Trialanne to help us. . . . Yes, I should manage."

"And so," commented Flandry, "we just, all of us, go on falling through sweet damn all until somebody condescends to make something happen."

"That's the way of it," agreed Grimes.

~ Chapter 17 ~

THEY, ALL OF THEM, went on falling through sweet damn all.

They swept past The Outsider's Ship, which was still dimly visible, although the derelicts in orbit about it were not. Neither was Flandry's *Vindictive*. The imperial captain complained rather bitterly that he was unable to communicate with his ship. Both Grimeses growled, simultaneously, that it was the fault of his culture for developing neither psionic communications nor the Carlotti system. Both Mrs. Grimeses were inclined to commiserate with Flandry. Relations aboard *Faraway Quest II* were becoming strained. Aboard *Wanderer* there were not the same problems. There was only one of each person, and there were no outsiders.

Out they fell, the four ships, out into the ultimate night.

Druthen and Captain Blumenfeld made an occasional attempt at evasion, which was countered with ease by the pursuers. Once Blumenfeld, using the Carlotti equipment, tried to reason with Grimes—either or both of him—and with Irene, who had been hooked into the conversation.

Blumenfeld was an older and stouter version of von Donderberg, and he was more of the politician and less of the space officer. His accent was not so heavy. He appeared in the screens of *Faraway Quest II* and *Wanderer* by himself, a fatherly-grandfatherly, almost, figure, smoking an elaborate pipe with a porcelain bowl. It was a pity that his cold, very cold, blue eyes spoiled the effect.

"Come now, Commodore," he said, "we are both reasonable men. And you, Kaiserin, are a reasonable lady. What do any of us gain by this pointless chase?"

"You gain nothing," Grimes told him. "Furthermore, you are intruding in Rim Worlds' territorial space. I order you, legally, to hand my ship and my personnel back to me, and also Dr. Druthen and his people so that they may be dealt with by our courts. . . ."

"*You* order, Commodore?" asked the other Grimes softly.

"Yes. I order, Commodore. *Faraway Quest I* is mine, and Druthen and his accomplices will be my prisoners."

"Speak up, Commodores," put in Blumenfeld jovially. "Do I detect a slight dissension in your ranks? And you, Kaiserin, do you acknowledge the right of these gentlemen to give orders? And you, Captain Sir Dominic Flandry? What is your view?"

"We'll settle our own differences after you have been disposed of," growled Irene.

"I second that," said Flandry.

Captain Blumenfeld puffed placidly at his pipe. Grimes wondered what tobacco it was that he was smoking. The man seemed to be enjoying it. At last he said, through a wreathing blue cloud, "My patience is not inexhaustible, Commodore. Or Commodores. I am addressing, however, whichever one of you it is who commanded the *Faraway Quest* aboard which I have placed my prize crew. The good Herr Doktor Druthen has made certain proposals to me regarding the prisoners. I was horrified, and told him so, in no uncertain terms. But . . ." There was a great exhalation of smoke. "But . . . I have thought about what he said to me. I still do not like it." He shrugged heavily.

"Nonetheless, my loyalty is to the Duchy, not to citizens of a Confederacy that the Duchy still has not recognized. It may—note that I say 'may,' Commodore, not 'will'—it may be expedient to use those prisoners as a lever to force a certain degree of compliance from you." Again he shrugged. "I shall not like doing it—assuming, that is, that I am obliged to do it. And I shall not resort to painful or . . . messy methods. Just a simple shooting, to be watched by all of you. And then, after a suitable interval, another. And then, if it is necessary, another."

He smiled coldly. "But there is no real urgency. You will be given time to think it over, to talk it over. Three days' subjective time, shall we say? Call me on this frequency. Over. And out."

The screen went blank, but the other screen, that showing *Wanderer*'s control room, stayed alive.

"Well?" demanded Irene harshly. "Well?"

"Suppose," said Grimes, "just suppose that I do knuckle under, to get my people back, my ship back. Suppose that I, as the ranking officer of the Rim Worlds Confederacy, do allow him prior rights to The Outsider. . . . What about *you* and *you*, Commodore Grimes, and you, Captain Flandry?"

"I shall abide by your decision, John," said the other Grimes.

"Speaking for the Federation," said Sonya, "I shall be with you."

"You beat me to it," said Maggie Lazenby.

"I'll have to think about it," stated Irene.

"As tour charterer," Smith told her, "I have *some* say. A great deal of say. I sympathize with Commodore Grimes. But it's a matter of evaluation. Are the lives of a handful of people of greater importance than the lives of the millions of oppressed men and women and children who look to GLASS for help?"

"Anybody mind if I shove in my two bits' worth?" asked Flandry. "I owe allegiance neither to the Federation nor to the Confederacy and certainly not to GLASS. I swore an oath of fealty to the emperor." He looked at Irene's face in the screen, and added, "My emperor. But my sympathies are with the commodore."

"Thank you, Sir Dominic," said Grimes.

"Wait till you see the bill. Furthermore, sir, I would remind you that you have at your disposal equipment and personnel which I have not. The same applies to you, ma'am. You have your espers. Can't you make full use of them?"

"I would remind you, Sir Dominic," said Mayhew, "that my wife is among the prisoners aboard the *Quest*."

"All the more reason why you should pull your finger out. All of you."

You arrogant bastard, thought Grimes.

"Sir Dominic's talking sense," said Sonya. "*We* have the telepaths.

Adler hasn't. Furthermore, one of *our* telepaths is aboard *your Quest*, John. There must be something that Clarisse can do to help herself. And the others."

"It's all we can do to get through to her," objected Mayhew. "There's too much interference from Lassie. . . ."

Sonya muttered something about a poodle's brain in aspic. Then she said, "Why don't you silence the bitch? Lassie, I mean. There's three of you here: Metzenther and Trialanne aboard *Wanderer*, and yourself. You told us once—remember?—that thoughts can kill."

"I . . . I couldn't, Sonya. . . ."

"Damn it all!" exploded Grimes. "Do you put that animal brain before your wife? What sort of man are you?"

"But . . . but Lassie's so . . . helpless."

"So is Clarisse, unless we do something to help her—and fast. It is *essential* that she be able to keep us informed as to what Druthen is thinking, and von Donderberg . . . and with that psionic interference snuffed out you should be able to keep us informed as to Captain Blumenfeld's intentions. You must do it, Ken."

"Yes," agreed the telepath slowly. "I . . . must. Metzenther and Trialanne will help. They have already told me that."

"Then go to it," ordered Grimes.

Not for the first time he thought, *They're odd people. Too bloody odd. But I suppose when you live inside your pet's brain, and it lives inside yours, you feel more intensely for and about it than any normal man feels for his dog. . . . There'll be guilt involved, too. . . . You'll blame yourself for its absolute helplessness. . . .*

He watched Mayhew stumbling out of the control room, his features stiff, too stiff. He saw the sympathy on the face of Grimes II, and rather more than a hint of a sneer on that of Flandry.

Grimes II looked at his watch. He said, "There's nothing much that we can do, Commodore, until your Commander Mayhew reports results. I suggest that we all adjourn for dinner."

"An army marches on its stomach," quipped Flandry. "I suppose that the same saying applies to a space navy."

"I've never known John to miss a meal," Sonya told him, "no matter what the circumstances."

Women . . . thought Grimes—both of him.

"You said it," agreed Maggie Lazenby.

Chapter 18

THIS WAS THE FIRST PROPER, sit-down meal that anybody had
enjoyed for quite a while. Not that Grimes really enjoyed it. He was
used to eating at the captain's table—but at the head of the board. To
see himself sitting there, a replica of himself, was . . . odd. He derived
a certain wry pleasure from the fact that this other Grimes, like
himself, was not one to let conversation interfere with the serious
business of feeding. He did not think, somehow, that Maggie
appreciated this trait any more than Sonya did.

There were five of them at the commodore's table. Grimes II was
at the head of it, of course, with Maggie Lazenby at his right and Sonya
at his left. Grimes I sat beside Maggie, and Flandry beside Sonya. The
imperial captain was a brilliant conversationalist, and the two women
were lapping it up. He made his own time track sound so much more
glamorous than the time tracks of the two Grimeses—which, in any
case, differed only very slightly from each other. He made the two
commodores seem very dull dogs in comparison with his flamboyant,
charming self. And, in spite of the nonstop flow of outrageous
anecdotes, his plate was clean before any of the others.

The meal, Grimes admitted, was a good one. Grimes II kept an
excellent table, and the service, provided by two neatly uniformed
little stewardesses, matched the quality of the food. There was wine,
of which Grimes II partook sparingly, of which the others partook
not so sparingly. Grimes thought, with disapproval, *That man*

Flandry is gulping it down as though it were lager . . . then realized that he was doing the same.

At last they were finished, sipping their coffee. Grimes—both of him—pulled out his pipe. His wife—both of her—objected, saying, "John! You *know* that the air conditioners can't cope with the *stink*!" Flandry, sleek and smug, lit a cigar that one of the stewardesses brought him. The ladies accepted lights from him for their cigarillos.

Grimes, from the head of the table, looked at Grimes with slightly raised eyebrows. He said, "I'm going up to Control, Commodore, to enjoy my pipe in peace. The officer of the watch mightn't like it, but he daren't say so. Coming?"

"Thank you, Commodore."

He (they) excused himself (themselves), got to his (their) feet. Flandry and the wives were enjoying liqueurs with their coffee and hardly noticed their going. Grimes II led the way out of the dining saloon, which, as a public room in a much larger ship, was luxurious in comparison with that aboard *Faraway Quest I*. Indoor plants, the lush, flowering vines of Caribbea twining around every pillar. Holograms, brightly glowing, picture windows opening onto a score of alien worlds. Grimes paused before one that depicted a beach scene on Arcadia. Maggie was an Arcadian. He looked closely to see if she were among the naked, golden-skinned people on the sand and in the surf. But what if she was? He grunted, followed his counterpart into the axial shaft.

The control room seemed bleak and cold after the warm luxury of the dining saloon. The officer of the watch got to his feet as the two commodores entered, looked doubtfully from one to the other before deciding which one to salute. But he got it right. Outside the viewports was—nothingness. To starboard, Grimes knew, were his own ship and *Adler*, and beyond them was Irene's *Wanderer*—but unless temporal precession rates were synchronized they would remain invisible. One of the Carlotti screens was alive. It showed a bored-looking Tallentire slumped in his chair, his fingers busy with some sort of mathematical puzzle.

"Any word from our tame telepaths yet, Mr. Grigsby?" asked Grimes II.

"No, sir. Commander Mayhew did buzz me to tell me that he and the people aboard *Wanderer* are still trying but aren't getting anywhere."

"Mphm." Grimes slumped into an acceleration chair, motioning to Grimes to follow suit. He (they) filled and lit his (their) pipes. "Mphm."

"There must be a way," said Grimes thoughtfully.

"There always is," agreed Grimes. "The only trouble is finding it."

The two men smoked in companionable silence. Grimes I was almost at ease but knew that he would be properly at ease only aboard his own *Faraway Quest*. He looked around him, noticing all the similarities—and all the differences. From the control room he went down, in his mind, deck by deck. And then . . . and then the idea came to him.

"Commodore," he said, "I think I have it. Do you mind if I borrow your O.O.W.?"

"Help yourself, Commodore. This is Liberty Hall. You can spit on the mat and call the cat a bastard."

Grimes winced. So that was the way it sounded when he said it. He caught the attention of the watch officer. "Mr. Grigsby . . ."

"Sir?"

"Ask Commander Mayhew to come up here, will you?"

"Aye, aye, sir."

The young man spoke into a telephone, then said, "He's on his way."

"Thank you."

When Mayhew came in the two commodores were wrapped in a pungent blue haze. "Sir?" asked the telepath doubtfully, looking from one to the other. "Sir?"

"Damn it all, Ken," growled Grimes. "*You* should know which one of us is which."

"There was a sort of . . . mingling."

"Don't go all metaphysical on me. I take it that you've made no headway."

"No. We just can't get through to Lassie. And it takes effort, considerable effort, to maintain Clarisse in a state approaching full awareness."

"But you are getting through to her."

"Yes."

"Good. Now tell me, Ken, *where* is she? Yes, Yes—I know bloody well that she's aboard my *Faraway Quest*—but where aboard the *Quest?* In your living quarters—or in your watch room?"

"In . . . in the watch room, sir. She hates Lassie, as you know, but she went to the watch room to maintain better communications when we left the ship to go aboard the Shaara derelict. The watch room is fitted up as a living cabin, and Druthen and his crowd left her there after the take-over."

"That makes things easier, a lot easier. Now, get in touch with your cobbers aboard *Wanderer*. . . ."

"I already am." Mayhew's voice was pained.

"Punch this message through, the three of you. *Stop Lassie's life-support system.*"

"You can't mean . . ."

"I do mean. It's the only way to quiet that helpless hound of yours. With that source of telepathic interference wiped out we might be able to learn something. After all, it's only short-range work. You don't need an amplifier."

"But . . ."

"*Do it!*"

"All right, Sir." Mayhew's face was white and strained. "But you don't understand. If I could do it myself, kill Lassie, I mean, it wouldn't be as bad. Because . . . because Clarisse has always hated Lassie. She'll . . . she'll enjoy it. . . ."

"Good for her," said Grimes brutally. "And have Mr. Metzenther inform Captain Trafford of what's going on."

He visualized Clarisse's slim fingers switching off the tiny pumps that supplied oxygen and nutrient fluid to the tank in which floated that obscenely naked brain—but only a dog's brain—and, suddenly, felt more than a little sick.

He said, "I think I'll go below, Commodore."

"As you please, Commodore," replied Grimes II. "I shall stay up here. There should be information coming through at any time now. If things start happening, this is my place."

"Too right," agreed Grimes. "And there's an old saying about two women in the same kitchen. Two shipmasters in the same control room would be at least as bad."

Chapter 19

HE MADE HIS WAY down from the control room to the deck upon which the master's quarters and the V.I.P. suite—in which he and Sonya had been housed—were situated. The general layout was very similar to that of his own ship. There was no extra accommodation in this compartment; everything was on a larger scale.

Absentmindedly he paused outside the door that had above it, in gold lettering, CAPTAIN. It was ajar. He had started to enter when he realized his error, but too late for him to pull back. He could see through into the bedroom. His wife was there, sitting up in bed, reading. The spectacles that she was wearing enhanced her nakedness.

His wife?

But she might have been. On another time track she was. "Come in," she not quite snapped. "Don't dither around outside." He went in.

She put down her book and looked at him gravely, but there was a quirk at the corners of her mouth. She was very beautiful, and she was . . . different. Her breasts were not so full as Sonya's but were pointed. Her smooth shoulders were just a little broader.

She said, "Long time no see, John."

He felt a wild, impossible hope, decided to bluff his way out—or in. He asked gruffly, "What the hell do you mean?"

She replied, "Come off it, John. She's put her mark on you, just as

I've put my mark on him. Once you were identical, or there was only one of you. That must have been years ago, round about the time that we had the fun and games on Sparta. Remember?"

Grimes remembered. It had been very shortly after the Spartan affair that he and Maggie had split brass rags.

"Furthermore," she went on, "my ever-loving had the decency to buzz down to tell me that he'd be in Control all night, and not to wait up for him . . ."

"But Sonya . . ."

"Damn Sonya. Not that I've anything against her, mind you. We've known each other for years and have always been good friends. But if you must know, John, she and I have just enjoyed a girlish natter on the telephone, and she's under the impression that you're sharing *my* John's sleepless vigil."

Get the hell out of here, you lecherous rat! urged the rather priggish censor who inhabited an odd corner of Grimes' brain.

"Don't just stand there," she said.

He sat down at the foot of the wide bed.

"John! Look at me."

He looked. He went on looking. There was so much that he remembered vividly, so much that he had almost forgotten.

"Have I got Denebian leprosy, or something?"

He admitted that she had not. Her skin was sleek, golden gleaming, with the coppery pubic puff in delicious contrast, the pink nipples of her breasts prominent. He thought, *To hell with it. Why not?* He moved slowly toward her. Her wide, red mouth was inviting. He kissed her—for the first time in how many years? He kissed her and went on kissing her, until she managed to get her hands between their upper bodies and push him away.

"Enough . . ." she gasped. "Enough . . . for the time being. Better shut the outer door . . . and snap on the lock. . . ."

He broke away from her reluctantly. He said, "But suppose *he* . . ." he could not bring himself to say the name ". . . comes down from Control. . . ."

"He won't. I know him. I should, by this time. The only thing in his mind will be the safety of his precious ship." She smiled. "And, after all, I am an ethologist, specializing in animal behavior, the human animal included . . . ."

Grimes asked rather stiffly, "I suppose you knew that I would be coming in?"

"I didn't know, duckie, but I'd have been willing to bet on it. The outer door was left ajar on purpose."

"Mphm." Grimes got up, went into the day cabin, shut and locked the door. He returned to the bedroom.

She said, "You look hot. Better take off your shirt."

He took off his shirt. It was a borrowed one, of course. And so was the pair of trousers. So were the shoes. (He had boarded this ship, of course, with only the usual long johns under his space suit.)

Borrowed clothing, a borrowed wife. . . . But was it adultery?

Grimes grinned. What were the legalities of the situation? Or, come to that, the ethics?

"What the hell are you laughing at?" she demanded.

"Nothing," he told her. "Everything."

She said, "I'll do my best to make this a happy occasion."

It was. There was no guilt, although perhaps there should have been. There was no guilt—after all, Grimes rationalized, he had known Maggie for years; he (or one of him) had been married to her for years. It was a wild, sweet mixture of the soothing familiar and the stimulating unfamiliar. It was—right.

They were together on the now rumpled bed, their bodies just touching, each of them savoring a fragrant cigarillo.

Grimes said lazily, "After all that, I'd better have a shower before I leave. I don't suppose I—he—will mind if I use his bathroom. . . ."

She said, "There's no hurry. . . ."

And then the telephone buzzed.

She picked up the handset. "Mrs. Grimes . . ." she said drowsily, with simulated drowsiness. "Yes, John. It's me, of course. Maggie. . . . Yes, I *did* lock the door. . . ." She covered the mouthpiece with her hand, whispered, "Get dressed, and *out*. Quickly. I'll try to stall him off." Speaking into the telephone again, "Yes, yes. I know that I'm the Commodore's wife and that nobody would dream of making a pass at me. But have you forgotten that *wolf*, Sir Dominic Flandry, who's aboard at *your* invitation, duckie, is *prowling* around your ship seeking whom he may devour? And you left me all by myself, to sit and *brood*, or whatever it is you do up there in your bloody control room. . . . No, Sir Dominic didn't make a pass at me, but I could tell by the way he was looking at me. . . . All right, then. . . ."

Grimes was dressed, after a fashion. As he walked fast toward the door, he saw that Maggie was punching the buttons for another number on the ship's exchange. She called over her shoulder, "Wait a moment!"

"Sorry. See you later."

He went out into the alleyway. He hesitated outside the door to his own quarters. Dare he face Sonya? It would be obvious, too obvious, what he had been doing, and with whom.

The door opened suddenly—and Grimes was staring at Flandry, and Flandry was staring at him, staring and smiling knowingly.

"You bastard!" snarled Grimes, swinging wildly. The punch never connected, but Flandry's hand around Grimes' right wrist used the momentum of the blow to bring Grimes sprawling to the deck.

"Gentlemen," said Grimes II coldly. "Gentlemen—if you will pardon my misuse of the word—I permit no brawling aboard my ship."

Grimes I got groggily to his feet assisted by Flandry. They looked silently at the commodore. He looked at them. He said, "Such conduct I expected from you, Captain Flandry. But as for you, Commodore Grimes, I am both surprised and pained to learn that your time track is apparently more permissive than mine."

At last Grimes felt the beginnings of guilt. In a way it was himself whom he had cuckolded, but that was no excuse. And what hurt was that during this night's lovemaking it had been his own counterpart, himself although not himself, who had been the odd man out. He knew how this other Grimes must be feeling.

He thought, *I wish I were anywhere but here.*

He said, "Believe me, Commodore, I wish I were anywhere but here." Then he grinned incredulously, looking like a clown with that smile on a face besmeared with lip rouge. "And why the hell shouldn't I be?"

"If I had any say in the matter you would be, Commodore. You *and* Captain Sir Dominic Flandry." He made it sound as though the honorific were a word of four letters, not three.

"You just might have your wish, Commodore. Tell me, have you received any reports from Commander Mayhew and the other PCOs?"

"This is no time to . . ."

"But it is. The success of our mission, the safety of our ships; these matters, surely, are of overriding importance. . . ."

"He's right, you know," said Sonya, who had appeared in the doorway, looking as though butter would not melt in her mouth.

"Shut up!" snapped Grimes. "You keep out of it."

"He's right, you know," said Maggie, cool and unruffled, who had just joined the party.

"Shut up!" snapped Grimes II. "You keep out of it."

"He's right, you know," drawled Flandry.

Grimes II snarled wordlessly. Then, "As a matter of fact, your Mayhew and his mates did get Clarisse to . . . to turn off the amplifier. They're trying to sort out the psionic impressions that they're getting from *Adler* and your *Faraway Quest*, now that the interference has been . . . switched off. I was thinking of calling you to let you know, but there was no urgency, and I thought you needed your sleep. Ha, ha."

"So now we work out a plan of campaign . . ." murmured Grimes I.

"Yes. In the control room. It'll be some time before I feel like setting foot in my own quarters again. And might I suggest that you two officers and gentlemen get yourselves looking like officers, at least, before you come up."

Grimes looked doubtfully at Sonya. Then he turned to Flandry. "Do you mind if I make use of your toilet facilities, Sir Dominic?"

"Be my guest, Commodore." Then, in almost a whisper, "After all, I was yours—and you were his."

Grimes didn't want to laugh, but he did. If looks could have killed he would have died there and then. But women have no sense of humor.

Chapter 20

WANDERER **AND** *FARAWAY QUEST II* synchronized temporal precession rates, and *Wanderer* closed with the *Quest*, laying herself almost alongside her. It was a maneuver typical of Irene's spacemanship—or spacewomanship—and when it was over Grimes I looked closely at Grimes II's head to see if his counterpart had acquired any additional gray hairs. He thought wryly, *Probably Maggie and I have put a few there ourselves . . .* It was essential, however, that the meeting of the leaders be held aboard one of the ships; *Adler* would do her best to monitor a conversation conducted over the Carlotti transceivers.

So there they all were in *Faraway Quest's* control room: the two Grimeses, their wives, Sir Dominic, Irene, Trafford, Smith (inevitably), Mayhew and Metzenther. Somehow Grimes I found himself in the chair.

Slowly and carefully, he filled and lit his pipe. (The other Grimes produced and lit a cigarette. *Subtle,* thought Grimes. *Subtle. I didn't think you had it in you, John . . .*) After he had it going well he said, "All right. I think we can take it as read that our PCOs have silenced the dog, and that they—including, of course, Clarisse—are now doing some snooping into the minds of our mutual enemies. Correct?"

"Correct, sir," answered Mayhew.

"Good. Then report, please, Commander."

The telepath spoke in a toneless voice. "Clarisse is well, although her mind is not yet operating at full capacity. As far as she can determine, as far as we can determine, all the other members of *Faraway Quest's* crew are unharmed. As yet.

"Insofar as their captors are concerned, we have found it advisable to concentrate on key personnel: Dr. Druthen, Captain Blumenfeld and Commander von Donderberg, who is still the senior prize officer aboard *Quest*. Dr. Druthen is not quite sane. He is ambitious. He thinks that the Duchy of Waldegren will appreciate his brilliance, whereas the Confederacy does not. His mother, who exercised considerable influence over him during his formative years, was an expatriate Waldegrener. Druthen, too, has strong sadistic tendencies. Had it not been for the restraining influence of von Donderberg the lot of the prisoners would have been a sorry one. He is still urging Blumenfeld to use them to blackmail us into giving him a free hand with *The Outsider*.

"Now, von Donderberg. The impression you gained from that talk with him over the Carlotti radio is a correct one. Like many— although not all—naval officers, he regards himself as a spaceman first and foremost. The prisoners happen to be wearing the wrong uniform, but they, as far as he is concerned, are also spacemen. He hates Druthen, and Druthen hates and despises him.

"Finally, Captain Blumenfeld. Once again, sir, you summed him up rather neatly. He is essentially a politician, with a politician's lack of conscience. He would stand on his mother's grave to get two inches nearer to where he wants to be. As a spaceman he is, at best, merely competent—but the success of this mission would put him at least two steps up the promotion ladder. He would play along with Druthen if he thought that he could get away with it, but realizes that maltreatment, or even murder of *Faraway Quest's* rightful crew could lead to an outbreak of hostilities between the Duchy and the Confederacy. He knows that his government would welcome this rather than otherwise, but fears, as they fear, that the Confederacy's Big Brother might step in. Should he get the 'all clear' from Waldegren—we gained the impression that the Duchy's political experts are hard at work evaluating the possibility of Federation intervention—he will tell Druthen to go ahead."

"Meanwhile, he is hoping that there will be dissension in our ranks. That was why he gave us time to think things over; not long, but long enough." He looked at Smith. "As you know, at least one of us present puts his own interests before the well-being of *Faraway Quest*'s crew."

"Mphm." Grimes puffed thoughtfully at his pipe. Then, "Do you concur, Mr. Metzenther?"

"Yes, Commodore. Commander Mayhew has summarized the findings of all four of us."

"And now you know," said Grimes II, who did not seem to be enjoying his cigarette, "what are you going to do about it? Not that you can do much. You haven't a ship of your own, even though . . ."

"Even though I'm carrying on as though this were my own ship?" asked Grimes. "In a way, she is. Just as . . ."

"She's not. And neither is Maggie."

"Shut up!" snapped the wife referred to. "Shut up! This is no time to let your personal feelings get in the way of important business."

"You should have thought of that last night," her husband told her.

Flandry laughed.

"Just what has been going on aboard this rustbucket?" asked Irene curiously, looking at Sir Dominic speculatively.

"It's a pity that you weren't here," he told her, while Sonya looked at him nastily.

"Just a slight domestic problem," said Grimes airily.

"Some people's idea of what's *slight* . . ." snarled Grimes II.

"Don't forget that I, too, am an injured party." Flandry laughed again.

"Please . . ." pleaded Grimes. "Please. We're getting no place at all with this petty squabbling." He turned to Mayhew. "You've given us the general background. It's obvious that we have to do something before Blumenfeld gives Druthen the okay, or before Druthen acts off his own bat. I've already thought of something that we—that Clarisse especially—can do. I take it that there are writing materials in your watch room aboard *my Quest*?"

"Of course."

"And writing materials are also drawing materials. . . ."

"Yes. But to call up some peculiar deities or demons at this juncture could make the situation worse than it is now."

"Who mentioned deities or demons?" Grimes saw that Flandry, Irene and Trafford were looking at him curiously, as were his alter ego and Maggie Lazenby. He said slowly, "I suppose I'd better put you in the picture. Clarisse is more than a mere telepath. She is descended from a caveman artist who, displaced in time, was found on Kinsolving's Planet many years ago. He, it seems, had specialized in painting pictures of various animals which, consequently, were drawn into the hunters' traps. Clarisse inherited his talent. . . ."

"Impossible," said Grimes II flatly.

"Not so, Commodore. I've seen it happen. Ken Mayhew has seen it happen. So has Sonya."

"It's true," she agreed soberly.

"So Clarisse could be a sort of Trojan horse . . ." murmured Flandry.

"You're getting the idea. Of course, there's one snag. Each time that she's . . . performed she's been under the influence of some hallucinogenic drug."

"And the rest of you," sneered Smith.

"No. Most definitely not. The main problem now is to get her suitably high."

"That's no problem," said Mayhew. A great load seemed suddenly to have dropped from his thin shoulders. He had something to do at last—something to help to save Clarisse. "That's no problem. Two telepaths who are married have more, much more in common than any pair of nontelepaths. There is far greater sensitivity, far more . . . sharing than in any common marriage. If I get high on anything at all, so will Clarisse. If I go on a trip, so will she."

"Good," murmured Grimes. "Good. So buzz the quack and tell him what you need to put your mind in the proper state. Try to get instructions through to Clarisse. All she has to do is sketch us, one by one, and we'll be with her. . . ." He looked rapidly around the control room. "Not you, Ken. I'm sorry, but you'll be too muzzy with dope.

What about you, Mr. Metzenther? Good. And you, Flandry? And myself, and Sonya. . . ."

"Count me in," Irene said gruffly. "I still don't believe it, but if it works I'd like to be in the party."

"And me," said Trafford, although not overenthusiastically. "Tallentire can look after the ship."

Smith did not volunteer.

Maggie Lazenby was about to, Grimes thought, but lapsed into silence as her husband looked at her long and coldly.

And Grimes II said, "I'll not be sorry to see some of you off my vessel and back aboard your own ships."

~ Chapter 21 ~

THIS SHOULDN'T BE HAPPENING, thought Grimes. *Magic—and what else can it be called? in the control room of an interstellar ship.* . . . But this was the Rim, where the Laws of Nature, although not repealed, were not enforced with any stringency. This was beyond the Rim.

He looked at Mayhew as the telepath regarded dubiously the little glass of some colorless fluid that he was holding. "This," the too-jovial ship's doctor had assured him, "will give you hallucinations in glorious technicolor and at least seven dimensions. . . ." Grimes looked at Mayhew, and everybody else looked at Mayhew. The PCO quipped, "Now I know how Socrates must have felt."

"Get on with it, Ken," urged Grimes.

"I'm drinking this muck, not you. All right, then. Down the hatch." He suited the action to the words.

His prominent Adam's apple wobbled as the draught went down. He licked his lips, enunciated slowly, "Not . . . bad. Not . . . too . . . bad." An odd sort of vagueness crept over his face. His eyes went out of focus. He wavered on his feet, groped almost aimlessly for a chair, slumped down into it.

Grimes whispered to Metzenther, "Clarisse—is she ready? Are you and Trialanne standing by to help?"

"Of course, Commodore."

Mayhew said with surprising clarity, "The black lambs of Damballa. But they shouldn't. No."

251

Never mind the bloody black lambs, thought Grimes testily.

"Clarisse . . ." Mayhew's voice was very soft, almost inaudible. "Clarisse. You shouldn't have killed Lassie."

"Damn Lassie," muttered Grimes.

"A man's best friend is his . . . is his . . . is his . . .? But the black lambs. And no sheep dog. Yes."

Metzenther looked toward Grimes. He whispered reassuringly, "It'll not be long now, Commodore. She's started on her pictures. And they won't be of black lambs. Black sheep, more likely."

"You can say that again," grunted Grimes II. Grimes I allowed himself a smile. Let Metzenther enjoy his play on words, and let the other Grimes make what he liked of it. It didn't matter. He would soon be back aboard his own ship. He looked down at the Minetti automatic pistol that he was holding, ready, in his right hand. (Luckily, his counterpart shared his taste in personal weaponry—as in other things.) He, he was sure, would be the first to be pulled aboard the *Quest.* After all, he knew Clarisse, had known her before Mayhew had. He took one last look around at the other members of the boarding party. All were armed. Sonya, Trafford and Metzenther wore holstered laser handguns; and Irene, two ugly looking pistols of .50 caliber. Flandry had something that looked as though it had been dreamed up by an illustrator of juvenile science fiction thrillers.

Grimes remembered the two occasions on which he had seen Clarisse at work. He recalled, vividly, that bare, windswept mountaintop on Kinsolving, with the black sky overhead, the Galactic Lens a misty shimmer low on the horizon. He visualized, without any effort on his part, the floodlit easel with its square of canvas, the pots of pigment, the girl, naked save for a scanty scrap of some animal pelt, working with swift, sure strokes on her brushes.

Sudden doubt assailed him.

Those had been ideal conditions. Would conditions aboard the hijacked *Faraway Quest* be as ideal?

Mayhew seemed to be completely out, sprawled loosely in his chair, his eyes closed, his mouth slack. A thin dribble of spittle crawled down his chin. Had the telepath taken too much of whatever concoction it was that the doctor had prepared? Was Clarisse similarly unconscious?

Metzenther smiled reassuringly at the commodore, whispered, "Any time now. . . ."

Flandry, overhearing, snorted his disbelief.

Grimes turned to admonish him, and . . .

Flandry was gone.

～ Chapter 22 ～

FLANDRY WAS GONE.

Grimes wondered why there had been no miniature clap of thunder as the air rushed in to fill the vacuum caused by his abrupt departure. Had the exactly correct volume of atmosphere been teleported from the room in which Clarisse was imprisoned to fill the space that the imperial captain had occupied? What did it matter, anyhow? Magic is an art, not a science.

Flandry was gone—and who next?

Grimes was more than a little hurt. He had known Clarisse for years. Sonya had known her for almost as long. And yet she called a stranger to her. She had met Sir Dominic only once; he must have made an impression on her.

He turned to the others. "Well, it seems to be working. But why *him*?"

"Why not?" asked Sonya sweetly. "He's resourceful. He's tough."

"And he's out of *my* hair," added Grimes II. He did not say aloud that he hoped that other people would soon be out of his hair. He did not need to.

Mayhew, still unconscious in his chair, twitched. He looked as though he were having a bad dream.

"Is she all right?" demanded Grimes of Metzenther.

"Yes, Commodore," answered the telepath. "Yes." He looked as though he had been about to say more but had decided against it.

"Can't you tell her to get the rest of us shifted across?"

"I . . . I will try. But you must realize that teleportation is a strain upon the operator."

"Damn it all, this is urgent."

"I know, Commodore. But . . . she will not be hurried."

"Druthen, von Donderberg . . . Do *they* know that Flandry is aboard the ship?"

"No. And with von Donderberg actually in charge everything—including the prisoners' meals—is very much to timetable. There is little chance that Clarisse and Sir Dominic will be disturbed."

Disturbed? thought Grimes. An odd choice of words. . . .

"You must be patient, Commodore," said Metzenther.

Grimes was never to know if it was his own imagination, or if the telepath had deliberately planted the picture in his mind. But he *knew* what was happening, what had happened. He saw Clarisse, her clothing cast aside the better to emulate her savage forebears, working at the sketch she was making on a signals pad. She saw the picture growing out of her swift, sure stylus strokes, the depiction of Sir Dominic. What subconscious desires had been brought to the surface by the drug that Mayhew had taken, the effects of which he had shared with her?

And then . . .

And then Flandry was with her.

Flandry, the unprincipled, suddenly confronted with a beautiful, naked, available and willing woman.

If Metzenther had not put thoughts, impressions into Grimes' brain he had read the commodore's mind. He said, telepathically, "Mayhew will never know. We shall make sure of that."

"But . . . but how can she?" asked Grimes silently.

He got the impression of quiet laughter in reply. "How could you? How could Sonya? How could Maggie? Some of us—even you, Commodore—have regarded this straying into other continua as a sort of a holiday. A pubic holiday . . . Forgive me. That just slipped out. And Clarisse has been under strain as much as any of us, more than most of us. What's more natural than that she should greet her deliverer in the age-old manner? Are you jealous, Commodore?"

Frankly, yes, thought Grimes. He grinned ruefully.

"What the hell do you find so amusing?" asked Sonya sharply.

"Oh, er . . . I was just wondering where Sir Dominic had finished up. As we both of us know, this talent of Clarisse's is rather . . . unreliable."

"You have an odd sense of humor," she told him. She was beginning to look anxious.

There were no pictures in Grimes' mind now. He was rather thankful for that. But still he did not know how long it would be before Clarisse resumed her magical activities. He knocked his pipe out into one of the large ashtrays that were placed all around the control room. He refilled it. He lit it.

"Please, John," said Clarisse, "not in here. It's dreadfully stuffy."

She was, as he had visualized her, naked. She was standing at the desk, adding the last touches to the sketch she had made of Grimes. Flandry was seated on the bunk. He was fully clothed.

But . . .

"Wipe the lipstick off your face, Sir Dominic," said Grimes coldly.

~ Chapter 23 ~

CLARISSE IGNORED THE EXCHANGE. She tore the sheet upon which she had portrayed Grimes off the pad, put it to one side. She started a fresh sketch. The commodore peered over her smooth, bare shoulder as she worked. The likeness was unmistakable.

"Now!" she whispered intently.

Grimes was almost knocked off his feet as Irene materialized. She exclaimed cheerfully, "Oops, dearie! Fancy meeting *you* here!" And then, to Clarisse, "Hadn't you better put something on, ducks? All these *men* . . ."

"I work better this way," she was told.

"Ssshh!" hissed Grimes. "This cabin . . . bugged . . ."

"It was," remarked Flandry, in normal conversational tones. "And very amateurishly, if I may say so."

"So you did, at least, take precautions before . . ." Grimes began.

"Before *what*?" asked Flandry, smiling reminiscently. "I always take precautions, Commodore."

Clarisse blushed spectacularly, over her entire body. But she went on sketching.

Sonya appeared, looking around her disapprovingly. *What's been going on here?* she asked silently. Then it was Trafford's turn, and finally Metzenther's. The little cabin was uncomfortably crowded. Grimes didn't like the way that his wife was sitting close beside Flandry on the bunk. She, obviously, didn't like the way that he was

257

being pressed between Irene's flamboyance and Clarisse's nudity. Somebody knocked over the tank in which the psionic amplifier was housed. It did not break, but the cover came off it, allowing the stagnant nutrient solution to spill on the deck. It smelled as though something had been dead for a very long time.

Sonya sniffed. "And now what do we do?" she demanded. "I'd suggest that Clarisse get dressed, but I realize that it's almost impossible in these circumstances."

"This is *your* ship, Commodore," said Flandry.

"Mphm. When is your next meal due, Clarisse?"

"I . . . my watch . . . with my clothes. On the bunk . . ."

Flandry rummaged in the little pile of garments and found the timepiece. He announced, "It is 1135 hours, this ship's time."

"Twenty-five minutes," said Clarisse.

"So we wait," said Grimes. "It'll not be for too long. Then we overpower whoever brings the tray and any other guards and take over."

Flandry laughed jeeringly. "Brilliant, Commodore. Really brilliant. And if anybody fires into this dogbox he'll get at least four of us with one shot."

"Have you any better ideas, Captain?"

"Of course," Flandry replied smugly. "If I am not mistaken, those weapons being toted around by Sonya, Captain Trafford and Mr. Metzenther are laser pistols. They are not used much in my continuum, but you people seem to like them. A laser pistol can be used as a tool as well as a handgun. A cutting tool . . ."

"So we break out, rather than wait to be let out."

"A truly blinding glimpse of the obvious, sir."

Trafford was nearest the door. "Go ahead, please, Captain," said Grimes.

The little man unholstered his weapon. He pulled out a slender screwdriver that had been recessed in the butt of it. Carefully, not hurrying, he made adjustments to the power settings. He replaced the screwdriver.

Grimes took a pencil from Clarisse. He managed to shove his way through the crowd to stand beside Trafford. He drew a rough circle on the smooth, painted metal panel of the door. He said, "The lock should be there, Captain. If you burn around it . . ."

"I'll try, Commodore."

The narrow beam of intensely bright light shot from the muzzle of the pistol. Metal became blue white incandescent immediately but was reluctant to melt. The structural components of a starship are designed to withstand almost anything. Trafford removed his finger from the trigger, used the screwdriver to make further adjustments. Then he tried again.

Grimes had foreseen what was going to happen. After all, as Flandry had pointed out, this was *his* ship. Grimes should have warned the others, but this chance to see the silly grin wiped off Sir Dominic's face was not one to be passed over.

The air in the watch room became stiflingly hot, and acrid with the fumes of burning paint and metal. And then . . .

And then there were bells ringing, some close and some distant, filling the echoing shell of *Faraway Quest* with their clangor. A klaxon added its stridency to the uproar. From the nozzles of the spray system jetted a white foam that blanketed everything and everybody. Flandry cursed, but he could never hope to match Irene's picturesque obscenities and blasphemies.

The door sagged open.

Grimes, pistol in hand, shoved past Trafford, out into the brightly lit alleyway. Sonya, looking like a figure roughly hacked from white foam plastic, was behind him, then Trafford, then Irene. Metzenther staggered out supporting Clarisse, who looked as though she had just emerged from a bubble bath.

"You bloody fool," gasped Flandry, who was last to emerge. "You bloody fool! You should have known. . . ."

"I did know," snapped Grimes. "Pipe down, damn you!"

The fire-extinguishing foam was pouring out into the alleyway. Grimes motioned to the others to follow suit, dropped to his knees, let the cool, not unpleasantly acrid froth almost cover him. How long would it be before the fire-fighting party was on the scene? When *Quest*'s own crew had been running the ship scant seconds would have elapsed; but Druthen and his scientists and technicians were not spacemen, and at least one of the three officers put aboard from *Adler* would be remaining in the control room.

Somebody, somewhere, switched the alarms off. So they realized that there was a fire. And without that incessant noise it was possible to think, to give orders.

"Keep covered," said Grimes. "They'll not see us until it's too late." He added, in a disgruntled voice, "The bastards are certainly taking their time. Billy Williams and his crowd would have had the fire out half an hour ago!"

"Glumph," replied Sonya through a mouthful of foam.

They were here at last, rounding the curve in the alleyway: a tall figure in a space suit, the spiked helmet of which made it obvious that he was a member of the Waldegren Navy, four men in civilian space armor, pushing a wheeled tank.

"Lasers only," whispered Grimes. "Fire!"

Lasers are silent—but they are dreadfully lethal. Grimes hated to have to do it—but the fire fighters must be given no chance to warn Druthen and von Donderberg in Control. Druthen's men were hijackers, and their lives were already forfeit. The universal penalty for this crime is death. The Waldegrener was acting under orders, but he had no business aboard Grimes' ship. What happened to him was just his bad luck.

Grimes stood up slowly in the waist-high foam. He looked at the five silent figures. They were dead all right, each of them with his armor neatly pierced in half a dozen places. There was no blood, luckily, and luckily nobody had employed the effective slashing technique, so the suits were still reasonably intact.

Five of them, he thought, trying hard to fight down his nausea. *Seven of us. Flandry can wear the Waldegren space suit—it'll fit him. Then myself. And Sonya. Irene? Metzenther? Trafford? Clarisse?*

He said, "Get the armor off them. It's a made-to-order disguise."

Trafford, Flandry and Sonya went to work. The smell of charred meat and burned blood was distressingly evident. Suddenly, Sonya beckoned to Grimes. He went to look down at the stripped figure. It was a woman. She was—had been—one of the junior technicians. Grimes remembered her. He had referred to her, in his thoughts, as a hard-faced little bitch. Feeling sorry for this would not help her now.

He walked slowly back to where Clarisse was standing, patches of foam slipping slowly down her smooth skin, others still clinging to the salient points of her body. He whispered, pointing, "You know her?"

"Yes."

"Wear her suit. Speak into the suit radio, using her voice. . . . You can do that?"

"Of course."

"Report that the fire is under control. Should Druthen or von Donderberg feel uneasy about anything you, as a telepath, will know the right things to say to put their minds at rest. Say that we are returning topside to report as soon as the fire is out. Get it?"

"Yes."

"Then get suited up."

She obeyed him, assisted by Sonya and Irene. She spurned their suggestion that she should wear the dead woman's long johns. Grimes didn't blame her, although he winced at the thought of the unlined inside of the suit chafing her unprotected skin.

Then Grimes, too, stripped to his skimpy underwear, could not bring himself to put on a dead man's next-to-the-skin union suit. Neither could Sonya. But the corpse robbing worried neither Irene nor Flandry.

The bodies were concealed in the congealing foam, which hid, too, the tools taken from the belt pouches of the fire party. Those same pouches served as holsters for the weapons of Grimes and his people. It was decided that Trafford and Metzenther, who had been unable to disguise themselves, would stay in the watch room. They would be safe enough there, especially since Metzenther should be able to give ample advance warning of the approach of any hostile persons.

Then, speaking in a voice that was not her own, Clarisse said into her helmet microphone, "Sadie Hawkes reporting to Dr. Druthen. The fire's out. Nothing serious. That stupid bitch was burning papers for some reason or other."

"Is she hurt?" Druthen's voice did not betray much, if any, concern.

"Naw, Doc. We just slapped her round a little, is all."

Von Donderberg's voice came through the speakers. "Lieutenant Muller."

"Sorry, Commander," Clarisse told him. "The lieutenant slipped on the foam an' caught his helmet a crack. His transceiver's on the blink."

"Where is the prisoner now?" inquired Druthen.

"We left her in her bubble bath to cool down. Ha, ha."

"Ha, ha," echoed Dr. Druthen.

Ha, ha, thought Grimes nastily.

✺ Chapter 24 ✺

GRIMES LED THE WAY into the control room. (After all, this was his ship.) He was followed by Flandry, whose right hand hovered just over the butt of his energy pistol, then by Sonya, then by Irene. Clarisse caught up the rear.

Druthen and von Donderberg swiveled in their chairs to face the returning fire-fighting party. The scientist was fatly arrogant. The Waldegrener looked more than a little frayed around the edges. *It's your own fault,* thought Grimes. *If you aren't fussy about the company you keep. . . .*

Grimes and the others stood there. Druthen and von Donderberg sat there. Grimes knew that he should act and act fast, but he was savoring this moment. Druthen, an expression of petulant impatience growing on his face, snarled, "Take your bloody helmets off! Anybody'd think there was a smell in here." His words, although distorted by the suit diaphragms, were distinct enough.

"There is," replied Grimes. "You."

The scientist's face turned a rich purple. He sputtered, "Mutinous swine! Von Donderberg, you heard! *Do* something!"

Von Donderberg shrugged. There was a flicker of amusement in his blue eyes.

Grimes said, "Mutiny, Dr. Druthen? I am arresting *you* for mutiny and piracy." He fumbled for his Minetti, but the little pistol, unlike the heavier weapons carried by the others, was not suitable for use by a man wearing space armor with its clumsy gloves.

263

But Flandry's odd-looking weapon was out, as were Sonya's and Irene's pistols. Druthen stared at them helplessly, von Donderberg in a coldly calculating manner. "You will note, Herr Doktor," remarked the Waldegren officer, "that there are neat holes in those space suits, holes that could have been made by laser fire at short range." He seemed to be speaking rather louder than was really necessary. "It would seem that our prisoners somehow have escaped and have murdered my Lieutenant Muller and four of your people." He turned to face Grimes. "You will surrender."

"I admire your nerve," Grimes told him.

"That is not one of the prisoners!" exclaimed Druthen. "It's that bastard Grimes! But that's impossible!"

"It's not, Doctor. It's not." The commodore was really enjoying himself. "You sneered at me—remember—for carrying a practicing witch on my Articles of Agreement. . . ."

The practicing witch screamed, "John! The Carlotti set! It's on! *Adler*'s seeing and hearing everything!"

And *Adler*'s temporal precession rate was synchronized with that of *Faraway Quest*. No doubt her cannon and projectors were already trained upon their target. No doubt boarding parties were already suited up and hurrying into the warship's airlocks.

Grimes swore. His gloating could easily have ruined everything. He dived for the Mannschenn Drive remote controls. He heard pistol fire as somebody, Irene probably, switched off the Carlotti transceiver in an effective but destructive manner. Von Donderberg got in his way, grappled him. The Waldegrener was a strong man and agile, whereas Grimes was hampered by his armor. His body was a barrier between the commodore and the Mannschenn Drive control console. Brutally, Grimes flailed at him with his mailed fists, but von Donderberg managed to get a firm grip on both his wrists. Grimes tried to bring his knee up, but he was too slow and the foul blow was easily avoided.

It was Irene who settled matters. (After all, this was not *her* ship.) Her heavy pistols barked deafeningly, the slugs just missing Grimes (intentionally, he hoped) and von Donderberg. The face of the control panel splintered; otherwise the immediate results were unspectacular.

But down in the Mannschenn Drive room the duty technician watched aghast as the great, gleaming rotors ran wild, precessing faster and faster yet, tumbling down and into the dark dimensions uncontrolled and uncontrollably. Beyond the control room viewports, the image of *Adler* glowed with impossible clarity against the blackness, then flickered out like a snuffed candle flame. Throughout the ship, men and women stared at familiar surroundings and fittings that sagged and fluoresced, that wavered on the very brink of the absolute nothingness. Belatedly, alarm bells started to ring, but their sound was a thin, high shrilling, felt rather than heard.

Abruptly, shockingly, normalcy returned as the Drive shut itself off. Colors, forms and sounds were suddenly . . . drab. The irregular throbbing of the inertial drive was harsh and irritating.

Grimes, still straining against von Donderberg, snapped, "Shut that bloody thing off!" Apart from the Waldegren commander and his surviving officer—wherever *he* was—there were no spacemen among those who had hijacked the ship. Free fall would not worry Grimes and his boarding party overmuch, but it would be, at the very least, an inconvenience to the planet lubbers.

The annoying vibration ceased. *What next?* Grimes asked himself. It was hard to think clearly. That blasted von Donderberg was still putting up a fight, and Sonya and Clarisse, who had come to the commodore's aid, were more of a hindrance than a help. "Irene!" he called. "Check the indicator! Are all AT doors shut?" (The airtight doors should have automatically at the first signs of main drive malfunction.)

"Yes," she replied at last. "There's a switch by itself in a glass-fronted box. . . . It's labeled LOCK. . . ."

"Got it. . . ."

"Then throw it!"

Grimes heard the little crash of shattering glass, heard Irene say, "Locked."

Sonya had a space-suited arm across von Donderberg's throat. The man was starting to choke; his face was turning blue, his eyes were protruding. Suddenly he relinquished his hold on Grimes' wrists. The two women hustled him to an acceleration chair, forced him down into it. They held him there while Irene, using a length of flex that she had found somewhere, lashed him into the seat. Druthen had already been similarly dealt with by Irene and Flandry.

"Mphm," grunted Grimes. The situation was, for the time being, under control. Slowly he removed his gloves, then took his pipe from one of the pouches at the belt of his space suit. He filled it and lit it, ignoring Sonya's "Not *now*!" He stared at Druthen, demanded, "Where are the prisoners?"

"Find out!" came the snarled reply.

From the intercom speakers came a growing uproar. "Doctor Druthen, what's happened?" "We're shut in, let us out of here!" "Doctor, there's no gravity!"

"We can do without that," said Grimes. Sonya switched off the system. Then, "Where are the prisoners, Druthen?"

Again the scientist snarled, "Find out!"

"And that is just what we intend to do, Herr Doktor," remarked Flandry. He pulled that complicated-looking weapon from a makeshift holster at his belt, looked at it thoughtfully, said regretfully, "Not quite subtle enough. . . ." From another pouch he took out a knife, drew it from its sheath. It was only small, but it gleamed evilly. "Perhaps a little judicious whittling . . ." He murmured. "Where shall I start?"

Von Donderberg, who had recovered his voice, croaked, "Remember that you an officer and gentleman are. A civilized man."

"Who says that I'm civilized, Commander? Come to that—who dares say that either you or the learned Herr Doktor are civilized? You, sir, are a pirate. He is either a mutineer or a hijacker or both— but this is no time to discuss legalities. H'm. Your hands are nicely secured to the arms of your chair, Doctor. Perhaps if I pry off your fingernails, one by one . . ."

"Flandry, you wouldn't!" expostulated Grimes.

"Wouldn't I, Commodore? You may watch."

"But I know where they are," said Clarisse. She added tartly, "What the hell's the good of having a professional telepath around if you don't make use of her?"

"Why must you spoil everything?" asked Flandry plaintively.
Von Donderberg laughed mirthlessly and Druthen fainted.

℘ Chapter 25 ℘

YES, CLARISSE KNEW WHERE THEY WERE. It was an obvious enough place anyhow, the empty cargo compartment, right aft, in which Grimes had intended to stow whatever fantastic artifacts could be plundered from The Outsiders' Ship. Sonya, taking with her the electronic master key that would allow her passage through the locked airtight doors, went to release them. She was accompanied by Irene and would pick up Trafford and Metzenther on the way. She assured Grimes that if she encountered any of Druthen's people she would shoot if she had to. Irene growled that *she* would shoot, period. But there was not much risk. Metzenther would be able to give them ample warning of what hostile action, if any, awaited them in any compartment that they were about to enter.

Grimes switched on the second Carlotti transceiver—luckily the ship was fitted with two of the sets—and raised *Faraway Quest II* without any difficulty. She was no longer ahead, relatively speaking. *Adler* had turned, and *Quest II* and *Wanderer* had turned with her, and all three ships were racing back toward *The Outsider* on a reciprocal of their original trajectory.

"So you've got your ship back, Commodore," commented the other Grimes, looking out from the little screen. "Your Commander Mayhew, and Trialanne aboard *Wanderer*, have been keeping us informed."

"There's a little mopping up yet, Commodore," said Grimes. "But it shouldn't take long. I suggest that you and *Wanderer* slow down to allow me to catch up."

"*Wanderer* can if she likes, Commodore, but I'm not going to. *Adler's* going like a bat out of hell, and has the heels of us. Mayhew tells me that she's using some experimental accelerator, for the first time. Unluckily he's a mechanical and mathematical moron, so he can't get anything but absolute gibberish from the mind of *Adler's* engineer officer. But I know that it's Blumenfeld's intention to race us to *The Outsider* and then to seize and to hold it against all comers, waiting for reinforcements."

"What about *Vindictive?* Captain Flandry's ship?"

"What, indeed?" echoed Flandry.

"We can't warn her," said Grimes II. "That stupid culture she comes from has never developed the Carlotti system, or used telepaths. . . ."

"I resent that," snarled Flandry.

Grimes II seemed to notice him for the first time. "Sorry, Captain. I didn't realize that you were listening. But can *you* warn your ship?"

"No, I can't. But my men have very itchy trigger fingers."

"They'll need 'em. But switch on your other set, Commodore. Mr. Smith in *Wanderer* would like a word with you."

"I can't. Commodore, will you tell Mr. Smith that his Mrs. Trafford switched off my other set rather permanently? The same applies to the remote control panel of my Mannschenn Drive."

"Then switch over to *Wanderer.* I'll just stick beak."

Grimes made the necessary adjustments, found himself looking at Smith. Tallentire was well in the background.

"Commodore," said Smith, "you realize that neither we nor the other Commodore Grimes can afford to wait until you have effected repairs and adjusted trajectory. *Adler* must be stopped. I, as the charterer, have assumed effective command of *Wanderer.* I do not see either Captain Trafford or Mrs. Trafford in your control room. Could you ask them to speak with me?"

"They're not available at the moment," said Grimes.

"They bloody well are!" Irene contradicted him.

Suddenly the control room had become crowded with people:

Sonya, Irene, Trafford, Metzenther, Billy Williams, Carnaby, Hendrikson, Major Dalzell and Daniels. Williams reported to Grimes, "Commander Davis and his juniors have gone straight to the engine room, Skipper. They'll let you know as soon as they can get her started up." He went to where Druthen and von Donderberg were lashed in their chairs. "An' what shall we do with these drongos?"

"Take 'em away and lock 'em up, as soon as we can get round to it."

"Captain Trafford, Mrs. Trafford," came Smith's insistent voice from the Carlotti speaker.

"Yes!" snapped Irene.

"You and Captain Trafford should be aboard this ship. But you're not. So I had no option but to order Mr. Tallentire to press the chase."

"You . . . *ordered*?"

"Yes. I ordered."

"He *is* the charterer," pointed out Trafford.

"All right. He's the bloody charterer. And so what?"

"Blumenfeld must be stopped," insisted the little captain. "Waldegren, in any continuum, cannot be allowed to get its hands on *The Outsider*'s secrets."

"You'll never stop us now!" bragged von Donderberg.

"Shut up, you!" growled Billy Williams.

Irene turned back to the Carlotti transceiver "All right, Smith. Press the chase. But, as owner, I appoint Mr. Tallentire master—until Captain Trafford's return. Mr. Tallentire will act as *he* sees fit. Get it?"

"As you wish." Smith managed to convey the impression of being supremely unconcerned.

"I will talk with Mr. Tallentire now."

Tallentire's face replaced that of Smith in the screen. He looked far from happy. "Yes, ma'am?"

"You are acting captain. Put the interests of the ship before those of Mr. Smith. Press the chase. Make use of your weaponry as requisite. You will revert to your normal rank as soon as we are back on board. That's all."

Somehow a junior engineer had managed to insert himself into the crowded control room. He elbowed his way toward Grimes. "Sir, Commander Davis told me to tell you that you can start inertial and Mannschenn Drives as soon as you like. He's been trying to raise you on the intercom, but the line is dead."

"It's switched off," Grimes admitted. "But we'll get it working again to the engine room. . . ." Daniels had anticipated him, handed Grimes a microphone. "Commodore here, Commander Davis. The remote control panel of the Mannschenn Drive is . . . out of order. You'll just have to get your instructions by telephone. Good." He turned to Carnaby. "Get ready to put the ship on the reciprocal heading—straight for The Outsider. We may be a little late for the start of the party, but we should be there before it's over . . ."

Flandry, Irene and Trafford looked at him with some animosity. "It's all right for you," growled the ex-empress. "You've got a ship now, and we haven't."

"Can you get us back to where we belong?" Flandry asked Clarisse, a little desperately.

"I . . . I don't know . . ." she admitted. "I've never tried *sending* anybody anywhere before."

"You'd better try now," Grimes told her." Or as soon as we have things sorted out." He didn't want Sonya and Flandry in the same ship.

~ Chapter 26 ~

THE COMMODORE'S QUARTERS still retained the distasteful traces of Druthen's occupancy, but the cleaning up could wait. Grimes forced himself to ignore the untidiness: no less than his own, but *different*—the scars left by smoldering cigarette ends on table tops; the sticky rings that showed where slopping over glasses had been set down. Sonya had wanted to do something about it at once, if not before, but Grimes had restrained her. "It is essential," he said firmly, "that Sir Dominic, Irene, Captain Trafford and Mr. Metzenther be returned to their own ships as soon as possible. . . ."

"And it is equally essential—to me, anyhow—that Ken be brought back here as soon as possible," Clarisse told him.

"Mphm. I see your point. But first of all both Captain Flandry's *Vindictive* and Captain Trafford's *Wanderer* must be put in a state of full fighting efficiency, so as to be able to cope with *Adler*. I would suggest that you deal with Sir Dominic first."

"Thank you," said Flandry.

"It will be a pleasure, Captain. Well, Clarisse?"

"I don't know how it can be done . . ." muttered the girl. "I don't know *if* it can be done. . . ."

"Rubbish!" snorted Irene. "If you can pull, you can push. It's as simple as that."

"Then why don't *you* try it?"

"It's just not my specialty, dearie. I'm just a rough-and-tough ex-mate out of the Dog Star Line."

"To say nothing of being a rough and tough ex-empress," commented Sonya acidly. "Shut up, unless you have something constructive to contribute."

"What I said *was* constructive."

"Like hell it was."

"Ladies, ladies . . ." murmured Flandry soothingly. Then, to Clarisse. "As I see it, your talent works this way. You're in the right, drug-induced frame of mind. You paint or draw a picture of whatever animal or person you wish to pull into the trap or ambush, concentrate—and the result is instant teleportation. . . ."

"You've oversimplified a little, Dominic, but that's about it."

"All right. Now suppose you sketched, to the best of your ability, the inside of my control room aboard *Vindictive*. . . ."

"I've never been aboard your ship, Dominic."

"But you've been inside my mind."

Oh, thought Grimes. *Have you, indeed? But I suppose that a telepath wants more than mere physical contact. . . .*

"Yes."

"This is what I want you to do. You must order from the ship's doctor whatever hallucinogen it is you need. And then, when you are ready, I'll visualize the control room of my ship, in as exact detail as possible, and you put it down on paper. . . ."

"And what," asked Grimes, "if *Vindictive*'s control room is brought to Captain Flandry, instead of the other way round? I seem to recall a law of physics that I learned as a child: Two solid bodies cannot occupy the same space at the same time."

"Let me finish, Commodore. After she has drawn the control room she will put me in it. . . ."

"Yes, Dominic," whispered Clarisse. "I think it will work. I'm sure it will work."

"As long as somebody's sure about something . . ." grumbled Grimes. "Now, I think that we have some neo-mescalin in our medical stores. It was you who insisted that we carry some. . . ."

"That is correct. If you will have it sent up . . .?"

Grimes called the doctor on the intercom, and then Billy Williams in Control. "Commander Williams," he said, "unless it is a matter of utmost urgency we are not, repeat not, to be disturbed."

"You won't be, Skipper. We're the also-ran in this race—an' I'm afraid that *Adler*'s the odds-on favorite! Of course, *Vindictive* might pip her at the post."

"We're trying to insure that she does," said Grimes, breaking off the conversation.

Slowly, without embarrassment, Clarisse removed her clothing, ignoring Irene's, "Is that necessary?" and Sonya's, "You're only jealous." She took the small glass of opalescent fluid that Grimes handed her, drained it. In her nudity she was more witch than mere woman. She was . . . untouchable. (*But that bastard Flandry hadn't found her so, thought Grimes.*) Her face was solemn, her eyes looking at something very far away. And yet it was Sir Dominic at whom she was looking. At whom? Through whom? Beyond whom?

She was stooping slightly over the table upon which a sheet of paper had been spread, upon which the colored pens had been laid out. With her gaze still intent upon Flandry she commenced to draw with swift, sure strokes. The picture was taking shape: acceleration chairs, consoles, screens, the remote controls of machinery and weaponry, all subtly unlike anything that *Quest*'s and *Wanderer*'s people had ever seen before. *Different ships, different long splices,* thought Grimes, recalling an ancient Terran seafaring proverb. *Different universes, different interstellar drives . . .*

Tension was building up in the Commodore's day cabin as the naked Clarisse stared at Flandry in his glittering uniform; as Flandry stared at Clarisse. As far as he was concerned, as far as she was concerned they were alone. Under her weaving hands the sketch was becoming three dimensional, real. Were the lights dimming? Was the irregular beat of the inertial drive, the thin, high whining of the Mannschenn Drive becoming fainter? Was the deathly cold of interstellar space pervading the ship?

There is one law of nature that is never broken—magic notwithstanding: *You can't get something for nothing.* A transfer of a solid body across a vast distance was about to take place. Such a transfer, whether by wheels, wings or witchcraft, involves the use of energy. There was energy in many usable forms available within the hull *of Faraway Quest*. It was being drawn upon.

Grimes stared at the picture on the table. The lights—red, green, blue and amber—on the panels of the consoles were glowing, and some of them were blinking rapidly. The darkness beyond the viewports was the utter blackness of intergalactic space. Something swam slowly into sight beyond one of the big transparencies—the dome-shaped Shaara derelict.

And then ...

And then there was a man there, standing in the middle of the hitherto deserted control room, the details of his face and figure growing under the witch artist's flying fingers. It was unmistakably Flandry, and he was stark naked save for his belt and his holstered pistol.

Grimes looked up from the sketch to stare at the emptiness where Flandry had been standing. He was ... gone. But not entirely; his uniform, a small bundle of black and gold, of rainbow ribbons, was all that remained of him.

Irene said—was it to Sonya or to Clarisse?—"At least you've something to remember him by, dearie."

Clarisse, her face cold and hard, snatched the sheet with the sketch off the table, screwed it up into a ball, threw it toward the disposal chute. She did not miss. She moved swiftly around the table, picked up the empty uniform, then stuffed it down the chute after the crumpled paper. Grimes made as though to stop her—after all, an analysis of the cloth from which Flandry's clothing had been cut could have told a great deal about the technology of his culture—then decided against it. He would be able to swap information with Sir Dominic after *Adler* had been disposed of. Nonetheless, he was sorry that he had not said goodbye properly to the man, thanked him for all his help. (But Flandry had helped himself, in more ways than one. ...)

The witch girl was ready to resume operations. A fresh sheet of paper was on the table. She said nothing aloud to Metzenther, but the two telepaths must have been in communication. He came to stand beside her, was obviously feeding into her mind the details of *Wanderer*'s control room. Again the detailed picture grew.

Irene asked. "Would you mind if I kept my clothes on, Clarisse? Public nudism never appealed to me."

Sonya said, cattily, "I don't think female nakedness interests her."

Nor did it. When Irene vanished she left nothing behind—and neither did Trafford nor Metzenther.

And now, at last, Clarisse was working for herself. For the last time the lights dimmed, the temperature dropped, the shipboard sounds were muffled. Grimes looked at the flattering portrait of Mayhew that had appeared, then at Sonya. He said, "I think we'll see what's happening topside, my dear." And, as Mayhew materialized, just as they were leaving, "It's good to have our ship to ourselves again."

~ Chapter 27 ~

THEY HAD THEIR SHIP to themselves again, but she was a ship alone. Far ahead of them now were their allies—allies only as long as it was expedient for them to be so—and their enemies. There was communication still with *Faraway Quest II* and with *Wanderer*, by Carlotti radio and through the telepaths. There was no word from *Vindictive*; but as Irene, Trafford and Metzenther were safely back aboard their own vessel, it could be assumed that Flandry was safely back in his.

Grimes, pacing his control room (three steps one way, three steps the other unless he wished to make complicated detours around chairs and banked instruments) was becoming more and more impatient. For many years he had thought of himself as a man of peace—but in his younger days, in the Federation's Survey Service, he had specialized in gunnery. If there was to be a fight he wanted to be in it. Apart from anything else, should he not be present at the moment of victory over *Adler* his prior claim to *The Outsider* would be laughed at by Irene, by Smith, by Flandry and even by his other self. And his engines were not developing their full capacity.

The emergency shutdown of the Mannschenn Drive had affected the smooth running of that delicate, complex mechanism. It was nothing serious, but recalibration was necessary. Recalibration can be carried out only on the surface of a planet. And even if there had been any planets in the vicinity—which, of course, there were not— Grimes could not afford the time.

So *Faraway Quest* limped on while, and at last, the reports started coming in from ahead of her. *Wanderer* thought the *Vindictive* was engaging *Adler*. One of the officers aboard *Faraway Quest II* had broken the code that *Adler* was using in her Carlotti transmissions to base, and Grimes II reported that Blumenfeld was screaming for reinforcements.

Wanderer and *Faraway Quest II* were now within extreme missile range of the engagement but had not yet opened fire. To do so they would have to revert to normal space time. Metzenther, aboard *Wanderer*, reported through Clarisse that he and Trialanne were monitoring the involuntary psionic transmissions of the personnel of both ships presently engaged in the fighting, and that Flandry was emanating confidence, and Blumenfeld a growing doubt as to the outcome of the battle. Each ship, however, was finding it difficult to counter the unfamiliar weapons being used by the other, and each ship was making maximum use of the cover of the derelicts in orbit about The Outsider.

Wanderer had emerged into the normal continuum and had launched missiles.

Faraway Quest II was engaging *Adler* with long-range laser.

Somebody had scored a direct hit on The Outsiders' Ship itself. And that was all.

~ Chapter 28 ~

THE CARLOTTI TRANSCEIVER was dead insofar as *Wanderer*, *Faraway Quest II*, and *Adler* were concerned. There were no psionic transmissions from *Wanderer*, no unintentional emanations from the crews of the other ships.

What had happened? Had the allies launched their Sunday punch against *Adler*, and had *Adler*'s retaliatory Sunday punch connected on all three of them? It was possible, Grimes supposed, just barely possible—but wildly improbable.

"Are you sure you can pick up absolutely nothing?" he demanded of Mayhew and Clarisse. (There are usually some survivors, even when a ship is totally destroyed, even though they may not survive for long.)

"Nothing," she replied flatly. And then—"But I'm picking up an emanation. . . . It's more an emotion than actual thought. . . ."

"I get it too," agreed Mayhew. "It's . . . it's a sense of strong disapproval."

"Mphm. I think that I'd disapprove strongly if *my* ship were shot from under me," said Grimes.

"But . . . but it's not *human* . . ." insisted the girl.

"Mr. Carnaby," Grimes barked at his navigator. "What do you get in the MPI? Is The Outsiders' Ship still there?"

"Still there, sir. And, as far as I can make out, only four vessels in orbit about her. . . . There could be a cloud of wreckage."

279

Possibly a couple of the derelicts, thought Grimes. Possibly *Adler*, or *Wanderer*, or the other *Quest*, or *Vindictive*. Possibly a large hunk blown off The Outsiders' Ship herself. Possibly anything.

He said, "We will stand in cautiously, proceeding under Mannschenn Drive until we are reasonably sure that it is safe to reenter normal space time. Meanwhile, Mr. Hendrikson, have all weaponry in a state of instant readiness. And you, Major Dalzell, have your men standing by for boarding operations. Commander Williams, see that the boats are all cleared away."

"What is a killer ape?" asked Clarisse suddenly.

"This is hardly the time or place to speculate about our probable ancestry!" snapped Grimes.

"I am not speculating, Commodore. It is just that I picked up a scrap of coherent thought. It was as though a voice—not a human voice—said, 'Nothing but killer apes.'"

"It's a pity we haven't an ethologist along," remarked Grimes. And where was Maggie Lazenby, the Survey Service ethologist whom he had known, years ago, whom he knew, now—but when *was* now?—as the other Grimes, captain of the other *Faraway Quest*? Where was Grimes? Where was Irene? Where was Flandry? He didn't worry about Blumenfeld.

He went to look at the MPI screen. It was a pity that it showed no details. But that large, rapidly expanding blob of luminescence must be *The Outsider*; those small sparks the derelicts. Carnaby said, in that tone of voice used by junior officers who doubt the wisdom of the procedures of their superiors, "We're *close*, sir."

"Yes, Mr. Carnaby. Mphm." He took his time filling and lighting his pipe. "All right, you may stand by the intercom to the engine room. Stop inertial drive. Half-astern. Stop her. Mannschenn Drive—stop! Mr. Hendrikson—stand by all weapons!"

And there, plain beyond the viewports, was *The Outsider*, coldly luminescent, unscarred, not so much a ship as a castle out of some fairy tale told when Man was very young: with towers and turrets, cupolas and minarets and gables and buttresses, awe-inspiring rather than grotesque. And drifting by, tumbling over and over, came one of the derelicts, the Shaara vessel aboard which the conference had been held. It had been neatly bisected, so that each of its halves looked like one of those models of passenger liners in booking agents' display windows, cut down the midship line to show every deck, every compartment.

"We will continue to orbit *The Outsider*," said Grimes. "We will search for survivors."

"Commodore," said Mayhew. "There are no survivors. They are all . . . gone."

"Dead, you mean?"

"No, sir. Just . . . gone."

~ Chapter 29 ~

THEY WERE . . . gone. *Wanderer* and *Adler*, *Faraway Quest II* and *Vindictive*. They were gone, without a trace, as though they had never been. (But had they ever been?) There was wreckage in orbit about *The Outsider*—the shattered and fused remains of the Dring cruiser: a whirling cloud of fragments that could have come only from that weird, archaic and alien ship that had never been investigated, that would never now be investigated. And Grimes' flag, the banner of the Rim Worlds Confederacy that he had planted on The Outsiders' Ship, was gone too. This was a small matter and was not noticed until, at last, Grimes decided to send away his boarding party. Until then the search for survivors had occupied all his attention.

Faraway Quest had the field to herself.

"We will carry on," said Grimes heavily, "with what we came out here to do." And his conscience was nagging him. Surely there was *something* that he could have done for Flandry, for Irene, for the other Grimes. All of them had helped him. What had he done to help them? What had he done to help Maggie? But space was so vast, and space time, with its infinitude of dimensions, vaster still; and the lost ships and their people were no more than microscopic needles in a macrocosmic haystack. Too, he told himself, some clue to their fates might be found within that enormous, utterly alien hull.

So it was that Grimes, suited up, stood in the airlock of the *Quest* with Sonya and Williams and Major Dalzell. *The Outsider* had . . .

permitted the ship to approach much closer than she had before; there would be no need to use the boats for the boarding party. The door slowly opened, revealing beyond itself that huge, gleaming construction. It looked neither friendly nor menacing. It was . . . neutral.

Grimes made the little jump required to break magnetic contact between boot soles and deck plating, at the same time actuating his suit propulsion unit. He knew, without turning to watch, that the others were following him. Swiftly he crossed the narrow moat of nothingness, turning himself about his short axis at just the right time, coming in to a landing on an area of The Outsider's hull that was clear of turrets and antennae. He felt rather than heard the muffled clang as his feet hit the flat metal surface. Sonya came down beside him, then Williams, then Dalzell.

The commodore looked up at his ship, hanging there in the absolute blackness, faint light showing from her control room viewports, a circle of brighter light marking the reopened airlock door. He could see four figures jumping from it—the sergeant of marines and three privates. Next would be Mayhew, with Engineer Commander Davis; Brenda Coles, the assistant biochemist; and Ruth Macoby, assistant radio officer. It was a pity, thought Grimes, that he had not crewed his ship with more specialist officers; but it had been assumed, of course, that Dr. Druthen and his scientists and technicians would fill this need. But Druthen and his people, together with von Donderberg and his surviving junior officer, were prisoners in the empty cargo hold in which Faraway Quest's crew had been confined.

"We're being watched," whispered Sonya, her voice faint from the helmet transceiver.

They were being watched. Two of the antennae on the border of the clear area were turning, twisting. They looked unpleasantly like cobras poised to strike.

"Not to worry," Grimes assured her. "Calver mentioned the very same thing in his report."

The sergeant and his men were down now. The eight humans were tending to huddle. "Break it up!" Dalzell was barking. "Break it up! We're too good a target like this!"

"So is the ship, Major." Grimes told him.

"Sorry, sir." The young marine did not sound very penitent. "But I think we should take all precautions."

"All right," said Grimes. "Scatter—within reason." But he and Sonya stayed very close together.

Mayhew, Davis, Coles and Macoby came in. The telepath identified Grimes by the badges of rank on his space suit, came to stand with him and Sonya.

"Well, Ken?" asked the commodore.

"It . . . it knows we're here. It . . . it is deciding. . . ."

"If it doesn't make its mind up soon," said Grimes, "I'll burn my way in."

"Sir!" Mayhew sounded horrifed.

"Don't worry," Sonya told him. "It's opening up for us."

Smoothly, with no vibrations, a circular door was sliding to one side. Those standing on it had ample time to get clear of the opening, to group themselves about its rim. They looked down into a chamber, lit from no discernible source, that was obviously an airlock. From one of its walls, rungs spaced for the convenience of human beings extruded themselves. (And would those rungs have been differently spaced for other, intelligent, space-faring beings? Almost certainly.)

Grimes reported briefly by his suit radio to Hendrikson who had been left in charge. He knew without asking that Mayhew would be making a similar report to Clarisse. Then he said, "All right. We'll accept the invitation." He lowered himself over the rim, a foot on the first rung of the ladder.

The Outsider's artificial gravity field was functioning, and *down* was down.

There was ample room in the chamber for all twelve of them. They stood there silently, watching the door slide back into place over their heads. Dalzell and his marines kept their hands just over the butts of their handguns. Grimes realized that he was doing the same. He was wearing at his belt a pair of laser pistols. He spoke again into his helmet microphone. His companions could hear him, but it became obvious that they were now cut off from communication with the ship. Captain Calver, he remembered, had reported the same phenomenon. It didn't really matter. Mayhew said that he could still reach Clarisse and that she could reach him.

"Atmosphere, Commodore," said the biochemist, looking at the gauge among the other gauges on her wrist. "Oxygen helium mixture. It would be safe to remove our helmets."

"We keep them on," said Grimes.

Another door in the curving wall was opening. Beyond it was an alleyway, a tunnel that seemed to run for miles and flooded with light. As was the case in the chamber there were no globes or tubes visible. There was nothing but that shadowless illumination and that long, long metallic tube, like the smooth bore of some fantastically huge cannon.

Grimes hesitated only briefly, then began to stride along the alleyway. Sonya stayed at his side. The others followed. Consciously or unconsciously they fell into step. The regular crash of their boots on the metal floor was echoed, reechoed, amplified. They could have been a regiment of the Brigade of Guards, or of Roman legionaries. They marched on and on, along that tunnel with no end. And as they marched the ghosts of those who had been there before them kept pace with them—the spirits of men and of not-men, from only yesterday and from ages before the Terran killer ape realized that an antelope humerus made an effective tool for murder.

It was wrong to march, Grimes dimly realized. It was wrong to tramp into this . . . this temple in military formation, keeping military step. But millennia of martial tradition were too strong for him, were too strong for the others to resist (even if they wanted to do so). They were men, uniformed men, members of a crew, proud of their uniforms, their weapons and their ability to use them. Before them— unseen, unheard, but almost tangible—marched the phalanxes of Alexander, Napoleon's infantry, Rommel's Afrika Korps. Behind them marched the armies yet to come.

Damn it all! thought Grimes desperately. *We're spacemen, not soldiers. Even Dalzell and his Pongoes are more spacemen than soldiers.*

But a gun doesn't worry about the color of the uniform of the man who fires it.

"Stop!" Mayhew was shouting urgently. "Stop!" He caught Grimes' swinging right arm, dragged on it.

Grimes stopped. Those behind him stopped, in a milling huddle—but the hypnotic spell of marching feet, of phantom drum and fife and bugle, was broken.

"Yes, Commander Mayhew?" asked Grimes.

"It's . . . Clarisse. A message . . . Important. I couldn't receive until we stopped marching. . . ."

"What is it?" demanded Grimes.

"The . . . ship . . . and Clarisse and Hendrikson and the others. . . . They're prisoners again!"

"Druthen? Von Donderberg?"

"Yes."

Grimes turned to his second-in-command. "You heard that, Commander Williams?"

"Yair. But it ain't possible, Skipper. Nary a tool or a weapon among Druthen an' his mob. We stripped 'em all to their skivvies before we locked 'em up, just to make sure."

"How did it happen?" Grimes asked Mayhew sharply.

"The . . . the details aren't very clear. But Clarisse thinks that it was a swarm of fragments, from one of the blown-up derelicts, on an unpredictable orbit. The *Quest* was holed badly, in several places . . . including the cargo hold. Mr. Hendrikson opened up so the prisoners could escape to an unholed compartment."

"Any of us would have done the same," said Grimes slowly. He seemed to hear Sir Dominic Flandry's mocking laughter. "But what's happening now?"

"Von Donderberg has all the *Quest*'s weapons trained on *The Outsider*, on the airlock door. If we try to get out we shall be like sitting ducks."

"Stalemate . . ." said the commodore. "Well, we've a breathable atmosphere in here—I hope. So that's no worry. There may even be water and food suitable for our kind of life. . . ."

"But they're coming after us. The airlock door has opened for them! They're here now!"

"Down!" barked Dalzell, falling prone with a clatter. The others followed suit. There were dim figures visible at the end of the tunnel, dim and very distant. There was the faraway chatter of some automatic projectile weapon. The major and his men were firing back, but without apparent success.

And at the back of Grimes' mind a voice—an inhuman voice, mechanical but with a hint of emotion—was saying. *No, no. Not again. They must learn. They must learn.*

Then there was nothingness.

～ Chapter 30 ～

GRIMES SAT ON THE HILLTOP, watching Clarisse work.

She, clad in the rough, more-or-less-cured pelt of a wolflike beast, looked like a cavewoman, looked as her ancestors on this very world must have looked. Grimes looked like what he was—a castaway. He was wearing the ragged remnants of his long johns. His space suit, together with the suits of the others who had been so armored, was stowed neatly in a cave against the day when it would be required again—if ever. Other members of the party wore what was left of their uniforms. They were all here, all on what Grimes had decided must be Kinsolving's Planet, twenty men and thirteen women.

And, some miles away, were Druthen and von Donderberg and their people. They were still hostile—and in their tribe were only five women, two of them past childbearing age. They had their weapons still—but, like *Faraway Quest*'s crew, were conserving cartridges and power packs. Nonetheless, three nights ago they had approached Grimes' encampment closely enough to bring it within range of their trebuchet and had lobbed a couple of boulders into the mouth of the main cave before they were driven off by Dalzell and his marines.

All of them were on Kinsolving's Planet.

It was Kinsolving's Planet ages before it had been discovered by Commodore Kinsolving, ages before those mysterious cavemen had painted their pictures on the walls of the caves. (Perhaps the ancestors of those cavemen were here now. . . .) The topography was all wrong. But by the time that Man pushed out to the rim of the galaxy, old mountain ranges would have been eroded would have sunk, seas would roll where now there were plains, wrinklings of the world's crust would bring new, towering peaks into being.

But that feeling of *oddness* that Grimes had known on his previous visit (previous, but in the far distant future) to this planet still persisted. On Kinsolving *anything* could happen, and most probably would.

Was it some sort of psionic field induced by The Outsiders' Ship? Or had *The Outsider* been drawn to that one position in space by the field? Come to that—who (or what) were *the Outsiders?* Do-gooders? Missionaries? Beings whose evolution had taken a different course from that of Man, of the other intelligent races of the Galaxy?

And we, thought Grimes, *are descendants of the killer ape, children of Cain. . . . What would we have been like if our forebears had been herbivores, if we had not needed to kill for food—and to protect ourselves from other predators? What if our first tools had been tools, peaceful tools, and not weapons? But conflict is essential to the evolution of a species. But it could have been conflict with the harsh forces of Nature herself rather than with other creatures, related and unrelated. Didn't some ethologist once refer to Man as the Bad Weather Animal?*

But They, he thought, as he watched Clarisse, squatting on her hunkers, scratching industriously away with a piece of chalky stone on the flat, slate surface of the rock, *but They have certainly thrown us back to our first beginnings. We didn't pass the test. First of all there was the naval battle—and I wonder what happened to* Wanderer, Vindictive, *the other* Quest *and* Adler. . . *First of all there was the naval battle, and then the brawl actually within the sacred precincts. Calver and his crew must have been very well behaved to have been accepted, nonetheless. Perhaps, by this time, the stupid pugnacity is being bred out of Man, perhaps Calver was one of the new breed. . . .*

"Stop brooding!" admonished Sonya sharply.

"I'm not brooding. I'm thinking. I'm still trying to work things out."

"You'd be better employed trying to recall every possible, smallest detail of your beloved *Quest*. Clarisse knows damn all about engineering, and if she's to succeed she must have all the help we can give her."

"*If* she succeeds. . . ."

"John!" Her voice betrayed the strain under which she was living. "I'm not cut out to be an ancestral cavewoman, or any other sort of cavewoman. I was brought up to wear clean clothes, not filthy rags, to bathe in hot water, not a stream straight off the ice, to eat well-cooked food, not greasy meat charred on the outside and raw inside. . . . Perhaps I'm too civilized—but this is no world for me." She paused. "And here we are, all of us, relying on the wild talent of a witch, a *teleporteuse*, who's been at least half poisoning herself by chewing various wild fungi which might—or might not—have the proper hallucinogenic effect . . ." She laughed bitterly. "All right—the artists in her ancestry did have the power to pull food animals to them. She has it too, as well we know. But will it work with a complex construction such as a spaceship?"

"It worked," Grimes told her, "with complex constructions such as human beings. And Clarisse is no more an anatomist or a physiologist than she is an engineer."

"Commodore," Mayhew was calling. "Clarisse needs your help again!"

Grimes got to his feet. Before he walked to where the artist was at work he slowly looked from his vantage point around his little kingdom. To the north were the jagged, snowcapped peaks, with their darkly forested foothills. To the south was the sea. To east and west were the rolling plains, with their fur of coarse, yellowish grass, their outcroppings of stony hillocks and boulders. From behind one of the distant hills drifted the blue smoke of Druthen's fires.

"Commodore!" called Mayhew again.

"Oh, all right."

He walked over the rocky hilltop to that slab of slate, to where Davis, Williams, Hendrikson and Carnaby were clustered around Clarisse. The sketch of *Faraway Quest* was taking shape, but it was vague, uncertain in outline. How many attempts had there been to date? Grimes had lost count. Earlier drawings had been obliterated by sudden vicious rain showers, had been rubbed out in fits of tearful anger by the artist herself. Once, and once only, it had seemed that a shimmering ship shape, almost invisible, had hung in the air for a microsecond.

Grimes looked at the faces of his officers, his departmental heads. All showed signs of strain, of overmuch concentration. Williams, who was responsible for maintenance, must have been making a mental tally of every rivet, every welded seam in the shell plating. Davis would have been visualizing machinery; Hendrikson, his weapons; Carnaby, his navigational instruments.

But . . .

But, Grimes suddenly realized, none of them had seen, had *felt* the ship as a smoothly functioning whole.

"Ready?" he asked Clarisse.

"Ready," she replied in a tired, distant voice.

And Grimes remembered. He remembered the first commissioning of *Faraway Quest* and all the work that had gone into her, the maintenance and the modifications. He relived his voyage of exploration to the Galactic East: his landings on Tharn, Grollor, Mellise and Stree. He recalled, vividly, his discovery of the antimatter systems to the Galactic West, and that most peculiar voyage, during which he and Sonya had come together, which was made as part of the research into the Rim ghost phenomena.

All this he remembered, and more, and his mind was wide open to Clarisse as she scratched busily away with her rough piece of chalk—and hers was open to him. It was all so vivid, too vivid for mere imagination, for memory. He could actually have been standing in his familiar control room. . . .

He was standing in his familiar control room.

But that was impossible.

He opened his eyes, looked around in a slow circle.

He saw the jagged, snowcapped peaks to the north, with their darkly forested foothills. He saw the glimmering sea to the south. To east and west were the rolling plains, with their fur of coarse, yellowish grass, their outcroppings of stony hillocks and boulders.

From behind one of the distant hills drifted the blue smoke of Druthen's fires.

But . . .

But he was seeing all this through the wide viewports of *Faraway Quest*.

He walked, fast, to the screen of the periscope, adjusted the controls of the instrument so that he had an all-round view around the ship. Yes—his people, his crew were there, all of them staring upward. He did not need to increase the magnification to see the wonder on their faces.

"Mphm," he grunted. He went to the panel on which were the controls for the airlock doors. He punched the necessary buttons. The illuminated indicators came on. OUTER DOOR OPEN. INNER DOOR OPEN. RAMP EXTRUDING—to be replaced by RAMP DOWN.

Meanwhile . . .

He put his eyes to the huge binoculars on their universal mounting. Druthen and von Donderberg must have seen the sudden appearance of the ship. She would mean a chance of escape for *them*. Yes, there they were, two dozen of them, running. The sun glinted from the weapons they carried—the guns with their hoarded ammunition, their carefully conserved power packs.

It was a hopeless sortie; but desperate men, more than once, have achieved miracles.

Grimes sighed, went to the gunner's seat of the bow 40-millimeter cannon. He put the gun on manual control. It would be the best one for the job; a noisy projectile weapon has far greater psychological effect than something silent and much more deadly. He flipped the selector switches for automatic and H.E. He traversed until he had the leaders of the attackers in the telescopic sights. Druthen was one of them, his bulk and his waddling run unmistakable. Von Donderberg was the other.

Grimes sighed again. He was genuinely sorry for the Waldegrener. In many ways he and Grimes were the same breed of cat. Only Druthen then . . .

He shifted his sights slightly. But the explosion of a high-explosive shell might kill, would probably injure von Donderberg. Solid shot? Yes. One round should be ample, if Grimes' old skill with firearms still persisted. And it would be a spectacular enough deterrent for the survivors of Druthen's party.

Still Grimes hesitated. The hijackers would be marooned on Kinsolving; nothing would make him change his mind about that. But even if they didn't deserve a chance their children, their descendants did.

And, on a primitive world such as this, the more outstandingly bad bastards contributing to the gene pool the better.

Again he flipped the ammunition selector switch, then lowered his sights. He stitched a neat seam of bursting incendiary shells across the savannah, well ahead of Druthen and von Donderberg. The long grass was highly and satisfactorily flammable. The raiding party retreated in panic. By the time that those of them who possessed space armor got back to their camp to put it on, no matter how they hurried, *Faraway Quest* would be gone.

"All aboard, Skipper," reported Williams from behind Grimes. "Take her up?"

"Take her up, Commander Williams," ordered the Commodore.

~ Chapter 31 ~

"SET TRAJECTORY, SIR?" asked Carnaby.

Grimes looked out through the viewports, toward the opalescent sphere that was Kinsolving, toward the distant luminosity of the Galactic Lens.

"We have to go *somewhere*, John," said Sonya sharply.

"Or somewhen," murmured Grimes. He said, in a louder voice, "We'd better head for where *The Outsider* was, or will be, or is. We have unfinished business."

But it didn't really matter. For the time being, nothing really mattered.

He had his ship again.

THE
WAY BACK

❧ Chapter 1 ❧

"SET TRAJECTORY, SIR?" asked Carnaby briskly.

Commodore Grimes regarded his navigating officer with something less than enthusiasm. The young man, thin features alert under the sleek, almost white head of blond hair, long fingers poised over the keyboard of the control room computer, was wearing what Grimes always thought of as his eager-and-willing expression. The Commodore turned slowly away, staring out through the viewports at the opalescent sphere that was, that had to be, Kinsolving's Planet, and beyond that world to the far distant ellipsoid of luminosity, pallidly agleam against the blackness, that was the Galactic Lens. There was no hurry, he thought, no need for an immediate decision. He had his ship again and his own people around him, and little else mattered.

"We have to go *somewhere*," said Sonya sharply.

"Or somewhen," Grimes murmured, more to himself than to her, although he faced her as he spoke. He sighed inwardly as he saw the impatience all too evident in her expression, her wide, full mouth already set in sulky lines. Sonya, he knew all too well, did not like ships, her rank as commander in the Federation's Survey Service notwithstanding. She regarded them merely as an unfortunately necessary means of transportation from Point A to Point B. There was something of the claustrophobe in her make-up, even though it was well concealed (from everyone but her husband), well controlled.

To her the little, artificial planetoids were prisons, to be escaped from as soon as possible . . .

"Mphm," grunted Grimes. Slowly, carefully, he filled and lit his pipe. He realized, as he went through the familiar, soothing motions, that he would have to remind the catering officer to make a thorough check of the consumable stores remaining. *Faraway Quest*, with her hydroponic tanks, yeast, tissue culture and algae vats, was a closed ecological system, capable of sustaining the lives of her crew almost indefinitely—but luxuries could well be very soon in short supply. For example, there were not any tobacco plants among the assorted flora in her "farm." *And was there tobacco growing anywhere in this Universe? And would anybody recognize it if it were found in its natural state?* There was no Botanist carried on the *Quest*'s Articles.

"Sir?" It was Carnaby again.

Persistent young bastard! thought Grimes, but without malice. He said slowly, "I suppose we could head back to where The Outsider is, or was, or will be." He chuckled mirthlessly. "After all, we have unfinished business . . ."

"Sir?"

The commodore looked severely at the young officer. Why was he dithering so? He was the navigator, wasn't he? Up to now he had been an exceptionally good one.

"Where *is* The Outsider, sir?"

Put the Macbeth and Kinsolving suns in line astern, thought Grimes, *and keep them so. Run out fifty light years on the leads . . .* He thought the words but refrained from saying them aloud. Those steering directions had been valid when *Faraway Quest* had lifted from Port Forlorn only a few weeks ago—as Time had been measured by her chronometers, experienced by her people. But the Clock had been put back—not by minutes, hours, days or even centuries, but by millennia. *Faraway Quest* was lost—in Time and Space. Grimes could envisage dimly the sluggish writhings of the matter-and-energy entity that was the Galaxy, the crawling extension of the spiral arms, the births and the deaths of suns and planets. Was there yet Earth, the womb and the cradle of Humanity? Did Man—in this Now—already walk upon the surface of the home world, or were the first mammals still scurrying in terror under the great, taloned feet of the dinosaurs?

"I have the Kinsolving sun, sir," announced Carnaby.

"If we're correct in the assumption that the world we've just left *is* Kinsolving," Grimes remarked.

"But I can't identify Macbeth," concluded the navigator.

"We have to go somewhere," insisted Sonya.

Major Dalzell, commanding the *Quest*'s marines, made his contribution to the discussion. He was a smallish man, with something of the terrier dog in his appearance and manner. Somehow he had found time to change into an immaculate, sharply creased khaki uniform. He said, "We know, sir, that Kinsolving is habitable . . ."

"It's just that we're rather fussy about whom we share it with," drawled Williams. The big Commander, like Grimes and most of the others, was still in his grimy long-johns, the standard garment for wear under a space-suit. Even so, in the slightly ludicrous attire, with no badges of rank or service, he looked as much a spaceman as the smartly dressed major looked a soldier.

"There's no need to *share*, Commander Williams," said Dalzell. "My men are trained land fighters. Too, we have the ship's artillery."

"We have," agreed Hendriks. The burly, bearded, yellow-haired gunnery officer was a little too fond of his toys, thought Grimes.

"A world is a world is a world . . ." whispered Sonya thoughtfully.

Grimes said tiredly, but with authority, "Let Druthen and von Donderberg keep their bloody planet. They're welcome to it. After all—we have a ship, and they haven't."

"And a ship," Sonya told him, "is built to go places. Or had you forgotten?"

"But where, Mrs. Grimes?" demanded Carnaby. "But *where?*"

"Mphm." Grimes relit his pipe. He turned to Mayhew, the psionic communications officer. "Can you . . . hear anything. Ken? Anybody?"

The tall, gangling telepath grinned, his knobby features suddenly attractive. "I can pick up the people we left on Kinsolving, even though there's only a handful of 'em. If thoughts could kill, we'd all be dead!"

"And . . . The Outsider?"

"I'm . . . I'm trying, Commodore. But the range, if the thing is still where we last saw it, is extreme. From outside—not a whisper."

"And from inside?" Grimes waved towards the viewport through which the distant, glimmering Lens could be seen.

"A . . . A murmuration . . . There's life there, sir. Intelligent life . . ."

"Our kind of life?"

"I . . . I cannot tell. The . . . emanations are from too far away. They are indistinct."

"But there's *something* there," stated rather than asked Grimes. "Something or somebody capable of coherent thought. Mphm. Mr. Daniels?"

"Sir?" The electronic communications officer looked up from his transceiver. His dark, slightly pudgy face carried a frustrated expression. "Sir?"

"Any joy, Sparks?"

"Not a squeak, sir. I've tried the N.S.T. set and the Carlotti. Perhaps if I went down and tried again with the main, long-range equipment . . ."

"Do that, and let me know if you have any luck."

Meanwhile, the *Quest* was falling out and away from Kinsolving's Planet. She was going nowhere in particular—but on this trajectory she would come to no harm (Grimes hoped). She was consuming power, however, even though only her inertial drive was operating, and to no purpose.

The commodore came to a decision. "Mr. Carnaby," he ordered, "set trajectory for Earth. Once there we shall have determined where we are, and we should be able to make at least an intelligent guess as to *when*. Bring her round now."

"But, sir . . . Earth . . . How shall we find it? We don't have the charts, the tables, and the ship's data banks weren't stocked with such a voyage in mind.

"Even if we hit the right spiral arm we could spend several lifetimes hunting along it . . ."

"We'll find a way," said Grimes, with a confidence that, oddly enough, he was beginning to feel. "We'll find a way. Meanwhile, just line her up roughly for the middle of the Lens!"

He sat back in his acceleration chair, enjoying the sound of the big directional gyroscopes as they were started up—the almost inaudible vibration, the hum, the eventual whine—the pressure that drove his body into the deep padding as centrifugal force became an off-center substitute for gravity. Then, with the Galactic Lens wanly gleaming in the center of the circular viewport overhead that was set in the stem of the ship, the gyroscopes, their work done, fell silent—and instead of their whine there was the thin, high keening of the Mannschenn Drive, whose own rotors were now spinning, precessing, ever tumbling down the dark dimensions, dragging the ship and all aboard her through the warped continuum. As the temporal precession field built up there was the queasiness of disorientation in Time and in Space and, felt by all the *Quest's* people, the uncanniness of *déjà vu*. But, as far as Grimes was concerned, there was neither revelation nor precognition, only a sudden loneliness. Later he was to work out to his own satisfaction the reasons for this, for the almost unbearable intensity of the sensation. He was alone, as he never had been before. In his own proper Time there was the infinitude of Alternate Universes—and, out on the Rim of the expanding Galaxy, the barriers between these Universes were flimsy, insubstantial. In this strange Now into which he, his ship and his people had been thrown by The Outsider there were no Alternate Universes—or, if there were, in none of them was there another *Faraway Quest*, another Grimes. He was alone, and his ship was alone.

Suddenly sound and color and perspective snapped back to normal. Ahead shimmered the Galactic Lens, iridescent and fantastically convoluted. It was the start of the voyage.

Grimes said cheerfully, "It is better to travel hopefully than to arrive."

"That's what *you* think," grumbled Sonya.

⤳ Chapter 2 ⤳

GRIMES, the acknowledged Rim Worlds' authority on Terran maritime history, knew of The Law of Oleron, knew that it dated back to the earliest days of sail, yet had been nonetheless invoked as late as the Twentieth Century. Insofar as Grimes was aware no space captain had passed the buck downwards in this manner—but there has to be a first time for anything. In any case he, Grimes, would not be passing the buck. He had made his decision, to steer for Earth, and he was sticking to it. He hoped, however, that somebody in *Faraway Quest's* crew would be able to come up with an idea, no matter how fantastic, on how to find the Home Planet in the whirlpool of innumerable stars, with never a Carlotti beacon among them, towards which the old ship was speeding at many times the velocity of light.

"The Law of Oleron?" asked Sonya as she and Grimes, in the Commodore's day cabin, were enjoying a quiet drink before going down to the meeting, which had been convened in the main lounge. "What the hell is it? Put me in the picture, John."

"It's an old law, a very old law, and I doubt if you'll find it in any Statute Book today. *Today?* What am I saying? I mean what *was* our today, or what will be our today, before The Outsider decided that it had had us in a big way. You had a ship, one of the early sailing vessels, in some sort of predicament—being driven onto a lee shore, trapped in an ice pack, or whatever. The Master, having done all that he could, but to no avail, would call all hands to the break of the poop and say, 'Well, shipmates, we're up Shit Creek without a paddle. Has any of you bastards any bright ideas on how to get out of it?'"

"I'm sure that he didn't use those words, John."

"Perhaps not. Probably something much worse . . . And then, when and if somebody did come up with a bright idea, it was put to the vote."

"A helluva way to run a ship."

"Mphm. Yes. But it had its points. For example, during the Second World War, Hitler's war, back on Earth, the Swedes, although neutral, carried cargoes for the Anglo-Americans. Their ships sailed in the big, allied convoys across the Atlantic. One such convoy was escorted by an auxiliary cruiser called *Jervis Bay*, a passenger liner armed with six-inch guns and smaller weapons. The convoy was attacked just before dark by a German pocket battleship, much faster than *Jervis Bay* and with vastly superior fire power. The convoy scattered—and *Jervis Bay* steamed towards the enemy, all guns blazing away quite ineffectually. As far as she was concerned the surface raider was out of range—but as far as the surface raider was concerned she, *Jervis Bay*, was well within range. But by the time the auxiliary cruiser had been sent to the bottom, most of the merchantmen had made their escape under cover of darkness."

"Where does this famous Law of Oleron come into the story?"

"One of the merchant ships was a Swede. She ran with the others. And then, when the shooting seemed to be over, her master decided to return to pick up *Jervis Bay's* survivors. He would be running a big risk and he knew it. The national colors painted on the sides of his ship would not be much protection. There was the probability that the German captain, if he were still around, would open fire first and ask questions afterwards. The Swedish master, if he embarked on the errand of mercy, would be hazarding his ship and the lives of all aboard her. So he called a meeting of all hands, explained the situation and put the matter to the vote. *Jervis Bay's* survivors were picked up."

"Interesting." Sonya looked at her watch. "It's time you were explaining the situation to *your* crew."

"They already know as much as I do—or should. But I hope that somebody comes up with a bright idea."

What had been done and what had happened to date was recorded in *Faraway Quest*'s log books, on her log tapes and in the journals of her officers. It was, putting it mildly, a confused and complicated story. Not for the first time in his long and eventful career Grimes had been a catalyst; things, unpredictable and disconcerting, had happened about him.

He had been recalled to active duty in the Rim Worlds Navy to head an expedition out to that huge and uncanny artifact known sometimes as The Outsiders' Ship, and sometimes simply as *The Outsider*. The *Quest* had carried, in addition to her Service personnel—most of them, like Grimes himself, Naval Reservists—a number of civilian scientists and technicians led by a Dr. Druthen. Druthen and his people had turned out to be agents of the Duchy of Waldegren, a planet-nation with which the Confederacy, although not actually at war, was on far from friendly terms. Waldegren had sent the destroyer *Adler* to support Druthen and to dispute Grimes' claims to *The Outsider*.

The arrival on the scene of armed Waldegrenese, in addition to Druthen and his hijackers, would have been bad enough—but there were further complications. It seemed that The Outsiders' Ship existed, somehow, as a single entity in a multiplicity of dimensions. It was at a junction of Time Tracks. Another *Faraway Quest*, with another Commodore Grimes in command, had joined the party, as had the armed—heavily armed—yacht *Wanderer*, owned by the ex-Empress Irene, who had once ruled a galactic empire in a yniverse unknown to either of the Grimeses. And there had been a Captain Sir Dominic Flandry in his *Vindictive*, serving an empire unknown on the time tracks of either of the two Confederate commodores or the ex-empress. There had been flag-plantings, claims and counter-claims, mutiny, piracy, seizure and, eventually, a naval action involving *Faraway Quest II*, *Vindictive*, *Wanderer* and *Adler*. This had been fought in close proximity to *The Outsider*—and *The Outsider* had somehow flung the embattled ships away from it. They had vanished like snuffed candles. And then Grimes I, with the hijackers overpowered and imprisoned, had arrived belatedly on the scene in his *Faraway Quest* and had boarded the huge vessel, if vessel it was, the vast, fantastic hulk, and had been admitted into the enormous construction that looked more like a gigantic fairy-tale castle adrift in nothingness than a ship.

Druthen and his surviving followers had escaped from imprisonment in the *Quest* and had also boarded *The Outsider*. A fire fight had broken out between the two parties. And then . . .

And then the alien intelligence inside *The Outsider*, that perhaps was *The Outsider*, had thrown them out. Literally. It had cast them away in Time as well as in Space and they had found themselves marooned on what seemed to be Kinsolving's Planet, the so-called "haunted world," somewhen in the distant Past, before the appearance of that long-extinct human or humanoid race who had left, as the only evidence for their ever having been, the famous cave paintings.

Perhaps Druthen and the men and women in his party were the ancestors of those mysterious artists.

"And that," concluded Grimes, "is my story, and I stick to it." There were a few polite chuckles. "Have I left anything out? Anything at all that might have some bearing on our present predicament? Speak up!"

"No, sir," replied a single voice, echoed by a few others.

Grimes, seated at a chair behind a small table on the platform that was a flange at the base of the axial shaft, looked down at his people, at the thirty-odd men and women who composed the *Quest*'s crew. They were seated in a wedge-shaped formation, a logical enough disposition in a compartment with a circular deck plan. The burly, slovenly Williams and the slim, elegant Sonya were at the point of the wedge, the others fanned out behind them, in rough order of rank and seniority. The back row of seats was occupied by the ship's messgirls and by Dalzell's Marines, uniformed in white and khaki.

Like a slice of pie, thought Grimes, *complete with crust* . . . And then, most irrelevantly, *Sing a song of sixpence, A rocket full of pie* . . .

But *Faraway Quest* was not, strictly speaking, a rocket, although she was fitted with auxiliary reaction drive, used sometimes in emergencies.

The commodore noticed that Mayhew, seated three rows back with his wife and assistant, Clarisse, was grinning. *Damn these telepaths!* he thought, but without viciousness. *Get out of my mind, Ken!*

Didn't know you were a poet, Commodore, the psionic communications officer replied, the words forming themselves in Grimes' mind.

Mphm, thought Grimes, and "Mphm," he grunted aloud. He surveyed the faces turned up to look at his. They all seemed to be wearing a brightly expectant expression. So they were expecting him to produce the usual bloody rabbit out of the usual bloody hat . . .

But you usually do, John . . . Mayhew told him telepathically.

I need help, replied Grimes. *Don't think that I've forgotten that Clarisse got us our ship back.* And, to himself, *That's an idea!*

He said aloud, "I need not remind you how much we owe to Ensign Mayhew and her psionic talents, especially her ability to teleport persons and even, at the finish, such a large construction as this ship. It has just occurred to me that it may be possible for us to reach Earth by being teleported there. What do you say, Clarisse?"

A frown cast its shadow over her rather plump, pretty face. She said slowly, "I'm sorry, sir. But it can't be done."

"Why not?" demanded Grimes. "You dragged the ship from wherever she was, brought her to us on Kinsolving."

"My technique worked then," she admitted. "But only just . . ."

Yes, thought Grimes, *her technique had worked—but, on that crucial occasion, only just.* Hers was a talent that must have been fairly common in the very remote Past, when science was undreamed of and what is called Magic still worked. She could trace her descent from a caveman-artist—a painter who, by his vivid depictions of various animals, drew them into the snares, the ambushes, to within range of the thirsty spears of the hunters. But first the picture had to be drawn. Clarisse, telepath as well as teleporteuse and with the aid of her telepathic husband, had succeeded at last in producing a true representation of *Faraway Quest*, drawing upon the intimate knowledge of the specialist officers, the heads of departments and the members of departments. And Grimes, the *Quest's* master over many years, had, at the finish, supplied from his own mind the essential *feel* of her. *The soul of her,* he thought.

"I would have to paint a picture of Earth," she said. "Or of some part of Earth intimately known to some of you, or to one of you." She added, "I have never been to Earth . . ."

And which of us has? Grimes asked himself. *Sonya was there, on a cruise, not so long ago. And I was born there. But the rest of us . . . Rim Worlders, Franciscans, you name it, anything and everything but Terrans . . .*

"You are a Terran, Commodore," said Clarisse.

"It's many years since I was there," said Grimes. "I've so many memories, of so many worlds . . ."

"I can help you find the right ones," said Mayhew.

Mphm. It's worth trying. We can't lose anything. Yet, somehow, Grimes felt no confidence in the scheme, despite his certain knowledge that the girl's talent was a very powerful one, that her technique had worked on several occasions.

He said, "Commander Williams, organize the necessary materials—easel, paint, canvas. And you, Doctor, make up a dose of whatever hallucinatory drug was used before." He turned to Mayhew. "Ken, I'm letting you into my mind. I want a picture, as clear and detailed a picture as possible, of the apron at Port Woomera . . ." He corrected himself. "No. Make it the Central Australian Desert, roughly midway between Ayers Rock and Mount Olga."

"And what was wrong with your first idea?" asked Sonya.

"Plenty. If Clarisse's technique works again we could find ourselves coinciding in Time and Space with a Constellation Class battlewagon. The result would be measured in megatons. The desert's the safest bet, and the Olgas and the Rock are good points of reference . . ."

Sonya still looked doubtful. "Even a tourist coach . . ."

"I've thought of that. I shall visualize the way that things look during the rainy season. As I recall it, there weren't any tourists around then."

He looked down at the upraised faces of his people. He did not need to be a telepath to read their thoughts: *The old bastard's pulling it off again!*

But he could not feel confident.

Clarisse's talent worked across Time as well as Space—there had been the odd business of the Rim Gods, and the equally odd Hall of Fame adventure—but . . .

~ Chapter 3 ~

IT WAS A GOOD PAINTING.

Clarisse stood before it, sagging with exhaustion, an incongruous figure among her smartly uniformed shipmates, spatters of paint on her naked upper body, smears of pigment on the bedraggled fur kilt that was her only garment. She had dressed the part, that of a cavewoman artist. She had played the part, with a massive dose of hallucinogenic drugs to put her in the proper trance state while she worked. Mayhew, her husband, was beside her, supporting her now that she had finished. She slumped, tired, against him. A dribble of dull red ran from the brush that she still held down his right leg.

But the magic hadn't worked. It had worked before, more than once. It had called the old gods of the Greek pantheon from that distant past when men had believed in them, it had evoked the Mephistopheles of fantasy rather than of religion, it had teleported Grimes and those with him from *Faraway Quest II* to his own *Faraway Quest*. It had drawn *Faraway Quest* herself from the unimaginable nothingness into which she had been flung to the surface of Kinsolving's Planet. Now it had failed to transport the *Quest* from the Rim of the Galaxy to Earth.

There was no need for Grimes to speak. Gently Mayhew led his wife away from the easel so that the commodore could see, in full detail, what had been painted.

Yes, the scene was just as he remembered it. There was the desert, green rather than red, carpeted with the growths that flourished briefly during the wet season. The sky was overcast, with drifting veils of rain, except to the westward, where there was a flaring orange sunset, silhouetted against which were the blue domes—blue only by contrast—of the Olgas. To the east, sullenly smouldering against the grey sky, was the great hulk of Ayers Rock . . .

But . . .

But this was how it had looked in Grimes' own Time. This was how it *would* look—how many years, how many millennia in the future? The domes of Mount Olga, products of erosion . . . Mount Olga, a mass of red conglomerate, plum-pudding-stone, shaped by century after century of wind and rain . . . And even the Rock itself, the granite monolith, could not have resisted the working tools of Time, the great sculptor.

How did the Rock and the Olgas look *now*?

And *when* was *now*?

"Nothin' seems to have happened, Skipper," commented Williams.

"It's not too late to go back to Kinsolving, sir," said Major Dalzell.

Grimes looked at the faces looking up at him. He knew what they were thinking. He had failed to deliver the goods. Mutiny, he realized suddenly, was far from impossible. The marines would be loyal to their own officer rather than to a mere spaceman, no matter what his rank. Hendriks would probably go along with the major. And the others? Personal loyalty would influence most of them, but not all. Williams he could count on, and Mayhew, and Clarisse, and Carnaby . . . Yes, and Daniels. But altogether lacking was the support given to any captain by Interstellar Law, by the Regulations of his own navy, or by the provisions of his own Merchant Shipping Act. The Age of the spaceship—or, at any rate, of the human-owned, -operated and -manned spaceship—lay far in the future. The crew of this particular spaceship might well feel fully entitled to make up their own rules as they went along.

Dalzell seemed to be on the point of saying something further, and those around him were turning towards the major expectantly. Grimes spoke loudly, more to attract and to hold their attention than because he had anything of importance to say.

He said, "This, of course, was only the first attempt. There will be others. The main trouble is that we do not know, yet, just *when* we are. There *is* an Earth waiting for us." *And how can you be so sure of that, buster?* jeered a little voice in his mind. "There *is* an Earth waiting for us," he repeated firmly. "The only thing to be determined is just what period of its history it has reached." He was warming up. "Perhaps we shall be privileged to see the glory that was Greece." He allowed himself a smile as he quoted from Kipling, "When Homer smote 'is bloomin' lyre . . .'"

"Homer?" asked Williams. "An' who was he, Skipper?"

Sonya, beside him, collapsed in helpless laughter.

"Did I say anything funny?" asked Grimes coldly.

"No . . . It was something I remembered."

"And what was it?"

"Nothing important. Just absurd. It just came into my mind. When I was last on Earth I spent some time in the north of England. The people there still have all lands of archaic sports, including pigeon racing. The birds are specially bred for their homing instinct. Oh, anyhow, I heard this story. About a christening. The parson asked the father what name he was giving his son, and the man said, 'Homer.' 'Ah,' said the parson, 'you, like me, are an admirer of the great Greek poet . . .' 'No,' the father replied, 'I keep pigeons.'"

"Ha," commented Grimes. "Ha. Ha."

"I thought that it was quite funny at the time," Sonya told him defensively.

Nobody else does, that's for certain, Grimes thought, looking down at *Faraway Quest*'s people. *And what the hell does Carnaby want?*

"Sir," asked the navigator, "didn't you once tell me about a similar sort of bird that was used in an automatic steering system, for surface ships, on Tharn?"

"Not quite automatic steering," Grimes said. "But the birds were, in effect, used as compasses."

Carnaby turned to Mayhew. "Commander, you're our expert on all forms of E.S.P. Do human beings have a homing instinct?"

"Yes," replied the telepath. "Not all, but some."

Is there an Earthman in the house? thought Grimes. Yes, there was, and he was it.

You will have to allow yourself to be placed under hypnosis, said a voice, Mayhew's voice, in his brain.

But who'll mind the shop, Ken?

Sonya, and Billy Williams . . . And Clarisse and myself. We'll manage.

What about Dalzell and his bully boys? And Hendriks?

I'm keeping tabs on them, John. They'll not be able to pull any surprises.

What about your Rhine Institute's famous Code of Ethics?

I'll worry about that when there is *a Rhine Institute . . .*

Grimes spoke aloud once more. He said, "Mr. Carnaby has given us what may be the solution to our problem. I have seen the records of all of you, so I know that I am the only Earthborn person aboard this ship. At times, in the past, I have prided myself on my sense of direction. I may or may not possess a homing instinct. I hope, most sincerely, that I do. In any case, I have to leave the . . . er . . . technicalities in the capable hands of Commander Mayhew . . ."

Mphm, he thought. *That bloody major would still like to have things* his *way, but Hendriks seems to be coming round . . .*

Put it to the vote, John, came Mayhew's soundless voice.

"Nonetheless," Grimes went on, "there are those of us who think that we should return to Kinsolving. I propose, therefore, that a decision be reached by a show of hands. All those who think that we should return, please indicate!"

Only Dalzell and his men raised their hands.

"Those in favour of continuing towards Earth?"

The Marines were outvoted. There were no abstentions.

And Grimes wondered what odd sort of rabbit he would be pulling out of the hat this time.

≫ Chapter 4 ≪

GRIMES WAS NOT A GOOD SUBJECT for hypnosis. For him the words of the long-dead poet had always held special meaning: *I am the master of my fate, I am the captain of my soul.* And for so many years he had been a captain, literally as well as figuratively. Even as a junior officer in the Federation's Survey Service he had been in command—only of small ships, but in command nonetheless.

Too, this was more, much more, than mere hypnosis. The telepath would be actually entering his mind, working from the inside. Psychic seduction or psychic rape . . . Whatever label was attached to it would make it no more pleasant from the viewpoint of this particular victim.

Luckily Grimes and Mayhew were friends, very old friends. Luckily Grimes trusted, fully, his psionic communications officer. Even so, he didn't like it. Even so, it had to be done.

The commodore sat in the master chair in the control room, the one from which one man could be in full and complete charge of every operation, every function of the ship. It was only on rare occasions that a captain did exercise such direct, personal control; in normal circumstances there were officers to do this and to do that, to watch this screen and those tell-tale lights. But, Mayhew explained, it was essential that now Grimes, more than ever before, must feel himself to be no more (and no less) than the brain, with *Faraway Quest* as his mechanical body.

Grimes sat in the master chair, with controls, set in the armrests, under his finger tips, with other controls in the waist-high console before him. Behind the console, facing him, stood Mayhew. To one side sat Sonya, with Williams and Carnaby. Mayhew had been insistent that no other members of the *Quest*'s crew be present, had been reluctant to admit even the commodore's wife, his second-in-command, his navigator. "But," Grimes had insisted, "if things go wrong, very wrong, there will be people here capable of taking over at once."

Mayhew held out a small tumbler of clear fluid. He said, "Drink this, John."

"What is it, Ken?" asked Grimes suspiciously. "Something fancy in the hallucinogenic line that the Quack brewed up?"

"No." The telepath grinned. "Just a mild sedative. You're too tense . . ."

"Down the hatch!" toasted Grimes, taking the glass and raising it to his mouth, gulping the contents. He said accusingly, "There should have been an ice cube and a hint of bitters. I like my gin—but not neat and warm . . ."

"It's the effect that matters, not the flavor," remarked Mayhew smugly. "And it's made you drowsy, hasn't it? You've had very little sleep of late, and you're tired. Very tired. Why not admit it? Yes, you are tired . . ." Subtly the telepath's voice was changing. At first it had been pleasantly conversational, now a note of insistent suggestion was becoming more and more evident. Grimes thought, *I shouldn't have had that large, neat gin* . . . Stubbornly he tried to visualize a mug of very hot, very black coffee, then dismissed the image from his mind. He was in this of his own free will, wasn't he? It was just that he hated to make himself subject to another's control.

"You are very tired, very tired . . . Why not relax? Yes, relax. Visualize your body part by part, member by member . . . Let every muscle, every tendon go slack, slack . . ."

S.O.B., thought Grimes smugly. *He'll tell me next to try to raise my arm, and I'll decide that it's just not worth the bother . . . But I wish that I didn't have the sensation of somebody scratching around inside my mind like an old hen . . .*

"Relax, relax . . . Visualize your body, part by part . . . Your right foot . . ."

And Grimes realized that he was visualizing his foot, in every detail—the bones, the sinews, the muscles, the slightly hairy skin, the toes and the toenails, even the texture of the encasing sock and the glossy polish of the black shoe.

He thought defiantly, *There are better feet to visualize,* and allowed his regard to stray to the neatly shod Sonya, to the long, smooth legs gleaming below the hem of her brief uniform skirt. But his own, uninteresting, utilitarian rather than handsome foot persisted in his mind's eye.

"You cannot feel your foot any longer, John. You cannot move your foot. Perhaps it is not *your* foot . . . Whose foot could it be? *What* foot could it be?"

And . . . And it was not a human foot any longer. It was a scaly claw, scrabbling on a filthy wooden deck . . .

Grimes was no longer in the control room of *Faraway Quest;* he was in the master compass room of a primitive steamship on Tharn, one of the worlds of Rim Runners' Eastern Circuit. He was looking (as he had looked, long ago) with pity and disgust at the living compass, at the giant homing bird, its wings brutally clipped, imprisoned in its tight harness from which the spindle extended upwards, through deck after deck, to the bridge, to the binnacle in the bowl of which quivered the needle, always indicating the Great Circle course to the port of destination, to the coastal town in which was the nest where the bird had been hatched and reared. The illusion was fantastically detailed; the thin, high keening of the Mannschenn Drive faded to inaudibility, the irregular beat of the inertial drive became the rhythmic thudding of an archaic reciprocating steam engine . . .

And then . . .

And then Grimes was no longer looking at the bird. He was the *bird.* He was dimly aware of the feel of the deck underfoot— unyielding timber instead of sand or grassy soil—and more strongly aware of the constriction of the harness about the upper part of his body. Suddenly there was a greater awareness. It was as though every atom of calcium in his bones had been replaced by those of iron. It was as though, somewhere ahead, there was a huge, fantastically powerful magnet—but not exactly ahead, that was the worst of it. He cried out with the pain of it as supernal forces twisted his body. (He learned later that his cry was the squawk of a bird.)

He thought defiantly, *But I am a man. I am an Earthman.*

A scrap of half-forgotten verse drifted into his brain, *Earthmen, shape your orbits home* . . . Home . . . And again the scrap of verse, *The green hills of Earth* . . . The green hills and, vivid against the dark verdure, a flight of white pigeons . . . Wings beating, beating . . . And the noise in his ears was no longer the steady stamping of a triple-expansion engine, but the drumming of wings. Wings—and a skein of geese dark and distant against the cloudless blue sky. Wings—and the migrating flock maintaining its course over the black, foam-streaked sea, through the blizzard . . .

The blizzard and the whirling flakes, glowing white, incandescent against the darkness, the snowflakes that were stars, multitudinous, brightly scintillant in the ultimate night . . .

The blizzard, the whirling blizzard of stars, and through it, beyond it . . .

Home.

Again there was the wrenching of his bones, his nervous system, his entire body. That supernaturally powerful magnetic field was not ahead, was not in the direct line of flight. Something, thought Grimes, would have to be done about it. He was, he knew, a bird, a huge bird, a metal bird with machinery in lieu of wings. His hands went out to the console before him. Williams and Carnaby were out of their chairs, tense, ready to take over. There were so many things that could go wrong, that could be done with a dreadful and utterly final wrongness. Nobody knew, for example, just what would happen if an alteration of trajectory were carried out while the dimension-twisting Mannschenn Drive was in operation . . . (It had been tried from time to time with small, unmanned, remote- or robot-controlled craft, and such vessels had vanished, never to return.)

But Grimes, temporarily a homing bird, was permanently a spaceman.

Under his hand the inertial drive fell silent, the ever-precessing rotors of the Mannschenn Drive sighed to a stop. There was the weightlessness of free fall, succeeded by the uncomfortable, twisting pull of centrifugal forces as the directional gyroscopes hummed and then whined, dragging the *Quest* about her short axis on to the new heading.

The persistent tug on Grimes' bones lessened but did not die—but now that it came from the right direction the sensation was more pleasant than otherwise.

He restarted the inertial drive and then the interstellar drive.

He heard Williams' voice coming from a very long way away, "Cor, stiffen the bleedin' crows! I do believe that the old bastard's done it!"

Grimes smiled. He knew that the word "bastard," in Williams' vocabulary, was a term of endearment.

☙ Chapter 5 ☙

INWARD, HOMEWARD BOUND sped the old *Quest*. Only she and her master, Grimes, were of actual Terran origin—but humans, no matter where born on any of the man-colonized worlds of the Galaxy, speak of Earth as home. Inward, homeward she sped through the warped continuum, falling down the dark dimensions, deviating now and again from her trajectory to avoid plunging through some sun or planetary system. Once course had been set, however, there was little for the commodore to do. He would *know*, Mayhew assured him, when the star directly ahead was Sol. "But how do I know," demanded Grimes, "just how far we have to go before planetfall?"

"You don't," said the telepath. "You can't. Oh, you might feel the strength of the pseudo-magnetic field—I have to use language that you nontelepaths understand—increase, but even that's not certain."

Sonya remarked acidly that she had read somewhere that it is better to travel hopefully than to arrive. Grimes, the acknowledged Rim Worlds' authority on Terran maritime history, talked about Columbus. *He* had known that those islands which, after weeks of voyaging, had loomed on his western horizon were part of the East Indies. And he had been wrong.

Columbus, said Mayhew, wasn't navigating by homing instinct.

"How do you know he wasn't?" asked Grimes. "After all, if he'd kept on going he'd have finished up back where he started from . . ."

"Like hell he would!" scoffed Sonya. "Neither the Suez Canal nor the Panama Canal was in existence then. Even I know that."

"He could have rounded Cape Horn," her husband told her, "just as Magellan and Drake did, only a few years later, historically speaking . . ."

Nonetheless, thought Grimes, *he had something in common with Columbus. The admiral of the Ocean Sea, driving his tiny squadron west and ever west into the Unknown, had been threatened with mutiny. And what, now, was the state of crew morale aboard* Faraway Quest?

Mayhew answered the unspoken question. "Not bad, John. Not bad. Most of the boys and girls trust you." He laughed. "But, of course, they don't know you as well as I do."

"Or I," added Sonya.

The commodore scowled. "You're ganging up on me. Billy Williams should be here, to even the odds."

"He's an extremely conscientious spaceman," said Sonya. "A hull inspection is far more important, in his book, than a few drinks and some social chitchat with his captain before dinner."

"And so it should be," Grimes told her firmly. "All the same, I wanted him here. He's my second-in-command, just as you are supposed to be my intelligence officer . . ."

"Not *your* intelligence officer, John. I hold my commission from the Federation's Survey Service, not the Navy of the Rim Worlds Confederacy."

"And neither the Federation nor the Confederacy is in existence yet—and won't be for a few million years. But I wanted you to flap your physical ears, just as I wanted Ken to flap his psionic ones."

"Nothing to report, sir," replied Sonya smartly. "The troops are well fed and happy, Commodore, sir. The last batch of jungle juice that the biochemists cooked up has met with the full approval of all hands and the cook. Even Mr. Hendriks seems to be happy. He's doing something esoteric to the fire-control circuits so that he'll be able to play a symphony, using his full orchestra, using only the little finger of his left hand. He hopes."

"I know. And I'm taking damn good care that it never gets past the drawing board. And the bold major?"

"He and his pongoes seem to be monopolizing the gym. I'll not be surprised if they start wearing black belts as part of their uniforms."

"Mphm. I could wish that some of the others were as enthusiastic keep-fitters . . . And what is *your* story, Ken?"

"I've been . . . snooping," admitted the telepath unhappily. "I realize its necessity, although I don't like doing it. Throughout the ship, insofar as I have been able to discover, morale is surprisingly high. After all, it's not as though Kinsolving were a very attractive planet, and we *are* going somewhere definite. But . . ."

"But what?"

"Hendriks isn't happy."

"My heart fair bleeds for him."

"Let me finish. Hendriks isn't happy. That's why he's shut himself up with his toys, to play by himself in a quiet corner."

"I suppose he's sulking because he wasn't allowed to play at master gunner on Kinsolving's Planet."

"That's only one of the reasons. Mainly he's sulking because his fine new friends won't have anything more to do with him."

"You mean Dalzell and his marines?"

"Yes."

"Interesting. And what about the major and his bully-boys?"

"I don't know, John."

"You don't know? Don't tell me that your conscience got the better of you."

"No, it's not that. But Dalzell and his people aren't spacemen; they're Marines. Soldiers."

"And so what?"

"Did you ever hear of the Ordonsky Technique?"

"No . . ."

"I have," said Sonya. "If I'd stayed on the Active List of the Intelligence Branch I would have taken the tests to determine whether or not I was a suitable subject." She added a little smugly, "Probably I would not have been."

"I don't think that you would, Sonya," Mayhew said. "As a general rule it works only on people whose I.Q.s are nothing to write home about. I'm not at all surprised that it was effective on the Marine sergeant and the other ranks, but on Dalzell . . . It all goes to show, I suppose, that it doesn't take all that much intelligence to be a soldier. Do what you're told, and volunteer for nothing . . ."

"At times," remarked the commodore, "that has been my own philosophy. But this Ordonsky. And his technique . . ."

"A system of mental training that makes the mind impenetrable to the pryings of a telepath. Almost a sort of induced schizophrenia. One part of the mind broadcasts—forgive the use of the term—nonsense rhymes, so powerfully as to mask what the rest of the mind is thinking. The use of the technique was proposed as a means whereby military personnel can be made immune to interrogation of any kind after capture. It involves a long period of training, combined with sessions of deep hypnosis. It does not work at all well, if at all, on people accustomed to thinking independently. I had heard, as a matter of fact, that the top trick cyclists of the Rim Worlds Marine Corps had been playing around with it."

"This is a fine time to tell us. So you just don't know what my brown boys are thinking, is that it?"

"That's it, John. Dalzell's defenses went up as soon as he felt the first light touch of my mental probe. So did those of his men. They're not talking to Hendriks any more, they're just not sharing their childish secrets with him. So . . ."

"So we bug the marines' mess deck," said Sonya.

"Do we?" asked Grimes. "Do we? Dare we? Would we? Can I order Sparky Daniels to plant bugs all through the bloody ship? Oh, I could—but what would *that* do to morale?"

"I'm no bug queen," Sonya told him, "but I think I could knock up a couple or three with materials to hand. *And* plant them, without being spotted."

"All right," said Grimes at last. "You can try—as long as you promise me that you can do it with no risk to yourself. But it wouldn't at all surprise me to find out that some bright marine has done a course in anti-bugging."

He was not surprised.

~ Chapter 6 ~

TAKE A PERSONALIZED FINGER-RING-type transceiver and plant it some place where it cannot easily be seen but from where it can pick up normal, or even whispered, conversation—and you have a quite effective bug. Have a receiver-cum-recorder tuned to the frequency of the transceiver, continuously monitoring—and you're in business. Take a corporal of marines who has done a few courses in electronics and who has been ordered by his superior officer to be alert for bugging—and you're not in business for long.

Sonya, accompanying Grimes and Williams on Daily Rounds, had managed to plant two of her special finger-rings, one of them among the glittering flowers and fruit of the Eblis jewel cactus that was the pride and joy of the marines' mess deck—they regarded the thing as a sort of mascot—and the other in a ventilation duct in Dalzell's cabin. A couple of recorders, locked in the commodore's filing cabinet, completed the assembly.

Grimes, Williams, Mayhew and Sonya listened rather guiltily to the results of the first (and only) day's monitoring.

Male voice: Hey, boys! Old Spiky's sprouted a new jewel!

Another voice: How did you find it, Corp?

First voice: Easy. The bloody thing's radiatin' like a bastard. The major thought that there might be somethin' like this left lyin' around. For once he was right.

Another voice: Ain't no flies on the major. Can I have a look at it,

Corp? Thanks. Oh, here's a thing, an' a very pretty thing, an' who's the owner of this pretty thing?

Another voice: Need you ask? The bleedin' duchess, that's who. Mrs. snooty ex-Federation Survey Service Grimes.

Another voice: Careful. She's not so "ex." She's still a commander on their Reserve List . . .

First voice: An' so bleedin' what? I'll spell it out to you. One—we're members of the Marine Corps of the Confederacy . . .

Voices: We're the worst curse of the universe, We're the toughest ever seen, And we proudly bear the title of A Confederate marine!

First voice: Pipe down, you bastards. Let me finish. One—we're members of the Marine Corps of the Confederacy. Two—the Federation ain't liable to happen for another trillion years or so.

Another voice: An' neither's the Confederacy, Corp.

First voice: But we're here, ain't we? Gimme that ring back, Timms. I'm takin' it to the major. Thanks. But first . . . Ah. That's fixed *you.*

There was nothing more on that tape but a continuous faint crackling. The other recorder at first played back only the small sounds that a man would make alone in his quarters. There was the clink of glass on glass and the noise of liquid being poured. There was a sigh of satisfaction. There was an almost tuneless humming. Then there was the sharp rapping of knuckles on plastic-covered metal.

Major: Come in, come in. Oh, it's you, Corporal.

Corporal: Yessir. I found this, sir. Mixed up in Old Spiky, it was.

Major: Is it working?

Corporal: It *was* working, sir.

Major: Oh. Oh, oh. And I always thought, until now, that the commodore was an officer *and* a gentleman. This shakes my faith in human nature. First of all, that bloody commissioned tea-cup reader, and now *this.*

Corporal: Careful, sir.

Major: You mean . . . ?

Corporal: Yes, sir.

Major: Why the hell didn't you say so before?

And that was all, save for minor scrapings and scufflings that told of a search being made. It was not a long one; presumably the Corporal had some sort of detecting equipment. And then the second transceiver went dead.

Sonya sighed, "Oh, well. It was a good try."

"A try, anyhow," said Grimes.

"An' you'd better not try again," warned Williams. "Come to that, it'll be as well if you don't come with us again on Rounds—not in Marine country, anyhow. Those bastard's be quite capable of rigging a booby trap, just out o' spite. Somethin' that'd look like a perfectly normal shipboard accident." He laughed. "There's an old saying. Listeners never hear good o' themselves! We learned the truth of that!"

"We also learned," said Mayhew, "that our brown boys aren't as smart as they think they are. If they were really bright they wouldn't have let us know that they'd found the bugs." Then he muttered something, in a hurt voice, about "commissioned tea-cup readers."

"But we're no forrarder," said Grimes glumly.

And you can say that again, he told himself. In the old days, the good old days of wooden ships and sail, the Marines had been the most trusted and most trustworthy personnel aboard a vessel, being berthed between the quarterdeck and the seamen's mess decks, a sea-borne police force, ever on guard against mutiny.

But now . . .

Then the commodore allowed himself a faint smile. After all, a certain Corporal Churchill had been among the *Bounty* mutineers.

"What are you grinning about?" demanded Sonya.

"Nothing," he said. "Nothing at all, Mrs. Bligh."

✥ Chapter 7 ✥

INWARD, HOMEWARD BOUND sped the old *Quest*, boring through the warped continuum, dragged down the dark dimensions by the tumbling, ever-precessing rotors of her interstellar drive. Inward she ran, in from the Rim, in from the frontier of the ultimate dark—and yet, paradoxically, inward to the Unknown. Past suns—yellow, and white, and blue, and ruddy, dwarfs and giants—she scudded, driving through the stellar maelstrom like a bullet through a snowstorm. Planetary systems she passed in her flight—and on none of them, so far as could be determined, had intelligence yet engendered advanced technology. There was life, said Mayhew, on most of those worlds—and intelligent life on some of them. There was life, intelligent life, but, so far as he could determine by his monitoring of stray, random thoughts, none of those races had yet progressed beyond the level of the nomadic hunter, the primitive agriculturalist—and none of them had yet produced a trained telepath. Daniels, the electronic communications officer, was less definite than his psionic rival. He was able to say that nobody in the worlds that they passed was using the Carlotti Communications System or its equivalent but told Grimes that the *Quest*'s Mannschenn Drive would have to be shut down before any NST—normal space-time—radio signals could be received. Mayhew, however, had been so firm in his opinions that it was obvious that such an investigation would be only a waste of time.

And so we're the first . . . thought Grimes. *The first spaceship . . .* A fragment of archaic poetry came into his mind.

We were the first that ever burst
Into that silent sea . . .

Then he remembered the fate of Coleridge's Ancient Mariner. *There had just better not be any shooting of albatrosses,* he told himself firmly.

Inward sped the *Quest,* and the commodore realized that her voyage would soon be over. He could feel, in his bones, that Earth was getting close. Not the next sun, nor the next, but the one after that would be Sol. He didn't know how he knew—but he *knew.*

Nonetheless, he wanted to be able to rely upon more than a hunch. He told Carnaby to have all of *Faraway Quest's* surveying instruments in readiness. "Look for nine planets," he said. "Or possibly ten . . ."

"*Ten,* sir? I thought that the Solarian System had only nine planets."

"So it does—in *our* Time. But this is not our Time. The so-called Asteroid Belt, the zone of planetary debris between the orbits of Mars and Jupiter, was once a sizeable world. Perhaps, *when* we are now, it is still a sizeable world . . ."

"Nine planets, then, sir. Possibly ten. Any other special features?"

"You've never been to Earth, have you, Mr. Carnaby?"

"No, sir."

"As you should know, the sixth planet—or possibly, the seventh—is one of the wonders of the universe. Saturn is not the only gas giant, of course, neither is it the only planet with rings—but it is the most spectacular."

"A ringed planet, then. And earth itself? Any special thing to look for?"

"Yes. One satellite. One natural satellite, that is. A big one. More of a sister world than a moon."

"Should be easy enough to identify, sir. But there's just one more point. There aren't any charts of Earth in the ship's memory bank."

"We didn't know that we should be coming this way, did we?

But I think that I shall be able to draw some maps of sorts from memory. How much use they'll be depends on how far back we are in the Past . . ."

"Surely the effects of erosion shouldn't be all that great, sir."

Grimes sighed. Carnaby was a good spaceman, an excellent navigator—and a trade-school boy. He was qualified, very well qualified to guide a ship between worlds, but knew nothing of the forces that had shaped, that were still shaping, those worlds. His specialized education had taught him his job and no more. Of what use to a navigator was knowledge of cataclysmic epochs of mountain building, of the effects of climatic change with consequent variation in sea level, of continental drift?

He said, "We might be able to recognize Earth from the maps that I draw. If we don't, it just might not be my fault."

But Earth was, after all, quite recognizable.

≈ Chapter 8 ≈

SATURN, HOWEVER, was the first member of Sol's family approached closely by *Faraway Quest*. The huge planet was not quite as the Commodore remembered it; the rings were even more spectacular than they had been (would be) in his proper time. It was while he and most of his crew were admiring the fantastically splendid sight that Daniels, able at last to listen out on his NST equipment, reported the reception of radio signals that seemed to be emanating from one of the inner worlds.

Reluctantly, Grimes, accompanied by Sonya and Mayhew, left the control room, went down to the compartment in which the main receivers and transmitters were housed. He stood beside the little radio officer who, hunched over his controls, was making fine adjustments, listening intently to the eerie whisperings that drifted from the speaker. They could have been music; there was an odd sort of rhythm to them. They could have been speech, something so prosaic as a weather report or a news bulletin. One thing was certain; they issued from no human throat.

Grimes turned to Sonya. "What do you make of it?"

"What am I supposed to make of it?" she countered.

"I'm asking you. You're the family linguist."

"It's no language that I've ever heard, John."

"Mphm." After all, thought Grimes, he had been expecting rather too much from his wife. He turned to Daniels. "Can you get a bearing, Sparky?"

"I'm trying now, sir . . . 177 relative . . . 180 . . . 185 . . . Damn it, it keeps changing . . ."

The commodore laughed. "'Relative' is the operative word. We're in orbit about Saturn, you know, maintaining a fixed attitude relative to the planet's surface . . ." He pulled his empty pipe from his pocket, played with it. He would liked to have filled and lit it, but tobacco, now, was severely rationed. He visualized the planetary setup as he had studied it in the *Quest's* big plotting tank. At this moment the ship was still on the sunward side of Saturn. Inward from her, almost in a straight line, were Mars and Earth. Radio broadcasts—from Earth? In a nonhuman language? Had there, after all, been pre-human cultures, civilizations? Intelligent dinosaurs, for example? Had it been such a good idea to return to Earth?

But what about Mars? A few artifacts had been found on that world, if artifacts they were. Time-corroded and -eroded they could well have been no more than fragments of meteoric metal roughly shaped over the millennia by natural forces. There had been the so-called Venus of Syrtis Major, a piece of alloy resembling bronze that had the likeness, the very crude likeness, to a woman, that bore far less semblance to the form of a woman than did the famous Colossus of Eblis, the huge, wind-sculptured monolith in the Painted Badlands of that world, to the figure of a man.

"Ken," said Grimes to Mayhew, a little reproachfully, "Sparky's picking up someone. Or something. What have *you* to report?"

The telepath flushed. "I've already told you, sir, that there's life, intelligent life, human life in towards the sun from our present position."

"That . . . noise isn't human," said Sonya.

"No . . ." admitted Mayhew. His face assumed a faraway expression. Grimes did not need to be told what he was doing. He would be mobilizing his department, putting it on full alert. He would be talking—wordlessly, telepathically—to Clarisse, still in the control room, informing her and instructing her. He would be awakening his psionic amplifier, the naked brain of a dog that floated in its tank of nutrient fluids in his quarters. Soon the three brains—the man's brain, the woman's brain and the dog's brain—would be functioning as one powerful receiver, reaching out from the ship, sensitive to the faintest whisper. Psionic transmission and reception was practicable across light years; surely Mayhew and his team would be capable of picking up signals from a source only light minutes distant.

Mayhew said, his voice barely audible, "Yes. There is a . . . whispering. I . . . I was not listening for it, until now. I was—forgive me for borrowing your technicalities, Sparky—tuned in to the psionic broadcast from Earth. That's human enough. Raw emotions: hate, fear, lust. Thirst and hunger. The satisfaction of animal appetites. *You* know. But there *is* something else. Not fainter. Just on a different . . . frequency. I can *feel* it now. It's more . . . civilized? More . . . intellectual. How can I put it? Yes . . . This way, perhaps. Once, I was present at a chess tournament. All the Rim Worlds masters were competing, and there were masters from other worlds. I shouldn't have . . . snooped, but I did. I couldn't resist the temptation. It was . . . fascinating. To *feel* those cold minds ticking over, playing their games many moves in advance, their universe no more (and no less) than tiers of checkered boards, inhabited only by stylized pieces . . ."

"Chess," said Grimes, "is a very old game."

"I used chess," Mayhew told him, "only as an analogy."

"Never mind the parlor games," snapped Sonya. "What you're trying to tell us, Ken, is that there's a highly developed civilization in towards the sun from where we are now. Right?"

"Right."

"And it could be on Earth?"

"I . . . I don't think so. The images, the images that I can pick up, the visual images, the sensory images, are . . . vague. The people are humanoid, I think. But not human. Definitely not human. And I get the impression of a world that's mainly desert. A dying world . . ."

"Mars?" murmured Grimes. Then, more definitely, "Mars."

The return to Earth could wait, he thought. On the home planet there would be, as yet, no organized science, no scientists. On Mars, if Mayhew were to be believed (and there was no reason why he should not be), there would be no shortage of either. Scientists, even alien scientists, could do more to help *Faraway Quest's* people than high priests or shamans.

He said, "We set trajectory for Mars. The Martians may not be human, but they'll be more our kind of people than Stone Age savages on Earth."

"You hope . . ." said Sonya sardonically.

"I know," he replied smugly.

"I . . . I'm not so sure . . ." whispered Mayhew.

～ Chapter 9 ～

PROVIDED THAT NORMAL CARE is exercised, the interstellar drive may be employed within the confines of a planetary system. Grimes had no doubts as to the ability of his officers to handle such a not-very-exceptional feat of navigation. So, after the lapse of only one Standard Day of ship's time, *Faraway Quest* was hanging in orbit above the red planet Mars.

Looking out through the control room viewports at the ruddy globe he wondered, at first, if there had been some further displacement in Time. Mars looked as it had looked when he had last seen it—how many years ago? There were cities, and irrigation canals with broad strips of greenery on either side of them, a gleaming icecap marking the north polar regions. There were the two little moons, scurrying around their primary.

Said Mayhew, "*They* know we're here . . ."

Demanded Grimes grumpily, "And who the hell are *they*, when they're up and dressed?"

"I . . . I don't know yet . . ."

"Doesn't much matter," contributed Williams, "as long as they tell us that this is Liberty Hall and that we can spit on the mat and call the cat a bastard!"

"Mphm," grunted Grimes around the stem of the empty pipe that he was holding between his teeth. "Mphm." Then, speaking almost to himself only, "What the hell happened—will happen—to those people? The cities, the canals—and damn all there when Man first landed but a very few dubious relics . . ."

"Perhaps *we* happened to them," said Sonya somberly.

"Come off it. We aren't as bad as all that."

"Speak for yourself," she told him, looking pointedly towards Hendriks, who was seated at the console of his battle organ.

Grimes laughed. "I don't think, somehow, that one ship, only a lightly armed auxiliary cruiser at that, could destroy a flourishing civilization with its own high level of technology." He gestured at the telescope screen, where Carnaby had succeeded in displaying a picture of one of the cities. It was as though they were hanging only a few hundred feet above the taller towers. "Look at that. The people who erected those buildings are at least our equals as engineers!"

Tall and graceful stood the buildings, the essential delicacy of their design possible only on a low-gravity planet. Glass and stone and glittering metal filigree, the materials blended in a harmony that, although alien, was undeniably beautiful . . . The sweeping catenaries of gleaming cables strung between the towers, some of which supported bridges, but most of which were ornamental only or filling some unguessable function . . . Green parks with explosions of blue and yellow and scarlet, and all the intermediate shades, that were flowering trees and shrubs . . . The emerald green of the parks, and the diamond spray of the fountains, arcing high and gracefully in shimmering rainbows . . . *Surely,* thought Grimes, *an extravagance on this world of all worlds!* The people, walking slowly along their streets and through their gardens, even from this foreshortened viewpoint undeniably humanoid, but with something about them that was not quite human . . .

"Carlotti antennae," said Daniels suddenly. "Odd that we didn't receive any signals from them while we were running under Mannschenn Drive . . ."

Yes, Carlotti antennae—or, if not Carlotti antennae, something indistinguishable from them. Mounted on the higher towers were the gleaming ovoids of metal, each like a *Mobius strip* distorted into elliptical shape. But they were motionless, not continually rotating about their long axes.

"Could be a religious symbol . . ." suggested Grimes at last. "After all, we have—or will have—crosses, and stars and crescents, and hammers and sickles, and what else only the Odd Gods of the Galaxy know . . . Why not a *Mobius strip*?"

Mayhew began to speak, slowly and tonelessly. "They have telepaths. They have a telepath. He . . . He is entering my mind. There is the problem of language, you understand. Of idiom. But his message is clear."

"And what is it?" the commodore demanded.

"It is . . . It is that we are not wanted. It is that those people cannot be bothered with us. To them we are an unnecessary nuisance, and one that has cropped up at a most inconvenient time."

Grimes' prominent ears reddened. He growled, "All right, we're a nuisance. But surely we're entitled to tell our story, to ask for assistance."

"What . . . What shall I tell them, sir?"

"The truth, of course. That we're castaways in Time."

"I'll . . . I'll try," said Mayhew doubtfully.

There was silence in the control room while the commodore and his officers looked at Mayhew and Clarisse. The two telepaths sat quietly in their chairs, the woman's right hand in her husband's left hand. The face of each of them wore a faraway expression. Their eyes were half closed. Clarisse's lips moved almost imperceptibly as she verbalized her thoughts.

Then Mayhew said, "It is no good. They want nothing at all to do with us. They tell me—how shall I put it?—they tell me that we are big enough and ugly enough to look after ourselves."

"Try to persuade them," ordered Grimes, "that it will be to their advantage to allow us to land. There must be some knowledge that they do not possess which they can gain from us—just as we hope to gain knowledge from them . . ."

There was another long silence.

Mayhew said at last, "They say, 'Go away. Leave us to our own devices.'"

Grimes knew that he had often been referred to in his younger days as a stubborn bastard, and on many occasions latterly as a stubborn old bastard. He had never been offended by the epithet. It was his nature to be stubborn. He was prepared to hang there in the Martian sky, an artificial, uninvited satellite, until such time as these Martians condescended to talk to him. Surely there must be some among their number capable of curiosity, of wondering who these strangers were and where they had come from.

"They say," said Mayhew, "'go away.'"

"Mphm," grunted Grimes.

"They say," said Mayhew after a long interval, "'go away, or we will make you.'"

"Bluff," commented Grimes. "Tell them, or tell your telepathic boyfriend, that I want to talk to whoever's in charge down there. Whoever's *really* in charge."

"Go away," whispered Clarisse. "Go away. Go away. The message is still '*Go away.*'"

"Tell them . . ." began Grimes—and, "Look!" shouted Williams.

Coming at them on an intersecting trajectory was a spacecraft. ("It isn't showing on the radar, it isn't showing on the radar!" Carnaby was saying to whoever would listen.) It appeared to be large, although, with no means of determining its range, this could have been an illusion. It was an odd-looking construction, with wide, graceful wings. There were no indications of rocket exhaust.

"Like a bird . . ." somebody murmured.

So they've finally condescended to notice us, thought Grimes smugly. Then another thought crossed his mind and he turned to Hendriks. But he was too late to give the order, *Hold your fire!* that trembled on his lips. Invisible but lethal, a laser beam slashed out from the *Quest*, shearing a wing from the Martian ship. She fell away from her trajectory, the severed plane tumbling after her. She spiraled away and down, down, falling like a leaf towards the distant planetary surface.

. . . With my crossbow I shot the albatross . . .

But this was no time for quoting archaic poetry to oneself. While Mayhew whispered, unnecessarily, "*They* are annoyed . . ." the commodore barked his orders. "Inertial drive—maximum thrust!" Acceleration slammed him deep into the padding of his chair.

"Mannschenn Drive—start!" He did not know what weaponry the Martians had at their disposal and had no intention of hanging around to find out.

The gyroscopes of the Mannschenn Drive whined querulously as their rate of revolution built up to its maximum. Precession was initiated. Outlines wavered and colors sagged down the spectrum as *Faraway Quest* lurched into the warped continuum engendered by her temporal precession field.

Astern of her, harmless yet spectacular, there was a great flare of actinic light, a near miss. Intentional or accidental? But Hendriks' shooting had been intentional enough.

"I saved the ship," the gunnery officer was saying. "I saved the ship."

"That will do, Mr. Hendriks," Grimes told him coldly. "I will see you after we've set trajectory."

"Hendriks saved the ship," Dalzell was saying, in a voice louder than a whisper.

I wish I had an albatross to hang around each of your bloody necks, thought Grimes viciously.

~ Chapter 10 ~

HENDRIKS had been stubbornly unrepentant. Hendriks had said, "But, sir, attack is the best means of defense." And Grimes realized that it would be practically impossible for him to inflict any punishment, that in these abnormal circumstances his disciplinary powers were little more than a fiction, still subscribed to by the *Quest's* people—but for how much longer? He was their captain, their leader, only so long as they continued to accept him as such. If it came to a showdown, on how many of his crew could he count? On Sonya, of course, and on Williams, on Mayhew and on Clarisse, on Carnaby . . . Certainly not on Major Dalzell and his marines. Probably not on Commander Davis and his assistant engineers. Possibly on Sparky Daniels . . .

To maintain any sort of control at all the commodore had to keep on doing things, had to continue pulling metaphorical rabbits out of that metaphorical top hat. He was like a man who has to keep running to avoid falling over. Well, he certainly had run. He had run in from the rim of the Galaxy to the Solar System, he had run from Saturn to Mars, and from Mars to Earth.

There was no doubt that the world beneath them was the home planet. The outlines of the continents, discernible through the breaks in the cloud cover, were as Grimes had sketched them from memory. It was obvious that *Faraway Quest* had been thrown back into the comparatively recent Past, geologically speaking. The polar ice caps seemed to be a little more extensive than they had been (would be) in Grimes' proper-time, but there was no excessive glaciation. Probably the sea level, was not quite the same, and the mountains might be a little higher—but this was Earth.

Carnaby, acting on the Commodore's instructions, had put the ship into a twenty-four-hour orbit, equatorial, on a meridian that roughly bisected the great, pear-shaped mass of Africa. Then, using the inertial drive, he pushed her downwards and northwards. The Mediterranean Sea, with the Italian boot aiming a kick at the misshapen Sicilian football, was unmistakable, in spite of the drifting cloud formations. It would be early autumn down there, perhaps not the best season in which to make an exploratory landing—but it was in this hemisphere that civilization would, perhaps, be found. The Pyramid builders? The glory that was Greece, or the grandeur that was Rome? Mayhew, unethically reading Grimes' thoughts, allowed himself a faint grin. "No, John," he said softly. "There aren't any pyramids yet, and there's no Acropolis. But there are cities. Of a sort."

"And ships," said Grimes. "There must be ships. I hope that it's not too late in the year to find any of them at sea . . ."

"And where the hell else would you find ships?" demanded Sonya tartly.

"In port, in snug harbors," replied Grimes. "Sitting the winter months out in comfort. In the early days of navigation men always avoided coming to grips with the weather."

She said something unkind about wooden ships and iron men.

Grimes, taking over the controls from his navigator, ignored her. Down he drove *Faraway Quest*, down, down. Carefully, he adjusted his line of descent, aiming for the eastern shore of the Mediterranean, for an imaginary dot on the sea roughly midway between Cyprus and the Palestinian coast. Were Tyre and Sidon in existence yet? Had the Phoenicians emerged as one of the pioneering seafaring nations?

Down he drove the ship, down, down. She was in atmosphere now, falling through the first tenuous wisps of gas, but slowly, slowly. *Faraway Quest* shuddered and complained as the medium through which she was being driven became denser, as upper-atmosphere turbulence buffeted her. But she had been designed to withstand far greater stresses. Through the high cirrus, the filmy mares' tails, she dropped, faster now, but still well under control. White-gleaming cumulus was below her now, a snowy complexity of rounded peaks and shadowy canyons—below her and then, seconds later, all about her, a pearly mist obscuring the viewports.

They cleared suddenly—and there was the sea. Even from this height, white ridges of foam could be seen on the slate-blue surface. And . . . And what was that dark speck?

Grimes checked *Faraway Quest*'s descent, held her where she was, then turned the controls over to Carnaby. Williams already had the big telescope trained and focused and the picture was showing on the screen. Grimes looked at it. Yes, it was a ship all right. Graceless, broad-beamed, with a single mast, stepped amidships, a low poop from which jutted a steering sweep. Other sweeps, six to a side, were flailing at the water. She seemed to be making heavy weather of it.

"Keep her as she is," said Grimes to Carnaby—and then, to Williams, "She's all yours, commander. Look after her till I get back." There was no need for any further orders. The Commodore had assumed that a solitary surface ship would be sighted and had planned accordingly. He, personally, would take one of *Faraway Quest*'s pinnaces down to make an inspection at closer range, accompanied only by Sonya and by Mayhew. The pinnace was capable of functioning as a submarine—after all, the *Quest* was a survey ship and carried the equipment necessary for the exploration of newly discovered planets. From the pinnace Grimes would be able to observe without being observed. And even if he were seen by a handful of ignorant seamen, what of it? The pinnace would merely be yet another sea monster to be added to the probably long list of those already reported.

He left the control room and, followed by Sonya and Mayhew, made his way down to the boat bay.

Slowly and carefully Grimes eased the little craft out and away from the parent ship. He looked at the *Quest* as she hung there, just below the cloud base. He had hoped that the dull silver of her hull would blend with the light gray of the cloud—but, at this range at any rate, she was glaringly obvious. It was unlikely that any of the mariners would look up and see her, but it was possible. The Commodore called Williams on the pinnace's transceiver and, seconds later, the grumble of *Faraway Quest's* inertial drive deepened to a muffled roar as she rose to hide herself in the vaporous cover.

Grimes brought the pinnace around in a wide arc, intending to land in the sea astern of and to leeward of the laboring ship. It was unlikely that anybody would be looking aft. As he closed her he began to appreciate the situation. The mast was canted at a drunken angle; one or more stays must have parted. From the yard fluttered rags of canvas, untidy pennants in the gale. So her sail had been blown to shreds just before she was dismasted . . . And what was the primitive captain doing, or trying to do, now? Grimes put himself in that seaman's place. Yes, he was hove to, doing his best to keep his bows to the wind and sea. *All very well and good,* thought the commodore, *when you have reliable main engines, but not so easy when your only motive power consists of sweeps manned by exhausted rowers . . .*

But there was the sea, only a few feet below the pinnace, and a very nasty sea it looked, too. Grimes put the little craft into a steep dive, felt his seat belt bite deeply into his body as her forward momentum was checked, as she plunged into the curling crest of a wave. But he had to get down; only a few feet under, the surface conditions would be much calmer. The whine of the pumps was audible above the hammering of the inertial drive as water was sucked into the ballast tanks. Briefly the control cabin viewports were obscured by a smother of white spray that was replaced by a blue-green translucency. The violent rocking motion eased to a gentle swaying.

Grimes extruded the periscope on its long mast. The screen came alive, showing the white-crested seas and, finally, the squattering hulk of the little surface ship. *I'd rather be here than there,* thought Grimes. He put the laboring vessel right ahead, then rapidly closed the range. As he watched, exasperation began to take the place of sympathy. Didn't that shipmaster know the rudiments of seamanship? These might be very early days in the history of sea transport but, even so, several millennia must have elapsed since the first men ventured out from the shore in coracles or dugout canoes. He muttered something about people who would be incapable of navigating a plastic duck across a bathtub.

"And what has he done wrong—or what isn't he doing right?" asked Sonya who, although no telepath, possessed more than her fair share of wifely intuition.

"It's a case of what he isn't doing at all," grumbled Grimes.

"All right. You're the expert. What should he be doing?"

"He's in trouble," Grimes told her.

"A blinding glimpse of the obvious."

"Let me finish. He's in trouble. Unless he can keep that unhandy little bitch's head to the sea he'll be swamped . . ."

"I'm no seaman, my dear, but even I can see that that is what he's doing."

"Yes, yes. But there's a way of doing it that does not involve his oarsmen pulling their hearts out. I thought that the technique was as old as ships, but I must be wrong. Oh, well, I suppose that somebody had to invent it."

"And what is this famous technique?"

"The sea anchor, of course."

"Isn't the sea too deep here to use an anchor?"

Grimes sighed. "A sea anchor is not the sort of anchor you were thinking of. It's not a hunk of iron or, as it probably is in these times, stone. Ideally it's a canvas drogue, not unlike the wind-sock you still see used on some primitive air-landing strips. It's paid out from the bows of a ship on the end of a long line. It is, or should be, completely submerged and not affected by the wind. The ship, of course, is so affected and is blown to leeward of the sea anchor, which has sufficient grip on the water to keep her head up to wind and sea. If you haven't a proper drogue, of course, almost anything will do, as long as it's only just buoyant and has sufficient surface to act as a drag." He glared at the periscope screen. "And there's that nong, sweating his guts out on his steering oar while his crew, at the sweeps, must be on the point of dropping dead with exhaustion. Damn it all, I hate to see a ship, any ship, in trouble! If only I could tell the stupid bastard what to do . . ."

"You can, John," said Mayhew quietly.

Grimes laughed. "All right, all right, so that skipper's not the only stupid bastard around here. I forgot that you can transmit as well as receive. Do you think you can get a message to him?"

"I'm . . . I'm trying now. I'm . . . inside his mind. I don't like it much. He's terrified, of course. And it's not only a healthy fear of the elements, but also a superstitious dread . . . He didn't make the proper sacrifices before pushing out on this voyage, and he knows it. The wine that he poured out on to the altar was very cheap and inferior stuff, almost vinegar . . . And the goat that had its throat cut was diseased and no good for anything else . . ."

"Mphm. So if you're going to do anything, do it properly or not at all. But can you get through to him, Ken?"

"I'm . . . I'm trying. He *feels* something. He's rationalizing, if you can call it that. He thinks, if you can call it thinking, that the sea god is condescending to answer his grovelling prayers. But the superstition . . . It's sickening!"

"Never mind that. He's typical of his day and age. *Be* a sea god! Prod him up the arse with your trident and make him *do* something!"

Mayhew managed a sickly smile. He said, "I don't like doing it, but it's the only way . . ." He whispered, vocalizing the thoughts that he was striving to transmit, *"Hear, and ye shall be saved . . . Heed, and ye shall be saved . . ."*

"Good," said Grimes. "Keep it up. As soon as you're through to him, *tell* him. You heard me explaining the sea-anchor technique. He won't have a drogue, of course, but anything at all will do. Anything."

There was a long silence, broken at last by the telepath. "It's hard, John, trying to explain modern seamanship to that primitive savage."

"*Modern* seamanship?" scoffed Grimes. "This is going back to the first, the very first beginnings of seamanship!"

"Perhaps the idea of a sacrifice . . ." whispered Mayhew.

"General Average!" laughed the commodore. "A pity we haven't got a Lloyd's underwriter along to sort it out!" Then, "You *are* getting through, Ken. One of the two men on the steering oar has just gone below . . . Yes. And a sweep on either side has been shipped . . ."

He watched the periscope screen with gleeful anticipation. So the primitive shipmaster was experiencing a long overdue rush of brains to the head—and he, Grimes, Honorary Admiral of one of the surface navies of Tharn, holder of an Aquarian Master Mariner's Certificate of Competency, was responsible. Sonya glared at him as he began to sing, softly and tunelessly, an archaic Terran sea chantey:

"Blow the man down, bullies, blow the man down. Way, hey, blow the man down! Blow him away right to Liverpool town—Oh, give us the time to blow the man down!"

Yes, here they came on deck, a half dozen of them, dragging something. *Take it for'ard, you unseamanlike cows,* muttered Grimes. *Not aft . . .* Then he decided that the skipper probably knew what he was doing; it could be that his clumsy vessel would ride better, would ship less water if brought up to the sea anchor with the weather astern. But what was happening in the poop? Mutiny? There seemed to be some sort of scrimmage in progress.

Ah, at last. The seamen, acting as one, were lifting what looked like a bundle of rags. *"Not big enough . . ."* muttered Grimes. *"Not nearly big enough . . ."* They lifted the bundle of rags and dropped it over the stern. *"And where the hell's your sea-anchor line?"* demanded Grimes furiously.

Then, just before a hissing rain squall blotted out all vision, the commodore and his companions saw that the thing jettisoned was a man.

⮾ Chapter 11 ⮽

THERE WAS ONLY ONE THING to do, and Grimes did it. But he could not be too hasty; for him to surface right alongside the laboring ship would be out of the question. She was making slow headway against the sea, however, gradually pulling away from that small, dark figure struggling in the water. The periscope was useless in the heavy, driving rain, so the pinnace's fantastically sensitive radar was brought into operation.

On the screen were two targets, one large and one small, and the smaller target was showing only intermittently in the clutter. The range between the two blips was opening. The commodore adjusted his speed to maintain his distance off from the larger target, steered so as to come directly beneath the smaller one. It was tricky work, but somehow he managed it. Suddenly there was a distinct shock, a continued vibration. Grimes guessed what it was. A drowning man will clutch at a straw—and a periscope standard is considerably more substantial.

Grimes started to blow his tanks, but as soon as the pinnace rose into the layer of turbulence just below the sea surface the motion was dangerously violent. He tried to correct it with the pinnace's control surfaces, but it was impossible to do so. Hastily he turned to the inertial drive controls, switched from *Ahead* to *Lift*. The unrhythmic hammering of the engine was deafening in the confined space of the little vessel's cabin and she went up like a rocket, lurching far over as a sea caught her, but recovering. Was the man still there? The lens of

344

the periscope could be swivelled so that the upper hull could be inspected. This was done—and the screen showed a huddled mass of dark rags wrapped around the base of the standard.

"We have to bring him in," said Grimes.

"By 'we,'" said Sonya, "you imply 'you.'" She unstrapped herself from her seat, and Mayhew followed suit.

"Be careful," warned Grimes.

"Good and careful," she said.

The upper hatch slid open and fresh air—cool, humid, salty—gusted in, and with it a spatter of chilly rain. But after the weeks of canned atmosphere, it was like sparkling wine after flat water. Grimes inhaled deeply and gratefully, watched Sonya clamber up the short ladder and vanish, followed by Mayhew. He heard her voice, faint but clear over the whining of the wind, the drumming of the rain, "Don't be afraid. Nobody's going to hurt you . . ." Surely that pitiful heap of human jetsam would understand the tone if not the words themselves.

Then, from Mayhew, "He's terrified . . ."

"And so would you be. *Help* me, Ken. Get into his mind or whatever it is you do, and tranquilize him . . ."

"I'm . . . I'm trying, Sonya . . ."

"Then try a little harder. His hands are *frozen* onto the periscope . . ." She continued in a crooning voice, "You're safe now . . . Just relax . . . We've got you . . ."

Another voice replied—high-pitched, gabbling. Grimes thought that he distinguished the word *elohim*.

"Yes . . . yes . . . hold on to me . . . *Give me a hand, Ken, or we'll both be overboard*! Yes . . . yes . . . hold on now . . . Carefully . . . Carefully . . . This way . . ."

First one of Sonya's shapely legs appeared through the circular hatch, then the other. Her feet sought and found the ladder rungs. Her buttocks in her rain-soaked skirt came into view, descended slowly. Between her upper body and the ladder, moving feebly, were a pair of bare feet under skinny calves. She was holding the man so that he could not fall, and Mayhew, above her, had a tight grip on the castaway's wrists and was lowering him as required.

They got him down at last. He collapsed onto the deck, huddling there in the pool of sea water that ran from his ragged clothing. Grimes turned in his chair to look at him. He was obviously a Semite; in this part of the world that was to be expected. He was paralyzed with terror—and that was not surprising. He stared up at his rescuers while his hands clawed at his black, straggling beard. He was trying to say something, but words would not, could not come.

Mayhew said, "I'm getting some sense out of his mind, John, but not much. He's too frightened. He thinks we're angels or something . . ."

"Mphm." Grimes turned back to his controls, shutting the hatch then cutting the lift. The pinnace fell to the sea, submerged rapidly to periscope depth as the pumps sucked water into the ballast tanks. It was not a moment too soon. The rain squall was almost over; in another two or three seconds the little spacecraft would have been clearly visible from the surface ship.

Yes, she was still there, clearly visible through the thinning veils of rain. She was still there, and riding much more easily. This must have been the clearing squall. The wind was dropping and the sea was much less rough and, very soon in this land-enclosed expanse of water the swell would be diminishing. The shipmaster would not be needing a sea anchor now.

"I've got . . . something . . ." said Mayhew. There was something odd about his voice.

"Out with it, Ken," ordered Grimes.

"He . . . he was a passenger aboard that ship. Some kind of preacher. He was bound for . . . Ninevah. His name . . ."

"I don't think you need to tell me," said the commodore. And he thought, *But we have a temporal reference point. Once we get back on board the* Quest, *with her data banks, we shall be able to pinpoint ourselves in Time.*

Chapter 12

"WELL," demanded Grimes irritably, "what have you found out? We haven't much time left, you know. Sonya insists that our friend be put ashore on a deserted beach not one second later than three days after his rescue . . ."

"We must keep to the script," stated Sonya firmly.

"Script? What script? Damn it all, I hoped that by rescuing Jonah we should be able to find out just *when* we are—and what do we find? What does our data bank, our fabulous electronic encyclopedia have to tell us? Just that the Book of Jonah is only a legend, a piece of allegorical fiction, and that the Great Fish symbolizes Dagon or some other ichthyological deity. What does it matter if we keep him aboard the *Quest* three days, three weeks, or three months? Or three years . . ."

"We mustn't tamper with history," she said.

"History is always being tampered with," he grumbled.

"Yes. But not at the time when it's actually happening."

"There has to be a first time for everything," he said. But he realized that they were all against him. None of the *Quest*'s crew was religious—but they all had their superstitions. Holy Writ is Holy Writ. And here, under heavy sedation in the ship's sick bay, was living proof that there is more to the Bible than mere mythology.

"Better stick to the script," said Williams.

"It would be the wisest course," agreed Carnaby.

347

Grimes looked around at the faces of his other senior officers, saw that all of them were in favor of returning the castaway to land. He couldn't help grinning. So the unfortunate man was a double Jonah, as it were, first thrown overboard from the surface vessel, now to be ejected from the spaceship. But it was a pity. Further probing by Mayhew and Clarisse could well have turned up information of value.

"So we put him down," said the Commodore heavily, at last. Then, to Mayhew, "But you must have found *something* out, Ken . . ."

"Given time," murmured the telepath, "we can promise to crack any nut you throw onto our plate. But we haven't had the time." He paused. "How shall I put it, sir? Like this, perhaps. Just imagine that *you* are trying to question somebody with whom you share a common language, but that this somebody is so terrified that he screams wordlessly, without so much as a second's break . . . That's the way it is. Oh, we can read thoughts, to use the common jargon, but it helps a lot when those thoughts are reasonably coherent. His are not."

"So he's *still* terrified?"

"Too right he is. Try to look at it from *his* viewpoint. He's in the belly of a great fish. He has every right to be terrified."

"Like hell he has. He's being pampered better than any VIP passenger aboard a luxury liner. Specially cooked meals, served by our most attractive stewardesses . . ."

"Whom he regards as succubi just waiting for the chance to dig their painted claws into him to drag him down to Hell . . ."

"But can't you and Clarisse get into his mind, to calm him down?"

"Don't you think that we haven't tried, that we still aren't trying? Given time, we should succeed. But three days just aren't long enough."

"And the three days are almost up," said Sonya, looking at her watch.

Grimes sighed, got up from his seat, led the way from his quarters to the control room. He looked at the periscope screen, but *Faraway Quest* was above the clouds; nothing was visible but a restless sea of gleaming white vapor. But Carnaby had constructed a chart and proudly showed it to the commodore. "We're here," he said, stabbing with a pencil point at the dot with the small circle around it. "*Here*" appeared to be over the sea. "And there," he added, "is the city . . ."

Grimes took the pencil. "And we land," he said, "here. As far as we could see before the cloud covered things it's a nice little well-sheltered bay. And it should be no more than three days' not-very-strenuous walk from the coast to the city. I suppose that it *is* Ninevah?"

Nobody answered him.

"Mphm." He played with the dividers, measuring off the distance. "I still think that it would save trouble all round if I took the pinnace down after dark and landed our passenger right at his destination."

Sonya quoted solemnly, "And the Lord spake into the fish, and it vomited out Jonah upon the dry land. And the word of the Lord came unto Jonah the second time, saying, Arise, go into Ninevah, that great city, and preach unto it the preaching that I bid thee. So Jonah arose, and went unto Ninevah, according to the word of the Lord. Now Ninevah was an exceeding great city of three days' journey . . ."

"Is the amphibian ready, Commander Williams?" asked Grimes.

"All ready, Skipper," replied Williams.

"Then let's get it over with," said the commodore.

He handled the small craft himself, bringing her down from the mother ship in a steep dive, levelling off just before he hit the water, landing on the sea about half a kilometer from the shore. He had decided against landing on the beach itself; perhaps to have done so would have constituted a deviation from the script. The little bay was not as sheltered as it had looked from the air; there was a moderate westerly swell running and the pinnace wallowed sickeningly. Grimes was not at all surprised to hear somebody in the passenger cabin abaft him being violently ill. He felt sorry for the native, assuming (correctly) that it was he; the combination of seasickness with overwhelming terror must be almost unbearable. Then he ignored the miserable sounds and the unmistakable reek of vomit, concentrated on running in at right angles to the line of breakers. The aerial survey had shown that there were no submerged reefs to worry about—but it would do the pinnace and her occupants no good at all if she were allowed to broach to, if she were rolled over and over and dumped violently onto hard sand. He applied lift so that the craft became barely airborne; in the unlikely event that there were any observers ashore this would not be obvious.

He skimmed over the surf, steering for a tall, solitary palm tree. He roared over rather than through the shallows. Then, gently, he cut the inertial drive, dropped down to the dry sand with hardly a jar. He turned in his seat, saw that Sonya and Mayhew were standing and were supporting the native between them. The poor devil was in a sorry state, looking at least half dead with fear and nausea. But his troubles were almost over. (Or were they just starting?)

"Take him out, John?" asked Sonya.

"Yes, as long as you're sure that it's according to the Book."

"It has to be," she said coldly.

The midships door opened and the little ramp extended itself. Sonya and Mayhew guided the man—he looked like little more than a bundle of filthy rags—towards the opening. He seemed in no condition for a forty-kilometer walk—but he, too, would have to follow the script.

With blessed solidity under his bare feet, with familiar sights around him, he recovered fast. But he fell prone, trying to embrace the earth. At last he sat up, looking down at his hands, through which he was dribbling a stream of golden sand. There was an incredulous smile on his dark, bearded face—a smile that swiftly faded as his regard shifted upwards, as he saw the beached amphibian still there. Hastily he looked away, staring inshore, drawing renewed strength from the prosaic (to him) spectacle of rolling dunes, clumped palm trees and a serrated ridge of blue mountains on the horizon. He got shakily to his feet and started to walk, with surprising vigor, heading inland, away from the accursed sea and its denizens.

"Another satisfied customer," muttered Grimes.

Sonya and Mayhew got back into the pinnace and as soon as the craft was sealed the Commodore lifted her and set course for the waiting *Faraway Quest*.

⸺ Chapter 13 ⸺

BACK ABOARD the *Quest* Grimes went straight from the boat bay to his quarters, accompanied by Sonya and Mayhew. He sent for Williams and Clarisse. She, of course, did not need to be told all that had happened; she had been in telepathic communication with her husband throughout. And it did not take long to put Williams into the picture.

Then, "I intend to land tomorrow morning, at dawn," announced Grimes.

"Will it be wise?" queried Sonya. "As I've said before, and as I keep on saying, we must not tamper with history."

"Have we done so?" countered her husband. "Shall we do so? This last episode has established, I think, that we are already a part of history."

"Never mind history, Skipper," put in Williams. "You look after yourself, and let history look after itself. I'm tellin' you this: unless the boys an' girls get some sort o' break, you're goin' to have a mutiny on your hands."

"As bad as that, Billy?"

"As bad as that. For days now we've been hangin' over one little spot of empty ocean, with nothin' to look at but sea an' clouds. It's even worse than bein' in orbit. It's a case of so near an' yet so far."

"Ken?"

"I should have told you before, John, but I thought you knew. In

351

any case, I've been keeping my prying to a minimum. And you don't have to be a telepath to be aware of the unhappy atmosphere that's permeating the ship. You don't have to be a mind reader to overhear remarks such as, 'He and his pets get down to the surface any time they want to. Why shouldn't we?'"

Grimes grinned humorlessly. "I know, I know. That's why I've decided to make a landing."

"I still say that it's risky," stated Sonya flatly.

"How so?"

"It's obvious. Or should be. *There* . . ." she made a down-sweeping gesture . . . "we have a world whose civilizations, such as they are, are very little advanced beyond the Stone Age. Here we have a ship packed almost to bursting with the technology of *our* Time. What sort of impact shall we make?"

"A very light one," said Grimes, "if I set the old bitch down with my usual consummate skill."

She waited until the others had stopped laughing then said coldly, "You know very well what I meant."

"Yes. I know. And I still say, 'a very light one.' Only the very crudest technology would mean anything to those people down there. Anything beyond it will be, so far as they're concerned, magic . . ."

"And isn't that just as bad, if not worse?"

"No. Remember that Terran mythology is full of legends of gods who visited Earth from beyond the stars. Quite possibly some—or most—of those legends are based on fact. Quite possibly *we* are part of the mythology. Quite possibly? No. We *are* part of the mythology."

"Jonah . . ." said Mayhew.

"Yes."

"But how do you know," argued Sonya stubbornly, "that our Jonah was *the* Jonah? After all, it must be a very common name in this here and now. Perhaps the *real* Jonah was rescued from a watery grave a couple of centuries ago. Or perhaps it won't happen for another hundred years."

"Please don't stretch the long arm of coincidence to breaking point," the commodore admonished her.

"But there is such a thing as coincidence. And I still think that by too-intimate contact with the people of this period we're liable to shunt the world onto a different Time Track."

"And so, to coin a phrase, what?" he demanded.

"Then quite possibly we shall never be born. Not only shall we find it impossible to return to our own Time but we must just . . . vanish. We shall never have been."

Grimes laughed. "And you can say that, quite seriously, after all the peculiar strife, Time-trackwise, that we've been in already . . . Really. What about my carbon copy whom we met, not so long ago? Even though *his* ship wasn't a carbon copy of *my* ship . . ."

"And *his* wife far from being a carbon copy of yours. So you'd prefer Maggie Lazenby to me, is that it?"

"I never said anything of the kind. And what about that poor old Commander Grimes, passed over for promotion but still in the Survey Service, commanding that utterly unimportant base . . ."

"I seem to remember that Maggie was mixed up in that affair, too."

"And so were you." Grimes was playing with his battered pipe, wishing desperately that he had the wherewithal to fill it. (Had tobacco grown around the Mediterranean Basin in ancient times, as well as in North America? It would be worth finding out.) "Get this straight, Sonya. There's no possibility of our cancelling ourselves out. From every second of Time an infinitude of world lines stretches into the Future. Some, perhaps, are more 'real' than others. Or more probable. All will be real enough to the people living on them. And we were—or will be—born on at least one of those tracks. At least one? Now I'm talking nonsense. In any case, I'm pretty sure that we shall not influence the course of history. After all, you can't have steam engines until it's steam-engine Time."

"And what fancy theory is that?"

"It's more than a theory. The steam engine is a *very* ancient invention. But it was hundreds of years before anybody thought of putting it to work. When Hero made his primitive steam turbine there was no demand for mechanical power. And there'll be no demand for our sophisticated machinery in this Time.

"We land tomorrow."

"That will be the wisest course of action, John," said Mayhew slowly. "So far, all hands are still with you, but there's considerable discontent. All hands? All hands, that is, with the exception of those bloody Pongoes. What they are thinking, I don't know. But they are a minority and quite incapable of taking over the ship."

"You say, 'so far.'"

"Yes. So far. As long as you let your people get away from this tin coffin for a while they'll remain loyal. If you don't, if you keep them cooped up, anything might happen."

"I still don't like the idea of landing," said Sonya stubbornly. "I think that it's asking for trouble."

"Whatever we do is asking for trouble," Grimes told her. "We could return to Mars—and get ourselves blown out of the sky. We could scour the Universe and die of old age before we found another habitable planet. Earth, after all, is Home—and we have come Home. Let's make the best of it."

"You're the boss," she said resignedly.

～ Chapter 14 ～

THE ISLES OF GREECE ...

That phrase, that scrap of half-remembered verse, possessed a magic insofar as Grimes was concerned. And there were the memories, too, of that odd planet called by its people Sparta, that Lost Colony with its culture modelled on that of the long-dead City State. He would have liked to have seen what the real Sparta was like ... He could have made his landing in Egypt or in Palestine, in Italy or in Spain, in Carthage—but he decided upon Greece. He was unable to recollect his Terran geography, even with the mind-probing assistance of his telepaths, and the ship's data bank was no help at all, but it didn't matter. The outlines of the Archipelago were unmistakable enough, even if he could not say just where Sparta or Athens stood, or would stand. He relied upon his instruments to select what appeared to be a good landing site—flat, between sea and mountains, on the bank of a small river. The descent at sunrise was standard survey practice; the almost level rays of light would show up every irregularity and then, once the landing had been made, there would be a full day to get settled in—or during which to decide to get the hell out.

Slowly, carefully, Grimes brought *Faraway Quest* down through the still, clear morning air. As the ship lost altitude he could see streamers of blue smoke rising almost vertically a little to the north of where he had decided to land. Cooking fires? A village? Carnaby stepped up the magnification of the periscope screen and the huddle of huts along a bend in the river could be seen clearly.

And what of the villagers? Surely they must have heard by this time the uncanny thunder beating down from a clear sky; surely they must have seen the great, gleaming shape dropping down from the heavens. *And had this event, or similar events, given the ancient Greek dramatists their favourite, labor-saving gimmick, the* deus ex machina? Grimes smiled at the thought. It was odd, though, that this convention existed only in Greek drama.

Yes, there were people. And they had come out into the open, were not cowering under cover. They were standing there, outside their huts, staring upwards. Grimes was tempted to use his reaction drive to give them a show for their money, but restrained himself. A sudden display of dazzling, screaming fire could well engender panic. It was amazing that there was no panic already.

Not allowing his attention to stray from his instruments, his controls, he asked, "And what do they make of us, Ken?"

Mayhew replied, "They think that we're gods, of course. They're frightened, and have every right to be, but are determined not to show it . . ." The psionic communications officer laughed briefly. "I admire their attitude towards gods in general, and towards us in particular. Superhuman, but not supernatural. Their deities are, essentially, no more than better than life-size men and women . . ."

"And no less," said Grimes. "And no less . . ."

It occurred to him that he, himself, would be regarded as a god by these aborigines. A sort of minor Zeus, perhaps—or not so minor. He regarded the prospect with a rather smug equanimity. He would not complain. After all, wasn't he a commodore, a master astronaut *and* a master mariner? At long last he would be getting his just due.

He chuckled briefly to himself, then concentrated on landing the ship. He focused his attention on a spot to sunward of a great, quartzite boulder that was casting a long, black shadow over grass that was more brown than green. His sounding radar told him that the ground was solid enough to support the great weight of the ship. It was not quite level, but the tripedal landing gear was self-adjusting.

And there, plain in the screen, was a good target—a patch of grass that, for some reason, was more yellow than brown or green. Was it grass or was it a myriad of small flowers? The distinction was of no importance; Grimes applied a hint of lateral thrust and brought the natural beacon exactly into the center of the cartwheel sight. He was almost down. Altitude dropped from tens of meters to meters, then to less than a meter. The ship hung there for long seconds, her inertial drive grumbling to itself irritably. Slowly, slowly she settled. There was the slightest of jars, an almost undetectable rocking motion as the huge recoil cylinders of her landing gear took the shock, as her long axis maintained the vertical. The irregular beat of the drive faded to a mutter. Yes, she was solid enough in the vaned tripod.

"Finished with engines," said the commodore.

"Go an' see them?" asked Williams. "Or let them come to see us?"

"Mphm . . ." grunted Grimes. He looked at the screen, which was now depicting the village on which the big telescope had been trained. He watched the people. They were tall, well proportioned; their scanty clothing or lack of any clothing at all made this obvious. Blond hair predominated among both men and women, although a substantial minority of the villagers were darkly brunette. All the grown men were bearded. They stood there, men, women and children, in a loose group, staring at the shining tower that had fallen miraculously from the skies. Even the dogs—shaggy, wolflike beasts—were staring. The other domestic animals—sheep, were they, or goats?—were going about their business as usual.

The commodore looked at them, feeling a certain envy. Here was the myth of the Noble Savage made flesh and blood. Here were people who were fitting ancestors to the Hellenes who later (how much later?) were to populate this land.

He said, prosaically, "How about getting some fresh air into this tin can, Commander?"

"Ay, ay, Skipper!" replied Williams, cheerfully. He used a telephone to give the necessary orders to the engineroom. Within seconds the fans were no longer circulating the spaceship's too-many-times used and reused atmosphere but were drawing directly from outside. Somebody sneezed. The scent of pine trees was strong and mingled with it was a spicy, unidentifiable aroma.

At the village there was activity. People were going back into their huts and then reappearing. What would become a small procession was starting to assemble. There was a big man, taller than his fellows, who had put on crude body armor of leather, who was carrying a short, broad sword that gleamed like gold (that had to be bronze) in the morning sunlight. There were half a dozen other men, also armored, bearing flint-headed spears. There was a shambling giant— not as tall as the leader but much broader, heavily muscled—with the shaggy skin of some animal draped carelessly about his thick waist, the fur of it almost matching the hairiness of his own pelt. He was armed with a club, a roughly trimmed branch from a tree. And there were musicians—two pipers with primitive bagpipes, three drummers with skin-covered sections of hollowed-out log slung before their bodies. Their drumsticks—bones, they looked like—gleamed whitely.

Somebody in the control room extruded and switched on an exterior directional microphone. The rhythmic thud and rattle of the drums came beating in, and the thin, high skirling of the pipes. For the benefit of any among his people boasting Scottish ancestry, Grimes remarked that *that* music hadn't changed much over the centuries.

Williams asked, "Are you *sure* this is Greece, Skipper?"

"I can't see any kilts," contributed Carnaby, who was more interested in the women bringing up the rear of the procession than the men. "Not even a sporran . . ."

"Mphm," grunted Grimes, with a this-has-gone-far-enough intonation. With his officers he looked at the screen. The villagers were marching steadily towards the ship, led by the big, armored man and the skin-clad giant. They were followed by the musicians, behind whom were the spearmen. Bringing up the rear came the women, naked, all of them, moving with the grace that comes naturally to those accustomed from childhood to carrying burdens on their heads. And these women were so burdened—with big jars, with baskets. One had the carcass of some small animal, a kid or a lamb.

"Sacrifices?" Grimes asked Mayhew.

"No, Commodore. Not exactly . . . These are *awkward minds* . . . They're transmitting, after a fashion, but there doesn't seem to be a receiver among the bunch of them. Sacrifices? Peace offerings, I'd say."

"An odd sort of reaction from a bunch of primitives . . ."

"Not so odd, perhaps. They've yet to evolve a theology, with all the trimmings. As I said before, their gods, such as they are, are superhuman rather than supernatural . . ."

"And I suppose I'd better go down to receive these . . . peace offerings."

"I . . . I think so . . ."

Briefly Grimes pondered the advisability of changing into dress uniform with its stiff linen, frock coat, fore-and-aft hat and ceremonial sword. But such regalia would be meaningless to these people—and, besides, the air temperature outside the ship was already twenty-five Centigrade degrees, and rising. His shorts and shirt would have to do, and his best cap with the scrambled egg on the peak of it, the golden laurel leaves, still undimmed by time. (And wasn't it in Greece where the laurel wreath, as a mark of honor, first originated?)

He said to Williams, "All right, Commander. Have the after airlock door opened, and the ramp down." And to Hendriks, "Extrude your light armament to cover the immediate vicinity of the ship. And I'm warning you, don't be trigger happy. Fire only on direct orders from myself or Commander Williams—" Finally, "I'd like a Guard of Honor, Major. Yourself and six of your most reliable men. Yes, wear your dress helmets, but with normal tropical khakis."

"And weapons?" asked Dalzell, adding "sir" as an afterthought.

"Mphm. Stunguns only."

"I'd suggest projectile pistols. Apart from its lethal qualities a fifteen-millimeter makes a nice loud bang."

"Stunguns only," repeated Grimes firmly. "*If* they are required, and *if* they aren't effective, Mr. Hendriks will be able to make enough noise with *his* toys to keep you happy."

The major made no reply, saluted with deliberate sloppiness and stalked out of the control room. *Another unsatisfied customer* . . . thought Grimes. But the ruffled feelings of his marines were the least of his worries.

He went down to his quarters to collect his cap. He watched Sonya as she changed from her short uniform skirt into sharply creased slacks. He said nothing, guessing that it was her reaction to the unashamed nudity of the native women. Like the majority of married men he had long since ceased to expect logical behavior from his wife.

"Ready?" he asked.

"Ready," she replied.

He led the way down to the after airlock.

⚘ Chapter 15 ⚘

SLOWLY GRIMES STRODE down the ramp, keeping step to the throb and rattle of the not-now-distant drums. The mad skirling of the approaching pipes was painful. He forced himself to ignore it. Sonya marched beside him, and Mayhew kept step a little to the rear. Behind them came Dalzell and his marines, six of them, all big men. The drabness of their uniforms was obscured by the glitter of their accoutrements—the highly burnished brass, the medals with their rainbows of colored ribbons.

When he had rough, solid ground under his feet the Commodore halted. Sonya stood at his right hand, Mayhew at his left. Behind them stood Dalzell and his line of space soldiers. At the sight of these beings emerging from the ship the procession halted; the drums missed a beat or two, the pipers paused their shrill squealing. But the two big men in the van came steadily on, one holding his gleaming sword aloft, the other with his club carried casually over his shoulder. After their initial hesitation the others followed, but without the apparent arrogant confidence of their leaders.

Grimes stood his ground. He hoped that the marines had their stunguns ready.

No more than six feet from the spacemen the armored man came to a halt. The giant made another step and then shuffled clumsily backward to stand beside the other. The drums and (mercifully) the pipes fell silent. The spearmen and the gift-bearing women grouped themselves behind the others.

The commodore stared impassively at the armored man—wearing, Sonya told him later, his best Admiral-Hornblower-on-the-quarterdeck expression. The native stared impassively at the commodore. *And is it up to me,* Grimes asked himself, *to say, "Take me to your leader?" But he* is *the leader. Obviously.* The crude armor could not hide the superb proportions of his body. The bronze helmet and the bronze sword were conspicuous badges of rank.

And then the chief's sword hand moved. Sonya uttered a faint gasp. Dalzell snapped an order to his men. "Hold it!" whispered Mayhew urgently. "Hold it, Major!" And to Grimes, "It's all right, sir . . ."

The right hand, holding the sword, moved—but only to transfer the weapon to the left hand, which let it drop, holding it with the point down. The right hand, empty, was raised, palm out, in salute. Grimes responded, bringing the edge of his own right hand smartly to the peak of his cap. *And what now?* he wondered. *I suppose I graciously accept the gifts.*

"Not yet, sir," said Mayhew.

"Do they want to see first what we are going to give them?"

"No. It's rather more complicated. We have to prove our superiority."

"That shouldn't be hard," said Grimes, conscious of the towering bulk of his ship behind him, of the might of her weaponry. "In fact it should be obvious."

"I'm not so sure . . ." murmured Sonya. "I'm not so sure . . ." She was looking at the handsome figure of the chief with something like admiration. And then Grimes realized that it was not the chief at whom she was so looking; it was at the uncouth, shambling giant beside him.

"Mphm," grunted the commodore dubiously.

The native leader said something in his own language. His voice was deep and musical, the words had a rhythm to them.

Mayhew murmured, "This is not an exact translation, but I'm picking up his thoughts as he speaks. Our champion will have to fight their champion."

Grimes looked at that big, bronze sword. Even now, held

negligently in its owner's left hand, it appeared nastily lethal. He asked, "Can I use whatever weapon I wish? Do I have the choice of weapons?"

Mayhew replied, "It is not the king whom you have to fight, sir. He is not the champion on an occasion such as this. Herak, the man with the club, is the champion." He added, "And I think that it's supposed to be a fight with no weapons—or, to be exact, only with nature's weapons."

Relief dawned in the commodore's mind. The king had his champion to do his fighting for him. What was good enough for a king was good enough for the captain of a ship. But . . . But could he *order* anybody to take on that hirsute hunk of overdeveloped muscle? The king of a savage community wields powers that, over the centuries, have been lost by mere shipmasters . . .

Dalzell stepped forward to talk with his superior. He said, "I think I get the drift of it, sir. You'll want a champion to beat the hell out of this Herak, or whatever he calls himself. Unless, of course, you'd sooner do it yourself . . ."

"I'm not an all-in wrestler, Major."

"I thought not, sir. But all of my men are well trained in unarmed combat. I could call for a volunteer . . ."

"Do that, Major."

The volunteer was Private Titanov—and he was a genuine volunteer. He stripped rapidly to his skimpy underpants. Divested of his uniform he could almost have been the twin of Herak. Herak grinned ferociously at him and he grinned back. It was as much a snarl as a grin. Herak handed his club to one of the spearmen, dropped the animal skin that was his only garment to the short grass, kicked it aside with a broad foot. It was picked up by a girl, who clasped it almost reverently to her full breasts. The giant flexed his muscles; they crawled under the hairy skin like thick snakes. He drummed on his barrel chest with his great fists, threw his head back and howled like a wolf.

Meanwhile, the king was giving orders in an authoritative voice. His people formed a rough ring, about ten meters in diameter, in the center of which the champion took his place. Herak grinned again and lifted his right arm; it was as thick as the thigh of a normal man. His fist was clenched. He did not need his heavy club. This was weapon enough.

The king looked towards Grimes. He said nothing, but the expression on his handsome, bearded face was easy enough to read. *Are you ready? Is your man ready?* "Yes," said the Commodore. "Yes." He hoped that the other would, somehow, understand him.

The king transferred his gleaming sword to his right hand, raised it, brought it down with a slashing motion. The drummers rattled briefly and noisily. The pipers emitted a short, strident squeal.

"Go, Titanov, go!" ordered Dalzell.

"Go, go, go!" chanted the other marines.

Titanov went. He advanced slowly, crouching, massive shoulders hunched. He reached the perimeter of the ring. A man and a woman moved apart to allow him ingress. The woman detained him briefly, putting out her hand to finger, curiously, the material of his shorts. At least that is what Grimes, who had his prudish moments, hoped that she was doing. Titanov broke away, kept on coming. In spite of his bulk, his motion was like that of a great cat. His arms were hanging loosely at his sides, his fists were clenched. Not that this meant anything; a karate chop is deadlier than a punch. Then he was within range of Herak's right fist—which, suddenly, swept down like a steam hammer. Had it connected, the marine's brains would have been spattered over the grass.

But it did not connect. Titanov skipped backwards with surprisingly delicate grace, like a ballet dancer—and he kicked, high, with deadly precision. Herak screamed, dreadfully and shrilly. He fell face forward on to the turf, clutching his genitals. His shoulders heaved as he noisily vomited.

Grimes heard Dalzell barking orders, realized that the major feared that the foul fighting of his man might well precipitate hostile action on the part of the villagers. He grasped Sonya's arm, intending to spin her around and shove her towards the ramp at the first sign of trouble.

Mayhew laughed softly. "Don't worry, John. It was a fair fight as far as they are concerned. They accept the decision."

"More than I'd do in their shoes . . ."

"They're not wearing any."

The women had crowded around Titanov, embracing him, almost mobbing him. One of them had produced a wreath of green leaves from somewhere and had crowned him with it. Evidently the felled champion was not popular.

"Titanov!" snapped Dalzell. Then, in a louder voice, "Titanov!"

"Sir?" replied the Marine at last.

"Come back here and get dressed. At once!"

"Sir."

Titanov managed to extricate himself from his female admirers. They let him go reluctantly. He walked slowly back towards the ship. He had lost his underpants, but did not seem to be at all embarrassed.

Chapter 16

"AND WHAT NOW?" Grimes asked Mayhew. He looked with pity towards the groaning Herak, still huddled on the grass, now in a fetal position. He said, "Perhaps I should send for the doctor to do what he can for that poor bastard . . ."

"No, sir. I advise against it. I have an idea that the local wise woman or witch or whatever will be out soon from the village to take care of him . . ."

"And what's the king saying?"

"He's ordering his women to present the gifts to you."

"Oh. And what do I do?"

"Accept them graciously. Smile. Say something nice. *You* know."

"Mphm. I think that can be managed. And do I reciprocate?"

"Only to the king, sir. His name, I think, is Hektor . . ."

"And what would he like?"

"He's rather hoping, sir, that you'll present him with something fancy in the way of weapons . . ."

"Firearms are out of the question," snapped Grimes testily. He was feeling out of his depth. On a normal survey voyage there would have been a horde of specialists to advise him—experts in linguistics, sociology, zoology, botany, geology . . . The list was almost endless. Now he had not so much as a single ethologist. He was lucky to have two excellent telepaths; their talent helped him to surmount, after a fashion, the language barrier.

"Your dress sword . . ." suggested Sonya. "I never did like that anachronistic wedding-cake cutter."

"*No.*"

"If I may make a suggestion, sir," said Dalzell, "my artificer sergeant has been amusing himself making some rather good arbalests—crossbows. He thought that such weapons could be useful if, at some time, we ran completely out of ammunition for our projectile rifles and pistols . . ."

"Thank you, Major. One of those should do very nicely . . ."

Dalzell spoke into his wrist-transceiver, then said to Grimes, "The arbalest will be down in a couple of seconds, sir."

"Good."

The king was approaching slowly, his gleaming sword once again held proudly aloft. Behind him marched the women with the jars and the baskets, the slaughtered lamb, balanced on their heads. They moved gracefully, their naked bodies swaying seductively as they walked. Some of them were blondes and some brunettes, and the skins of all of them were a lustrous, golden brown. Grimes—and the other men—watched them with undisguised admiration.

Sonya said sharply, "Beware the Greeks when they come bearing gifts!"

"Ha!" snorted Grimes. "Ha! Very funny."

"But rather apt, my dear."

The king stood to stiff attention, a little to one side of the line of advance of the gift-bearers. Slowly the leading woman, a statuesque blonde, approached Grimes. With both hands she lifted the jar from her head and then, falling to her knees with a fluid motion, deposited it on the grass at the commodore's feet. She got up, bowed, then turned and walked away.

"You didn't thank her," said Sonya. "But no doubt your mind was on other things, although not higher things . . ."

"I think that's oil in the jar," said Mayhew. "Olive oil."

Grimes was ready for the other women. As each of them made her presentation he smiled stiffly and murmured, "Thank you, thank you . . ." Some of the baskets, he saw, contained grain and others held berries. Probably, he thought, some of the jars would contain wine or beer. He began to wonder what it would be like . . .

"Sir, sir!" It was Dalzell's artificer sergeant. "The crossbow, sir."

"Oh, yes." Grimes took the weapon in his right hand. It was heavy, but not overly so. He examined it curiously and with admiration. There was a stirrup at the head wide enough to take even a big foot. For cocking it there was not a small windlass, as was used in the first arbalests, but an ingeniously contrived folding lever. The construction was metal throughout. Modern in design and manufacture as it was, it would never be the superb rapid-fire weapon that the longbow became (was to become) but it was powerful, and deadly, and accurate . . . The king had approached Grimes, was standing over him. Eager anticipation was easy to read in his bearded face.

"Would you mind demonstrating, Sergeant?" asked the commodore, handing the crossbow back to the man.

"Certainly, sir." The sergeant lowered the stirrup to the ground, put his right foot into it, then heaved upwards with both hands grasping the cocking lever, grunting with the effort. There was a sharp *click* as the pawl engaged. He then took a steel quarrel from the pouch at his belt, inserted it into the groove. He raised the skeleton butt to his shoulder. He kept it there, but looked puzzled. "What's me target, sir?" he asked.

The king guessed the meaning of the words even if he did not know the language in which they were spoken. He smiled broadly, pointed to the unfortunate Herak. The defeated wrestler had managed to sit up, was being attended to by a filthy old hag in a tattered skin robe who was holding a crude, clay cup of some brew to his lips.

The sergeant would have been quite capable of using this target—but, "No," ordered Grimes firmly. "*No.*"

"But I could shoot the mug outa her hands, sir . . ."

"You're not to try it. Use that!" *That* was a small, yellow-white boulder about two hundred meters distant.

"But it'll damage the quarrel, sir."

"That's too bad. Aim. Shoot!"

"Very good, sir," responded the man in a resigned voice.

The taut wire bowstring twanged musically. The short, metal shaft flashed in the sunlight as it sped towards the rock. It hit in a brief, sudden explosion of glittering dust. And when this cleared the boulder was seen to be split in two; sheer good chance had guided the projectile to a hidden fault line.

The king rumbled obvious approval. He thrust his sword into the ground, held out both his big hands for the new toy. He took hold of it lovingly and then, with almost no fumbling, succeeded in cocking it. The sergeant handed him a bolt. Grimes moved as unobtrusively as possible so that his body was between the native ruler and what probably would be his choice of targets.

But there was a herd of goats drifting slowly over the grassy plain towards the ship. The king grinned again, took careful aim on the big, black buck in the lead. He seemed to be having a little trouble understanding the principle of the sights with which the weapon was fitted, but at last pulled the trigger.

It was another lucky shot, catching the hapless animal squarely in the head, between the horns.

What have I done? Grimes asked himself guiltily. But surely the bow was already in existence, and the introduction of the arbalest into this world, even though it might be a few centuries too early, would make very little difference to the course of history.

"We have a satisfied customer, sir," said Dalzell smugly.

"Mphm," grunted Grimes.

Chapter 17

AFTER THE EXCHANGE OF GIFTS—the crossbow, a few knives, a couple of hammers and a saw for the baskets of produce and the jars of oil, beer and milk—the natives returned to their village. Grimes wondered if he and a party should accompany them, but Mayhew advised against it. "They wouldn't object, John; they're essentially too courteous. But the party's laid on for tonight, and they have to get things ready . . ."

"What party?" asked Grimes.

"Do you expect a gilt-edged invitation card?" Sonya asked him.

"I suppose not." He turned again to the telepath. "So there's to be a feast, is that it?"

"Yes. In our honor."

"Then the samples of the local foodstuffs will be useful. Major Dalzell, please have these gifts delivered to the biochemist, and tell him from me to go into a huddle with the Quack to find out if we can enjoy the wine and food of the country without serious consequences . . ."

"Yes, sir."

"And, Major . . ."

"Sir?"

"There is to be no, repeat no, fraternizing with the natives. I shall give the same order to Commander Williams regarding the spacemen and women of the ship's complement."

"Understood, sir."

Grimes could not help noticing the expressions on the faces of Dalzell's marines. If looks could have killed, he would have had only another second to live. Titanov glowered even more ferociously than his mates.

"And what about tonight's ... er ... feast?" asked the major.

"I'll let you know later," said Grimes. He heard one of the men mutter, "One o' those officers-only bun struggles, I suppose ..." But it would not be, he had already decided. It would all too probably be the sort of affair at which any staid, respectable senior officer should be conspicuous by his absence.

Back aboard the ship Grimes called Williams, Mayhew and Clarisse into his quarters. He said, "We know *where* we are. We still don't know *when*."

"Wasn't there a Bronze Age?" asked Williams. "The sword that the chief or king or whatever he is was carrying looked like bronze ..."

"An Age is an Age is an Age," remarked Sonya. "In other words, it's not a mere two or three weeks."

Grimes grunted irritably. His wife was right, as she usually was. The Bronze Age, following the Stone Age, had lasted for quite a while. But when, roughly, had it started? He, Grimes, did not know, and he doubted very much if anybody in the ship knew. *Faraway Quest's* data banks were stuffed almost to bursting with information on just about everything but ancient Terran history.

"This period," said Sonya, "must be towards the beginning of the Bronze Age ..."

"How do you make that out?" asked Williams.

"Metal artifacts are so scarce as to be the perquisites of the rulers. The local king has a bronze sword. The spears of his soldiers are tipped with stone."

"Could be," admitted Grimes. "Could be. On the other hand, this may be a backward, poverty-stricken little kingdom. Just as in *our* day and age not every world can afford the very latest in sophisticated weaponry."

"There are precious few planets that can't," she told him. "Guns before butter has been a working principle of Man for all the millennia that he has been Man. It was a working principle ages before that mad German dictator—Hitler, wasn't it?—coined the phrase."

"So we can assume," said the commodore, "that bronze artifacts are rare as well as being expensive."

"You can assume all you like, my dear, but that does seem to be the way of it."

"Mphm. two thousand B.C.? three thousand? I read up on Greek history after I got involved in that Spartan Planet affair, but I'm afraid that not much of it stuck in my memory. In any case, I never could remember dates. This land, as I recall it, was settled by a variety of peoples, some coming by sea and some by land. Our friends in the village seem to be land nomads who have settled down in one spot, who are living in permanent wooden houses rather than tents. But they should have horses, and we haven't seen any . . ."

"Horses," said Sonya, "have been known to die. Perhaps some epidemic in the past wiped all their horses out, so they had to stay put and make the best of it."

"But they should have cattle," persisted Grimes.

"Not necessarily. They have sheep, and goats . . ."

"And figs," added Williams. "And some very small pears . . ."

"How do you know?"

"I looked in the baskets when the pongoes brought them aboard."

"I hope," said Sonya, "that you did no more than look."

"I was tempted," admitted the commander. "But I've no desire to come down with a case of the squitters. I hope that the local tucker *is* passed fit for human—our sort of human—consumption."

"Yes," said Grimes, "I do, too. We have this feast tonight. Have you any idea, Ken, what's being laid on for us?"

"It'll be a barbecue," answered the telepath. "Already they're slaughtering lambs and kids . . ."

"Sounds a bit of all right," commented Williams, licking his lips.

"I'm sorry, Billy," Grimes told him, "but you won't be among the guests."

"Have a heart, Skipper!"

"I'm sorry, and I mean it. But somebody has to watch the shop. I shall require a skeleton crew remaining on board—you, in command in my absence, and Hendriks, in case any show of force is required, and either the chief or the second engineer . . . And such ratings as you consider necessary."

"Talking of the engineers—the chief wants to have a grand overhaul of the inertial drive. He was telling me that it'll not be safe to lift off until he's satisfied himself that everything is as it should be."

"We'll see how things go tonight," said Grimes. "If I'm reasonably happy he can take things apart tomorrow. Meanwhile, arrange a meeting of all hands for 1600 hours."

Faraway Quest's people were in a restive mood when they assembled in the main lounge at 1600 hours. This was understandable. Outside the ship there was an unspoiled world, bathed in sunshine. Inside the ship there were the same old drab surroundings, and the subtle scents of thyme and asphodel, mingled with the aroma of distant pines, drifting through the ventilation system, made their virtual imprisonment harder to endure.

However, Grimes, when he mounted his platform, had the attention of the meeting.

He opened proceedings briefly, then said, "You will all be pleased to learn that the samples of foodstuffs and liquor brought on board have been passed as fit for human consumption. It will be necessary, however, for all hands to receive a broad spectrum antibiotic injection to ensure their continuing good health while on this world. This will also lessen the possibility of our transmitting any diseases to the natives, although after our long spell in space we should be practically sterile." He smiled briefly. "In the surgical sense of the word, of course. Mphm.

"As many of you are already aware there will be a feast in the village tonight. I am given to understand that we shall be the honored guests. Save for a shipkeeping skeleton crew—the duty list will be posted by Commander Williams—we shall all attend. Rig of the day—of the evening, rather—will be Number Seven. Major Dalzell will see to it that his men wear the marine equivalent. Side-arms will be worn only by officers of lieutenant commander's rank and up, although Marine other ranks will carry stunclubs. Weapons, however, are not, repeat not; to be used unless in circumstances of extreme provocation.

"All hands attending the feast will behave in a gentlemanly . . ." he grinned . . . "or ladylike manner. Remember that we are ambassadors. Do not partake too freely of the local liquor—or, if you do, do not fail to counteract the effects with antidrunk tablets that you will all be carrying. Do *not* molest the native women. And as for you, ladies, try to avoid too close contact with the native men.

"And do not forget that even though you are away from the ship you are still subject to discipline.

"That is all."

He heard somebody mutter, "With old Pickle Puss keeping an eye on us it's going to be a fine party. I don't bloody think!"

∾ Chapter 18 ∾

THE SUN WAS WELL DOWN and the silvery sliver of the new moon, swimming in the afterglow, was about to lose itself behind the black peaks to the west'ard when the invitation to the feast was delivered. From the village marched a small procession—six men bearing aloft flaring pine-knot torches, four drummers, two pipers. All of them were wrapped in cloaks of sheepskin against the evening chill. They paraded around the ship to the squealing of their pipes and the rattle of their drums.

Said Grimes sourly, "It *could* be a serenade . . ."

Mayhew told him, "I'm picking up their thoughts. It's a traditional melody, John. It could be called *Come To The Party . . .*"

"To be played on the typewriter?" asked Sonya. Then, "Now is the time for all good men to come to the party."

"And can we take our quick red foxes and lazy brown dogs with us?" wondered Grimes aloud. He got up out of his chair, reached for and put on his third-best uniform cap. He was wearing Number Seven uniform—tunic and trousers of tough khaki drill over a thick black sweater, black kneeboots. It was the standard wear for shore excursions in rough country in less than subtropical temperature. For an occasion such as this promised to be the cloth had the big advantage of being stain-resistant.

Before leaving his quarters he said to Williams, "I don't anticipate any trouble, Billy. But if there is, we'll yell for help on our personal transceivers."

"I'll be listening, Skipper. Have a good time."

The commodore led the way down to the after airlock, followed by Sonya, Mayhew and Clarisse. The others were assembling there— ship's officers and ratings, Dalzell and his Marines. They stood to one side to allow Grimes to be first down the ramp.

As he stepped on to the ground the torch bearers advanced and then, with their flambeaux, made a beckoning gesture. They turned about and, flanked by the pipers and the drummers, began to march back towards the village. The commodore and his party fell in behind them, then a larger contingent of men and women led by Carnaby, finally the major and his men.

It was rough going in the deepening dusk; the fitful flare of the torches was more of a nuisance than a help. Luckily most of the boulders were well clear of the short grass and glimmered whitely. Nonetheless, Grimes was thankful for his stout boots.

On they marched to the barbaric music, towards the dark huddle of houses among which fires flared and flickered ruddily. Downwind drifted the tang of wood smoke, the aroma of roasting meat. Grimes realized that he was starting to salivate. Nobody could have described *Faraway Quest* as a hungry ship—but after a very few weeks, tank-grown food loses its essential flavors, its individuality.

Suddenly drummers and pipers fell silent, but there was still music. They were singing in the village, a song in which male and female voices blended in compulsive rhythm.

"And what is that?" Grimes asked Mayhew.

"A . . . a welcome . . ." The telepath tripped over a rock and would have fallen flat on his face had Clarisse not caught him. "A welcome reserved for heroes or for superior beings . . ."

"Gods?" asked Grimes.

"As I keep saying," replied Mayhew, "these people regard gods as sort of older brothers. Powerful, but not quite omnipotent, and with all sorts of all-too-human weaknesses . . ."

"That last part is true as far as we're concerned!"

They were very close to the village now. The low houses stood in black silhouette against the glare of the fires—which must be, Grimes decided, in some sort of central square. The noise of singing was loud.

And then he saw a huge figure, dark against the unsteady firelight, advancing to meet them. The torch bearers and the musicians stepped to one side to make way for the newcomer. It was the king, Hektor. In one hand he held not his sword but the arbalest, in the other a huge mug. He thrust this at Grimes, who had to use both his hands to grasp it.

"Drink it. All of it," urged Mayhew in a whisper.

The commodore lifted the vessel to his lips. He toasted briefly, "Down the hatch!" He sipped—then decided ruefully that this was something he would have to get over with quickly. He liked beer, and this was beer, but . . . It smelled musty and tasted mustier. It had an unpleasantly thick consistency, and there were semisolid bodies suspended in it.

He gulped and swallowed manfully.

He muttered, "Garrgh!"

But he finished the muck in one draught. At least, it was alcoholic . . .

The king was leading the way now to where the feast was already in progress. It was, decided Grimes, quite a party. There were at least six huge fires burning in the village square; two of them were blazing, affording illumination, the other four were beds of red coals over which the spitted carcasses of animals dripped and sizzled, spurts of yellow flame marking the fall of each spatter of hot fat. The older women were attending to the cookery; the younger ones came dancing out to meet the party from the ship. A trio of beauties, more naked than otherwise, surrounded the commodore, and one of them hung a garland of rather wilted flowers about his neck.

"And which one are you giving the apple to?" whispered Sonya.

But these were no pale-skinned animated statues. These were shapely girls, very human, whose sun-browned skins gleamed ruddily in the firelight. The blonde who had presented the garland, greatly daring, threw her slim yet strong arms around Grimes' shoulders, brought her face close to his in a gesture of invitation. He hesitated only for a second, then kissed her full on the mouth. Her lips were greasy; it was obvious that she had been sampling one of the roasts of lamb—but, Grimes told himself, they tasted far better than that vile beer had and were just as intoxicating.

"Down, boy, down!" growled Sonya.

Reluctantly the commodore disengaged the girl's arms from his neck, put his own hands on her shoulders and turned her away from him. He could not resist the temptation to speed her on her way with a friendly slap on the buttocks. She squealed happily.

They were led by the villagers to places around the fire—Grimes and his party, Carnaby and the men and women with him, Dalzell and his marines. They sat on the threadbare grass, not too comfortably, yet pleasantly conscious of the heat from the flames. Men and women brought them mugs of drink. The commodore sipped his dubiously; it was wine this time, much too sweet but a vast improvement on the beer. And there was coarse bread in thin, flat cakes, and rough hunks of hot meat, lamb and kid, thyme- and onion- and garlic-flavored. There was the continual drumming, and the singing, and—almost inaudible in the general uproar—the squealing of the pipes.

There was dancing.

There was a circle of girls weaving sinuously about a huge, naked, bearlike man crowned with a wreath of green leaves, laughing shrilly as he reached out and tried to grab them. It must be Herak, Grimes thought at first, and was pleased that the defeated wrestler had made a good recovery. Herak? No, it was the marine, Titanov.

He nudged Sonya.

"Do you see what I see?"

"What of it?" she countered.

"He . . . He's going native . . ." And he thought, *This won't do at all, at all. Have to put a stop to it . . .* He realized that his thinking was getting muzzy and fumbled for the no-drunk tablets in his pocket, swallowing two of them.

He got unsteadily to his feet, walked with careful deliberation to where Dalzell was reclining on the grass like a dissolute Roman, attended closely by two women. One of them was feeding him with bite-sized pieces that she was tearing from a leg of lamb, the other was holding a mug to his lips at frequent intervals.

"Major!"

"Commodore . . ."

"That man of yours. The wrestler . . ."

"What man? Where?"

"There . . ."

But as Grimes pointed he realized that Titanov was gone—and with him, presumably, had gone the dancing girls. But there was a little heap of uniform clothing not far from Dalzell, and a stunclub was on top of the garments.

"What about *that?*"

"The fire's hot, Commodore. Thinkin' of gettin' stripped off myself . . ."

"But . . ."

But the fire *was* hot, and it was bloody absurd wearing this heavy khaki . . . Grimes had unbuttoned his jacket when his ears were assailed by a strident blast of music. He turned to look at its source. One part of his mind was horrified—another, almost as strong, part accepted what he saw as being right and proper. Strutting by came one of his stewardesses. He remembered her name, Maggie Macpherson. She was wearing nothing but her kneeboots and jauntily angled forage cap, and she was playing a set of the native bagpipes, and playing them as well as such instruments can ever be played. He even recognized the tune, the traditional *Scotland The Brave*. After her pranced a small procession—three of her fellow stewardesses, a quartet of junior engineers, a half-dozen villagers, three of whom were children.

He thrust out a detaining hand. "Miss Macpherson!"

The music squealed to a dying-pig finish.

"Miss Macpherson, what is the meaning of this?"

"What is the meaning of what, sir?"

"You . . . You aren't properly dressed . . ."

"I'm wearin' me cap, sir . . ."

"Gie us *The Scottish Soldier*, Maggie!" shouted one of the engineers.

"John!" It was Mayhew, his voice urgent.

"What is it, Ken?"

Grimes could not hear the telepath's reply for the renewed skirling of the pipes. "Speak up, man!"

"It's the wine, John," almost shouted Mayhew. "Not the same wine as we had analyzed. Something in it. Mushrooms, I think . . ."

"Could be . . ." muttered the commodore. Whatever it was, the drug was converting what had been a feast—a rather rough one, admittedly—into an orgy. The scene illuminated by the fitful flaring of the fires could have been painted by Hieronymus Bosch. And yet Grimes was feeling revulsion only because he thought that he *should* be feeling revulsion. But as long as he kept his uniform on, that part of his personality which he regarded as "the commodore" would remain in the ascendancy.

He demanded, "Can you and Clarisse control my people?"

"It's all we can do to keep ourselves in control . . . Carnaby is still more or less in possession of his senses, and Brenda Cole . . . Apart from them . . . But you must *do* something, John. There're our weapons lying around for anybody to pick up . . ."

And where the hell was Sonya? Grimes looked around for her, but could not see her. Accompanied by Mayhew, he hurried back to where he had left her. Her jacket was on the grass, and her slacks, her belt with the holstered pistol—and, beside them, what looked like a wolfskin breech-clout and something that gleamed metalically. It was the steel arbalest.

But he, Grimes, was responsible for the entire ship's company, not just for one woman, even though she was his wife. (And, he knew very well, she was quite capable of looking after herself.) First of all he would have to put a stop to this . . . this orgy, and then there would be some sorting out.

He raised his wrist transceiver to his mouth.

"Commodore to *Quest*. Commodore to Commander Williams. Do you read me? Over."

It was a woman's voice that answered. Grimes remembered that Ruth Macoboy, the assistant electronic communications officer, was among Williams' shipkeepers.

"*Quest* here, Commodore. Bill—Commander Williams, I mean— is coming to the transceiver now."

"Williams here, Skipper. Anything wrong?"

"Plenty, Bill. First of all, get Hendriks to plaster the village with

Morpheus D. Don't open fire, though, until I give the word. We shall be getting away from the place as soon as we can. Send somebody from the ship to meet us with half a dozen respirators. Got that?"

"Have got, Skipper. Hendriks can load his popguns, but he's not to fire until you say so."

"Correct. We're on the way out now."

Clarisse appeared with Carnaby and Brenda Coles in tow. They seemed to be sober enough, but rather resentful. And then, to Grimes' surprise and great relief, Sonya came running up to them, her legs indecently long and graceful under the black sweater. She gasped, "That . . . lout!"

"Never mind him. Out of here. Fast."

"But . . . My clothes . . ."

"Come *on*, damn you!" Grimes grabbed his wife by the arm, hurried her out of the village.

Behind them somebody was wordlessly shouting, the bellowing of a frustrated animal. Then something whirred between Grimes and Sonya, narrowly missing both of them. A quarrel, the commodore realized; a bolt from Hektor's arbalest. There was a second missile—another very near miss—and a third.

"Down!" ordered Grimes, suiting the action to the word. He spoke into his wrist transceiver, "Commodore to *Quest*. Fire!"

From the fighting top of the distant ship came a flickering of pale flame and then, after what seemed a long interval, a series of sharp reports. The projectiles from Hendriks' guns wailed overhead and, almost immediately, came the dull thuds as the gas shells burst precisely over the village. Grimes could visualize that heavy, soporific vapour settling, oozing downwards through the air, permeating every building, every nook and cranny.

Abruptly the wild singing and the shouting died and the drums fell silent.

But a lone piper—was it Maggie Macpherson? It had to be—persisted for long minutes, an eldritch lament that blended perfectly with the thin, cold drizzle that was beginning to fall.

But even she must, in the end, inhale, and then there was complete silence.

Chapter 19

WILLIAMS CAME OUT FROM THE SHIP in one of the work boats, a flying craft that was little more than a platform fitted with a powerful inertial drive unit. He was using his searchlight, and Grimes and the others stood up and waved as he drifted towards them. He brought the ungainly thing down to a soft landing a meter or so from where they were waiting, then asked, "What the hell's been happening, Skipper?"

The commodore found it hard to reply. He was almost overcome by a lethargy far deeper than that resulting from overindulgence in alcohol. But, with a great effort, he forced himself to reply. He finished, "And things were . . . getting out of hand. Only one thing to do . . . Put everybody to sleep . . ."

"Sure you didn't get any o' the gas yourself, Skipper? You sound pretty dopey to me."

"It was . . . the drug."

"So you think you were all drugged?"

"*Think?*" snapped Grimes testily. "I *know* we were drugged." He remembered vividly the taste and the smell of that beerlike drink, its consistency. Lucky he hadn't liked it, had downed only one mug of the muck. A concoction brewed from sacred mushrooms for special occasions? That assumption made sense.

"And what do we do now, Skipper?"

Grimes pulled himself together, gave orders. He and the others put on respirators, clambered aboard the workboat. Williams restarted the drive then cruised slowly, at low altitude, towards the village. The engine was horridly noisy in the quiet night, but nobody would hear it; the effects of the Morpheus D would take at least six hours to wear off. The fires were still burning in the village square but they were now little more than mounds of red embers, and in the glare of the searchlight no more than gray cinders. Grimes looked down and ahead anxiously; he was suddenly afraid that some of the anaesthetized revellers might have fallen into the beds of red-hot coals. But nobody had done so. The tangles of limbs and bodies were all well clear of danger.

Williams landed the raft in a narrow lane just away from the square. Grimes, followed by the rest of the party, jumped down to the ground. The drizzle had misted his goggles and he doubted if he would be able to tell, even with the aid of the powerful hand torch that Williams had given him, who were members of his own crew and who were natives. Nudity makes for anonymity.

The first body he came to was that of Maggie Macpherson. There was no mistaking her for anybody else. She still had the bagpipes, clasping the instrument to her breasts. It looked as though she were giving suck to some bloated little arthropoidal monster. Her uniform cap was, somehow, still on her unruly red curls. She still had her boots on. Grimes laughed—not an easy action to perform while wearing a respirator, but possible. This could be simple after all, so long as the others had shown the same respect for uniform regulations as had the Scottish girl.

And so it turned out to be, although some of the tangles took some sorting out. *Faraway Quest*'s crew hadn't died with their boots on—but they had been doing all sorts of other things when the anesthetic gas hit them. At one stage Williams muttered, "I should have brought a camera . . . What a marvelous picture this would make! Twelve people in six poses . . ."

"Pipe down and get on with the bloody job!" growled Grimes. "It's quite bad enough without your making a joke of it!"

But it was Williams who knew how many bodies to look for and who kept a tally of those piled aboard the raft. It was Williams who said that Titanov was still missing, and who overrode his superior's suggestion that the marine be left to stew in his own juice. The big man was found at last, in one of the houses. An untidy heap of six naked girls had to be lifted off him before his body could be carried outside.

Another tally was made—of the weapons that had been recovered. Officers' side-arms and the marines' stunclubs were loaded aboard the workboat, together with a pile of discarded clothing. From this latter Sonya recovered her own uniform, got into it hastily.

Then, "We have to find the king," said Grimes.

"Why?" asked Williams.

"Because the bastard shot at us. I'm taking back his crossbow."

Carrying torches, the two men walked slowly through the sleeping village. For what seemed a long time they searched in vain. At last their lights showed two giant, huddled bodies, were reflected from gleaming steel.

One of the unmoving men was Hektor, and he was dead, his skull messily crushed. The other was Herak, with the crossbow, which he had used as a club, still in his hands.

The king was dead—and who would be the next king?

That, Grimes told himself, was no concern of his.

~ Chapter 20 ~

IT WAS A LONG NIGHT, and a wearing one, and Grimes was still feeling muzzy from the effects of the mushroom beer. So was Sonya, and so were Carnaby and Brenda Coles, although the navigator and the assistant biochemist had done little more than to take experimental sips of the stuff. Williams, of course, was exhibiting the infuriating, cheerful competency of the virtuously sober—but if it had not been for his efforts the sleeping crew members would never have been tucked away in their own quarters before daylight. Even so, the flush of dawn was bright in the east when the job was finally over.

Grimes turned in all standing, taking off only his jacket and his boots. He did not sleep in his bedroom—relations between him and Sonya were, naturally, rather strained, although it seemed doubtful if the late king had actually *done* anything—but on the settee in his day cabin. As his head touched the cushion he was using as a pillow he went out like a light.

When he woke up it was as though somebody had switched that figurative light back on. He was suddenly aware that someone was standing over him. He opened his eyes, realized that he was looking almost directly into the muzzle of a large-caliber projectile pistol. At this close range it was like the business end of a forty-millimeter cannon.

Behind the gun, he realized eventually, was Dalzell, who was grinning wolfishly.

385

"Major!" demanded Grimes. "What is the meaning of this?"

"Not major, Commodore," replied the marine. "Not any longer. You will address me as Your Majesty."

He must have had a skinful, thought Grimes. *He's still hallucinating like a bastard . . . I shall have to be tactful . . .* He said, "Would you mind putting that thing down?"

"Your Majesty," prompted Dalzell. "Yes, I would mind. And get this into your stupid skull—from now on *I* give the orders."

This was too much. "Have you gone mad?" roared Grimes.

"No, Commodore. Just a sudden rush of sanity to the head. That mushroom beer or whatever it was last night cleared my brain. I am seeing things in their proper perspective. What the hell's the use of beetling all around the Galaxy, not even knowing what we're looking for, when there's a kingdom—the nucleus of an empire—right here and now, just for the picking up?"

"I still say that you're mad."

"Careful, Commodore. Or Mr. ex-Commodore. I hold the ship."

"*You?* You're not a spaceman."

"I have the military power. And Hendriks is with me—he's a master astronaut, for what that's worth, as well as being the gunnery officer. And Sparks. And the engineers. And the Quack, and all the tabbies . . ." He laughed at the alarm that must have shown on Grimes' face. "No need to get too worried—yet. We haven't killed any of your pets. We might still find a use for them."

"My . . . pets?"

"The two tame telepaths. Williams. Carnaby. Their popsies."

"Their . . . popsies?"

"Really, Commodore. You surprise me. Your own ship— although not any longer!—and you don't know all that's going on aboard her. Ruth Macoboy and Brenda Coles, that's who. Williams and Carnaby are loyal to *you*—the Odd Gods of the Galaxy alone know why!—and the two wenches are loyal to their boyfriends. It's as simple as that."

Grimes watched the pistol hopefully, but with all the time that Dalzell was talking, it did not waver so much as a fraction of a degree.

Then—"What's simple?" asked Sonya coldly. She was standing in the doorway to the bedroom, dressed still in her black sweater and khaki trousers, holding Grimes' Minetti. The deadly little automatic was pointing straight at the major.

Dalzell laughed. He remarked in a very reasonable voice, "If you pull *your* trigger, Mrs. Grimes—or, if you like, Commander Verrill—reflex action will cause me to pull mine. Not that it much matters as, in any case, your ever-loving husband will get his fair share of the burst intended for me. Furthermore . . ." He pursed his lips and whistled softly. Grimes did not have to turn his head to see that two Marines had entered his day cabin.

"So . . ." murmured Sonya regretfully.

"So drop your gun, Mrs. Grimes. Or Commander Verrill. Better make it Mrs. Grimes. A commander's commission in the Terran Survey Service doesn't pile on many Gs here and now, does it?"

"Better do as the man says," muttered Grimes at last.

"As the *man* says? You forget yourself, Commodore. As the *king* says."

"The major has promoted himself," explained Grimes mildly.

Surprisingly Dalzell took this in good part. He grinned, then said, "There was a vacancy, and I applied for the job. I displayed my qualifications—noisy ones, and quite spectacular . . ." His face hardened, took on a vicious twist. "On your feet, Commodore! I've wasted too much time yapping to you. My men will escort you to the empty storeroom we're using as a brig."

"I shall need . . ." began Sonya.

"You need nothing. You'll get food and water, and there's a disposal chute for your personal wastes. Shake the lead out of your pants, the pair of you!"

Grimes sighed. A man and a woman, unarmed, against at least three armed men, all of whom were trained fighters. He almost wished that Sonya had used her pistol, disastrous as the results would have been. Now the weapon was on the deck, out of reach.

"All right," he said, rolling off the settee. "All right."

Grimes and Sonya made their slow way down through the ship. Save for their escort they saw nobody. Were the crew members avoiding him of their own volition or had they been ordered so to do by Dalzell? Not that it mattered. The major, judging from his attitude, was very firmly in the saddle.

They came at last to the storeroom, one of those on the farm deck. It was ideal for its purpose—that of a jail cell—as it was more of a utility compartment than a storeroom proper, and had been used as a handling room for meat from the tissue-culture vats. There were benches, and washing facilities. Even with six people in it there was no overcrowding. The other four were Williams, Carnaby, Ruth Macoboy and Brenda Cole. The commander's rugged face was badly battered. He, at least, had put up a fight. He growled sardonically as the commodore and Sonya were thrust into the prison, "Welcome aboard, Skipper. This is Liberty Hall; you can spit on the mat and call the cat a bastard!"

Grimes ignored this. "Where are Ken and Clarisse?" he demanded.

"Stashed away somewhere else, I reckon. They musta been pounced on first, so that they couldn't warn us. Not that they could have warned us about Dalzell an' his bloody pongoes, thanks to that fancy antitelepathic conditioning of theirs."

"But the others. The real crew members. Ken must have had some warning, surely. A mutiny doesn't just happen, out of thin air."

"Gotta be a first time for anything, Skipper—an' this it. Don't forget that all of you were as high as kites on that fancy mushroom juice. Could be, too, that the muck damped out Ken's talents rather than enhancing 'em. But Ken an' Clarisse ain't here, that's for certain. Which is a bloody pity. If they were, we might cook somethin' up between us . . ."

And they can hear *us,* thought Grimes, *but we can't* hear *them. I could suggest that they teleport themselves here, but unless Clarisse has sketching materials to hand—which she won't have; Dalzell's no fool— there's no way at all that it can be done . . .* There was a faint dawning of hope. *But isn't there?* Grimes had read of prisoners using their body wastes, their blood even, to write or draw or paint.

A vivid picture formed itself in his mind. Wherever they were, the two telepaths were not very far away and, with a pooling of powers and a great expenditure of psionic effort, transmission of a sort would be possible to the brains of nontelepaths. Had they been in the same cell as Grimes it would have been relatively easy, of course—but not, in those circumstances, necessary.

Grimes, then, saw quite clearly the interior of a storeroom not unlike the one in which he was imprisoned. There were two benches, on each of which was a mattress. On one of the benches Mayhew was stretched supine, on the other one was Clarisse. Each of them was secured firmly to his bed by manacles at wrists and ankles.

And Clarisse could function as a teleporteuse only when she was able to paint the people to be moved or the locations to which they were to be shifted.

∾ Chapter 21 ∾

THEY MUST HAVE BEEN in their prison for all of three weeks.

They had no means of telling time; Dalzell had seen to it that they were stripped of any and all personal possessions of use or value, including their wristwatches. Meals came at irregular intervals. There was enough to sustain life, but with very little surplus. And always the food consisted of sandwiches so that there were never any table utensils that might be used as tools or weapons—not that knives or forks would have been any good against the machine pistols carried by the guards.

Time dragged.

Grimes grew a beard. He could not see it—there were, of course, no mirrors—but had to take Sonya's word for it that it was not becoming. Williams grew a beard, and it suited him. Carnaby was one of those who had undergone permanent depilation.

Sonya, although she tried very hard to maintain appearances, lost her elegance. Brenda Coles, never very elegant to start with, lost weight. Ruth Macoboy, skinny rather than slim at all times, began, with her long, unkempt black hair to look like a fairy-tale witch. The tempers of the women soured as their appearance deteriorated.

Especially trying was the lack of privacy. At first, jokes were made about it, but, as the days wore on it became no laughing matter.

Meanwhile, what was happening?

Insofar as the ship was concerned, some not-too-far-off-the-beam guesswork was possible. It seemed obvious that Davis, the chief engineer, was striking troubles with the overhaul of the inertial drive unit. This would have taken no time at all had there been shoreside workshop facilities available—but here, of course, such were nonexistent. Through decks and bulkheads, all day and every day, drifted the noise of spasmodic hammering, but never the irregular beat that would tell of a test running of the engines.

And outside the ship?

Now and again Mayhew and Clarisse would succeed in transmitting a telepathic picture of events to Grimes, a relay of a picture which they, themselves, had picked up from some member of a shore party. The commodore watched, with helpless horror, what seemed to be an execution in the main square of the village—three white-bearded old men against a wall, a firing squad of Dalzell's marines. Laser rifles were used, set at medium beam to ensure a spectacular incineration. Grimes watched, too, as those same marines dragged six girls out of a house, carried them away somewhere out of the sight of the original viewer. Again he was horrified—then realized with disgust that the young women were putting up only a token resistance.

Dalzell figured, too, in these waking visions. Every time that the major appeared he was wearing dress uniform, but with something that looked more like a crown than a helmet on his head. Some of the time he was supervising the building of what had to be a new palace—three-storied and with a sort of steeple to give it additional height, towering high over all the other houses in the village, including that which had been occupied by Hektor. At other times he was drilling his army—the marines and also a sizeable force of young native men. These latter now had spears tipped with metal instead of obsidian, and short swords that gleamed like steel. That persistent hammering, Grimes decided, was probably not entirely due to the engine overhaul. Some of the engineers must be working as armament artificers.

Grimes was not the only one to pick up the psionic broadcasts made by Mayhew and Clarisse. Sonya shared them, as did Williams. Carnaby, Ruth Macoboy and Brenda Coles did not, but listened intently to what the others told them.

"That bloody pongo," swore Williams, "is having himself one hell of a good time!"

"We most certainly are not," stated Sonya.

"But what does he intend to do with us?" asked Carnaby, of nobody in particular. Then, to Grimes, "You've made a study of this sort of thing, sir. Piracy, mutiny and all the rest of it. In the old days, I mean. At sea."

"I suppose I have, James," admitted the commodore.

"What usually happened to the victims of mutiny or piracy?" The young man looked as though he regretted having asked the question, but persisted with it. "What usually happened?"

Grimes had already given the matter considerable thought. He said, "It varied. It all depended on how bad a bastard the pirate captain or the leader of the mutineers was, and on how bad his men were. Some victims were made to walk the plank—which was not as funny as it sounds. It must have been a rather nasty method of execution. Some were marooned, on desert islands. Some—like Bligh of the *Bounty*—were cast adrift in open boats . . ."

"*They* had a chance . . ." muttered Carnaby.

"After this prison," remarked Sonya, "a desert island would seem like paradise."

"Depending, of course," Grimes told her, "on its location and on its natural resources. Here, we are sheltered from the weather and are getting adequate food."

"A defeatist attitude, John."

"Mphm. Perhaps. Don't forget that many a person has wished himself out of the frying pan and found himself in the fire."

"But Dalzell must have *some* intentions as far as we're concerned," persisted Sonya.

"But are they good ones?" asked Williams.

Probably not, thought Grimes. *Almost certainly not.* A thought insinuated itself into his mind—from outside was it? put there by Mayhew or Clarisse? A public trial, followed by a public execution . . . Would Dalzell dare? Perhaps the major would consider a trial too risky, but the execution would make it plain to all hands that *he* now was the leader.

"And were you thinking what I was thinking?" asked Sonya. "Yes."

"Me too," growled Williams.

"Did . . . did you receive something?" asked Brenda Coles.

"I'm not sure," Grimes told her. "I think we did." He tried to grin. "I think that Dalzell will turn out to be one of the really bad bastards."

"An' that brings me," put in Williams, "to something that I've been wanting to say for a long time. He, the major, has to do something about the Skipper and Sonya and meself. He can't afford to have us running around loose. But there's no reason at all why young James an' Brenda an' Ruth should be for the high jump. Next time that the pongoes bring us our tucker we can ask 'em to tell Dalzell that the three of you are willing to be faithful and loyal servants of his Majesty. You all have skills that he'll be needing."

"No," said Carnaby.

"*No*," said the two girls.

"If you have any sense," Grimes told them, "you'll say 'yes.'"

"*No!*" they told him. And they refused to be persuaded.

It was some hours later when the door to the storeroom opened.

And about time, thought Grimes irritably. The next meal wasn't due; it was considerably overdue. Even those unappetizing sandwiches would be welcome.

But no packets of sandwiches were tossed in through the barely opened door, which remained open. Grimes got to his feet, feeling the beginnings of hope. *Release?* Then his brief elation faded. This could only be a squad of marines to lead him and the others to their execution.

"All right," he said. "Let's get it over with."

A voice replied—a woman's voice, unfamiliar yet oddly familiar. It said, "Quickly, John. You must seize the ship."

"Who the hell . . . ?" demanded Grimes. He was at the doorway in two swift steps. He was staring at a stranger, a naked, fair-haired girl, obviously one of the women from the village. She stared at him. It was as though, he realized suddenly, somebody else were looking at him from behind her eyes.

"There is no time to lose, John. Dalzell and most of the crew are at a feast in the village. There is only a skeleton watch on board."

"Who . . . Who are you?"

The woman laughed, then replied, "Believe it or not, I'm Ken. Elena, here, is susceptible to telepathic control. She was kept on board to keep the watchkeepers company. They've been having their own party. When they passed out she collected the keys."

It made sense—or as much sense as psionic technology ever made. But it was a pity, thought Grimes, that Mayhew hadn't used this borrowed body to pick up a few hand weapons on the way down. Even so, he and the loyalists would have the advantage of surprise. Once in the control room he would have the ship's armament at his disposal; within minutes he would plaster the village with Morpheus D.

"Now you're cooking with gas!" remarked the woman approvingly in a voice that sounded more and more like Mayhew's.

"What about you and Clarisse?" asked Grimes.

"Never mind about us. Elena will release us while you're on the way to Control. But *hurry!*"

"You heard?" demanded the Commodore, turning to his cellmates. "Then come *on!*"

He brushed past the girl, ran out into the alleyway. He made his way to the axial shaft, pushed the button for the elevator. Indicator lights flashed; the cage had been only two decks below, at the marines' messdeck. The door opened, the freed prisoners scrambled in, followed by the native woman.

"Let me—let Elena—off at the boat-bay compartment," said Mayhew through her mouth. "We're in one of the storerooms there."

"We'll wait for you there," said Grimes, pushing the right button.

"No. Get up to the control room as fast as you can. The officer of the guard woke up and is looking for Elena . . ." There was a pause. "*And* his keys. Never mind us, John. Carry on straight up."

After a second's hesitation Grimes cancelled the boat-bay compartment stop. But there was, unfortunately, no way of controlling the speed of the elevator. Its cage *was* a cage, in every sense of the word. Once the shipkeepers realized what had happened, what was happening, the prisoners would be prisoners again, trapped between decks.

The elevator jolted to a halt, just as the stridency of alarm bells shrilled throughout the ship. But luck was with Grimes and the loyalists. Whoever had cut the power had done so hastily, without checking the location of the cage. It had stopped at the level of the boat-bay compartment.

"Out!" ordered Grimes as Williams strained at the manual door control. "Out!" The floor of the cage was half a meter above deck level, but that did not matter. The compartment, now, was sealed off from the rest of the ship by the airtight doors, but that did not matter either. There was no egress either up or down, forward or aft—but there was still *out*.

Number Three was the nearer of the several bays. "Number Three Boat!" snapped Grimes. "How is she, Bill?"

"Fine, Skipper, last time I checked. She can take us anywhere."

"Then open her up. We'll take her."

He ran behind Elena to the storeroom where Mayhew and Clarisse were confined. He snatched the bunch of magnetic keys from her hand; Ken, as he knew very well, always fumbled pitifully with even the simplest magnetic devices, and when he was controlling another's body the fumbling would be even more pronounced. He opened the door, saw Mayhew and Clarisse stretched on their benches, manacled at wrists and ankles. He released them, was briefly surprised at the agility with which they swung off their beds. But, of course, Dalzell would have allowed them to exercise under guard; he would have had uses for them.

Grimes had no need to tell the telepaths of his intentions. They followed him without question to the boat bay. As they were about to board the craft the commodore asked suddenly, "Where's Elena?"

"She ran off as soon as I got out of her mind. She's frightened. She's hiding . . ."

"Can't you control her again? We can't leave her to face the music."

"I'm . . . I'm trying, John. But she has a strong mind. She's . . . fighting back . . ."

"What's that noise?" asked Sonya sharply.

Faintly, but audible now that the alarm bells had stopped ringing, was the wailing of a siren, an externally mounted horn. It would not be long before Dalzell and the mutineers returned from the village. And surely, thought Grimes, not even the major would blame the native girl for the escape of the prisoners. *But I wouldn't like to be in the shoes of the shipkeepers!* he told himself with grim satisfaction.

"All systems Go!" shouted Williams. "It's time we went!"

The commodore clambered into the boat, took the pilot's seat. He sealed the hull. He pressed the remote control button that should open the external door of the bay. Nothing happened; he was still looking out through the forward viewport at an unbroken sheet of metal. Whoever was in the control room had had enough sense to actuate all locking devices throughout the vessel.

But a lifeboat is a lifeboat, designed to get away from a distressed ship in practically every foreseeable combination of adverse circumstances. *The emergency break-out*, thought Grimes, *should be working.* It was. When he pushed the red button one explosive charge blew the door outwards, and another one threw the boat clear of the ship. Had the inertial drive failed to function she would have hit the village like a projectile—as it was, she blundered noisily skyward, pursued by a stream of tracer fired by somebody who was obviously not Hendriks.

"He, whoever he is," commented Williams scornfully, "would make a good gunnery officer . . . He'd make a good gunnery officer weep!"

"Don't complain," Sonya told him.

~ Chapter 22 ~

THE BOAT WAS SPACEWORTHY enough. All its equipment was in good working order and it was fully stocked with emergency provisions. Grimes had no doubt of its capability to transport him and the loyalists to Mars, or to anywhere else in the Solar System. The *Quest*, with her main engines immobilized, could not pursue. Unfortunately, the ship's armament, both main and secondary, was still in working order.

Grimes turned to Mayhew. "Ken," he said urgently, "try to tune in to Hendriks. Get inside his mind, find out what he's doing, what he's going to do . . ."

"I . . . I'm already in touch. I'm picking up his thoughts. Dalzell is telling him to swat us out of the sky."

"Hell!" muttered the commodore. And it would be hell, a brief, searing and spectacular inferno if one of *Faraway Quest*'s missiles found the lifeboat. A near-miss would be enough to destroy her. Her inertial drive unit was hammering flat out, but she could not hope to outrun the vicious rockets. It would be many, many minutes before she was safely out of effective range.

Grimes glanced nervously out of the viewports, saw that the others were doing the same. There was nothing to see; there would be nothing to see until the boat broke through the heavy overcast. Unless . . . Perhaps a blinding flash, and then oblivion.

Mayhew was speaking softly. "He . . . he is telling Dalzell that the

397

self-guiding missiles are inoperable . . . But . . ." there was amazement in the telepath's voice . . . "but I think that he is lying . . ."

Grimes felt the beginning of hope. Perhaps Hendriks was not, after all, a murderer.

"*Fire* . . ." whispered Mayhew.

"Wait for it!" exclaimed Williams with spurious heartiness. "Wait for it!"

"We've no bloody option, Bill," remarked Grimes resignedly. He suppressed the temptation to throw the boat violently off course; to do so might convert a miss into a near-miss or even into a direct hit. He would stand on, trusting in whatever decency remained in the gunnery officer's makeup.

Then it happened.

Below and to starboard the clouds were rent apart by the explosion, by a brief and dreadful burgeoning of scarlet fire. The ambient mists vanished, flash-dried by the searing heat of the blast. The boat was driving upwards towards the domed ceiling of a roughly globular cavern of clear air in the center of which a man-made sun had been born, had lived briefly and had died. The first shock wave hit her and, even through the insulation, the doomsday crack of it was deafening. The first shock wave hit her, and then the secondary, and then the tertiary, slamming her to port and up. Grimes, sweating, fought the controls, somehow keeping the little craft steady on her heading. She was buffeted by the turbulence engendered by the detonation of the missile's warhead; it seemed that surely she must break up, spilling her people into the incandescent nothingness.

Up, Grimes pushed her. Up, up . . .

And she was clear of the overcast, although only those who had not been temporarily blinded by the blast could see the bright stars in the black sky overhead, the yellow moon, lopsided, in its last quarter, low on the eastern horizon.

Below them was the cloud—towering cumulus, vaporous peaks and pinnacles that grew and shifted and toppled, that swirled around and above the point where the rocket had burst.

"*Fire* . . ." whispered Mayhew again, echoing Hendriks' thought and spoken word.

Grimes said nothing. He knew that he must gain altitude, and yet more altitude, and even then there would be no safety. The inertial drive snarled in protest but kept going.

This time it was a salvo of three missiles, all of them well short of the target. This must have been, the commodore realized, intentional on Hendriks' part, just as the first miss must have been intentional—although too near for comfort. The rockets burst where the boat *had* been, not where she was now. They flared dazzlingly beneath the surface of the cloud mass, turning the shadowy canyons into deep rivers of flame.

Mayhew started to laugh. It was not hysterical mirth. It was genuine amusement.

"Share the joke, Ken," snapped Sonya. "We need something to cheer us up."

"That last salvo," said the telepath, "consisted of four missiles . . ."

"I counted only three explosions," Carnaby told him.

"There were only three explosions, James. The fourth missile was a dud."

"So what?" demanded the navigator. "None of them came near us."

"That is so. But . . . But Hendriks is the gunnery specialist, and Dalzell is only a glorified infantryman. Hendriks told the major that the first round was the ranging shot—which it most certainly was. Then, to the observers in the ship, the bursts of the second salvo, well in the clouds and practically simultaneous, looked like a single explosion. The radar showed something falling out of control and tracked it down to the sea. Hendriks knew that it was his dud missile. Dalzell thought, as he was meant to think, that it was us . . ."

"If Hendriks is so bloody loyal," growled Williams, "why isn't he here?"

"Because he doesn't want to be, Billy. He thinks he has a future on Earth . . ."

Grimes, who had been listening, chuckled. "And so he could have. After all his given name is Thor . . ."

"Very far-fetched," commented Sonya. "And what about the others? Do none of them go down in history? Or mythology . . ."

"Those two hulking marine privates . . ." suggested Brenda Cole. "Those twin brothers . . . Their name is Rome . . ."

"Romulus and bloody Remus? Oh, no. *No.*"

"And why not, Sonya?" asked Grimes. "Come to that, the Second Engineer's name is Caine. William Caine or Bill Caine . . . Tubal Cain or Vulcan?"

His wife snorted inelegantly. "At least," she said, "you will not realize *your* secret ambition. You will not go down in history as Zeus, father of the gods. Let us be thankful for small mercies."

The commodore sighed. He realized wryly that his display of regret was at least half genuine. He checked the instruments, then set the controls of the boat on automatic. She would fly herself now, driving up and clear through and out of the atmosphere, until such time as course could be set. He motioned Carnaby to the seat next to his. He pointed out through the wide forward viewport to where Mars gleamed ruddily, almost a twin to the equally ruddy Antares only a few degrees to the south.

He said, "There she is, James. We've a toy computer that's little more than an electric abacus and precious little else in the way of navigational gear. We haven't even got an ephemeris. Do you think you can get us there?"

"I do, sir," replied Carnaby confidently.

"But why Mars?" demanded Sonya. "We should be safe enough from Dalzell and his mob in Earth's southern hemisphere—especially since he thinks that we've all been killed . . ."

"Hendriks *knows* that we haven't been. He's given us our chance, but he wouldn't welcome us back. Am I correct, Ken?"

"You are, John. I'll tell you what he was thinking. 'And that's the last I'll see of that cantankerous old bastard! He'll not do much good for himself among the Australian aborigines . . .'"

"So Australia is definitely *out*," said Grimes. "And the Martians *may* be willing to help us."

"That'll be the sunny Friday, Skipper," said Williams. "But we'll give it a go."

"We'll give it a go," agreed Grimes.

～ Chapter 23 ～

A LIFEBOAT IS DESIGNED to save and to sustain life; comfort is a minor consideration. Nonetheless, Grimes and his seven companions were lucky. The boat was certified to accommodate fifty persons; there were only eight people aboard it, so there was room to stretch and for the maintenance of some degree of privacy. There were six toilets—two forward, two aft and two amidships—all of them part and parcel of the boat's life-support systems. In this respect the loyalists were almost as well off as they had been aboard the ship. There was a stock of the versatile, all-purpose plastic sheeting in one of the lockers, more than enough for the improvisation of separate sleeping quarters. Grimes did mutter something about "bloody gypsy tents," but nobody took him seriously. The initial supply of fresh water—which would be cycled and recycled many times before planetfall—was ample for all requirements. The food supply—mainly dehydrated concentrates—was adequate, highly nutritious and boring.

The power cells, always kept fully charged, had provided the energy needed to push the boat up clear of the atmosphere and into orbit. The initiation of the fusion reaction which was the craft's main power source took time, care and patience. The reactor's controls were so designed that anybody able to read and to follow instructions would be capable of starting the thing going, however—an absolute necessity in a vehicle which might well (as on this occasion) number no qualified engineers among its crew.

There was, of course, a powerful inertial drive unit, but neither reaction drive nor interstellar drive. But there was Carlotti equipment in addition to the normal space time transceiver. The boat was incapable of making an interstellar voyage, although any deep space ship picking up the initial distress call (if any) from the parent vessel or from the boat itself would be able to home on the Carlotti transmitter. Voyages within a planetary system, however, were quite practicable. That from Earth to Mars, Carnaby estimated, would occupy a mere fifty days.

He told the others this while they were eating—"enjoying" would be the wrong word—their first meal in the lifeboat.

"A *mere* fifty days?" exploded Sonya. "In *this* sardine can!"

"Don't complain," Grimes told her. He went on to speak of the much longer voyages, in much worse conditions, that had been made in open boats on Earth's seas. "And at least," he concluded, "there's no danger of our having to resort to cannibalism."

"Isn't there?" demanded Sonya. She looked with distaste at the pallid mess in the bowl of her spoon. "Isn't there? After a few weeks of this . . . *goo* we might feel like it!"

"Cheer up, Sonya," Williams admonished her. "The first fifty years are the worst!"

"I said 'days,' not 'years,' Commander," corrected Carnaby.

"Fifty days . . ." said Grimes thoughtfully. "Ample time to get ourselves organized—but not too much time. To begin with we must try to get it through to the Martians that we come in peace. That's your department, Ken and Clarisse. Try to get in touch with that local telepath again. Play the poor, helpless castaway angle for all you're worth!"

"And poor, helpless castaways is just what we are," commented Sonya.

"Mphm. Not so helpless, as long as we have a ship of sorts under us. But there's no point in telling the Martians that. Now, has anybody else any suggestions?" He added, looking at his wife, "Constructive ones, that is."

"I was rather wondering, sir," asked Ruth Macoboy diffidently, "if I should try to get in touch too. Our NST transceiver, on a tight beam, has a very long range . . ."

Grimes considered this. He said at last, "We're up against the language barrier, Ruth. Ken and Clarisse, working with ideas rather than words, aren't . . . Mphm. But a beamed signal, even if it's no more than a repetition of a Morse symbol, will tell them that we're coming, that we aren't trying to slink up on them, as it were . . ."

"Assuming that *they* are tuned in and listening," said Sonya.

"They probably will be," said Grimes, "once the telepathic contact has been established." He thought, *It doesn't matter, anyhow. The main consideration is keeping as many people as possible fully employed on a voyage like this. In some ways—in one way—Bligh was lucky. During his boat voyage after the Bounty mutiny he charted everything along his track.*

"Can't anything be done about the food?" asked Sonya.

Grimes turned to Brenda Coles. "That's your department, Brenda. What has *Faraway Quest*'s Assistant bio-chemist to suggest?" He grinned. "My apologies. As far as this boat is concerned, you're *the* bio-chemist."

The small, plump blonde smiled back at him. "This *is* rather grim, isn't it? But I hope that the next meal will be better. There's a supply of flavoring essences in the galley—chicken, steak, lobster, and coffee, chocolate, vanilla . . . The trouble is that I've never been much of a cook . . ."

"*Your* department, then, Sonya," said Grimes. "Ruth will measure out for each meal what we need in the way of proteins, vitamins and whatever to keep us functioning. You will try to turn these basic requirements into something palatable."

"Chicken mole . . ." murmured Sonya thoughtfully.

"And what's that?" demanded Williams. "I've heard rabbit referred to as underground chicken . . ."

"Really, Bill," she said reprovingly. "Chicken mole is a Mexican dish. Chicken with mole sauce. The mole sauce is made mainly from bitter chocolate."

"Gah!" exclaimed Williams.

"And the other main ingredient of the sauce," Grimes told him, "is dried chicken blood. Mphm. I don't think, somehow, that we shall be having chicken mole on the menu. Anyhow, do your best, ladies.

And remember that there's no risk of the customers deciding to patronize another restaurant . . ."

"There's always the risk of their murdering the chef!" said Williams cheerfully.

But it wouldn't come to that, Grimes hoped. His people would be keeping themselves occupied during the seven long weeks of the voyage. Williams there was no need to worry about—*he* would always find something useful to do. And as long as Carnaby could navigate, *he* would be happy. And if time did hang heavily, in spite of everything, there was the games locker, with chess, Scrabble and the like, as well as packs of playing cards and sets of dice. This would be no luxury cruise, but it could have been a lot worse.

Chapter 24

IT WAS A LONG, long drag from Earth to Mars.

They had made much longer voyages, all of them, but in conditions which, compared to those in the lifeboat, were fantastically luxurious. There had been organized entertainment and ample facilities for self-entertainment. There had been a well-varied menu and meals had been occasions to look forward to. In the boat meals were something to be gotten through as expeditiously as possible. In spite of the skill of Sonya and Brenda, in spite of the wide variety of flavorings, the goo was still goo. Texture is as important as taste and appearance.

Of them all, Carnaby was the happiest. Grimes almost regretted that the navigator had been one of the officers remaining loyal to him. He, the commodore, had always loved navigation, had always maintained that it was an art rather than a science. But he had always maintained, too, that it is rather pointless to keep a dog and to bark oneself. So . . . So Carnaby was the navigating officer. Carnaby was a direct descendant of those navigators who, in the days of sail on Earth's seas, had been called "artists." Grimes helped Carnaby when he was asked to, but this was not very often.

Out from Earth's orbit, in a widely arcing trajectory, swept the boat, its inertial drive unit hammering away with never a missed beat. Through the interplanetary emptiness—the near-emptiness—it flew, with the ruddy spark that was Mars at first wide on the bow but, with every passing day, the bearing closing. Carnaby was shooting at a moving target and, ideally, his missile (of which he was part) would arrive at Point X at precisely the same second as its objective. From a mere spark the red planet expanded to an appreciable disc, even to the naked eye. Astern, on the quarter, the blazing sun diminished appreciably.

Meanwhile Ken and Clarisse Mayhew rarely stirred from the little tent of plastic sheeting that they had made their private quarters—but they were not idle. Now and again Grimes would hear their soft voices as they vocalized their thoughts, their psionic transmissions. *Castaways calling Mars . . . Castaways calling Mars . . . Do you hear me? Come in please. Come in . . . Come in . . .* The radio-telephonic jargon sounded strange in these circumstances, but its use was logical enough.

On they drove, on, and on.

Mars was a globe now, an orange beach ball floating in the black sea of space, its surface darkly mottled, the polar frost cap gleaming whitely. It was time, Carnaby announced, for deceleration. He and Grimes took their places at the controls, turned the lifeboat about its short axis until the thrust of the drive was pushing them away from the planetary objective instead of towards it. It would be days, however, before the braking effect was fully felt.

And then Mayhew came out from his tent and said, "John, I have them. I have the same man that I had before, when they gave us the bum's rush . . ."

Grimes made the last adjustment to his set of controls, said to Carnaby, "She's all yours, James." Then, to Mayhew, "Any joy, Ken?"

"I . . . I think so, John. They aren't overjoyed to learn that we're on our way to them, but they realize, I think, that we have no place else to go. We can land, they say, as long as we don't get underfoot."

"Decent of them. No, I'm not being sarcastic. After the exhibition that Hendriks put on the last time that we were out this way it's not surprising that they don't want to know us. Mphm. Well, I suggest that you go into a huddle with Ruth—frequencies and all that—and try to get them to set up some sort of radio beacon for us to home on. We'll set this little bitch down exactly where they want us to . . ."

"Into the jaws of a trap, perhaps," suggested Sonya pessimistically.

"No, Sonya. They aren't that sort of people," Mayhew told her.

"I sincerely hope that you're right."

"I am right," he said shortly. "In fact, now that they have learned quite a lot about us, they are hinting that they may be able to help us. After all, their level of technology is a high one."

"From you," she said, "that *is* praise."

"Machines have their uses," he admitted.

And Grimes thought, *Can they get us back to where and when we belong? Science or black magic—what does it matter as long as it gets the right results . . .*

∾ Chapter 25 ∾

SLOWLY THE BOAT DROPPED DOWN through the clear Martian sky, its inertial drive muttering irritably, riding the beam of the radio beacon that had been set up on the bank of one of the minor canals. The line of approach took them well clear of any city, although a sizeable metropolis could just be seen, a cluster of fragile towers on the far northern horizon. There were no villages within view, no small towns. There was only the desert, ochre under the bright sunlight, with a broad, straight band of irrigation sweeping across it from north to south, a wide, dark green ribbon down the center of which ran a gleaming line of water.

In some ways this Mars was not unlike the terraformed Mars that Grimes had known (would know). The air was a little thinner, perhaps, and there was less water—but it was, even so, utterly dissimilar to the almost dead world upon which the first explorers from Earth had made their landing. Nonetheless, this was a dying world. There was an autumnal quality in the light, bright though it was . . . *Rubbish*! he told himself angrily. But the feeling persisted.

The commodore had the controls, and Carnaby was visibly sulking. Grimes was more amused than otherwise by his navigator's reaction to his taking charge at the finish. Meanwhile, he watched the needle of the improvised radio compass, keeping the boat exactly on course. Carnaby had done well, he thought, very well—but he, Grimes, was entitled to his fun now and again. Carnaby had done well, and so had all of the others. Clarisse and Ken Mayhew were mathematical morons, but the minds of Carnaby and Ruth Macoboy had been opened to them, and the telepaths, working with their opposite numbers on Mars, had been able to cope with the task of setting up a radio-navigational system. Fortunately mathematics is a universal language, and the basic laws of physics are valid anywhere in the known Galaxy . . .

"There's a light!" called Carnaby, who was in the co-pilot's seat, pointing.

Yes, there was a light, winking, brilliantly scarlet against the dark green. The commodore switched his attention from the radio compass to the visual mark. With his free hand he picked up the binoculars, studied the landing place. There were buildings there, he saw, although they seemed to be little more than plastic igloos. But there was no sign of an airstrip or a landing apron. This did not much matter, as the boat would be set down vertically—but Grimes was reluctant to crush what looked like a crop of food plants during his landing.

"It's all right, John," said Mayhew. "They aren't worried about this last harvest. They will not be needing it."

"Mphm?" But if Mayhew said so, then this was the way it was.

Grimes reduced speed as he lost altitude, coming in at little more than a crawl. The downthrust of the drive produced a wake of crushed vegetation. This effect could have been avoided by coming in over the canal itself—but it was too late to think about that now. In any case, he had Mayhew's word for it that it didn't matter. Finally he dropped the boat to the ground no more than a meter from the flashing beacon. He looked out through the ports at the cluster of plastic domes. What now?

A circular doorway appeared in the skin of the nearer one. A figure appeared in the opening. It was not unmanlike, but was unhumanly thin and tall, and the shape of the head was cylindrical rather than roughly spherical. But it had two arms, two legs, two eyes and a mouth.

"Dwynnaith," said Mayhew. "He is here to meet us . . ."

"Where's the red carpet?" demanded Williams.

Mayhew ignored this. "His people may be able to help us. But, first, he wishes to inspect the boat."

"Tell him," said Grimes, "that this is Liberty Hall, that he can—"

"I'm rather tired of that expression," interrupted Sonya.

"Just convey the correct impression, then," Grimes said. "And tell him that we're sorry not to be able to receive him on board with the proper hospitality."

"That," Mayhew assured the commodore, "is the very least of their worries. At this particular point of their history they regard us as a nuisance. Luckily, some of their mathematicians are intrigued by our predicament and have decided to help us." He smiled slightly. "By helping us they are also getting us out of their hair."

Grimes pushed the buttons that would open the door and extrude the ramp. He remarked, as he did so, "I was brought up never to look a gift horse in the mouth. As long as they help us I shall be grateful, and not worry about their motivation."

Dwynnaith clambered into the boat. He was all arms and legs, and his garments of metal and plastic gleamed like the chitinous integument of an insect. He exuded a vaguely unpleasant dry, musty odor. He creaked as he moved. He ignored Grimes, Williams, Carnaby, Sonya, Ruth Macoboy and Brenda Coles, went straight to Mayhew and Clarisse. He extended a three-fingered hand on the end of a spidery arm, touched first Mayhew and then Clarisse lightly on the forehead. They responded, although they had to reach up to return the salutation.

Escorted by the human telepaths, he made his slow way aft until he came to the boat's Carlotti transceiver. He stared at the instrument with his huge lidless eyes for at least a minute, then touched the antenna with his left hand. The elliptical Mobius Strip rotated slowly about its long axis in response to the impulse of his thin finger. He looked at it, standing in motionless silence, for about five minutes. It was impossible to read any expression on that almost featureless face.

"Well?" asked Grimes at last. "Well?"

"I—we—think that it is well, John," said Mayhew. "He is reporting what he is observing to his colleagues in the city. They, in turn, are passing the information on to the mathematicians . . ."

But what the hell, Grimes asked himself, *has our Carlotti transceiver to do with their helping us?* Then he remembered—or did the picture come from outside his mind?—the towers of the city they had seen, each of which had what looked like a Carlotti antenna at its highest point.

Mayhew spoke again. "We are to stay here, John, until sent for. We can live aboard the boat or in the temporary dwellings, as we please. Meanwhile *they* would like to take our Carlotti set to the city to study it and—as far as I can gather—make the necessary modifications. If Ruth will unbolt it from the bulkhead . . ."

"Modifications?" demanded Grimes. "What modifications? And what for?"

"I'm no wiser than you are, John. All that I know is that it's somehow important. They must have it if they're to help us. They haven't the time to produce a similar, suitably miniaturized instrument of their own."

"Do as the man says, Ruth," ordered Grimes. "Or do as the Martian says."

As Mayhew and Clarisse escorted Dwynnaith from the boat she had assembled her tools ready to start work.

Chapter 26

DWYNNAITH returned to the city in a blimplike airship that came out for him. Carnaby, watching the clumsy-seeming contraption approaching, said, "A gasbag? A dirigible balloon? I thought these people were highly advanced, but . . ."

"And what's wrong with it, James?" Grimes asked him. "Why consume power just to stay aloft when, with aero-static lift, you do it for free?"

"But the speed of the thing . . . Or the lack of speed, rather . . ."

"If you're in no great hurry," said the commodore, "an airship is at least as good as any other form of transport."

The Martian, still silent, was obviously communing with Mayhew. Then the telepath said, "He wants us to keep well away from the beacon, John."

"Why, Ken?"

"I'm . . . I'm not quite sure. Some mechanical technicality about anchoring . . ."

It was a pity, thought Grimes, that Mayhew was such a moron in all matters concerning machinery. But, probably, the airship would be lowering some kind of grapnel. It made sense. He and the others moved well away from the immediate vicinity of the still-flashing beacon.

The airship was by no means as primitive as it had seemed from a distance. As it approached it lost altitude, and Grimes could see the silvery mesh that enclosed the ballonnettes tightening, compressing the gasbags, reducing buoyancy. Here was no wasteful valving of gas. The ship came in very slowly at the finish, its single, pusher airscrew just ticking over. When it was almost directly over the beacon it stopped. There was a loud *thung!* and a metal projectile shot out and down from the gondola, burying itself in the soil. As it did so the grapnel arms opened, to grip firmly. The mooring line—a flexible wire, pencil-thin—tightened as a winch in the airship took the strain, hauling it down for the last few meters. Then it floated there, riding quietly to the slight breeze, the skids of its undercarriage just clear of the tops of the green plants.

Dwynnaith stood a little apart from the humans, issuing what sounded like a rapid-fire stream of orders. So he *could* speak, and so the airship's crew were not telepaths, thought Grimes. His voice was painfully shrill, as were the voices that answered him from inside the gondola. It was like the chirping of insects, or of birds. *Like birds?* wondered the commodore, the beginning of a wild surmise taking vague shape in his mind. Like birds? Somehow that tied in with the autumnal feel in the air. There was some correlation—but what?

Dwynnaith clambered with anthropoidal agility up a short ladder that was extended from the open door of the gondola. Grimes noted that as his weight came on it the gasbag was allowed to expand in compensation. He stood in the doorway which, although narrow, was quite wide enough to accommodate both himself and one of the crew members. The two attenuated beings were obviously waiting for something.

"The Carlotti transceiver . . ." said Mayhew.

The dismantled instrument was handed up and taken inside. The door slid shut. Abruptly the anchor jerked from the ground, its blades retracting. The airship bounded upwards, turning in a wide arc as it did so, flew steadily northwards. Soon it was no more than an almost invisible dot in the clear sky.

"And what happens now?" asked Carnaby.

"We wait," said Mayhew.

"For what?" demanded Sonya.

"If I knew, I'd tell you," replied the telepath testily.

So they waited.

They decided to live in the plastic domes that had been set up for their use; the temporary, inflatable dwellings offered far more comfort and privacy than the cramped quarters of the lifeboat. The furniture—beds and chairs and tables of a sort, also inflatable—must have teen especially made with human proportions in mind. There was no heating, although this did not much matter as the double skin formed adequate insulation against the coldness of the Martian night, and there was a good supply of blankets woven from some synthetic fibre. There was no lighting, but portable lamps could be brought in from the boat. There were no cooking facilities, but the lifeboat's galley could be used for the preparation of meals. No food was provided, but the boat's stores were very far from being exhausted.

There was food growing all around them, of course. The boat carried the means whereby spacemen stranded on an alien planet could test local foodstuffs to determine their suitability or otherwise for human consumption, and Brenda Coles was a qualified biochemist. She announced that the beanlike crop among which they were sitting was not only edible; it was highly nutritious. Unfortunately the flavor was vile, and nothing could be done to kill the taste.

Grimes said, after an experimental nibble and hasty spitting out, "Perhaps we *would* have been better off in Australia . . . Even witchety grubs'd taste better than this!"

He was not, after the first day or so, happy. There was so little to do. He would have liked to have taken the boat to make a detailed exploration of the countryside—but this, Mayhew assured him, would most certainly not be approved by the Martians. "We must stay here, John," he said firmly. "We must be ready to go to the city as soon as they send for us. Bear in mind that we are uninvited guests and that we must do nothing, nothing at all, to antagonize our hosts."

"But they *will* help us?"

"They think that they will be able to help us."

And with that Grimes had to be satisfied.

Of them all, only Brenda Coles seemed to be reasonably content. She was only a biochemist, not a xenobiologist, but she possessed a smattering of xenobiology and occupied herself by attempting to catalogue the flora and fauna in the vicinity of the camp. Carnaby helped her, although not with over-much enthusiasm. He complained, out of her hearing, "Damn it all, I'm a navigator, not a butterfly hunter!"

Not that the butterflies, so-called, *were* butterflies. They were winged arthropods of a sort—but arthropods are not warm-blooded, and these things were. In spite of this they had not survived the millennia prior to Man's first landing on Mars—but neither had much of anything else, plant or animal. Perhaps the great meteor shower which formed the craters had wiped out practically all life on the Red Planet—or would wipe out all life.

"But what about the cities?" asked Grimes, when this theory was advanced. "You can't tell me that each meteor had the name of a city written on it. There must have been *something* left for men to find."

"But there wasn't," said Williams.

"No. There wasn't—save for a couple or three dubious artifacts."

"I think . . ." began Mayhew hesitantly, "I think that we arrived just before some sort of mass migration . . . An old world, senescent, and its people moving on to greener, fresher pastures . . ."

Carnaby picked up the home-made butterfly net that he had been using, pretended to strum it as though it were a guitar.

"I've laid around and played around, this old town too long," he sang.

"Summer almost gone, winter comin' on . . .

"I've laid around and played around this old town too long,

"And I feel I gottagotta travel on . . ."

"Mphm," grunted Grimes. "Yes, there is that sort of feel in the air. But . . ." Then he, too, sang, in spite of Sonya's protests.

"There's a lonesome train at six oh eight a-comin' through the town,

"A-comin' through the town, an' I'll be homeward bound,

"There's a lonesome train at six oh eight a-comin' through the town . . .

"An' I feel I gotta travel on . . ."

"No one's stopping you," said his wife acidly.

"You don't get the point. When you board that lonesome train you don't take the town with you. You leave it behind. You leave town, in fact."

"What are you drivin' at, Skipper?" asked Williams.

"I . . . I don't quite know. When I was a kid, when I was a cadet at the Survey Service Academy, we were supposed to read selected twentieth century science fiction. Wild stuff, most of it, and well off the beam most of the time. And yet, after years, some of it sticks in my memory. There was one story about an invention called, I think, the spindizzy. It was a sort of antigravitational device that lifted entire cities and sent them whiffling around the Galaxy as enormous spaceships with closed economies . . .

"What if the Martians have something of the kind in mind? What if those antennae on the towers of their cities, like Carlotti antennae, aren't for communication but are something on the same general lines as our Mannschenn Drive? After all, both the Mannschenn Drive and the Carlotti Communication System do funny things to Space and Time . . . Mphm. It could be that they've taken our Carlotti set so they can modify it so it can be used as an interstellar drive for the boat . . ."

"And if they have, if they can," asked Sonya, "where do we go to? And, come to that, why?"

Carnaby started to sing again.

"Sheriff an' police a-comin' after me,

"Comin' after me, a-comin' after me . . .

"Sheriff an' police a-comin' after me,

"An' I feel I gotta travel on . . ."

Nobody thought that it was very funny.

~ Chapter 27 ~

THE SUMMONS CAME an hour before sunrise.

Mayhew woke Grimes and Sonya, while Clarisse called the others. Grimes asked, struggling into his clothes, "So this is it?"

"This is it, John."

"What is this *it*?" demanded Sonya grumpily.

"I . . . I don't know. *They* seem determined not to let me have a detailed picture. But you must be able to *feel* it . . . An atmosphere of tense expectancy . . . The bustle of embarkation . . ."

Sonya sniffed audibly, then said, "Fort Sumter has been fired upon. My regiment marches at dawn."

"I don't get it . . ." said Mayhew, after a puzzled pause.

"I do," Grimes told him. "But get into the boat, Ken. And we'll leave none of our own gear behind. Come to that, we may as well take these blankets. They might come in useful . . ."

Grimes and Sonya, muffled against the cold, emerged from the dome into the pre-dawn darkness. There was a thin, chill wind, and overhead the sky was clear, the stars bitterly bright. To the east the horizon was black against the first pale flush of day and a bright planet blazed with a greenish effulgence. Earth . . . And what were the mutineers doing, wondered the commodore. And what was happening, what would happen, to his ship, to the old *Quest*? Grimes looked away from the distant home world to the west, where tiny Phobos was slowly rising. Deimos, even tinier, was among the stars somewhere, undistinguishable from them. He had no time to waste determining its exact location. And to the north was the glare of the city lights.

Lights were coming on in the lifeboat. The loud grumbling of the inertial drive unit shattered the early morning calm. Williams must be already aboard, ensuring that all was in a state of readiness.

Grimes and Sonya hurried to the boat, clambered in through the open door. Yes, Williams was there, in the co-pilot's seat, and Clarisse, Mayhew, Carnaby, Brenda and Ruth were in their places.

"All right," said the commodore. "Let's go." He eased himself into his chair. "To the city, I suppose, Ken?"

"To the city. We are to land in the central plaza."

The hammering of the inertial drive became louder as Grimes lifted the boat. She lurched, steadied. Below her the canal was a ribbon of faintly gleaming silver in the starlight. Ahead the city was a star cluster on the black horizon, individual lights now visible through the dim-glowing haze.

As they flew on, the rosy pallor in the east spread slowly over the entire sky and the ocherous desert reflected the growing luminosity. Abruptly, a point of dazzling light appeared over the low hills, expanded rapidly. The sun was up, and the towers of the city stood stark and black in the pearly morning mist, but only for an instant; the clarity of their first appearance dimmed to a quivering insubstantiality. Grimes remembered again that story which he had read so long ago; what was its title? *Cities in Flight?* Something like that. He laughed briefly. *Just a trick of the light,* he told himself.

They flew on—and, quite suddenly, were rattling over the pinnacles of the outermost towers. On each of them gleamed the elliptical Mobius strip, but the antennae were motionless. Over broad avenues they flew, slowly now, over the graceful bridges that spanned the wide streets, that connected tower to tower in a complex mesh. There was traffic abroad—beetlelike vehicles, small knots of pedestrians, most of whom paused briefly to look upwards at the noisy flying boat.

They came to the central plaza, which was circular in plan, paved with lustrous pink stone, and ornamented by a central fountain and a profusion of flowering shrubs. To the north of the fountain a space had been cleared for them—shrubs removed, their beds flattened. So that there could be no mistake, a little red-flashing beacon indicated their landing site.

"I suppose this is where they want us," said Grimes.

"It is," Mayhew told him.

"Mphm. I think I can wriggle us in without knocking anything over," said Grimes.

Cautiously he brought the boat down. There was just room for her between the beds of shrubs and the stone benches. When her landing gear crunched on the paving he cut the drive. He said, unnecessarily, "Well, we're here."

Sonya muttered something about a blinding glimpse of the obvious but she, with the others, was staring out through the viewports. From ground level the towers were even more impressive than they had appeared from the air. They soared like fountains, flash-frozen to immobility. They, and the connecting bridges, were an arching spray of intricately interlacing stone and metal. Over all, glittering gold in the sunlight, were those enigmatic antennae.

"Company," announced Williams prosaically.

Grimes pulled his regard away from the fantastic architecture, looked to where the commander was pointing. Walking slowly towards the boat came a small procession, six Martians, all of them tall, attenuated, all with those almost featureless elongated heads, all of them looking more like insects than men. Two of them carried between them the Carlotti transceiver. It looked just as it had when it had been dismantled, but it was impossible to see what changes had been made to the components concealed by the casing.

"Dwynnaith is with them," said Mayhew. His lips went on moving, silently, as he put his thoughts into words. Then, "We are to accompany him to the assembly hall. The others will fit the . . . the apparatus back into the boat."

"Very well," said Grimes at last. He did not like the idea of letting strangers, aliens, loose in the lifeboat without himself or one of his people there to see what was being done, but realized that he had no option. "Very well."

Mayhew and Clarisse were first out of the boat. They went through the head-touching ceremony with Dwynnaith. The other Martians looked at the humans with an apparent lack of curiosity, conversed among themselves in eerie, chittering voices. Grimes was last on the ground. He waited until the telepaths seemed to have completed their silent conversation, then said, "We're all ready, Ken."

"Good. The Council is waiting for us."

The Council was waiting for them in a great hall on the ground floor of one of the towers. It was a huge room, with a vast expanse of polished floor, a high, vaulted ceiling, a platform against one wall. There was neither ornamentation nor furniture, save for the eight inflatable chairs for the humans, incongruous in the vastness. Six of these chairs were on the floor before the platform, the other two were on the platform itself.

On the dais stood the members of the Council—ten of them, all tall, all attenuated, each one indistiguishable, to human eyes, from any of the others. Dwynnaith joined them on the platform, accompanied by Mayhew and Clarisse. He stood behind their chairs as they seated themselves.

"Is it all right for us to sit?" asked Grimes.

"That is what the chairs are for, John," replied Mayhew.

The humans seated themselves. They looked up at the grave Martians, the Martians looked down at them. The silence was becoming oppressive. Grimes wished that he had his pipe with him— and that he had something with which to fill it.

Mayhew spoke again—but it was not, somehow, his voice. Just as he had controlled the girl Elena, Grimes realized, somebody or something was now controlling him. His face was the face of a humanoid robot, mobile yet not really alive.

He said, "I, Gwayllian, Moderator of the Council, have studied and learned your language. It is not possible for my vocal cords to form the necessary sounds, therefore I speak through the mouth of Mayhew. You will forgive me if my vocabulary is in any way deficient."

"You're doin' fine," remarked the irrepressible Williams.

"I thank you. But you will please not interrupt. The time fast approaches when we, when we all, must . . . go. But before our departure you should know what is about to happen.

"The first time that you came to this world, which you call Mars, we wanted nothing of you. Your landing, in your ship, would have interfered with our preparations for the . . . voyage. You were, with all the resources of your own technology at your disposal, quite capable of . . . looking after yourselves. The second time that you came, as fugitives, our preparations were almost complete. You were in no way a menace to our plans. Our engineers, our mathematicians, our scientists could spare the time to consider your problem. The solution of it was an amusing mental exercise.

"But, as a beginning, I must tell you who and what we are.

"We are not of this world. Many millennia ago our people lived on another planet, many light years from here. The name of the sun, the star, around which it revolved would be meaningless to you; besides, that star is no more. We—our ancestors—escaped before our sun became a nova. Our ships dispersed. One ship found this planet which, as it was then, was almost a twin to the one which we had abandoned. Slowly, over the centuries, we rebuilt our civilization. But slowly, over the long centuries, this world was dying. Rejuvenation of the planet was considered; this would have been a far from impossible feat. But our astronomers warned of an inevitable, coming catastrophe. An extrapolation of the orbits of Mars, as you call this world, and of sundry planetoids made it obvious that a disastrous meteoric bombardment could not be avoided.

"Yet we did not wish to leave this planet, even though we still possessed the technology for faster-than-light travel between the stars. It had become home. We did not wish to leave our cities, which had grown up with us. But there was a way. There was a way to avoid the inevitable wreck, to save our cities as well as ourselves. And we took it."

He's getting his tenses mixed, thought Grimes. He said—some comment seemed to be expected—"So you will convert your cities into FTL spaceships . . ."

"Not *will*," replied Mayhew in that voice which was not his own.

"Not *will*, but *did*. And not space ships, but time ships. We went back in Time to a period just prior to the landing of our ancestors, so that they found the civilization which they, themselves, had founded already well established and flourishing. We have repeated the cycle now a thousand times, on each occasion with only minor variations.

"You will be such a variation—and a very minor one."

Somewhere a great bell was tolling, slow, measured strokes.

A countdown, thought Grimes, *a temporal countdown* . . . He said desperately, "Suppose that we don't want to come with you?"

"You and your people may stay if you wish. You may hope to survive the meteoric storm which will wreck this world, or you may return to Earth. But do not forget that we offer you hope."

"Give it a go, Skipper," urged Williams. "Give it a go. What have we to lose?"

"Nothing," said the Moderator of the Council through Mayhew. "Nothing, but there may be—there just may be—much to gain. And now you will return to your boat."

⧼ Chapter 28 ⧽

THEY HURRIED BACK TO THE BOAT.

It lay there, in the center of the plaza, glistening in the fine spray that was blowing over it from the fountain. The Martian technicians had finished their work and were gone. The Carlotti transceiver was back in its old place. It was Sonya who noticed that the blankets they had brought from the encampment had gone. It seemed a matter of no great importance—but, thought Grimes, it looked as though it had been decided that they were to take no local artifacts with them to wherever—or whenever—they were being sent.

"Button up, Skipper?" asked Williams.

"Yes, we'd better," Grimes told him.

The doors slid shut, sealing the hull.

What was going to happen now? That great bell was still tolling with slow, solemn deliberation, measuring off the remaining minutes of time. The plaza was deserted, as were the streets and the bridges. There was a brooding atmosphere of tense expectancy.

Grimes said, more to himself than to anybody else, "I wonder if we're supposed to switch on the Carlotti . . ." He walked slowly to the instrument, put out his finger to the On-Off button. But it was no longer there. The panel was featureless. "Ruth!" he called. "Come here! What do you make of this?"

Then the bell stopped, and the silence was like a heavy blow. "Look!" shouted Carnaby. "Look!"

They looked. Atop the towers surrounding the plaza the antennae were starting to rotate, slowly at first, about their long axis, the sunlight flashing from the polished, twisted surfaces. And—"Look!" cried Ruth Macoboy. The miniature antenna of the Carlotti transceiver was rotating too, in synchronization. Slowly at first, then faster and faster, the sun was setting, falling back towards the eastern horizon. Abruptly there was deep shadow as it was obscured by the towers. Then there was twilight, but morning not evening twilight, come again. There was twilight, and night, and day, with the sun rising in the west and setting in the east.

Night followed day and day followed night, faster and faster, a flicker of alternating light and darkness that became too fast to register on the retina, that was seen as a gray dusk. Overhead the sun was a wavering band of yellow light in the sky, with Phobos as a narrower, dimmer band. The stars were streaks of silver.

Yet the buildings surrounding the plaza were still substantial, were glowing with a hard luminosity. The whirling antennae at their pinnacles flared like torches in the dimness.

For hours this went on.

It was fascinating to watch, at first, but the fascination wore off. One can get used to anything in time. Brenda Coles left the port beside which she was seated, went into the little galley. She returned with mugs of instant coffee, which all of them sipped gratefully. It was not very good coffee, but the very ordinariness of what they were doing was psychologically beneficial. They talked a little, in disjointed sentences. They wondered what was going to happen next, more for the sake of idle speculation than in the hope that any questions would be answered thereby.

Said Grimes, "I hope that we are able to watch the first colonists landing. I'd like to see what sort of ship they have . . ."

Williams said, "It must be about time for our learned friends to start putting on the brakes . . . I don't know *when* we are—but at this rate we shall be slung back to the birth of the Solar System . . ."

"Our Carlotti antenna is still spinning as fast as ever," commented Ruth Macoboy. "They must have fitted it with new bearings . . ."

"Mphm?" grunted Grimes. He looked into his empty mug. "Any more of this vile brew, Brenda?"

"I'll get some for you, Commodore."

"Don't bother. A short stroll to the galley will stretch my legs."

He got to his feet. He glanced out through the nearest viewport. The mug dropped from his hand, bounced noisily on the deck.

"What's wrong?" asked Sonya sharply.

"Something," he said at last. "Something is very much wrong!"

He thought bitterly, *The bastards! They said all along that they didn't want us, and now they've got rid of us!*

No longer were the towers of the city visible from the viewports. Outside was just a featureless landscape, although overhead the sun and the larger moon still were arches of light in the gray sky. The boat was still falling through Time, but the city must have been left many years in the future. And that city, Grimes realized, had been to the boat no more than a temporal booster, analogous to the first stage of a primitive space rocket, a booster that had given the small craft escape velocity from Now.

"Ruth," he said, "stop that bloody thing!"

"I . . . I can't, Commodore. There are no controls . . ."

"Open it up. Take a hammer to it. An axe . . ."

"No," said Mayhew. *"No."*

"And why not?"

"Can't you see, John? This is intentional . . ."

"I know bloody well it's intentional. Your long-headed friends put over a far better marooning stunt than even Dalzell could have managed. We must stop this blasted time machine before it's too late, and then we return to Earth . . ."

"And get nibbled by dinosaurs, John?" asked Sonya. "No, thank you. Hear Ken out before you do anything rash."

"We must have faith . . ." persisted the telepath.

"Faith?"

"They meant us no harm, John. They were doing their best for us. They gave us a chance to get back to our own Time . . ."

"Looks like it, doesn't it?"

Grimes glared through the port. Was that water out there, a vast, sullen sea? How far back had they come? Seas on Mars? Was that water, or was it barren rock, glowing incandescently, flowing like water? Was it molten rock—or a fire mist?

Was it a fire mist—or nothingness?

The nothingness before the birth of the worlds, of the suns, of the universe itself . . .

There is no place to go, thought Grimes.

"There is no place to go," he said.

"But there will be," stated Mayhew with an odd certainty. "There will be, or there was. There must be."

"I'll make some more coffee," said Brenda Coles.

～ Chapter 29 ～

TIME, subjective Time, passed.

The boat hung in a formless nothingness, an empty void. And yet, Grimes knew, she was not in a vacuum. She was afloat in a vast sea of hydrogen atoms, the building blocks of the universe. She was afloat, and she was adrift. To have started the inertial drive would have been pointless; there was no place to go. Furthermore nobody, not even Carnaby, was mathematician enough to work out the possible consequences. The antenna of the modified Carlotti transceiver was still whirring about its long axis, and who could say what the resultant would be if motion in Space were added to the motion in Time?

She hung there, motionless, a tiny bubble of light and life in the all-pervading nothingness. She hung there, while her crew went about the dreary business of staying alive apathetically, gulping at regular intervals their unappetizing meals, maintaining, without enthusiasm, the machinery that ensured their continued survival. Brenda Coles was beginning to look worried, however. Their stores, although ample to begin with, would not last forever. She reported the dangerous depletion of foodstuffs to Grimes.

He said, "We shall have to ration ourselves."

"Luckily," remarked Sonya, "that is no great hardship."

"Not with this tucker," agreed Williams.

"I think," said Carnaby hesitantly, "that we may be getting somewhere at last. Or somewhen . . ."

"Masterly navigation, James," said Williams. "If you can find your way through this interstellar fog you're a super genius!"

Carnaby took offense. "Nobody could find his way in *this*, Commander, and you know it. But it seems to me that there's the start of a definite luminosity . . ."

"The heat death of the Universe in reverse . . ." murmured Grimes. "The wheel always comes full circle, no matter which way it's spinning . . ."

"James is right," stated Brenda Coles firmly. "It *is* getting lighter."

There was an intense, dreadful flare of radiation, dazzling, blinding, but lasting for only an infinitesimal fraction of a second. When at last Grimes was able to reopen his watering, smarting eyes, he thought that what he was seeing was only a persistent after image, a wavering band of dull crimson light that bisected the blackness outside the viewport. But it did not fade; it seemed, instead, to be growing steadily brighter.

"The sun . . ." he whispered.

"The sun . . ." murmured Williams. "This is where we came in."

"No. Not yet. But we have to think about stopping that infernal contraption the Martians planted on us. Not yet, but as soon as conditions outside seem capable of supporting life . . ."

"Still desert, by the looks of it," Williams said. "Sand. Nothing but sand . . ."

Sand, nothing but sand, and then a hint of green under the blue-gray sky, the yellow sun. Sand, and the green area spreading . . . The greenness spreading, flickering through its seasonal changes, but spreading . . . And was that a cluster of white buildings? They appeared briefly, and were gone, but there were others, larger ones where they had stood, their outlines firmer, more solid.

Again there was the flickering that they had experienced at the start of this voyage, the rapid alternation of light and dark as day followed night, as day followed night, the periods growing longer, hours passing in seconds and then in minutes . . .

The antenna of the Carlotti transceiver was rotating more slowly now, its shape could clearly be seen. It was slowing down, slowing down, and the rate of temporal regression was slowing with it. It was slowing down, spinning lazily, stopping . . .

There was a muffled explosion. Acrid smoke billowed from the cabinet.

But Grimes hardly noticed. He was staring out of the port at a familiar sight. The boat was resting on a concrete apron, clean and bright under the noon sun. Along the perimeter were spaceport administration buildings; from a flagstaff atop the control tower flew the blue, star-spangled flag of the Interstellar Federation. And there were ships—one of the Federation's Constellation Class cruisers, a couple of Serpent Class couriers.

"Where are we?" Carnaby was asking. "Where are we?"

"Still on Mars." Grimes told him. "The neatly terraformed Mars that I used to know when I was in the Survey Service. Marsport, the Survey Service base . . ." He started to cough as the smoke from the explosion reached him. "Open her up, Bill. The air's quite good. It was when I was here last, anyhow."

He stayed aboard until all the others were out of the boat, then joined them on the concrete apron. He looked at them, deploring the scruffiness of their appearance—and his own, he knew, was equally scruffy. But it could not be helped, and it did not matter.

An immaculately uniformed officer was walking towards them. He looked at them with a distaste that he could not quite hide. He stared at the Rim Worlds Navy insignia, the stylized wheel, on the stem of the boat and his eyebrows lifted in amazement.

He asked, "Where are *you* from? And who gave you permission to land?"

"We are castaways, Commander," Grimes told him. "We request assistance."

"And you look as though you need it. And aren't you a long way from your own puddle?"

"That will do, Commander," snapped Grimes, but his authorative manner was wasted. The officer was looking at Sonya, hard.

He said, "I know you. Commander Verrill, isn't it? But we'd heard that you were dead, that you'd vanished on some crazy expedition out on the Rim. But what are you doing here?"

She said, "I'm not quite sure myself. But my husband, Commodore Grimes, is in charge." She stressed the title of rank. "I suggest that you ask him, after he has had time to get cleaned up and has made his report to his superiors, and to yours."

The Federation Survey Service commander was humbly apologetic. "Sir, I have seen photographs of you, but I never recognized you . . . *The* Commodore Grimes. But you were lost, with your ship, *Faraway Quest*. On the Rim of the Galaxy. Surely you never came all the way here in *that* . . ."

Grimes cut him short. "It's a long story, and I'm not sure that you'll believe us, even if we tell it to you. Meanwhile, please take us to whoever's in charge. My officers and myself are in need of food, fresh clothing, and possibly medical attention. Oh, and you might put a guard on the boat—although I doubt if we will be able to learn anything from the Carlotti transceiver *now*."

"Come this way, sir." The commander was obviously bursting with curiosity, but restraining it with an effort. "I'm sure that Captain Dell will be happy to make all arrangements for your comfort . . ." Then, "But how *did* you get here?"

Grimes sighed. He would be answering questions and writing reports for far into the foreseeable future. He would have to explain, or explain away, the loss of a unit of the Rim Worlds Navy. He would have to tell the stories of two mutinies—that by Druthen and that by Dalzell. When he got back to the Rim he would have to face a Court of Inquiry.

"How *did* you get here, sir?" persisted the annoying young man.

"We took the long way back," said Grimes at last.

THE
DUTCHMAN

⫷ Chapter 1 ⫸

GRIMES WAS PACKING his overnight bag without much enthusiasm.

"Do you have to go?" asked Sonya.

He replied rather testily, "I don't have to do anything. But the lightjammers have always been my babies and I've always made a point of seeing them in and seeing them out."

"But Coldharbor Bay? And in midwinter? There are times, my dear, when I strongly suspect that I married a masochist."

"If only you were a sadist we'd live happily forever after," he retorted. "And if you were a masochist you'd be coming with me to Port Ericson."

"Not bloody likely," she told him. "Why you couldn't have arranged for your precious lightjammers to berth somewhere in what passes for the Tropics on this dismal planet is beyond my comprehension."

"There were reasons," he said.

Yes, there were reasons, one of the most important being that a lightjammer is a potential superbomb with a yield greatly in excess of that of the most devastating nuclear fusion weapon. The essential guts of a star-sailor is the sphere of antimatter, contraterrene iron, held suspended in vacuum by powerful magnetic fields. In theory there is no possibility that the antimatter will ever come in contact with normal matter—but history has a long record of disasters giving

dreadful proof that theory and practice do not always march hand in
hand. The terminal port for the lightjammers, therefore, was located
in a region of Lorn uninhabited save by a handful of fur trappers. It
would have been at the South Pole itself but for the necessity for open
water, relatively ice-free the year around, to afford landing facilities for
the ships.

The first of these weird vessels, *Flying Cloud,* had been an
experimental job designed to go a long way in a long time, but with a
very low power consumption. The most important characteristic of
antimatter—apart from its terrifying explosive potential—is antimass.
A ship with a sphere of contraterrene iron incorporated in her
structure is weightless and inertialess. With her sails spread to the
photon gale she can attain an extremely high percentage of the
velocity of light but cannot, of course, exceed it.

The crew of *Flying Cloud* had been, putting it mildly, a weird mob.
Somehow they had become obsessed with the idea of turning the
vessel into a real faster-than-light ship. (The conventional starship,
proceeding under inertial drive and Mannschenn Drive, is not faster
than light, strictly speaking; she makes light-years-long voyages in
mere weeks by, as it has been put, going ahead in space while going
astern in time.) This desirable end they attempted to achieve by means
of a jury-rigged rocket drive, using home-made solid fuel, just to give
Flying Cloud that extra nudge.

Fantastically, the idea worked, although it should not have. Not
only did it work, but there were economically advantageous side
effects. The lightjammer finished up a long way off course, plunging
down to apparently inevitable destruction on Llanith, one of the
planets of the antimatter systems to the galactic west of the Rim
Worlds. But a transposition of atomic charges had taken place. She
now was antimatter herself, whereas that contraterrene iron sphere
was now normal matter.

Flying Cloud had landed on Llanith and had been welcomed by
the people, human rather than merely humanoid, of that world. She
had remained on Llanith until the Llanithian scientists and engineers
had worked out just what had happened and why. (The attitude of the
scientists at first had been that it couldn't possibly have happened.)

Then, after modifications had been made to her control systems and the makeshift rocket replaced by a properly designed reaction drive, she had returned to Lorn, carrying not only a sample shipment of trade goods but passengers from the Llanithi Consortium.

And Rim Runners, the shipping line of the Rim Worlds Confederacy, had a new trade.

Grimes sat in the forward cabin of the Rim Runners' atmosphere ferry that somebody had called—the name had stuck—The Commodore's Barge. He was not handling the controls himself. His old friend and shipmate Billy Williams, master of the deep space tug, *Rim Malemute,* was piloting. Grimes was admiring the scenery.

The landscape unrolling beneath the barge was spectacular enough but cold and forbidding. Lake Misere was well astern now and the craft was threading its way over and through the Great Barrens, skirting the higher, jagged, snowcapped peaks, its inertial drive snarling as Williams fought to maintain altitude in the vicious downdrafts. The big man cursed softly to himself.

Grimes said, "You would insist on coming along for the ride, Billy."

"I didn't think you'd make me drive, Skipper."

"Rank has its privileges."

"No need to rub it in. If it's all the same to you I'll take this little bitch down through the Blackall Pass. It's putting on distance, but I don't feel like risking the Valley of the Winds after what we've been getting already."

"As you've been saying, you're driving."

Williams brought the Barge's head around to port, making for the entrance to the pass. The opening was black in the dark gray of the cliff face, a mere slit that seemed to widen as the aircraft came on to the correct line of approach. And then they were plunging through the gloomy, winding canyon—the tortuousness of which was an effective wind baffle, although the eddies at every bend made pilotage difficult. The echoes of the irregular beat of the inertial drive, bouncing back from the sheer granite walls, inhibited conversation.

They broke out at last into what passed for daylight in these high latitudes, under a sky which, on this side of the ranges, was thickly overcast. Only to the northwest, just above the featureless horizon of the Nullarbor Plain, was there a break in the cloud cover, a smear of sullen crimson to mark the setting of the Lorn sun.

They flew steadily over the desolate tundra through the gathering darkness. The lights of Port Erikson came up at last, bright but cheerless. Beyond them Grimes could see the tiny moving sparks of white and red and green that must be the navigation lanterns of the small icebreaker that, in winter, was employed to keep Coldharbor Bay clear of floes and pack ice.

"Too bloody much seamanship about this job, Skipper," remarked Williams cheerfully.

"No such thing as too much seamanship," retorted Grimes huffily. He pulled the microphone of the VHF transceiver from its clip. "Astronautical Superintendent to Port Erikson. Can you read me? Over."

"Loud and clear, Commodore. Loud and clear. Pass your message. Over."

"My ETA Port Erikson is ten minutes from now. Over."

"We're all ready and waiting for you, Commodore."

"What's the latest on *Pamir?*"

"ETA confirmed a few minutes ago. 2000 hours our time."

"Thank you, Port Erikson. Over and out."

Ahead was the scarlet blinker that marked the end of the airstrip. Williams maintained speed until the flashing light was almost directly beneath the barge, until it looked as though they must crash into the spaceport's control tower. With only seconds to spare he brought the aircraft to a shuddering halt by application of full reverse thrust, let her fall, checked her descent a moment before she hit the concrete.

Grimes decided to say nothing. After all, he himself was frequently guilty of such exhibitions and all his life he had deplored the all-too-common *Don't do as I do, do as I say,* philosophy.

Grimes and Williams waited in the control tower with Captain Rowse, the harbormaster. (In a normal spaceport his official title would have been port captain, but a normal spaceport does not run to a harbor, complete with wharfage and breakwaters.)

"She's showing up now," announced the radar operator.

"Thank you, Mr. Gorbels," said Rowse.

The VHF speaker came to life. "*Pamir* to Port Erikson, *Pamir* to Port Erikson. Am coming in. Over."

Grimes recognized the voice, of course. Listowel had been master of the experimental *Flying Cloud* and was now in command of *Pamir*. A good man, not easily panicked, one who would have been just as at home on the poop of a windjammer as in the control room of a spaceship.

The commodore moved so that he could look up through the transparent dome that roofed the control tower. Yes, there she was, her navigation lights bright sparks against the black overcast, white and ruby and emerald, masthead, port and starboard. (Her real masts were retracted, of course, and her sails furled. She was driving herself down through the atmosphere by negative dynamic lift, a dirigible airship rather than a spaceship.) Faintly Grimes could hear the throb of her airscrews, even above the thin whining of the wind that eddied about the tower.

The ship was lower now, visible through the windows that overlooked Coldharbor Bay. Grimes lifted borrowed night glasses to his eyes, ignoring the TV screen that presented the infrared picture. The slim, graceful length of her was clearly visible, picked out by the line of lighted ports. Down she came—down, down, slowly circling, until she was only meters above the dark, white-flecked waters of the bay. From her belly extended hoses, and Grimes knew that the thirsty centrifugal pumps would be sucking in ballast.

"*Pamir* waterborne," announced Listowel from the VHF speaker. "Am proceeding to berth. Over."

Grimes, Williams and Rowse shrugged themselves into heavy overcoats, put on fur-lined caps. The harbormaster led the way to the elevator that would take them down to ground level. They dropped rapidly to the base of the tower. Outside it was bitterly cold and the wind carried thin flurries of snow. Grimes wondered why some genius could not devise earflaps that would not inhibit hearing—his own prominent ears felt as though they were going to snap off at any moment. But during berthing operations it was essential to hear as well as to see what was going on.

The three men walked rapidly to the wharf, breasting the wind—little, fat Rowse in the lead, chunky Grimes and big, burly Williams a couple of steps in the rear. The shed lights were on now, as were the position-marker flashers. Beside each of the latter waited three linesmen, beating their arms across their chests in an endeavor to keep warm. The berthing master, electric megaphone in his gloved hand, was striding up and down energetically.

Pamir came in slowly and carefully, almost hidden by the cloud of spray thrown up by the turbulence induced by her airscrews. She was accosting the wharf at a steep angle at first and then turned, so that she was parallel to the line of wharfage. The wind did the rest, so that it was hardly necessary for Listowel to use his line-throwers fore and aft. She fell gently alongside, with her offshore screws swiveled to provide transverse thrust against the persistent pressure of the southerly.

She lay there, a great, gleaming torpedo shape, gently astir as the slight chop rolled her against the quietly protesting fenders. The hum of motors, the threshing of airscrews, suddenly ceased.

From an open window in his control room Listowel called, "Is this where you want me?"

"Make her fast as she is, Captain," called the berthing master.

"As she is," came the reply.

A few seconds later a side door opened and the brow extended from the wharf, stanchions coming erect and manropes tautening.

Grimes was first up the gangway. After all, as he had said to Sonya, the lightjammers were his babies.

Listowel received the boarding party in his day cabin. With him was Sandra Listowel, who was both his wife and his catering officer. Rim Runners did not, as a general rule, approve of wives traveling in their husband's ships in any capacity, but Sandra was one of the original *Flying Cloud* crew and had undergone training in that peculiar mixture of seamanship and airmanship required for the efficient handling of a lightjammer. Grimes often wondered if she had, over the years, become like so many of the wives of the old-time windjammer masters, a captain *de facto*—though he did not think that Ralph Listowel would allow such a situation to develop.

Captain Listowel had changed little over the years. When he rose to greet his visitors he towered over them. He had put on no weight and his closely cut hair was still dark, save for a touch of gray at the temples. And Sandra was as gorgeous as ever, a radiant blonde, not quite as slim as she had been but none the worse for that. Her severe, short-skirted, black uniform suited her.

Listowel produced a bottle and glasses. He said, "You might like to try this. You look as though you need warming up. It's something new. Our Llanithi friends acquired a taste for scotch and a local distiller thought he'd cash in on it. What he produced is not scotch. Even so, it's good. It might go well on Lorn and the other Rim Worlds."

Grimes sipped the clear, golden fluid experimentally, then enthusiastically. "Not bad at all." Then: "You'd better have some more yourself to soften the blow, Listowel."

"What blow, Commodore?"

"You've a very quick turnaround this time. As you know, *Herzogen Cecile* is tied up for repairs on Llanith—and I'd still like to know just how Captain Palmer got himself dismasted."

"I have his report with me, Commodore."

"Good. I'll read it later. And when *Lord of the Isles* comes in to Port Erikson she's being withdrawn for survey. Which leaves you and *Sea Witch* to cope." He grinned. "As they used to say back on Earth in the days of sail, 'Growl you may, but go you must.' "

"But we're still in the days of sail, Commodore," said Listowel. "And as one of the sailing ship poets said, 'All I ask is a tall ship and a star to steer her by.' "

"Very touching, Ralph, very touching," commented Sandra Listowel. "But I'm sure that the chief stewards of the oceangoing sailing ships had their problems, just as I have." She turned to Grimes. "Last time we were in Port Erikson, Commodore, we enjoyed our usual two weeks alongside—but even then we sailed without all our stores. How will it be this time?"

"Better," promised Grimes. "I'll light a fire under the tail of the Provedore Department back at Port Forlorn." He allowed Listowel to fill his glass. "Did you have a good trip, Captain?"

"Yes. Even so—"

"Even so what?"

"I think you might keep us informed, sir, of these other lightjammers, the experimental ones, cluttering up the route between Lorn and Llanith."

Grimes stared. "What are you talking about, Listowel?"

"We averted collision by the thickness of a coat of paint. Captain Palmer, in *Herzogen Cecile,* also had a close shave. His emergency alteration of course was so violent that it carried away his N and E masts with all their sails. He limped to Port Listowel on Llanith on S and W only."

"Why didn't he report it? The circumstances, I mean."

"He must have read your last circular, Commodore."

Grimes' prominent ears burned as he flushed angrily. But Listowel was right. He, Grimes, had written that circular under pressure from the Rim Worlds Admiralty—which body was, as he had put it, passing through a phase of acting like small boys playing at pirates. The fleet was out—or had been out or would be out—on deep space maneuvers. Masters and officers were reminded that the Carlotti bands were continually monitored by potentially hostile powers. Therefore no report of any sighting of Rim Worlds Navy warships was to be made over these channels, whatever the circumstances. And so forth.

"We are the only people with the Erikson-Charge-Reversing Drive," went on Listowel. "So we assumed that what we saw was an experimental warship. One of ours. Palmer assumed likewise."

Grimes made a major production of filling and lighting his pipe. He said through the swirling cloud of acrid blue smoke, "The Navy doesn't have any lightjammers, yet. They want some, just in case we ever fail to see eye to eye with the Llanithi Consortium. But the first ships of the line, as they are to be called, are still on the drawing board."

Listowel murmured thoughtfully, "Nevertheless we saw something—and it as near as dammit hit us. What was it, Commodore?"

"You tell me," said Grimes. "I'm listening."

Chapter 2

LISTOWEL WAS SAYING, "We were bowling along under a full press of sail and the Doppler Log was reading point eight nine seven, so it was nowhere near time to light the fire under our arse—" He coughed apologetically. "That, sir, is the expression we use for starting the reaction drive—"

"I gathered as much," said Grimes. "But go on."

"We were just finishing dinner in the main salon. I had Llawissen and his two wives—he's the new Llanithi trade commissioner, as you know—at my table. We were making the usual small talk when I noticed that the little red warning light in the chandelier had come on."

"Sounds very fancy," commented Williams.

"You should have done more time in passenger ships, Billy," Grimes told him. "That signal is to tell the master that he's wanted in control, but for something short of a full-scale emergency. Carry on, Captain."

"So I excused myself, but didn't leave the table in a hurry. Still, I lost no time in getting to the control room. Young Wallasey, the third mate, was O.O.W. He said, 'We've got company, sir.' I said, 'Impossible.' He pointed and said, 'Look.'

"So I looked.

"We had company all right. She was out on the starboard beam, just clear of E topmast. She was only a light at first, a blueish glimmer,

441

a star where we knew damn well no star should be, could be, hanging just above the distant mistiness of the Lens.

" 'Anything on the radar?' I asked.

"There wasn't—and these ships aren't fitted with Mass Proximity Indicators."

"No need for them," grunted Grimes, "unless you have Mannschenn Drive."

"So—there was nothing on the radar, which is what made me think afterward that this vessel must have been an experimental warship. The light was getting brighter and brighter, suggesting that the ship—I had already decided that it must be a ship—was getting closer.

"I got the big mounted binoculars trained on it. After I got them focused I could make out details, although that fuzzy, greenish light didn't help any. Some sort of force field? But no matter. I'd say that it—she—wasn't as big as *Pamir* or any of the other commercial lightjammers. She had an odd sort of rig, too. Instead of having four masts arranged in a cruciform pattern she had three, in series. And the sails—what I could see of them—had reflective surfaces on both sides instead of on one side only, as is the case with ours.

"And she was getting too bloody close on a convergent course. That was obvious, radar or no radar. Wallasey was calling her, first on the Carlotti set and then on NST, but getting no reply. There wasn't time to break out the Morse lamp. Whoever dreamed that we'd need it in deep space?

"So I said to hell with this and altered course, turning my W sails edge on to the Llanith sun. It was only just in time. That bastard was so near that I could see a line of ports with what looked like the muzzles of weapons sticking out of them. If she'd opened fire I wouldn't be here to tell the tale."

"Nor would any of us," commented Sandra Listowel.

"And only you and the officer of the watch saw this—thing?" asked Grimes.

"I'm not in the habit of throwing tea parties in my control room during emergencies, Commodore."

"Sorry. And presumably Captain Palmer saw something similar?"

"He did."

"But finish your story, Captain. What happened next?"

"Nothing. As I've told you, I altered course. And when next I was able to snatch a glance out of the ports she was gone. Like a snuffed candle, Wallasey told me."

Grimes grunted. He was thinking matters over. While he had discovered the antimatter systems to the Galactic West he had never visited their worlds. And he had never sailed in the lightjammers—though these ships were his brain children. He could afford the time for a voyage to Llanith—although his best policy would be to make all arrangements for the conduct of affairs during his absence first and to inform Rim Runners' management afterward.

Not that this last mattered really. The Rim Worlds Navy would be interested in this story of alien lightjammers on the Lorn-Llanith trade route—and Grimes, as a commodore of the Naval Reserve, had often in the past been called back to active duty to investigate strange occurrences. He had been called the Confederacy's odd-job man for reasons. And Sonya would be in this too—she still held her commission in the Intelligence Branch of the Federation Survey Service.

Grimes said to Rowse, "I'd like to borrow your office, Captain. I've a pile of telephoning to do. Oh, Captain Listowel, would you mind having accommodation ready for Mrs. Grimes and myself? We shall be making the next round trip with you."

"And what about me, Skipper?" asked Williams plaintively.

"I'm sorry, Bill, but there just aren't any senior masters kicking around loose at the moment. So, as of right now, you're appointed Port Forlorn Astronautical Superintendent, acting, temporary."

"Not unpaid?" demanded the big man.

"Not unpaid," agreed Grimes.

Williams' manner brightened.

Grimes called Admiral Kravitz first. The Officer Commanding Rim Worlds Navy was not pleased at being awakened from a sound sleep, but after he had listened to Grimes' story he was alert and businesslike. He glowered at Grimes from the telephone screen.

"These reports. They're utterly fantastic. Can you trust these masters of yours? Couldn't they have been seeing things?"

"They saw something," said Grimes. "In the case of *Pamir,* the intruder was seen by Captain Listowel and his third officer, Mr. Wallasey. In the case of *Herzogen Cecile,* the chief and second officers were in the control room as well as Captain Palmer. All the stories tally, even to minor details."

"Is there any—ah—excessive drinking aboard your ships? Any addiction to hallucinogenic drugs?"

"No." Grimes' ears were reddening. He countered with: "Are you sure that the Navy hasn't any experimental lightjammers?"

"You know bloody well we haven't, Grimes. Oh, all right, all right. Have your free trip at the taxpayers' expense. Don't forget to send the bill for your fare in to the Rim Worlds Navy."

"And my commodore's pay and allowances, sir?"

"Take that up with the Accounts Department, Grimes. You know how to look after yourself. Call me again at a civilized hour tomorrow morning after you've got things organized.

"Good night."

Grimes allowed himself a small grin. He was in an if-I'm-up-everybody's-up mood. He called Sonya. She, too, exhibited extreme displeasure at being disturbed at, as she put it, a jesusless hour. But her displeasure was replaced by enthusiasm. By the time the call was concluded she had decided what she would pack for herself and for Grimes and assured him that she would be at Port Erikson within twenty-four hours.

There was another call Grimes would like to have made, but unluckily Ken Mayhew, one of the few remaining psionic communication officers in the Rim Worlds, was not on Lorn. He was spending a long holiday on Francisco, of which planet his wife was a native. A good PCO, Grimes often said, was worth his weight in Carlotti transceivers—but not all PCOs were good and in the vast majority of interstellar ships the temperamental telepaths had been replaced by the time-space-twisting Carlotti radio equipment. But a Carlotti transceiver could not read minds, was incapable of that practice, frowned upon by the Rhine Institute but exercised nonetheless and known variously as snooping and prying. If *Pamir* had carried a psionic radio officer much could have been learned about the strange lightjammer. As it was, nothing—apart from the details of her appearance—was known.

Grimes went to the guest bedroom that had been provided for him in the Port Erikson staff accommodation block and settled down to read the reports—Listowel's as well as Palmer's. He would like to have discussed them with Rowse and Williams, but the port captain was organizing the round-the-clock stevedoring activities and Williams, who loved ships, was no doubt making a nuisance of himself to *Pamir's* officers.

The reports told Grimes little more than he had already learned from Captain Listowel's spoken account.

Grimes and Sonya were guests in *Pamir's* control room when she sailed from Port Erikson at local noon, three days later. The southerly had persisted, had freshened and was holding the ship against the wharf. The pivoting airscrews would be hard put to it to provide sufficient transverse thrust to pull her out bodily from the berth. But the little icebreaker was also a tug and was given a forward towline by *Pamir.*

Mooring lines were let go fore and aft, were swiftly winched inboard. The pivoted offshore airscrews began to spin faster and faster, their whirling blades flickering into invisibility—but they were doing little more than holding the ship against the wind.

"Take her out, *Bustler,*" ordered Listowel into his VHF microphone.

"Take her out, Captain," came the cheerful acknowledgment.

The towline grew taut, scattering a glittering spray in the thin sunlight. *Bustler's* diesels thumped noisily and black smoke shot from her squat funnel to be shredded by the stiff breeze. Grimes went to an open window on the port side of the control room, looked out and down. There was a gap now between the wharf fenders and the side of the ship forward, a gap that was slowly widening. But what was happening aft? What about the projecting venturi of the reaction drive, the after control surfaces? Wasn't there a possibility—a probability—of their fouling the wharf gantries? But Listowel, standing in the middle of his control room, didn't seem to be worrying about it. And, after all, the ship was his.

The stern was coming off, too, under the tug of the airscrews, although not so rapidly. There was clearance between the tail fins and the nearest wharf structure—not much, but enough. And then the port propellers, unpivoted, whirled into motion, giving headway and accentuating the swinging moment, *Pamir* turned to starboard slowly but determinedly, a white and green jumble of brash ice piling up along that side. She came around into the wind and the starboard screws pivoted as she turned, giving headway instead of lateral thrust.

Astern the distance between ship and wharf was widening rapidly.

"Let go, *Bustler*," ordered Listowel and then, to Grimes, "I'm always afraid that one day I'll forget and drag that poor little bitch with me all the way to Llanith."

"Is there any market there for used tugs or icebreakers?"

"Button her up, Mr. Wallasey," said Listowel.

The third officer pressed buttons. The wheelhouse windows slid shut.

And about time, Grimes thought. Icy drafts had begun to eddy about the compartment.

"Dump ballast."

The ship lifted as the tons of water gushed out from her tanks, rising faster and faster, stemming the wind, until Coldharbor Bay, directly beneath her, seemed a puddle beside which a child had set a huddle of toy buildings—until far to the south the Ice Barrier, a coldly gleaming wall of pearly white, lifted over the black sea horizon.

She lifted like a rocket, but without noise and without crushing acceleration effects. She soared into the clear sky, the color of which deepened from blue to purple, to black. Below her the planet was no longer a vast, spread-out map—it was a globe, with seas and continents half-glimpsed through the swirling cloud formations, with the dark shadow of the terminator drifting slowly across it from the west.

The chief officer came into the control room to report all secured for space. Other reports came over the intercom. Listowel acknowledged them and then, smiling, turned to his guests. "Well, Commodore and Mrs. Grimes, how do you like it so far?"

"I envy you, Listowel. You've a fine ship and you know how to handle her."

"Thank you, Commodore." He said to the third officer, "Make the usual warning, Mr. Wallasey." Then, to Grimes: "Seats and seat belts, sir. I have to swing her to the right heading now."

The maneuver was routine enough in any interstellar ship, the turning of a vessel about her axes until she was lined up with the target star. Somewhere amidships the big, directional gyroscopes grumbled, hummed and then whined, and centrifugal force gave the illusion of off-center gravity. The great globe that was Lorn seemed to fall away and to one side, and its sun drifted aft. Ahead now was only the blackness of intergalactic space, although the misty Lens was swimming slowly into view through the side ports. Then, coming gradually toward the center of the cartwheel sights, appeared the distant cluster of bright sparks that were the antimatter stars. The gyroscopes slowed almost to a stop, grumbling, as Captain Listowel made the last fine adjustments. They halted at last.

The master looked up from his sighting telescope, murmured, "She'll do." Both hands went to the console before him. He said, "Look out through the side ports and aft, Commodore. This is worth watching."

It was.

From the control room—which, like the bridge of a sea-going ship or the conning tower of a submarine, was a superstructure—there was a good view astern. Grimes could see the engine pods, four to a side, their now motionless four-bladed airscrews gleaming in the harsh sunlight. He could see the stubs of three of the masts—W to port, N on the centerline and E to starboard. S, of course, was beneath the hull and not visible, except in the periscope screen. But those stubs were stubs no longer. They were elongating, extending, stretching like impossibly fast growing, straight-stemmed trees. And as they grew they sprouted branches, foliage—the yards and the sails. The royals at the head of each mast were fully spread before the process of telescopic elongation was completed.

There was disorientation then, visual confusion, upset balance as the star wind filled the sails. What had been up was up no longer. Aft was still aft, but it was also "down." Chairs swung in their gymbals, as did some of the instruments. Other equipment was cunningly designed so that it could be used from almost any angle.

Grimes realized what was happening but, twisting his body awkwardly in the chair, still stared in fascination aft and down through the polarized glass of the viewports. He had seen the sail plan of this ship, of course, had helped to draw it up; but this was the first time he had watched a lightjammer actually making sail. He mentally recited the names of the courses. He had insisted the old nomenclature be used. Northsail, lower topsail, upper topsail, topgallant, royal . . .

He turned away at last, asked, "Do you usually make sail all in one operation, Captain?"

Listowel laughed. "Only when I have guests in the control room."

Sonya laughed, too. "John would prefer to see all hands out in spacesuits, clambering in the rigging like monkeys."

"The good old days, eh?" Listowel unsnapped his seat belt. "Roll and go. Hell or Llanith in ninety days—and the sun's over the yardarm."

Grimes took one last look at that splendid suit of sails, black against the glare of the Lorn sun, before he got up to follow Listowel and Sonya from the control room. He realized that he would have to get his spacelegs back. In this inertialess ship, in spite of the already fantastic acceleration, the distinction between up and down was a matter of faith rather than of knowledge.

They enjoyed their drinks—more of the Llanithian whisky—in Listowel's comfortable day room, where Sandra joined them.

"How are the customers?" her husband asked her.

"There's only one this trip," she told him. She flashed a smile at the guests. "I don't count the commodore and Mrs. Grimes as real passengers."

"Who is it?" asked Grimes. "Anybody I know—or should know?"

"Perhaps you should know her, sir. She's a missionary."

"Why wasn't I warned?" demanded Listowel.

"I'm warning you now, Ralph."

"What's her name? What nut cult is she trying to peddle?"

"She's the Reverend Madam Swithin. Rather an old dear, actually. She's a missionary for the United Primitive Spiritualist Church."

"And she thinks she'll be able to convert the Llanithi?"

"She'll probably convert some of them. After all, given the right conditions you can convert anybody to anything."

"But United Primitive Spiritualism—" muttered Listowel disgustedly.

"They have something," Sonya told him. "I've had some odd experiences and so has John."

"I only hope she's not at my table," said the master.

"Where else could I put her, Ralph? After all, she is a person of some importance in her church. I couldn't put her with the junior officers."

"I'm sorry about this, Commodore," Listowel said.

"Don't worry, Captain. We'll survive somehow," Grimes told him.

The Reverend Madam Swithin was, as Sandra had said, rather an old dear, but the sort of old dear whose idea of conversation is asking endless questions. Yet it could be said in her favor that she enjoyed the excellent food prepared by Sandra and served by the efficient stewardess and that she did not belong to one of those sects that regard alcoholic beverages as sinful. It took her some little time to get things sorted out, however. She knew that a commodore is superior to a captain and so assumed that Grimes was master of *Pamir*. She asked him why he wasn't wearing uniform. Then she asked why *Pamir* wasn't named according the general Rim Runners Principle, with the "Rim" prefix.

Grimes told her, "In these vessels we've tried to revive the names of the old sailing ships, the Terran windjammers. Unluckily most, if not all, of the most famous names are being used by Trans-Galactic Clippers—*Thermopylae* and *Cutty Sark* and so on."

"Are Trans-Galactic Clippers lightjammers like this one, Commodore?"

"No, Madam Swithin. But the original clippers were very fast sailing ships and long after sail had vanished from the seas the name 'clipper' was still being used by the operators of other forms of transport—road services, airlines and so forth. One of the first little ships to fly to Earth's moon was called *Yankee Clipper*."

"How interesting, Commodore. The usage gives one a sense of continuity, don't you think? And now, Captain, when do you think you're getting this clipper of yours to Llanith?"

"ETA is just three weeks subjective from now."

"You said 'Hell or Llanith in ninety days,' " Sonya reminded him.

"Ninety days objective," He told her. "But only three weeks as we shall live them, Mrs. Grimes."

"And is there really any danger of the ship's getting wrecked? Not that I'm frightened, of course. I know that there is no death."

Sandra joined them at the table, bringing coffee. "Don't worry, Madam Swithin. That 'Hell or Llanith' is just an expression that Captain Listowel picked up from a book about the famous windjammers. There was a captain on the trade between England and Australia who used to say, 'Hell or Melbourne in ninety days!' "

"And as *I* was saying, dear, such a sense of continuity. So fascinating to think that you sailing ship captains are reincarnations of the old sailing ship captains. The wheel has come full circle and you have been reborn—"

Listowel was beginning to squirm uncomfortably in his chair. The junior officers at their tables—obviously listening—were starting to look amused. Grimes endeavored to steer the conversation on to a fresh tack.

"And when, Captain," he asked, "do you start the reaction drive?"

"A week from now, Commodore, as soon as we have point nine recurring on the Doppler Log. Then we have a week of full acceleration and FTL flight. Then we have to decelerate. And then, all being well, we're there."

All being well, thought Grimes. *But if all is well, I shall have made this trip for nothing.*

~ Chapter 3 ~

SHE WAS A FINE SHIP, this *Pamir,* and most efficiently run—but, to one accustomed to a conventional starship, uncannily quiet.

Grimes missed the incessant, noisy, arrhythmic hammering of the inertial drive, the continuous thin, high keening of the Mannschenn Drive. Here the only mechanical noises were the occasional sobbing of a pump, the soft susurrus of the forced ventilation.

On she drove, running free before the photon gale. The Rim stars astern were ruddily dim—the suns of the Llanithi Consortium blazed intensely blue ahead. And on the beam, mast and sails in black silhouette against it, glowed the great Lens of the Galaxy, unaffected by either red or blue shift.

The needle of the Doppler Log, after its initial rapid jump, crept slowly around its dial. *Point eight, point eight five, point eight seven five . . .* Grimes tried to imagine what the ship must look like to an outside observer, tried to visualize the compression along the fore and aft line. But to see her at all that mythical outside observer would have to be in another ship traveling in the same direction at the same speed—and then, of course, he would observe nothing abnormal.

And what would happen if *Pamir* hit something—even only a small piece of cosmic debris—at this fantastic velocity? So far the lightjammers had been lucky—but what if their luck suddenly ran out? The question, as far as her crew was concerned, was purely academic. They would never know what hit them—although after weeks or months or years the brief flare would be visible in the night skies of Lorn and Llanith.

At last came the time for the final acceleration—and the reversal of atomic charges. Again Grimes and Sonya were guests in the control room, watching with fascination. Listowel explained, "This isn't half as bad as that moment when the temporal precession field of the Mannschenn Drive is initiated. Oh, you'll feel something. We all do. Just a microsecond of tension and, at the same time—as the charges are reversed—what we call a scrambled spectrum. But there's none of the dithering about in and on alternate time tracks that we experienced when we first discovered the effect."

"Just as well," grunted Grimes. "Alternate time tracks are among my pet allergies."

Listowel was watching the log screen, which gave him far finer readings than the dial, to six places of decimals. Grimes and Sonya watched, too.

999993 . . . The crimson numerals glowed brightly. 999994 . . . 999995 . . . The 6 was a long time coming up . . . Ah, here it was. 999997 . . . 999998 . . . There was another long delay. Then the final 9 appeared briefly but flickered back to 8.

"Go, you bitch, go," Listowel was whispering.

999999 . . .

"It's holding, sir," whispered one of the officers.

"I have to be sure . . . Now!"

After the long days of quiet sailing the screaming roar of the rocket drive, carried by and through the metal structure of the ship, was startlingly loud. There should have been brutal acceleration, but there was not. There was not physical sense of acceleration. Yet Grimes felt as though he, personally, were striving to lift some impossibly heavy weight. He felt as though he were pressing against some thin yet enormously tough film that stubbornly refused to break.

Then it burst.

There was real acceleration now, driving him down into the padding of his chair. He was dimly aware that Listowel—a strange Listowel, who looked like a photographic negative, whose shorts-and-shirt uniform was black instead of the regulation white, whose face had become oddly negroid—was doing things, explaining as his hands moved over the console. His voice, normally light, was a deep, grumbling bass. "Have to pivot the sails, Commodore. Edge on, or we'll be taken aback—"

Suddenly things snapped back to normal.

Color and sound were as they should be and the acceleration had eased to a fairly comfortable one gravity. Grimes took mental stock of himself. Yes, he was still Commodore John Grimes of the Rim Worlds Naval Reserve, astronautical superintendent of Rim Runners. And he was still aboard *Pamir*. He turned to look at his wife, who smiled back at him rather shakily. And Sonya was still Sonya.

So far so good.

And the log screen?

Blue numerals now—1.000459 . . . 1.000460 . . . The final *1* flashed up and then, in steady succession: 2, 3, 4, 5 . . .

All my years in deep space, thought Grimes, *and this is the first time I've* really *traveled faster than light . . .*

"So we are all antimatter now, Captain?" asked the Reverend Madam Swithin that evening at dinner. She did not wait for a reply, but went on, "But what about our souls, our essential essences?"

"I'm afraid, madam, that that's rather outside my province," replied Listowel.

"And what do you think, Commodore?"

Grimes grunted through a mouthful of steak.

"But the Llanithi have souls," the missionary went on. "Otherwise I should not be traveling to their worlds."

A rather uncomfortable silence was broken by Sonya. "Tell me, Madam Swithin—do you ever, in your séances, establish communication with the departed spirits of nonhuman entities?"

"Frequently, Mrs. Grimes. One of our mediums has as her control a Shaara princess, who last enjoyed material existence five hundred Standard Years ago. And recently, during a service in our church in Port Farewell, a spirit spoke through the officiating medium and said he was—that he had been, rather—a people's marshal on Llanith. What is a people's marshal, Captain?"

"It's roughly equivalent to a police commissioner on our worlds, madam," replied Listowel.

Sonya sipped from her wine glass, then asked, "One thing has always rather puzzled me, Madam Swithin. One of the doctrines of your church is reincarnation. How does that fit in with that large number of disembodied spirits who are always present at your séances to say their pieces?"

The motherly little woman smiled sweetly at Sonya. "There is reincarnation, as we believe—as we *know*—Mrs. Grimes. But the soul is not reincarnated into a new body immediately after its release from the old one. In the case of ordinary people the delay is not a long one. It is the extraordinary people, the outstanding personalities, who often have to wait for centuries, or until a suitable vehicle for their rare psyches has become available—"

"In other words," said Grimes, who was becoming interested, "until the genes and chromosomes have been suitably shuffled and dealt."

"What a good way of putting it, Commodore. I must remember that." She looked at Grimes as though she were viewing him as a potential and valuable convert—which, Grimes realized, he could be. *Why can't I keep my big mouth shut?* he asked himself. "You will agree, Commodore, that a special sort of character is required for the captain of a ship?"

Grimes made a noncommittal sound.

"And that an even more special kind of character is required for the captain of a sailing ship—"

"I did," admitted Grimes cautiously, "bear certain qualities in mind when I appointed the masters and officers to these lightjammers—and not all of those I selected passed the rather rigorous training."

Listowel muttered something about bumbling around in blimps over the Great Barrens, but subsided when Grimes glared at him.

"And how many lightjammers does your company operate, Commodore?"

"At the moment, four, *Pamir, Herzogen Cecile, Lord of the Isles* and *Sea Witch*. As the trade expands we shall require more tonnage, of course. *Preussen* and *Garthpool* are on the drawing boards. And the Rim Worlds Navy has the plans for at least three sailing warships."

"Four ships. And five more sometime in the future. But what of the thousands of sailing captains who must have lived in the days when their vessels were the only long-distance transport on Earth? Many of those souls must still be waiting for reincarnation."

"One of my ancestors might be among them," said Grimes.

"Really, Commodore?"

"Yes. He was a Barbary Corsair—but before that he was master of an English ship in the Mediterranean trade. A forced convert to Islam who decided to play along and do as well for himself as possible—"

"Are you sure that he was never reincarnated, John?" asked Sonya. "Some of the less savory episodes in your past haven't been far short of piracy."

"I might be able to find out for you, Commodore," said Madam Swithin eagerly. "I am more of an administrator than a medium, but I do have powers—"

"Thank you," Grimes told her. "But I think I'd rather not know."

Pamir drove on, no longer scudding before the photon gale but riding the thunder of her rocket drive. Ahead was an impossible star cluster—the suns of the Llanithi Consortium blue-blazing, the Rim suns sullenly smoldering embers. Astern was—nothing. On she drove, outrunning light, until the time came for deceleration.

The reaction drive was shut down and, at his controls, Listowel carefully pivoted his sails. Northsail, eastsail, southsail and westsail he turned, trimming them so that the radiance from the Llanithi stars was striking their reflecting surfaces at an oblique angle. Grimes, watching the Doppler Log screen, saw the numerals change from 25.111111 to 25.111110 to 25.111109 . . .

All four lower courses were now exerting full braking effect and the lower topsails were trimmed, squared. 23.768212 . . . 23.768000 . . . 23.759133 . . . Upper topsails next. 19.373811 . . . Topgallantsails . . . The log was winding down rapidly and ahead one of those vividly blue stars was a star no longer, was beginning to show an appreciable disk. Now the royals. *12*.343433 . . . 11.300001 . . . 10.452552 . . . 8.325252 . . . 5.000000 . . . 2.688963 . . .

So far there was no sensation. The ship was inertialess, her structure and crew protected from the forces that should have exploded them through the darkness and emptiness in a blazing flare of energy.

1.492981 . . . 1.205288 . . . 1.200438 . . . 1.113764 . . . 1.000009 . . .

The countdown was slowing,

1.000008 . . . 7 . . . 6 . . . 5 . . . 4 . . . 3 . . . 2 . . . 3 . . . 2 . . . 1 . . . 2 . . . 1 . . .

1.000000 . . .

As when the light barrier had been broken, there was the feeling of unbearable tension. Something snapped suddenly. The stars ahead diminished in number, although those remaining were still blue. Astern, dim and distant, the Rim Stars reappeared.

And the figures in the screen were now in red light: 999999 . . . 999998 . . . 999997 . . .

"Sir." Willoughby, the chief officer was pointing. Out to starboard, just abaft the beam, was a star where no star should or could be—a point of greenish radiance that steadily brightened.

"Captain! Commodore!" It was Madam Swithin's voice. What the hell was she doing in the control room?

"Mr. Wallasey," said Listowel to his third officer, "please escort this lady down to her cabin."

"But, Captain," cried the missionary, "this is most important."

"So is that," he said, pointing. "I've no time to spare for—"

"That," she interrupted him, "is what is important."

"Mr. Wallasey—" began Listowel.

"Let her stay," said Sonya sharply. It was more of an order than a request. "Let her stay."

The young officer looked uncertainly at his captain, at the commodore, at the commodore's wife. He looked again, questioningly, toward Listowel. But the master's full attention was on the strange light. It was closing on a converging course. And there was something solid, or apparently solid, in the center of that glowing circle of blue-green mist. A ship? Grimes had found a pair of binoculars, had them to his eyes.

Yes, a ship.

Madam Swithin was speaking again, but the voice was not her own. It was male and had a strange, guttural accent. And the language was one that Grimes did not understand, although it seemed to be of Terran origin. German? No, he decided. Although there were similarities.

"Who are you?" Sonya was asking. "Speak so that we may understand."

"I cannot rest. I must not rest. Effer. To sail der seas vas I condemned, for all eternity, vhereffer and vheneffer dere are ships—"

The seas? wondered Grimes. *But space is a sea . . .*

He could make out the hull now through his glasses—high-pooped, with a tall forecastle. He could see the line of black-gaping gunports and the three masts with the square sails at fore and main, the staysails and the spritsail, the lateen sail at the mizzen . . .

This was no lightjammer.

"Kapitan!" that deep, urgent voice was commanding, "Starboard der helm! Starboard der helm!"

But an alteration of course to starboard would make a collision between *Pamir* and this apparition inevitable.

"Kapitan! Starboard der helm!"

And in the old days when the helm, the tiller, had been put to starboard both rudder and ship had turned to port, Grimes remembered from his reading. Even after the invention and introduction of the ship's wheel those topsy-turvy steering orders had persisted for quite a long while.

In the old days, the days of the windjammers . . .

And hadn't there been a legend about a Captain Van . . . What was his name? A Dutchman?

He laughed softly. "A ghost," he murmured. "A ghost."

Listowel laughed with him. "A bloody Rim ghost. I should have known. I've heard enough about them. Phantom ships from alternate universes—"

"Kapitan! For der luff of Gott, starboard!"

Listowel laughed again, contemptuously, "That thing can't hurt us. I'll not risk my spars and sails, my ship, for a silly, blown-away phantasm!"

A spurt of orange flame leaped from the archaic ship's forward gunport, followed by billowing dirty white smoke. The Dutchman had fired a warning shot.

"Listowel, bring her around to port at once," ordered Grimes.

"I'm not running from a ghost ship with ghost cannon, Commodore."

"Bring her around, damn you!"

"And you can't order me in my own control room—"

"Legally I can't—but I do order you." Had Grimes known how to handle the lightjammer he would have tried to push the younger man from the controls. But he did not know. The only thing in his mind that could be of value in this situation was his memory of the old sailors' tales.

"Kapitan! Starboard der helm!" It was a despairing cry in that strange male voice from the lips of the medium.

"He's warning us, Listowel!" cried Grimes. "The old legends—you've read them. I've seen your bookshelf. The appearance of the Flying Dutchman before disaster . . . The ships Vanderdecken were saved from disaster by a ghost ship's warning! Come to port, Captain! Bring her around to port!"

Realization dawned on Listowel's face. With a muttered oath he dropped his hands to the console. He worked fast now that it was almost too late—with desperate urgency. He trimmed the east sails, not bothering about precise angles, bringing all five of the great vanes around as fast as the trimming motors would let him, presenting their light-absorptive surfaces to the radiation of the Llanith sun. *Pamir* lurched as she fell off to port. The mast whipped violently and the royal was ripped from its yards, flapped ahead and away from the ship like a bat into hell. But the rest held as the ship pivoted about her short axis.

And Grimes, looking out to starboard, saw the Dutchman vanish like a snuffed candle—but not before he had glimpsed the tall figure on the poop, his long beard streaming in the wind (here, in interstellar space, where there were no winds but the star winds!), his right arm raised in a gesture of farewell.

"Well," muttered Listowel shakily. "Well—" Then: "Is it all right for us to resume course, Commodore?"

"I—I suppose so," replied Grimes. In a stronger voice he said, "I shall ground the lightjammers until a thorough survey has been made of this sector of space. There was something there. Something we just missed."

On the deck where she had fallen, where Sonya was supporting her head and shoulders, Madam Swithin began to stir. Her eyes opened, stared around her. "Where am I? What happened? How did I get here? I came all over queer and I don't remember any more—"

"Everything is all right," Sonya told her.

"Thank you, dear. Thank you. I shall be feeling better in a couple of jiffs. But I'd be ever so grateful if somebody could bring me a nice cup of—" The expression faded from her plump face and her eyes went vacant. That strange male voice—although now little more than a dying whisper—finished the sentence.

"—Holland gin," it said.

THE
LAST HUNT

≈ Chapter 1 ≈

GRIMES STOOD AT THE WIDE WINDOW of his office, which overlooked the Port Forlorn berthing apron, watched the starship *New Bedford* coming in. She was a stranger to the Rim Worlds. According to Lloyd's Register she was owned by the Hummel Foundation of Earth. The Foundation, Grimes knew, had been set up for the intensive study of xenobiology—its Interstellar Zoo, covering hundreds of square miles of Australia's Central Desert, was famous throughout the Galaxy. Almost equally famous was *New Bedford*'s master, Captain Haab. He was both master astronaut and big game hunter—an unlikely combination, but a highly successful one.

And what was Captain Haab doing out on the Rim?

Grimes could guess.

Slowly *New Bedford* dropped down from the clear sky—her arrival had coincided with one of Port Forlorn's rare fine days. She gleamed dazzlingly in the bright morning sunlight. As she gradually lost altitude the beat of her inertial drive rose from an irritable muttering to a noisy, unrhythmic drumming, frightening the snowbirds—which at this time of the year infested the spaceport—into glittering, clattering flight.

The commodore picked up binoculars, studied the descending ship. He already knew that she was modified Epsilon Class, but was interested in the extent of the modifications. She looked more like a warship than a merchantman, the otherwise sleek lines of her hull broken by turrets and sponsons. Most of these seemed to be recent additions. She must have been specially fitted out for this expedition.

No doubt, Grimes thought, Captain Haab would be visiting him as soon as the arrival formalities were over and done with—it would be more of a business than a courtesy call. But everything was ready. The files of reports were still in Grimes' office, the spools of film, the three-dimensional charts with their plotted sightings and destructions. If Haab wanted information—which he almost certainly would—he should have it.

New Bedford was almost down now, dropping neatly into the center of the triangle marked by the brightly flashing red beacons. Already the beetlelike ground cars of the spaceport officials—port captain, port health officer, customs—had ventured on to the apron, were waiting to close in. But Haab, with all the resources of The Hummel Foundation behind him, would have no trouble in obtaining inward clearance.

New Bedford was down at last. Her inertial drive complained for the last time, then lapsed into silence. A telescopic mast extended from high on her hull, at control room level, and from it broke out a flag that fluttered in the light breeze. It was not, Grimes realized, the houseflag of The Hummel Foundation, a stylized red dragon on a green field. This standard was white and blue.

Miss Walton, Grimes' secretary, had come to stand with him at the window. "What a funny ensign—what is it supposed to be? It looks like an airship, a blimp in a blue sky—"

The commodore laughed. "I think that the blue is supposed to represent sea, not sky. And that's not a blimp—"

"What is it, then, Commodore?"

"It could be a white whale," Grimes told her.

"Captain Haab to see you, sir," announced Miss Walton.

Grimes looked up from his desk where he had been blue-penciling the stores requisition sent in by the chief officer of *Rim Percheron*. "Show him in," he told his secretary.

The girl returned to the office followed by Haab. The master of *New Bedford* was a tall man, thin, towering over the little blonde.

There was an oddly archaic cut to his tightly fitting black suit, to his stiff, white linen and black stock. His face was gaunt and deeply tanned between his closely cropped black hair and black chin beard. His eyes were a startlingly pale blue. He walked with a peculiarly jerky motion and from his right leg came a strange faint clicking noise.

Grimes rose to his feet, extended his right hand. "Welcome to Port Forlorn, Captain."

Haab took the commodore's hand in his own almost-skeletal claw. "Thank you, sir."

"Sit down, Captain. Tea? Coffee?"

"Coffee if I may, Commodore. Black."

"Will you attend to it, please, Miss Walton? Black coffee for two. And did you have a good voyage out, Captain?"

"A quiet voyage."

"First time I've seen anybody from The Hummel Foundation out here. Of course, we haven't much in the way of exotic fauna on the Rim. Not on the man-colonized planets, that is. Most of our animals were raised from Terran stock."

"I'm not concerned with any of the life-forms actually on the planets, Commodore."

A grin softened Grimes' craggy face. "I can guess what you're come for, Captain—" Miss Walton brought in the coffee tray, set it on the desk. Grimes said to the girl, "Would you mind having the projection room ready? You know the films we shall want—those that the Admiralty lent me."

"The ones shot on the Lorn-Llanith route, sir?"

"Of course."

"Very good, sir. Oh, would you mind if I asked Captain Haab a question?"

"Go ahead, Miss Walton."

The girl addressed herself to *New Bedford*'s master. "I'm interested in flags, sir. What is the one that you have flying from your ship?"

Haab smiled thinly. "It's my own personal broad pennant. The Foundation allows me to wear it."

"But what is it, Captain?"

"A white whale," replied Haab.

"As I've already told you," grunted Grimes. "And now will you get those films ready?"

"And could you fill me in while we're waiting?" Haab asked Grimes.

"Of course, Captain. I'll start at the beginning."

"As you know," said Grimes, "we operate lightjammers on the run between the Rim Worlds and the Llanithi Consortium. The lightjammers are the only ships that can have their atomic charges reversed so that they can land on the antimatter worlds without blowing themselves—and anybody else within ten thousand miles—to glory. The lightjammers had been running into trouble—a strange vessel kept appearing on a collision course, shoving them away to hell and gone off trajectory—"

Haab smiled. "You'll probably be hearing from the Rhine Institute about that. But The Hummel Foundation is concerned with living beings, not ghosts, not even such famous ghosts as the Flying Dutchman."

"Just as well. Since the Navy started cleaning up the shipping lanes old Vanderdecken has been conspicuous by his absence. Maybe he's found a home on Atlantia. They still go in for sail in a big way there.

"Well, after the first reports came in I decided I'd better see for myself, so my wife and I took passage from Lorn to Llanith in *Pamir*. At that time it was thought that the Flying Dutchman was another lightjammer, a foreign ship snooping on our trade routes. But we had with us the Reverend Madam Swithin of the United Primitive Spiritualist Church going out to Llanith as a missionary. Thanks to her we found out what the Flying Dutchman was and that Vanderdecken was warning us about something.

"So I grounded the lightjammers and sent a report to Admiral Kravitz, urging him to make a full-scale investigation. He did. Luckily our fleet was out on maneuvers at the time so it all fitted in with the war games that were being played. Instead of the usual Redland versus Blueland it was the armed might of the Confederacy versus the Menace from Intergalactic Space. Mphm."

Haab registered strong disapproval. "Not a hunt," he growled, "but a military operation—"

"Of course. If one of our lightjammers had run into a herd of those things—or even a single one—there would have been a shocking mess. Don't forget that the Erikson Drive ships, unlike the Mannschenn Drive jobs, remain in normal space-time while accelerating to the velocity of light and return to NST when decelerating. The energy eaters—"

"Is that what you call them?"

"What else? The energy eaters were a menace to navigation and they were dealt with as such."

"I still don't like it."

"You're not master of a lightjammer, Captain. Oh, all right, all right, you're a big game hunter as well as being a shipmaster. But the EEs don't have nice, horned heads that you can hang on the wall. They don't have pretty pelts that can be made into fireside rugs."

"I want a living specimen."

"I doubt if your marvelous zoo in Central Australia would be able to accommodate it."

"A zoo need not be on a planetary surface, Commodore. The plans for an orbital zoo have been drawn up, with lines of magnetic force among a grouping of small artificial satellites forming the bars of a cage. If I capture a specimen the Foundation will have everything ready for its reception when I get it back to Earth."

"*If* you capture a specimen. The Navy's doing a good job."

Haab inhaled deeply from the villainous black cigar that he was smoking as a countermeasure to Grimes' foul pipe. He withdrew the thing from his mouth and his right hand, holding it, rested on his knee. Grimes sneezed. There was more than tobacco smoke in those acrid fumes.

He said hastily, "You're setting yourself on fire, Captain."

The other man looked down at the little charred circle in the cloth of his trousers, beat out the embers with his left hand.

Grimes said, "You must feel deeply on the subject. You didn't notice that you were burning yourself."

"I do feel deeply, Commodore. But this leg's prosthetic. I lost the original on Tanganore when a harpooned *spurzil* took retaliatory action. The Tanganorans fitted me out with this tin leg and, by the time I got back to Earth where I could have had a new flesh-and-blood one grown, I'd gotten used to it. In any case, I couldn't spare the time for a regeneration job."

"Tanganore? That's in the Cepheid Sector, isn't it? And what is a *spurzil?*"

"A sort of big-armor-protected whale. White."

"And now you're hunting Moebius Dick himself."

"Moebius Dick, Commodore?"

"I thought that your private flag was supposed to represent the original Moby Dick."

"No. It represents the *spurzil* that took a piece of me. It's a reminder to myself to be careful. But *Moebius* Dick?"

"Wait until you've seen the films, Captain Haab."

Grimes sat with Haab in the darkened projection room and Miss Walton started the projector. Slowly the screen came alive and in it glowed words: OPERATION RIMHUNT. FOR EXHIBITION TO AUTHORIZED PERSONNEL ONLY.

The credit titles were succeeded by a spoken account of what was happening, by some quite good shots of lightjammers arriving at and departing from Port Erikson, by an excellent shot of *Herzogen Cecile* making sail. The voice of the commentator said, *But these ships, the pride of our Merchant Navy and the first vessels successfully to trade with the antimatter Llanithi Consortium, discovered that all was not plain sailing."* Grimes contrived to wince audibly. *"A new menace appeared on the trade routes and only by taking violent evasive action were the lightjammers able to escape certain destruction.*

"No mention of Vanderdecken," commented Haab.

"Our Navy refuses to believe in ghosts," Grimes told him. "Their psychologists have a marvelous theory that the Flying Dutchman was no more than a projection of our own precognitive fears, a visual presentation of a hunch."

The commentator went on: *Commodore John Grimes of the Rim Worlds Naval Reserve—also astronautical superintendent of Rim Runners—was a passenger aboard the lightjammer,* Pamir. *He was in her control room when the master, acting upon a hunch, trimmed his sails in order to make a large alteration of course to port—*

"I like that!" snorted Grimes. "I had to bully the stubborn bastard into making that alteration."

—deciding that there must have been some unseen danger ahead of the ship, Commodore Grimes made a report to Admiral Kravitz, recommending that a thorough survey be made of the trade routes between Lorn and Llanith. At the time the fleet was out on maneuvers off Eblis and the frigates Rim Culverin *and* Rim Carronade *were detached to carry out investigations in the neighborhood of Llanith.*

The last shot of a lightjammer under sail faded from the screen, was replaced by one of a conventional warship proceeding under Mannschenn Drive, obviously taken from a sister ship. In the background glowed the warped, convoluted galactic lens, an oval of luminescence twisted through and into an infinity of dimensions. The outline of *Rim Culverin* herself was hard and clear.

Arriving at the position in which, according to Commodore Grimes' report, the danger was thought to exist, Rim Culverin *and* Rim Carronade *reduced to cruising speed and initiated a search pattern. Both vessels, of course, had their Mass Proximity Indicators tuned to maximum sensitivity. Eventually a target was seen in the screens, the indications being that it was something extremely small, with barely sufficient mass to register. It must be pointed out, however, that collision with a dust mote at a speed close to that of light could have serious consequences—*

"How do your lightjammers guard against that?" asked Haab.

"We don't. Cosmic dust is something that we don't have any of out on the Rim."

"What about hydrogen atoms? Wouldn't they be as bad?"

"We don't have any of those either—or the operation of lightjammers would be impossible. But look!"

—inertial drive only, Rim Culverin *and* Rim Carronade *approached the target with caution. Radar had been put into operation when the ships made their reentry into normal space-time and proved more effective than the Mass Proximity Indicator had been. The original target was resolved into a cluster of targets, each presenting an echo in the screen equivalent to that given by a small ship, such as a scout.*

Furthermore, as the range decreased to a hundred kilometers and less, the targets could be seen visually.

In the screen was what looked like a star cluster, bright against the intergalactic nothingness.

"The cautious approach was continued—"

The effect now was more like a swarm of fireflies than a star cluster. The points of light were in rapid motion, weaving about each other in an intricate dance. The ship from which the film had been taken was approaching the shimmering display—probably magnification was being stepped up at the same time. If it were not—then the approach was far from cautious.

Each of the dancing lights possessed a definite shape.

"Haloes," murmured Haab.

"Not haloes," Grimes told him. "Look more closely, Captain."

Nonetheless, haloes they could have been, living annuli of iridescence—but twisted haloes. As they rotated about their centers they flared fitfully, seemed to vanish, flared again.

"What do they remind you of?" asked Grimes.

"The antenna of a Carlotti beacon or transceiver," replied Haab after a moment's thought. "But circular, instead of elliptical—that's what I thought when I saw the stills that the Survey Service passed on to the Foundation. It's more obvious when you see the things in motion."

"In other words," said Grimes, "a Moebius Strip. But watch."

The voice of the commentator came up again. *Rim Culverin dispatched a drone to make a closer investigation—*

There was a shot of the little craft—a spaceship in miniature, bristling with a complex array of scanners and antennae—pulling out and clear from the parent ship. *Rim Carronade's* camera tracked her until she was too distant for details to be distinguished. Then this picture was replaced by the one seen by the probe's electronic eyes. The small unmanned craft was making a close approach to one of the whirling rings of light. The enigmatic thing was almost featureless, although flecks of greater luminosity on its surface were indicative of its rotation. It was a Moebius Strip made from a wide, radiant ribbon. It flared and dimmed like an isophase beacon with a period synchronized with that of its revolution. It could have been a machine—yet it gave the impression that it was alive. It filled the screen, spinning, pulsing—and then there was blackness.

The commentator said in a matter-of-fact voice, "The drone went dead. It had not been destroyed, however. Powerful telescopes and radar aboard both ships could still pick it up. But it was obvious that all its electronic equipment had suddenly ceased to function.

It was obvious, too, that the cluster of mysterious entities was approaching the frigates at high velocity. Captain Laverton, aboard Rim Carronade, *ordered a withdrawal from the scene.* Rim Carronade *and* Rim Culverin *proceeded west, first at normal cruising speed, then increasing to maximum inertial drive acceleration. But the hostile beings steadily decreased the range.* Rim Carronade *and* Rim Culverin *were obliged to open fire with their stern-mounted laser cannon—*

ᨒ Chapter 2 ᨒ

THE SCREEN SHOWED the false star cluster again, but its individual components were no longer dancing about each other, maintaining a globular formation—they were holding a steady trajectory. They were no longer alternating between light and darkness. Every now and again they would flare into increased brilliance, which did not diminish.

Realizing that laser was an encouragement rather than a deterrent," the commentator went on, "Captain Laverton decided to take evasive action and ordered the starting of the Mannschenn Drive units aboard his ship and Rim Culverin, *reasoning that once the frigates were out of synchronization with normal space-time the hostile entities would be unable to press home their attack. At first it seemed that these tactics would be successful, but after a lapse of no more than fifteen seconds the things reappeared at even closer range than before, obviously matching temporal precession rates. Captain Laverton returned to normal space-time briefly—and in the few seconds before he restarted his Mannschenn Drive, just as the entities reappeared off* Rim Carronade's *quarter, launched a torpedo with a fission warhead fused for almost instant detonation. This defensive action was successful.*

The screen displayed a fireball of incandescent plasma, expanding and thinning, the obvious aftermath of an atomic explosion in deep space. Through the cloud of glowing gases could be seen only a mere half-dozen of the entities—earlier there had been at least fifty of the things.

Returning to NST, Captain Laverton observed that the majority of the creatures had been destroyed and that the few survivors were sluggish and—he thought erroneously—badly injured. Two were dispatched by laser fire. The remaining four retreated rapidly, eluding the frigates.

The first phase of Operation Rimhunt was over.

"The next spool, sir?" asked Miss Walton.

"Not just yet, if you don't mind," replied Haab. Then: "I beg your pardon, Commodore. But I'd like to talk about what we've just seen first."

"Talk away, Captain." Grimes refilled and lit his pipe. "Talk away."

"As you know, Commodore, I've seen the stills and read the reports that your navy passed on to the Federation Survey Service, that the Survey Service, in its turn, passed on to the Foundation. I was present at most of the conferences of the Foundation's boffins. I didn't understand all they were saying, but I caught the general drift. The energy eaters, as they dubbed them, are just that. Their peculiar Moebius Strip configuration ensures that their entire surface is exposed to any source of radiation. According to *our* mathematicians they must be susceptible to magnetic fields—so the cage that our people are designing should work. The creatures are also susceptible to beamed Carlotti transmissions, which could be used to prevent a caged entity from escaping by desynchronizing with normal space-time."

Grimes grunted affirmatively.

"And as we have just seen—they can be killed. Killed by kindness." Haab chuckled dryly. "Throw the energy of a nuclear blast on to their plates and they're like a compulsive eater digging his grave with a knife and fork."

"Mphm."

"But *I* don't want to kill them. I want to capture one, or more than one, to take back to Earth. I want to save a specimen of this unique life form, probably not a native of this galaxy, before the species is hunted to extinction."

"Then you had better get cracking," Grimes told him without much sympathy. To him a menace to navigation was just that. "At last report there's probably only one of the things left."

"Moebius Dick," murmured Haab.

They watched the remainder of the films of Operation Rimhunt, which could as well have been called Operation Search and Destroy. The use of fission weapons, stumbled upon by Captain Laverton, remained effective, but it had to be improved upon. The energy eaters were intelligent—just how intelligent no one knew, probably no one ever would know. After the almost complete wiping out of that first cluster they tended to run from the Confederacy's warships. Magnetic fields, set up by two or more vessels, were an invisible net from which not all of the entities escaped—and those that did so made their getaway by desynchronization. Time-space-twisting Carlotti beams were employed by the hunters and this technique seemed to inhibit temporal precession.

"Butchers," muttered Haab at last. "Butchers."

"Exterminators," corrected Grimes. "But both butchers and exterminators are essential to civilization. What about all the animals you have killed in your profession? Can you afford to talk?"

"I can, Commodore. In the first place, I've gone after living specimens far more than I have dead ones. In the second place, the odds have never been stacked against the quarry in my hunts—as they have been in this operation of yours."

Grimes grunted. "I'm not a hunter. If I really wanted a dinner of grilled trout I'd be quite capable of tossing a hand grenade into the stream. If I have an infestation of rats or mice I go out and buy the most effective poison on the market."

"I seem to recall," said Haab, "that you once used a fusion bomb to destroy a rat-infested ship."

"Yes. I did. It was necessary."

"Necessity," murmured Haab, "what sins are committed in thy name? But let's agree to shelve our differences. Do you think I could see the charts of sightings and—ah—victorious naval actions?"

"Let's have them, please, Miss Walton," said Grimes.

Grimes later entertained Haab in his home. After the captain had returned to his ship, Grimes' wife, Sonya, said "So that's the great hunter."

"I hope you were impressed," said Grimes.

"Impressed? Oh, I suppose I was in a way. But the man's a monomaniac. Hunting is his whole life."

"But you can say in his favor that he's more concerned with capturing than killing."

"Is that so much better?" she demanded. "Have you ever seen The Hummel Foundation's zoo?"

Grimes had seen it many years ago when he had been a very junior officer in the Survey Service. He had thought at the time that those animals from Earth-type planets had been comparatively lucky, they had been allowed a limited freedom in the open air. The beings from worlds utterly unlike Earth had been confined in transparent domes, inside which the conditions of their natural habitats had been faithfully reproduced in all respects but one—room to run, fly or slither.

He said, "I think I know what you mean."

"I should hope you do," she replied. "I'd sooner be dead than in a cage."

"Haab's only doing his job."

"But he needn't enjoy it so much."

"Are we so much better?" he queried. "Here are these creatures, drifting in from the Odd-Gods-of-the-Galaxy-know where. They may be intelligent, but have we tried to find out? Oh, no—not us. All we did find out is how to destroy them."

"Don't come over all virtuous, John. You were the first to start screaming about menaces to navigation on the Lorn-Llanith route. Now your precious lightjammers can come and go as they please. And that's what you wanted."

The following morning he received a call from Admiral Kravitz. "I'm putting you back on the Active List, Grimes."

"Again, sir? My paperwork piled up when I made the voyage in

Pamir and I'm still trying to shovel my way through the worst of the drifts."

"I want one of our people along in *New Bedford* as an observer. You are the obvious choice for the assignment."

"Why me?"

"Why not you? You were keen enough to make a voyage in *Pamir* when it suited you. Now you can make a voyage in Haab's ship when it suits me."

"Does Captain Haab know I'll be along?"

"He has been told that he will have to have a representative of our navy aboard when he lifts from Port Forlorn. He has only one spare cabin in his ship—a dogbox—so you'll not be able to have Sonya along. Still, it should be an interesting trip."

"I hope so," said Grimes.

"With you among those present, it will be." The admiral chuckled. "But I have to ring off. I'll leave you to fix everything up with Haab. Let me know later what's been arranged. Over and out."

Grimes rose from his desk. "Miss Walton," he said to his secretary, "I shall be aboard *New Bedford* if anybody wants me. Meanwhile, you can call Captain Macindoe at his home—he's due back from leave, as you know—and ask him to come in to see me after lunch. He'll be acting superintendent in my absence."

"Not B—Not Commander Williams again?" asked the girl disappointedly.

"No. Billy Williams, as you almost called him, is better at looking after his precious *Rim Malemute* than keeping my chair warm. What the pair of you were doing when I was away in *Pamir* and on Llanith I hate to think." He grinned, then made his way out of the office.

He looked with fresh interest at *New Bedford* as he walked briskly across the apron. His earlier curiosity about her had been academic rather than otherwise, but now that he would be shipping out in her he was beginning to feel almost a proprietorial concern.

He stared up at the dully gleaming tower that was her hull, at the sponsons and turrets that housed her weaponry, at the antennae indicative of sophisticated electronic equipment of a nature usually found only in warships and survey ships. But she was both, of course.

Her normal employment could be classed as warfare of a sort and as survey work—also of a sort.

Grimes marched up the ramp to the after airlock. His way into the compartment was barred by an officer who asked curtly, "Your business, sir?"

Grimes' prominent ears started to redden. Surely everybody in Port Forlorn knew who he was. But this ship, of course, was not a regular visitor and her personnel were not Rimworlders.

He said gruffly, "Commodore Grimes to see Captain Haab."

The young man went to a telephone. "Fourth mate here, Captain. A Commodore Grimes to see you . . . Yes, sir. Right away." Then to Grimes: "Follow me, sir."

The elevator carried them swiftly up the axial shaft. Haab's quarters were just below and abaft the control room. The master rose from his desk as Grimes was ushered into his day cabin. "Welcome aboard, Commodore. Thank you, Mr. Timon, you may carry on." When the officer had left Haab asked, "And what can I do for you, Commodore Grimes?"

"I believe, Captain, that you've already heard from our admiralty."

"Indeed I have. They're insisting that I carry some snot-nosed ensign or junior lieutenant with me as an observer—"

"Not an ensign or a lieutenant, Captain."

"Who, then?"

Grimes grinned. "Me."

Haab did not grin in return. "But you're not—"

"But I am. I'm a reserve officer back on the Active List as and from this morning."

"Oh?" Haab managed a frosty smile. "I'm afraid I can't offer you much in the way of accommodation, Commodore. This is a working ship. There's a spare cabin the mate has been using as a storeroom—he's getting it cleaned out now."

"As long as there's a bunk—"

"There is—but not much else." Haab's grin was a little warmer. "But I am neglecting my duties as a host." He walked to the little bar that stood against the bulkhead under the mounted head of some horrendously horned and tusked beast Grimes could not identify. "Perhaps you will join me in a sip of *mayrenroth?*"

"It will be my pleasure." Haab filled small glasses with viscous, dark-brown fluid and Grimes accepted his, raised it. "Your very good health, sir."

"And yours, Commodore."

The drink was potent, although Grimes did not much care for its flavor. He said, "This is an unusual—ah—spirit."

"Yes. I laid in a supply when I was on Pinkenbah. The natives ferment it from the blood of the *mayren,* a big, carnivorous lizard."

"Fascinating," said Grimes, swallowing manfully. "I suppose your ship is well stocked with all manner of foods and drinks."

"She is," Haab told him.

∽ Chapter 3 ∽

NEW BEDFORD lifted from Port Forlorn on a cold, drizzly morning, driving into and through the gray overcast. Grimes was a guest in her control room and, he was made to feel, a very unwelcome guest. Haab was coldly courteous, but his officers managed to convey the impression that they resented the presence of the outsider and were demanding silently of each other, *What is this old bastard doing here?*

New Bedford went upstairs in a hurry. Word had come through to Port Forlorn that *Rim Arquebus* was not only tracking what was believed to be the last of the energy eaters but had already made two unsuccessful attempts to destroy the creature. Haab had protested and had been told this sector of space was under the jurisdiction of the Rim Worlds' Confederacy and that he, his ship and his people were only there on sufferance. The attitude adopted by his government did not make things any more pleasant for Grimes.

Haab wasted little time setting trajectory once he was clear of Lorn's Van Alens. He lined his ship up on an invisible point in space some light years in from the Llanith sun, then put his inertial drive on maximum acceleration, with his Mannschenn Drive developing a temporal precession rate that Grimes considered foolhardy. Foolhardy or not, the discomfort was extreme—the erasing weight of three gravities acceleration combined with the eerie sensation of always being almost at the point of living backward.

Apart from these discomforts she was not a happy ship. Her

people, from the master down, were too dedicated. They lived hunting, talked hunting, thought hunting and, presumably, dreamed hunting. Grimes was allowed into a conversation only when it was assumed that he would make some contribution to the success of the expedition—and this was not often.

One night, at dinner, Haab did ask him for his views on the energy eaters.

"How intelligent do you think they are, Commodore?"

Grimes put down the fork with which he had been eating some vaguely fish-tasting mess, about which he had not dared to inquire. The implement clattered loudly on the surface of the plate—the high acceleration took some getting used to. He said, "You've seen all the reports, Captain Haab?"

"Yes, Commodore Grimes. But you must have formed an opinion. After all, the energy eaters are in your back garden."

Grimes decided that he might as well talk as eat—he would not be missing much. "I don't suppose I need to tell you about the Terran shark, Captain. He has, however, been described as a mobile appetite. He just eats and eats without discrimination, often to his own undoing. He just hasn't the sense to consider the consequences. Right?"

Haab looked to Dr. Wayne, his biologist. Wayne grinned and said, "The commodore hasn't put it in very scientific language, but he's not far off the beam."

"Then," Grimes went on, "we have human beings who are compulsive eaters. They often are far from being unintelligent—yet they cannot control themselves, even though they know that they are digging their graves with knives and forks. The energy eaters are more intelligent than sharks. They may be as intelligent as we are but we don't know. Intelligent or not, they are handicapped."

"Handicapped? Just how?" demanded Haab.

"Unlike human compulsive eaters they have no control over their intake. If there is raw energy around they absorb it, whether they want to or not. They know, I think, that the absorption of the energy generated by a nuclear explosion will be fatal—but if they are in the vicinity of such a blast they cannot help themselves. Sorry—they can help themselves, but only by exercising their power of temporal precession. And by the time they found this out they were almost extinct."

"Then Moebius Dick will give us a good fight," commented the mate. "He has survived in spite of everything that the navy has thrown at him."

"The commodore isn't very interested in lighting fish," said Haab. "He told me that he fishes for trout with hand grenades."

"I believe in getting results," said Grimes, conscious that the officers and specialists around the table were looking at him coldly.

New Bedford sped through the warped continuum, homing on the continuous Carlotti signal that Grimes had persuaded the captain of *Rim Arquebus* to transmit. The warship was remaining in the vicinity of the last sighting of Moebius Dick and had received orders from the admiralty to cooperate with Haab. Coded signals had been made to Grimes and, reading them, he had gained the impression that Captain Welldean of the *Arquebus* was far from happy. But Grimes' heart did not bleed for Welldean. Welldean was in his own ship with his own people as shipmates and his own cook turning out meals to his own taste. No doubt his feelings had been hurt when he had been ordered to abandon his own hunt and to put himself under the command of a reserve officer. But he was not an unwelcome guest aboard somebody else's vessel.

At last the tiny spark that was *Rim Arquebus* showed up just inside the screen of the Mass Proximity Indicator. Speed was reduced and eventually both drive units were shut down. *Rim Arquebus* hung there, five kilometers from *New Bedford,* a minor but bright constellation in the blackness.

Welldean's fat, surly face looked out from the screen of the NST transceiver at Grimes and the others in *New Bedford*'s control room.

"Have you any further information, Captain?" asked Haab.

Welldean replied in a flat voice, "The EE emerges into NST at regular half-hourly intervals, remaining for ten minutes each time, presumably to feed on the radiation emitted by my ship. Pursuant to instructions—" he seemed to be glaring directly at Grimes—"I have made no hostile moves. Would the commodore have any further orders for me?"

"None at the moment, Captain," Grimes told him. "Just stand by."

"Rim Arquebus standing by," acknowledged Welldean sulkily.

"When will Moebius Dick—" Haab was interrupted by a shout from his mate.

"There she blows!"

The energy eater had appeared midway between the two ships. It was huge, brilliantly luminous, lazily rotating. Grimes paraphrased wryly, *He who eats and runs away will live to eat some other day* . . . This thing had eaten and run away, eaten and run away and it had grown, was a vortex of forces all of a kilometer across. It would never fit into *New Bedford*'s capacious hold, a compartment designed for the carriage of alien life forms, some of them gigantic. But this did not matter. The cage of beams and fields would be set up outside the ship, but still within the temporal precession field of the Mannschenn Drive.

Grimes, a mere observer aboard a vessel that was not his own, felt superfluous, useless, as Haab and his officers went into the drill that had been worked out to the last detail. The mate, Murgatroyd, would remain on board in charge of the ship—and Haab, with the second, third and fourth mates, would go out in the one-man chasers. Haab was already in his spacesuit—the small craft were no more than flying framework, unpressurized—and his prosthetic leg, through some freak of sound conductivity, clicked loudly as he moved. In his armor, with that mechanical noise accompanying every motion of his legs, he was more like a robot than a man, even though his chin beard was jutting through the open face-plate of his helmet.

"Good hunting, Captain," said Grimes.

"Thank you, Commodore." Haab turned to his mate. "You're in charge of the ship, Mr. Murgatroyd. Don't interfere with the hunt." Then, to Grimes: "Will you tell Captain Welldean to keep his guns and torpedoes to himself?" Welldean's heavy face scowled at them from the screen of the NST transceiver.

"Moebius Dick has gone," announced Murgatroyd.

"When he surfaces again, we shall be in position," Haab told him as he left the control room.

Murgatroyd looked at Grimes. *There's nobody else to talk to,* he seemed to be thinking, *so I may as well pass the time of day with you.* He said, "The Old Man always brings 'em back."

"Alive?" queried Grimes.

"When he wants to," replied the mate.

Then he laughed. "He hasn't much choice as far as that thing's concerned. If it's dead it's—nothing." Even in free fall he contrived to give the impression of being slumped in his seat. An incongruous wistfulness softened the rough, scarred, big-featured face under the coarse, yellow hair.

"You wish you were out in one of the chasers," Grimes stated rather than asked.

"I do. But somebody has to mind the shop—and it always seems to be me. There they go, Commodore."

Four bright sparks darted into the emptiness between *New Bedford* and *Rim Arquebus.* As they reached a predetermined position they slowed, stopped, then slid into a square formation. Moebius Dick should reappear at the center of the quadrangle and then, at Haab's signal, each of the little crafts would become a fantastically powerful electromagnet and each would emit the beamed Carlotti transmissions, effectively netting the energy eater in time and space.

Murgatroyd and Grimes stared into the screen of the Mass Proximity Indicator. Four little points of light marked the positions of the chasers, a much fainter one denoting the presence of the energy eater.

"Master to *New Bedford?*" crackled from the speaker. "Check position, please."

"*New Bedford* to master," replied Murgatroyd. "You are exactly in position. Over."

"*Rim Arquebus* to Commodore Grimes," put in Welldean. "Do you wish me to take any action when the EE surfaces?"

"Haab to Grimes. You are only an observer. And that goes for your navy, too. Over."

"The old man gets tensed up," remarked Murgatroyd, with the faintest hint of apology in his voice."

"*Rim Arquebus* to Commodore Grimes. My weaponry is manned and ready," persisted Welldean.

"So is mine." Murgatroyd chuckled, waving a big hand over his fire-control console.

The minutes, the seconds, ticked by. Grimes watched the sweep second hand of the clock. He had noted the time of Moebius Dick's disappearance. The half-hour was almost up. When that red pointer came around to 37 . . .

"Now!" yelled the mate.

Moebius Dick was back. The enormous circle of gyrating luminescence had reappeared in the center of the square formed by the chasers. From the NST speaker came the low-pitched buzz and crackle of interference as the solenoids were energized. The energy eater hung there, quivering, seeming to shrink within itself. Then it moved, tilting like a processing gyroscope.

Haab's voice could be heard giving orders: "Increase to six hundred thousand gausses. To six-fifty—seven hundred—"

From one of the chasers came a bright, brief flare and from the speaker a cry of alarm: "Captain, my coil has blown!"

"Master to second and fourth mates—triangular formation."

Moebius Dick was spinning about a diametric axis, no longer a circle of light but a hazy sphere of radiance. The energy eater was rolling through the emptiness, directly toward one of the three still-functioning chasers. The small craft turned to run. *Rim Arquebus* stabbed out with a barrage of laser beams. In *New Bedford*'s control room Murgatroyd swore, added his fire to that from the frigate. It was ineffective—or highly effective in the wrong way. The monster glowed ever more brightly as it absorbed the energy directed at it, moved ever faster. The chaser turned and twisted desperately, hopelessly. The other chasers could not pursue for fear of running into the fire from the ships. There was nothing that they could have done, in any case.

"The old man's boat—" muttered Murgatroyd. "I guess it's the way he wanted to go—" His hand fell away from the firing stud. Moebius Dick was rolling over Haab's small and fragile craft.

Grimes, on the NST VHF, was ordering, "Hold your fire, *Rim Arquebus!* Hold your fire!"

Welldean's voice came back: "What the hell do you think I'm doing?" Adding, as a grudging afterthought: "Sir."

The lights of the chaser flared briefly through the luminous, swirling haze that enveloped them, flared and died. But something, somebody, broke through the living radiance. It was the space-suited Haab, using his personal propulsion unit to drive him back to his ship.

He broke through and broke away and for a second or so it seemed that he would succeed. Then Moebius Dick was after him, overtaking him, enveloping him. From the NST speaker came a short, dreadful scream. The globe of flame that was the energy eater seemed to swell, was swelling, visibly and rapidly, assuming the appearance of a gigantic, spherical fire opal. The three surviving chasers retreated rapidly.

Dark streaks suddenly marred the iridescent beauty of the sphere, spread, rapidly covering the entire surface. Where Moebius Dick had been there was only nothingness.

No, not nothingness.

Floating in the darkness, illumined by the searchlights of the three small craft, was the lifeless, armored figure of Captain Haab.

"They'll bring him in," muttered Murgatroyd. "I'll take him back to Earth for burial. Those were his wishes."

"*Rim Arquebus* to *New Bedford*," came Welldean's voice. "Do you require medical assistance? Shall I send a boat with my surgeon—"

"We've a Quack of our own," snarled Murgatroyd, "and a good one. But even he won't be able to do anything. The old man is dead."

"It was his leg that saved him," said Grimes to Sonya when, back at Port Forlorn, he was telling her the story of the hunt.

"How do you make that out?"

"Well, perhaps it wasn't his leg, but all of us came to the conclusion that it was, as it were, the last straw that broke the camel's back."

"Make your mind up, John. I'd gotten used to the idea that Moebius Dick was a sort of latter-day white whale—and now you refer to him as a camel!"

"You know what I mean—I'm talking about the item that finally made him lose control. Moebius Dick had been feeding well over a period of quite some weeks. Every time *Rim Arquebus* heaved a torpedo at him he'd skim the cream off the fireball and then vanish, being too intelligent to overeat. But all life forms tend to act unintelligently when infuriated and he was no exception. When he broke out of Haab's electromagnetic net he was no more than a dangerous, vicious animal. He was being pumped full of photons by the concentrated laser fire from the two ships—and it meant as little to him as a stream of bullets means to a charging carnivore. He 'killed' Haab's chaser, gulping all the energy from its machinery. He would have killed Haab himself—Haab was in a state of complete paralysis when he was brought on board—if he hadn't started his meal on the Captain's leg.

"You know that the Tanganorans are famous for their powered prosthetic limbs, don't you? Haab's right leg was a beautiful machine with its own, built-in power plant—cells with a working life of a least twenty Standard Years after installation, a slow, rigidly controlled fission process. Moebius Dick got that twenty years' worth of energy in one bite."

"Critical mass or critical charge—or whatever?" murmured Sonya. "But Haab's anagrammatic namesake wasn't as lucky with *his* peg leg."

"What the hell are you talking about?"

"Or was he more than just a namesake?"

"I still don't get you."

"You must remember that talk we had with the Reverend Madam Swithin about reincarnation. How she told us that—according to the tenets of her Church—some souls have to wait around for centuries until the shuffling of chromosomes and genes produces just the right body, with just the right brain and psychological make-up, for their next embodiment. It makes an odd sort of sense, doesn't it? Captain Ahab, the whaler—Captain Haab, the hunter—"

"But Ahab was only a fictional character!" Grimes, protested to his wife.

"Aren't we all finally?" she asked reasonably. "Those of us who deserve being made into legends?"

ON THE ACCOUNT

~ Chapter 1 ~

COMMODORE GRIMES sat at his desk, looking down at the transcript of a Carlottigram from Port Listowel. *Lord of the Isles,* one of the lightjammers on the run between the Rim Worlds and the Llanithi Consortium, was overdue. She, using her own Carlotti equipment, had beamed a final message to Port Forlorn before breaking the light barrier. Once the speed of light had been exceeded she was in a weird, private universe of her own—stranger even than the private universes of ships running under the space-time-twisting Mannschenn Drive—and unable to communicate with any planetary base or any other ship. Toward the end of her voyage she had made her routine reduction of speed to a sublight velocity and had started to send her ETA to the Carlotti Station on Llanith. She had gotten as far as giving her name and then, according to the Llanithi Carlotti operator on watch, had experienced what seemed to be interference on the band in use. Nothing more had been heard from her. And now she was all of ten days overdue.

The communicator buzzed sharply.

Grimes pressed the button that would admit the incoming call. The screen lit up and on it appeared the fleshy, ruddy face of Admiral Kravitz.

"Ah, Grimes."

The commodore repressed the temptation to counter with, *And whom the hell else did you expect?* Legally speaking, the admiral was not his superior officer except when Grimes was called back to Active Duty with the Rim Worlds Navy, but there would be no sense in antagonizing the man.

"Sir?" Grimes replied curtly.

"This *Lord of the Isles* business, Grimes?"

"You have a transcript of the signal from Port Listowel, sir?"

"Of course. We do have an Intelligence Branch, you know. What do you make of it?"

"I don't like it. Especially coming right after the vanishing of *Sea Witch* under very similar circumstances."

"What are you doing about it, Grimes?"

"I could ask you the same question, sir."

"We cleaned up the energy eaters for you, Grimes, and we made a clean sweep. *Rim Culverin* has been maintaining a patrol ever since the conclusion of Operation Rimhunt and has reported no further invasion of our territorial space by those entities." The admiral paused, then went on: "I'm not altogether happy about those lightjammers of yours, Grimes. As you know, we're having some built for the Navy, but I'm beginning to feel like trying to get the program canceled. They aren't safe. Sailing ships, indeed, in *this* day and age?"

"They're the only ships we have capable of trading with the Llanithi Consortium."

"At the moment, Grimes, at the moment. But our boffins are working on some other, simpler way of achieving a reversal of atomic charges."

"With what success, sir?" asked Grimes innocently.

Kravitz flushed. "None so far. But give them time, give them time. Meanwhile—"

"Sir?"

"Meanwhile, Grimes, I am recalling you to Active Duty. As long as the so-called ships of the line are still on our drawing boards we have to maintain an interest in sailing vessels. Furthermore, I have learned from your employers—from Rim Runners—that all further sailings of the lightjammers have been suspended until such time as the mystery of the disappearance of *Lord of the Isles* and *Sea*

Witch has been cleared up. They are agreeable to the requisitioning and commissioning of *Pamir* as an auxiliary cruiser. You will sail in her."

Grimes grinned. "Thank you, sir. But I have to tell you that I'm not qualified in sail."

"*Pamir*'s people are—and they all, like yourself, hold reserve commissions. Listowel's a full commander, isn't he? You'll be in overall charge of the ship and the expedition, but he can be your sailing master. We'll be putting aboard regular Navy personnel—gunnery specialists and the like. Satisfied?"

"Gunnery specialists?"

"You never know when weapons are going to come in handy, Grimes. It's better to have them than to be without them."

Grimes had to agree. He knew as well as anybody that the Universe was not peaceful and that Man was not its only breaker of peace.

Not at all reluctantly Grimes handed over his astronautical superintendent's duties to Captain Barsac, one of Rim Runners' senior masters. But it was with a certain degree of reluctance that he left his comfortable home in Port Forlorn for Port Erikson, the lightjammers' terminal. Sonya refused to accompany her husband. She detested cold weather. Port Forlorn's climate was barely tolerable. Only Esquimaux, polar bears or penguins—assuming that the immigration or importation of these from Earth could be arranged—would feel at home at Coldharbor Bay in Lorn's Antarctica.

Pamir was alongside at Port Erikson. The cargo she had brought from Llanith had been discharged but she had not commenced to load for the return voyage. As yet the advance party from the Admiralty Yards was still to arrive, although accommodations—looking like black, partially inflated balloons grounded in the snow—had been set up for them.

Grimes, accompanied by Captain Rowse, the Port Erikson harbormaster, went aboard *Pamir*. He was received by Ralph Listowel, the lightjammer's master.

"Glad to have you aboard, sir," said Listowel.

"Glad to be aboard, Commander."

Listowel scowled. "That's right, sir. Rub it in. I suppose you'll be taking over my quarters."

Grimes grinned. "No. You're to be my sailing master—and, as far as I'm concerned, this is still your ship and you're still the master of her. You've quite palatial passenger accommodations. That'll do me."

Listowel's scowl faded from his lean, dark face. "Thank you, sir. But what is going on?"

"Your ship has been requisitioned—and you and your officers have been called up for Active Duty in the Rim Worlds Navy."

"I know that. But what *is* going on?"

"I was hoping that you'd be able to tell me."

Listowel waved his visitors to seats, took a chair himself. He said, "Let's face it, Commodore. To date the lightjammers have been lucky, fantastically lucky. Even in *Flying Cloud,* where we had to make up the rules as we went along, we all came through in one piece. But sooner or later luck runs out."

"You think that's what happened to *Sea Witch* and *Lord of the Isles?*"

"There are so many things that could happen. When we're running under sail, building up to a velocity just short of that light, we could hit something—"

"And the flare of the explosion would be seen from Llanith."

"All right, all right. Something could go wrong with the magnetic suspension of the sphere of anti-iron—"

"And with matter and antimatter canceling each other out the burst of released energy would be even more spectacular."

"Yes, Commodore. But what if it happened at trans-light speed? We know very little of conditions outside the ship at that velocity. Would the explosion be witnessed in this universe—or in the next universe but three?"

"Mphm. You have something there, Listowel. Even so, we've two ships missing, one after the other. There's an old saying: Once is happenstance. Twice is coincidence. Three times is enemy action."

"There hasn't been a third time," said Listowel.

"Yet," pointed out Grimes. "But there's still the apparent jamming of *Lord of the Isles'* last call to be considered."

Back in Rowse's office Grimes asked for the manifests of the cargoes carried by the two missing ships. It was possible that there had been some item of freight which, at trans-light speeds and with the reversal of atomic charges, had become chemically or physically unstable with fatal consequences. This was an idea worth considering. But no radioactives had been listed. No industrial chemicals, dangerous or otherwise, had been listed. Mainly the freight carried in each ship had consisted of luxury goods—preserved foodstuffs, liquor, fine textiles and the like. A few shipments of machine tools and some drugs had also been part of the cargoes.

One drug in particular—Antigeriatridine—caught Grimes' attention. The substance was not manufactured on any of the Rim Worlds. It came from Marina, a planet in the Pleiades Sector. It was an extract from the glands of an indigenous sea slug and could not be synthesized. It was fantastically expensive and, on most worlds, was controlled by the state, rationed out only to deserving citizens. It was Marina's main source of income, exported to any planet that could afford to pay for it. In recent years the Llanithi Consortium had been placed on Marina's list of customers. Transshipment for Llanith was made from Lorn.

Grimes' memory carried him back to the long ago days when he had been a newly commissioned ensign in the Federation Survey Service. He had played a part in bringing the pirates who had captured the merchant vessel *Epsilon Sextans* to book. *Epsilon Sextans* had been carrying Antigeriatridine, which had made her a worthwhile prey.

Perhaps Admiral Kravitz's insistence that *Pamir* be armed made sense.

But piracy?

It was not the continued existence of the crime itself that Grimes found hard to comprehend, but rather the actual mechanics of it. Piracy was not unknown along the spaceways, but both predators and victims had always been conventional starships, with inertial drive and Mannschenn Drive and auxiliary rocket power for use in emergencies. Under inertial drive only, maintaining a comfortable one G acceleration, a ship could build up almost to the speed of light if she took long enough about it. But, as soon as possible, she usually ran under Mannschenn Drive which, in effect, gave her FTL velocity. In these conditions she was untouchable unless the vessel attacking her succeeded in synchronizing her own rate of temporal precession. The captains of warships—and of such vessels as have from time to time sailed on the plundering account—were reasonably competent in the practice of this art.

But it would be impossible for a ship proceeding under inertial drive only to match velocities with a lightjammer under sail. And a ship running under Mannschenn Drive would have to return to the normal space-time continuum before her weapons could be brought to bear on a lightjammer—and, once again, the matching of velocities would be impossible.

Hijacking was a form of piracy, of course.

Grimes turned from the missing ships' cargo manifests to their passenger lists. The names meant nothing to him, neither those of Rim Worlds citizens nor of Llanithans. No doubt the police could help him in this respect. Perhaps one or more of those passengers had a criminal record. But the hypothesis made little appeal to him. He just could not imagine the officers of either of the vessels submitting meekly—and he could not imagine any passenger being able to handle a lightjammer. Sail spacemanship was an art rather than a science and the only practitioners of the art—Grimes told himself—consisted of the handful of Rim Runners' personnel trained and qualified for lightjammers.

He filled and lit his pipe, looked down at the manifests and passenger lists on the desk. He had a hunch that the manifests meant more than the passenger lists—no more than a hunch, but his hunches were often right. Any ship—even a pirate ship—anywhere in space between Lorn and Llanith and in position to receive the beamed Carlotti transmissions from one planet to the other, would be able to read the routine signals sent immediately after the lift-off of one of the lightjammers. Date and time of departure—passengers carried—a listing of freight aboard. Nothing was encoded. There had never been any need for secrecy until now.

Only the actual mechanics of attack, seizure and boarding puzzled him.

He called Sonya and told her that she had better come to Port Erikson. "You're the intelligence officer in this family," he said. "This job calls for intelligence." Reluctantly she agreed to join him.

The following morning he stood in the Port Erikson control tower, looking out through the wide windows at the bleak landscape. *Pamir* was alongside at her wharf, a great, dull-gleaming torpedo shape on the dark water. The sleekness of her lines was broken only by the pods that housed her airscrews and their engines. Out on Coldharbor Bay a small tug, *Bustler,* was chuffing busily back and forth, functioning as an icebreaker, keeping the harbor clear of any accumulation of ice heavy enough to impede surface maneuvers. Grimes had decided that *Pamir* must keep to her original schedule, which meant that her conversion to an auxiliary cruiser would be a skimpy one. There would be time for the installation of an extra generator and the fitting of two batteries of laser cannon, but no more.

A familiar voice issued from the traffic controller's transceiver. "Pinnace *Firefly* to Port Erikson. Do you read me? Over."

"Loud and clear, *Firefly.* Pass your message. Over."

Grimes went to stand by the traffic control officer. He heard Sonya say, "My ETA Port Erikson oh-nine-four-five hours, your time. Over."

So neither she—nor Admiral Kravitz—had wasted any time. And Sonya was doing her own piloting, which was typical of her.

"I have her on the screen, sir," announced the radar operator.

Grimes went to the window overlooking the Nullarbor Plain, almost featureless under the blanket of snow. It was one of the rare clear days, and on the horizon stood the distant, jagged battlements of the Great Barrens. And was that a tiny, glittering speck in the pale sky? Yes. It expanded rapidly and even in the control tower, through the thick glass of the windows, the irritated snarl of an inertial drive unit operating at maximum capacity was distinctly audible.

"That's her," said Captain Rowse.

"That's her," agreed Grimes. He shrugged into his heavy cloak, put on his cap and went down to the airstrip to meet Sonya.

"The trouble with you, John," she said, "is that you've read too much of the wrong kind of history. Wooden ships and iron men and all that sort of thing. Pieces of eight. Broadsides of carronades. The Jolly Roger. Oh, there have been space pirates, I admit. But I still get my share of the bumf issued by the Federation Survey Service's Intelligence Branch—and I can tell you that today there just aren't any pirates. Not that sort of pirate, anyway. There's still the occasional hijacking."

Grimes' prominent ears flushed. He indicated with his hand the passenger lists. He said, "I've asked the Port Forlorn chief of police if any of these people have criminal records. He assures me that none of them have and that everybody aboard *Lord of the Isles* and *Sea Witch* was a little, innocent woolly lamb—"

"He'd know, wouldn't he?" She herself was flushed, her fine features literally glowing under the glossy auburn hair. "And you have all these bright ideas and drag me out here, where all the brass monkeys are singing falsetto, to join you in this comfortless shack to help you think."

"Not comfortless," said Grimes. The quarters that he had been given were commodious and comfortable enough, although lacking in character. ACCOMMODATION, MARRIED COUPLE, FOR THE USE OF . . .

"Well, what do you intend doing? Put me in the picture."

"*Pamir* will sail on time, having loaded the cargo that's been booked for her. That will include a shipment of Antigeriatridine. The usual routine signals will be made once she has lifted off. And then we wait to see what happens next."

"We?"

"I suppose you'll be coming along."

"I might as well get a free trip to Llanith out of it."

"All right. You. Me. Ralph Listowel and his officers. The gunnery officer from the Navy who'll be looking after the laser batteries. The two dozen or so marines who'll be traveling as passengers."

"Anybody would think that you were contemplating embarking on a career of piracy yourself."

Grimes laughed. "Why not? After all, one of my ancestors sailed on the account."

"And what happened to him?"

"He was eventually hanged from his own yardarm."

She joined him in his laughter. "Then you'd better be careful. After all, the lightjammers are the only ships that run to masts and yards!"

❧ Chapter 2 ❧

PAMIR WAS READY FOR SPACE.

The extra generator had been installed, as had been the batteries of laser cannon. Stores for the voyage and the cargo had been loaded. The passengers were embarked. Grimes and Sonya, together with Major Trent, the marine officer, and Lieutenant Fowler, the gunnery officer, sat with Listowel and his wife, Sandra, in the master's day cabin.

Listowel sipped his coffee rather glumly. He asked Grimes stiffly, "Have I your permission to cast off, sir, at the arranged time?"

"Of course, Listowel. You're the master still. The rest of us are just along for the ride."

"It's a ride I'm looking forward to," put in Fowler enthusiastically. He was a young giant with short-cropped yellow hair, the perpetual schoolboy so common in all the armed services. "It'll give me some time in sail and I'll be all set for our own ships of the line when they come out."

"It's not a free ride we're here for," commented the major sourly.

"More coffee anybody?" asked Sandra cheerfully.

"No thanks," replied Listowel, looking at his watch. "It's time we got the show on the road."

"Can I come up to Control, sir?" asked Fowler.

"Of course, Lieutenant. You're welcome on the bridge. And so are you, Major."

Grimes and Sonya went along with the others. They had witnessed *Pamir*'s departure from the control position before, but it was so unlike the lift-off of a conventional spaceship as to remain fascinating. This time there was no need to use the tug, no need for the transverse thrust of the airscrews. The wind, what little there was of it, was northerly, blowing the ship bodily off from the wharf, the brash ice piling up along her lee side but not impeding her. When she was well out into the bay water, ballast was dumped and—the sphere of antimatter giving her positive buoyancy—she went up like a balloon or a rocket—silently. Within seconds she was driving through the low cloud ceiling and then had broken through into the clear upper air. Fast she rose—and faster—into blackness, while below her Lorn became an opalescent globe hanging in nothingness.

The directional gyroscopes rumbled and whined, rumbled again and then lapsed into silence. She was steadied on course now, with Lorn to one side and the Lorn sun astern. The tiny cluster of stars— the antimatter suns around which revolved the planets of the Llanithi Consortium—was directly ahead.

The control room guests crowded to the side ports of the bridge, looking aft to watch as Listowel made sail. The stubs of the telescopic masts extended themselves rapidly, sprouting yards as they elongated. The yards and the great sails, spreading to catch the star wind, the royals, the topgallants, the upper topsails and the lower topsails, the main courses . . . The polarized glass of the viewports dimmed the glare of the sun and black against it stood the driving surfaces, filling to the photon gale. The inertialess ship was already scudding before it and the Doppler Log was clicking and flashing like a clock gone mad.

"Roll and go," murmured Listowel.

"Wonderful!" breathed Fowler.

Major Trent only grunted, then said, "I'd better get down to see to my men."

Fowler said, "And I'd better check my cannon."

"We'll not be needing them yet," Grimes told him.

The ship drove on, steadily accelerating.

It was like the first voyage that Grimes and Sonya had made in *Pamir*—and yet, in some ways, unlike. The atmosphere on board was different, mainly because there were no civilian passengers. Major Trent and his marines were passengers of a sort, of course—there was little that they could do about the ship until such time as their professional services would be required. But Trent maintained his own standards of discipline and there was altogether too much heel-clicking and saluting. And Listowel's officers were all too conscious of their temporary standing as commissioned personnel of the Rim Worlds Navy, serving aboard an auxiliary cruiser of that same service. Their captain didn't like it.

He complained to Grimes over a quiet drink in the commodore's quarters: "Damn it all, sir, I'm just a shipmaster and my people are my mates and engineers and all the rest of it. But now I have Mr. bloody Willoughby putting on airs and graces and expecting to be addressed as Lieutenant Commander every time anybody talks to him."

Grimes chuckled. "It doesn't matter. He can call himself what he likes—he's still a very good chief officer."

"Even so—" Then Listowel managed a wry chuckle of his own. "All right. I'll let him and the others have their fun. But it still reminds me of small boys playing at pirates."

"Talking of pirates—" Grimes pulled a key from his pocket and unlocked a drawer of the desk that was part of the cabin's furniture. "I asked you in for a talk as well as a drink. You remember that coded Carlottigram that came through for me on the teletype this morning?" He took a sheet of paper out of the drawer.

"This contains the decode, top secret—your eyes only. To Be Destroyed By Fire Before Reading—and all the rest of it. When it comes to playing childish games the Admiralty is at least as bad as anybody else. And this message concerns us all in this vessel.

"Navy has an intelligence service, you know. According to Sonya it's not a patch on the Intelligence Branch of the Federation Survey Service, but its officers do flap their ears and twitch their little pink noses now and again. Unluckily, Admiral Kravitz didn't get his paws on their reports concerning the Duchy of Waldegren until after we'd sailed."

"Waldegren?"

"Yes. It seems that our people managed to plant some monitor buoys in the territorial space of the Duchy. I've heard those gadgets described as miracles of miniaturization. See all, hear all, and punch it all back to Port Forlorn on tight-beam Carlotti in one coded parcel before the automatic self-destruction. And that, of course, occurs when anything approaches within ten kilometers.

"Well, there's been something going on around Darnstadt—the fortress planet, so-called. There's a photograph of a lightjammer under sail. There are monitored signals—both Carlotti and NST." He tapped the sheet of paper. "Kravitz sent me translations of some of the messages. 'Clear of atmosphere, making sail.' 'Arrange berthage for prize.' The sort of things you send just after departure and just prior to arrival."

"I don't take any prizes, Commodore."

"You might yet." Grimes looked at his watch. "Time we went to see Mr. Fowler get a prize for good shooting."

"Didn't you specialize in gunnery yourself, sir, when you were in the Survey Service?"

"At one time, yes. But I never had a practice shoot at point eight the speed of light. This should be interesting."

"Surely no more so than any other practice shoot, Commodore. As far as the target rocket and the ship are concerned, there'll be no great relative velocities. The target will just run parallel to us once it's been launched. If it took evasive action it would drop astern too fast for Fowler to get a shot at it. We're still accelerating, you know."

"Mphm?" Grimes locked away the message. "Let's go to watch the fireworks."

The watchkeeper—Denby, the second officer—and all off-duty officers were in the control room. Sonya was there, too, as was Sandra. Major Trent was there, accompanied by his sergeant. Wallasey, the third officer, was assisting Lieutenant Fowler. The gunnery officer sat at his fire control console. Young Wallasey was at the smaller set of controls, part of the ship's normal equipment, from which signal and sounding rockets were handled. He was managing to look at least as important as Fowler.

"Let battle commence!" whispered Grimes to Sonya.

Fowler overheard this and scowled. But he said nothing. Commodores, even commodores on the Reserve List, were entitled to their pleasantries at the expense of mere lieutenants.

"Targets in readiness, Mr. Fowler," reported Wallasey.

"Thank you, Mr. Wallasey," replied Fowler stiffly. Then, to Grimes: "Permission to commence practice shoot, sir?"

"This is Captain Listowel's ship, Mr. Fowler," said Grimes.

The young man flushed and repeated his question to Listowel.

"Carry on, Mr. Fowler."

"Fire one," he ordered.

"Fire one," repeated Wallasey.

Grimes, looking aft with the others, saw the gout of blue flame, intensely bright against the black backdrop with its sparse scattering of stars, as the missile was ejected from its launching tube. It fell away from the ship on a slightly divergent course, pulling ahead, but slowly, at first.

"Open the range, Mr. Wallasey," ordered Fowler.

"Range opening. One kilometer. Two. Four. Ten—"

The rocket now was only a bright spark against the darkness.

Fowler worked at his console. Abaft the control room but forward of the masts and sails the quadruple rods of the starboard laser battery turned and wavered like the hunting antennae of some huge insect.

"Fire—" muttered Fowler to himself. A faint glow showed at the tips of the rods, nothing more. Here there was no air, with its floating dust motes, to be heated to incandescence. Out to starboard the bright spark persisted, neither extinguished nor flaring into sudden explosion.

Fowler muttered something about the calibration of his sights, then ordered, "Close the range."

"Range closing, Mr. Fowler. Ten. Nine. Eight—damn!"

"What's wrong?"

"Burnout." The bright spark had vanished now.

"All right. Fire two."

"Fire two."

The second missile was thrown from its tube.

"Range, Mr. Wallasey?"

"One kilometer. Opening."

"Hold at one kilometer." Then, to himself: "It's right in the sights. I can't miss—"

"But you're doing just that," remarked Grimes.

"But I can't be!" Fowler sounded desperate. "With a single cannon, perhaps. But not with a battery of four. And the sights can't be out."

Grimes grunted thoughtfully. Then: "Tell me, Mr. Fowler, has anybody ever tried to use laser in these conditions before?"

"From a lightjammer, you mean, sir? From a ship traveling at almost the speed of light?"

"Yes."

"You know that this is the first time, sir."

"And it's been an interesting experiment, hasn't it? Oh, I could be wrong, but I have a sort of vision of photons being dispersed like water from the spray nozzle of a hose. Perhaps if the ship were not accelerating the tight, coherent beam would be maintained . . . Is there a physicist in the house?"

"You know there's not," said Sonya sharply.

"Unfortunate, but true. So in these conditions our laser is about as effective as a searchlight and we've nobody to tell us what to do about it."

Fowler was slumped in his seat, a picture of dejection. He was a gunnery officer whose weapons were as lethal as toy pistols. "Cheer up," Grimes told him. "I've a job for you."

"But what is there for me to do, sir? As you've pointed out already, I'm not a physicist."

"But you are a weapons specialist." Grimes turned to Wallasey. "How many rockets have you left?"

"Six, sir."

"Then I suggest that you and Mr. Fowler, assisted by the engineering staff, convert them into weapons."

"What about warheads?"

Grimes sighed heavily. "You'd never have made a living as a cannoneer in the early days of artillery, Mr. Fowler. Those old boys used to cast their own cannon and mix their own powder—and they didn't have the ingredients that we have aboard this ship. Ammonium nitrate, for example—one of the chemical fertilizers we use in the hydroponic tanks. We should be able to cook up something packing far more of a wallop than gunpowder."

"You're convinced that we shall need weapons, John?" put in Sonya.

"I'm not convinced of anything. But somebody once said— Cromwell, wasn't it?—'Trust in God, and keep your powder dry.' Furthermore, my dear, this vessel is rated as an auxiliary cruiser, a unit of the Rim Worlds Navy. Our lords and masters of the Admiralty have, in their wisdom, equipped her with weaponry. We have discovered that this weaponry is useless. So—we improvise."

"I'm surprised," she said, "that you don't follow in the footsteps of your piratical ancestor and fit *Pamir* out with a couple of broadsides of muzzle-loading cannon."

A slow smile spread over Grimes' rugged features. "Why not?" he murmured happily. "Why not?"

All deep space ships carry a biochemist. In large passenger vessels and warships he is a departmental head, but usually he is one of the officers who has been put through a crash course and looks after the life-support systems in addition to his other duties. *Pamir*'s biochemist was Sandra Listowel, who was also purser and catering officer. Even a full-time, fully qualified biochemist is not an industrial chemist. Sandra most certainly was not. Nonetheless, she succeeded— losing her eyebrows and a little more than half of her blond hair in the process—in brewing up a batch of what Grimes referred to as sort-of-kind-of amatol. After all, cooking oil is not toluene. Lieutenant Fowler, given the freedom of the engineer's workshop, was told to produce a half-dozen impact fuses. He was a good worker and not unintelligent but sadly lacking, Grimes concluded, in initiative. He was a good gunnery officer only when he had all the resources of a naval arsenal behind him.

Grimes, however, loved improvising. Many years ago, when he had been Federation Survey Service lieutenant, commanding the courier *Adder,* he had made some missiles, using large plastic bottles as the casings and black powder as the propellant. After a browse through the chemical fertilizers in the "farm's" storerooms he decided that he had the necessary ingredients for more black powder. He wanted something relatively slow-burning for the weapons he had in mind.

He had seen *Pamir*'s manifest of cargo on the completion of loading. One item was a consignment of metal piping with a bore of 100 millimeters. Fortunately this was easily accessible in the hold. It was backbreaking work to lug the heavy sections out of their stowage and to the ship's workshop, but Major Trent's marines were able to accomplish this without too much grumbling. The pipe sections were cut to size, each two and a half meters in length. One end of each of the tubes was sealed with a heavy, welded flange. The crude cannon, eight of them, were beginning to take shape.

There was no time to introduce too many refinements. *Pamir* had broken through the light barrier, was well away on the second leg of her voyage. It was when she decelerated, to complete the passage to Llanith under sail, that the pirate would strike. This was a probability if not a certainty. The evidence indicated that this was what had happened to *Lord of the Isles* and *Sea Witch*.

Grimes discussed the prospect with Listowel, Willoughby, Major Trent and Sonya. He said, "Let's face it. The principles of our lightjammers aren't secret. We're the only people who have had such ships simply because we're the only people with inhabited antimatter systems in our sector of space. But there have been articles a-plenty in both scientific and shipping journals. And the Waldegrenese can read."

"Waldegren?" asked Trent.

"Yes. Waldegren. The Duchy has a bad record of harboring pirates." He spread a chart on Listowel's desk. "Now, just suppose that Waldegren is monitoring our traffic with Llanith on the Carlotti bands. Oh, I know that the beam between our two systems doesn't pass near any of the worlds of the Duchy—but a small relay station, possibly fully automated, could have been planted anywhere along the line of sight. *If* we knew just where to look for it we could find it. Mphm. Well, one of our lightjammers lifts off from Lorn. The routine message is sent. ETA and all the rest of it. Cargo such and such, consigned to so and so. Then the pirate—a lightjammer, of course— lifts off from Darnstadt . . . So far I've told only two people of the contents of the signal I received from Admiral Kravitz—Captain Listowel, of course, and Sonya. She helped with the decoding. But it all ties in. There has been lightjammer activity in the Duchy—and what would Waldegren want lightjammers for?"

"Piracy," said Listowel.

"Still, we must be careful. We aren't at war with Waldegren. The evidence indicates, however, that Waldegren has built at least one lightjammer. After all, the essential guts of such a ship, a sphere of antimatter, aren't all that hard to come by. There are other antimatter systems besides the Llanithi Consortium. But where was I? Oh, yes. The pirate lifts off from Darnstadt, sets course and adjusts speed so as to intercept our ship as she decelerates to sublight velocity. She jams the Carlotti bands, attacks, seizes."

"And what about the passengers and crew?" asked Listowel.

"If they're lucky, Captain, they'll be prisoners on Darnstadt. That's why we want to take prisoners ourselves."

"The pirate," said Trent, "will probably be armed with rockets, or projectile cannon. Not laser—unless the Waldegren scientists have worked out some way of making it effective at near-light speeds. Quick-firing cannon, I'd say."

"Quicker than your muzzle-loaders," said Sonya to Grimes.

"Almost certainly," he agreed. "But surprise is a good weapon."

≈ Chapter 3 ≈

AS *PAMIR* SPED THROUGH the nothingness the work of arming her progressed. Ahead of her blazed the stars, those toward which she was steering and those whose laggard light she was overhauling. Filters and shields protected her crew from the dangerous radiations that were a resultant of her velocity. Yet there was still visible light, harsh, intensely blue, light that should not have been seen but that, nonetheless, seemed to penetrate even opaque plating.

But apart from the watch officers nobody had time to look out into space. Those cannon had to be finished and mounted. There was black powder to be mixed and tested, the charges to be packed in plastic bags. There were the springs to be contrived to carry and dampen the recoil of the guns. There were bags of shot to be made up.

Pamir, fortunately, was so designed as to make the mounting of archaic cannon practicable. As a lightjammer, handled inside a planetary atmosphere like an airship, she was fitted with ballast tanks which, of course, were emptied on lift-off. Grimes decided to place his batteries, each of four guns, in the port and starboard wing tanks. To begin with, two crude airlocks were made and welded to the manhole doors leading into the compartments. Spacesuited and carrying laser tools the chief officer and the engineer went into the tanks, first to cut the gunports, then to strengthen the frames to take the weight of the artillery, the thrust of the recoil. The gun mountings were then passed in and welded into place.

The pieces themselves slid in cradles and, on being fired, would be driven back against powerful springs, locking in the fully recoiled position. Loading was fast enough—first the bag of powder, then the shot, with a ram-rod to shove all well home. Firing would have to be deferred until the guns were run out again. For firing Grimes had first considered electrical contacts, then some sort of flintlock. He was amused by his final solution—touch-hole and slow match. Even though hand lasers were the slow matches—within the confines of the ship they worked well enough—the principle was a reversion to the very earliest days of firearms.

Then there was the drilling of Trent's marines. They took it all cheerfully enough, making a game of it.

Finally Grimes was satisfied with the rate of fire—although none of the guns had yet actually been fired—under simulated conditions.

Grimes checked personally the ready-use lockers for the bagged charges, the lockers for the improvised shot, the arrangements for passing more ammunition through into the tanks should it become necessary, communications. But there was one more problem. A row of gunports, with the muzzles of guns protruding, is easily detectable. He decided that the cannon would be retained in the fully recoiled position until just before firing and the ports concealed by sheets of plastic. He ordered, too, that the laser batteries be withdrawn into their recesses. They were of no use, anyhow.

"Deceleration stations," Listowel ordered.

"Make that action stations," said Grimes quietly. "I'm taking over now, Captain."

"So I'm just your sailing master," Listowel commented, but cheerfully enough. "At your service, Commodore." He pressed the bell push. A coded clangor sounded and resounded, short long, short long, short long—the Morse A. Fowler fidgeted in his seat at the console, the one from which he would fire and, hopefully, direct the sounding rockets, each of which was now fitted with a high-explosive warhead. The batteries of muzzle loaders were manned. Spacesuited marines were standing by the drainpipe artillery, three to a gun. Handy to the airlocks over the manhole doors were the ammunition parties.

"Cut reaction drive."

"Cut reaction drive, sir."

The muted thunder of the rockets suddenly ceased.

Slowly, carefully, as though this were no more than a routine deceleration, Listowel trimmed his sails, pivoting them about the masts so that the light from the glaring Llanithi stars, almost dead ahead, was striking their reflecting surfaces at an oblique angle. It had to be done gradually. If *Pamir* were suddenly taken aback she would be dismasted. The Doppler Log was starting to wind down. 25.111111 . . . 25.111110 . . . 25.111109 . . . The lower courses were turned to exercise full braking effect. The lower topsails next—the upper topsails—the top gallants. Speed was dropping fast. Inside the inertialess ship there was no sensory hint of the titanic forces being brought into play, forces that in a normal vessel would have smeared ship and crew across the sky in a blaze of raw energy.

The log was still winding down, although the count was slowing.

1.000007 . . . 1.000005

1.000003 . . . 1.000001 . . .

1.000001

1.000001

1.000000

Now there was sensation, a feeling of unbearable tension. Something had to give. Something, somewhere, snapped suddenly. Ahead the sparse scattering of stars diminished in number. The Rim suns—astern in actuality—suddenly flickered out, reappeared in their proper relative bearing.

"Mr. Wallasey," said Listowel, "make the routine ETA call to Llanith."

He looked inquiringly toward Grimes, who said, "Yes. We maintain routine—until somebody or something interferes with it."

Wallasey was having his troubles. From the switched-on Carlotti transceiver issued a continuous warbling note.

"Interference—" he muttered.

"Jamming," amended Grimes. "This is it, Captain. Any moment now." He looked around the control room. Fowler was tense over his console, as was Denby, the second officer, at the radar. Wallasey was still twiddling knobs at the Carlotti set. Sonya and Sandra were sitting quietly in their chairs, apparently taking only a mild interest in the proceedings—but either woman, Grimes well knew, could spring into action at an instant's notice. And Sandra, after all, could handle a lightjammer almost as well as her husband.

There was nobody else on the bridge. Willoughby was below, in charge of the damage control party, and Major Trent was looking after the guns manned by his men.

"Target," reported Denby. "Green seventy-five. Range fifty kilometers. Closing."

"Thank you, Mr. Denby. Keep us informed," said Grimes.

"Green now seventy-five, still. Positive altitude five degrees, increasing."

"Range?"

"Forty—and closing."

Grimes spoke into the microphone that carried his voice through the ship and into the gunners' helmet speakers. "This is the commodore. The enemy has been sighted. She is closing fast. From now on there will be frequent changes of trajectory. Stand by to open fire on command. Over."

Trent's voice came in reply, "All is ready, sir. Guns loaded, but not yet run out."

"Don't run them out until you get the order to fire, Major."

"Green seventy-four, sir. Range thirty, closing. Positive altitude seven degrees. Increasing slowly."

"Captain," said Grimes, "roll us seven degrees to port. I want to keep our friend exactly on the plane of our ecliptic. We can't aim the guns individually—we have to aim the ship. Understand?"

"Understood, Commodore." The directional gyroscopes rumbled briefly as *Pamir* was turned about her long axis.

"And now, Captain, start altering course to port. Just behave as you would normally in trying to avoid a close quarters situation."

Looking through the viewports Grimes saw the sails being trimmed. With the light from the Llanith sun as the wind, *Pamir* was being steadied on to a starboard tack.

"Green eighty-five, opening. Range twenty-five, holding. Altitude zero."

Grimes got up from his chair, went to the big binoculars on their universal mount. He had no trouble picking up the intruder. Her suit of sails made her a big enough target.

He said, "Mr. Wallasey, don't bother any more with the Carlotti set. Try calling on NST."

"Very good, sir." The third officer turned to the normal space-time transceiver, equipment suitable for use only at short ranges. "What shall I say, sir?"

"*Pamir* to unidentified vessel. What ship? What are your intentions? You know."

"*Pamir* to unidentified vessel," said Wallasey, speaking slowly and distinctly. "Come in, please."

Almost immediately a voice replied, "Unidentified vessel to *Pamir*. Maintain your present course and speed. Open your airlocks to receive my boarding party." There was a slight accent. Waldegren? It sounded like it.

Listowel turned to Grimes, "What now, Commodore?"

Grimes grinned. "If we didn't have ladies present I'd tell him to get stuffed. Pass me the mike, Mr. Wallasey." Then he said, in what Sonya referred to as his best quarterdeck voice, "*Pamir* to unidentified vessel. Identify yourself at once. And sheer off. You are getting in my way."

"Unidentified vessel to *Pamir*. Open your airlock doors. Prepare for boarding party. Do not offer resistance. Over."

"Mphm," grunted Grimes, releasing the pressure of his thumb on the transmit button of the microphone. "I want you to turn away, Listowel. You are master of an unarmed merchant vessel. You can't fight, so you run. Put the Llanith sun dead astern. As long as he sees us doing all the right things he'll be lulled into a sense of security."

Driving surfaces pivoted about their masts, the east sails presenting their black sides to the source of light, the west sails their reflective sides. The ship came around fast. And then, on all four masts, the reflective surfaces were spread to catch the full force of the photon gale.

"Bearing green one six five. Altitude zero. Range nineteen. Closing."

"Must have hung out the crew's washing," commented Listowel. "I'm afraid that I can't squeeze any more out of *Pamir.*"

"It doesn't matter," Grimes told him. "We want her to catch up." He looked astern through the binoculars. *Pamir*'s sails cut off the glare from the Llanith sun and the raider was clearly visible on the starboard quarter. Like *Pamir* she was a four-master, with a cruciform rig, but additional triangular sails had been set between the masts. Running free this would give her a decided advantage.

"Range fifteen. Fourteen. Closing."

"Sir?" asked Fowler appealingly.

"No," said Grimes. "Not yet. We must consider the legalities. She must fire the first shot."

"But those legalities would only apply, sir, if we were a merchant vessel. But we aren't. We're an auxiliary cruiser of the Rim Worlds Navy—"

"A space lawyer yet!" commented Grimes admiringly. The young man was right, of course. He, Grimes, should have played heavy commodore as soon as contact had been made with the pirate, demanding her unconditional surrender. He might have done just that if he had a real warship under his feet. He decided that, after all, his own way of playing it was the best, especially since the other ship obviously had the heels of *Pamir.* He said, "You can play with your rockets as soon as I give the word, not before. And when you do use them, try for the enemy's rigging, his masts and sails."

"Bearing green one five oh. Closing. Range nine. Closing."

"This is the commodore. Action will be opened shortly. It seems likely that the starboard broadside will be the first to be used."

"Unidentified ship to *Pamir.* You've been asking for trouble. You are about to get it. Over."

"You have our permission to tell him to get stuffed, John," said Sonya sweetly.

"Bearing green one two five. Range seven. Closing."

Shortening sail, thought Grimes, watching through the binoculars. *There're those tri-s'ls or whatever he calls 'em coming in. And I can see ports opening. Boat bays? Or gunports?*

A gout of yellow flame spurted from one of the openings in the raider's hull, just abaft the masts. A long time later, it seemed, there was an explosion ahead of *Pamir,* about half a kilometer distant, a sudden rose of pale fire burgeoning in the blackness. So the pirate was using projectile weapons.

"Unidentified vessel—" the joke was wearing thin—"to *Pamir.* That was the last warning. Surrender or take the consequences."

"Bearing green ninety. Range five, four, three—closing."

No identification marks, thought Grimes, studying the other vessel through the powerful glasses. *Could be one of ours, save for a few, subtle points of difference . . .*

He said to Fowler, "All right, Lieutenant. You may open fire."

He saw the first rocket flash from its launching tube, trailing a wake of blue flame, spinning a flimsy filament of incandescence over the shortening distance between the two ships. It got a little over halfway, and then a stream of tracer came hosepiping from a gunport, met it, eroded it into ragged and harmless fragments of spinning debris. The warhead didn't explode.

"Rapid fire!" ordered Grimes. "Get the other five rockets out and on the way as quickly as possible. Don't bother guiding them in. One might get through."

None did. The pirate's machine gunners were fast.

"Range one. Point seven five. Point five."

"Resistance is useless," came the voice from the NST transceiver.

"Starboard broadside, fire," said Grimes into the intercom microphone.

He was not altogether prepared for what happened. He was expecting to see the enemy's sails shredded, his masts cut down, by the shot that he had prepared, the same sort of shot that had been used so effectively during the days of sail on Earth, the bags of scrap metal, nuts and bolts, lengths of metal chain. He had forgotten, though, that one of the old men-o'-war never, when firing a broadside, fired all guns simultaneously—they were fired in quick succession.

Pamir lurched. It was more than a mere lurch. It was as though a giant palm had swatted her on her starboard side. The north and south masts were carried away, each of them falling to starboard as the ship was driven to port by the recoil, the yards of each of them ripping the sails of the east mast, becoming inextricably entangled with the rigging.

"You got her, sir!" Fowler was yelling. "You got her!"

Grimes, who had been knocked down by the violent lateral acceleration, got groggily to his feet, staggered to the starboard viewports. The raider was, indeed, in a sorrier state than *Pamir*. In addition to the damage to her rigging there were gaping holes in her shell plating, through some of which smoke and flame flared explosively, like rocket exhausts. Her control room ports were bright with the ruddy glare of an internal fire. She was spinning slowly about her long axis. The one undamaged main spar, the east mast, which had been on her starboard side, shielded from *Pamir*'s guns, lifted into view as she rolled, lifted, then dipped toward the other ship—and held steady, a long, metal lance. Freakishly, then, the rotary motion ceased. Perhaps a survivor was still exercising some sort of control, was determined to exact vengeance before his death. And on the far side air, mixed with the gases of combustion, was still escaping into the vacuum, inexorably driving the total wreck on to the near-wreck.

"Range closing," Denby was saying, over and over again. "Range closing. Range closing."

"Reaction drive!" ordered Grimes. "Get us out of here!" He could visualize the end of that long spar driving through *Pamir*'s shell plating and piercing the vacuum chamber in which the sphere of antimatter was suspended in the strong magnetic fields. It was not a nice thing to think about.

Listowel made no reply. The captain was slumped in his seat, unmoving.

Sandra was shaking her husband violently. "Ralph! Wake up! Wake up!" Then, snarling wordlessly, she pulled him from his chair, letting him drift to the deck. Before she was properly seated in his place her long fingers were on the controls. She snarled again, then snapped, "Something's wrong, Commodore!"

"Starboard broadside," ordered Grimes into the intercom microphone. "Fire!" That should push them away and clear from their dying attacker.

"The guns are off their mounts," came a hysterical voice. "We have casualties—"

Denby was still calling out range figures—in meters now—but it was not necessary. The shattered, burning raider was too close and was getting closer.

"Roll her, Sandra!" shouted Grimes.

"But our east mast is some protection—"

"It's not. Roll her, damn you!"

"Roll her," repeated Sonya. "He knows what he's doing." She added quietly, "I hope."

The gyroscope controls and the gyroscopes themselves were still working. There was the initial rumble as the flywheels started to turn, then the low hum. The drifting wreck slid slowly from view, dipping below the starboard viewport rims—but if Denby's radar readings were to be credited disaster was now only millimeters distant.

Grimes ordered, "Rotate through ninety degrees. Let me know when you're on eighty-five."

The next few seconds could have been twice that many years.

"Eighty-five," stated Sandra at last.

"Port battery—fire."

Again *Pamir* was slammed by that giant hand and was swatted clear of the dying raider's murderous sidelong advance. The tracks of the two ships diverged—but not fast enough, thought Grimes. He said urgently, "I don't care how you do it, Sandra, but get some of our sails trimmed to catch the light from Llanith. We must get out of here, and fast!"

"But we should board," said Sonya. "There may be survivors. There will be evidence. The fire will burn itself out once the atmosphere in the ship is exhausted."

"Not that sort of fire. Do something, Sandra."

Using the gyroscopes she turned the ship, at last getting the sails of the one surviving mast trimmed to the photon gale. Astern the wreck dwindled in a second to the merest point of light—and then, briefly, became a speck of such brilliance as to sear the retinas of those who watched. It had happened as Grimes had been sure that it must happen. The casing of the sphere of antimatter had been warped by the heat of the fire—or, perhaps, had been buckled by an explosion. Contact with normal matter had been inevitable.

The pirate was gone, every atom of her structure canceled out.

The pirate was gone and *Pamir* was drifting, crippled. It was the time for the licking of wounds, the assessment of damage before, hopefully, limping into port under jury rig. Men aboard *Pamir* had been injured, perhaps killed. It had been an expensive victory. And Grimes knew that it would not have been so expensive had he remembered to fire the guns of his broadside in succession instead of all at once.

He realized that Fowler, the gunnery officer, was saying something to him. "It was brilliant, sir, brilliant, the way you fought the action—"

He replied slowly, "We won. But—"

"But?" The young man's face wore a puzzled expression.

"But you can't make an omelet without breaking a few eggs," contributed Sonya rather too brightly.

"But you should be able to make one without blowing up the kitchen," was all that Grimes was able to manage in way of reply.

RIM
CHANGE

❧ Rim Change ❧

I'M A SORT OF EXCEPTION that proves the rule.

And that, oddly enough, is my name—George Rule, currently master in the employ of the Dog Star Line, one of the few independent shipping companies in the Federation able to compete successfully with the state-owned Interstellar Transport Commission. When I was much younger I used to be called, rather to my embarrassment, Golden Rule. That was when my hair, which I tend to wear long, and my beard were brightly blond. But, given time, everything fades, and my nickname has faded away with my original colouring. In uniform I'm just another tramp master—and the Odd Gods of the Galaxy know that there are plenty of such in the Universe!—and out of uniform I could be the man come to fix the robochef. It's odd—or is it?—how those engaged in that particular branch of robotics tend to run to fat . . .

But this exception business . . .

The space services of the Rim Confederacy are literally crawling with officers who blotted their copy books in the major shipping lines of the Federation and various autonomous kingdoms, republics and whatever, and even with a few who left certain navies under big black clouds. The famous Commodore Grimes, for example, the Rim Worlds' favourite son, isn't a Rim Worlder by birth; he was emptied out of the Federation Survey Service after the *Discovery* mutiny. (It was Grimes, by the way, who got *me* emptied out of Rim Runners, the Confederacy's state shipping line, many years ago.)

I am a Rim Worlder by birth. I'm one of the very few spacemen who was born an Outsider and who now serves in the Insiders' ships, the very opposite to all those Insiders who, for reasons best known to themselves, came out to the Rim. I was one of the first cadets to pass through the Confederacy's space training college at Port Last, on Ultimo. I started my space-going career as Fourth mate of the old *Rim Mammoth* and then, after I gained my Second Mate's Certificate, was appointed third mate of *Rim Tiger*. Captain—as he was then—Grimes was master of her. He was a real martinet in those days.

Now that I'm master myself I can appreciate his reasons for wanting to run a taut ship. The affair aboard *Discovery* must still have been vivid in his mind and probably he was thinking that if he'd been less easy going the mutiny would never have happened. I didn't take kindly to the sort of discipline that he tried to impose. *Rim Mammoth* had been a *very* happy ship; the *Tiger* was far from it. Looking back on it all, any third mate of mine who tried to get away with the things that I tried to get away with would get a rough passage and a short one.

Anyhow—it was after I'd scrambled aboard at Port Fortinbras, very much the worse for wear, about two microseconds prior to lift-off—I was called into the Sacred Presence. Before he could start on me I told him what he could do with his Survey Service ideas. Then I told him what he could do with his ship. I told him that I wasn't at all surprised that *Discovery*'s officers had done what they did . . . And so on.

I don't blush easily, but the memory of that scene induces a hot flush from my scalp to the tips of my toes. I was lucky, bloody lucky, not to have been pushed out through an airlock without a spacesuit. (At the time we were, of course, well on our way to Port Forlorn.) Oh, I was escorted to the airlock after our landing on Lorn, taken to the shipping office and paid off, and told that it was extremely unlikely that Rim Runners would ever require my services again.

But I was lucky:

I got a job.

I got a job that took me away from the Rim.

I got a job that exercised a certain civilizing influence (badly needed, I admit now) on me.

You may remember when Trans-Galactic Clippers used to include the Rim Worlds in the itinerary of their Universal Tours. One of their big ships—*Sobraon*—was in, and her fourth officer, who had incurred multiple injuries in a rented air car crash, was in hospital. The post was mine, I was told, until such time as a regular TG man was available to relieve me.

I took it, of course, hastily affixing my autograph to *Sobraon*'s Articles of Agreement before Captain Grimes could breathe a few unkind words into the ear of Captain Servetty, who was to be my new boss. And it was with great relief that I watched, from the Clipper's control room, the lights of Port Forlorn fading below us as we lifted. I decided, then, to make the most of this second chance. I decided, too, that I'd not return to the Rim Worlds, ever.

There was nothing to hold me; I was an orphan, and had never gotten on with the various aunts and uncles on either side of my family. I'd had a girl, but she'd ditched me, some time back, to marry a wind turbine maintenance engineer. This broken romance had been one of the reasons—the main reason, perhaps—why I'd been such a pain in the neck to old Grimes. As the Universal Tour proceeded, everything that I saw—the glamorous worlds such as Caribbea, Electra and all the rest of them—stiffened my resolution. The Rim Worlds were so dreary, and the planets of the Shakespearean Sector were little better.

This was before Grimes, commanding *Faraway Quest,* had discovered the worlds of what is now known as the Eastern Circuit—Tharn, Mellise, Grollor and Stree. All that we had then were Lorn, Faraway, Ultimo and Thule—and, of course, Kinsolving's Planet and Eblis. But nobody ever went near either of those.

Sobraon knocked quite a few corners off me. There's a saying that you often hear, especially in star tramps, that Trans-Galactic Clippers is an outfit where accent counts for more than efficiency. Don't you believe it. Those boys may convey the impression of taking a cruise in daddy's yacht, but they're superb spacemen. They play hard at times—but they work hard.

I played with them—and I like to think that I pulled my weight when it was time to work. I was genuinely sorry when I paid off at

Canis Major—Dogtown to we Sirians—the capital city of the Sirian Sector. There was a new fourth mate, a Company boy, waiting for us there, so Captain Servetty had to take him on. He told me, though, that if I cared to fill in a TG Clippers application form he'd see to it that it received special consideration. I thanked him, of course, and I thought about it. I didn't have to think very hard about the repatriation to the Rim Worlds to which I was entitled. I took the money in lieu and decided to treat myself to a holiday.

It was while I was enjoying myself at New Capri that I met Jane. She too was on holiday—on annual leave, as a matter of fact. She was at that time a purser with the Dog Star Line. It was largely because of her that I became a kennelman myself; I became a naturalized Sirian citizen shortly after we married. She gave up spacefaring when our first child was on the stocks.

Oh well, it's nice having your wife aboard ship with you—but it's also nice to have a home, complete with wife and children, to come back to. You can't have it both ways. And most of the time I got ships that never wandered far from Dogtown, and was contented enough as I rose slowly—but not too slowly—through the ranks from third to second, from second to chief and, finally, from chief officer to master.

But now, after all these years, I was coming back to the Rim.

The Dog Star Line ships spend most of the time sniffing around their own backyard, but now and again they stray. *Basset* had strayed, following the scent of commerce clear across the Galaxy. At home, on Canis Major, I'd loaded a big consignment of brassards and self-adjusting sun hats for Arcadia. I must find out some time how those brassards sold. They were made with waterproof pockets for smoking requirements, small change, folding money &c &c. The Arcadians, who practice naturism all the year round, have always seemed to manage quite well with a simple bag slung over one shoulder.

At Ursa Major (the Arcadians have a childish love of puns) I filled up with the so-called Apples of Eden, a local fruit esteemed on quite a few worlds. These were consigned to New Maine. And what would one load in Port Penobscot? Need you ask? Smoked and pickled fish, of course, far less fragrant than what had been discharged. This shipment was for Rob Roy, one of the planets of the Empire of Waverley.

The cargo we loaded on Rob Roy was no surprise either. The Jacobeans, as they call themselves, maintain that their whisky is superior to the genuine article distilled in Scotland. It may be, it may not be; whisky is not my tipple. But the freight charges from the Empire of Waverley to the Rim Confederacy are far less than those from Earth to the Rim.

So *Basset* had followed the scent of profit clear from the Dog Star to the Rim, and now it looked as though the trail was petering out. On the other legs of the voyage, Head Office, by means of Carlotti radio, had kept me well informed as to what my future movements would be. On my run from Rob Roy to Lorn they had remained silent. And Rim Runners, my agents on Lorn, had replied to my ETA with only a curt acknowledgement. I didn't like it. None of us liked it: we'd all been away from home too long.

Probably I liked it less than my officers. I knew the Rim Worlds; I could think of far nicer planets to sit around awaiting orders.

We found the Lorn sun without any trouble—not that we should have had any trouble finding that dim luminary. Even if we hadn't been equipped with the Carlotti Direction Finder, and even if the Rim Worlds hadn't been able to boast the usual layout of Carlotti Beacons, we'd have had no trouble. There's the Galactic Lens, you see, and it doesn't thin out gradually towards its edges; the stars in the spiral arms are quite closely packed. (I use the word "closely" in a relative way, of course. If you had to walk a dozen or so light years you wouldn't think it was all that close.) And then there's that almost absolute nothingness between the galaxies. Almost absolute . . .

There's the occasional hydrogen atom, of course, and a few small star clusters doing their best to convey the impression that they don't really belong to the galactic family. The Rim Confederacy is one such cluster. There are the Lorn, Faraway, Ultimo, Thule, Eblis and Kinsolving suns. To the Galactic East there's a smaller cluster, with Tharn, Grollor, Mellise and Stree. To the west there's a sizeable antimatter aggregation, with a dozen suns. So, as long as you're headed in roughly the right direction when you break out of the Lens, you have no difficulty identifying the cluster you want.

You have the Galactic Lens astern of you. When the space-time-twisting Mannschenn Drive is running it looks like an enormous, slowly squirming, luminescent amoeba. Ahead there's an uncanny blackness, and the sparse, glimmering, writhing nebulosities that are the Rim suns seem to make that blackness even blacker, even emptier. And that emptiness still looks too damned empty even when the interstellar drive's shut down and the ship's back in the normal Continuum.

I could tell that my officers were scared by the weird scenery—or lack of it. I was feeling a bit uneasy myself; it was so many years since I'd been out here. But we got used to it after a while—as much as one can get used to it—and here we were at last, dropping down through the upper atmosphere of Lorn. The landing was scheduled for 0900 hours, Port Forlorn Local Time. We couldn't see anything of Port Forlorn yet, although we had clearance from Aero-Space Control to enter and were homing on the radio beacon. Beneath us was the almost inevitable overcast, like a vast snowfield in the sunlight, and under the cloud ceiling there would be, I knew, the usual half-gale (if not something stronger) probably accompanied by rain, snow, hail or sleet. Or all four.

"How does it feel to be coming home, sir?" asked my chief officer sarcastically.

"My home's in Canis Major!" I snapped. Then I managed a grin. "If you'll forgive my being corny, home is where the heart is."

"You can say that again, Captain," he concurred. (He was recently married and the novelty hadn't worn off yet.)

I took a last, routine look around the control room, just to make sure that everybody was where he was supposed to be and that everything was working. Soon I'd have to give all my attention to the inertial drive and attitude controls and to the periscope screen; inevitably I'd have to do some fancy juggling with lateral and downthrusts. Rugged, chunky Bindle, the chief officer, was strapped in the co-pilot's chair, ready to take over at once if I suffered a sudden heart attack or went mad or something. Loran, the second, was hunched over the bank of navigational instruments, his long, skinny frame all awkward angles and the usual greasy black cowlick obscuring one eye. His job was to call out to me the various instrument readings if, for some reason, such data failed to appear on the periscope screen. Young Taylor, the third, an extraordinarily ordinary-looking youth, was manning the various telephones, including the NST transceiver with which we were in communication with Aero-Space Control. In most Dog Star Line's vessels this was the radio officer's job, but I had found that our Sparks, Elizabeth Brown (Betty Boops, we called her) was far too great a distraction. Even when she was wearing a thickly opaque uniform blouse (she preferred ones which were not), her abundant charms were all too obvious.

We fell steadily, the inertial drive grumbling away in its odd, broken rhythm, healthily enough. We dropped into the upper cloud levels, and at first pearly gray mist alternated with clear air outside our viewports. And then, for what seemed like a long time, there was only dark, formless vapour. The ship shuddered suddenly and violently as turbulence took her in its grip. The changing code of the blips from the radio beacon told me that I was off course, but it was early yet to start bothering about corrections.

We broke through the cloud ceiling.

Looking into the screen, stepping up the magnification, I could see that there had been few changes during my long absence. The landscape, as always, was gray rather than green, almost featureless, although on the horizon the black, jagged peaks of the Forlorn Range loomed ominously. There were the wide fields in which were grown such unglamorous crops as beans and potatoes. There was the city, which had grown only a little, with the wind turbine towers and the factory chimneys in the industrial suburbs, each smokestack with its streamer of dirty white and yellow vapour. Yes, it was blowing down there all right.

And there was the spaceport, a few kilometers from the city. I could see, towards the edge of the screen, the triangle of bright red flashing beacons on the apron. They were well to leeward, I noted, of the only other ship in port. This, I had been told, was *Rim Osprey*. There would be enough clearance, I thought hopefully, although I wondered, not for the first time, why port captains, with acres of apron at their disposal, always like to pack vessels in closely. I applied lateral thrust generously, brought the beacons to the exact centre of the screen.

At first it wasn't too hard to keep them there, and then we dropped into a region of freak turbulence and to the observers in the Port Forlorn control tower it must have looked as though we were wandering all over the sky. An annoying voice issued from the NST speaker, "Where are you off to, Captain?"

"Don't answer the bastard!" I snarled to Taylor.

I had control of her again and, as well as maintaining a steady rate of descent, corrected the ship's attitude. We dropped rapidly and the numerals of the radar altimeter display were winding down fast. I was coming in with a ruddy blush—but that, I had learned years ago, was the only way to come in to Port Forlorn. I said as much to Bindle, who was beginning to make apprehensive noises. "Try to drop like a feather," I told him, "and you'll finish up blown into the other hemisphere . . ."

I heard Loran mutter something about a ton of bricks, but ignored him.

There was little in the screen now but dirty concrete and the flashing beacons, marking the triangle in the centre of which I was supposed to land—but only when my stern vanes were below the level of the top of the control tower did I step up downthrust. The ship complained and shuddered to the suddenly increased power of the inertial drive.

I was beginning to feel smug—but what happened then wiped the silly grin off my face. I had been leaning, as it were, into the wind—and suddenly, as we came into the lee of the administration block, there was no longer any wind to lean against. Worse still, there was a nasty back eddy. I reversed lateral thrust at once, of course, but it seemed ages before it took effect. The marker beacons slid right to the edge of the screen, right off it. Then, with agonizing slowness, they drifted back, not far enough . . .

But we were down. I felt the slight jar and the contact lights came on. I cut the drive. *Basset* trembled and sighed as she sagged down into the cradle of her tripedal landing gear, as the great shock absorbers took the weight of her. With a steady hand—but it took an effort!—I fished a packet of Carib panatellas out of my breast pocket, struck one of the long, green cylinders and stuck the unlit end between my lips. (I almost did it the wrong way round, but noticed just in time.) I checked all the tell-tales, saw nothing wrong and ordered quietly, "Make it Finished With Engines."

Nobody acknowledged the order. I looked around indignantly. All three officers were staring out through one of the viewports. "Gods! That was close! Bloody close!" the mate was muttering.

I stared through that viewport myself. Yes, it had been close. Another metre over towards the administration block and one or other or our stern vanes would have torn down the side of the other ship, ripping her open like a huge can opener. I unsnapped my belt, walked a little unsteadily to join the officers at the viewport. We could look directly into our neighbour's control room. A junior officer, the shipkeeper, was staring across at us. His face was still white. It had reason to be.

"Port Forlorn Control to *Basset,*" came from the speaker of the NST transceiver. "Do you read me?"

"Loud and clear," I replied automatically into the microphone.

"Port Forlorn Control to *Basset.* You are far too close to *Rim Osprey.* For your information, she is not a lamp-post." *Funny bastard,* I thought. "You will have to shift. Oh, by the way, you also destroyed two of our marker beacons when you set down. Over."

I shrugged. It's a rare master who hasn't rubbed out the occasional marker beacon. And, after all, they're cheap enough. (But *Rim Osprey* wouldn't have been cheap if I'd hit her. But I hadn't hither. So what?)

Finally, after the ground crew had set out new beacons, I tackled the ticklish job of shifting ship. I managed it with no damage except for a slightly dented vanepad and a long scratch on the concrete apron. *(Straight as though drawn with a rule,* the mate remarked. I forgave him, but it wasn't easy.)

When we had reberthed to the port captain's approval, customs and port health boarded to clear us inwards. Both officials were quite amazed to find that my place of birth, as shown on the crew list, was

Port Forlorn. They had to say, of course, that I had gone to the dogs. My agent—Rim Runners' Port Forlorn branch manager—made the same feeble joke. Finally we got down to business. He said, "I've nothing for you at the moment, Captain. My last instructions from your owners were to try to arrange some sort of charter for you locally . . ."

I told him, rather plaintively, "But I want to go home . . ."

He replied cheerfully, "But you *are* home. Lives there a man with soul so dead, and all that. Don't you have friends or relatives here? And you were in Rim Runners once, weren't you?"

"I was," I admitted.

"Then you must know Commodore Grimes, our astronautical superintendent. He's in Port Forlorn now, as a matter of fact . . ."

"The commodore and I didn't part on the best of terms," I said carefully.

"Time wounds all heels," he told me. "Shall I tell him you're here?"

"Perhaps not," I said.

"He'll know anyhow, Captain. He always likes to look through the crew lists of strange ships that come in here." He laughed. "He could be looking for *your* name!"

"I should have changed it when I changed my nationality," I said. "But I doubt if he'll want to see *me* again."

Oddly enough—or not so oddly—nobody went ashore that day. The weather was partly to blame; shortly after our final berthing a cold driving rain had set in. Too, all the way to Lorn I'd been telling everybody how drab and dreary the Rim Worlds are, and they must have at least half-believed me.

And then, after dinner that night, a little party started in the wardroom. We were all relaxing after the voyage and we had a few drinks, and a few more, and then . . . You know how it is. And, as always, we finished up in full voice, singing our company's anthem.

All the big outfits have one, usually some very old song with modern words tacked on to the antique melody. In the Waverley Royal Mail they have their own version of *Fly, bonny boat, like a bird on the wing*. In TG Clippers it's one of the ancient Terran sea chanteys, Sally Brown. *(Way, hey, roll and go!)* Rim Runners have a farewell song from some old comic opera. *(Goodbye, I'll run to find another sun/Where I may find/There are hearts more kind than the ones left behind . . .)*

And ourselves, the Dog Star Line? The choice is obvious.

"How much is that doggy in the window? (Arf! Arf!)
"The one with the great big glass eyes . . .
"How much is that doggy in the window?
"I think she looks ever so nice
"I don't want a Countess or a Duchess,
"I don't want an Empress with wings . . ."
(This, of course, a dig at the Waverley Royal Mail Line.)
"I don't want an Alpha or a Beta . . ."
(The two biggest classes of ship in the Interstellar Transport Commission.)
"Or any of those fucking things!
"How much is that doggy in the window? (Arf! Arf! Arf!)
"The one with the Sirius look,
"How much is that doggy in the window?
"Please put my name down in her book!"

We were all happily arfing away, with a few yips and bow-wows, when the mate noticed a visitor standing just outside the wardroom door. "Come in, come in!" he called. "This is Liberty Hall! You can spit on the mat and call the cat a bastard! But . . ."

We took the cue and roared in unison, "Beware of the dog!"

"That last," remarked a voice, familiar after many a year, "makes a very welcome new addition."

I turned slowly in my chair to look at him. At first I thought that the old bastard hadn't changed a bit.

Then I saw that his hair was gray now, matching his eyes, and that his face had acquired a few new wrinkles. Otherwise it was as it always had been, looking as though it had been hacked rather than carved out of some coarse textured stone and then left out in the weather. His ears were the same prominent jug handles of old.

"Don't let me interrupt the party, Captain Rule," he went on, slightly emphasizing the title. "I had some business with *Run Osprey,* and then I thought that I'd call aboard here to see you. But it can wait until the morning."

I got to my feet, extended a slightly reluctant hand. He shook it. "Good to have you aboard, sir," I said in the conventional manner. "Will you join us in a small drink?"

He grinned. "Well, if you twist my arm hard enough . . ."

I introduced him around and found him a chair. If he was bearing no malice—and he had far more reason to than I did—then neither was I. He was very soon completely at home.

Betty Brown—wearing one of her transparent shirts and a skirt that was little more than a pelmet—and Sara Taine, my purser, sat— literally—at his feet, getting up now and again to bring him savouries or to freshen his drink. *I* didn't get that sort of service, I thought resentfully, and this was *my* ship . . . He had a fine repertoire of songs and stories, far more extensive than any of ours. Well, he should have done. He had been around so much longer.

At last he raised his wrist and looked at his watch. He said, "Thank you for the party, but I must be going . . ."

"The night's only a pup, Commodore," Bindle told him.

"It was a bitch of a night when I came aboard," he replied, "and probably still is. Raining cats and dogs . . ." He laughed. "Your Dog Star Line brand of humour seems to be catching . . ."

"Just one more before you go? One for the road?" urged the mate.

"No. Thank you. I don't want to find myself in the doghouse when I get home. Goodnight, all. Goodnight. Goodnight . . ."

I saw him down to the after airlock.

He told me, "I'll be seeing you in the morning, Captain Rule, if it is convenient."

"Would you mind answering a question before you go, sir?" I asked him.

"I'll try. What is it?"

"I've always rather suspected, sir, that you were instrumental in getting me that berth in *Sobraon.* After all, Captain Servetty didn't have to take *me,* of all people. And he must have known why I was . . . available . . ."

"He did know, Captain. He asked me if he should sign you on. I told him that you had the makings of a good officer, but that he'd have to keep a close eye on you."

I said, "If I hadn't been such a self-centered puppy I'd have known that you were still getting over the *Discovery* business . . ."

He said, "Let's forget about it, shall we? It was all so long ago, and so very far away . . ." Suddenly he looked old, then recovered, equally suddenly, his appearance of ageless strength. "Goodnight, Captain Rule." Our handshake, this time, was really sincere. "I'll see you in the morning."

Wrapping his rather flamboyant cloak about his stocky figure he strode down the ramp, ignoring the wind and the rain, let himself into his squat, ugly little ground car, and then was gone in a flurry of spray.

"That Commodore Grimes isn't anything like the ogre you made him out to be," said Sara Taine when she brought me in my tea tray the next morning. "I'm looking forward to seeing him again. What time will he be coming aboard?"

I said severely, "He's married. Very happily, I believe."

She frowned. She had one of those thin, serious faces, under sleek, gleaming black hair, on which a frown sits rather well. She complained, "All the attractive men in my life are married. You, and Peter Bindle, and now your old pal Commodore Grimes . . ."

"What about the engineers?" I asked her. "What about the second and third mates? Or the Quack?"

"Them!" she snorted, then grinned softly, "If I wasn't such a good friend of Jane's . . ."

"Don't tempt me, Sara. The way this voyage is dragging on I shouldn't require so very much tempting."

She had been sitting on the bed, sipping her own cup of tea. She got up, moved to a chair. "That will do, Captain Rule. As I've said, Jane and I are good friends. I want us to stay that way. But it is a pity that she has such archaic ideas about sex, isn't it?" She put her cup back on the tray with a clatter, got up and went out of the bedroom, leaving me to deal alone with the business of getting up to face the day.

Showered and dressed I made my way down to the wardroom for breakfast. There were no absentees; the doctor had insisted that each of us take a neutralizer tablet before retiring. As you know, they're very effective—but by the time you need them you're in such a state you can't be bothered to take them. That's one of the beauties of having a party aboard ship; you have your own medical practitioner on hand to prescribe as required . . .

Canvey, the interstellar drive engineer, asked what everybody else was intending to ask. He got in first. "Was that only a social call last night, Captain, or did Commodore Grimes have any information about our next loading?"

And then Terrigal, reaction drive engineer, stated rather than asked, "He's coming aboard again this morning, isn't he?"

I told them, "The Commodore is Rim Runners' astronautical superintendent, not their traffic manager."

"But he still piles on a lot of gees, doesn't he?" said Canvey.

"I suppose he does," I admitted. I helped myself liberally from the dish of Caribbean tree-crab curry on the table, hoping that it would taste as good as it looked and smelled. (It did. Sara was as good a cook as she was a purser, and even the most sophisticated autochef—which ours wasn't—gives of its best only when imaginatively programmed.) I asked, "How is the crab holding out, Sara?"

"It isn't," she said. "This is the last of it."

"I tried to make a tissue culture," put in Dr. Forbes, who was biochemist as well as medical officer, "but it died on me . . ." He looked more like a professional mourner than ever as he imparted the bad news.

"Then I hope they send us home by way of Caribbea," I said.

"So there *is* a chance of our getting home," persisted Canvey. He was one of those little, gray, earnest men who always seem to be persisting.

"I'll believe it when we crunch down in Dogtown," said Porky Terrigal glumly, making sure of his second helping of the fragrant curry.

"You must have heard *something*, Captain . . ." went on Canvey.

"I'm just the master," I told him. "Nobody ever tells *me* anything."

Breakfast over, I went back up to my quarters. Bindle brought me a morning paper; somebody in Rim Runners' dock office had been thoughtful enough to send copies on board. I lit a cigar, skimmed through it. It was deadly dull. (Other people's local rags are always dull—but this, *The Port Forlorn Confederate,* had been my local rag once . . .) I noted that *Basset* was listed in the shipping information column as having arrived. I noted, too, that the date of her departure was given as "indefinite". I knew that already.

I read that the Confederacy's Department of Tourism was thinking about reestablishing the holiday resort on Eblis. I read about the Burns Night party that had been thrown by the ambassador of the Empire of Waverley. Obviously he couldn't have been waiting for our consignment of Waverley scotch. I read about the Rim Rules football match between the Port Forlorn Pirates and the Desolation Drovers. I found it hard to raise any interest in the account of the game. Even when I had been a Rim Worlder myself I hadn't been all that keen, and on most of the worlds of the Sirian Sector, *the* game is Old Association, the only *real* football. Finally I found the crossword. It wasn't one of the cryptic variety, just a collection of absurdly simple clues that a retarded child of five could have solved in four minutes. It only took *me* three and a half.

There was a knock at the door. I threw the paper aside, got out my chair to welcome Commodore Grimes.

He took the seat I offered him, pulled out of his pocket an ancient and battered pipe that looked as though it was the very one that he had always smoked when I last knew him. It smelt like it, too. Sara Taine came in with a tray of coffee things. She seemed disposed to hang around with flapping ears, and looked hurt when I told her, "That will be all, thanks, Sara."

Grimes said, "Quite comfortable quarters you have, Captain Rule."

"Yes," I agreed. *"Basset* and her sister ships are an improvement on the Commission's basic Epsilon design. We have our own yards now in the Sector, of course, and build our own vessels . . ."

"Passenger accommodation?" he asked.

"I can take a dozen, in single-berth cabins. More if people are willing to double up."

"Mphm." He looked at me through the cloud of acrid smoke that he had just emitted. I countered with a smokescreen of my own. "Mphm. You know, of course, that we have our own Survey Ship, *Faraway Quest . . .*"

"I've heard of her, sir."

"Well, the *Quest*'s out of commission. Will be for some months yet. Oh, she's old, I admit, but even I didn't know that there were so many things wrong with her until she came up for Survey . . ." He relit his pipe, which had gone out, using one of the archaic matches that he still affected. "You know Kinsolving's Planet, of course?"

"I know of it, Commodore. I've never been there."

"I have," he told me. "Too often. The things that have happened to me there shouldn't happen to a dog. Well, the Port Forlorn University wants to send another expedition to Kinsolving. Normally I'd have been their bus driver, in *Faraway Quest.* But she, as I've told you, is grounded. And our Navy won't lay a ship on for a bunch of civilian scientists, psychic researchers at that.

"And all of our merchant tonnage, the Rim Runners fleet, is heavily committed for months to come. Do you get the picture?"

"I'm beginning to," I admitted reluctantly.

"Do I detect a certain lack of enthusiasm, Captain Rule? I can't say that I blame you. Oh, well, it shouldn't be hard to arrange a charter whereby we man the ship with our own personnel, while you and your boys and girls are put up in hotels at the Confederacy's expense."

"I stay with my ship," I told him. "And I'm pretty sure that all my people will be of the same mind."

"Good. I was expecting you to say that. So . . . *If* the charter is arranged—it's not definite yet—you'll be carrying half a dozen scientists, two qualified psionicists, the Kinsolving's planet advisor and his wife. The advisor is me, of course. Sonya—my wife—doesn't like that world any more than I do, but she maintains that I'm far less liable to get into trouble if she's along . . ."

"What *is* wrong with Kinsolving?" I asked.

"You're a Rim Worlder born," he said. "You know the stories."

Yes, I knew the stories, or some of them. Kinsolving had been colonized at the same time as the other Rim Worlds, but the colonization hadn't stuck. The people—those of them who hadn't committed suicide, been murdered or vanished without trace—were taken off and resettled on Lorn, Faraway, Ultimo and Thule.

They all told the same story—oppressive loneliness, even in the middle of a crowd, continuous acute depression, outbreaks of irrational violence and, every night, dreams so terrifying that the hapless colonists dreaded going to bed. One theory that I remembered was that Kinsolving is the focal point of . . . forces, psychic forces. Another theory was that around the planet the fabric of our Universe is somehow strained, almost to breaking point, and that some of the alternate Universes aren't at all pleasant by our standards. But you don't have to go to Kinsolving to get the feeling that if you make an effort you'll be able to step into another Continuum; that sensation is common enough anywhere on the Rim. But it's on Kinsolving that you know that no effort at all is necessary, that a mere sneeze would suffice to blow you out of the known Universe into . . . into Heaven? Maybe, but the reverse would be more likely.

"Kinsolving," said Grimes softly, "is a sort of gateway . . . It's been opened quite a few times, to my knowledge. I'd as lief not be involved in its opening, but . . ." he shrugged . . . "it seems to be my fate always to be involved with the bloody planet."

There was a heavy silence, which I thought I'd better break. "The professional psionicists you mentioned . . . ?"

"Old friends of mine," he told me. "Ken Mayhew. One of a dying breed. He was a psionic communications officer long before the Carlotti System was dreamed of. He still holds his commission in the Rim Worlds Naval Reserve. And Clarisse, his wife. A telepath and a teleporteuse. Both of them know Kinsolving."

"And does this Mayhew," I asked, "still cart his personal amplifier around with him? I can remember the old-time PCOs and how they used to make pets of those obscene, disembodied dogs' brains . . ."

"Ken used to keep his poodle's brain in aspic," said the commodore, "but not any longer. He and Clarisse work as a team. She amplifies for him when he's sending or receiving, and he for her when she's teleporting."

"And the scientists? Any weirdos among them?"

"Oddly, enough, no. They study psychic phenomena without being in any way psychic themselves. They've cooked up some fantastically sensitive instruments, I understand, that can measure the slightest variations of temperature, atmospheric pressure, electrical potential and whatever. They have their own theory about Kinsolving, which is that the planet is actually haunted, in the good, old-fashioned way. And for a ghost to appear and speak and throw things around it must get energy from somewhere. A drop in temperature, for example, indicates that energy is being used." He laughed, rather mirthlessly. "It makes a change from all the other ideas about Kinsolving—multidimensional universes and all the rest of it . . ."

"And what are *your* ideas about it, sir?" I asked.

"Kinsolving," he said, "is a world where anything can happen and almost certainly will."

The charter was arranged; our Canis Major Head Office was happy enough that profitable employment had been found for *Basset*. We, *Basset*'s crew, were not so happy. We were all a long way from home, and too long a time out, and this excursion to Kinsolving would inevitably delay our departure from the Rim Worlds for the Sirian Sector.

There was one slight consolation: we were not kept hanging around long on Lorn. One day sufficed for the discharge of our inward cargo. It was a matter of hours only to ready the passenger accommodations for occupancy. There was the routine overhaul of all machinery, which took four days, and while this was in progress extra stores were taken on and the crates and cases containing the scientists' equipment loaded. On the morning of the sixth day the passengers boarded.

Ken and Clarisse Mayhew I had already met at Grimes' home, where he and Sonya, his wife, had had us all to dinner. Ken was a typical telepath, one of the type with which I have become familiar in the days when the only FTL communication between ships and between ships and planet-bases stations was through the PCOs. He was tall, inclined to be weedy, with mousy hair, muddy eyes and an otherworldly appearance. Clarisse was another kettle of tea, not at all conforming to the popular idea of a psionicist. She was a very attractive girl with brown hair and brown eyes, strong featured, although a mite too solidly built for my taste. Sonya Grimes, however, was the sort of woman for whom I could fall quite easily; tall and slim, with a thin, slightly prominent nose and a wide mouth, remarkable violet eyes, sleek auburn hair. Her figure? She could have worn an old flour sack and made it look as though it had been imported at great expense from Paris, Earth.

The commodore and his wife were guests in the control room during lift-off. Sonya was a spacewoman, I had learned earlier, and although married to a Rim Worlder she still retained both her Federation citizenship and her Survey Service commission. Grimes, I could see, was just itching to get his own paws on the controls. (He had confided to me that, at times, he found the life of a deskborne commodore more than a little irksome.) But he sat in one of the spare chairs, well out of the way, watching. I don't think that he missed anything. Sonya was beside him. She laughed when we went through our own Dog Star Line ritual after the routine checks for spaceworthiness.

The junior officer present—young Taylor, the third—demanded in a portentiously solemn voice, "What is the Word?"

We all roared in reply, "Growl you may, but go you must!"

Sonya, as I have said, was amused. She whispered to her husband, "I'm beginning to find out why this company's ships are called the chariots of the dogs . . ." I knew what she meant. That twentieth-century book, *Chariots of the Gods,* is still regarded as a Bible by those people who believe in the Old Race who started all the present civilization extant in the Galaxy.

Aero-Space Control gave us clearance to lift, wished us *bon voyage.* We climbed into what was an unusual phenomenon for Lorn, a clear sky. Soon the spaceport was no more than a huddle of model buildings far below us, with three toy ships on the apron. *(Rim Kestrel* and *Rim Wallaby* had come in before our departure; *Rim Osprey* was due to leave, for the worlds of the Eastern Circuit, later in the day.)

The little bitch was handling well. I took her up easily, not trying to break any records. I heard Sonya murmur, "George isn't like you, John. He doesn't show off using his auxiliary reaction drive when there's no need for it . . ." Grimes replied with a far from expressionless *mphm.*

Lorn, with its wide, dreary (even in the sunlight) plains, its jagged, snowcapped mountains, diminished below us, became a mottled globe, gray-brown land, green-blue water, white snow. Still we drove upward, through and clear to the Van Allens.

The inertial drive was shut down and the directional gyroscopes grumbled into life, swinging the ship about her axes, bringing her head around to point almost directly at the target star, the Kinsolving sun, a solitary spark in the empty blackness. On the ship's beam glowed the iridescent lens of the Galaxy, spectacular and, to those of us not used to seeing it from outside, frightening. I steadied her up on the target, making a small allowance for drift. I restarted the inertial drive and then started the Mannschenn Drive, the space-time-twister.

As on every such occasion I visualized those gleaming rotors spinning, precessing, fading as they tumbled down the warped dimensions fading yet never vanishing, dragging the ship and all aboard her into that uncanny state where normal physical laws held good only within the fragile hull. There was the long second of *déjà vu* during which time seemed to run backward.

Inside the control room colours sagged down the spectrum and perspective was distorted, and all sounds were as though emanating from a distant echo chamber. Then all snapped back to normal, although the thin, high whine of the drive was a constant reminder that nothing was or would be normal until we were at our destination. And there was nothing normal outside the ports, of course. Ahead the Kinsolving sun was a writhing, multicoloured nebulosity, and on the beam the Lens was a pullulating Klein flask blown by a drunken glass blower. It looked as though it were alive. Perhaps it was alive. Perhaps only with the Mannschenn Drive in operation do we see it as it really is . . .

I dismissed the uneasy thought from my mind. I said to Bindle, "Deep space routine, Mr. Mate."

"But who will keep the dog watches?" asked Taylor.

"You're all watchdogs," I replied.

"More of your ritual?" asked Sonya interestedly.

"Yes," I admitted, feeling absurdly embarrassed. "I suppose it does sound rather childish to an outsider . . ."

Grimes laughed. "I remember one ship I was in when I was in the Survey Service. The cruiser *Orion.* We called her *O'Ryan,* of course, and everybody had to speak an approximation to Irish dialect, and *our* song, just as *Doggy in the Window* is your song, was *The Wearin' of the Green* . . ."

"Still rather childish," his wife said, but her smile took any sting out of the words.

Grimes said, "Well, Captain Rule, are you coming down to meet the customers?"

I said, "I suppose it's one of the things I'm paid for."

The customers—the passengers—were in their own saloon. Ken and Clarisse Mayhew I had already met, of course, the others, until now, had been no more than names on the passenger list. There was a Dr. Thorne—I never did get it straight what exactly he was a doctor of—and his wife. They were Jack Spratt and Mrs. Spratt in reverse, he a bearded, Falstaffian giant, she a gray, wispy sparrow. There were two, almost identical young men; mousy, studious, bespectacled. Their names were Paul Trentham and Bill Smith. The two young women could have been their sisters, but were not. One was Susan Howard, the other Mary Lestrange. They were friendly enough—not that they overdid it.

Sara, ever efficient, had seen to it that the bar in the saloon was well stocked. Thorne took over as barman; the drinks soon dispelled the initial stiffness of this first meeting. I rather took to the leader of the expedition and he to me. I felt that I would be able, without giving offense, to ask him a question that had been bothering me slightly.

"Tell me, Doctor," I put to him, "why don't you have any mediums along? You have two psionicists, sure, but they are, essentially, communications specialists, and by communications I don't mean communications with the dear departed."

He laughed, a little ruefully. "One thing that our researches have taught us is this. There are many, many phony mediums. Even the genuine ones sometimes, although not always intentionally so."

"What do you mean, exactly?"

"Look at it this way. A genuine medium is determined to deliver the goods. If the goods aren't forthcoming, because conditions aren't right, perhaps, then he or she would just hate to disappoint the customers. Quite possibly subconsciously—but now and again consciously—fake results are delivered. The main trouble, I suppose, is that the average medium doesn't have it drummed into him, all through a long training, that high standards of professional ethics must be maintained. A graduate of the Rhine Institute, however—such as Ken Mayhew—is bound by the Institute's code of ethics. He is therefore far more reliable than any medium."

"But you do believe in spiritualism, don't you?"

"I believe that there are hauntings. I believe that Kinsolving's Planet is haunted. I—we—want to find out by whom. Or what."

"I seem to be spending my life finding out," grumbled Grimes. "But every time I get a different answer."

"Perhaps you're a catalyst, Commodore," suggested Mrs. Thorne.

"And perhaps Captain Rule is a dogalyst," said Sonya.

I tried to laugh along with the rest at the vile pun—jokes about the Dog Star Line are all right when *we* make them, but . . .

The voyage was a relatively short one. It was like all other voyages, except that at the latter end of it we should not be landing at a proper spaceport with all the usual radio-navigational aids. There would be no bored voice coming from the NST speaker, talking us down. There would be no triangle of beacons to mark our berth on the apron. Come to that, there would be no apron. The spaceport had become a sizeable crater when *something* had destroyed the Franciscan ship, *Piety,* a while ago.

Grimes had brought his charts with him. Together we studied them. He advised me to make my landing in the old sports stadium, on the shore of Darkling Tarn, not far from the city of Enderston, the ruins of which stood on the east bank of the Weary River. Those colonists had shown a morbid taste in place names . . . That applied to all the Rim Worlds, of course, but Kinsolving took the prize for deliberately miserable nomenclature.

The commodore acted as pilot when we finally made our approach; he had been on Kinsolving before, more than once, and he possessed the local knowledge. I handled the controls myself, of course, but he was in the chair normally occupied by Bindle, advising.

We were making an early morning descent—always a wise policy when landing on a world without proper spaceport facilities. The lower the sun's altitude, the more pronounced the shadows cast by every irregularity of the ground. Too, when an expedition arrives at sunrise it has all the daylight hours to get itself organized. Left to myself, I'd have arrived when I arrived and not bothered about such niceties. It was Grimes, with his years of Survey experience behind him, who had urged me to adopt Survey Service S. O. P.

So we were coming down after a few hours of standing off in orbit. Already there was enough light for us to be able to make out details of the landscape beneath us. There was the Weary River—and with all the twists and turns it was making it was small wonder that it was tired! There was the Darkling Tarn—looking, Grimes said, like an octopus run over by a steamroller. Bindle loosed off the sounding rockets that, at Grimes' insistence, had been added to our normal equipment. Each of them, in its descent, left a long, unwavering smoke trail: there was no wind to incommode us.

Each of them released a parachute flare that drifted down slowly. As we ourselves dropped, the picture in the periscope screen expanded. We could see the city at last, a huddle of overgrown ruins. We could see the stadium, an oval of green that was just a little lighter in tone than the near-indigo of the older growth around it. One of the flares had fallen just to one side of the sports ground and started a minor brush fire; the smoke from it was rising almost directly upwards.

At least it would be easier landing here than at the proper spaceport on Lorn . . . Grimes guessed my thoughts. "The ground's level enough, Captain Rule," he told me. "Or it was, last time I was here."

"Any large animals?" I asked.

"Just the descendants of the stock brought by the original colonists. Wild pigs and cattle. Rabbits. They'll all have sense enough to bolt for cover when they hear us coming down."

In the periscope screen the ground looked level enough. I maintained a slow but steady rate of descent, slowed it to the merest downward drift when there were only metres to go. At last the contact lights flashed on. I cut the inertial drive. The silence, broken at first by the sighing of the shock absorbers and the usual minor creakings and groanings, was oppressive. I looked at the commodore. He nodded, and said, "Yes, you can Make it Finished With Engines." Before I did so I glanced at the clinometer. The ship was a little off the vertical, but only half a degree. It was nothing to worry about.

"So we're here," whispered Sonya. "Again." I didn't like the way she said it.

"Shore leave?" asked Bindle brightly. "Of course, we shall want an advance from the purser first, sir."

"Ha, ha," I said. "Very funny." I looked out through the viewports. This didn't look like a world on which there would be any need for money. It didn't look like a world on which to take a pleasant walk.

Oh, the day was bright enough, and such scenery as was in view was pretty enough, in a jungly sort of way, but . . . it was as though a shadow was over everything, dimming colours and bringing a chill to the air that bit through to the very bones. The sunlight streaming through the viewports was bright, dazzlingly so, to the outer eye— but as far as the inner eye was concerned it could have been the rays of a lopsided moon intermittently breaking through driving storm clouds. I'm not a seventh son of a seventh son or any of that rubbish, and if I applied for admission to the Rhine Institute for training they'd turn me down without bothering with the routine tests, but I do have my psychic moments.

A premonition of impending doom, I thought. I liked the feel of it. I thought it again.

"If you don't mind, Captain Rule," said Grimes, "I'll assume command until such time as we lift off again. The ship is still your charge, of course, but all extra-vehicular activities are my pigeon."

"As you please, sir," I said a little stiffly. He was doing no more than to confirm, in front of witnesses, what had already been decided—but it was essential that my officers have no doubt as to who was boss cocky of the expedition. "Your orders, sir?"

"Please pass the word for everybody, ship's officers and civilian personnel, to assemble in the wardroom for briefing. I shall just be repeating what I have told you all time and time again during the voyage—but this is a world on which you can't be too careful. This is a planet on which anything might happen, and probably will."

I reached for the microphone and gave the necessary orders.

The wardroom was crowded with everybody packed into it, but there was seating for everybody. Grimes, nonetheless, remained standing. He said quietly, "Of all of us here, only Commander Mayhew, Mrs. Mayhew, Commander Verrill and myself have set foot on Kinsolving before . . ."

Commander Verrill? I wondered, then realized that he meant Sonya.

"As we have told you," he went on, "this is a dangerous world, a very dangerous world. You have heard the story of what happened to the Neo-Calvanist expedition when an attempt was made to invoke the Jehovah of the Old Testament. I was among those present at the time, as was Mrs. Mayhew, and the crater where the spaceport used to be bears witness to the destruction of their ship, *Piety.* You have heard what happened when our own expedition, a little later, tried to repeat that foolhardy experiment. That time there was only one victim—me. And then there was the landing made by the Federation Survey Service's ship, *Star Pioneer,* aboard which Commander Verrill and myself were passengers. That time the pair of us got into trouble . . ."

"Of course," Sonya said sweetly, "I wasn't worrying myself sick about you the other times . . ."

"Mphm. Anyhow, this a smaller expedition than the previous ones and I therefore insist that when excursions are made from the ship there is to be no splitting up; nobody is to go wandering off by himself on some wild goose—or wild ghost—chase. Personal transceivers will be carried at all times. Ship's personnel, acting as escorts to the scientists, will be armed. Captain Rule and all of his officers hold commissions in the Sirian Sector Naval Reserve and are trained in the use of weaponry . . ."

Ha! I thought. *Ha bloody ha!* I remembered, all too well, our practice session at the Navy's small-arms range shortly before our lift-off from Dogtown. "Miss," the exasperated petty officer instructor had said at last to Betty Boops, "if you *really* want to hurt anybody with that pistol creep up close and hit him over the head with it . . ." And most of the rest of us including myself, weren't much better. Only Sara, the purser, made a fair showing.

"Compared to the rest of you," the P.O. had said, "she's Annie Oakley." He went on, turning to Betty, "And you, Miss, are Calamity Jane." Sara had been quite pleased . . .

Grimes continued, "You civilian ladies and gentlemen are not to set foot off the ship without your . . . watchdogs. Is that understood, Dr. Thorne?"

"Understood, Commodore," replied the scientist laconically.

"Good. I don't know about the rest of you, but my belly is firmly convinced that my throat's been cut. I propose that we all enjoy breakfast before getting the show on the road."

There were, as a matter of fact, two shows to be gotten on the road. One was the small party leaving the ship on foot to poke around the stadium and its environs, the other one flew to the city in the pinnace that we had on loan from the Rim Worlds Navy and that we earned in lieu of one of our own boats, which had been left in Port Forlorn. Like any ship's boat it was not only a spaceship in miniature but could be used as an atmosphere flier. Unlike a merchantship's boat, it was armed, mounting a heavy machine gun, a small laser cannon and a rocket projector.

Grimes and Sonya were in the boat party, as were Ken Mayhew, Dr. Thorne, Rose, his wispy wife, Sara Taine and myself. Sara was pleased at having real guns to play with—somehow she had appointed herself gunnery officer of the pinnace—and was hoping that she would have a chance to use them. I was hoping that she wouldn't.

We boarded the boat in its bay. The commodore took the controls, the rest of us disposed ourselves around the small cabin. The inertial drive unit grumbled into life and we lifted from the chocks and then, with the application of full lateral thrust, shot out through the open port into the bright sunlight. Grimes took us round the ship in an ascending spiral. Bindle, who was minding the shop, waved to us from the control room. We were close enough to see his envious expression.

Grimes levelled out, headed for the city. It was not easy to see from this relatively low altitude; when we had been looking down on it the street plan had been obvious enough, but from a height of a mere one hundred metres it looked only like an unusually lumpy piece of jungle in the distance. Oh, there were a few ruined towers, prominent enough, but they were so overgrown that they could have been no more than freak geological formations.

I tried to enjoy the flight. I should have enjoyed it; the bright sunlight was streaming through the ports, the scenery over which we were skimming was unspoiled, I had enjoyed a good breakfast and my after-breakfast cigar was drawing well. And yet . . . for no reason at all—apart from a quite illogical feeling of unease—I kept looking aft. I noticed that the others—apart from Grimes—did so too. (But Grimes had his rear viewscreen above the console.) A fragment of half-remembered verse kept chasing itself through my mind. How did it go?

Like one that on a lonesome road
Doth walk in fear and dread,
And having cast a glance behind
Durst no more turn his head,
Because he knows a fearsome fiend
Doth close behind him tread . . .

Something like that, anyhow. And, in any case, there wasn't any fearsome fiend in our wake. I hoped.

Grimes tapped out his pipe and refilled and relit it for about the fifth time. Sara Taine checked, yet again, the pinnace's fire control panel. (*But could you shoot at ghosts?* I wondered. Had anybody had the forethought to substitute silver bullets for the normal machine-gun ammo?) Dr. Thorne cleared his throat and, speaking loudly to be heard over the irritable snarl of the inertial drive, asked Mayhew, "Do you *feel* anything, Ken?"

"I suspect," replied the telepath, speaking slowly and carefully, "that something out there doesn't like us . . ."

"A normal state of affairs on this world," grumbled Grimes.

"Are there likely to be any manifestations, Commodore?" said Thorne.

"Anything, no matter how unlikely, is likely here," was the reply.

Cheerful shower of bastards! I thought.

Rose Thorne—people do tend to be given unfortunate names, although the lady's parents couldn't have been expected to know that she'd marry whom she did—had opened the case that she had carried aboard with her and was tinkering with fragile looking instruments. She was finding out, I supposed, if there were any variations in temperature, gravitational or magnetic fields or whatever. Presumably she discovered no anomalies. In any case, she said nothing. And Ken Mayhew had a very faraway look on his face, was staring into nothingness, a nothingness in which . . . something stirred. That was the impression I got. Cold shivers were chasing themselves up and down my spine.

"Cheer up, George," Sonya admonished me. "The first time here is the worst."

"Not for me it wasn't," grunted the commodore. "Although every time was bad."

"My first time was bad," stated Sonya.

We were over the outskirts of the city now, following a broad street through the cracked surface of which trees and bushes had thrust. On either side of us were the buildings, creeper-covered houses with empty windows peering like dead eyes through the tangled greenery. I found myself thinking of ancient graveyards—cemeteries in which the victims of massacre had been buried and commemorated, and then, after many years, forgotten. Something, disturbed by our noisy flight, scuttled below and ahead of us, finally diving into a doorway.

"Hold your fire, Sara," said Sonya sharply. "It's only a hen."

"Nothing wrong with roast chicken," I said. "The fowl in the tissue culture vats has long since lost whatever flavour it had . . ."

"There wouldn't have been much left for roasting if I'd let fly with the MG," Sara told me.

It was a feeble enough joke, but we all laughed nervously.

We came to a sort of square or plaza. There was a group of statuary—once a fountain?—in the middle of it, but so overgrown that it was impossible to see if the figures had been men or monsters. They looked like monsters now. Around the plaza were ruined towers, their outlines blurred by what looked like—was, in fact—Terran ivy. Those colonists had brought a fair selection of Earth flora and fauna with them, some of which had survived and flourished.

Grimes set the pinnace down carefully, very carefully, selecting an area that did not have any sturdy bushes and saplings thrusting up through the paving. We landed with hardly a jar. Reluctantly, it seemed, he turned off the drive. We could hear ourselves think again. This was not the relief that it should have been. The silence, after the arrhythmic snarl and thump of the motor, seemed about to be broken by . . . something. By what?

"Well," said the commodore unnecessarily, "we're here."

"You know the city," said Thorne. "Wasn't there—isn't there— some sort of temple . . ."

"I don't want to go *there* again," said Sonya determinedly.

Grimes shrugged. "It's as good a place to start our . . . investigations as any. After all, we *are* here to investigate . . ." he remarked. He turned to Mayhew. "You're the psionicist, Ken. What do you think?"

The telepath seemed to jerk out of some private dream, and not a pleasant one. "The temple . . ." he murmured vaguely. "Yes . . . I remember. You told me about it. . ."

"Where is this temple?" asked Thorne.

"We shall have to walk," Grimes told him. "It's not on the plaza. It's in a little alley . . . I'm not sure that I'll be able to find it again . . ."

"I can lead you there," said Mayhew.

"You *would!*" muttered Sonya.

So the telepath was picking something up, I thought. He would home on it, as a navigator homes on a radio beacon. I was beginning to feel as the commodore's wife was obviously feeling about it. Deciding to throw in my two bits' worth I asked, "Shall we leave somebody to guard the pinnace?" Sara scowled at me. She was the obvious choice. She would be no more keen on going outside than any of us, but she most certainly did not want to be left alone.

"It will not be necessary, George," said Grimes. "We will, of course, notify the ship of our intentions. And Ken will maintain his telepathic hook-up with Clarisse. And, before leaving, each of us will leave his hand impression so that the outer airlock door can be locked after us . . ."

This we did. The door would now open if any of us placed either hand—or only fingertips—on the plate set in the hull beside the entrance. One by one we jumped down to the mossy paving stones. There was an unpleasant dankness in the air in spite of the sunlight, a penetrating chill. Yet, according to the thermometer that Mrs. Thorne produced from her capacious shoulder bag, it was mild enough, a fraction over twenty six degrees, too warm for the heavy, long-sleeved shirts, long trousers and stout boots that we were wearing.

Mayhew took the lead, with Grimes, projectile pistol in hand, walking beside him. Sonya and I, immediately behind, followed his example, although she favoured a laser hand gun. The Thornes followed us. Sara, carrying a submachine gun, brought up the rear. The telepath led us over the broken pavement, deviating from his course as required to avoid clumps of bushes and the occasional tree, but heading all the time to where a wide street opened off the plaza. It looked more like some fantastically fertile canyon than a manmade thoroughfare. The leaves of the omnipresent ivy glistened in the sunlight, glossy greens and a particularly poisonous-looking yellow. There were other creepers too, native perhaps, or importations from other worlds than Earth, but they were fighting a losing battle against the hardy, destructive vine.

We walked slowly and cautiously into the wide street. It must have been an imposing avenue before the abandonment of the city, before burgeoning weeds blurred its perspective and obscured the clean lines of the buildings on either side of it. I tried to visualize it as it had been in its heyday—and succeeded all too well. Everything . . . flickered, flickered then shone with an unnatural clarity. I cried out in alarm as I stared at the onrushing stream of traffic into which we were so carelessly walking. A gaudy chrome and scarlet ground car was almost upon on us, the fat woman driving it making no move either to swerve or to brake her vehicle. I grabbed Sonya's arm to drag her to one side, to safety. She cried out—and her sharp voice shattered the spell. Again there was the brief flickering and when normal vision returned I could see that nothing was moving in the street save ourselves. There was no traffic, no homicidal ground car. But there was a low mound ahead of us looking like a crouching, green furred beast. Freakishly, the lenses of its headlights had not been grown over and were regarding us like a pair of baleful eyes. And had I seen the ghost of the machine, I wondered, or of its driver?

Sonya was rubbing her arm and glaring at me. The others had stopped and were staring at me curiously.

"Did you *see* something, George?" asked Thorne.

I said slowly, "I saw this street as it must once have been, at its busiest. We were right in the middle of the traffic, about to be run down." I pointed at the derelict, almost unrecognizable car. "We were almost run down by . . . that. Or its ghost."

"The ghost of a *machine?*" demanded Thorne incredulously.

His wife, looking at an instrument she had taken from her bag, said, "The graph shows a sudden dip in temperature . . ."

"But a *machine!*" repeated the scientist.

"Why not?" countered Grimes. "Life force rubs off human beings on to the machinery with which they're in the most intimate contact. Ships, especially . . . And a car is, in some ways, almost a miniature ship . . ." He turned to Mayhew. "Ken?"

The telepath replied, in a distant voice, "I . . . I feel . . . resentment . . . In its dim, mechanical way that thing loved its mistress. It was abandoned, left here to rot . . ."

"Did *you* see anything?" persisted Thorne.

"I saw the same as George did," admitted Mayhew. "But I knew it wasn't it . . . real."

We resumed our trudge along the overgrown street. Everybody, I noticed with a certain wry satisfaction, gave the abandoned car a wide berth. We walked on, and on, trying to ignore the brambly growths that clutched at our trouser legs as though with malign intent.

"Here," announced Mayhew.

We could just make out the entrance to a side alley, completely blocked with a tall, bamboolike growth with tangled strands of ivy filling the narrow spaces between the upright stems.

"Shall I?" asked Sonya.

"Yes," said Grimes, after a second's thought.

While Sara watched enviously the commodore's wife used her laser pistol like a machete, slashing with the almost invisible beam. There were crackling flames and billows of dense white smoke. Coughing and spluttering, with eyes watering, we backed away. I couldn't help thinking that a fire extinguisher would have been more useful than most of the other equipment we had brought along.

But only the bamboo burned; the surrounding ivy was too green to catch fire once the laser was no longer in use. At last the smoke cleared to a barely tolerable level and we were able to make our way forward. The embers were hot underfoot, nonetheless, but our boots were stout and the fabric of our trousers fireproof.

We found the church.

It was only a small building, standing apart from its taller neighbours. It was a featureless cube. Well, *almost* a cube. I got the impression that the angles were subtly, very subtly, wrong. Unlike the buildings to either side of it, it was not overgrown. Its dull gray walls seemed to be of some synthetic stone. The plain rectangular door was also gray, possibly of uncorroded metal. There were no windows. Over the entrance, in black lettering, were the words: TEMPLE OF THE PRINCIPLE.

Grimes stared at the squat, ugly building. I could see from his face that he was far from happy. He muttered, "This is where we came in."

"This," Sonya corrected him, "is where we nearly went out . . ."

They had told me the story during the outward passage. I knew how they had investigated this odd temple, and found themselves thrown into an alternate existence, another plane of being on which their lives had taken altogether different courses. It had not been a dream, they insisted. They had actually lived those lives.

"Something . . ." Mayhew was muttering. *"Something . . .* But what? *But what?"*

"And what was the principle that they . . . er . . . worshipped?" asked Thorne, matter-of-factly.

"The Uncertainty Principle . . ." said Grimes, but dubiously. "You know, the funny part is that in none of the records of the abandoned colony is there any mention of this temple, or of the religion with which it was associated."

"The worshippers must have . . . left," Sonya said, "before the other colonists were evacuated."

"But where did they go?" asked Thorne.

"Or *when,*" said May hew. *"To* when, I mean."

Grimes filled and lit his pipe, then almost immediately knocked it out again, put it back in his pocket. He pushed the door. I was expecting it to resist his applied pressure but it opened easily, far too easily. He led the way inside the temple. The others followed. I was last, as I waited until I had raised Bindle on my personal transceiver to tell him where we were and what we were doing. He—always the humorist—said, "Drop something in the plate for me, Captain!"

I was expecting darkness in the huge, windowless room, but there was light—of a sort. The gray, subtly shifting twilight was worse than blackness would have been. It accentuated the . . . the *wrongness* of the angles where wall met wall, ceiling and floor. I was reminded of that eerie sensation one feels in the interstellar drive room of a ship when the Mannschenn Drive is running, the dim perception of planes at right angles to all the planes of the normal Space-Time continuum. Faintly self-luminous, not quit in the middle of that uncannily lopsided hall, was what had to t the altar, a sort of ominous coffin shape. But as I stared at it, the planes and angles shifted. It was, I decided, more of a cube. Or more *than* a cube . . . A tesseract?

Rose Thorne was pulling instruments out of her capacious bag. She set one of them up on spidery, telescopic legs. She peered at the

dial on top of it. "Fluctuations," she murmured, "slight, but definite
. . ." She said in a louder voice, "There something *odd* about the
gravitational field of this place . . ."

"Gravity waves?" asked her husband.

She laughed briefly. "Ripples rather than waves. Undetectable by
any normal gravitometer."

Thorne turned to Grimes. "Did you notice any phenome like this
when you were here before, John?"

"We didn't have any instruments with us," the commodore told
him shortly.

"And what do *you* feel, Ken?" the scientist asked Mayhew.

But the telepath did not reply. Looking at him, the way that was
standing there, his gaze somehow turned inward, I was reminded of
the uneasy sensation you get when a dog sees something—or seems
to see something—that is invisible to you. "Old . . ." he whispered.
"Old . . . From the time before this, and from the time before that,
and the time before and the time before . . . The planet alive, alive and
aware, a sentient world . . . Surviving every death and rebirth of the
universe . . . Surviving beyond the continuum . . ."

It didn't make sense, I thought. *It didn't make sense.*

Or did it?

His lips moved again, but his voice was barely audible.
"Communion. Yes. Communion . . ."

He took a step, and then another, and another, like a sleepwalker.
He paced slowly and deliberately up to—*into*—the dimly glowing
tesseract. He seemed to flicker. The outline of his body wavered,
wavered and faded. Then, quite suddenly, he was gone.

The metallic click as Sara cocked her submachine gun was
startlingly loud. I still don't know what she thought she was going to
shoot at. I did know that in this situation all our weapons were utterly
useless.

"We have to get Clarisse here," said Grimes at last. "She's the only
one of us who'll be able to do anything." He added, in a whisper, "If
anything can be done, that is . . ."

We had to go outside the temple before we could use our personal transceivers. Clarisse was already calling; she *knew,* of course. She was already in *Basset*'s second boat, which was being piloted by young Taylor. Grimes told him to try to land in the street just by the mouth of the alley. There were more obstructions there than where we had set down, in the square, but speed was the prime consideration. I walked, accompanied by Sara, to the proposed landing site, my transceiver set for continuous beacon transmission so that Taylor could home on it.

We heard the boat—the inertial drive is not famous for quiet running—before we saw it. Taylor came in low over the rooftops, wasting no time. He slammed the lifecraft down to the road surface, crushing a couple of well-developed bushes and knocking a stout sapling sideways. I shuddered. I didn't like to see ship's equipment— especially *my* ship's equipment—handled that way. The door midway along the torpedo-shaped hull snapped open. Clarisse jumped out.

She brushed past us, unspeaking, ran into the alley, clouds of fine ash exploding about her ankles. Sara and I followed her. Clarisse hesitated briefly at the temple doorway, exchanging a few words with Grimes and Sonya, then hurried inside. When the rest of us joined her we found her standing by the altar, motionless, her face set and expressionless. In the dim light she looked like a priestess of some ancient religion.

Then she spoke, but not to any of us.

"Ken," she whispered, obviously vocalizing her thoughts. "Ken . . ." She smiled suddenly. She was getting through. "Yes . . . Here I am . . ."

"Where is he?" demanded Grimes urgently.

She ignored the question. Suddenly, walking as Mayhew had walked, she stepped into that luminous shape, that distorted geometrical, multidimensional diagram. We saw the outline of her body through her clothing, her shadowy bone structure through her translucent flesh, and . . .

Nothing.

Thorne broke the stunned silence. "Did you observe the meter while all this was happening?" he asked his wife.

You cold-blooded bastard! I thought angrily, then realized that the scientists' instruments might provide some clue as to what had happened.

"No," she admitted, then stooped over the gravitometer, pressed a button. "But here's the print-out."

We could all see the graph as she showed it to him. There were the slight, very slight irregularities that she had referred to as gravitational ripples. And there were two sharp and very definite dips. The first one must have registered when Mayhew disappeared, the second when Clarisse vanished.

So *It*, whatever *It* was, played around with gravity. *A sentient planet,* I reflected, *ought to be able to do just that . . .*

"Rose," said Grimes, "watch your gravitometer, will you?"

She shot him a puzzled look, but obeyed. The commodore brought something small out of his pocket. It was, I saw, a box of matches. He tossed it towards the tesseract. Nobody was surprised when it, too, vanished.

"The field intensified," reported the woman. "Briefly, slightly, but very definitely."

"So . . ." murmured Grimes. "So what?" He turned to face us all. "We must get Ken and Clarisse out. But how?"

Nobody answered him.

Having waited in vain for a reply he continued. "Twice, while on this blasted planet, I've been shunted . . . elsewhere. Each time I got back. I still don't know how. But if I could, they can." He gestured towards the altar. "That thing's a gateway. A gateway to where—or *when!*" He addressed me directly. "You've an engine room gantry aboard your ship, George. And there are drilling and cutting tools in the engineers' workshop."

"Yes," I told him.

"I'd like them here. Mphm. But there'll be only a few metres of wire on your gantry winches. We could want more, much more . . ."

I remembered, then, something which had been a source of puzzlement to me for a long time. "In the storeroom," I told him, "are two funny little hand winches, with reels of very fine wire. There's a lot of wire. Nobody knows what those winches are for. But . . ."

"But they might come in handy now," said Grimes, suddenly and inexplicably cheerful. "I think I know what those winches are— although what they're doing aboard a merchant spaceship is a mystery. In the Survey Service, of course, we had things like them, for oceanographic work . . ."

"You're losing me, sir," I said.

"I could be wrong, of course," he went on, "but I've a hunch that these will be just the things we need. I'd like one of them out here at once. The other one, I think, could be modified slightly. Your engineers can study the simple workings of it, and then fit it with a motor from your gantry . . ."

I suppose that he knew what he was talking about. Nobody else did.

We went outside the temple to use our transceivers to get in touch with Bindle, back aboard the ship. Grimes put him in the picture and then gave him detailed instructions. As well as the first of the odd little hand winches and the cutting tools he wanted a sound-powered telephone, with as much wire as could be found.

Then the commodore and myself went to the mouth of the alley to await the return of Taylor with the first installment of equipment. The boat came in at last and we boarded it at once and were promptly carried to the flat roof of the building. Under my watchful eye the third officer made a very cautious landing—but that rooftop, by the feel of it, could have supported the enormous weight of an Alpha Class liner. We unloaded the tools and the reel of wire, then Taylor lifted off and returned to the ship.

Grimes looked at the wire reel and laughed. He said, "And you really don't know what this is, George?"

"No," I told him.

"Was your ship ever on Atlantia?"

"A few times, I think, but never when I was in her."

"And one of those times—probably the last time—she overcarried cargo," went on Grimes. "And the good Dog Star Line mate buried those leftover bones in the back garden, thinking that they might come in handy for something, some time. This is a sounding machine, such as the Atlanteans use in their big schooners, and such as we, in the Survey Service, use for charting the seas of a newly discovered world. But our machines have motors."

"I thought that all sounding was done electronically," I said.

"Most of it is," the commodore told me, "but an echometer can't bring up a sample of the bottom . . . Yes, this is a sounding machine. Armstrong Patent."

"Is that the make of it?"

Grimes laughed again, obviously amused by my ignorance. I rather resented this. It was all very well for him; he was one of the experts, if not *the* expert, on Terran maritime history. And not only did he hold a Master Mariner's Certificate in addition to his qualifications as a master astronaut—he had actually sailed in command of a surface vessel on that watery world Aquarius.

"Armstrong Patent," he said, "is the nickname given by seamen to any piece of machinery powered by human muscle. And they're a weird mob, the Atlanteans, as you may know. They have a horror of automation even in its simplest forms. They pride themselves on having put the clock back to the good old days of wooden ships and iron men. But they do import some manufactured goods—such as this." He looked at the dial set horizontally on top of the winch. "And there's two hundred fathoms of piano wire here. That's about three hundred and sixty five metres." He pulled a cylinder of heavy metal from its clip on the winch frame. "And here's the sinker. About ten kilograms of lead, by the feel of it."

"Oh, I see," I admitted. (Well, I did, after a fashion.)

"Mphm." Grimes was studying the legs on which the machine stood, the feet of which were designed so that they could be bolted to a deck. "Mphm . . ." He straightened up, then walked to the edge of the flat roof. I followed him. There was no parapet. I stayed well back; I don't suffer from acrophobia—I'd hardly be a spaceman if I did—but I always like to have something to hold on to. And it looked a long way down. The temple hadn't looked all that high from the ground, but in its vicinity perspective seemed to be following a new set of rules.

Grimes was shouting down to his wife after a futile attempt to use his personal transceiver. Apparently the inhibitory field was as effective on the roof as inside the building. "Sonya, we want some timber. Yes, timber! Two good, strong logs, straight, each at least two metres long and fifteen centimetres thick . . . Yes, use your laser to cut them!"

When she had gone, accompanied by the others, he determined the centre of the flat roof by pacing out the diagonals. Where these intersected he put down his precious pipe as a marker. I brought him the laser cutter—one with a self-contained power pack. He held it like the oversized pistol that it resembled, directing the thin pencil of incandescence almost directly downward.

At first it seemed the surface of the roof was going to be impossible to cut; the beam flattened weirdly at the point of impact, spreading to a tiny puddle of intense light, dazzlingly bright even though it was in the full rays of the sun. And then, quite suddenly, without any pyrotechnics, without so much as a wisp of smoke, there was penetration.

After that it was easy. Grimes described a circle of about one-metre diameter but left a thirty-degree arc uncut. He switched off and put down the cutter, then retrieved his pipe. When it was safely back in his pocket he extended a cautious fingertip to the cut in the roof. He looked puzzled. "Cold, stone cold," he whispered. "It shouldn't be. But it saves time."

I fetched the pinch bar and we got one end of it under the partially excised circle, then levered upwards. It came fairly easily, and did not spring back when the pressure was released. I took a firm hold on the smooth edge and held it while Grimes completed the cut.

When the disc was free it was amazingly light, even though it was all of four centimetres thick. I put it to one side and we looked down.

The altar—I may as well go on calling it that, although I was sure by now that it had no religious significance—was almost directly below us. Its alien geometry glimmered wanly. I'd been expecting, somehow, to find myself looking down into a hole, a very deep hole, but such was not the case. It was just as we had seen it from ground level, a distorted construct of slowly shifting planes of dim radiance. But we knew that if we fell into it we should keep on going.

Somebody was calling. It was Sonya, back from her wood-cutting expedition. We went to the edge of the roof. She and Sara were carrying one suitable looking log between them, the Thornes another. She shouted, "How do we get these up to you?"

Grimes did something to the winch handles of the sounding machine so that the wire ran off easily. He pulled as much as he needed off the reel, lowered the end of it over the edge of the roof to the ground. Sonya threw it around the first of the logs in a simple yet secure hitch. We pulled it up. It wasn't all that heavy, but the thin wire bit painfully into the palms of our hands. Then we brought up the second one.

We used the laser cutter to trim the logs to square section, adjusting the beam setting carefully before starting work. We didn't want to cut the roof from under our feet. Then we arranged the two baulks of timber so that they bridged the circular hole. We lifted the sounding machine and set so that it rested securely on the rough platform. Grimes shackled the heavy sinker to the end of the wire, left it dangling. "Mphm . . ." he grunted dubiously. He had found, clipped inside the frame of the winch, a small L-shaped rod of metal on a wooden handle. He asked, "Do you know how this works?"

I didn't. I'm a spaceman, not a seaman.

"This," he told me, "is the feeler. Normally there's a good lead from the sounding machine so that the wire runs horizontally from the reel to a block on the taffrail or on the end of the sounding boom. Whoever's working it holds the feeler in one hand, pressing down on the wire—and he knows when the sinker has hit bottom by the sudden slackening of tension. Then he brakes. Obviously we can't do that here. So you, George, will have to exercise a lateral pull with the feeler. Yell out as soon as you feel the wire go slack."

We took our positions, myself crouching and holding the feeler ready, he grasping both winch handles. He gave them a sharp half-turn forward and the sinker dropped, and the wire sang off the drum. It was plain that we hadn't found bottom on the floor of the temple. Out ran the gleaming wire, out, out . . . I heard Grimes mutter, "Fifty . . . One hundred . . . One fifty . . ." And what would happen when we came to the end of the wire?

It went slack suddenly. "Now!" I shouted as I went over backwards.

Somehow I was still watching Grimes and saw him sharply turn the handles in reverse, braking the winch. When I scrambled to my feet he was looking at the dial. "One hundred and seventy three fathoms," he said slowly. "One hundred and seventy three fathoms, straight down . . ." He grinned ruefully. "That was the easy part. Gravity was doing all the work. The hard part comes now!"

I didn't know what he meant until we had to wind up all that length of wire by hand. We waited a little while, hoping that Mayhew and Clarisse would be able to attach a message of some kind to the sinker, and then we took a handle each and turned and turned and turned. The pointer moved anticlockwise on the dial with agonizing slowness. We had both of us worked up a fine sweat and acquired blisters on the palms of our hands when, at long last, the plummet lifted slowly through the hole in the roof. There was more than just the sinker attached to the wire. There was a square of scarlet synthesilk that, I remembered, Clarisse had worn as a neckerchief at the throat of her khaki shirt. And knotted into it was the box of matches that Grimes had dropped into the altar.

There was something wrong with it. It took me a little time to realize what it was—and then I saw that in order to read the brand name—PROMETHEUS—one would require a mirror.

The Thornes had a pad and a stylus among their equipment. We used the sounding machine wire to bring these up to the roof, then attached them to the sinker and sent them down to wherever Mayhew and Clarisse were trapped. This time Grimes applied the brake when he had one hundred and sixty fathoms of wire down and walked out the rest by hand. Then we waited, Grimes smoking a pipe—his matches still worked in spite of the odd reversal—and myself a cigar. This would give the psionicists time to write their message and, in any case, we felt that we had earned a smoko.

We thought of asking Sonya to use the boat that we had left in the plaza to bring others of the party up to the roof to lend us a hand, then decided that, for the time being, it was better to have them standing by on the ground. To begin with, there was the problem of radio communication with the ship to be considered.

Our rest period over, we sweated again on what the commodore had so aptly called the Armstrong Patent machine. At last the sinker rose into view. Attached to it was a sheet torn from the pad. Grimes detached it carefully but eagerly, then grunted. Mayhew's handwriting, at the best of times, was barely legible, and a mirror image of his vile calligraphy was impossible. And nobody had a mirror. I suggested that Grimes hold the sheet of plastic up against the sunlight. He did so, then muttered irritably, "Damn the man! If he can't write, he should print!"

Squinting against the glare I looked over Grimes' shoulder. At least, I thought, we should be thankful for small mercies; Mayhew had written on only one side of the sheet. I could just make out: *Safe, so far, but no communication. It*—the "it" was heavily underlined—*will receive but not transmit. I can't get inside its mind. It wants to know about us but does not want us to know about it. It's draining us. Can you get us out?*

(It took us far longer to read the message than it has taken you.)

"This piano wire is strong," Grimes told me. "The weight of a human being is well below its safe working load, let alone its breaking strain. But I don't fancy winching Ken or Clarisse—Clarisse especially—up by hand."

I was inclined to agree.

Grimes wrote a short note to Mayhew, using the reverse side of the sheet on which the telepath's message had been penned. He printed in large block capitals: HELP BEING ORGANIZED. GRIMES. We sent it down attached to the sinker.

And then Taylor appeared with additional equipment, bringing the boat down to a landing almost at the edge of the roof. Also with him were Thorne's assistants—Trentham, Smith, Susan Howard and Mary Lestrange. The mousey quartet showed signs of pleasurable excitement. *A few turns on the hand winch,* I thought sourly, *would wipe the silly grins off their faces.* Betty was with them. She had brought a sound-powered telephone set, a large reel of light cable and a tape recorder. And there was the second sounding machine, to which a motor from the engine room gantry had been attached. Porky Terrigal, the reaction drive engineer, had come along with it to make sure that nobody misused his precious machinery. There were also thermo-containers of hot and cold drinks and boxes of sandwiches, a couple of coils of strong plastic line that Bindle had sent along thinking that they might come in useful (they did) and a spidery-looking folding ladder that would give us access from the roof to the ground, and vice versa.

The boat had to stay in position, as the power to the sounding machine winch would be fed from its fusion unit. Luckily, the rooftop was wide enough to accommodate all the extra people and gear without crowding. Sonya and Sara came up to join the party, leaving the Thornes standing watch below.

Grimes turned the four young scientists to on the hand winch. By the time they got the sinker up to roof level they had lost their initial enthusiasm. The message was easier to read this time. To begin with, Mayhew had taken the hint and printed the words and, secondly, Susan Lestrange produced a small mirror from her shoulder bag. It said: WOULD LIKE A LITTLE MORE TIME. CAN YOU SEND TELEPHONE? KEN.

We sent the telephone, and with it some food and drink. Betty hooked an amplifier up to the instrument at our end of the line. We waited anxiously, far from sure that things would work. What if what had been happening to the written word also happened to the spoken word? Then, after what seemed an eternity of delay, we heard Mayhew's voice. "Thanks for the tucker, John! It's very welcome. All the others seem to have died of thirst and starvation . . ."

"What others?" asked Grimes.

"Clarisse here," came the reply. "Ken can't talk with his mouth full. We're safe, so far. But I'll try to put you in the picture. It feels like a huge control room, like a ship's, but much, much bigger. Only there are no controls as *we* know them, no banks of familiar instruments . . . This is a great, cavernous space with lights shifting and pulsing . . . We *know* that it all means something, that it isn't mere, random activity, but what? But *what?* Maintaining stasis over uncountable millennia . . . Staying put in Time and Space while the Universe around it dies and is reborn . . ." A note of hysteria crept into her voice. "*It . . . It* has sucked us dry, of all we know, even of knowledge that we did not dream that we owned. And now *It* isn't interested in us anymore. We can take our places with the . . . others . . ."

"What others?" demanded Grimes.

Mayhew came back on the line. "There are bodies here. Not decayed but . . . desiccated. Sort of mummified. Some human. Some . . . not. There's . . . something not far from us with an exoskeleton. Something not from *this* Universe. And there are two things like centaurs . . . The arthropod thing is holding a machine of some kind . . . It could be a complicated weapon . . . And there's all the time the slow, regular pulse of the coloured lights washing over everything, and there's something that's like a gigantic pendulum, but not of metal, but of radiance . . . I can *feel* it rather than see it . . ." He paused. "It's like being a tiny insect in the works of some vast clock, only the wheels and the gears and the pendulum aren't material . . ."

Clarisse cried, interrupting, "But can you imagine a clock ticking backwards?"

Thorne had climbed up the rooftop. He said, "I heard all that. We must try to bring up some . . . specimens."

"All that I'm concerned with," Grimes told him, "is bringing our friends up."

"It would be criminal," said the scientist, "to miss this opportunity."

"It will be criminal," said Grimes, "to risk two lives any further. How do we know that the . . . gateway will stay open? No; we get Clarisse and Ken out of there *now!*"

The wire of the hand-powered sounding machine had been reeled in by this time and, under Grimes' supervision, the one with the electric motor was set up in its place. To the sinker the commodore attached one of the coils of light plastic rope. He said into the telephone, "You remember that book of mine you borrowed on bends and hitches and knots and splices, Ken? You should be able to throw a secure bowline on the bright with the line I'm sending down to you . . . Yes, you sit in it . . ."

"But can't he send up something, *anything,* first?" pleaded Thorne.

"No, Doctor." Grimes was adamant.

"I overheard some of that," came Mayhew's voice. "I think we should. That lobster thing, and the contraption it's holding in its claws . . . I could carry it up with me . . ."

"Mayhew is speaking sense," commented the scientist.

There was a long wait. Then, "It's heavy," came the voice from the speaker. "Damned heavy. We can't shift it . . ."

"Then leave it," Grimes ordered. "The sinker and the plastic line are on their way down to you now. I'm using the electrically powered machine, so I'll have you and Clarisse up in no time."

"You have *two* machines?" asked Mayhew.

"Yes. Why?"

"I'll send Clarisse up first. Send the wire down again, and I'll have made a sling with what's left of the line and put it round the . . . *thing*. Then you bring *me* up with the hand-powered winch, and you can use the stronger one to lift the specimen . . ."

"Well?" demanded Thorne.

"All right," Grimes agreed reluctantly.

It took no time at all to extricate Clarisse. Grimes had sent Taylor down to the temple, accompanied by the two girl scientists, to pull her clear of the altar and then down to the floor as soon as she emerged. She joined us on the roof. I looked at her and tried to remember on which of her cheekbones that beauty spot had been . . .

We sent the wire down again. Mayhew telephoned that he had the end of it, was making it fast to the sling that he had managed to get around the body of the weird alien. We then shifted the electric winch to one side, replacing it with the hand-powered one. Grimes was worried that the two sounding wires might become entangled, but the sinker dropped with the same speed that it had done on the prior occasions.

Mayhew said that he was seated in the bowline and ready to come up. Trentham and Smith manned the winch handles. It was brutally hard work; the winch was not geared. After a while Grimes and I had to spell them. And then Thorne and Terrigal took a turn. Mayhew was bringing his end of the telephone up with him and was keeping us informed. "Like swimming up through a sort of gray fog . . ." he said. "I'm putting my hand out, but there's nothing solid . . . I can see the other wire . . . I can touch *that,* but it's all that I can touch . . . Looking up, I can see a sort of distorted square of white light . . . It's a long way off . . ."

Yes, it was a long way. A long way for him, and a bloody long way for those of us who were doing all the work. I hoped that Dr. Thorne was enjoying his turn at the winch; it had been his idea that a specimen be brought up. If he hadn't insisted Mayhew would have been whisked to safety with the same speed as Clarisse.

We heard Taylor's shout from below at last, just as Mayhew himself reported that he was being lifted into the temple. We came back on the winch after the third mate had caught his swinging feet and was lowering him safely to the floor. Once he was out of his harness he came up the ladder to join us on the rooftop.

Now that the operation was almost over I realized, suddenly, how time had flown. It was almost sunset, and a chill breeze was blowing from the east. In a matter of minutes it would be dark. Kinsolving has no moon and here, on the Rim, there would be precious little starlight.

Grimes said, "I think we should defer any further operations until tomorrow morning."

Thorne said, "But there are lights in the boat. A searchlight . . ."

Mayhew said, "John, do we *want* that . . . thing? I've a feeling that the gateway may be closing again, at any second."

"Oh, all right," said Grimes resignedly. He turned to me, "Let's get the electric winch back on to the platform."

We did so. Then he told me, "It's your equipment, George, operated by your personnel. Over to you."

I thought, *You buck-passing old bastard!* But what he had said made sense. I gestured to Terrigal at the winch controls, made the Heave Away! signal. The piano wire tightened. I looked over Terrigal's shoulder and could see the pointer on the dial begin to move. I visualized that bundle of—something—being dragged across the floor of the . . . Cavern? Control room? The winch hadn't got the weight yet.

Then it took the strain and almost coincidentally the sun set. The light breeze was chillier still and there was almost no twilight. Somebody switched on the lights in the boat, including the searchlight, which flooded the rooftop with a harsh, white radiance. The winch groaned. Terrigal complained, "I can't be held responsible for any damage to the machinery . . ."

"Keep her coming!" I told him. I was more concerned about the baulks of timber upon which the sounding machine was resting than with the machine itself. But engineers, in my experience, always tend to be slaves to rather than masters of their engines.

There was an acrid taint in the air from overheated metal and insulation and the wire, a filament of incandescent silver in the searchlight beam, was beginning to sing. But the pointer on the dial was moving—slowly, slowly, but moving.

I asked, "Can't you go any faster?"

"No, Captain. I'm on the last notch now. And I don't like it."

"Better get people cleared away from here, George," Grimes told me. "If that wire parts it's going to spring back . . ."

"And what about *me?*" demanded Terrigal.

"If you're scared—" I began.

"Yes, I am scared!" he growled. "And so would you be if you had any bloody sense. But I wouldn't trust any of you on this winch!"

All right, all right—I *was* scared. And it was more than a fear of a lethally lashing end of broken wire. It was that primordial dread of the unknown that has afflicted Man from his first beginnings, that afflicts, too, the lower orders of the animal kingdom. The darkness around the brilliantly lit rooftop was alive with shifting, whispering shadows. Most of our party, I noticed, had already taken refuge in the boat, a little cave of light and warmth that offered shelter, probably illusory, from the ultimate night that seemed to be closing around us. Only Grimes, Sonya, Sara and myself remained in the open—and, of course, Terrigal at the winch controls.

The winch was making an eerie whining noise. The smell of hot metal and scorching insulation was much stronger. And the wire itself was keening—and was . . . stretching. Surely it was stretching. Surely that shining filament was now so thin as to be almost invisible.

"Enough!" ordered Grimes. "Avast heaving!"

The engineer brought the control handle round anticlockwise, but it had no effect. He cried, "She won't stop!"

"Mr. Taylor," shouted Grimes into the boat, "switch off the power to the winch!"

"The switch is jammed!" came the reply.

"She won't stop! She won't stop!" yelled Terrigal, frantically jiggling his controls.

The light was dimming, sagging down the spectrum, and outlines were wavering, and frightened voices sounded as though they were coming from an echo chamber. The thin high keening of the overtaut wire was above and below and through all other noises. Sonya and Sara were wrestling with the power cable, tugging at it, worrying it like two dogs fighting over a bone, trying to drag it out of its socket in the boat's hull. It resisted all their efforts.

"Let's get out of here!" snapped Grimes. "Into the boat, all of you!"

Terrigal abandoned his winch, but not before aiming a vicious kick at the control box. He scurried into the little airlock. The two women followed. Grimes and I made it to the door in a dead heat; he pushed me inside then followed hard after me. As soon as we were all in, Taylor, forward at the controls, slammed the inertial drive into maximum lift, not bothering to close the airlock doors first. We started to rise, then stopped with a jerk, heeling alarmingly to port. The power cable to the winch was holding us down. But it would soon part, I thought. It must part. It was only a power cable, not a heavy-duty mooring wire.

It didn't part. It . . . stretched. It shouldn't have done, but it did. And we lifted again, slowly, with the inertial drive hammering like a mechanical riveter gone mad. I clung to the frame of the open door and looked down. I saw the sounding machine dragged up and clear from the circular hole in the roof, with the shining filament of wire still extending straight downwards.

Terrifyingly, the city around the temple was coming to life—but it wasn't the city that we had explored. The human colonists had laid out their streets in a rectangular plan; these streets were concentric circles connected by radial thoroughfares. And there were the tall, cylindrical towers, agleam with lights, each topped with a shining sphere. Unsubstantial they seemed at first, but as I watched they appeared to acquire solidity.

Grimes saw it too. He shouted to Taylor, to Terrigal, to anybody who was close enough to the fusion generator to do something about it, "You have to cut the power to the winch! We're dredging up the Past—and we shall be in it!"

"Just show me how, Commodore!" cried the engineer. "Just show me how! I've done all that *I* can do—short of stopping the jenny!"

And if he did stop the generator we should fall like a stone. *If* he could stop it, that is.

An aircraft came slowly into view, circling us warily. It was huge, a cylindrical hull, rounded at the ends, with vanes sticking out at all sorts of odd angles. It was like nothing that I had ever seen and possessed a nightmarishly alien quality. There were tubes protruding from turrets that could have been, that almost certainly were guns, and they were trained upon us. What if the alien commander—I visualized him, or *it,* as being of the same species as the lobsterlike being whose body we had been attempting to recover—should open fire? What would happen to us?

Nothing pleasant, that was for sure.

But we had weapons of our own; we could, at least, defend ourselves if attacked. Sara, I was sure, would enjoy being able to play with her toys. And Sara, I suddenly realized, was beside me in the cramped little airlock, holding her submachine gun. I said to her, "What use do you think that will be? What's wrong with the heavy armament?"

She replied obscurely, "I can't bring it to bear." I couldn't see why she couldn't. That blasted flying battleship was staying well within the arcs of fire of the laser cannon and the heavy machine gun, and a guided missile would home on her no matter where she was relative to us.

Sara opened fire. Bright tracer flashed out from the muzzle of the gun, but not towards the huge flying ship. It may have been the first round of the burst that hit the power cable, certainly it was one in the first half-dozen. There was an arcing sputter of blue flame and the boat, released from its tether, went up like a bat out of hell.

And below us the weird city out of Time flickered and vanished.

✎ ✎ ✎ ✎

I turned to Grimes. "You said, sir, that the things that happen on Kinsolving's Planet shouldn't happen to a dog. And they shouldn't happen, either, to respectable employees of the Dog Star Line."

He managed a grin, then went, "Arf, arf!"

DOGGY IN THE WINDOW

⁓ Doggy in the Window ⁓

DURING ALL MY YEARS as a Rim Worlder and as an officer in Rim Runners I'd never made a landing on Kinsolving's Planet; come to that, I'd never come within extreme guided-missile range of that world. Now, as a naturalized Sirian and a captain in the Dog Star Line, I was not only on Kinsolving but stuck there. It shouldn't have happened to a dog.

I sat glumly in *Basset*'s control room, mulling things over in my mind. Commodore Grimes sat with me, presumably similarly employed, although his main preoccupation seemed to be keeping his vile pipe alight. There was nothing that either of us could do here, in the ship's nerve centre, but it was a refuge from the others, from the incessant bombardment of questions to which we had no answers.

I looked out through the wide viewports. The time was late afternoon and the peculiar quality of the sunlight was making the yellows and greens of the jungly landscape look positively poisonous. And, I was sure, the scenery did not look the same as it had looked on the occasion of our dawn landing the previous day. Bindle, my chief officer, swore that he had not shifted the ship during our absence from her and I did not doubt his word—but there were low hills where no hills had been before and the ruins that we could see in the distance looked nothing at all like the crumbling, overgrown remains of Enderston.

Grimes said, speaking around his pipe, "*It* knows that we're here. *It* doesn't mean to let us go . . ."

It was the world of Kinsolving itself, a planetary intelligence that, somehow, had survived cycle after cycle, that had retained *Its* identity through death after death, rebirth after rebirth of the universe. Or so Grimes' psionic communications officer, Mayhew, the highly trained and qualified telepath, had told us.

And what was I, no longer a Rim Worlder, doing in the middle of this essentially Rim Worlds mess, I asked myself. It was all right for the commodore and his people to get mixed up in these affairs, but not for *Basset* and her crew. *If* the Rim Worlds survey ship, *Faraway Quest,* hadn't been laid up . . . *If* the Dog Star Line's *Basset* hadn't come out to the Rim on a tramping voyage and then found herself temporarily unemployed . . . *If* she hadn't been chartered to do the job that, normally, would have been handled by *Faraway Quest,* carrying Grimes and his small expedition to Kinsolving . . . *If, if, if . . .*

But we had been so chartered. Then, very shortly after our landing on Kinsolving, investigations had been initiated in and about the weird Temple of the Principle, the "only building in Enderston that, somehow, had remained immune to the general decay. Mayhew had fallen into (?), through (?) the . . . altar (?), plunging to . . . somewhere (?), somewhen (?). Clarisse, Mayhew's wife and fellow psionicist, had followed him. We had rescued them, using two deep sea sounding machines—essentially winches with many metres of piano wire on their drums—that were items of overcarried cargo, originally consigned to Atlantia. We had rescued them but, in the process, seemed to have dredged up the remote Past. Or had we dragged ourselves back in Time?

Bassett was, of course, equipped with Carlotti radio. Our transceiver was powerful enough to put us into direct communication, given favourable conditions, with our home office in Canis Major, let alone any of the Rim Worlds. But our signals, although being beamed with extreme accuracy, did not seem to be getting through. Certainly nothing was coming through to us. And we should not be able to keep up our attempts at electronic communication for much longer. What energy remained in our power cells would have to be carefully conserved.

The Carlotti system has, to a great extent, replaced psionic communications but on most planets there are still trained telepaths, most of them in the employ of the armed forces of their worlds. Mayhew had remained in touch with his colleagues in the Rim Worlds Navy until the landing on Kinsolving. Now, he had reported to Grimes, it was as though he had suddenly become a deaf mute. But it was selective deafness and dumbness. He could still communicate wordlessly with Clarisse. He could still pick up the thoughts of the rest of us—although, in accordance with the Rhine Institute's Code of Ethics, he was not supposed to. And he was still conscious of the alien intelligence that brooded somewhere in the heart of the planet.

Meanwhile we were stranded. We would have lifted, run for home—assuming that home was still there—but we were . . . stuck. There was nothing at all wrong with our hydrogen fusion generator but, according to my engineers, Canvey and Terrigal, no power was getting through to the inertial drive unit or to the firing chambers of the reaction drive, or even to the ship's auxiliary machinery. They had talked learnedly of induction and more abstruse matters—but all that it boiled down to was that we were being drained of every last erg produced by the generator. As I have said, we still had the power cells—but their endurance was limited.

"*It* doesn't mean to let us go," said Grimes again.

"And what are *Its* reasons?" I asked.

"I've only a human mind," he said, with a wry grin. "I can only guess how a planetary intelligence would think. From what Mayhew has told us it seems to be a machine of some sort, a super-robot. Perhaps it was built, originally, by beings not unlike ourselves. Then it got . . . uppity. I've had experience with uppity robots in the past— but never such an enormous and enormously powerful one. But *It's* not a god."

"Perhaps not, sir," I agreed dubiously. "But it'll do until a real god happens along."

"Mphm," he grunted. "You know, Clarisse did raise *real* gods once, on this very planet, the deities of the ancient Greek pantheon. Or were they real? I'm not so sure now. Could they have been manifestations of *It*, built up from data extracted from our memories? If that was the way of it, then *It* has a sense of humour, and that makes *It* all the more dangerous . . ."

"Dangerous?" I asked.

"Too right. Even we have a weakness for black humour, and sick humour. And practical jokes can be very malicious. Practical jokes perpetrated by a being with godlike powers might be wildly funny to *It*, but fatal to us."

"Pratfalls can be fatal," I agreed.

"You've hit the nail on the thumb, George." He looked at his watch. "Your efficient purser should have the afternoon tea laid on by now. Shall we go down, or ask her to send ours up here?"

"We'll go down," I said. "Just to show the flag . . ."

Afternoon tea was on in the officers' wardroom, a compartment large enough to accommodate, with not too much crowding, both ship's personnel and passengers. Everybody was there. Porky Terrigal, the reaction drive engineer, was working out his frustrations on a huge tray of the sweet and savoury pastries that Sara had produced. Nobody else was eating much and I gained the impression that most of those present would have preferred something much stronger to drink than the hot, innocuous brew from the big silver pot. But we could not afford the risk of taking anything that would dull our perceptions, slow our reaction times. Kinsolving was a world on which anything might happen and probably would.

Dr. Thorne—bulky, bearded—heaved himself up from his deep chair as we entered. "Ah, Commodore Grimes, Captain Rule . . ." He waved his cup vaguely in our direction and drops of tea spattered onto the already-stained shirt bulging above his belt. "And may I—we— ask if anything of consequence has emerged from your deliberations?"

"You may ask, Doctor," replied Grimes mildly. He accepted the cup of tea that Sara Taine poured for him, thanked her. He went to the small settee on which Sonya, his wife, was already seated, took his place beside her.

"Well?" demanded Thorne.

"You asked if you might ask," Grimes told him. "I gave my permission. So ask."

The scientist glared at him, then said, "Has anything of consequence emerged from your deliberations?"

"No," said Grimes. "Meanwhile, have any of you ladies and gentlemen anything to contribute?"

"We've tried rigging bypass circuits," said Terrigal through a minor blizzard of pastry crumbs, "but the wires might as well have been solid insulation."

"And I've taken the Carlotti transceiver down, checked every part, and reassembled it," stated Betty Boops, the radio officer. "It should be working perfectly. But there just don't seem to be any stations to send to or receive from."

"Tonight, if the sky is clear," said Loran, second officer and navigator, "I shall be able to observe the stars, such as they are out here on the Rim. Then I shall be able to determine if there has been any shift in Space."

"Or Space-Time," said Sonya somberly. "John and I have been on this world before. We've had . . . experiences."

Time travel yet, I thought glumly. Oh, I know that every time we use the Mannschenn Drive to make an interstellar passage it's time travel of a sort—but, at least, we don't arrive before we've started . . .

"Ken?" asked Grimes, addressing Mayhew.

The tall, wispy telepath started. His thoughts had obviously been very far away. "Oh. Yes. I was trying to get some idea of the local fauna. This place should be overrun with the descendants of the Terran animals brought here by the original colonists. It was, when we landed yesterday. Terran life forms. Our relations, not too distant ones. I could . . . hear them without any trouble. I know what it feels like to be a rabbit. But they aren't here now. No pigs. No rabbits. No hens. The life that *is* here now I can't get into. I can pick up . . . feelings, primitive, on the lowest level, but they're too alien. Fear, hunger, lust . . . But which is which?"

"And *It?*" asked Grimes.

"*It* has closed *Its* mind to me. But I know that *It's* watching us."

"Mphm," Grimes grunted thoughtfully. Then he addressed Sara Taine. "Miss Taine, is this ship habitable?"

From the very start she had made it obvious that Grimes was one of her pets, but she flared angrily. "Of course, Commodore."

"Dr. Forbes?"

"As, among my other duties, biochemist I must reply in the affirmative, sir." Forbes looked so miserable that I should not have been surprised if he had said that *Basset* was no more than an anteroom to the grave—but Forbes always looked miserable.

"Mr. Canvey? Mr. Terrigal?"

Porky Terrigal answered, "All of our auxiliary machinery is working perfectly, Commodore, even if the drives aren't."

"From the power cells, of course."

"Of course."

It was Bindle, the chief officer, who realized suddenly what Grimes was driving at. He said, "And once the cells are dead, so is the ship."

"So," stated Grimes, "we must do our utmost to conserve electricity. To begin with, ventilation. I'm afraid I must ask you, Captain Rule, to have a few holes cut in the skin of your ship." He read my expression without difficulty. "Don't worry. The charterers will make good any and all damage."

I said stiffly, "I don't see the necessity for piercing the shell, Commodore Grimes. With the airlock door open *and* the cargo ports we shall have through ventilation."

"Shall we?" he asked. "The way I see it, none at all through the forward part of the ship, where we need it most. We don't sleep in the storerooms, cargo holds and engine spaces, you know. Too, open cargo ports would be an invitation to anything large and nasty to walk, crawl or fly in."

"An electric defense and alarm system . . ." began Bindle.

"Power-consuming," said Grimes. He turned back to me. "I suggest a conventional, trimmable cowl-type ventilator at control-room level. It will have to be so designed that the shaft can be sealed quickly if and when we are able to get upstairs."

"Cutting holes in the shell plating will consume power," I told him, enjoying my feeble triumph, although not for long.

"Yes, Captain, it will. But sooner or later the cells are going to be drained, anyhow, and we might well be stuck on this world for a very long time." Then he asked suddenly, addressing *Basset*'s ship's company in general, "Do you Sirians go in for barbecues?"

"Of course," answered at least four people, not quite achieving synchronization."

"Good. As and from breakfast tomorrow all meals, with the exception of dinner, will be cooked outside. The evening meal will be a cold one, starting tonight if Miss Taine has the materials."

"Why?" she asked.

"Because I don't want a fire after sunset that might attract nocturnal predators. Come to that, I don't want any lights showing outside the ship, for the same reason." He got to his feet and addressed us all. "We'll spend the remaining hours of daylight preparing ourselves for a long stay. And we'll start conserving power right now, by switching off every nonessential light strip. With a bit of luck we shall have the back of the job broken before dark, and in the morning we'll go to the city and see if that temple is still there."

"I was afraid that you were going to suggest that," said Sonya.

I didn't sleep at all well that night. The ship was too quiet. I missed the sussurus of the forced ventilation, the occasional sob and whine of a pump. And I was conscious of the alien smells—of night-blooming flowers, of rotting vegetation—that drifted through our alleyways, eddied through the open doors of our cabins. In one way the unfamiliar aromas were reassuring, however. They were evidence that the officer of the watch was alert and, in addition to keeping a lookout, was trimming the ventilator on to the shifting breeze. The main cause of my insomnia, however, was worry. I had allowed my ship to be made unspaceworthy. Her shell had been pierced, was no longer airtight. I had been assured by my engineers that an hour's work, at the outside, would suffice to restore the integrity of the hull, but I still didn't like it. Apart from anything else, such work should be carried out to the requirements and satisfaction of a Lloyd's surveyor—and where was such an official to be found on Kinsolving?

Sometime in the small hours, I took a long, hard look at myself and found the spectacle amusing. Often in the past, before I attained command, I had laughed at shipmasters whose main exercise of the imagination was to find something to worry about. And there was enough to worry about without dragging Lloyd's of London into it.

I dropped off then, and it seemed that I was almost immediately awakened by Sara. She was bearing not the usual tea tray but a glass of some fruit juice, unchilled. She told me, "The kettle's boiling outside, George. If you want tea you'll have to take your place in the queue by the fire."

I said, "This will do. But it could be colder."

She said, "The refrigerator consumes power. It must be used as little as possible."

The refrigerator was not the only power-consuming equipment in the ship. My morning shower was cold. I like a cold shower when I happen to want one, which is rarely. This was not one of those occasions. I was in a rather bad temper when I joined the others by the fire a few metres from the airlock. But I enjoyed my breakfast—a slab of steak grilled on a steel plate over the hot coals, a mug of tea that had acquired a pleasantly unfamiliar smoky tang. This sort of living would be very nice until the novelty wore off.

Both boats—our own lifeboat and the pinnace that was on loan from the Rim Worlds Navy—were inoperative. Each of the small craft had its own hydrogen fusion power unit, and each of these units behaved in the same inexplicable manner as the big one in the ship. Power was being generated but just wasn't getting as far as the boats' inertial drive or even, in the case of the Rim Worlds Navy pinnace, as far as the laser cannon.

So, if we wished to revisit the city, we should have to walk. To *revisit* the city? As I have said, it didn't look the same as it had done. It looked further away than it had been. Unluckily, the night had been overcast, so Loran had been unable to make any astronomical observations. We knew only that we were on Kinsolving. We did not know where or when Kinsolving was now. Perhaps, in the city, we should find out.

A party was organized. Grimes, of course, was the leader. Sonya was with him. Reluctantly Dr. Thorne and his wife decided to stay with the ship. The scientist was a realist and knew that he was not fit enough for the march through the jungle. I thought myself that Rose Thorne could have coped—she was one of those wispy little women who're fantastically tough under their seemingly frail exteriors—but she was loyal to her husband. Bill Smith and Susan Howard were to represent the scientists. They looked fit enough, both of them, in their mousy way. Ken Mayhew was in the party but Clarisse was staying aboard *Basset*. This would ensure that we were in psionic contact at all times with our base. I was going along, much to Bindle's disgust. He complained that he had been confined to the ship ever since the landing. I told him that there must be somebody there capable and qualified to take *command* during my absence. Finally Sara, our weapons expert, completed the party. Her accurate shooting had saved us all when, with one short burst, she had severed the wire that tethered us to a dimension where we did not belong.

(As a matter of fact, she had told me, in confidence, that her shooting had not been all that marvelous. "Imagine a pistol range," she said. "Imagine a standard target, complete with bull's eye. You're trying to hit the bull. To use big gun phraeology you're having to both lay and train. Then you have the card set up edgewise to you. You split it. Everybody thinks it's marvelous shooting. But it's not—because you don't have to worry about gunlaying. Training is all that counts . . .")

So we set out. Luckily, we had laid in a stock, as recommended by Grimes, of tough drill clothing and heavy boots before lifting off from Port Forlorn. Luckily, we had loaded all sorts of other equipment that I, in my innocence, had thought that we should never need. But I'm a merchant spaceman, pure and simple, whereas Grimes had been brought up in the Federation Survey Service. The FSS, in spite of its name, is more of a fighting navy than anything else but its personnel are, now and again, required to do actual survey work such as exploration. So we had machetes for hacking our way through the jungle and magnetic compasses to ensure that we hacked away in the right direction.

Before starting out we took a careful bearing of the city from the control room. Grimes noted that a prominent tree that we should be able to see from ground level was on this line of sight. Then, standing directly below the ship, he took another bearing of this tree. I asked him why he was doing this.

He replied, "There's such a thing as magnetic deviation, George. In the control room our compasses were affected by all manner of fields, some permanent, some residual. Outside the ship the effect is not so great—although I hope that it's not enough to throw us out too badly . . ."

We set off, Grimes in the lead, holding his compass, Bill Smith and Susan Howard, wielding machetes almost expertly. Now and again he would pause to let the two young scientists go ahead to clear a way. Sonya and myself, submachine guns cocked and ready, followed. Then came Ken Mayhew—armed, but with his weapon slung—and Sara Taine, her automatic carbine in her capable hands. We had one laser pistol, carried by Grimes in a holster, but it was not to be used unless it was absolutely essential. We did not know when, if ever, we should be able to recharge its power cell. (Come to that, when our ammunition for the projectile weapons was exhausted there would be no way of replacing it. The commodore had already suggested to the engineers that they might try to manufacture some arbalests . . .)

It was hot under the trees, hot and damp. We were ankle-deep in decayed vegetation that squelched unpleasantly as we walked. The trees were . . . trees. I'm no botanist. Their tall, straight trunks, exploding many metres above ground level into clouds of green and yellow foliage, were obscured by broad-leaved, sharp-spined creepers that, stretching horizontally between the trees, formed a natural barbed wire entanglement. We did not see any large animal life although we heard things scuttling in the undergrowth. There were flying things—insects?—but they did not come near us. There was something else—reptile? mammal?—that could almost have been a scale model of an ancient biplane. We were not able to make a close examination of it, nor did we much wish to.

We pressed on, sweating profusely. After a while Sonya and I relieved Bill Smith and Susan Howard at the head of our little column.

Grimes, as navigator, was exempt from machete work. Mayhew, as our psionic lookout, was likewise exempt. So was Sara; if there were any chopping to be done with a submachine gun she was the one best qualified to do it. I soon began to wish that I loo was exempt from the manual work. Those strands of creeper not only looked like barbed wire, they were almost as tough. We should have brought along a whetstone. I said as much to the commodore. He grunted, muttering that a man cannot think of everything. His wife—her hands were as blistered as mine—told him tartly that to think of everything was his job. He made no reply.

At last we became aware that the trees were thinning out. More direct sunlight was striking through the high foliage and there were quite long stretches not obstructed by that infernal, thorny creeper. Too, the ground was drier underfoot and the dead leaves were crackling rather than squelching. Under the leaves was a hard surface. We paused and Sonya and I squatted, clearing the dead vegetation away with our hands. What we uncovered was, we decided at length, artificial—but old, very old sort of concrete it could have been weathered and stained with exudations. It was a dirty yellow rather than gray.

"Follow the yellow brick road," said Grimes. He was obviously quoting from some work unfamiliar to me. Sonya and Mayhew rewarded him with a small burst of laughter. He sang untunefully, "We're off to see the Wizard . . ." There was more laughter while Sara, the two young scientists and myself looked at him uncomprehendingly.

We marched on. It was not hard to follow the road. It was almost an avenue, with the tall trees on either side of it. Had it been straight we should have seen the city long before we did. The first sight we had of it as we rounded a wide bend was a lofty tower, a structure that must have been loftier still before its upper levels had crumbled, had fallen to a heap of rubble around its base. There were more towers, a vista of them before us. None was intact. They were like guttered candles, their flames long extinguished. This was, I realized, the city that we had seen, but briefly, when making our escape from the temple.

Guttered candles ...

The towers on the outskirts of the city had been smashed, those towards the centre had been ... melted. As we walked along the radial street, surprisingly free of vegetation, we realized that the heat, whatever had caused it, had been of greater intensity towards the centre of the town. I'm a merchant spaceman but I'm also a naval reserve officer. I know something about weapons. I've taken all the required courses, seen the films. I didn't have to ask Grimes what destructive agent had been unloosed here—how long ago? Already I'd have been willing to predict what we would find at ground zero. I did not think that it would have been damaged by blast or radiation. We marched on.

Apart from half-melted rubble from the towers the streets—the ringroads and the radial thoroughfares—were remarkably free of debris. There were not, as there had been in that other city in this place, *our* city, the carcasses of long-abandoned vehicles. Grimes suggested that we investigate one of the towers before we pressed on further. We did so, entering cautiously through an open door that obviously had not been designed for use by beings even remotely human. It was too low, too wide. The beams of our torches augmented the daylight that seeped through the dust-encrusted windows. The ground level seemed to be no more than a sort of vestibule. In the centre of it was a group of statuary. Possibly it had once been an ornamental fountain. Two many-limbed beings were locked either in combat or copulation. They were, Mayhew told us, like the dead arthropod that he and Clarisse had found in that weird cavern at the heart of the planet, that we had tried to drag out and up with one of the sounding machines. Statues of the beings who had built—and destroyed?—this city, or of familiar or mythological animals? (Alien travelers coming upon some long-deserted human city might assume, from the evidence of statuary in public places, that such beings as mermaids and mermen actually once existed.)

"These were the people," said Mayhew slowly. "Arthropods, like giant Terran crabs. But that should not be surprising. After all we, in *our* universe, are familiar enough with the Shaara. And they're arthropods."

Grimes said, "It's easy to accept the idea of beelike beings building lip a technological civilization. But crabs or lobsters . . ."

"Why not?" asked Mayhew. He shone the beam of his torch on to one of the statues. "Look at the way in which these forelimbs terminate in handling tools—some for coarse, heavy work, some for the most delicate operations. Everything from shifting spanners . . ." the light shifted . . . "to micrometers. One hand—if I may call it a hand—for building a steam engine, another for repairing a lady's watch . . ."

"Mphm," grunted Grimes. "And do you *feel* anything, Ken? Did these beings leave any . . . record? Any . . . ghosts, like the ghost that George saw in the city, the other city, the first time?"

"They may have done, John—but I can't . . . receive. How shall I put it? It's like expecting a Carlotti receiver to pick up a Normal Space-Time transmission, or the other way round. This place was lived in, once. I can tell you that much. But it was so long ago that the . . . records have faded, and even if they hadn't . . ."

We looked at the statues a little while longer. The group compelled interest but it was not the sort of thing I'd have liked to have lived with. And then we went slowly up the ramp that, following the curvature of the inner wall, took us up to the next level. There were living quarters there. There was furniture that might, conceivably, have been beds and chairs. There were what could have been bathrooms—or kitchens. There was one room that could have been a playroom or a workroom, and in this, on a low table, was a beautiful ship model. It was a greatly scaled down replica of the airship that we had seen, a little less than a metre in length, a cylinder, hemispherical at its ends, with a profusion of vanes protruding at odd angles, with what could have been gun turrets.

We took photographs—I should dearly have loved to have taken that airship model and not merely its picture, but we were already loaded with weapons and other equipment—and then made our way out of the ruined tower and continued our march to the city centre. We did not have much time to spare; the sun was approaching the meridian and we were determined to be back aboard *Basset* before dark.

The commodore had put his compass away. Mayhew was now our direction finder. He was homing in on the temple—or whatever form it had assumed in this otherwhen universe.

We found it without difficulty. It was as we had seen it before—a featureless, subtly distorted cube. It stood by itself, at the intersection of imaginary diagonals drawn between four towers—or what had, once, been towers. Now they were little more than shapeless mounds of slag. Not far from the building was a little pile of bright, twisted metal. It looked somehow familiar. We walked to it cautiously, inspected it. It was the wreckage of one of the sounding machines that we had used to rescue Ken and Clarisse. It was the one that the boat had dragged up from the roof of the temple by the power lead. A length of insulated cable was still plugged into it, and from the winch drum extended a tangle of piano wire. But the door of the temple was no longer rectangular but more nearly an ellipse. And the lettering over it was in no familiar script but an indecipherable scrawl. It looked, I thought, like the record left by the claws of a crustacean on damp sand.

"Here's your sounding machine, George," said Grimes. "Or one of them. I wonder if the other one is still on the roof . . ."

"If we could get there we could find out," I said shortly. There was no way of scaling those featureless walls.

"We can go inside the temple," said Grimes.

"Do we want to?" asked Sonya sharply.

"What did we come out here for?" he countered. Then, to Mayhew, "Ken, do you *feel* anything now?"

"No more than before," replied the telepath. "*It* is aware that we are here. What *Its* intentions are I cannot say."

We went to the door. We pushed it. It showed no signs of giving. And then somebody thought of applying a sidewise pressure. The panel moved then, reluctantly at first and then easily, sliding clear of the oval opening. We entered the temple.

There was light of a sort in the huge, windowless room, a gray, shifting twilight. As before there was the *wrongness* of the angles where wall met wall, ceiling and floor. There was the distortion of Space, of Space-Time. When we spoke it was like being inside an echo chamber—not that any of us did much speaking. The . . . the altar was still there—but why should it not have been? The altar—coffin or tesseract, or both, shining wanly with a light that, somehow, was not light, a dead, ashy radiance.

But there were changes. The shape of the door, and the inscription over it. And the hole that we had cut in the roof was no longer there, and there were no marks on the smooth ceiling to show that it ever had been. (In this Time and Space it never had been.)

"What now?" asked Sonya.

"What now?" repeated Grimes. "Well, I suppose we find out if the . . . altar is still functioning." He asked sardonically, "Any volunteers? No? Then can somebody spare something that we can throw into the gateway to the interior?"

"Your pipe," suggested his wife. He said, "I was brought up never make sacrifices to strange gods. And that *would* be a sacrifice . . . talking of sacrifices—any virgins among those present?"

Susan Howard blushed painfully. Sonya said sharply, "That wasn't funny, John."

"My apologies, Miss Howard." Grimes could turn on the charm when he wanted to. "Believe me, I had no idea . . ."

Grimes had opened his pack, taken from it the little parcel of sandwiches that was to be his midday meal. He said, "And now I must apologize to you, Sara. But I can spare one of these dainties; since I have been aboard *Basset* I have been eating too much. Which shall it be? The cheese, I think . . ."

He tossed the little square of filled bread into the tesseract. It faded, vanished.

"So . . ." he murmured.

"What now?" demanded Sonya.

"We go outside, sit down, enjoy our lunch, and then return to the ship."

"You mean to say that we've come all this way just to watch you waste good food?"

"We must be back before dark, my dear. Our expedition has not been altogether fruitless. We know that we have suffered dimensional displacement. We know that the temple still exists, and that the gateway to *It* is still open."

"And we know that *It* likes cheese sandwiches," said Sara. "At least, it didn't spit out the one you fed it . . ."

We all laughed. There was precious little to laugh about so we made the best of what we had.

We left the temple. We sat down on the ground a respectable distance from the building, made a sketchy meal of sandwiches and coffee from our vacuum flasks. When we had finished I walked over to the twisted wreckage of the sounding machine. It looked as though somebody had tried to turn it inside out, not altogether unsuccessfully. Suppose that this had happened to us . . . I thought. But it hadn't, so why worry about it? Or—the idea sent a cold chill down my spine—perhaps it had, and we didn't know about it, whereas that metallic tangle would look the way it had looked in *our* universe . . .

Then the others got to their feet and we started the march back to the ship. I hoped that she would still be where we had left her. Mayhew, reading my thoughts, assured me that she would be.

We came to the outskirts of the city, to the tower that we had entered earlier. I said to Grimes, "Wait a couple of minutes, Commodore."

"What for?" he asked.

"That airship—or spaceship—model. I'm going to pick it up. I think that we should examine it properly when we get back to *Basset*."

He said, "You'll be carrying it. It's your idea, so you do the work." He relented slightly. "If it's too heavy we'll distribute your other bits and pieces among the rest of us."

Sara accompanied me into the building. She hadn't fired a shot all day and was, I was sure, hoping that something would spring out at us from the shadows. She was disappointed. I was not. The beautiful little ship model was where we had last seen it. (There was no reason why it shouldn't have been, but on Kinsolving one takes nothing for granted.) I picked it up. It was heavy, too damned heavy. Holding it carefully in my arms I made my way down the ramp, followed by Sara. It seemed to me that it was not so heavy as it had first been and assumed that it was because I had adjusted to the weight and the awkwardness. When I was outside the others gathered round to look at it, to admire it. It gleamed brightly in the sunlight, its vanes like metal mirrors. There was surprisingly little dust on it.

"It could almost be a lightjammer," said Grimes at last. "If the sails were larger . . ."

"Lightjammer or not," I quipped, "it's certainly not light . . ."

But wasn't it? There was almost no strain on my arms now. And what was that vibration that I could feel? What was the almost inaudible hum that I could hear? And was I the only one hearing it? Somehow it reminded me of being in the control room of a ship, listening to the quiet song of her machinery, main and auxiliary, conscious that the vessel was part of me, no more (and no less) than an extension of my own body. A touch of a finger, and she would lift . . . She lifted.

I was as amazed as the others. I stood there, mouth open, gazing at the glittering machine rising slowly into the clear sky.

"Captain Rule," said Mayhew sharply, "bring it back."

"But how, Ken? How?"

"The same way that you got it up," he told me. "You're in a control room. *Your* control room. You are the ship. The ship is you . . ."

Fantastically, I was looking down at the group outside the ruined tower, on the fringe of the jungle. I could see my own face among the upturned visages. And that was my marker beacon for the landing. I came down slowly, carefully; I hadn't got the feel of this vessel yet but knew that distortion of the vanes would reduce their power-collecting efficiency. Where that knowledge came from I did not know. It was just there. I was more concerned about the possibility of damage to the ship than to myself, notwithstanding the fact that my body was the target that I was aiming for.

The little ship settled gently into my outstretched arms. *A nice piece of pilotage,* I thought smugly. And then I stared at the thing that I was holding like a baby. *What the hell was happening? And what was I doing, and how the hell was I doing it? Was this model a toy, a robot toy, at least partly sentient?*

"Not a toy," said Mayhew. "Not a toy, but a simulator . . ."

"A simulator?"

Mayhew laughed softly. "Yes. And you, Captain, were the first spaceman with whom it's been in contact for the Odd Gods of the Galaxy alone know how many millennia. You've heard of imprinting?"

"Of course. But this is a . . . machine, not an animal."

"And aren't animals machines?" countered Mayhew. "Including ourselves."

This was cheating, I thought. It was the sort of argument that one might expect from a materialist, but not from one whose profession, to many people, smacked of the supernatural.

"So the builders of this city were, in some ways, more advanced than ourselves," said Grimes. "So they could control their machines directly by thought . . . Mphm. I wonder if that thing will take my orders . . . I'm a shipmaster, like you, so there should be some affinity . . ."

He stared at the ship model, scowling with concentration. "Lift," I heard him mutter. *"Lift!"*

Nothing happened.

Sonya tried, then Sara, then the two young scientists, and finally Mayhew. The model stayed snugly in my arms. After they had all given up I sent the thing aloft, drove it around above our heads in a tight circle, made it dive and soar and, finally, hover.

"It's your pet," Grimes admitted. "It's your . . . doggy."

"It's a pity," said Sonya, "that the engineers will have to take it to pieces to see what makes it tick."

"Why should they?" I demanded.

She said, "It's obvious that, somehow, this toy converts radiation into power, usable power. Antigravity, perhaps. And power is just what we need right now."

I said, "And if my ham-handed mechanics ruin this machine without finding out what makes it work—don't forget that I know them better than you do—we shall be no better off than we are now. On the other hand, if we keep it intact we shall have a means of lugging supplies from the ship to wherever we need them. I . . . I feel, somehow, that it will be capable of lifting quite a big weight."

"Mphm," grunted Grimes. "Perhaps we can find out right now just what it can do."

"No," I said. "That will have to wait until we get back to the ship. The engineers will have to make some sort of harness that will fit around the hull without damaging, or even touching the vanes. Don't ask me how I know—I just do—but those surfaces must be at exact angles each to the other."

"Oh, well," said Grimes, "at least you won't have to carry it back to the ship. So you can have your rifle and machete back . . ."

But there was one consolation. As I was fully occupied during the march in steering the model through the forest—I kept it below treetop level—I was exempt from the task of hacking a way through the undergrowth. We had expected that this would not be necessary, that we would be able to keep to the path that we had cleared on our way out to the city, but those vines, in a few hours, had repaired the damage that we had inflicted upon them. The severed ends had reunited themselves. The tangle was even worse than it had been before.

We got back to the ship just before sunset. The others already knew what we had done and seen; Mayhew had been in contact with Clarisse throughout and she had passed on the information.

They were all eager to see the model flying machine—and were all disappointed to discover that it could be handled by nobody except myself. The engineers, of course, were itching to get their greasy paws on it, into it. Grimes and I told them that it was too potentially valuable to us to risk its being rendered inoperative by clueless tampering. If they wanted to do something useful, I said, they could make a sort of harness to fit around its fuselage, the straps of which must not make even the slightest contact with any of the vanes.

I put the model, the simulator, through its paces in front of an admiring (possibly) and envious (definitely) audience. I had really gotten the feel of it during our inarch back from the city. I wished that I had a real ship to play with this way. In such a vessel pilotage would be unalloyed pleasure . . .

Inevitably the thing acquired a name—two names, in fact. It was Bindle who referred to it as a winged *wurst*. It had never occurred to me until then that the hull was sausage shaped. And Betty Boops called it "the captain's doggy". It wasn't long before some genius came up with a new verse to the Dog Star Line's anthem which everybody had to sing, with the usual *arf, arf!* accompaniment.

> *How much is that doggy in the window?*
> *It looks like a sort of a wurst;*
> *You* can't *have that doggy in the window,*
> *Because the Old Man saw it first!*

Very funny, I thought. *Very funny. But they were jealous, that was all.*

We had our evening meal and then I put my doggy through more trials in the darkness. It functioned as well as it had done in broad daylight. Either it had very efficient storage batteries or there was enough radiation, even from the night sky of the Rim, to keep it going. The two engineers watched wistfully. I decided that, to be on the safe side, I would take my pet to bed with me.

The next morning we set out early. The party was as before but we had an easier time of it; the harness that the engineers had devised from wires and webbing allowed us to hang most of our equipment from the little ship.

It looked absurd—imagine a balloon with a basket far larger than the gasbag—but it worked. And we knew, having made the experiment, that the machine could lift two people together with their equipment. One of those persons would have to be me—the captain's doggy was a one-man dog—and the other was to be Sara. It was possible that some fast and accurate shooting might be necessary.

We hacked our way through that blasted jungle again. Sonya remarked that it was a pity that I had not found a robot bulldozer. We came at last to the city. We ignored the ruined towers, went straight to the temple. I brought my doggy to ground level and we unloaded the equipment. Then I arranged the dangling slings to form a sort of seat and went for my first flight. It was very little different from the other flights that I had handled from ground level. I just . . . *thought* myself into the air, just thought myself to the roof of the temple. It was very little different, after all, from handling a big ship, except that

I wasn't having to use my hands to actuate the controls on a panel. I didn't bother to land on the rooftop, just hovered over it. The smooth surface was unmarked. There was no sign of the other sounding machine. But it didn't matter. We now had something far better than those primitive winches.

I returned to the ground, extricated myself from the harness.

We walked into the temple. I brought my doggy in after us. We looked at the altar. Grimes asked, "Are you sure that you don't mind risking it, George?"

I didn't feel especially heroic, but somebody (I supposed) had to go down to where Mayhew and Clarisse had gone. Somebody had to try to find out what made this planet tick. The only reason why it had to be me was that I was the only one with control over a means of transportation.

Sara and I assembled the pieces of equipment that we should need. A sound-powered telephone, with a sufficiency of wire. Two powerful torches. A laser pistol each. A projectile pistol for myself, a submachine gun for Sara. Ammunition. A camera. Food pellets. (I hated the things, but they were easily portable nourishment should it be required.) Water flasks.

Hung around with gear like Christmas trees we strapped ourselves into the harness. I must confess that I rather enjoyed this forced close bodily contact with Sara. She seemed to read my thoughts, murmured, "George . . . At last!"

I said, "Secure all for lift-off."

She replied, "All secure, captain."

Grimes said, "No heroics, George. If you're at all in doubt, get the hell out."

"He's a poet and doesn't know it," quipped Sonya.

Then, obedient to my unspoken command, the little ship lifted, raising us from the floor. I looked up, was relieved to see that there was still ample clearance between it and the roof of the temple. I applied lateral thrust and we drifted slowly over the altar, then hovered. I looked down. If I hadn't been an experienced spaceman I'd have changed my mind about making the descent. It was like—much too like—space as seen from the viewports of a ship running under

Mannschenn Drive. There was the slowly shifting . . . formlessness, the darkness that was deeper than darkness should ever be, the ultimate night.

"Ready?" I asked Sara.

"Ready," she whispered.

We dropped slowly. Grimes and Sonya, Mayhew and Bill and Susan, stood there, watching us go. They looked like reflections of themselves in the distorting mirrors of a fun fair, but not at all funny. Their greatly elongated bodies wavered like candle flames in a draught, shimmered and faded. Grimes raised his hand and his arm seemed to stretch to an impossible length. Sonya said something and her voice was no more than a faraway sighing, long drawn out, like wind soughing drearily over a field of rocks and snow.

Then they were gone. They were gone, whirled away into the far distance, fading, diminishing, tumbling down and through the dark dimensions. They were gone—but we, ourselves, did not seem to be moving. Around us was nothingness, but I sensed the fast approach of solidity from below. I realized that the model was equipped with the same sensory devices—radar?—as a full-sized ship, and that those sensors were . . . mine.

I slowed our rate of descent so that we were falling gently as a feather. My boot soles made gentle contact with a hard surface. I said, "We're here."

Sara complained, "You may be, but I'm not. Even when I stretch my toes are only just touching."

I brought the doggy down a few more centimetres.

Mayhew had told us of a vast chamber with shifting, pulsing lights. And that is where we were. Stalactites and stalagmites of iridescence were its pillars and its roof was one enormous rainbow, the colours of which swept in steady procession up from the far distance to one side of us, setting in the far distance to the other. You know those coin-in-the-slot synthesizers that provide music in some taverns? That was the general effect. Mayhew and Clarisse, being in direct telepathic contact with the godlike planetary intelligence, had been awed. Sara and I, nontelepaths, were awed too—but mingled with our awe was a touch of contempt for the gaudiness, the . . . *kitsch* of it all.

"Not very neat," she whispered, "but definitely gaudy."

We looked around us. There, and there, and there were the desiccated bodies of the explorers who had perished here from time to time in the Past, a Past so remote that it was unimaginable. There were the centauroid beings. There were other things that were more or less human. There was the arthropod, like a huge crab, like the creatures which had been immortalized in enduring metal in that group of statuary. Attached to it was a bright, tangled filament, piano wire, the sounding machine line by which we had tried to drag it to the surface.

A voice sounded in the single receiver of my headset. "George! Are you all right? Report, please."

"We're all right, Commodore," I replied. "We're in the cave described by Ken. There are the lights, and the bodies. How much wire have you for the telephone? We shall want to move around."

He said, "We can splice on at least another kilometre if we have to. Keep on reporting, will you?"

"Wilco," I said.

I thought of unbuckling Sara and myself from the harness so that we could continue our exploration on foot, then decided against it. We would be able to cover a far greater distance in far less time using my doggy. Obedient to my unspoken command it lifted us clear of the floor of the cave, flew towards a pillar of pulsing light that seemed, somehow, to be an important part of the . . . machinery? I don't know why I thought that it was important, it was just a hunch. But when you've been using machines of various kinds all your life you develop a feel for them, even when you're not an engineer. And the first saboteurs must have known, instinctively, just where in the works to throw their wooden shoes to cause the maximum disruption.

Grimes spoke to me again. "Be careful," he said. "Ken tells me that *It* knows that you're down there. *It's* puzzled. *It* can't read your mind the same way that it read Ken's."

I said, "My nose fair bleeds for *It*."

We drifted slowly over the long-dead bodies. I paused above two of the humanoids. Before they dried out they must have been very like ourselves, I thought. Their faces were upturned; their expressions seemed to change, their limbs to stir under the continually shifting lights. *Humanoid?* Human, rather. A man and a woman, who must have been handsome before the skin was stretched so tightly over their bones. How long ago had they died? How had they died?

Reluctantly I came in to a landing. Sara and I unbuckled ourselves from the harness. The doggy hung there, humming faintly, like a faithful hound awaiting orders. We walked slowly towards the bodies. I knelt beside that of the man, pulled what was a weapon of some kind from the holster at his wide belt of metal mesh. It was a pistol, although not a projectile weapon. I found the firing stud and, foolishly, pressed it. Nothing happened, of course. Its power cell was very dead.

Sara removed a bracelet from the woman's wrist. She said, "This is like grave-robbing, but . . ." Then, "This must be a watch . . . There's a dial, but blank. And a stud that you press . . . And nothing happens."

"Batteries have a limited life span," I said. "Even when they're not being used, there's leakage. H'm. These people had a level of technology not dissimilar to our own. Their clothing could be plastic . . ." Both man and woman were wearing kilt and shirt, dull green in colour, heavy sandals. I lifted the hem of the man's kilt, rubbed it between my fingers. The material crumbled to a fine powder.

"Not dissimilar," agreed Sara, "and certainly not superior. I, for one, wouldn't like to walk around not knowing when I was going to do an involuntary strip act."

"This stuff is *old*," I told her.

"So's Doggy old, but she's functioning well enough."

"She's metal," I said.

"Metal, shmetal," she sneered.

"What are you arguing about?" demanded Grimes. He could hear my voice, of course, through the throat microphone but was getting only one side of the conversation.

I made a brief report.

"Get photographs," he ordered. "Clothed, then unclothed."

"You want us to strip the corpses?" I asked, shocked.

"They won't mind," he said callously.

"I'm not some sort of ghoul, or necrophiliac, Commodore," I protested.

"This is a scientific expedition," he said.

"I'm not a scientist," I told him.

"You're under charter to a scientific expedition, Captain Rule. And the terms of the charter party, which you signed, require that you render every assistance to the scientists."

He was right, of course. I told Sara what he wanted and we got the first of the photographs. Then we set about the distasteful task that I couldn't help thinking of as desecration, Sara removing the woman's clothing, myself the man's. Fortunately, there was very little handling involved; the plastic material disintegrated at a touch, leaving only the metallic belts, sandal buckles and the like. The male, allowing for desiccation over the aeons, looked normal enough. So did the female, apart from a pair of secondary nipples under her breasts. There was no body hair on either of them—but many human peoples practice depilation and, come to that, extra pairs of breasts aren't all that uncommon.

We put the metal articles into the specimen bag and then got back into the harness. Obedient as ever, Doggy lifted and headed towards our original objective. There were no more corpses between us and that pillar of multicoloured light. There was no reason for us to stop, to delay the . . . the confrontation?

Mayhew's voice came through the earpiece. "George *It's* aware of you. Be careful."

Now he tells me, I thought.

"George I think you'd better turn back!"

Then Grimes, "Captain Rule, return to the surface. That's an order."

I said to Sara, "They're scared of something. They want us to return."

She replied, "Then we return." I heard the sharp click as she cocked her submachine gun. "I've a feeling myself that we've outstayed our welcome."

Doggy came round in a wide arc. We should have no trouble finding our way to the . . . the exit; all that I had to do was follow the cable of the sound-powered telephone. Doggy came round in a wide arc—and kept on coming, steadying up, once again, on the pillar of light.

"Come round, you little bitch," I muttered. "Come *'round,* damn you." It was happening the way it sometimes happens with big ships, no matter what you do, no matter what you try they seem to exhibit a will of their own. And was Doggy exhibiting a will of *her* own? I did not think so. She was *mine,* or had been mine, but now some other intelligence was taking over from me in that miniaturized control room.

I . . . concentrated. I couldn't turn her again, but I could—but for how much longer?—check her progress towards the column of luminescence. She wanted to obey me—I felt—but a stronger will than mine was taking her over. It was she and me against . . . *It.* Two against one. A human mind and a low-grade robot intelligence against a near-deity. But it wasn't a real god, I told myself. It was only a robot with all a robot's limitations. (And so was Doggy, come to that, a very minor robot, and I was only a human.)

She was faithful to me. I was the prince who had awakened her from her aeons'-long slumber. She was imprinted on me. She was trying to obey my orders. But *something* had hold of her leash and was . . . pulling. She had all four paws dug in yet was slowly being dragged forward.

"Bail out," I ordered Sara.

She unsnapped her buckles, dropped to the ground. I followed her. We stood there helplessly watching Doggy's struggles. She would jerk back half a metre and then, slowly, slowly, would lose all that she had gained, more. And I identified with her, as any shipmaster always identifies with his vessel. Oh, she was only a model, and she hadn't been made by beings even remotely humanoid but, from the start, there had been symbiosis.

"If we lose her," whispered Sara, "we've had it . . ."

Oddly enough that aspect of it all hadn't occurred to me until Sara put it into words. And then I felt fear, fear such as I had never known before in my entire career—and I admit that I've been scared stiff more than once.

Sara opened fire on the pillar of flame. It may have done some good—or harm, according to the viewpoint—but there were no visual indications that anything was being accomplished. The stream of tracer just lost itself in the greater luminosity of the column of light.

I pulled my own pistol from its holster. I realized, after I had it out, that it was the laser and not the projectile weapon. And what could it do that the heavy slugs could not?

But . . .

Hastily I set the weapon to wide beam. I took aim, pressed the firing stud. I aimed not at the flaming pillar but at Doggy. The dazzling light fell full on the vanes projecting from her sleek body. Radiation was what she fed on, what gave her strength. Perhaps . . .

"Turn," I whispered, vocalizing my thoughts. "Turn . . . Turn . . ."

She turned, not slowly, spinning on her short axis.

"Steady, now, steady as you go . . . Accelerate!" And, "Run!" I shouted to Sara. "Run! Follow the telephone line!"

We ran. Luckily the cavern floor was smooth, as most of my attention was devoted to Doggy. I had to stop her at the point where the telephone wire curved up from the horizontal to the vertical. The headset itself I tore off, dropped. There was too much risk of my becoming entangled in the wire.

Ahead of us, Doggy hesitated, started to swing back towards us. I could see that as yet she was nowhere near the opening of the shaft to the upper world. I gave her another burst from my laser pistol—and, her cells recharged, she came once again under my control.

We ran past the bodies of the two humans. Briefly I wondered if we should join them. We dashed through a curtain of cold, blue fire that suddenly rose from the cavern floor. Doggy, I saw, had reached the vertical telephone wire. She was waiting for us. Had I ordered her to do so? I could not remember.

Another curtain of fire, and another . . . A weapon, possibly, a weapon evolved for use against some life form other than ourselves. So it wasn't so bloody omniscient, omnipotent after all. These pyrotechnics, frightening as they were, weren't hurting us.

We were under the telephone cable—a filament stretching upwards into . . . nothingness. We were under the waiting Doggy. The high-pitched whine that she was emitting set my teeth on edge. *Down!* I thought imperatively. *Down!*

She dropped slowly. With fumbling fingers I caught the dangling harness, strapped Sara in and then myself.

Up . . . Up . . . Lift, you bitch! Lift!

We could feel the tension in the straps but our feet were still firmly on the ground. And something was happening in the cavern. Lights were flashing all around us and the "sky" was a terrifying sheet of multicoloured flame.

Lift! I commanded. *Lift!* The bodies of the other explorers, the long-dead beings who had preceded us, were on their feet, animated by some force that had taken control of them, were shambling towards us, stiffly, jerkily. The naked, skeletal man and woman . . . the centaurs . . . a thing like a big-headed dinosaur . . . the giant arthropod. Like robots they advanced, walking at first, then crawling as the stream of tracer from Sara's gun hosed into them, knocking them from their feet, shattering fragile limbs. And then only the great crab was left, its carapace split in a dozen places, but three of its spindly legs still functional and one horrid claw raised menacingly.

Doggy was whining and straining but she still could not lift our weight.

I pulled my laser pistol again. I hated having to do it. It was like (I imagine) flogging a faithful, willing but utterly exhausted horse. I let her have a burst of energy in the belly. She screamed. But we were rising at last, slowly at first then faster, faster, through a darkness that was utter emptiness rather than the mere absence of a light source. We were lifting. We . . .

With a dreadful certainty, I knew that we were falling again. Again I used my laser pistol. Again Doggy screamed.

And Sara screamed. An arm, attenuated, enormously long, was reaching for us, the fingers of the hand writhing like tentacles. She was swinging her gun around to bear upon this apparition. Just in time to prevent her from firing I caught her wrist. In spite of the distortion I had recognized the unusual ring on one of the fingers, a wide band cut from Carinthian black opal on which was mounted a spiral nebula in silver filigree. Sonya's ring.

Other arms stretched out for us, other hands. They caught hold of us, of the harness. They dragged us away from the altar, into the temple. We saw them standing around us, their faces pale, strained.

"Unbuckle yourselves!" Grimes shouted. "Hurry! Hurry!"

And there was need for haste. Doggy screamed for the last time as fire flashed from her miniature ports, from the tips of her vanes. She fell heavily, with a clattering crash, just missing Sara and myself as we scrambled clear from the tangle of webbing. There was a trickle of blue smoke from her, bearing the acridity of hot metal.

Grimes said, his voice shaky, "I thought you'd had it . . ." He went on, "But you're back . . ."

"Thanks to Doggy," I said. I looked down at the pitiful little heap of wreckage. "You know, if we get out of this mess I'm going to keep her at home, with my other souvenirs, in a glass case . . ."

"Doggy in the window," said Sara.

I was the only one who didn't think it funny.

GRIMES AND THE GAIJIN DAIMYO

Grimes and the Gaijin Daimyo

KITTY KELLY, BY THIS TIME, did not need to be told to make herself at home in Grimes' day cabin aboard *Faraway Quest*. The old ship had now been a long time, too long a time, on Elsinore while repair work on her inertial drive unit dragged on, and on, and on. Shortly after the *Quest*'s arrival at Port Fortinbras, Kitty had interviewed Grimes for Station Yorick and had persuaded him to tell one of his tall—but true—stories. The commodore, sitting at ease with pipe and glass to hand, had gone over well with Station Yorick's viewers. Soon he became a regular guest on Kitty's Korner, as Ms. Kelly's programme was called.

"And still you're here," she remarked brightly as she set up her recording apparatus, adjusting lenses and microphones.

"A blinding glimpse of the obvious!" he growled. *Still*, he thought, watching the raven-haired, blue-eyed, creamy-skinned girl in the emerald green dress that left very little to the imagination, *there were compensations, or at least one compensation—and she was it.* He would feel a strong twinge of regret when, at long last, *Faraway Quest* was again spacewordly and on her way.

"That's it," she said finally, getting briefly to her feet and then subsiding into an easy chair, facing Grimes in his, stretching her long, shapely legs before her. "Ready to roll. But pour me a drink first, Johnnie boy."

Grimes had learned not to wince at this appellation. (After all, during a long and, according to some, misspent life, he had often been called worse.) He went to his liquor cabinet, poured an Irish whisky for Kitty and constructed a pink gin for himself.

"Here's mud in your eye!" she toasted, raising her glass.

"And in yours," he replied.

After what was more of a gulp than a ladylike sip she switched on the audio-visual recorder. "And now, Commodore," she said, "can you tell us, in nontechnical language if possible, why your ship, the Rim Worlds Confederacy's survey vessel, *Faraway Quest*, has been so long on Elsinore?"

"Because my inertial drive is on the blink," he said.

"In what way?"

"First of all it was the governor. There were no spares available here. Too, the inertial drive unit is a very old one; it came with the ship—and she's no chicken! So there were no spares anywhere at all for this model. A new governor was fabricated in our workshops at Port Forlorn, on Lorn. It was shipped out here. Then my engineers had to turn down the shaft so that it would fit the bearings. The drive was tested—and the main thruster fell to pieces. And so on, and so on . . ."

"I'm only a planet lubber," she said, "but it seems to me that much time and money would have been saved if your *Faraway Quest's* inertial drive unit had been renewed, in its entirety, long before it got to the state that it's in now. After all, the Rim Worlds Navy, to which your *Quest* belongs, is not some penny-pinching star tramp outfit."

Grimes laughed. "Except in times of war, navies are as expert at penny-pinching as any commercial shipowner! And I often think that the only bastard who really wants to keep the old *Quest* running is me."

"You have been in her a long time, haven't you, Commodore?"

"Too right. She started life as one of the Interstellar Transport Commission's Epsilon Class freighters. When she became obsolescent, by the Commission's rather high standards, she was put up for sale. I happened to be in the right place at the right time—or the wrong place at the wrong time!—on the world about which her lay-up orbit had been established. Very temporarily I had too much money in my bank account. So I bought her, changing her name from *Epsilon Scorpii* to *Sister Sue*. She became the flagship—and the only ship—of my own star tramp company, Far Traveller Couriers. She replaced a deep space pinnace that I'd been running single-handedly, called *Little Sister*. Well, I tramped around for quite a while, making not-too-bad a living. It helped that the Federation Survey Service, into which I'd sort of been dragged back with a reserve commission, organized the occasional lucrative charter for me. And then, while I was trying to weather a rather bad financial storm, I drifted out to the Rim Worlds. At that time Rim Runners, the Confederacy's merchant fleet, were going through a period of expansion. They were buying anything—anything!—that could clamber out of a gravity well and still remain reasonably airtight. They offered me a good price for the ship and offered, too, to absorb myself and my people with no loss of rank or seniority while guaranteeing repatriation to those who did not wish to become RimWorlders . . ."

"But you became a RimWorlder, Commodore."

"Yes, Kitty. And the ship was renamed again—to *Rim Scorpion*. For a while I stayed in command of her. Then, at about the same time that I got a shore job, as Rim Runners astronautical superintendent, the ship had another change of name, to *Faraway Quest*. She was converted into a survey ship. Every time that she was required for survey work—which wasn't all that often—Rim Runners would second me to the Navy, in which I held, and still hold, a reserve commission. After all, I know the ship and, too, held command in the Federation Survey Service before I became an owner-master."

Kitty laughed sympathetically. "We can understand very well how much this ship means to you, Commodore." She laughed again. "Now I'm talking off the top of my head—but what a pity it is that you can't modify your Mannschenn Drive unit, your Time-twister, to take the ship back into the Past so that she can be refitted with a suitable inertial drive at a pre-inflation price. After all, there was that first story you told me, about the Siege of Glenrowan, when a modified Mannschenn Drive was used to send you back to 1880, Earth Old Reckoning, so that you could change the course of history."

"I didn't change the course of history," said Grimes stiffly. "I prevented the course of history from being changed."

"Ensuring," snapped Kitty, "that my ancestor, the sainted Ned himself, was awarded a hemp necktie."

"In any case," Grimes told her, "there was no *physical* Time travel. I was just sent back to occupy the mind of one of my own ancestors who was among those present at the siege."

"And so even though your interstellar drive, your Mannschenn Drive, does odd things to the Space-Time Continuum, even though FTL flight is achieved by having the ship, as you told me once, going astern in Time while going ahead in Space, physical Time-travel is impossible? But isn't it true that most governments have forbidden research into possible techniques for using the Mannschenn Drive for real Time-travel, physical as well as psychological?

"Have *you* ever been involved in such research?" She grinned. "After all, Commodore, there's not much that you haven't been involved in."

Grimes made a major production of refilling and lighting his pipe. He replenished Kitty's glass, and then his own. He settled back in his chair.

He said, "There was one rather odd business in which I played my part. In this very ship . . ."

She asked sweetly, "And did you interfere as you did at Glenrowan, changing the course of history?"

"I did *not* change the course of history on either occasion. I kept history on the right tracks."

"But have you ever thought that these are the wrong tracks, that we're living in an alternative universe that could never have come into being but for your interference?"

"I like being *me*," he told her, "and I'm pretty sure that you like being *you*. And we are *us* only because *our* history has made us what we are. In an alternative universe we might have no existence at all."

She laughed. "We're neither of us cut out to be philosophers, Commodore. Just do us all a favour and wear your storyteller's hat for the next hour or so."

"You're the boss," said Grimes. He got up, recharged glasses, refilled and lit his pipe, then settled down back in his chair. "You want a story. Here it is."

It was quite a few years ago, he said, more than just a few. It was when this ship was still called *Sister Sue* and I was both her master and her owner. It was during that period when the Federation Survey Service was still throwing charters my way like bones to a hungry dog. Very often I'd be carrying Survey Service cargoes from Earth to the various Survey Service bases throughout the Galaxy.

This was such an occasion. A cargo of *sake* and soy sauce and assorted pickles to Mikasa Base, the personnel of which was then, and probably still is, Japanese. Rather unusually I was loading not at Port Woomera in Australia but at the new spaceport just outside Yokohama in Japan. I still think that spaceports should be well away from heavily populated areas but the Japanese wanted one of their very own and they got it. Of course there were very strict regulations—inertial drive only, when landing or lifting off. No, repeat and underscore no, use of reaction drive when in the spaceport vicinity. But my inertial drive wasn't in the same mess that it's in now and I was reasonably sure that shouldn't need a squirt of superheated steam in an emergency.

It was my Mannschenn Drive that got me into trouble.

Well, even though Japan is a very small target compared to Australia, I found it without any trouble, and found the spaceport and set down in the middle of the triangle formed by the marker beacons. And then, as so often happens, especially when governmental agencies are involved, it was a case of hurry up and wait. The cargo wasn't ready for me. This pleased me rather than otherwise. The ship was on pay, which meant that myself and my officers were on pay. I treated myself to a couple or three weeks leave and booked on a JAL airship from Narita to Sydney, changing there to a Qantas flight to Alice Springs. My parents were pleased to see me. My mother was her charming, hospitable self and my father, as always, was both a good listener and a good talker—and could he talk on his pet subject, history! As I've told you before he was an author of historical romances and always prided himself on the thoroughness of his research.

He asked me about my impressions of Japan and told me that he had visited that country, doing research for one of his novels, a few weeks prior to my arrival. "Yokohama," he said, "is handy for two shrines that you will find worth a visit. There's Admiral Togo's flagship *Mikasa,* in which he defeated the Russian Navy during the Russo-Japanese War, preserved for posterity as the English have preserved Nelson's *Victory.* And, on a hilltop on the Miura Peninsular, is the tomb of Will Adams and his Japanese lady wife . . ."

"Will Adams?" I asked. "But that's not a Japanese name, surely? Why should a foreigner be honoured by having his grave regarded as a shrine?" My father laughed. "Oh, Will Adams was a *gaijin,* a foreigner, when he first set foot on Japanese soil. He was the first Englishman—although not the first European—in Japan. He was an Elizabethan—the first Elizabeth, of course—sea dog. He was pilot major—senior navigator—of a small fleet of Dutch ships that sailed to Japan in an attempt to get some share of the trade that had become the monopoly of the Portuguese. Only one ship, Adams' ship, reached Japan. Adams was sort of adopted by the Shogun, the real ruler—the Emperor was little more than a figurehead—and was made a Samurai, and then a Daimyo, which translates roughly to Baron. He was known as the Anjin-sama—Pilot-lord—and as the Miura Anjin, after the estates on the Miura Peninsular that he was granted. He held the rank of admiral in the Japanese Navy . . ."

I said, "He must have been quite a character . . ."

"He was," agreed my father. "I hope to use him in my next novel. He's been used before, of course, but I think that I shall be able to introduce a new twist. But if you find out anything interesting about him when you're back in Yokohama, let me know, will you?"

"I will," I told him. "I'll ask Yoshi Namakura what she knows about him."

"Yoshi Namakura?" he asked.

"My chief Mannschenn Drive engineer. Oddly enough, in spite of her name, this is her first time in Japan. Her first time on Earth, too. I engaged her in Port Southern, on Austral, where her family have lived for generations. An attractive wench and clever with it. A list of letters after her name as long as my arm. Doctorates in mathematics and physics and the Odd Gods of the Galaxy alone know what else. And ardently

Japanese. Knowing Yoshi I'm sure that she'll have been making the rounds of the local shrines, pouring libations and clapping her hands and bowing . . ."

"I have often wished, John," said my mother, "that you did not have such a casual attitude towards religion."

"But I've always had the impression, Matilda," I told her, "that you're an agnostic."

"I am. But I try to avoid giving offence."

"Except when you want to," muttered my father.

"That's different, George," she snapped.

"I suppose that I was rather making fun of Yoshi," I admitted. "But she's such a *serious* person. But as far as Shinto is concerned I have far more respect for it than for many other faiths and I quite approve of the honouring of distinguished ancestors."

"You'd better honour me," said my father, "or I'll come back and haunt you!"

And that was that. The rest of my leave passed very pleasantly and it was with mixed emotions that, eventually, I made my way back to Yokohama. Mixed emotions? Yes. One's boyhood home holds a large place in one's affections but so does a ship, especially a ship that one both commands and owns.

It was early evening when I got back to the Yokohama spaceport. *Sister Sue* was the only ship on the ground. The loading gantries had been set up about her but were still idle. She stood there in black silhouette against the odd, lemon-yellow sky, a dark tower surrounded by an elaborate tracery of metal, looking like one of those intricate Japanese ideographs that you see on ornamental scrolls and screens.

Security was fairly tight and I had to identify myself to the spaceport gatekeeper and then, again, to the guard on duty at the foot of the ramp. Port regulations required that I employ him so I was pleased to find that he was taking his job seriously. In any case the charters, the Survey Service, would be picking up the bill for his wages. Once I was in the airlock I looked at the indicator screen to see who was aboard. The third officer was the shipkeeper. Normally, especially in a rather exotic port such as this, he would have been sulking in solitary state, feeling very hard done by. But, it seemed, he was not alone. Neither the chief Mannschenn Drive engineer nor the communications officer was off painting the town red. But surely Yoshi would have made friends in Yokohama or, even, discovered distant relatives. Perhaps, I thought, she was entertaining some such or one such on board.

I took the elevator up from the airlock to my quarters. On its way it passed the Mannschenn Drive compartment. And the Drive was running—the oscillating whine that it made whilst operational was unmistakable. Perhaps, I thought, Yoshi was recalibrating the controls, a job that can be done only when the ship is at rest on a planetary surface. Recalibration should not be carried out without the permission of the master. But so what? Billy Williams, my chief officer, had the authority to issue such permission during my absence. But I was uneasy nonetheless.

I stopped the elevator then went down again to the Mannschenn Drive compartment. The door into it was both shut and locked. I could hear the whine of the machinery inside and, very faintly, the sound of voices. I rapped on the door. And again, more loudly. *They must be deaf in there,* I thought.

In my pocket was my keyring and on it, among others, was *my* key, the master key that would give me access to any compartment in the ship. I took it out, fitted its flat surface into the recess designed for its reception.

The door slid open, making a sharp clicking sound as it did so. One of the two men intently watching the display in the screen that had been set up alongside the complication of slowly rotating, ever-precessing flywheels—had the Drive been working at full capacity it would have been suicidal to have looked directly at it—turned his head and grumbled, "Come in, come in, whoever you are. This is Liberty Hall. You can spit on the mat and call the cat a bastard." Then he saw who it was and muttered, "Sorry, sir. We weren't expecting you back just yet."

It was the third officer and with him was the electronic communications officer. I glared at the two young men and they looked back at me. They were more than a little scared. And I'd give the puppies something to be scared about.

"Where is Ms. Namakura?" I demanded. "What are the pair of you doing in the Mannschenn Drive room, running a machine that only qualified personnel are supposed to touch? The Odd Gods of the Galaxy alone know what damage you'll do with your tinkerings!"

"She . . . she *was* here, sir," stammered the third.

"Is she in her quarters? Get her back down here. At *once*."

"She . . . she's not there . . ." stammered the third.

"She's not *now* . . ." said Sparks.

"Are you mad?" I almost yelled, glaring at them. Somehow in the light that was coming from the screen the skin of their faces had an odd yellowish tinge and their eyes a peculiar slant to them. I remembered then that, like Yoshi Namakura, they both had Japanese blood, although, unlike hers, theirs was much diluted and their names were European. But the three of them, spaceman officer, communications officer, and Mannschenn Drive engineer, had always been as thick as thieves. There were those who suggested that they had a *ménage a trois* going. Perhaps they had, but what of it? A ship is not a Sunday School outing.

"Look at the screen, sir," said Sparks.

I looked. The picture was that of the poop of some sort of ancient sailing vessel, a galleon, a small one, at sea. In the background were five other ships of the same type, on parallel courses.

"So you got some new spools for the play master," I said. "But what's a playmaster doing here? Its proper place is in the wardroom."

"This is not a playmaster, sir, although it's adapted from one. Running in conjunction with the Drive it gives a picture of the Past."

I remembered that conversation with my father. "And now I suppose you'll try to tell me that you're picking up coverage of Will Adams' voyage to Japan." I laughed. "As I was told the story, only one of those Dutch ships got here."

"Those are not Dutch ships, sir," said Sparks. "Look!"

He did something to the controls under the screen, zoomed into that poop deck in the foreground. There was an almost modern-looking binnacle and there was a large wheel with one man at it, clad only in baggy trousers, steering the ship. He was obviously an Asiatic. Japanese? Chinese? But that wheel . . . It looked wrong. Just *when* had the wheel replaced the tiller? I was pretty sure that it had been well after Will Adams' time.

A man and a woman came into view—he a bearded European, tall, in a white shirt with ballooning sleeves, white trousers that flapped about his legs. Instead of a belt he wore a wide sash; thrust into it on one side was a sheathed sword, on the other a big, flintlock pistol. The woman was in what I thought of as traditional Japanese finery, with elaborately upswept hair. I recognized her, although I was more used to seeing her in uniform.

They were talking, this man and woman. What a pity it was that there was no sound—and lip reading is not one of my accomplishments. They paced slowly back and forth. Then the man sat on one of the two bronze cannons mounted on the poop and Yoshi subsided gracefully onto the wooden deck, leaning back against his legs.

"So far," Sparks told me, "this is the furthest into the Future that we can get a clear picture. But the ones of the finish of the voyage are getting clearer all the time . . ."

"The furthest into the *Future*?" I asked, bewildered.

"Perhaps I didn't make myself clear, sir. What I meant was the future as reckoned from the start of the voyage . . ."

"*What* voyage?"

Sparks fiddled with the controls. He got a clear picture of a seaport, a Japanese seaport, with the six galleons looking out of place among the smaller craft, with the wharf crowded with people, with armoured Samurai wielding long staffs to clear the way for those embarking aboard the ships, the tall European, attired now as a Japanese nobleman, his lady *(my* chief Mannschenn Drive engineer), the armoured Samurai of his personal guard . . .

And the ships cast off and their unfurled sails filled and the gaily coloured streamers of bunting (or of silk?) fluttered from their mastheads and orange flame and white smoke gushed from their gunports as a salute was fired to the emperor or the shogun or whoever it was who had come to see them off.

I thought again what a pity it was that there was no sound.

"And now," said Sparks, "the finish of the voyage . . ."

The picture was dim, distorted, the perspective all wrong, the colours sagging down the spectrum. But I recognized that coastline, that entrance to one of the world's—Earth's, I mean—finest harbours, with the sheer cliffs of the North Head and the less regular rock formations on the south side. The ships, the galleons, were standing in with a fair wind, guided by one of the small pinnaces that had carried out a preliminary survey.

"It's clearer than it was the last time we tried," said the Third Officer. "Do you realize what that means?" He sounded frightened.

So he was frightened and I was both puzzled and angry.

"Just what the hell is going on here?" I demanded.

There were swivel chairs in the Mannschenn Drive room and we sat in them, turning them so that we did not have to look at those ever-recessing rotors or the screen with its disturbing pictures. It was heavy work at first trying to drag the story out of them but, at last, the dam broke. Then it was hard for me to get a word in edgewise, to ask the occasional question, to try to get clarification of various points.

It was Yoshi, of course, who had made the modifications to the Mannschenn Drive unit. I suspect that she had been toying with such an idea for quite some time but, until her visit to the home of her ancestors, had lacked a strong motivation. Shortly after *Sister Sue*'s arrival at Yokohama spaceport, she had made the pilgrimage to Will Adams' burial place, had made Shinto obeisance at the shrine. The story of Adams fascinated her. The man was among those who, with only the slightest nudge, could have changed history. And why should not she, Yoshi Namakura, supply that nudge?

She had Sparks and the Third Officer eating out of her hand. They would help her. Although they did not share her knowledge of the workings of the Mannschenn Drive they could be trusted to follow her instructions and to monitor her progress. They were to snatch her back to her own Time should things go wrong. (But, as they were beginning to realize, *right* for her could be *wrong* for very many people, including themselves. People face death—they're doing it all the time—but how do they face the utter extinction of never having been at all?)

History is full of *Ifs*. *If* Napoleon had accepted the American inventor Fulton's offer to build him steam-driven warships . . . (imagine a squadron of steam frigates, wearing the French flag, at Trafalgar!). *If* Pickett's charge at Gettysburg had been successful, and the Confederacy had won the War Between the States . . . *If* that special train had been derailed, as intended, by Ned Kelly's freedom fighters at Glenrowan . . .

And *if* Will Adams, the Anjin-sama, had been allowed to build European-style ships—with improvements, the Japanese excel at improving things—armed with cannons, officered by Samurai . . . *If* an expedition under the command of the Anjin-sama, the master navigator, himself had pushed south on a voyage of exploration . . .

And *if,* I thought, on the some yet-to-become established Time Track he had pushed south, reaching Australia, founding a colony . . . history might be, would be changed on a grand scale. With the resulting population shifts, with the wars that didn't happen in *our* history books, with inventions made before their time or not made at all, many of us might never have been born. I'm an Australian, as you know. Would I, could I have happened in an Australia that had been a Japanese colony founded in the seventeenth century?

I demanded, "Why don't you bring her back? Why don't you snatch her back to our here and now from a time before she's had a chance to influence Will Adams and his sponsors?"

Sparks said, "We've tried, sir. But she told us to pull her back only if things went wrong. She must be carrying some device that will keep her where and when she is, no matter what *we* do, as long as things are going to *her* satisfaction."

"Then somebody," I said, "will have to go back to a Time before the fleet sets sail to throw a spanner in the works . . ."

"I'll go, sir," said the third bravely. "Sparks has to stay here to operate the controls."

"I'll go," I said, not feeling at all brave. Oh, I did not doubt the third officer's courage but, after all, he had been under Yoshi's influence and, too, had Japanese blood himself. (Was it my imagination or had he been looking more and more Japanese as we had been talking? Was it proof that *our* time line was fading out?)

"But . . ." objected both young men, yet I thought that I could detect a note of relief in their voices.

"Wait here," I told them. "Don't touch anything till I get back."

In my quarters I disguised myself as well as I could—by putting on a rather elaborately embroidered dressing gown over my shirt and trousers. From the ship's arms locker I took a stungun and a laser pistol, checking each to see that it was fully charged. I stuck both weapons in my dressing gown sash. I glanced in the mirror. I didn't look Japanese. I looked like a middle-aged shipmaster of European origin clad in a dressing gown hung around with incongruous weaponry. But I hoped that Sparks would be able to make me arrive at night—and the lighting in and around seaports wasn't all that good in those days. With any luck at all I should be able to do what I knew, with increasing certainty, I had to do, undetected.

I returned to the Mannschenn Drive room.

Sparks and the third stared at me in some amazement. I ignored this. I told Sparks what I wanted and he fiddled with the controls of the monitor screen, at last got what I wanted. Despite the midnight darkness it was quite a clear picture, the galleons, with their lofty masts, the furled sails glimmering palely on their spars, were alongside in the Japanese seaport. There were a few, a very few, lights aboard them. Ashore watchfires, around which moved dark figures. What little light there was threw glimmering reflections from polished spearheads.

"That will do," I said. "The night before sailing day. All stores—including powder—aboard. All hands ashore enjoying a last night in the arms of their lady loves . . ."

"What are you going to *do*, sir?" almost wailed Sparks.

"Never mind. I'm just going to do it. Or try to do it. Just get me back there, not too close to any of the sentries."

"I think I can manage that, sir. I put Yoshi down by the side of the road where the Anjin-sama was taking his morning ride, unaccompanied. Do you see that circle painted on the deck? Just stand in it. Look at the rotors."

I did as he directed, gave him last instructions. "As soon as I've shunted history back onto its right track, use the recovery procedure. For Ms. Yamakura as well as for myself. It should work on her this time. Things will have gone very badly wrong—from her viewpoint."

I looked at those blasted, precessing rotors. They seemed to be dragging me into some dark chasm that had opened in the Space-Time continuum. And their motion was subtly . . . *wrong*. Their precession was not confined to the fourth dimension, somehow involved more dimensions than merely four.

And then the night air was cold on my face. A light drizzle was falling. I was standing in a puddle that chilled my feet in their light shoes. I could smell the smoke of the watchfires and something spicy cooking over one of them. I was sorry that in these circumstances I could not sample whatever it was. Somewhere a stringed musical instrument was plaintively *plinking* away. The nearest group of sentries were talking in quite loud voices and laughing. I wondered what the joke was.

I pulled the stungun out of my dressing gown sash, walked as quietly as possible towards the ships. Towards the one that was third in line from the head of the wharf; she had fewer lights aboard her than did the others and that at her gangway was almost out. The gangway, a slatted, wooden ramp, rattled slightly as I set foot on it. I froze. But the other gangways were rattling too as the ships stirred in the slight swell that was coming in from seaward.

At the head of the gangway was a sentry. He was standing there, leaning on the bulwark, more than half-asleep. After a brief buzz from my stungun, he was wholly asleep but did not fall, propped up as he was.

I wished that I'd been able to study constructional details of the ships of this period. The powder magazine would be, I thought, amidships, well below decks. But aft there should be a storeroom, the lazarette, with flammables of various kinds—canvas and cordage and barrels of tar and oil. So I made my way towards the stern. I let myself into the officers' quarters in the sterncastle, hoping that none of them would be spending this last night aboard.

I used my laser pistol, at a very low setting, as a torch. At last I found what I was looking for two decks down: a small hatch. I lifted it, looked down into what seemed to be the bo's'n's store. There were coils of rope, bolts of canvas. There were barrels and there was the smell of tar. I aimed the pistol at one of the tar barrels, adjusted the beam. A viscous black fluid spilled out, igniting as it did so. The fire that I'd started needed no further help from me. I hoped that I'd be able to get out and clear before it reached the magazine.

I scampered up the ladders, pursued by the acrid stench of burning. At the head of the gangway the sentry was still unconscious. I slung him over my shoulder in a fireman's carry—he was only a small man, luckily—and got him away from immediate danger. After all, I bore no grudge against him. I bore no grudge against anybody. I was just trying to save my—*our*—universe. And my own skin.

That fire was spreading fast. The big windows of the stern gallery were glowing ruddily and the flames were roaring, louder and louder. There was bawling and shouting among the sentries on the wharf, a great deal of running around. I did my best to impersonate a chicken with its head cut off, reasoning that if I joined the general panic I might escape notice. Then I found cover in a narrow alley between two warehouses, stood and watched. The galleon was well ablaze by now, with lines of fire running up her rigging, spreading to the furled canvas on her spars. Somebody had organized a bucket party but by this time it was utterly ineffectual. There was only one thing to do— to get the remaining ships away and out from the wharf before the first vessel's magazine went up. But there was nobody there to do it; those sentries must all have been soldiers, not seamen.

The fire reached the magazine.

Oh, I've seen, more than once, the sort of Big Bang that can be produced by modern weaponry—but that particular Big Bang still, after all these years, persists in my memory . . . The strangely slow flare of orange flame and a somehow leisurely boom of man-made thunder . . . The blazing fragments scattered in all directions and other fragments, not yet burning, black in silhouette against dreadful, ruddy light . . . And the fires exploding in the rigging and on the decks of the other five ships—and on the roof of the warehouse beside which I was standing.

Somebody was addressing me urgently in Japanese. It was a tall, kimono-clad man, with pistols as well as a sheathed Samurai sword thrust into his sash. He was tall, as I have said, and bearded, and the language that he was using did not sound right from his lips. There was a kimono-clad woman with him. She stared at me wide-eyed.

"Captain!" she gasped. "What are *you* doing here?" What have you *done*?"

"What have *you* been doing, Yoshi-san?" I demanded.

Adams—it could have been none other—had one of his pistols out, was pointing it at me.

"Who is this," he asked, "that you know him? Some Spanish dog sent to frustrate me? Who are you, man, and who employs you? Should you make truthful answer I might spare your life."

And then, at the other end of the timeline, Sparks did what he should have done minutes before and I was standing in *Sister Sue*'s Mannschenn Drive room, with holes burned by flying sparks in my dressing gown, my face smoke-blackened. I moved out of the circle to look at the screen. Nothing could save those ships now. As I watched two of the others exploded.

I heard the third say to Sparks, "What about Yoshi?" and Sparks reply, "I'm trying."

And he got her.

She sprawled lifeless on the deck, in a pool of her own blood. A dagger was in her right hand. And one of those scraps of useless knowledge that one accumulates floated into my mind. Japanese ladies, wiping out some real or fancied disgrace, were not expected to carry out ritual self-disembowelment.

A mere throat-cutting would suffice.

But it wasn't all over yet. The two young men who had been Yoshi's accomplices were taking her death very badly. Before I could stop him Sparks had snatched the laser pistol from my sash. And he took his revenge. Oh, yes, Kitty, I know that I'm still here, but he took his revenge. He turned the destructive beam of the weapon onto the machine that had sent his lady back into the Past, to when and where she had met her death. He paid particular attention to the controls that she had installed. And I did not stop him. I did not try to stop him. It was better that Yoshi's knowledge died with her. The Present may be bad enough, but tampering with the Past would almost certainly make it worse, not better. The mere fact that we are here and now is proof that on *this* Time Track things have been working out not too badly.

"Having known a few Australians, including yourself," said Kitty, "I still think that a Japonified Australia might have been an improvement."

"You're entitled to your opinion," said Grimes stiffly.

AROUND
THE WORLD IN
23,741 DAYS

∾ Around the World ∾
in 23,741 Days

IF ANYBODY CARES to do his sums he will discover that this opening paragraph is being written on my 65th birthday and that when I made my own calculations Leap Years were taken into account. Sixty-five is, I think, as good an age as any for an autobiographical exercise. It is supposed to be retiring age—although the Union Steam Ship Company of New Zealand retires its people at the age of sixty-three and writers, of course, never retire. Come to that, I seem to have been on the Company's pay roll for quite long periods each year since I was turned out to grass. Still, sixty-five is a good vantage point from which to look backwards over the years and the miles. Such a lot has happened in the last six and a half decades and so much of it has been of absorbing interest to a science fictioneer. And so much of it all has been incorporated into my own writings.

My quite notorious unrequited love affair with airships, for example . . .

One very early—but remarkably vivid—memory I have is of a Zeppelin raid on London during World War I. can still see the probing searchlights, like the questing antennae of giant insects and,

Originally Published in *Algol*, Spring, 1978. Copyright ©1978 by *Algol* Magazine; reprinted by permission of *Algol*.

sailing serenely overhead, high in the night sky, that slim, silvery cigar. I can't remember any bombs; I suppose that none fell anywhere near where I was. It is worth remarking that in those distant days, with aerial warfare in its infancy, civilians had not yet learned to run for cover on the approach of raiders but stood in the streets, with their children, to watch the show.

I remember, too, the British dirigibles R33 and R34 which, in the years immediately after the (so-called) Great War were almost permanent features of the overhead scenery; the country town in which I spent most of my childhood—Beccles, in Suffolk—was not far from the airship base at Mildenhall. A little later, after I had commenced my seafaring apprenticeship, I saw *Graf Zeppelin*, then maintaining her regular trans-Atlantic service, a few times.

I have other aviation memories too. As a very, very small child I watched from my perambulator the British military aeroplanes—the old 'flying birdcages'—exercising on and over (not very far over!) Salisbury Plain. That was just prior to World War I. During World War II, home on leave, I watched fleets of heavy bombers streaming east to hammer German targets. Also, while on leave, I once again experienced air raids on London—including, towards the end of hostilities, those by the V1s, the flying bombs, and by the V2s. Quite a few people were inclined to get hostile when I was enthusiastic rather than otherwise about these latter weapons, claiming that they were, after all, no more (and no less) than working models of moon rockets.

War rockets—much smaller ones, of course—were among my toys during a long spell as armaments officer of a troopship. I liked them, of course, but they never liked me. Whenever I had occasion to use them the most horrid things would happen but never to the enemy . . .

But autobiographies should start at the beginning.

I was born on March 28, 1912, in the military hospital in Aldershot, England. If anybody should ask what a seaman was doing being born in an army hospital I can only reply that I wanted to be near my mother. My father, as a matter of fact, was a soldier in the Regular Army. He was one of the first of the many killed in the First

World War. I have no memory of him. Nonetheless, as the inheritor of his genes, I owe very much to him. Had he lived in a slightly later period he would certainly have been a fan, possibly a science fiction writer himself. I still recall my discovery, in the attic of his parents' house in a village called Brampton, in Huntingdonshire, of a trunk full of his books. Without exception these were all early science fiction and fantasy—the old, yellow-covered Hodder & Stoughton paperback editions of Rider Haggard, the *Strand Magazines* with serialised Wells and Doyle and another long-defunct periodical called *The Boys' Own Paper* with SF serials by lesser but still readable authors.

My father was a professional soldier and I became a professional seaman but, had he survived that utterly stupid clash between rival imperialisms, we should have had very much in common.

After my father's death in action my mother, with my younger brother and myself, went to live with her parents in Beccles, a small, quiet town on the River Waveney. I was exposed to education there and some of it must have caught—a smattering of mathematics sufficient to enable me to navigate a ship, a rough working knowledge of the principles of English grammar. Even now I feel slightly guilty when I, knowing full well what crimes I am committing, split an infinitive, start a sentence with a conjunction or finish one with a preposition.

My first school was the Peddars Lane Elementary School. In those days the free schools in England did little more than to prepare their pupils for entry into the lower echelons of the work force at the age of fourteen and to teach them to fear God and honour the King. Fortunately it was possible to win a scholarship to an establishment operating on a somewhat higher level. This I did, gaining entry to the Sir John Leman Secondary School. In the 1920s the secondary schools did not quite have the same status as grammar schools which, in their turn, were socially several notches below the private schools and the "public" schools. The class system of the England of those days was rigidly stratified. Nonetheless the Sir John Lemanites did tend to put on the dog, considering themselves a cut above the students at the local grammar school. After all, *our* swotshop had been founded way back in the days of Good Queen Bess by one of her merchant knights . . .

But I've said before—and I say again—that those who say that their schooldays were the happiest days of their lives either are bloody liars or have very short memories. Still, as most of us do, I got by. I was a dud at sports and, to this day, regard the sports pages of the daily and Sunday newspapers only as convenient wrapping for the garbage and save on the electricity bill whenever any sporting event—even cricket!—is shown on television. Luckily, too, the Sir John Leman School, although it had its football* and cricket events, never took sport seriously. It was known as a "swot school," the accent being on education.

My pet subjects were English, in which I always came top in examinations despite my vile handwriting; chemistry, in which I always came top in the practical examinations and second—because of my vile handwriting—in the theoretical ones; mathematics, geography and history, in all three of which I made consistently high scores. In those days there was no biology and physics was no more than instruction in such abstruse subjects as mechanical advantage. I was always bottom in scripture—schoolboy gropings towards an agnostic viewpoint were not encouraged—and very near the bottom in French. (To this day I have an intense dislike for that language.) However my consistently good marks in English and the various sciences ensured my steady upward progress.

Almost my final memory of the Sir John Leman School is that of a crucial point in my life. *If* I had not been brainwashed by my reading of English school stories, in which the myth of schoolboy honour was always perpetuated, *if* I had not assumed that Miss Deeley, the science mistress, would do the right thing by her teacher's pet, my subsequent career would have been entirely different. I should not, at this moment of time, be sitting in my caravan on the premises of a nudist club on the outskirts of Sydney writing this. I should never have experienced the very real joys and the occasional terrifying responsibilities of sea-going

---

*It was real football, Association (Soccer), not Rugby. I maintain that the notorious Rugby schoolboy who started the absurd game bearing the name of his scholastic institution by breaking the rules of the sport, picking up the ball and running with it, must have been none other but Flashman. It was just the sort of thing he would have done!

command. My World War II service would have been entirely different; should I have been a soldier, an airman, a back room boy? Probably I should have become a writer, a science fiction writer, but the Rim Worlds would never have been shown on the star charts of our mythology and Commodore Grimes, that twentieth-century Anglo-Australian shipmaster displaced in Time and Space, would never have inflicted his prejudices upon readers in just about every country from Japan to the Soviet Union, the long way around the world. There might have been a Doctor or Professor Grimes, chemical engineer of the far future turning base metals into gold or water into wine or whatever . . .

But to return to Miss Deeley and my first—but not my last—Big Black Mark . . .

There was a very important examination Those who passed would move up one form to sit for Matriculation the following year—and with Matriculation there would be the chance of a university scholarship. Those who failed to make the grade would have to stay put for another twelve months, to try again I *knew* that I should make my usual poor showing in French and Scripture. I *knew* that I should do well enough in my good subjects to achieve promotion Unfortunately (fortunately?) I was not yet wise in the ways of the wicked world.

(Am I now? Mphm?)

As I've already said, chemistry came in two parts: theoretical and practical. Theoretical Chemistry examination consisted of the working out of complicated (for those days) equations. Practical Chemistry was much more fun. Each candidate was issued with his own vial jar or dish of some fluid, goo or powder and was required to carry out standard analytical procedure to determine the composition of the test specimen. Acid or alkaline? Soluble or insoluble? Flammable or nonflammable? And so on and so on and so on.

In the laboratory were the usual benches, each with its two sinks, its pair of Bunsen burners, its duplicated vessels and instruments. During the examination, presided over by the science mistress, there was to be no, repeat, underscore and capitalize—NO—talking.

We all collected our specimens and took them to our benches, lit up our Bunsen burners. I was just about to apply heat to a small sample of the goo that I had been given when my benchmate—a rather dim lout called George Martin—looked apprehensively at the dish of blue powder that he was supposed to analyse and whispered, "What do I do with this?"

No, I didn't make the obvious rejoinder. I merely whispered back, "Shut up, you bloody fool!"

Miss Deeley—as I recall her she was a bespectacled, dried-up, spinster schoolmarm—pricked up her ears and demanded, "Were you talking, Chandler?"

I admitted that I had been, thinking that the clot Martin would at once confess (a) that he had initiated the conversation and (b) that I had given him no advice as to what to do with his specimen. But he remained silent. So much for schoolboy honour. Nonetheless I was not worried. I knew that Miss Deeley knew that I was the form's star chemistry student and would not be asking anybody's advice on how to carry out a simple task of analysis.

I had a shock coming. Oh, I was top in Practical Chemistry as always but all my marks were stripped from me because I had broken the No Talking Rule. This meant that owing to my extremely poor showing in my two unfavourite subjects—scripture and French—I should not be moving up a grade but would be obliged to mark time for another year.

Looking back on it all, putting it down on paper, I have suddenly realised that for many years I have thought of Miss Deeley—when I have thought of her—with unjustified harshness. I remember how more than once, as a subordinate, I have had my decisions overruled by superiors and how, as master, I have, at times, overruled my officers. Had Miss Deeley been in a position of overall command she would doubtless have conducted an enquiry and ascertained who said what to whom, and why. I think now that she was not allowed to do so and that it was the Headmaster, "Baddy" Watson, who was the author of my downfall. As well as acting in a supervisory capacity he conducted the Scripture classes and, furthermore, took them seriously. I must have been his *bete noir*. And then he was presented, on a silver tray, garnished with parsley, the Heaven-sent opportunity to smite the youthful infidel hip and thigh. He took it.

Not for the first time I say, with heartfelt conviction, "Thank God I'm an agnostic!"

Digressing slightly, now and again I argue with Susan, my second wife, about religion. She is an atheist. She accuses me of being, in my heart of hearts, religious in spite of my professed agnosticism.

I suppose that I am, really. I admit to being a Mobrist. MOBR is an acronym: My Own Bloody Religion. Take Swinburne's "Holy Spirit of Man," add Wells' "Race Spirit," flavour with infusions of Darwinism, Marxism and Buddhism, put into the blender, switch on and leave well alone except for, now and again, adding other ingredients such as Forteanism. And, even, Vonnegutism. So it goes.

Picking up the main thread once more—I did not matriculate. So I did not get the chance to sit for a university scholarship. So I did not become—as otherwise I probably should have done—an industrial chemist.

The prospect of having to seek for employment in a small country town in the England of the late 1920s did not appeal to me. Had I been in the possession of at least the matriculation certificate things would have been a lot easier; as it was my smatterings of education fitted me only for a job as an office boy or something similar. The only avenue of escape from the town—and from that stratum of society into which God had seen fit to place me—was the sea. So it was that shortly after my sixteenth birthday I was apprenticed to the Sun Shipping Company—called by its maritime personnel the Bum Shipping Company—of London.

Pause for the filling and lighting of my pipe and for reflection. *Is this*, I ask myself, *the autobiography of a writer or a seaman*? But the sea has been my life for so long and, as the late and great John W. Campbell once told me, my stories are "costume sea stories" rather than real science fiction. If I had not become a ship's officer and, eventually, master there would have been no John Grimes. If I had not served on some of the less pleasant trades of the Union Steam Ship Company of New Zealand there would have been no Rim Worlds.

When I first went to sea I was not yet a writer although I had become an avid reader of science fiction. I had discovered Wells in the school library. There were my father's books. There were the cheap Woolworth's editions of Jules Verne. There was Hugo Gernsback's *Science And Invention* with its Ray Cummings and A. Merritt serials and then, when Gernsback realised that a lot of readers were buying his first magazine only for the fiction, there was his new venture, the amazingly durable *Amazing Stories*.

I was hooked, from my early teens onwards, but it would be quite some time before my own private vision of the future would include a picture of myself as a science fiction writer. The pinnacle of my ambition—one never attained—was the captaincy of a Big Ship. I have served in such as an officer but have commanded only relatively small vessels.

In the 1920s—and the procedure is probably much the same today—entry into the British Merchant Navy could be made through a variety of channels. If your family was well-to-do you went to one of the posh pre-sea training schools: HMS CONWAY, HMS WORCESTER or the land-based Nautical Academy at Pangbourne. The big liner companies recruited their cadets from these. If your family was not well-to-do application was made to the Shipping Federation and if that body was satisfied that you had attained a reasonably good standard of education you were apprenticed to some tramp company as an STS—straight-to-sea— officer candidate. You could, of course, start your seafaring career on the lower deck, beginning as deck boy, rising to ordinary seaman and then to A.B. (able bodied seaman) and then, once you had completed the mandatory four years' sea service, sitting for the Certificate of Proficiency as Second Mate of a Foreign Going Steamship. Even though the Merchant Navy is far less class conscious than the Royal Navy the percentage of officers who have "come up through the hawsepipe" must be about the same in both services.

My first ship was *Cape St. Andrew*, a coal-burning tramp steamer of about eight thousand tons' deadweight capacity. Her owners named their vessels after headlands around the coast of South Africa, in which part of the world they had commercial interests not directly connected with shipping. They owned coal mines in Natal; whenever possible we bunkered with the Company's coal. They owned a crayfish canning factory, but this delicacy was far too good for the likes of us. They owned, too, a jam factory in England, and their canned conserves and preserves, definitely not in the luxury class, were always to be found in the storerooms of their ships.

Somehow I've gotten on to the subject of food so I'll stay on it for a while. Today's seamen take for granted things that, in my early days, would have been regarded as the wildest luxuries. Very few tramp steamers were equipped, in the '20s and '30s, with domestic refrigeration. They had, instead, a huge icebox on the poop which, prior to departure from a port, was stocked with blocks of ice and with fresh meat, fish and vegetables. For the first week the food would be quite edible. By the end of the second week it wouldn't be so good. During the third week people would be ignoring the meat and making do on boiled potatoes. Eventually the master—those old tramp captains really had their owners' interests at heart!—would reluctantly order that the remaining contents of the ice box be sent to feed the sharks and that the preserved foodstuffs be broken out. At first the canned meats and fishes would be, relatively speaking, gourmet fare but, before long, everything would taste of tin.

Other delicacies would be salt horse straight from the harness cask (salt beef, actually, pickled in brine) and dried, salted cod. These were not as bad as they sound. I am always disappointed by the sea pie cooked and served in modern ships in which fresh meat is used. A real sea pie consists of layers of salt meat, sliced potatoes and sliced onion encased and cooked in a suet dough—a sort of savoury steamed pudding, actually. It is good. And the salt cod, which is procurable even now, I still enjoy.

Then there was "gallery." This was marmalade. The legend was that the marmalade supplied to ships—to tramp ships especially— was made from the sweepings of orange peels from the galleries of theatres and music halls. It may well have been true.

But it wasn't the nicknames that, at first, put the apprentices off their food. In that ship we messed with the officers, at the foot of the long saloon table. The master sat at the head, of course, and carved the joint. I still haven't made up my mind regarding Captain Puzey. Was he a seaman who owned a farm (run during his absences by his wife) to supplement his salary or was he a farmer who came to sea to make the money to save his farm from bankruptcy? He rarely wore uniform and, whilst the ship was in temperate waters, clad himself in a sort of Farmer Giles outfit in rough tweed, complete with leather gaiters. And how did he (at first) put us off our tucker? Easily. Whilst carving the joint he would discourse learnedly upon the many and various diseases to which whatever animal it was that we were supposed to be eating was susceptible.

The vessels of the Sun Shipping Company carried lascar crews, recruited in Calcutta. As a result of this I acquired a taste for curry that persists still.

But life at sea isn't one long Cook's Tour unless you're a cook yourself (or Captain Cook). I was supposed to be learning the seaman's trade, not eating my head off. It has been said (probably it is still being said) that tramp steamer apprentices are no more than cheap labour; legally speaking they are (or they were, in my early days) apprentice seamen, not apprentice officers. Nonetheless, as well as chipping and scraping rust, washing paintwork, polishing brass, cleaning bilges and all the rest of it they are trained in the real seamanlike arts such as rope and wire splicing (this latter very much a lost art these decadent days!). They are required to study navigation, signaling, meteorology and all the rest of it.

One thing still sticks in my memory, still slightly rankles. As I have said, the vessels of the Sun Shipping Company carried lascar crews who were, of course, Moslems. If we were in any Asiatic port during a Moslem public holiday we, the apprentices, would rank as officers, not crew. If we were in any port during a Christian public holiday we would rank as crew, not officers. On the other hand the Chinese carpenter, who was a follower of Confucius, got *all* the holidays . . .

Oh, well, old Chippy was worth a damn sight more to the ship than we were. A fascinating character who claimed—truthfully, I think—to have been a pirate in his youth. (Piracy on the China Coast persisted until the Communists brought their own brand of law and order to China.) And he was certainly a bigamist in his later years with one wife in Canton and another in the Chinese enclave in Calcutta.

Cape St. Andrew was a round-the-world tramp rarely returning to

England. Calcutta was not officially her home port but she seemed to be there more often than anywhere else. Her main employment was the Calcutta coal trade—black diamonds from the Bengal mines to the small ports on the West Coast of India, to Colombo in Ceylon (as it was then called), to Madras on the East Coast, and further afield to Hong Kong and Whampoa, which was an anchorage port halfway up the Pearl River to Canton. (Attempts at piracy were still quite common on the Pearl River but nobody bothered us.) During my apprenticeship I was only in Australia once; we loaded a cargo of grain in Fremantle for Calcutta. I was only in the U.S.A. once; we loaded jute in Calcutta for New Orleans, then cotton in Houston, Texas, for Kobe, Osaka and Shanghai. (This, to date, has been my only visit to Japan but, as my Japanese fans are promising a Rim-Con in my honour I shall probably revisit that country, as an author rather than as a seaman.) Even though we seemed to steer clear of Japanese ports we were frequent visitors to Shanghai, usually with cargoes of sugar from Java. It was on one of these voyages that I was under fire for the second time in my life. (The first time, of course, was during that Zeppelin raid on London in World War I.) The Sino-Japanese War had broken out. (Or it may have been one of the preliminary skirmishes.) We were proceeding down river. There was an artillery duel between Japanese cruisers and the forts at Woosung. We had to pass between the combatants. The ships courteously ceased fire until we were clear, the forts did not. The trajectory of the projectiles was high enough so that there was no real danger but it wasn't a very pleasant sensation to hear those shells whistling overhead. (The next time that I was under fire I was aboard the vessel actually being shot at, but that was many years later.)

There were voyages to Rangoon and other ports in Burma to load rice for Java. There was a voyage to Odessa, in the Black Sea, to load or to discharge something or other; I forget now. My main memories are the bitter cold—it was midwinter—and of the International Seamen's Club where, bribed with music, rye bread and sausage and excellent heavy Ukrainian beer we listened to the usual Marxist propaganda spiels. Actually it was all just the same as the Church of England's Missions to Seamen with alcoholic beverages served instead of tea.

It was in winter, too, that we were in Trieste, in the Adriatic. The main memory is of the *bora*, the bitterly cold wind that sweeps down from the Italian Alps. A lazy wind, somebody said. It's too tired to go round you so it goes through you.

As well as the Calcutta Coal Trade there was the Calcutta Salt Trade. Salt, manufactured from sea water, was loaded either in Aden, at the entrance to the Red Sea, or Port Okha, on the North West Coast of India. Loading completed, the hatches would be sealed by the Customs. Discharge was at the Salt Moorings, river berths in Calcutta. Every ounce of the precious commodity would be weighed and tallied out under customs supervision and, at the close of each day's work, the hatches would be resealed. The rate of discharge depended upon the briskness or otherwise of the salt market. The reason for all this red tape was that in those days, the last years of the British Raj, salt was the one thing that everybody, no matter how poverty stricken, had to have and the customs duty on salt was the only way to ensure that the entire population contributed to the upkeep of the British administration and military forces in India.

So my apprenticeship went on. Apart from being shot at (well, over, actually) in other people's wars and the occasional China Sea typhoon it was a relatively quiet life. Finally, our time having been served, the other three brats and myself were shipped home as passengers from Calcutta in one of Harrison's cargo liners. (The Harrison Line was one of the companies maintaining a regular service between London and Calcutta.)

With others in the same age group but from varying backgrounds— tramps, liners, oil tankers—I attended the King Edward VII Nautical School, which also had boarding facilities, to complete my studies for the Second Mate's Certificate of Competency and managed to convince the examiners that I was a fit and proper person to hold such a qualification. Shortly thereafter I re-entered the service of the Sun Shipping Company as third officer.

I was still reading all the science fiction that I could lay my hands on but never dreamed that I would one day be writing the stuff.

My new (?) ship was *Saint Dunstan*. Actually she was owned by the Saint Line, which was a subsidiary of the Sun Shipping Company.

She was old, old and scruffy. (*Cape St. Andrew*, a new ship when I joined her, was by comparison a luxury liner.) She didn't get round as much as *Cape St. Andrew* did and, as I recall it, spent practically all her time on the Calcutta Coal and Salt Trades. I swotted hard and passed, in Calcutta, for my First Mate's Certificate of Competency without having to go to school first. (Actually the "First Mate's Ticket" was little more than a recapitulation of second mate's work with the addition of Ship Stability, applied hydrodynamics.)

It was while I was in *Saint Dunstan* that I somehow got bitten by the writing bug and, in Calcutta, purchased my first typewriter, an ancient but serviceable Remington portable which lasted me for many years. (I got bitten by other bugs, too. I sat down on a wicker-seated chair in the shop to try the machine out before buying it and the bed bugs in the wicker work had a real feast on the backs of my legs; it was during the Hot Weather and I was wearing shorts.) And yet I had no burning desire to become a science fiction writer, or any kind of fiction writer. My ambition—a weird one, I admit now—was to become a freelance journalist. I did succeed in selling short articles and occasional light verse to newspapers and to the British *Nautical Magazine*. None of this output has, so far as I know, survived. This is no great loss.

When the term of the ship's Articles of Agreement ran out I was among those officers who had no desire to sign on for another three years. I returned to the U.K. from Calcutta in a Brocklebank liner and, the times being what they were, found it hard to obtain suitable employment after I had taken a holiday. Nonetheless I did not regret leaving *Saint Dunstan*. In my career I have served in three outstandingly scruffy ships. *Saint Dunstan* was the first. Then there was the Shaw Savill Line's *Raranga*, one of the last of that company's coal burners, of which vessel I was second officer during the latter part of the Second World War. (But *Raranga* I rather liked. Apart from anything else she gave me the inspiration for "Giant Killer.") Finally there was the Union Steam Ship Company's *Kaimanawa*, of which I held command. Although she was oil-fired she was one of the last of the company's steam—as opposed to motor—ships. She had been built during World War II and looked as though she had been built during World War I. Her accommodation was primitive. Her hatches leaked. Her steam winches were so noisy as to make thought—let alone speech!—impossible during cargo-handling operations.

To return to the period immediately after my return to England from the Indian Coast . . . Times, although improving, were not yet good. For a while I, with two other shipless officers, was a tally clerk at Ford's Dagenharn plant in Essex. Then, my mother and brother having moved to that island, I was a kennelman in Jersey. (The British Channel Island, not the American state.) I must have learned quite a lot. In later years, when I was chief officer in the Shaw Savill Line, people shipping small animals out from England to Australasia would try to get them on to whichever ship I was mate at the time.

Then Shaw Savill were wanting officers. First they were asking for people with Master's Certificates who were from either Conway, Worcester or Pangbourne. They lowered their sights a little when none were forthcoming and asked for Master's Certificates only. They lowered their sights still more, their new requirements being First Mate's Certificates and Conway, Worcester or Pangbourne. Then it got down to First Mate's Certificates only. So it was that I signed on the old *Pakeha's* books as fourth officer.

After *Pakeha* there was the relatively new motor vessel *Karamea*. In those days the Shaw Savill Line, like the Union Steam Ship Company of New Zealand, favoured Maori names for its vessels although the "ics" (*Coptic*, I think, was the first) were beginning to creep in. It was while serving in her that I married for the first time. And it was in her that I was under fire for the third time, this being shortly after the outbreak of World War II.

War was declared shortly after we sailed from Wellington, New Zealand for England with a cargo of refrigerated foodstuffs. Immediately we, although a merchant vessel, came under the orders of the British Admiralty and were told to continue our voyage to the U.K. via the Panama Canal but to put into Kingston, Jamaica, to be equipped with guns and for convoy assembly. We put into Kingston, waited there for some time for our armament, which we never got, and eventually sailed as part of a small, unescorted for most of the time, unarmed convoy.

There was the Royal Mail cargo liner, *Loch Avon*. Her master was a captain in the Royal Naval Reserve (Retired) so was Convoy Commodore. *Karamea*'s master, Teddy Grayston, was a Commander R.N.R. (Rtd.) so was appointed vice commodore. There was a Union Steam Ship Company's vessel (I forget her name; she was with us only until we were clear of the Caribbean then proceeded to Canadian ports independently). There were two French ships: *Bretagne*, an old, twin-funneled passenger liner and *Oregon*, a modern motor vessel similar to *Loch Avon* and ourselves.

Whilst still in West Indian waters we had our first scare but were very relieved when the submarine sighted turned out to be an American one. We were, of course, listening to every news broadcast and it seemed that the first outburst of German submarine activity was over. We dared to hope for a quiet voyage home.

Meanwhile, Teddy had us on a war footing. Normally in merchant vessels the fourth officer keeps the chief officer's watch for him but I was put on day work as navigator, signals officer, black-out king and anything else that needed doing. There were four cadets; three of these were junior watchkeepers and the other one was my sidekick.

The convoy steamed steadily east, in line abeam, *Karamea* leading the port (but nonexistent) column, then *Loch Avon*, then *Bretagne*, then *Oregon* to starboard. Still there was no word of enemy submarine activity. But it was too good to last.

First there was a message from the British tramp steamer *Stonepool*. I remember it well for its *chutzpah*. It wasn't a plaintive squeal for help, it read: "Am engaging enemy submarine." But *Stonepool* had guns. None of us did. *Stonepool*, as a matter of fact, won her little battle.

The next message received by our Sparks was even more frightening. *Emil Miguet*, a large French oil tanker, had been torpedoed and abandoned by her crew. Furthermore, this had happened directly ahead of us on the course that we were making. The commodore reasoned, as I think that anybody in his position would have done, that the German submarine would, by now, be we away from the scene of the crime. He did not order any deviation from the convoy course. During the remaining hours of daylight, however, we carried out a heavy zig-zag and were ordered to resume this at first light the following morning.

At about 0200 hours. we passed the still-burning wreckage of *Emil Miguet* I didn't see it myself as I had turned in on completion of the day's duties, leaving word to be called at 0500 hours. so that I could obtain a morning star fix. I was called much earlier, by the second officer. "Wake up, Four Oh! A position, quick, for Sparks! *Loch Avon's* been torpedoed!"

Loch Avon, I learned later, had used an unshielded, all-round Morse lamp to make a signal to the other ships of the convoy regarding resumption of zig-zag, thereby attracting the attention o the officer-of-the-watch of the surfaced U-Boat which, actually, was directly ahead of *Karamea*. She positioned her self to fire a torpedo, successfully, and then, fortunately (for her) saw us bearing down upon her and put on a burst of speed. Our chief officer saw the submarine making off to starboard. His peacetime reaction was to alter course to port, to avoid, not to go hard-a-star board to ram. It was indeed fortunate that he did alter course (although an alteration to starboard would have been better) as a torpedo hurriedly fired from a stern tube missed our stem by inches.

It was quite some time, however, before we were able to hold any sort of post mortem on the morning's disasters. My first job was to run up a dead reckoning position and take it down to Sparks in the radio office. I returned to the bridge to find that the Old Man, in his capacity as vice commodore, had ordered the convoy to scatter. We maintained course as we were heading for the rendezvous position with a promised destroyer escort. *Oregon* cleared away to the south'ard and, we finally learned, made it safely to port. *Bretagne*, that poor old coal burner, plodded along behind us, sparks cascading from her twin funnels, dropping slowly astern.

Daylight came in slowly. The horizon was hard enough for me to get sights of suitable stars and to calculate our position. After Sparks had sent this off I returned to the bridge and was pottering around in the chartroom when the chief officer called, "Hoy! Four Oh! Signals! *Bretagne's* using a daylight Morse lamp!" Then, as I picked up my binoculars and stepped outside, "No, by Christ! It's shellfire!"

Shellfire it was: pale flashes all around the bridge of the old, gray ship, and then the slowly climbing column of water and smoke as a torpedo hit her amidships. There was another flash-range-from a low, dark, almost invisible shape and a shellburst well short of us.

Teddy Grayston altered course to put the submarine right astern and ordered our engineers to give us maximum speed. The U-Boat fired again, and again, correcting the range. All that her gunnery officer had to do to score a hit was bracket—and all that Teddy had do to bugger the bracketing was alter course towards each fall of shot. Meanwhile the second and third officers were in charge on deck, getting the boats swung out and stocked with extra blankets and provisions, getting some cases of gold bullion that were among our cargo out of the strong room and putting these in the boats, even placing the two little dogs that were also part of the cargo into the lifecraft. These tasks completed all they had to do was to keep all hands under cover.

By this time the sun was well up and, as chance would have it, directly on the port beam. I got out my sextant and took two good shots. It was an old but very good instrument, and heavy. When you are taking sights under fire a heavy instrument is advantageous rather than otherwise. The shaking of the hands is minimised. By sheer good luck we were steaming directly along a position line, which meant that any help steaming or flying along this same line would be sure to find us. (For some reason we, on the bridge, were sure that our rescuers would be Coastal Command's Sunderland flying boats; we were well within their range.)

I gave the new message form to Sparks then returned to the bridge. The shelling was continuing, with every miss a very near one. But there were other smells beside the acridity of exploding lyddite. The cooks were busy making steak and egg and bacon sandwiches—and nobody thought of sending any up to the people who were doing all the work.

My readers will know that Grimes is, now and again, referred to as Gutsy Grimes, the nickname derived from his appetite rather than his courage. There is, I suppose, something of me in Grimes. Anyhow, during a slight lull in the shelling, I asked the Old Man, "Do you think I might make some tea and toast for us all, sir?"

"Excellent idea, Chandler!"

I went down to the saloon pantry, switched on the boiler and the toaster. I found the largest teapot, some loaves of bread. There were five hungry mouths to feed—Teddy, the chief officer, two cadets and myself. I made an enormous pile of toast and was generous with the butter and the anchovy paste. I brewed the tea. I loaded everything, including cups and spoons and milk and sugar, on to a big tray. All the time I had been conscious that there was only a thin sheet of steel between me and the German projectiles; I had been much less unhappy when I could see what was going on.

During my return up top with the loaded tray I had to come out on to the lower bridge. The wind scooped the toast off the dish and on to the deck. I thought, *If we're going to die, a bit of dirty toast won't kill us.* I gathered up the toast, put it back in the tray and completed my journey without further mishap. (Later I told the story, in confidence, to the second officer. He told the Old Man. Teddy took me severely to task about it.)

Shortly after we had finished our delayed breakfast the Third Officer wandered up to the bridge. He said cheerfully to Teddy, "We're being followed, sir."

Teddy accorded him a laserlike glare from his monocle and snapped, "A blinding glimpse of the obvious, Owen."

"Look astern, sir."

Until now we had been scanning the sky ahead through our glasses, searching for the Coastal Command flying boats that must, surely, be on the way. Now we looked aft. There was the U-Boat, still slowly gaining on us. And, hull down, three gray pyramids, the upperworks of destroyers. Like ourselves the submarine's people had not been keeping a lookout astern. Had she dived in time she would have escaped. She did dive eventually and almost immediately was surrounded by a pattern of depth charges. She surfaced and surrendered.

When the shooting was over the chief steward came up to the bridge and addressed the captain. "Splice the main brace, sir?"

"Of course, Mr. Davis."

"Scotch, sir?"

There was another laserlike glare from Teddy's monocle. "Scotch,

Mr. Davis? What are you thinking of? Nelson's blood!" he thundered. "Nelson's blood!"

So rum it was.

The third officer took over the watch and the rest of us went down to the officers' smoking room for our main brace splicing. Mr. Moffatt, the chief officer, a few years previously had been second Officer of the old *Mamari* when she hit an iceberg off Cape Horn during his watch, in the small hours of the morning. He had seen it— there was some moonlight, I believe—but had assumed, until it was too late, that it was low cloud. Anyhow, Mr. Moffatt was tending to pat himself on the back for having saved *Karamea* by going hard-a-port as soon as he saw the submarine, even though he did not learn that a torpedo had been fired at us until well afterward.

Teddy brought his monocle to bear. (I've often wondered why that thing never melted.) "It's a bloody pity, Moffatt," he drawled, "that you aren't as good at ramming submarines as you are at ramming icebergs!"

And that's about all, I think, that I shall be writing about World War II. Oh, I could tell the tale of how I missed the wreck of the old *Matakana* by being landed in Panama, on the homeward passage, with chickenpox, which infantile ailment I must have caught from my current girlfriend in Wellington, who was a schoolmistress. And there was the time in the notorious *Raranga* when we were trapped in the ice, in Buzzard's Bay, and almost drifted on to the Hen and Chicken Shoal. Also in *Raranga* was a Night to Remember: a Western Ocean convoy slamming at full speed through an icefield in thick fog. In theory the escorting destroyers were picking up the bergs on their radar and laying calcium flares at the base of each one; in practice it didn't work out too well. Ice is a very poor radar target. There was my spell as armaments officer in the troopship *Mataroa* and the way in which my rocket weapons invariably failed to reciprocate my affection for them. And vivid in my memory is the occasion when the Bo's'n of the same ship almost wiped out the entire crew of the six-inch gun— and myself!—with a point thirty stripped Savage Lewis. And there was that event-crowded morning when the admiral took off his cap, threw it down on the deck and jumped on it . . .

Nonetheless World War II, as well as providing me with experience and material, as it did so many other writers, also got me into the right place at the right time. In days of peace New York just isn't among Shaw Savill's ports of call. In wartime, the ships of the Shaw Savill Line—like the ships of every other company—were required to go anywhere and everywhere.

Astounding Science Fiction had long been my favourite magazine. On one visit to New York I decided that I would like to meet the Great Man who edited the great periodical. I visited the editorial offices of Street & Smith and, having made my request to the receptionist, was ushered into the Presence. John received me cordially. We talked. He complained that as most of his writers were now in the armed forces of the U.S.A. he was very short of material. Perhaps I, as a Faithful Reader of very long standing, would care to contribute . . . I didn't take his suggestion seriously . . .

But . . .

Why not? I must have asked myself.

It was shortly after this that I left *Mataroa* to sit for my Certificate of Competency as Master of a Foreign Going Steamship. I had to go to school for this; I could have passed an examination in gunnery easily but, over quite a long period, had not been able to spare the time to continue my studies of navigation, seamanship, maritime law and all the rest of it. I passed and, shortly thereafter, was appointed as second officer to the old *Raranga*, a big, coal-burning, twin-screwed steamship. She had been torpedoed during World War I but had survived. She got through World War II unscathed although she once distinguished herself by shooting down a German bomber and a British fighter in the same action.

She was infested with rats. We kept a .22 rifle on the bridge so that, on moonlit nights, the officer of the watch could amuse himself sniping at the brutes. (The use of heavier armament, such as the 20mm machine guns, would have been frowned upon.)

Anyhow, the first time that I came into New York in *Raranga* I had my first short story ready for personal delivery to John Campbell. It was 4,000 words long and had taken me all of a fortnight to peck out on the ancient Remington. (Today that would be little more than a forenoon's work.) It was called "This Means War." It was about the captain of a Venusian spaceship who, making a landing on one of Earth's seas, is shot at by *everybody* and assumes that all this hostile fire is directed at him personally. The period, course, is during World War II.

I handed this masterpiece to and said that I'd better leave return postage with it. John assured me that there was no need for me to do so and that he would send it back. *Raranga* made her way to England in a very slow convoy. Awaiting me was a letter from Street & Smith. In it was a cheque.

Raranga was a frequent visitor to New York, sometimes calling there for bunkers on her homeward voyages from Australasia, sometimes loading refrigerated cargo there for the U.K. I became one of the Campbells' regular week guests, others being Lester del Ray, Theodore Sturgeon and George O. Smith. I became, too, one of Campbells' regular writers during the remainder of the war years. John always asked members of his team use pseudonyms when peddling his rejects to other magazines. I had two: George Whitley, for use in the U.S.A. and, a little later, the U.K. and Andrew Dunstan for use in Australia. Later, when John relaxed his house rules, it was not unusual for me to have two stories, under different by-lines, in the same issue of a magazine. It made my day, once, when I read a letter in somebody's correspondence column saying that Whitley was better writer than Chandler . . .

It was while I was in *Raranga* that I wrote what many people regard, as my best story—"Giant Killer." It was those rats that gave me the idea. The first version was written from viewpoint of the crew of a space who find this derelict adrift in some cockeyed orbit. Boarding her, they attacked by the ferocious mutated rodents. John read it then said, "No, won't do. Try it from the viewpoint of the original crew of the derelict." (That first version did sell to a projected English sf magazine that, however, never got off the ground due to the paper shortage.)

Version No. 2 was a real beaut. I'm still sorry that it never saw print. It was called "The Rejected," the title coming from the first verse of *The Internationale*. The spaceship was a Russian one, with brass samovars bubbling on the bulkheads and portraits of the Little Red Father decorating every crew space. She had a mixed crew. The navigator was having an affair with the catering officer, who was also captain's wife. The amount of vodka consumed by one and all would have fuelled a rocket to Far Centaurus. And, of course, I heavily stressed the irony of this mess of mutinous mutants seething under the comrades' feet.

John read it. He looked at me in sorrow than in anger. He said, "I would point out that *Astounding Science Fiction* is neither *Thrilling Romances* nor a monthly edition of *The Daily Worker*. Take it away— and do it again from the viewpoint of the rats!"

"*What?*"

"You heard me."

The next time in New York I had the first two thousand words completed. I took it out to one of the Campbells' weekend house parties. John read it, passed it to Ted Sturgeon. He read it, passed it to George O. Smith. He read it. They all demanded, "Where's the rest of it?"

I said, "There ain't going to be no rest unless John promises to buy it."

Peace broke out shortly thereafter. Until my promotion to chief officer I remained a very prolific short-story writer, contributing to magazines in the U.S.A. (there were so many of them!), the U.K. and Australia. Gradually the George Whitley and Andrew Dunstan by-lines were phased out, the former, however, being used for quite some time or stories that did not fall into the typical Chandler space opera pattern.

When I got my penultimate rise in the world I had far less time for writing although I was, by this time, toying with the idea of making the switch from short stories to novels. One such was in fact, written during my final years with Shaw Savill: *Glory Planet* (*my* title was *Glory Shore*), eventually published by Avalon, some years after its completion. When I wrote it very little was known about Venus. When finally it was published far too much was known. Impossible as it has turned out to be I still feel affection for the story locale that I created—a colony strung out along the banks of a long, long river, the people living in towns given the names of Terran riparian conurbations, travelling back and forth by sternwheel paddle steamers . . .

My first ship after World War II was *Coptic*, running for a time on charter to the U.S. Navy. Then there was *Tamaroa*, sister ship to *Mataroa*, running alternately as a peacetime troop transport and as a civilian passenger ship. Then *Empire Deben*, one of the spoils of war. A one-time German passenger liner—*Thuringia*, on the Western Ocean trade, *General San Martin* on the South American trade—she had spent the war years as a U-Boat depot ship. Under the British flag she was a peacetime troopship, owned by the Ministry of Sea Transport (all such vessels were named after British rivers) and managed by Shaw Savill.

Then there was *Cufic* there was *Doric*, which vessel I joined for her maiden voyage. She should have been a fine ship but she was not, mainly due to the appallingly low standard of workmanship in the yard where she was built.

My last ship in the Shaw Savill Line was *Waiwera*, in which I sailed for quite some time. She represents another crucial point in my life. If I had not served in that particular vessel it is highly probable that there would never have been any Rim Worlds or any Commodore Grimes to be a pain in the arse to the rulers of that far-flung Confederation.

It was while I was serving in *Waiwera* that I met the lady who became my second wife. She was travelling out as passenger from England to Australia but had no fixed intention of settling in that country. She was at my table in the dining saloon and, during the meal-time conversations, and at other times, we discovered that we had a great deal in common. But this is not *Thrilling Romances*. Suffice it to say that I resigned from the service of the Shaw Savill Line, emigrated to Australia and, after seeing what the various Australian shipping companies had to offer, joined the Union Steam Ship Company of New Zealand as third officer.

USSCo, although its Head Office was (and still is) in Wellington, New Zealand, in those days owned quite a large fleet of small vessels under the Australian flag. What made the company attractive to me was that the majority of officers were, like myself, refugees from the big English companies: Shaw Savill, the Blue Funnel Line, the Port Line, the Royal Mail, even Cunard. Our marine superintendent in Sydney had started life, as a seafarer, in the P & O. To American readers all the above may seem to be without great significance but the old established English shipping lines, before industrialisation replaced the now outmoded ideals of service, were practically private navies.

It was not long before I was back in my old rank, as chief officer. I served on Australian coastal trades, on the Bass Strait passenger ferry service, on the New Zealand coast, on the Pacific Islands trade, on the trans-Tasman service. I became used to and came to love relatively small ships. Relatively small? Some were *bloody* small, by anybody's standards.

And I started writing hard again, short stories and novelets at first. A spell on the Strahan Trade—back and forth between Strahan, a small port on the wild West Coast of Tasmania and Yarraville, a grimly and gimily industrial suburb of Melbourne—somehow gave me the idea for the Rim Worlds and for their major shipping company, Rim Runners, with a fleet officered by refugees from the big Terran spacelines. Rim Runners had to have an astronautical superintendent just as today's shipping companies have marine superintendents. That vacancy was filled by Captain (later Commodore) Grimes. At first Grimes was only a background character.

The Great Magazine Market Crash came just when I had nicely re-established myself as a short story writer. One of the reasons was the proliferation of paperback novels. So, like many others, I had to make the switch from short to long material. That was when the never-ending Grimes saga really got off the ground. It was some time, however, before he had a novel all to himself. My protagonist *should* have been one Derek Calver—but he was last seen heading in the general direction of the next galaxy and hasn't been heard from since.

Finally, having attained sufficient Union Steam Ship Company seniority, I was appointed to command. Somehow, when I made the transition from "Mr." to "Captain," Grimes made his from "Captain" to "Commodore." Much later, when I was a sort of honorary

Commodore, being the senior (but only) captain in a one-ship company (actually one of USSCo's subsidiaries) Grimes became an honorary Admiral of the Rim Worlds planets.

When Commodore Grimes was firmly established as a series character I took a leaf from the book of the late C. S. Forester and started to tell the story of Grimes' early life just as Hornblower's creator did regarding him. The first book was *The Road To The Rim*, dedicated to Hornblower. For quite a while two series were running concurrently: the somewhat elderly and cantankerous Commodore Grimes of Rim Runners, and the Rim Worlds Naval Reserve and the young Mr.—eventually Commander—-Grimes of the Federation Survey Service. There were novels, some of which were serialised in *If*. There were short stories, appearing in *If*, *Galaxy* and *Analog*, which later came out in book form.

All the time I was hinting that there was some Big Black Mark in Grimes' career, some crime or colossal blunder as a result of which he had been obliged to resign his commission in the Survey Service and emigrate to the Rim Worlds.

At last I decided to write the book that would fill the gap between his two careers. I didn't even have to think up a plot; there was one readymade. All that I did, essentially, was to retell the story of Bligh and the *Bounty*. The only real difference between real life and fiction was that Bligh survived his mutiny and went on to become, in the fullness of time, a rear admiral in the Royal Navy. Grimes— considerably less vindictive in his dealings with the mutineers than Bligh was—was obliged to make a fresh start.

I thought that I had filled the gap with *The Big Black Mark* but readers were not slow to tell me that I had done nothing of the kind. And not only readers . . . If anybody is to be blamed for the third Grimes series—Grimes, Survey Service drop-out, yachtmaster, owner-master, still to make his way to the Rim Worlds—it is Hayakawa Publishing of Tokyo. A few years back that company purchased Japanese paperback rights to all the Rim Worlds novels then in print. They had the bright idea of publishing these in the correct order insofar as Grimes' biography was concerned starting off with *The Road To The Rim*. Before they got around to printing *The Big Black Mark* they were demanding a direct follow-up to this book.

For various reasons the sequence in the U.S.A. has, once again, gotten out of order. *Star Courier* has been published by DAW before *The Far Traveller* (the novel, that is, not the *Analog* novelette). At the moment of writing I can report that *To Keep The Ship*, the follow-up to *Star Courier*, has been purchased by DAW and Hayakawa but not yet by my usual publishers in London.

Then there is the *Kitty And The Commodore* series, the first episode of which will be appearing in *Isaac Asimov's*. In this the somewhat elderly Commodore Grimes tells stories of his misspent youth to one Kitty Kelly who produces a programme called Kitty's Korner for Station Yorick, on Elsinore. Other episodes will be written between novels.

Looking over the above few paragraphs I realised that I made the transition from shipmaster and part-time writer to full-time writer. But the transition still is not complete. I would class myself now as part-time shipmaster and full-time writer. Since my retirement, I seem to have been spending quite a lot of my time in charge of laid-up ships and have been referred to as the Union Steam Ship Company's Commodore Baby Sitter. These last pages, as a matter of fact, are being written aboard out of commission vessel.

So far—like Grimes—I have been lucky. The first baby-sitting job ended just before the Aussiecon, the second shortly prior to my trip to the U.S. to attend the Expo-That-Wasn't, the third immediately before the QCon Brisbane. All being well I should be free to make a trip to Japan to meet my publishers and readers later this year.

Looking back over the decades and the miles I feel that I have very little cause for complaint. Things might not always have been for the best in the best of all possible worlds but they could have been a damn sight worse. And my earlier life, at least, there has be the element of unpredictability that helped to make things interesting. I recall a rather amusing incident from my youth, shortly after my first, round-the-world-a-couple-or-three-times in *Cape St. Andrew*. I was home on leave. It was during what passes for summer in England. With a couple of friends I went to spend the day at Great Yarmouth, a seaside resort on the east coast. On the beach there was the tent of a gipsy fortune teller. I had my fortune told. The lady assured me that I should never travel. Not so oddly I did not believe her prognostications. But if she had told me that I should finish up as an Australian shipmaster and an internationally known science fiction writer I should have been incredulous.

It would have been much neater if my second wife had been to see her fortune teller at exactly the same time, but it must have been quite a few years later. She, a girl raised in an entirely land-locked country, was told that she would one day marry a sea captain . . .

I'm glad that the second fortune teller—her fortune teller—was right. Apart from anything else, three of the four Ditmars that I have been awarded should really have gone to Susan.

The other one should have gone to Grimes.

Or Bligh.

~·~·~·~·~

Editor's note: A few years after this memoir was written and published in Algol, *A. Bertram Chandler was the Writer Guest of Honor at the 1982 World Science Fiction Convention, held in Chicago that year. Captain Chandler died on June 6, 1984.*

—*Hank Davis*